HANA DU ROSE

-THE HANA DU ROSE MYSTERIES-

by K T BOWES

HANA DU ROSE

The Hana Du Rose Mysteries

A New Zealand Mystery Romance

Copyright © 2013 K T BOWES

All rights reserved. No part of this book may be reproduced in any form by any electronic or mechanical means including photocopying, recording, or information storage and retrieval without permission in writing from the author.

ISBN: 978-0-9951190-1-7

Give feedback on the book at:

www.facebook.com/NZauthorKTBowes
www.ktbowes.com
admin@ktbowes.com
Twitter: @ktboweswrites

First Edition
Published by Hakarimata Press

Dedication

This novel is dedicated to my family.
So to those who have listened and
supported, endlessly read, critiqued and
made suggestions, your faith in me has
made it all worthwhile.
One day, Andy, the Audi R8 will be
yours…

PSALM 23:4

Yea, though I walk through the valley of the shadow of death, I will fear no evil: for thou art with me; thy rod and thy staff they comfort me.

-1-

The noise rose from a gentle hum to a roar as the couple appeared in the doorway. The scene inside the ballroom overwhelmed Hana. Shades of cream and lightest blue decorated it. Swags of cloth hung from the ceiling, creating a scene reminiscent of a Jane Austen style banquet. She and Logan stood paralysed in the doorway, Hana clutching her husband so hard her nails dug into the back of his hand. A 'Happy Birthday Hana' sign hung over the double doors, making her conscience pang with sickening guilt.

First to greet her was her daughter Izzie, who flew to her side and hurled herself at Hana. She gripped her mother in a suffocating bear hug and wouldn't let go, her sobs strange and alarming. Marcus balanced a sleeping baby Elizabeth over his shoulder. He leaned in and kissed Hana, squeezing his face past his wife's shoulder to get to her. "Hey there, he said, with a smirk which told Hana he knew everything. She glanced across at her daughter and Marcus shook his head. Turning to Logan, he pumped his hand with enthusiasm and Hana narrowed her eyes. Marcus needed no more co-conspirators.

Meeting and greeting their guests took Hana and Logan a while. Hana's school principal, moved forward to hug her. "Hello my dear, congratulations on reaching your mid-forties." Angus smiled at her obvious discomfort. "Now, now. You grow more beautiful with age, so we'll have none of that. Don't you agree Mr Du Rose?"

Logan smirked at Angus and nodded, flicking an appreciative glance at his elfin wife. Hana pursed her lips, feeling the blush rise to her cheeks at the memory of their passionate wedding night and Logan turned his attention back to the other guests. Hana saw the twinkle in his grey eyes and knew he read her mind too easily for a new husband. "Thank you, Angus." She smiled. "You're very kind."

The school principal gave a magnificent bow and moved away,

his brightly patterned Scots kilt swishing around his hairy knees. He wandered towards another knot of familiar people.

"Happy birthday, Hana." She winced as Peter North's garlic breath assailed her in a sloppy wet kiss on the cheek. Hana fought not to swipe her hand across her skin. He pressed a badly wrapped gift into her hands and she almost dropped it. "Henri bought it," he admitted without shame. "I dunno what you chicks want."

Hana heard Logan snort next to her as Pete delivered his greeting. Then she saw her husband's face disappear into the folds of Henrietta's voluptuous neck in a bear hug. Hana shuddered, anticipating her turn. "Hana, darling! How wonderful to be invited. Peteepoos got so excited. When was the last time you were here my sweet?"

"Couple of months ago." Pete scratched at a spot in his head. "Boris and me brought Loge's other vehicles back. I wanted to drive the Triumph, but I got the truck instead." His face dropped into an ugly pout and his girlfriend bellowed out an unholy laugh.

"Oh you sulky baby!" She ruffled Pete's remaining hairs with a meaty hand and led him away, enfolding him into her giant armpit.

"Gosh that was close," Hana hissed out of the side of her mouth to Logan. "Did you like your hug from Henrietta?"

"Loved it," Logan commented and shot Hana a sideways look of mischief. "I didn't realise the word enfold was onomatopoeic."

"Ugh! English teachers!" Hana scoffed as she greeted another wave of colleagues and friends. She felt a twinge of guilt as she welcomed guests who travelled miles to wish her well, in what until moments before had been a surprise birthday party.

"You look like ze bride and groom greeting ze wedding guests," Boris joked, in his thick German brogue and Hana cringed. Logan reached sideways and touched her fingers and the single tantalising stroke across her flesh was enough to galvanise her.

Henrietta bustled her large frame around, admiring everything in reach. "It's magnificent," she breathed to Pete. "Logan's family owns all this? But he never said."

Pete looked shifty and shot a nervous look at his friend. Henrietta nudged him and spoke behind her hand. "Peteepoos, this would be a wonderful place for our wedding reception. We must get a brochure on the way out."

Pete buried his face in his wine glass and looked frightened.

Logan greeted a man and woman with a tight smile and Hana's brow narrowed at the similarities between them. "Hey, bro', how's life in the fast lane?" Logan asked and the other man laughed.

"Tiring. Sticking the great and good of Auckland back together isn't all fun." He shook Logan's hand but Hana noticed a rigidity in the action. Their grey eyes and regal bearing acted as a familial uniform.

The woman didn't smile as she air-kissed Hana, expensive perfume wafting round her like a haze. Her embrace of Logan bore more sincerity. The three dominated the room with their tall figures and striking good looks.

Logan's parents proved attentive hosts. They ran around amongst other uniformed staff, fetching drinks and opening a buffet which occupied much of the far end of the room. Izzie stayed glued to Hana as the party got under way, making it difficult for anyone else to get near her. "I'm so pleased to see you, Mum," she gushed for the fifth time. She seemed emotional and overwhelmed and Hana grew worried by her unusual clinginess. She worried that she may have guessed her secret. Marcus drifted up still carrying Elizabeth and took his wife away, persuading her to go with him and get food. He winked back at Hana over his shoulder and her worry intensified.

Searching for Logan, Hana spied her son. She smiled at him, noting his reluctance to approach her. Anxiety rested on his shoulders, an uncharacteristic companion. Henrietta's large frame blocked Bodie's companions as Hana moved towards him, cutting her way around the crowd. The floor cleared as spotting the buffet, Pete grabbed Henrietta's hand and yanked her towards it. "Quick, food," he whooped and set off. The couple's absence opened the route between mother and son.

Then Hana saw him and inhaled a breath she couldn't release. A small boy around four held Bodie's hand, clinging to his fingers like a lifebuoy. His tousled black hair curled at the ends and dark skin covered a slight, delicate body. With thin little wrists sticking out of his shirtsleeves and enormous brown eyes, he sucked his thumb and stared around him, uncomfortable in the adult surroundings. Occasionally he glanced up at the slender, pale-skinned woman next to him, seeking reassurance from her presence. He popped his thumb from his mouth and took hold of her dress between his fingers. Touching the fabric, he found comfort and the thumb went back into his mouth with a flicker of satisfaction.

Hana walked with deliberate slowness, absorbing the moment and struggling to comprehend what she saw. Her late husband's huge brown eyes fixed on her from the face of the child and he watched her progress through the people milling around her. Hana's hands shook by the time she reached her son, suppressing emotions she couldn't name. His expression held fear and defiance as he greeted her with uncharacteristic awkwardness. "Mum."

Hana trembled and nodded to him, forcing her lips into a smile. Words failed her as she recognised the imminence of her own revelation and dreaded his reaction. "Hi, Bo," she stuttered, her sideways glance taking in the girl beside him. Hana offered her hand in a formal handshake and tuned in to the girl's fear and apprehension, felt as a tremor through their joined fingers.

"Hi, I'm Amy." Her eyes darted from Bodie to Hana and back again.

"Lovely to meet you." Hana maintained the rigid smile while suppressing a multitude of questions and accusations. She jerked her head towards the boy. "And who's this?" The mystery unfolded before her like a picnic rug laid on the ground. Bodie's time at police college seemed the happiest of his entire life, but his transfer to Whangarei during his probation period took her by surprise. It followed a period of darkness, the root of which he never confessed to his mother. Hana always suspected the involvement of a woman, but he'd kept the door to that cupboard closed from her prying.

Hana smiled at the small boy and her brow knitted. Bodie's secrecy had denied her the first few years of her grandchild's life. She wanted to yell and scream but refrained. Instead, she gave Bodie a look which made him feel like a child again. He swallowed his discomfort, preferring postponement to a scene.

Amy's gaze darted around the room, her fingers stroking a curl on her son's head. She nodded towards him. "This is Jas," she said, nudging the boy's arm. "Say hello, Jas."

The boy popped his thumb from his lips and fixed his brown-eyed gaze on Hana. "Hello, Jas," he said. He smirked and put his thumb back.

Bodie glanced down in horror and Amy winced. Hana fought the laugh bubbling in her chest. "Where do you work, Amy?" she asked, hating the inane conversation starter in such surreal circumstances. She winked at the child and he grinned around his thumb.

"I'm a cop," Amy ventured.

Hana smiled as her brain did mental gymnastics. "In Whangarei?"

"No, Hamilton."

Hana opened her mouth to speak and Bodie cringed, begging her with his eyes not to press further.

"Can we go now?" Jas fidgeted, sucking his thumb and peering down at shiny shoes poking from beneath his slacks. "My shoes is hurtin' me." His white shirt hung slack on one side and the neat bow tie at his neck tilted to a jaunty angle.

Hana dropped to her haunches to speak to him and he observed her with adult seriousness. The combination of his inherited features rattled her, Vik's eyes boring into hers as her new husband's voice sounded nearby. Hana held out her hand, offering a grown-up handshake. Jas took it, using the hand with the wet thumb. "I'm Hana," she said. "I'm very pleased to meet you."

He studied her long enough for Hana's bent knees to complain about the prolonged squat. Then he dropped his bombshell. "Nope, you're Granny and I'm Jas."

Bodie and Amy both inhaled in a horror reflex and Hana kept her face straight. "Is that right?" she said and he nodded. His thumb went back between his lips and the serene smile showed a disregard for the landmine he casually detonated.

Hana stood with care, her legs tingling. She smiled at the boy and pointed towards the buffet. "Why don't you help yourself to food, Jas?" She glanced at Amy. "If that's okay with Mummy?"

Jas looked for his mother's nod of approval before weaving towards the food table. The adults surged around him but he exhibited great courage, his lips lined in grim determination as he waited his turn and filled a plate. Avid concentration made the task appear laboured.

Hana's gaze flicked back to Bodie. Fear caused a wobble in his fingers as he ran a hand over his handsome face. His eyes pleaded for mercy and Hana acquiesced. "As long as we talk another time," she said, voicing her side of an unspoken conversation. She raised her eyebrows and he nodded.

"I promise."

"I'll hold you to it." Hana reached out and hugged him, instant love for the child overriding her disappointment in Bodie's behaviour. But the moral high ground made lonely terrain and Hana watched as Logan worked the room alone. He thanked people for coming and her heart clenched in fear. She needed to stop him announcing what they'd done.

"Hey, Bodie." Hana heard his voice and Logan's hand appeared to the side of her.

"Hi, Logan." Bodie's teeth ground in his jaw as he accepted the handshake. "This is nice. I don't think Mum's ever had a birthday party." Hana dropped her gaze as he delivered the unnecessary comment. "She's never wanted one."

"Oh yeah?" Logan's reply sounded half-hearted and Hana tensed. His fingers ran up her spine and onto her shoulder in an intimate, familiar movement. Bodie missed it, but Amy saw. A rosy flush lit Hana's cheeks.

"Can I steal you for a moment?" Logan's eyes twinkled with mischief and Hana read the undertone. He didn't mean for a moment, but a lifetime. He took Hana's hand and whisked her away, leading her to a stage beyond the food tables. Hana watched Jas' head bobbing up and down as he leaned forward to inspect the various offerings. Logan tugged at her fingers.

Hana's stomach flipped at the foot of the stairs and she took a ragged breath, trying hard not to look at her children. "Logan, please don't," she begged. "Not now. I can't do this."

"You don't have to," Logan replied, turning to face her, his body twisted on the stairs. "I'll do the talking." His brow furrowed. "I thought you wanted this."

Hana blew out through pursed lips, panic in her eyes. "I spent the last eight years explaining everything to my children in advance," she gasped. "I can't shock them this way."

Logan cocked his head, strands of dark fringe flipping into his eyes. "And you did a fantastic job, babe." He reached out and stroked her cheek. "They're just fine. Now it's your turn." He pulled her up the steps after him, strong fingers cupping her elbow..

"It's too public," she hissed, feeling people staring. "It's cruel."

Logan shook his head and tugged her towards the centre of the stage. "Life is cruel, wahine. But you're not. Cruel would be jilting me in my second wedding of the year." His smile held pain and Hana's breath caught in her chest.

"We're getting married again?" she asked, understanding dawning.

Logan nodded and raised his eyebrows. "Yep. Your son-in-law agreed to bless our marriage."

Hana kept her eyes down, staring at the beautiful parquet floor. Her flailing fingers tugged at the back of Logan's shirt, but he concentrated hard on getting his words right and ignored her. She suspected he didn't notice until his other hand reached around to seize hers and hold it in a crushing grip. "I don't need a weggie thanks," he whispered with a smile.

Silence filled the room and Hana heard her heartbeat resound in her ears. All faces turned towards her. Only Jas continued his busyness, choosing sandwiches from the buffet and munching on a cracker. Hana inhaled as Logan spoke. "I just learned that Hana's never had a birthday party," he said, looking across at Bodie. "And that it's not her thing." Hana gasped and Logan squeezed her fingers. "So I'll dispense with the singing of Happy Birthday on this occasion and cut to the other reason I've brought you from your warm homes to a party in the middle of nowhere." Logan drew in a breath and his voice carried across the room. "A short while ago, I asked Hana to marry me and she said yes." He smiled and his grey eyes softened. Hana watched her son's colour heighten and swallowed, anticipating trouble. Her hand sweated against Logan's.

Marcus stepped up to the stage and the gathered crowd gasped in realisation. Logan fell silent and Hana panicked at the spite in Bodie's eyes. Marcus took over, his tone steady and cajoling, easing the guests into acceptance. "I'd like you all to find a seat," he said, resting his hands on Hana and Logan's shoulders and speaking from between them. "And then I'll invite you to witness the marriage of Hana Singh Johal and Logan Du Rose."

Bodie started walking, his heels clicking against the wooden floor. Hana swallowed and saw a hand shoot out to stop him. Alfred Du Rose levered his bent body upright and halted Hana's son with the look on his face. He leaned close and she saw Bodie pale. "What did he tell him?" she hissed at Logan, her green eyes wild. "What did he say?"

Logan kissed her cheek and put his lips to her ear. His eyes flashed a warning. "He told him he's too late," he whispered. "And he is. Nobody else needs to know that."

Marcus waggled his eyebrows and Hana sighed. "I'm here to bless this marriage in the sight of God," he began and Hana clung to his words. "Logan's family are catholic but have graciously allowed me to conduct this service."

She shot a look sideways at Logan and he smirked. So many things she didn't know about him.

Hana sought her children's faces in the crowd, her heart beating an unhealthy rhythm and making her fight for breath. Bodie bent to wipe sauce from Jas' shirt, his face unreadable. Izzie stared at her with an intentness that freaked Hana out. She wanted to go to her daughter and reassure her, but needed to stay on the stage with her new husband and do the first thing he'd ever asked of her.

Marcus proved his worth as a cleric, engaging the shocked guests in his brand of pantomime. Hana cringed as he delivered a marriage service fit for the record books in terms of speed. "These guys are older than nubile sixteen-year-olds but their commitment to each other is undeniable," he said, pausing for effect. Hana inspected Logan's black cowboy boots with interest and felt him squeeze her fingers. "Marriage is for life and I'm convinced they both understand." Marcus spoke for a short time and Hana focused on her breathing pattern, regulating it so the pain in her chest eased. Marcus' words brought her back to the moment with a bump. "So, in the name of the Father, the Son and the Holy Spirit, Logan and Hana, I bless you and pray it's not too late for babies."

Logan's jaw dropped in shock and Hana winced. She daren't look at her children. "Marcus!" she hissed, watching his lips twist up in a smirk. He fixed a solid hand on her shoulder and pinned her in place. "Hana's new husband has a few words he wishes to add." Hana saw her escape route closing and her knees wobbled. She contemplated kicking both men, but figured she'd overbalance and entertain everyone in a way she didn't want.

Logan grappled in his trouser pocket next to her and Marcus leaned closer. "Stay here a second longer," he whispered and Hana groaned. "Behave, woman!" he hissed and winked at her.

Logan unfolded a piece of paper, smoothing it out on his thigh. Creased into quarters, the edges looked neat. Hana glanced over his shoulder and saw his precise, left-handed script. Logan began with a welcome and his mihimihi. "Tēnā koutou, tēnā koutou, tēnā tatou katoa." Hana listened to her husband's native language tumble eloquently from his full lips, rolling over her like a soft sheet. The paper fluttered at his side, not needed for the familiar detailing of his heritage. "Ko Tainui te waka," he said, naming the Tainui as the canoe which carried his forebears. He listed the river and mountain of his lineage, the natural landmarks which made him Logan Du Rose. His words strengthened Hana, those parts of him belonging to her by proxy. He spoke his native tongue to her in bed, lilting soft words, intoxicating and ethereal. As warm water, it soothed and refreshed her. Other times he spoke French, knowing it annoyed her British blood. Hana watched Logan's mouth move, fighting the urge to reach up and kiss his sensitive lips like she did earlier.

Logan's grey eyes turned in her direction and Hana jumped and tuned back in. He switched to English and lifted the paper in front of him. His fingers shook and the paper jerked. She wanted to tell him to stop, but couldn't. "Hana, we met twenty-six years ago on a dirty tube train in the middle of London and I fell in love with you then. I spent many wasted years looking for the beautiful redhead and when I gave up and returned home, there you were." Logan turned towards her and smiled. "You crawled around the car park on your knees for the contents of your handbag. You lost a lipstick and I lost my heart." He swallowed and Hana heard the collective titter from the guests. She sensed Bodie's animosity from across the room and stared at her shoes. "I tried all my best stalker antics to get near you and then one day you just sat next to me." He turned towards her and lifted their joined hands. "You've made me happier than I ever imagined possible."

Hana daren't look at any of the faces below the stage as everyone's eyes fixed on her. Logan's hand betrayed his nerves, but his voice spoke with confidence into the silence. "I promise to love and cherish you forever, Hana Du Rose." He turned to face her and his grey eyes conveyed his seriousness. "I want to be the first person you see in the morning and the last one you see at night. For as long as we're both alive, I want it to be as a married couple. I intend to make up for lost time and enjoy every moment with you. And I promise to tell you every day; you're beautiful."

A tear slipped down Hana's cheek at the unexpected bearing of Logan's soul. It felt raw and touching and cost him. She saw emotion sparkling in his eyes and gratitude flooded her. She gulped, knowing she couldn't better his words but wanting to at least match them. "You found me and showed me how much love I still have to give. Thank you for persevering with me." Hana gave a shy smile. "I know I didn't make it easy for you." She bit her lip and heard a snort from

Peter North. Henrietta slapped him on the forehead and the sound reverberated around the room. He rubbed it and she whispered her apologies, causing those nearby to smirk.

"I appreciate your love and faith in me. I'll never let you down, Logan. That's my promise to you."

Logan blinked in surprised at Hana's odd undertaking. But he didn't yet know how deep the broken fragments of her trust were buried. His palms felt warm against her shoulders as he kissed Hana's lips, dragging the action out with a sparkle in his eyes. Everyone clapped and Hana sighed with relief. A hint of terror surfaced at the thought of approaching Izzie and Bodie and she forced it back. Marcus read her fear as he moved away and answered her distress call. He took a step back onto the stage and whispered into her ear. "Izzie will be fine. It's me she's angry at." He sighed at Hana's look of confusion. "Because I knew and didn't tell her," he said. "I'll get the hiding, not you." He smirked and she watched him take heavy steps down to the dance floor.

Descending from the stage, congratulations swamped the couple and despite their surprise, the guests seemed genuine in their enthusiasm. Izzie punished Marcus by forcing him to carry a heavy, sleeping Elizabeth at the same time as eating his food. Hana watched them from a distance, anxiety distracting her. Bodie kissed Hana's cheek, his face unreadable. He shook Logan's hand but the action looked forced. Hana tried to work her son out, failing as always.

Music began in the background and the volume of chatter increased to compensate. Pete monopolised Logan, so Hana moved towards her daughter. Izzie glanced around the room without seeing, twisting her wedding ring in a nervous action. Hana touched her shoulder. "I didn't mean to shock you, Izz," she whispered. "I'm sorry." Her face pinched with fear and she offered her daughter the untouched glass of Baileys in her hand. Izzie refused with a shake of her head. "But it's your favourite. Are you mad at me?"

Izzie put her head down and covered her face with her hands. Hana's heart went into free fall. "I'm sorry, Izz. It's not how I meant it to be. I owe you an explanation. Sweetheart, look at me."

Izzie sniffed and a tear rolled down her olive cheek, diving into midair as another replaced it. Hana led her to a chair, placing the liqueur on the table between them. "Sit down, Izz," she said, guilt dulling her green eyes. "It's all my fault." Hana had promised herself she wouldn't apologise for her mammoth life choice, hearing her words condemn her as they tumbled out on an automatic loop.

Izzie sat, the tears coming thicker and faster. Hana moved alongside, enfolding her daughter in a wordless embrace. Alfred turned the main lights to low, creating a nightclub atmosphere. Hana and Izzie found solace in the darkness while he fought the switch for the strobe. Izzie broke away and searched her sleeve for a tissue, groaning at the wet patch on Hana's shoulder. "I've ruined your dress," she said, her hiccough heralding more tears.

Hana patted her thigh. "No, you haven't. It'll wash. Mop up and tell me how you feel."

Marcus walked towards them balancing Elizabeth. He turned away as he saw Izzie struggling with the tissue and Hana frowned at the action. He looked back at her and mouthed something she didn't catch. She sighed. "I think your husband's gone for more tissue," she said. "Or he's gone to eat something in the toilet. I can't be certain."

Izzie snorted and blew out the fragile remains of the tissue. "I hope he hurries."

Hana waited for her daughter to compose herself, licking her lips and running through possible questions and answers. Marcus returned with a whole toilet roll and plopped it in front of Izzie. He sat next to her as Elizabeth grew fractious and wriggly. "Can I have a cuddle?" Hana asked, reaching out.

Marcus' face morphed into a grin. "Sure, Hana. Just let me get rid of the baby."

"Smart ass!" Hana narrowed her eyes and took Elizabeth, settling her in her lap and kissing the blonde topknot. She breathed in the sweet smell of baby.

"Hey darlin', it'll be ok." Marcus turned his attention to Izzie and put his arm around her shoulders.

"I'm not speaking to you!" Izzie snapped, pushing him away. "How could you keep a secret as big as this?" She flapped her arms and Marcus ducked.

"Mitigating circumstances," he replied, kissing the side of her face and swiping a wedge of toilet roll for her to mop up with.

Hana cuddled the baby and waited for the recriminations to start. A glance at Logan found him on the other side of the room, head bowed as he spoke to Alfred. His neat backside looked firm in his expensive suit trousers. Muscular biceps flexed as he patted his father on the shoulder. Izzie inhaled and Hana tensed. "Mum, I'm pregnant."

Hana's concentration snapped back to her daughter, waiting for the unexpected words to filter into her brain. She frowned. "I thought you just said you were pregnant." Hana smiled, knowing it wasn't possible. Her gaze flicked across to Marcus. He smirked and Hana sighed. "The vasectomy didn't work then?"

Marcus waggled his eyebrows. "You can't keep a good man down."

"Wow." Hana kissed Elizabeth's crown. She smirked and Marcus narrowed his eyes.

"What?"

Hana shrugged and reached across to take Izzie's hand. "I bet that's a conversation I'm glad I missed." She winked at her daughter and Izzie glared at Marcus.

"Mum, at no point did he accuse me of cheating."

Marcus frowned and his body jerked upright. "It never occurred to me. I missed a golden opportunity to escape."

"Good," Hana replied, warning in her eyes.

Marcus stroked Izzie's shoulder and swallowed. Despite the bravado, Hana sensed his fear.

"Congratulations," she said, injecting joviality into her voice. "I know Elizabeth's small and it's unexpected, but we'll pray about it." She watched her daughter's face and realised her secret wedding hardly touched her. Her own anxieties negated any hostility towards her mother. Hana ached for her. She put on her mothering hat and responded to a different situation than the one she expected when she first sat down. "Let's explore what you're afraid of," she urged, her voice soft. "And we'll think of some solutions."

Hana turned Elizabeth towards her as she listened, pulling funny faces and rejoicing when the child returned her smile in a bonny display of gums. Elizabeth gurgled and beat the air with her tiny fists, leaning backwards into Hana's palms in jerky, excited movements. Izzie cried some more and Marcus explained her anxieties. "There's a high risk of another child with disabilities," he said, his shoulders slumping. He sighed and shook his head. "I feel I'm betraying Elizabeth speaking about her this way." He pressed his fingers to his eyeballs as though attempting to diminish his emotional pain. "We adore her. She's perfect to us and exactly the child ordained to be ours."

"I know." Hana's smile held understanding. "But her needs are demanding. I know how often Izz visits the hospital for routine appointments and how much time it takes. It's obvious that another pregnancy may compromise her ability to do that." Hana smiled at her daughter. "You're an amazing mother, Izz. I'm so proud of you. You've taken everything in your stride. Having Elizabeth and then moving south, you've done so well. You put your heart into everything and nobody could ask more of you."

Izzie sniffed and blew into the tissue again. "I went to an appointment last week so they could test Beth's hearing and I threw up." Her wail of misery made Marcus widen his eyes and clutch her closer into his side. Izzie's eyes ran as she looked across at Hana. "In the doctor's sink." She hiccoughed again and Hana melted.

"Poor girl. You said nothing."

"No, you didn't." Marcus' eyes narrowed. "I'm happy to come to the hospital with you."

"You work full time," Izzie complained. She waved her hand. "It's as though you work two full time jobs in reality. You're at the church at seven in the morning and I'm lucky if I see you before bedtime."

Marcus lowered his head and nodded. He turned to Hana, desperate to explain his neglect. "I'm sorry. Our congregation is older and many of them need home and hospital visits. I'll try harder to put Izzie first from now on." He swallowed and Hana saw the guilt in his eyes.

Izzie nodded. "Any new child to cope with alongside Elizabeth's demands will be exhausting. The possibility of another baby with Downs is out of range of my ability to imagine, let alone plan for." Izzie blew her nose again.

Marcus darted a nervous look at Hana and she contemplated being in his shoes for the last few weeks. She guessed it involved much crying and shouting. His face said he suspected Izzie was cranking up to another round and he didn't want a public repeat. "Let's talk about this another time," he suggested, looking to Hana for backup.

"That's a good idea," she agreed. "Let's not worry over things we can't change right this minute." Hana reached across and clasped her daughter's wet, writhing hand in hers, infusing her with love and security. "It'll be ok, Izz. Just as it was before."

Hana jumped as Jas plonked his plate on the table next to her. He clambered onto a chair and sat on his knees, pulling a sausage roll apart and popping the pastry into his mouth. In between swallowing, his thumb found its way between his lips and it seemed hard for him to decide which he needed most. Hana's heart quailed at the complete lack of recognition in Izzie's face and recognised another situation brewing. It became too late to head it off as the boy turned towards Hana. "Granny, is that my baby too?"

Hana took a deep breath, concentrating all her energy on the child to avoid looking at Izzie or Marcus. "Yes," she replied, turning Elizabeth towards him so he could see her better. "Do you like her? Her name's Elizabeth."

Jas popped his thumb in his mouth, watching the baby with interest. He answered like a politician, giving his answer great consideration. "Yes," he said. "I love her heaps and heaps. It's my job to look after her forever. We's cousins. I have a mummy and a daddy now, aye?" He fought a gooey egg sandwich which leaked over his fingers. With a look of disgust, he discarded it onto the tablecloth, "I'm gonna tell Jarad Smith all about my new fambly on Monday when I go back to kindy. He's got no daddy neither. He's gonna get jealous." After another suck of his thumb he leaned his face into Hana's. "Would it be okay if Jarad shared her?" Jas pointed at Elizabeth. "I don't want him to stop being my friend, but he ain't sharin' my new dad."

Hana smiled and nodded, still not getting eye contact with Izzie. Jas seemed oblivious to the chaos he wreaked every time he opened his mouth. Chaos laced with cuteness. "Do you want to see my bestest chicken spot?" he offered, "It's in my hair. Look."

"It's too dark in here," Hana said, smirking. "Maybe later?"

Jas nodded with enthusiasm and picked around on his plate for a while. Bored, he abandoned it in a sea of crumbs and detritus, making a beeline for his mother. He wove across the dance floor like a drunk.

Hana felt the tension without looking. It hung over their small table like a fog. Marcus smirked but Izzie's face held savage betrayal. "Seems to be a day for secrets," she spat. Glancing sideways at her husband, she narrowed her eyes. "I bet you knew, didn't you?"

Marcus patted his chest. "Penitent privilege, my dearest. What's told in the confessional is sacred."

"You don't have a confessional!" Izzie snapped and Marcus laughed and nudged her arm.

"Can I just remind you of your own secret, my love? The small matter of the wee bun in your oven."

"Different," Izzie maintained. "Not the same at all."

Marcus wiggled his eyebrows at Hana and she shook her head. "You seem to be everyone's confidante," she said with a smile. The expression faded from her face, leaving her complexion pale. He couldn't know everything. She hoped not. A wave of fear came from nowhere, snaking up her spine as the memories returned. Hana swallowed and concentrated on the child in her arms.

Logan's hand on her shoulder brought instant comfort and Hana sensed the dark cloud move aside at his bidding. "Please may I have the first dance with my wife?" he asked, his tone tender.

Hana smiled up at him and nodded with relief. "I'd love to," she replied.

A slow, romantic song crooned from the speakers either side of the stage and Logan led Hana onto a dance floor teeming with coloured spots of moving light. He held her close and edged her around the parquet floor. The sound of clapping and wolf whistling from their gathered friends drowned out the music during the first bars and quieted as other couples joined them. Hana heard the click of cameras and saw occasional flashes of light. She cuddled into Logan's chest, enjoying his proximity and the clean, musky scent surrounding him.

Logan bent his body into hers, holding her around her waist with his hands clasped in the small of her back. She felt his fingers brush sensuously across the bones of her spine and shivered. "That wasn't so bad was it?" he asked, his cheek against hers so she could hear him over the music which Alfred cranked up to a deafening volume.

"Nobody fainted or ran out." Logan raised his eyebrows, seeking endorsement like a child.

"No. Nobody ran out." Hana winced and glanced across at her son. His jaw looked fixed and Amy sat next to him cradling Jas. "I'm sure there's still time." She sighed and Logan smoothed his palms across her back. Her cheek nuzzled into his chest, feeling his heart beat through the tight shirt. She'd gained two extra grandchildren in the space of an evening, but the news would keep until later.

The first song ended and the next began. Logan kept hold of Hana, his breath warm on her cheek as they moved to the music, bodies pressed together in intimate closeness. She resisted the urge to slide her hand up his shirt now she knew what delights lay beneath.

A gentle Scots voice interrupted, "May I cut in?" Angus smiled as he held out his hand to Hana and Logan nodded, his eyebrow quirking upwards in amusement.

"Just this once," he warned, bowing to them both and leaving the dance floor. He looked back and winked at Hana, not moving much further before guests encircled him, seeking gossip to take back to the staffroom.

Angus took both Hana's hands and they resumed the dance as the music changed to another slow, melodic tune. Miriam wrestled the controls away from her trigger happy husband and resumed order. She set the volume to a more bearable decibel level and shooed him away. Pete ensnared Logan's reluctant sister and danced some hideous boogie at her feet, his eyes on the same level as her breasts. She didn't look amused but used her presence on the dance floor to shoot occasional, spiteful glances in Hana's direction. The chilling expression made her blood run cold.

"I hope you'll both be very happy." Angus dragged Hana's attention back to him, his expression sincere. The look in his eyes spoke of wistfulness. "Is it such a massive thing, starting again?"

Hana held his gaze, her nod just a hint of movement. "Yes," she replied. "Bigger than massive." Her mind cast back to the afternoon after Vik's death when Angus appeared fresh from his own grief, urging her to do nothing for a full year. He advised her to live with her memories until she'd dealt with them. "I waited as you suggested," she said, her voice soft. "But I didn't realise I'd got stuck waiting."

Angus tilted his head as though testing the gravity of her wisdom. "Oh." His face reflected his intensity as he hung onto every syllable, assessing his own journey through loss. "I think I may be stuck too." His orange brows knitted in concentration and regret. "I wasn't a good husband," he said, biting his lower lip. "I wonder if I'm stuck in a pattern of guilt. What do you think?"

Hana gaped in surprise. "You and Iris loved each other. I can't imagine she'd want you to live your life alone, not if it made you unhappy. Do what you think is best."

She saw the desperation in his eyes as he leaned closer. "But is it possible to love someone else as much as them, or do we settle for second best?" He asked the question and then cringed as the words emerged. Angus flapped his hand. "Don't answer that. It's none of my business whether you love Logan as much as you loved your wonderful Vikram. Forget I asked." His freckled face pinked to a painful hue and Hana winced at his embarrassment.

"We're friends, Angus. You can ask me that. I can tell you it's different." She stared at the floor as though the answer might be written there. "I hero worshipped Vik. He was a year older and yet, to some extent he parented me and the gap felt greater than twelve months. I'm older than Logan but feel more of an equal. He affects me in ways Vik never did. If I've learned one thing these last few months, it's not to compare them." Her mind wandered to Logan's expert lovemaking and a smirk lifted the corners of her lips. She sighed. "There's no roadmap to being a widow or widower, Angus. All we can do is walk the path and see where it leads."

Angus nodded, the action slow and deliberate. "I suspected I'd pushed you too hard. I encouraged you to let go of Achilles Rise and then everything seemed to go wrong for you."

"No." Hana shook her head, the fear of the blonde man returning for the first time in days. "That's nothing to do with my relationship with Logan. It started before I met him."

Angus leaned closer, his breath soft on her face. "But it intensified after."

Hana gaped and her breath locked in her chest. "What do you mean?"

"Nothing." Angus seized her wrist and forced her into a twirl beneath his arm. A sharp pain ran up Hana's arm and the partial healing felt undone. When she crashed back into his chest with a cry, he looked sorry. "Apologies," he said, his eyes flashing a warning. "Be careful, Hana. If you ever need help, you know where I am."

Hana opened her mouth and gaped at him in shock, unable to find the right words. Angus clicked his heels together and bowed like a fine Scottish gentleman. Then he left her standing in the centre of the dance floor alone.

Pete spotted the vacancy and boogied across to her, poking a finger up his bulbous nose. When he reached out for Hana, she pushed his hand away. "Don't even think about it!" she snapped.

"Liza dumped me." Pete shimmied his hips and looked ready to lay an egg. Hana took a step back. "She terrifies me," he added.

Hana nodded and looked around for Logan, seeing him standing next to his brother. Liza Du Rose hovered nearby as though waiting for an audience. Anger flitted across her attractive features.

Hana watched the strobe lighting twist and turn on the parquet at her feet and wondered if Angus' behaviour reflected jealousy. She'd escaped widowhood and he remained stuck in it alone. Pete continued to gyrate in front of her and a sudden tug on Hana's dress made her start. She looked into the eyes of her new grandson as he stared up at her, arms outstretched. "Dance?" he demanded, bouncing from foot to foot in anticipation.

"I'm figuring you hit the buffet table again?" Hana smiled at his eagerness. Jas grinned back through a mouth which bore the unmistakable signs of chocolate. A dribble of cola ran into the sauce stain on his shirt.

"I didn't hit nothing," his said, his expression showing fake affront. "It's naughty."

Hana bopped and shook with him for the next few minutes until he went a disgusting shade of pale green and clapped his hand over his mouth. At the perfect moment, Amy arrived and hastened him off to find a bathroom before the inevitable happened. They reappeared a while later with Jas looking better. He sat on his mother's knee and fell asleep.

Hana danced with numerous guests, all wanting to know the fine details of her relationship with Logan. Henrietta slapped her on the back and sent her sprawling into Pete. "I didn't know you'd met Logan in London!" she yelled over the music. "How romantic."

"Yes, very." Hana picked herself up and staggered to the side of the dance floor. Her gaze roved the room for Logan and she saw him in deep discussion with his sister. His face displayed anger and Hana cringed and avoided them. She observed her son as he sat next to Amy. Hurt and confusion marred her green eyes. The existence of the little boy ached like a raw wound, reminding her of the huge chunk of his life she'd missed. "Tonight isn't the right time," she whispered to herself.

"Pardon?" Logan's kiss on her neck made her jump and Hana turned.

"Your sister hates me." Her brows narrowed in fear and Logan stroked her cheek.

"Liza likes nobody. Don't let her bother you." Soft fingers on her shoulder caressed the line of Hana's dress and she sighed, pleasure reminding her nothing else mattered.

"Happy wedding day, beautiful." Logan's gentle kiss alighted on her cheek. He wrapped his arms around her and breathed out a contented sigh. "Who's the wee boy with Bodie?"

"Tell you later." Hana's reply sounded guarded. Logan leaned back to study the sadness in her face.

"Okay," he whispered, not needing to see the flash of warning in her eyes to know to leave the subject alone. "What do you want? Food or dance?" His easy smile pulled Hana from her turmoil.

"I'd love a glass of wine, please," she asked.

Hana danced with Alfred and accepted his kiss. "Welcome to the insane branch of the Du Rose family, kōtiro."

"Thank you for the party," Hana replied. "I feel guilty for the deception." She waved her arm to take in the beautifully decorated ballroom.

Alfred laughed. "Logan rang at the start of last week. We thought he wanted to throw youse a birthday party. We've even got a gift."

Hana's face flushed in shame as she muttered thanks. "It is my birthday in a few days' time," she reassured him.

Alfred leaned in and whispered, "Miriam sensed something was goin' on. She's been excited ever since the boy phoned. And she liked you when Logan brought youse home." His face darkened. "She thought she'd messed somethin' up for him."

Hana gulped and her face paled, remembering the awkward conversation. Alfred cocked his head at her imperceptible nod. "Logan knew things about me I didn't expect," she said, her voice wavering. "It took me by surprise." She banished the vision of the fourteen-year-old Logan, feeling a flush of desire as she caught his gaze across the crowded room. Logan's lips tilted upwards on one side and he winked.

Hana pouted, offering her husband a pair of sensual lips ripe for kissing. Pete's head popped up midpoint between them and his eyes widened at Hana's intercepted offer of intimacy. "Oh," he said, looking wrong-footed. "What about Henrietta and Logan?"

Hana snorted and Alfred asked her if she felt okay. "I'm fine thanks," she replied. "But Logan wants me for a moment." She excused herself and walked across the room towards her new husband. The thought of being one of a pair gave her immense pleasure. Logan met her half way and pulled her into his arms.

"Hey, babe. My bro' and big sis want to meet you officially." He turned Hana towards the imposing Du Roses and led her forward. Her walk slowed and she eyed the carbon copies of Logan, overwhelmed by their height and grace. Nervousness robbed her of thinking time between the questions Logan's sister fired at her and Hana spluttered out answers like she stood in a witness box.

Intimidating and abrupt, Liza cross examined her, grey eyes filled with venom. She leaned in close to Hana. "We thought we'd come to check you out. We didn't realise he'd already married you." She made no attempt at pleasantries. "If you hurt him, I'll make you sorry!"

Hana's eyes widened and she took a step back, the night tilting out of control at an alarming rate. She saw no twinkle in the grey eyes, no hint of joking in the austere features. Liza meant every word. Hana chose not to pursue the conversation, gripping Logan's fingers in hers and facing his brother instead. Liza's eyes bored into the side of Hana's face. A power dresser, she resembled Miriam in her facial features. She reached a long arm across Hana and ruffled Logan's hair, treating him as the little brother and staking her claim against Hana.

"You only just met me," Hana whispered. "You can't have formed a judgement already!"

"Oh, can't I?" Liza spoke without moving her lips or teeth, creating an action filled with menace. Hana's righteous indignation died an instant death and when Logan went to fetch another drink, Liza hit her with another barrage of pointed questions.

"What do you actually do for a living?"

"How did your first husband die?"

"Did he leave you well provided for?"

"What's your interest in my brother?"

There seemed no end to Liza's inquisition and the questions became more personal. Hana's snippy retorts stumbled from her lips without effect because if Liza realised she'd offended her, she didn't care.

Hana paused mid-sentence, trying to avoid discussing her financial solvency with a stranger. Logan pushed a glass of red wine into her fingers and blocked Liza. "Leave it!" he commanded. Animosity oozed from his flashing eyes and Hana caught a whiff of what brewed beneath the guise of happy families. She felt the tension in them both hike to frightening proportions and it made her head ache.

"You're being a fool!" Liza spat and Logan widened his eyes in warning.

"I know what I'm doing," he hissed. Liza pouted and the salvo of inappropriate questions stemmed. The look she gave Logan alerted Hana to some reason beneath her questioning.

"Don't come crying to me when she's ruined you!" she spat and moved off towards the buffet table.

Hana opened her mouth to demand an explanation from Logan but Michael stepped forward and engaged her in conversation. From the corner of her eye, Hana watched Logan struggle for control, his body ramrod straight next to hers. "I understand you work at a secondary school." Affability flowered in Michael Du Rose's face and Hana relaxed. A natural flirt, he diminished her anxiety and drew her into the conversation. Liza's barb loosened its grip and Michael's easy nature smoothed away the discomfort. Only Logan failed to let go, watching his brother through suspicious, narrowed eyes.

"Where do you work?" Hana asked.

Michael's handsome face broke into a smile. Broader than Logan, they otherwise resembled a matched pair side by side. But where Logan seemed dark and brooding, Michael behaved with open friendliness. "I've worked at Auckland's Emergency Room for the last ten years. I decided to go into medicine when I was twelve." His eyes flicked towards Logan and back to Hana. "I held someone's intestines in their split guts with my hands and enjoyed the adrenaline rush." He threw his head back and laughed but Hana cringed.

"That sounds painful," she said, siding with the victim. "Did they recover?"

Michael smirked and nodded. "Yeah. Lost a few metres of it but they recovered."

Hana shivered. "That's a horrid work story. My worst one is probably a paper cut."

Michael laughed again and Hana's smile drooped at the sight of Liza returning.

"Hey sis," he said to Liza as she pulled a sausage roll apart with her fingers. "How's life out at Mission Bay?"

"Fine," she grunted, feeding the crumbled remains through painted lips. Michael winked at Hana, his grey eyes sizing her up. Something about the look made the breath stutter in her chest. She knew in that moment he'd traded a wedding band for a steady procession of conquests. It made her nervous. Plainly used to dealing with drunks and rowdy, injured parties, he placated Liza with a well-timed question about her latest case and turned her attention away from Hana.

Logan inclined his head in a look of gratitude and pulled her away with a firm hand in the small of her back. "Sorry," he whispered. "I should've realised she'd go in for the kill."

"Why?" Hana's eyes widened in fear and the answer met her in Logan's eyes. "Oh. Because of Caroline?"

Logan inhaled as an irritated snort. "Please, let's not talk about her today."

Hana nodded in agreement but the Du Rose family dynamic perplexed her. She gleaned from the short but painful conversation with Liza that she and Caroline Marsh were friends. It rattled her. A family connection to Logan hindered her ability to expunge the woman from their lives and gave Caroline a reason to stick around. She wished for Rory's return like a shopaholic craving shoes. Caroline might remain at the school, but at least she'd leave Hana's office.

She cast around the room, looking for familiar faces and confused when she didn't see them. "Where's Rory and Sheila?" she asked, peering into the strobing gloom.

Logan halted at the edge of the dance floor. "I invited them." He shrugged. "I called Rory and he said they'd come."

"That's weird." Hana narrowed her brows. "Sheila loves a good party. I hope nothing's wrong."

"Hana, Hana, dance with me?" Pete snatched up her arm and whisked her away from Logan. She managed to hand over the wine glass before Pete yanked her back into the throng of dancers. She realised too late he hadn't offered out of any desire to spend time with her, but because a member of the sports department frolicked behind them with Henrietta. Both looked worse for wear.

After Pete stepped on her feet four times, Hana left him doing his loose-armed impression of John Travolta alone in the middle of the floor. She found space at a circular table and a waitress offered a tray of drinks as soon as she sat down. "Thank you," Hana said, giving the teenager a smile.

"You're welcome, Mrs Du Rose," the girl replied and Hana gaped in surprise. Gwynne watched her from across the table and laughed.

"You'll need to get used to that." He patted his new wife's hand on the tablecloth and she beamed up at him.

"I love being Mrs Jeffs," she replied with a coy smile.

"I suppose I will." Hana pushed the glass of wine in a circle using the stem. "I like how it sounds."

The new Mrs Jeffs grinned. "It suits you."

They turned their attention to the dance floor as Pete's antics drove the other dancers away, including Henrietta and the sports teacher. "Whatever happened with that incident?" Gwynne asked, breaking into the silence as Pete moved on to the 'Chicken Dance.'

"Which incident?" Hana asked and Gwynne's eyes widened.

"You mean there were more than just the mugging? Oh yeah, I guess there was the broken windscreen too." He turned to explain to his wife. "A woman and male teenager attacked Hana in the chapel car park after work one night. They tried to snatch her handbag. I was at a cricket meeting and we managed to grab the boy."

"That's awful!" Her eyes widened in sympathy. "I didn't know."

"Oh," Hana waved her hand in dismissal. "The police didn't contact me about that again. It disappeared into the ether, like everything else that happens to me." She leaned forward. "Did you know my car went missing a few weeks later?"

"No!" Gwynne sat back in his chair, surprise in his eyes. "I assumed you changed it for the big off-roader."

Hana shook her head. "That's Logan's. I borrowed it. I've replaced it now with a Honda. The cops don't know where my other one went. It disappeared from the garage I contracted to mend the bumper."

"Bumper?" Gwynne's eyebrows joined in the middle. "What did you do to the bumper?"

Hana swallowed. Her catalogue of incidents seemed ludicrous and unbelievable. The happiness of her marriage lost its glow as she overwrote it with misery. She couldn't let that happen. "Just a minor ding." She dismissed it with a casual wave of her hand. "But you guys caught the boy who mugged me, didn't you?" she asked. "I wonder what happened to him."

Gwynne snorted and sat back in his chair. "Court. Or at least I'd hope so. Nice kid. Terrible home life. I'm not sure who paid his fees, but they wanted something better for him than becoming a criminal. Mind you, when they come from that kind of background, they often regress into it."

Hana gaped. "You know him?"

"Didn't you?" Gwynne rubbed his face in confusion. He shrugged in dismissal. "I assumed you did but perhaps he never ventured into your part of the school. I acted as the Year 9 dean in his first year so I saw him a lot. Stupid kid. Heaps of potential wasted."

Hana started with such violence, the drink slopped from her glass and onto the table. She watched the liquid pool; concentration etched into her face. Gwynne's wife mopped at it with a napkin. "This isn't the right time to discuss it," she chided him. "Not on Hana's wedding day."

"Sorry." Gwynne winced. "I didn't think."

Hana shook her head. "It's fine. An Old Boy of the school. I never saw that coming."

Gwynne's wife made her excuses and headed to the bathroom. He leaned forward to apologise. "Just forget it," he said. "It sounds like your car became a liability and it's gone now."

Hana nodded and let him believe it, wishing she could too.

-2-

Logan and Hana bid their guests goodbye as the evening drew to a close and most of them travelled back to Auckland or Hamilton. Izzie seemed calmer as she and Hana hugged goodbye. "Where are you staying?" Hana asked, kissing Elizabeth's sleeping face.

"We'll drive up to Drury. It's half an hour from here." Izzie smiled. "Marcus' parents haven't seen Beth since we moved south, so we'll spend tonight with them and fly home tomorrow."

"Thank you for coming." Hana's face crumpled. "I appreciate how hard it is with a baby."

"You're worth it." Izzie's smile held a panicked quality and Hana's heart clenched.

She brushed her daughter's hair away from her caramel forehead. "Let me know if there's anything I can do to help."

Marcus squeezed Hana's arm as he kissed her cheek, giving her a knowing look which summed up the unspoken promise to look after Isobel. "Goodbye, Mrs Du Rose," he said and smirked. "Bless ya."

The staff from school left in dribs and drabs, uttering their congratulations. Logan kept his arm around Hana. "If I was a betting man, I'd wager everyone knows about our wedding before staff briefing on Monday," he whispered.

Hana's eyes narrowed in dreaded anticipation. Ethel Bowman's flaccid face and multiple chins wafted across her inner vision wearing a look of victory. The issue of Caroline's rage followed a close second.

"What's wrong?" Logan sensed her anxiety and his grip tightened.

"Oh, just imagining Ethel Bowman's reaction. She'll want to know why she wasn't invited and then she'll move onto claiming it as a matchmaking victory."

Logan shrugged. "That's easy. Tell her I organised the whole thing and she's welcome to moan at me if she wants. We both know she wouldn't dare." Logan took Hana's fingers in his and smoothed the skin surrounding her new wedding ring. "Let her hear from someone else how I've known and loved you for decades. Who cares?"

"Guess so." Hana smiled and rested her chin against his shirt, smiling up at him through relieved green eyes. "I'll send her to you then, shall I?" She didn't ask who she should send an apoplectic Caroline to.

"For sure." Logan kissed the end of Hana's nose. "You now have access to the most useful words in the English dictionary."

"What are they?" Hana cocked her head to one side like a little bird.

Logan narrowed his grey eyes and adopted a somber expression. "My husband wouldn't like it." He delivered the line with a sexy lift of his lips.

Hana snorted. "Oh that's awesome. I forgot about that sentence. Did you know there are others too?"

"There are?"

"Yeah." Hana nodded with confidence. "There's heaps. 'I must check with my husband,' and, 'I think my husband has plans for that weekend.' There's a whole range to choose from." She sighed. "It's gonna be amazing."

"Steady on!" Logan snorted. "You can't use me as the get-out for everything, woman."

"I can and will." Hana smiled with satisfaction. She glanced at her watch. "Gosh, we'll get back to Culver's Cottage really late."

"I booked us a room," Logan whispered, pressing his body into hers and moving his lips across the skin under Hana's earlobe.

"Aw that's so thoughtful," she breathed. "But what about poor Tiger? He must be going out of his kitty mind cooped up at home."

"It's ok Mum," Bodie interjected, seeking the newlyweds out to say goodbye. "I'm staying at your place tonight. He'll be fine. I checked on him earlier when I drove to get Amy."

"Oh, thank you." Hana's expression flooded with relief.

"Yeah." Bodie slanted his eyes and shot Logan a look of challenge. "We'll talk when you get back. What time are you leaving tomorrow?"

"I'm not sure." Hana glanced back at Logan and saw his jaw flex. He moved away to help his father dismantle a trestle table which fought the old man with its spindly metal legs.

"Watch your fingers Dad!" Logan took the table from his father and collapsed it. He tuned back in to Hana's body language whilst folding the next table. She looked tense. From Bodie's uncomfortable expression, Logan saw the conversation going downhill and hovered between involving himself and staying out of it. Hana's fingers clenched as she stood facing her son, releasing as he leaned in and kissed her cheek. She smiled and Logan exhaled the breath clogging up his chest.

She disappeared outside with Bodie and his companions, returning to the ballroom shivering. "It's frosty already," she announced. The table Alfred rolled across the parquet floor wobbled on its circular edge, threatening to squash him if he made a wrong move.

"First of many," Alfred called back, rolling the table into the cupboard. It picked up speed as it went through the double doors and a deafening crash followed. "Oh shit!" came the muffled voice. "Forgot that was there."

Logan ignored the banging and crashing from inside the cupboard and the sound of Alfred talking to a number of chairs and one round, stubborn table. He pushed his arms around Hana's shaking body and linked his fingers across her breasts. "Geez you're cold. What was that all about with your son?" He kept the question light but Hana felt his anxiety.

She shrugged. "He wanted to talk. He said it's urgent. I usually drop everything and listen, but I don't know when we'll be home tomorrow. He doesn't like not having me on speed dial anymore."

"We shouldn't be late," Logan replied, rubbing her back to warm her. "Will he wait?"

Hana sighed. "I don't know, Loge. Maybe. Maybe not."

"Sorry." Logan's breath felt warm against her neck and Hana pulled him closer. "When I asked Bodie to check the cat on Friday night, I expected him to come to the party alone. What's the story with that little kid? Is it some deep, dark Johal secret?"

"You could say that." Hana rolled her eyes and jerked at the sound of another deafening crash and a yell from Alfred.

"Sorry." Logan let go of her and raced towards the cupboard.

In the kitchen later, Miriam held a cold compress to Alfred's head and chastised him. "How many times have I told you to leave those damn tables alone? The staff have no trouble with them. It's just you!"

"There's a knack to it!" His attempt to defend himself played into her hands.

"Yes," she retorted, brandishing the compress like a brick. "And you don't have it!"

The wounded soldier sat on a chair in the warm kitchen, sulking as his wife examined the bruise on his head and poured brandy into a small tumbler. Alfred reached for it and received a slap on the back of his head. "Not for you," Miriam snapped. "It's for me. For my bad nerves, which you get on!"

Alfred's bottom lip protruded in a childish display of attention seeking and Hana watched in fascination as Miriam capitulated. She poured three more glasses and pushed one of them across, not near enough to show forgiveness, but enough to make him reach. Alfred downed it in a few quick swallows and smacked his lips. "For the shock," he muttered, winking at Hana.

Miriam shoved a glass towards her and Hana sculled it in one. She pushed her tumbler back for more and Miriam hesitated for a second before refilling it. Hana saw her bug her eyes at Alfred. "I'm not an alcoholic," Hana said, cradling the liquor in her hands and watching the colours change in the light. "But it's been one heck of a day."

Logan closed the kitchen door behind him, shaking his head at his father. "Nice mess you made of the cupboard," he grumbled. He noticed Hana staring at the brandy and raised an eyebrow. "But babe," he said, sounding disappointed. "I thought we agreed to keep your problem between us."

"What?" Hana's cheeks flushed and Logan's parents turned towards her, judgement in their eyes. His laugh sounded brutal in the silent kitchen. Hana pouted. "Not funny, Logan."

He shrugged. "You got trolleyed here last time," he said and Hana squirmed in discomfort. Logan noticed Miriam's expression and laughed harder. "It's a joke, Mum!"

Miriam frowned, her eyes narrowing to grey slits. "You never joke, son."

Hana groaned and put her hands over her face. Her feet ached and she longed for the oblivion that overindulging might bring. Miriam stroked the brandy bottle, reducing even that faint hope.

Logan declined Miriam's offer of the remaining glass. "Na, I'm good thanks." He watched Hana clench and unclench her jaw and realised he'd hurt her. "Hana's not an alcoholic," he said, quirking his left eyebrow upwards and aiming the comment at his mother. "Poor joke." He thumped into the chair next to Hana and draped his arm over her shoulders, studying her from beneath his long eyelashes. "You look tired, babe. Big night aye?"

Hana nodded. "Yeah." She bit back a retort about her drunken state, her mood jaded by the memory of three wasted drinks she didn't get to enjoy. Instead, she rested her head against him with a nod and sighed.

Logan jerked his head towards his mother. "Hone from the township helped put the cupboard back together." His tone sounded light as he leaned across to examine Alfred's head. "That looks sore. It's gonna hurt tomorrow."

Alfred pouted and looked even more pathetic. He pushed his glass towards the bottle, inching it there a fraction at a time as though expecting a guillotine to dismantle hand and glass. Miriam moved the bottle away and glared at her husband. "You shouldn't drink after a head injury."

"You gave me the first one!" Alfred complained, but Miriam ignored him with practiced ease.

He shrugged and pushed his bottom lip higher. His grey-eyed gaze fell on Logan. "It's only youse gets the sympathy, boy. Maybe I should get the curse."

Hana sensed the tension in the room hike and sat up, staring at Alfred in surprise. "What curse?"

"Alfred Du Rose!" Miriam shouted. "Shut your mouth!" Her voice wavered and Hana's eyes widened in fear. Logan's body stiffened next to her and she heard his sharp inhale. Alfred's jaw clenched in irritation and he pushed himself away from the table, creaking his old bones into a standing position.

"I'll finish the tidying," he stated, sounding cowed while his eyes flashed opposite emotions.

"I'll help." Logan eyed Hana sideways. "Will you be okay for a while?"

Hana nodded, the movement slow and non-committal. Her heart sped up in panic as she watched him leave the room. Miriam reached for her glass. Her fingers shook and slopped the refill over the sides. "So you went along with it then?" She sounded jaded, struggling for control as she ran arthritic hands across eyes which lost their childish liveliness to deep seated spite.

"I didn't just go along with it." Hana injected indignation into her voice. "I married Logan because I love him."

Miriam's grey eyes drilled into hers, ready to inflict harm at the sound of any wrong word. The little old lady act melted behind the face of a dreadful adversary.

"You seemed pleased." Hana tried to keep the whine from her voice.

Miriam snorted. "I am actually. I like you. You've a way to go before this family trusts you, but I believe that time will come." She nodded as she said the last sentence as though agreeing with herself. "I heard you met the other one." So much bile accompanied the mention of Caroline, Hana stopped with her glass halfway to her lips. The older woman's teeth gritted shut and her jaw flexed with passionate anger. Miriam launched into a vitriolic monologue. "You keep that bitch away from my boy!" she spat, her eyes widening in fury. "She dangled him like a fly on a spider's web. She's a toxic, spiteful piece of trash. Logan was her fall guy and the best thing he ever did was walk away when she humiliated him at the altar. It wasn't tears of sadness I shed. Alfie and I never felt so relieved. We're simple people, Hana. We don't ask for much, but respect from our whānau." Miriam paused for breath. "That bitch won't let a wedding ring get in her way, so you hold onto my boy tight."

Hana took a deep breath. "I share an office with her at work. I hoped she might leave us alone now."

Miriam scoffed and her drink sprayed across the table. "Sorry to disappoint you, girly. Married men are just her sort of challenge. The last sucker was wed to my niece." Miriam gripped Hana's arm, her fingernails digging into flesh. "Keep Logan away from her. Promise me? They aren't meant to be together. The old kuia said so. If I'm not around to stop her, you must!"

Hana nodded her head in a jerky motion, fear and dismay growing inside her chest. "Why wouldn't you be around?" she asked, her voice faltering.

Miriam shrugged. "I can't see the future kōtiro. You must be his rear guard."

Hana scoffed. "If Logan wants to cheat with Caroline, I won't beg him to stay." Her upper lip curled in disgust and the old woman baulked. Hana rose, unable to cope as Miriam bounced between gentle elderly mother-in-law and frantic-lunatic, dangerous to be around.

Hana pushed her chair back and edged sideways while Miriam downed another tot of spirit and swayed in her seat. Hana hovered by the door, not sure where her bedroom might be. She wanted to escape the crazy lady, but felt responsible for her in the absence of anyone else. "Nice looking boy, that one of yours," she heard Miriam sigh. "My Barry turned heads too, not handsome like Logan but fine-boned and gentle. A bit like your boy."

Hana swallowed, compassion overriding her desire to retreat. "I'm sorry," she whispered. "We aren't meant to bury our own children."

Miriam shook her head and poured another tumbler of brandy. It looked bigger than two fingers and Hana's brow knitted with anxiety. "We're not," the old lady agreed. "They should lower us into the ground." A tear hit the scarred wooden table and Hana inhaled. The compassionate side of her nature took charge. She knelt beside Miriam's chair and the old lady's shoulders heaved. Hana stroked her back, feeling the knotty spine poking through her blouse.

"I'm so sorry," she whispered. "I can't imagine how hard it was."

Miriam sniffed. "It's all my fault. I caused it."

"No. It's natural to blame yourself but it's not true."

"It is!" Miriam's eyes flashed a warning, insanity dancing across her expression. Hana rose and took a step back in alarm.

The sound of voices echoed in the corridor. Like the flick of a switch, Miriam composed herself. She rubbed her eyes and pushed grey hair out of her face. By the time Logan and Alfred re-entered the kitchen, she stood at the sink washing the last of the big saucepans.

"You ready for bed?" Logan touched Hana's hand, raising his eyebrows in surprise at the way she jerked away from him. Her silent, wooden nod unnerved him further. His gaze took in Miriam's frantic scrubbing and he jerked his head towards Alfred.

Upstairs in Logan's old bedroom, Hana found it hard to settle. She lay on her stomach with her arms wedged beneath a pillow and her face buried. Logan called to her from the bathroom. "You don't mind staying in here, do you?" Hana heard him rinse his mouth out after cleaning his teeth. "I just felt I wanted to be here with you. It's where I used to imagine finding you and starting our life together."

"It's fine," Hana conceded, covering her yawn. "I just want a bed. I don't care where it is."

Painted in neutral colours, the room boasted cream walls and an accent navy wallpaper behind the bed. Dark blue blackout curtains decorated the floor to ceiling windows. Logan emerged from the bathroom, the lamplight defining his muscular chest and a white towel wrapped around his waist. "It used to look crap in here," he said, flicking the light switch with his hand. "Ripped wallpaper and draughty window frames. I think my Uncle Reuben had this room before I was born."

He laid on the bed next to Hana and his fingers traced a line down her bare back. "I always sleep in here." Logan sighed and the awful thought rose into Hana's brain, escaping without filtering.

She sat up, exposing her naked breasts. "Please tell me you never shared this bed with Caroline." Her top lip creased upwards in disgust and she flipped her legs over the side of the bed.

"No!" Logan leaned across and grabbed her forearm. "She never stayed in this house."

Hana flapped her arm at the pillows. "I don't think I can sleep here." She wrested her arm free, feeling the familiar smart begin in her wrist. Standing, she took the sheets with her to cover herself and edged towards the window.

"Hana!" Logan knelt up on the mattress. "She never set foot in this room."

Hana stopped her backwards movement, searching Logan's face for truth. "Promise?" she demanded, her face twisted in misery.

"I promise." Pain flooded Logan's eyes and he let his hands drop to the mattress. "All I can ask you to do is trust me."

Hana's eyes narrowed. "I know but it's hard."

He nodded and settled onto the bed, leaning back against the pillows. His hands ran through his hair, hiding the misgiving in his face. "I won't hurt you, Hana," he whispered. "Not deliberately."

She snorted. "Nobody means to. They don't wake up in the morning and think, hey, I know, I'll cheat on my wife this morning."

"What?" Logan looked alarmed and he placed his feet on the rug next to the bed. When he stood, Hana took a step backwards.

He shook his head. "I don't cheat, Hana. Never have and never will. You're it, babe. There's no Plan B."

Hana shook her head. "Your mother thinks you might. With Caroline." The name choked in the back of her throat.

Logan closed his eyes and his jaw worked, creating a moving line through his cheek. "Then she's wrong!" he bit. "And I'm bloody disappointed in her."

Hana strayed backwards and the sheet slid from the mattress. Logan edged around the bed towards her as though cornering a frightened mare. He let his hands fall to his sides, minimising the threat. His voice sounded soothing and gentle. "I want you, Hana," he said, lulling her into a state of doubt. "Nobody else. I've wanted you my whole life. Come to bed with me." He bent and gathered the twisted sheet into his hands. Hana squeaked as he tugged it towards him, letting it feed through his fingers like a game of tug-of-war. She thrashed, but he reeled her in, hauling hand over hand until she needed to make the choice between decency and letting go. "Please believe me," he whispered and his breath against her cheek caused a shiver to run down her spine.

With every moment as Mrs Du Rose, Hana sensed the gnawing loneliness drain away and a long craved sense of companionship raise its head. She dared to wish she might be happy again. She swallowed and her eyes widened with conflict, emeralds flashing against the harsh spot lighting. Logan enticed her with promised security and the lure of his gorgeous body. Hana sighed. Only God knew the moment he'd take everything from her.

Logan's lips brushed against her cheek and his hands searched her body for familiar curves. He slid his fingers over her hipbone and tugged the sheet away. Hana let it fall and sank into his embrace, recognising a fight she'd never win. She abandoned thoughts of dead husbands, disapproving sons or vitriolic ex-girlfriends, succumbing to the rising pressure in her chest. It urged her to let go of everything belonging to the past.

Logan's brand of lovemaking proved slow, passionate and insistent, waking Hana's sleeping sexuality and increasing the craving. "I love you." His breath moved Hana's fringe as his mouth sought hers. He didn't give her time to answer, scooping her up and laying her on the bed. He poured his love into her soul and soothed her when she cried afterwards. Her heart welled with emotions she couldn't explain, knowing people like her didn't get second chances like this.

Hana woke in the dawn hours of Sunday, aware something troubled her but unsure what. Seeing Logan's outline next to her in the grey light reminded her she wasn't used to someone else in her bed. An icy breeze whistled through a gap in the window frame and she snuggled further into the blankets seeking warmth. Logan's arm under her head made her neck ache and she wriggled away. He disturbed and his breathing changed, his fingers snaking across the mattress until they contacted Hana's thigh. She held her breath as he exhaled as though finding reassurance in her presence. The beginnings of a snore blossomed and she smiled. Widowhood taught her how much she would've given to hear Vik snore next to her during the long, miserable nights after his death. She lay on her side and watched Logan's chest rise and fall, doubting her ability to be happy.

"I love you, Logan Du Rose." Hana reached out tentative fingers and stroked his cheek, feeling his stubble scratch her delicate pads. Her hand edged upwards towards the silken strands of his wavy hair. In the dim light, she overestimated and poked him in the eye. His hand clamped around her wrist like a vice and before she could blink, he spun her onto her back beneath him.

"What're you doing, wahine?" he growled and Hana cringed beneath him.

"I'm so sorry!" she gushed. "I wanted to stroke your hair."

Logan rolled off her, getting to his feet and striding into the bathroom. "That bloody hurt," he grunted.

Hana followed and hovered in the doorway, her fingers clinging to the wooden frame. The outline of defined muscle rippled over his back and shoulders as Logan ran cold water and scooped it onto his face. Silky boxer shorts rode low on his hips and Hana watched a long scar snake down the right-hand side of his body. Red and raised, it started inside his shorts below his right hip and ran upwards into his armpit. Hana ventured closer, intrigued by the jaggedness of the skin and the oddness of its healing. "I'm sorry," she repeated. "I didn't mean to hurt you."

Logan lowered his arm obscuring the ugly scar. He towelled his face and ran his hands through his hair. "No harm done," he said. Hana's lips pursed in guilt at the redness of his eye and she dragged a towel from the rail to cover her nakedness. His eyes narrowed and alertness filled his body at the cloth barrier she placed between them. "Why are you awake so early? Did something disturb you?"

Hana slid around the doorframe and back into the cold bedroom. "It's unfamiliar. Different noises."

"What kind of noises?" He followed, matching her step for step.

Hana huffed in impatience. "It doesn't matter. Just noises." Logan climbed onto the bed after her, his gaze predatory. "Snoring noises." She regretted it in an instant and his eyes flashed.

"I don't snore."

Hana shrugged and pushed herself between the sheets, the towel scratchy against her nakedness. "How do you know if you're sleeping?"

"Oh. I just assumed I didn't." Logan bit his lip and disappointment flicked across his face.

He settled on his side, adjusting the pillow and staring at the ceiling. The distance between them seemed insurmountable and Hana snuggled down with a sigh. She lay there for a while, jiggling around to get comfortable. Logan's breathing changed and she listened to rain pattering against the window and watched the dawn light grow stronger. Her mind ran through a list of the unspoken protocols for sleeping with a husband. She assumed it was not okay to wake him up to tell him about the rain. Having poked him in the eye after less than forty-eight hours of marriage, it seemed a little rude.

Hana closed her eyes and listened to Logan's shallow breathing. She tuned into it and hoped the rhythmic beat might help her sleep. She focused, counting the number of ins and outs, until he stopped. Then he started again. It continued for a while and there seemed no pattern to the periods of nothing. Growing anxious, Hana sat up and stared at Logan's back. Another period of eerie silence followed. Edging closer, she placed her ear near to his head, desperate for him to breathe. When he didn't, she panicked and prodded him in the back.

"What?" Logan scooted forward so fast; he tumbled from the bed and landed on the floor. Hana heard the bump and watched in horror as his hands gripped the mattress and he hauled himself upright.

"Sorry, sorry, sorry," she whined for the second time that night. "But you fell asleep and stopped breathing!"

"I didn't sleep, woman! I was trying not to snore." Logan rubbed his painful eye. "I need danger money to go to bed with you!"

"Thanks," Hana grumbled. "I've said I'm sorry."

Logan clambered into bed and they settled again. He clung to the furthest edge of the bed and Hana wriggled around in the ridiculous towel. She determined to stay awake until she could enjoy a shower without waking the whole hotel, but sleep took her anyway. Her dream plunged her into forgotten memories of Logan and the worst day of her life. The day she lost everything.

The Circle Line tube train slid through the tunnels of the London Underground at terrifying speeds. Hana glanced down at the filthy seat and focused her attention on a ratty hole between her and Vik. He shifted next to her, concentrating on dabbing nasty cuts on his dark eyebrow and lip. Both continued to ooze. Hana felt the knot in her chest and the tears on her cheeks. Her father's words rang in her brain. Whore. Slut. Disgrace. They melded together as a damning sentence, condemning her to burn in Hell. Her tears blurred the vision of her brother's angry fists pummeling Vik and she heaved in a breath. Hana reached out a hand and touched his thigh, wanting to connect with him. He shrugged her off and continued his dabbing.

The child in her womb jabbed an elbow into her ribs and Hana inhaled with pain. Despite everything, she loved the baby already and smoothed her fingers across the yellow fabric of her dress. The hard crown of a skull moved beneath her hand, offering reassurance and invoking a primeval sense of maternalism.

"The next station is Earl's Court. Due to maintenance works please change here for Ealing, Ruislip and Heathrow." Hana jumped at the voice issuing from the speaker above her head. She glanced sideways at Vik and he shook his head. Not this stop. She blew through pursed lips, wondering how much more misery she could take in one day. The memory of the sadness in her mother's eyes haunted her. She needed to know what to expect from Vik's Sikh family but he wouldn't meet her gaze.

The woman in the seats opposite reached into her pocket and drew out a handkerchief. Hana watched her through lowered lashes, scrubbing at her nose with her hand. Thick foundation covered a patch of swirls on the woman's chin and they fascinated her. Decorum dictated she look away and she forced herself. "Here, kōtiro." The woman leaned across and held out the handkerchief. She lifted her other hand and pointed to grey eyes which glittered in her own face. "Take it," she said and flapped the pale blue cloth.

Hana swallowed and reached out a shaking hand. She nodded in thanks and lifted the soft triangle of fabric to her eyes. The teenage boy shifted in his seat and frowned, removing his gaze from Hana and glancing sideways at the woman. He opened his mouth to speak and she shook her head. Dark curls identical to his slid from a bun at her nape. He closed his lips and his jaw flexed. His gaze settled back on Hana, intense and searching. Grey eyes bored into her soul and she shut him out, numbing herself against any more feelings as she looked away. She studied the underground map above the teenager's head and fear rose as they drew closer to their destination. To lose one family could be classed as careless but two would be foolish. As the speaker sounded above her head, announcing the end of life as she knew it, Hana opened her mouth and screamed.

"Hana, no, Hana. Geez, what's wrong?"

She gulped for air and batted his chest with her fists. It made no impact and Logan held her tighter. "The train," Hana garbled, running a hand over her flat stomach and reeling back in confusion. "It's gone."

"What train?" Logan soothed her with kisses to her cheeks. His body curled around her, forming a cage of protection.

"The baby's gone," Hana gasped and her fingers fluttered over her stomach.

"Shhhh." Logan held her and let her surface from sleep, asking no more questions which taxed his ability to understand the muddled answers. "You're safe," he whispered. "No trains, no babies. Just me and you." His fingers traced gentle circles across her bare back and shoulders. "Lie down." He pulled her with him as he lay back against the pillows, hauling her on top and covering them with the sheets.

Hana felt her heart rate slow and heaved out a breath, resting her cheek against the downy hair of Logan's chest. "I have nightmares," she whispered, her voice sounding cracked and strained. "I forgot to tell you."

"It's okay." Logan kissed the top of her head. "I'm not going anywhere."

The words sounded good to Hana's fractured heart and she pressed her lips against his chest. "Take my mind off it," she demanded, curling her fingers around the back of his neck.

Hana woke late to the sound of rain beating hard on the side of the building and spurting in rivulets down the windows. She opened her eyes with deliberate slowness, distracted by the sight of her unused nightdress draped over the headboard. Logan lay on his side facing away from her and Hana absorbed the warmth from his long back. The scratchy hotel towel felt bunched and uncomfortable beneath her hip.

With precise movements, Hana reached up and tugged at the corner of her silky nightdress, careful not to move the mattress. The material slithered down, landing over her face and making her stifle a sneeze. Slipping from the bed backwards, she slid into her nightie, feeling relief as she covered up the scars of motherhood. Her bladder urged her to seek the ensuite bathroom and she tiptoed around the bed, her eyes widening as Logan snuffled in his sleep. Too late she noticed his cowboy boots sticking out from under the bed. They winked out from beneath his discarded boxer shorts and Hana let out a yelp of pain as she hit the floorboards. "Oh!" she groaned, cradling her wrist in the other hand.

She heard Logan stir and winced, grappling for something to haul herself upright. Thinking she'd grabbed the footboard she pulled, hitting the ground a second time as swathes of duvet cover and sheets landed on her head.

"What are you doing, wahine?" Logan demanded, yanking the duvet off her face. Hana glanced up at his glorious nakedness and groaned with embarrassment. She buried her face in the crook of her good arm and cradled her wrist against her chest. "Hana?" He seized her by the shoulders and gave her a shake. "Are you okay?"

She nodded, her cheeks flushed pink. "Why did you marry me?" she whimpered.

Logan snorted and his lips curved upwards in amusement. "Because I love you and you're entertaining." He shivered and scooped her into his arms, lifting her without effort. "And now I'm freezing." His gaze darted sideways towards the bathroom and he smirked. "How about our first hot shower together?"

Hana gave a tiny nod and narrowed her eyes. "As long as you don't look too hard at my body."

Logan threw his head back and laughed. "I've got a licence which says I can look at whatever I want." Long strides took them towards the door. He set her on her feet and his brows knitted into a dark line. "Hana, why is your nightdress inside out?"

=3=

They enjoyed a breakfast of bacon and eggs with the family stragglers from the party. Miriam bustled around with purpose and importance.

"Is there any more bacon, Mum?" Michael asked from next to Hana, his mouth bulging with bread. Hana slid her gaze towards Logan as she felt him stiffen next to her, watching his jaw work against his cheek. His veiled tension unnerved her and her fork clattered against her plate. "Don't you want that?" Before she could answer, Michael's knife flipped her tomato onto his pile of food. Her appetite went with it.

"You're disgusting!" Liza pouted across from them, nibbling on an assortment of fruit next to a dollop of yoghurt. "You're a doctor. Don't you know how to protect your arteries?"

Michael laughed, dodging sideways as Miriam placed more bacon on his plate. She stared at Hana's abandoned cutlery with a narrowed brow. "I always eat well when I come home," Michael continued with a grin at his mother. Hana saw his gaze flick to the side of Logan's face as though baiting him. He noticed her watching and his brow furrowed. "Has my brother explained our weird family to you?" he asked, jerking his head towards Logan.

Hana shrugged and shook her head, feeling her ponytail swish across her back. "It's not relevant," she replied, her tone nonchalant. "I've married Logan, not his family."

"Good answer!" Michael nodded in appreciation. "He picked a woman with looks and brains. Well done Logan. I didn't think he had it in him, did you Liza?"

Liza's eyes narrowed and Hana avoided her gaze, sensing the condemnation with no need to see it written on her regal expression. The single rasher of bacon turned to ash in her throat. Liza leaned forward. "It takes a village to raise a child, Hana." Her grey eyes bored into Hana's face. "Like it or not, you've married this family and we shall hold you accountable."

"Accountable for what?" Hana glanced sideways at Logan and saw his jaw clench.

"Leave her alone!" he snapped and Liza recoiled in surprise.

Hana jumped at the barb in his voice and pushed her bottom harder into the back of her seat. She'd half-packed their belongings upstairs and wondered how long it might take her to sling the rest into the Honda. A speedy escape seemed preferable to the awful tension in the room. Logan rose to rinse his breakfast plate and Hana watched a chef beat eggs in a corner of the industrial kitchen. His white clad arms whisked in a frantic motion. Miriam leaned over a woman unloading the dishwasher. "Start on the bedrooms when you're done there," she said and received a nod in return.

Hana opened her mouth to excuse herself and Michael beat her to it. "Wouldn't you get paid more if you were a qualified teacher?" he asked, biting on egg yolk like a hungry bear.

"Probably." Hana wished to avoid a conversation with the potential to go downhill.

"Didn't you go to university?"

"Yes. I have an English Honours degree."

"So you could still do it."

"But I don't want to. I have no desire to teach." Hana felt colour rising in her neck, overheating her from the inside. Battling it worsened the flush. She kept her voice level. "What's the big deal about teaching?"

Michael shrugged, his expression nonchalant. "Just seems a bit dumb is all. Working in an office for peanuts when you could earn more."

"I've done just fine, thank you. I like my job and I'm financially secure. I'll be fine."

"Yeah, you will now!" Liza's barbed comment sounded loud enough for Hana to hear. The pecking festival left her breathless and disconcerted.

"What's that supposed to mean?" She gulped and looked to Logan for help, watching him turn and lean his bum against the counter. His arms folded across his chest and his face exuded thunder. Michael opened his mouth to start again.

"Shut it!" Logan's command carried across the large kitchen. A woman with a laden tray widened her eyes and stopped in her tracks, scurrying on when she realised he didn't mean her. Logan's eyes flashed and he gritted his teeth. "Quit cross-examining my wife. Or get out."

Hana gaped as nobody challenged him. Miriam placed toast racks into a tall cupboard with careful hands and remained silent. Michael shoveled food into his mouth and Liza slurped coffee opposite without comment. Logan reclaimed his seat next to Hana, stretching his long legs out in front of her and resting his boots on the beam between the stout table legs. He turned his body in towards her like a human shield and she shot him a look of gratitude. The atmosphere plummeted towards freezing point and she pondered her escape with more urgency.

Liza continued to observe Hana across the kitchen table. She resembled an eagle, circling the up draughts before plunging onto its prey with talons and hooked open beak. Hana understood her success in the law courts. The woman could sever heads from bodies without moving out of her seat. Her treatment of Miriam seemed cursory and Hana cringed as she fussed around her daughter for the price of an insincere smile.

"Will you stay another night?" Miriam asked, brushing Liza's shoulder with the back of her hand.

Liza glanced across at Logan in response and shook her head. "No. Big case starting tomorrow."

"Oh." Her mother's face sank into a haze of wrinkles and Hana felt a spark of compassion begin in her breast. Miriam turned to Michael. "Are you staying, tāne?"

He looked up from his plate and nodded. "Yeah, sounds good."

Miriam smiled with pleasure. "That's wonderful," she gushed.

Hana became aware of the female wait staff shooting looks between Logan and Michael. Logan ignored them but Michael promised assignations with his sultry grey eyes. They tittered in the corner of the room over the pretence of polishing cutlery and discomfort made Hana squirm in her seat. Michael winked at a teenage waitress and Logan narrowed his eyes. "Don't!" he snapped and Michael laughed, giving him a two fingered salute in a childish display of defiance.

Hana watched Logan's slender fingers tap a beat on the table. Veins and tendons disappeared into his shirt, wrapped around olive wrists like corded ropes. Hana followed their route with her eyes, knowing the capable muscular frame hiding beneath the expensive cloth. She imagined what he might use those hands for and felt her cheeks flush. Craving the safety of Logan's bedroom and the promise of more intimacy, she rubbed her fingers across his thigh and narrowed her eyes. His lips rose in one corner in a lopsided smile and a dimple appeared in his cheek. Hana watched from beneath her lashes and he winked in return. "I should finish packing," she whispered and watched him bite his lower lip.

Liza studied the exchange through hooded lids and heaved out an exaggerated sigh. Logan ignored her as he ran his hand along the outside seam of Hana's jeans, waking up the nerves in her thigh and leaning in for a kiss. "Need help?" he mouthed and Hana feigned coyness with a nonchalant shrug.

A car screeched outside, travelling too fast for the deep gravel surface. Wheels spun and stones peppered the long kitchen window as the vehicle slewed to a stop. Everyone jumped except Logan. He looked towards his mother. "Trouble?"

The slam of a car door and scrunch of footsteps followed. Miriam stood on tiptoe at the sink and peeped out through the long sash window. Her complexion blanched as she sought Logan with her eyes and gave him a look of helplessness. She sent a silent transmission and he left the room, gone before Hana could assess the situation with any clarity. A cool belt of air occupied his vacant space and her chest tightened. She heard his boot soles thud along the tiled floor, followed by the bang of the ornate front doors. Hana stood, shoving her chair with the backs of her knees. A dart of pain shot up her wrist as Michael gripped it one-handed, his fingers tight and uncompromising. His grey eyes flashed with veiled warning. "Leave it," he said, laying his fork down with his other hand. The steel behind his smile only hardened Hana's resolve.

"Let go of me!" She tugged her wrist and his grip tightened, drawing a hiss from between her teeth. "It hurts!" she snapped and slapped him around the face.

A collective gasp filled the room and Hana felt the eyes of the kitchen staff on her flushed cheeks. Cradling her wrist in her right hand, Hana fumbled her way through the heavy door and ran down the corridor. Her feet slapped against the tiles. She followed the sound of raised voices, one of them hysterical.

"She's gone, she's gone!" Tama stood at the bottom of the front steps, his back to Hana. She skidded to a halt at the top of the stairs and stopped the door banging behind her. Logan leaned his backside on the old car next to them, not attempting to quiet the teenager. A couple pulling a suitcase up the front steps gave the men sideways looks of concern. Hana offered a lame smile and moved sideways on the uppermost step to allow them to pass.

The door closed behind them and Hana watched the slump in the teenager's shoulders and knew what ailed him. Anka left, abandoning him like an unwanted pet. Her heart sank into her gut with sadness. "What a waste," she sighed, pressing her hand over her mouth. Anka sacrificed her job at the school, her marriage and children, her faith and friendships. All collateral damage as the promise of excitement faded against the bite of reality. Hana shook her head knowing Anka had torched every possible bridge back to her former life.

Tears of regret pricked her eyes as Hana stood in the wide doorway, the wind lifting her hair from her shoulders and tossing it around behind her. A wave of bitterness urged her to gather up the pea-sized gravel and throw handfuls into the air in temper. She hoped sex with the teenager made up for losing everything else, but doubted it.

Tama thrashed around in front of Logan, his body moving with stiffness and aggression. Hana heard him shift from begging to bargaining, his back towards her. "Please, tell me where she went. Your chick must know; they're friends."

"They were friends." Logan's voice remained calm. "You ruined that for her." He stared around the empty car park as though bored, his body language relaxed and unthreatening. Hana noticed how the family resemblance looked striking at close quarters and a doubt rose into her mind. "What do you want from me, Tama?" Logan asked.

His question acted as a catalyst and Tama's body folded from the waist. "Help me!" he exploded. "Tell me what to do."

Logan shook his head and Hana watched sympathy flicker in his expression. "I can't, mate. You've detonated your life like I said you would. I advised you not to move in with her and I asked you to stay in school. You did what you wanted and now you'll have to work through the consequences."

"Please!" Tama begged and Hana heard his voice rock with tears.

Logan stood and shifted his butt off the car. He shook his head. "Are you high, Tama? Did you take something?" His voice sounded level and Hana held her breath and backed towards the door.

"Screw you!" Tama spat. "Like you even care."

Logan's body language stiffened, his muscles flexing in readiness for trouble. "Stay at the bunkhouse and sleep it off," he advised, his voice calm and reasonable. "Make any trouble and I'll ask security to throw you out."

Tama reached out a hand, twisting Logan's shirt in his fingers as he passed. He dragged him close, almost overbalancing with the effort. "Where is she?" he yelled into Logan's face. "Tell me where that chick is. You know who I mean, don't you? The one you're banging. Where is she?"

Hana held her breath and Logan stopped walking. His body resembled a power pole, upright and immovable. Grey eyes flashed danger and he put his hand over Tama's fingers. "Let go of me and I won't break your face," Logan hissed. "But you ever speak about Hana like that again and I'll bury you. You just enjoyed your last free pass." He snatched his shirt free and sent Tama reeling backwards with a single push. Then he strode towards the stairs.

Hana shook as hatred boiled inside her against a man who slipped into her friend's life like a cuckoo and detonated it from the inside. Logan jerked his head to warn her to go inside, but she didn't move fast enough. Tama righted himself against the car door and turned to watch Logan walk away. He spotted Hana and lunged towards the stairs, garbled words erupting from his lips. "Where is she? You know where she is. Tell me where she went!"

Hana squeaked in fear as the frantic teenager lurched up the first step. She backed towards the door and fumbled with the handle. "Logan!" She shouted for help but he controlled the situation, intercepting Tama before he reached the next step. He dragged him backwards by the collar and Tama's lips parted in surprise.

"No!" Logan spun him around, leading him away from the steps. "Stay away from my wife!"

Hana told her feet to move and take her inside but they refused, keeping her on the smooth, flat terrace watching the awful scene unfold. She sensed her presence inflamed Tama's temper but couldn't tear herself away.

"Wife?" Tama screeched and his face crumpled in an ugly combination of misery and fury. "No! That's not fair!" He wrestled against Logan's grip on his collar and anger made him strong. Hana's feet took root on the landing, her heartbeat pounding in her ears and rendering her useless as the men struggled.

Despite the age gap, Logan got the upper hand and forced Tama's arm behind his back. The teenager grunted in pain. "I'll break it," Logan warned and Hana pressed her fingers to her lips. He shoved Tama towards the driver's door of the battered car, holding him upright as he pushed him against it. "I'll ask you again," he hissed. "Have you taken anything?"

"No!" Tama shouted into his face and Hana watched her husband recoil. His shirt strained tight as his torso bulged with muscle and his face remained hidden from her. Tama's cheeks paled and he quailed at whatever he saw in Logan's eyes. "I'm just upset." He swallowed. "She left me, Logan. What should I do?"

Logan took a step back and let go of Tama. Hana saw him shrug. "I don't know, mate. Dude, she used you, just like I said she would."

Without answering, Tama opened the car door and started to get in, fiddling around in his jeans for the keys. Shaking his head, Logan turned away and walked back up the stairs. His face oozed dark menace and Hana saw him as a stranger; a mysterious brooding force she didn't understand. She felt a wave of fear at the look in his grey eyes and held her breath.

Logan made it up the first two steps before Hana let out a strangled cry. "No!" she screamed and galvanised herself enough to move forward. She tripped down three steps and landed on her knees, unable to stop the spiteful backhander catching Logan a nasty blow across the left side of his body. A dull metallic clang cut through the air as he staggered backwards with a grunt of pain and almost fell. Hana screamed and crawled towards him, holding her arms over them both to protect them from the next blow. The crowbar whooshed through the air as Tama lifted it to shoulder height again. He hadn't finished.

Hana braced herself for the impact, needing to defend her husband. Logan's complexion slipped into a ghastly grey and he clutched his left arm close to his body. Tama cracked the metal bar against the concrete steps as Hana shoved her fist into his right leg, unbalancing him on the small ledge. "No!" she shrieked as Tama lifted the bar again, his face a mask of rage. She covered Logan with her body, cringing at the expected blow.

Hana saw shoes move past her vision. Tama's feet shifted backwards and he stumbled down the stairs, landing on his bum in the gravel. The metal bar flew wide. Michael Du Rose followed him and picked him up by the throat, slamming him backwards against the car. Hana lost interest as she felt Logan push against her. His breath came in rasps and she sat up, giving him air. She panicked at the look on his face, seeing beads of sweat break out on his forehead. Shaking arms held him as Michael shoved Tama back into the car and the engine started running. "Something broke, I heard it," Hana hissed, her voice breaking as she checked Logan's arm with inexperienced hands. "Let your brother check you out?"

"I'm fine!" Logan gritted his teeth and a strange look crossed his face. "He's not touching me. Don't say anything." His grey eyes dulled as he implored Hana to play along. She stood and helped him to his feet, supporting his weight up the stairs to the front door. A glance behind her showed Tama's face through the open driver's window. She saw a mix of emotions in his eyes and turned away sickened.

"I hate you so much!" she heard him scream at Michael, hatred in his wavering voice.

They made slow progress to the top of the stairs and a tourniquet gripped Hana's chest in a vice of breathlessness. "I don't know what to do," she whispered, leaning Logan against the door and reaching for her cell phone. She fumbled to unlock the screen in her haste and almost dropped it.

Long fingers with red varnished nails plucked it from her trembling hand and Hana exhaled in relief. "I need the cops," she stammered.

Liza's face creased in a sneer which involved every muscle. "We don't do things that way, pākehā. You need to learn the rules of the game!"

Hana recoiled in amazement, looking to Logan for direction. Liza singled her out as a white face amongst the brown and the racism shocked her. Logan's blank expression gave away nothing. He continued to shuffle towards the doorway, his left arm clasped to his side and every breath an effort. Miriam stood in their way and Hana grabbed her hand. "Do something!" she begged, recoiling at the blank look in the other woman's eyes. The silence deafened Hana and she swallowed as Liza slipped the phone into her jeans pocket out of reach. "You're sick," she gasped. She shook her head and supported Logan into the lobby. "You're all bloody sick."

Logan squeezed her shoulder and gave an almost imperceptible shake of his head. Hana pursed her lips and respected his wishes, keeping her anguished words inside. Nobody spoke and not one member of his gathered family tried to stop Logan's painful progress as he walked up the main staircase. Hana looked around at each of them in utter amazement, shaking her head in disgust. Then she followed him up the stairs, putting her energies into helping her husband.

Logan's breath came in short gasps at the top of the stairs. Reaching their room, he grappled with the keypad, punching the numbers in with a shaking hand. He shook his head at her offer of help. Inside, he collapsed onto the bed and lay there, ignoring her questions as though she wasn't there. "Let me help you!" Hana begged. "He broke a bone, Logan! I heard it!"

Silence met her pleas. Panicking, she paced the room and at the continued lack of response from Logan, packed the rest of their gear. "We need to get out of here," she muttered, hearing him groan in agony as he rolled onto his back. "They don't care!" she said, raising her voice. "They watched him hit you and wouldn't let me call the cops. What's wrong with them?"

Logan reached out a hand and the greyness in his face frightened her. Hana crouched next to his side. "What do you need?" she asked. "What can I do?"

"My wash bag," he murmured. "Can I have it?"

Hana wrenched it free of Logan's rucksack and helped him to a sitting position. Logan used his right hand to grapple around inside. "Let me do it," she said. "What are you looking for?"

Logan waved her away. "I'm good."

"I'll finish getting our stuff together." Hana ran around the room, checking for stray belongings. She found the green clip from her wedding day and pushed it into a pocket in the larger bag. Retrieving Logan's socks from under the bed, she put them with her own dirty washing. She looked around in time to see him shove something up his nose and faltered. "What's that?" she demanded, her fingers fluttering over the bag strap. "It's not drugs, is it?"

"It's a prescription," Logan said, shaking the bottle and repeating the exercise. His eyes watered and he dropped the bottle back into the bag. "It stops bruising."

"Like arnica?" Hana asked, dragging the bag towards the door. "Like that?"

Logan shook his head and ran a hand over his eyes. "No. That brings out bruising. I don't want that."

Hana plucked the bottle from the wash bag and Logan watched her sideways as she read the label. She didn't understand the chemical composition but recognised the pharmacy as local. Logan's name ran along the bottom of the label in capital letters and the date showed as recent. Her new husband watched her reaction. "It's nothing dodgy," he promised. "Can you drive?" He cracked open another bottle with his teeth and shook out the contents onto the bed.

Hana nodded and propped the bedroom door open with the bag. "For sure," she said and held out her hand.

"Thank you." Logan hauled himself from the mattress, popping four white painkillers into his mouth and swallowing without water.

"For what?" Hana's eyes searched his face, fear making her blind. She dived back and cleared up the tablets, shoving the remainder into the bottle and pushing it in her pocket. "For what?" she repeated, urgency in her voice.

Logan shook his head and winced at the action. "You tried to protect me with your hands," he said, his voice husky. He reached out and took her slender fingers in his. "He could've killed you."

Hana swallowed and tossed her head. "Can we go now?" she demanded.

Logan nodded and his expression softened. "I won't forget this, Hana," he said, his tone sincere.

"Nor will I!" she replied, her tone sarcastic.

Shock replaced Logan's smile as he grabbed his stomach and lurched towards the bathroom. He hurled himself to his knees and vomited into the toilet. Hana felt powerless, hovering in the doorway as he retched. She offered him a glass of water once he finished. "Drink this," she said, treating him as her child. "Sip it."

Logan exhaled, taking the glass and slurping the water. It ran down his chin and onto the floor, speckled with blood. He didn't speak, rising enough to perch his butt on the side of the wide bath. He cradled his arm and looked sick. Hana cleaned the toilet through a misplaced sense of guilt and then threw their remaining possessions into Logan's rucksack. "Up," she said to him as his colour returned. "We're leaving. Right now!"

Logan showed surprising reluctance and with his stomach empty of the sumptuous breakfast, looked less grey. "It's fine," he said, his words slurring. "We can't just run away."

"Are you freaking kidding me?" Hana shouted. "Don't change your mind. You asked me to drive and I need to get out of here."

Logan watched her dragging the bag. "Our stuff is mixed up," he said, brows knitting in discomfort. "I wanted it neat."

Hana snorted and added the rucksack to her load. "Our lives are mixed up!" she snapped. "I wanted that neat, so neither of us got what we desired."

"Mum's doing a roast lunch," Logan protested and Hana stared at him, her eyes wide with incredulity.

"I'm not staying now, so don't ask me to. I'll be in the car. Five minutes, Logan. That's how long I'll wait for you. Then I'm driving home and you'd better believe me. When I get there, I'm calling the cops."

Hana slung the rucksack over her shoulder and struggled with the heavier bag. It banged against her calves as she hauled it into the wide hallway. Her auburn hair escaped from her ponytail, swathing her shoulders in an amber carpet. Glancing backwards, she saw Logan standing where she left him. "I mean it Logan," she stated, her voice full of threat. "I'm leaving, with or without you."

Logan's eyelashes fluttered and he nodded. He pressed his right hand over his stomach to test his nausea and followed Hana out of the room. "I won't be long," he promised. "Wait for me." He turned right instead of left and walked the opposite way.

Hana wrestled the bag into the Honda and sat in the driver's seat, shaking from head to toe. Alarm bells sounded in her brain. "Oh God, I'm so sorry," she prayed to herself. "I've made a monumental mistake and now I can't ask you to help me." She drummed her fingers on the steering wheel and felt her insides churn. Logan never lied to her about his strange and volatile family, but he failed to impart the true picture of their odd and violent behaviour. Their lack of emotion terrified her.

Hana counted to one hundred and eighty as slowly as she could manage, reducing her racing heart rate as much as reaching the promised deadline. "Come on Logan!" She slapped the steering wheel and her wrist protested.

Passing the four-minute mark, she feared Logan wouldn't come. Not daring to think about the implications for her forty-eight hour marriage, Hana finished counting the final sixty seconds and started the engine. Her fingers shook against the key. Waiting a second longer with panic building, she saw him hobble towards the car and exhaled with relief. He worked hard to pretend he didn't nurse a serious injury, but Hana watched how he carried his left arm with care and maintained a rigid mask over his pain. He clambered into the Honda without using his left arm, reaching his right hand across his body to slam the door.

Nobody came from the house to wave them off. Biting at Logan in her anxiety, Hana snapped, "That was six minutes, not five! Don't you know the difference? You're the mathematician!" She shoved the gear lever into drive and shot away from the hotel, spraying gravel as she pulled out. Logan used his right arm to fasten his seatbelt, grunting as he pulled it around him. He indicated turns and direction changes with single word answers but rebuffed Hana's attempts to talk to him. She fought the urge to rant, shout and scream in the pattern of her previous marriage. Hindsight taught her to hold her tongue. It cost her.

They reached the outskirts of Huntly before Logan reached out and laid his right hand on Hana's thigh. His black lashes fluttered and high spots of colour showed on his cheeks. The sudden contact caused something tense inside her soul to snap like an elastic band and she turned her face away while hot tears slid down her cheeks. "Pull over," Logan commanded, indicating a wide lay-by ahead. Hana turned into it, the wheels skidding against loose grit. She sat with her hands gripping the steering wheel, fear and anger feeding her fragile nerves. Logan put his hand over hers, prying her fingers off the wheel. He fumbled undoing her seatbelt and pulled her towards him. "Sorry," he whispered. "I'm so sorry."

Hana dried her tears on her sleeve and restarted the engine, ignoring Logan's attempts to kiss her. "I'll drive," he offered, but Hana pushed his hand away.

Her glance in his direction held sarcasm. "I don't think so." She ignored the turn onto the Tainui Bridge, staying on the main highway and heading south. In Ngaruawahia, she pulled up in front of a neat wooden building. '24 Hour Accident and Emergency' flashed neon writing against the grey sky.

"Aw, come on, Hana! I just need a lie down. It's not bad; I'll be fine by tomorrow."

"Get out!" Hana held his door open.

"No!" Logan objected. He turned his body away from her and refused to engage, brows knitted and grey eyes flashing.

"Fine." Hana placed her hands on her hips. "Get out of your own accord or I'll fetch a wheelchair. You choose!"

Tired and in pain, Logan obeyed, closing the door with his backside and following Hana into the waiting room. "This is bloody ridiculous!" he grumbled. Sitting on a plastic chair, he put his head down and closed his eyes while Hana paid the fee. She appeared next to him with a green form and a pen. At the section asking for details of the accident, Hana paused and looked at Logan.

"What do I say?" she demanded. "I'm not lying."

He sighed. "Give it here." Balancing it on his knee, he wrote in a childish right-handed font. Hana watched him give details of a fall downstairs and shook her head in disgust.

"You promised you weren't a liar!" she hissed and Logan leaned close so he could whisper in her ear.

"Only with you," he whispered, his breath ruffling Hana's fringe. "I will never lie to you."

Logan went into the doctor on his own. He hovered in the doorway but she ignored him, not wanting further association with the day's events. Scrupulously honest, she felt tainted by a sentence of less than ten words which were all untrue.

Logan reappeared after three-quarters of an hour, wearing his arm in a sling. Hana read a banal celebrity magazine and remembered none of it. The screech of a toddler disturbed the waiting room, his head stuck in a terracotta flowerpot. Hana winced as his wails echoed in the pottery and exited the little drain hole at the top. She stared at the cover of the magazine and avoided thoughts of breaking him out with her stiletto heel. Logan looked at her sideways from under his long eyelashes. His nervous grey eyes showed he knew the argument hid just beneath the fragile surface of her hatred of public spectacles. Hana ground her teeth and maintained her silent vigil while the child wailed into his flowerpot.

"Logan Du Rose?" A pretty blonde nurse called him after ten minutes and he followed her out of sight, his long legs moving with grace across the waiting room. Again, he hovered at the doorway and Hana refused eye contact. She tapped an impatient fingernail on her knee and wished she could take herself back in time to the start of the year. She'd ignore the damned rat under her desk and save herself a heap of trouble. Her audible groan attracted the attention of other patients as she realised she'd have missed out on the best sex of her entire life.

Logan reappeared ages later, his arm in a sling and a black plaster cast stretching from his hand to above his elbow. Hana narrowed her eyes in victory, remembering the awful sound of bone cracking and feeling vindicated.

"There's an extra charge," the receptionist called as Hana followed Logan to the door. He pushed his right hand into his jeans and she waved him away. She handed over her visa card as the woman read out the list of Logan's medical procedures including x-rays and things she struggled to pronounce.

"A drip?" Hana demanded, recognising one of the words. "What kind of drip?"

The receptionist glanced at Logan and pursed her lips. "I can't discuss patient details with anyone else," she commented.

Logan waited for Hana and struggled to open the front door. She felt a numbness descend over her brain and couldn't bring herself to help him.

The scent of fresh flowers filled the house and Hana discovered a bouquet from Bodie in a vase on the kitchen table. He'd left them in the paper and the stems reached for the water in desperation. Hana fingered the delicate petals of a lily between her fingers while she read the note tucked into the wrapper.

'Sorry Mum! I didn't mean for you to meet Amy and Jas that way. I'll visit soon and we can talk about it. There's something else I need to tell you, anyway. It's important but face to face would be better. Happy Birthday for Tuesday, love Bo. Xxx'

Hana let out a deep breath, trying not to cry as she reached in her bag for her phone to send him a text. Not finding it, she checked her pockets as panic set in. It wasn't there. She thought back to the last time she used it as Tiger crept into the room and wound himself around her legs, mewing. "Your bowl's full, silly boy," Hana cooed as she smoothed his soft fur. "Have you really missed me? Where's my phone, boy?" A memory of Liza confiscating it snapped into her brain and Hana let out a groan of annoyance. "Noooo!"

Logan walked into the room and filled the kettle one-handed. "What's wrong?"

"My phone!" replied Hana, the whine evident in her voice. "Your sister confiscated it when I tried to call the police."

Logan grimaced. "Sorry." He reached into his jeans pocket and fished it out. "She gave it to me as I left."

Hana snatched it from his fingers, ignoring the stab of pain that crossed his face as she jarred his body. She walked into the hallway to text Bodie, wandering around the house seeking privacy.

'Thanks for the flowers, I love them. Text me when you get this. Love you Bo, Mum. Xxx'

Hana pressed the button to send her message and sat down on her old double bed, looking around her spare room. She thought back to her excited exit from Culver's Cottage just a few days ago, embarking on her new marriage with hope. "What have I done?" she sighed, running a hand over her face. Her mascara smudged and she examined the black line across her fingers. Anka's image floated across her mind's-eye, her slender hand waving from across the street from the registry office. The small wave and the tears made sense if she'd left Tama. Hana thought back to their rental house the night she borrowed her wedding outfit. Anka's odd behaviour added to the picture of a woman abandoning a hopeless situation. "Oh, Anka," she sighed. "What a bloody mess. And now you've dragged me into it."

At the thought of Tama, Hana closed her eyes in misery and flopped backward on the bed. The day's events made her body feel like a concrete block, weighed down by worry. Her wedding seemed like a farce and it mattered that nobody carried her over the threshold. Hana picked at a loose threat on the duvet cover, disappointment screwing up her face as she watched a small spider journey across the yellow stained ceiling.

A noise in the doorway caused her to open her eyes and lift her head. Logan balanced a cup of hot liquid that dribbled down the side with the awkward tilt of his cast. He held it out to her like a small boy offering a special toy, craving her approval. His grey eyes were the colour of smoke and his fringe fell over his eyelashes, bouncing as he blinked. Hana sat up and reached for the mug, wiping the drips away with her index finger and taking a long swallow of the tea. "Nice, thanks."

Logan sat on the bed next to her, causing the mattress to tip Hana towards him. They sat in silence for a while, Hana drinking and Logan wondering what to say to her. "I'm sorry," he began. "That was a stinking way for it to end, him turning up like that."

"Is Tama your son?" Hana voiced the concern which forced its way into her brain as the men squared up against each other. "You're very alike."

Logan's eyes narrowed. "No, Hana. No way."

Silence descended. It seemed Logan would only tell her his history if she asked for it. She tested the water. "Why are you so close to him? Sorry, I mean that in the past tense." She eyed his cast assuming the relationship would be over.

Logan watched Hana with unnerving intensity, his eyes searching her for trustworthiness. His gaze rested on the clincher, his ring on her finger. "Michael's his father." He sighed. "Guy's a douche bag."

"Oh!" Hana bit her lip, remembering how Tama told Michael he hated him. That, at least made sense. "So where does Kane, the alcoholic dad fit in?" she asked.

If Logan resented the questions fired at him, he didn't show it, responding with patience. Yet she knew she walked a tightrope. One question too many and he would shut down and leave her outside the Du Rose circle to flounder alone. "Kane dated Tama's mum. She always liked Michael, but nobody realised it progressed into anything. He was at medical school. It got messy and complicated and she stayed with Kane. Everyone found out, including Kane. He bought Tama up all wrong, on purpose. I tried to mentor the kid while I was here, but Kane beat the crap out of Tama five years ago and threw that little gem at him in the process. I paid for him to go to school in Hamilton then. My Uncle Reuben never let Tama's mother back onto the property after she left. I don't really know why. After Tama ran off with that stupid typist, I tracked him down and he told me some stuff I probably didn't want to hear. I spoke to Michael last night and he doesn't care. He's an ass hole. He always knew." Logan shook his head and finished his sentence with a worse swear word, indicating he didn't approve of his brother's carelessness towards his unintended offspring.

Hana served her next question while her husband seemed willing to answer. "What's the story with that big scar on your side? How did you get hurt? You're so weird about it; I know it wasn't an accident."

Logan ran his good hand over his face and through his hair before answering. His voice sounded calm but cold. Hana put her hand over his. "It doesn't bother me," she said. "I've kissed most of it and I know you don't have any feeling there. It affects nothing, but I want to know how it happened."

He provided only sparse details, his tone and face impassive and devoid of emotion. "We played a game. It's a stupid game and always led to something bad. Kane's foster-sister won a dare. She told Kane to stab me. He and Barry chased me through the bush until they caught me. Barry split me open with a machete and Mike carried me home. Kane thought it funny when he shined the torch on me and saw my guts spilling out. I was eleven."

"Barry?" whispered Hana. "Your own brother?"

Logan turned to sit sideways on the bed so he could face her. "Barry behaved like Kane, do you get it? He was one of them." His voice tapered off and he chewed his lip. Hana felt a wave of guilt for pushing him.

"It's fine, you don't have to tell me any more." She reached out and put her hand over Logan's writhing fingers. "I'm sorry. I shouldn't have asked."

He lay back on the bed, shifting his body so his head reached the pillows. The sling rubbed an uncomfortable red line around his neck. His left foot touched the floor, his right leg bent and Hana watched the rigidity in his body release. She knew she'd married a complete stranger.

Yet she sensed her attraction to him ripped out her insides every time she looked at his strong profile or stared into his bottomless grey eyes. Logan used his good hand to squeeze the point at the bridge of his nose and Hana saw pain written in the action. "They didn't care, did they?" she asked, imagining Logan's family going back to their breakfast like nothing happened. She sighed. "I'm amazed you're not more messed up than you seem. I'd sleep in a padded cell if they raised me."

Logan squinted against the sunshine filtering through the dirty window and smiled. "I'm guessing that's a compliment. It just doesn't sound like it."

"Sorry." Hana gave him a flicker of a smile. She held out her hand. "I'll help you into bed, you look shattered." She placed her empty cup outside on the hall floor to grab later and held Logan's hand, leading him into their bedroom with the beautiful four-poster bed. She intended to leave him to sleep while the doctor's painkilling injection did its job, but hadn't figured he could still undress her with such skill, using only one hand.

-4-

Hana sat at the kitchen table watching through the window as hawks soared above the trees, hunting. They seemed tireless, hovering and waiting. Their delicate, fluttering feathers resembled fingers at the end of their wings as they rode the up draught from the canopy, absurd patience on display. They plunged through the fauna like missiles and didn't reappear.

Hana's gaze strayed to a wooden ornament sitting on the windowsill. Bodie plonked it there during the move. The word HOME arched from the wood in calligraphy script. Hana sighed and picked at a knot in the table. "I'm a walking disaster," she whispered. "What am I doing?"

Her cup of tea cooled as she pondered the error of her ways. Common sense berated her for marrying a man she didn't know and joining a family which terrified her. Tiger plonked himself on the windowsill, eyeing the sparrows on the fronds of a Nikau palm near the house. He glanced at Hana as she sipped her drink. "You're not meant to be up there." The cat licked the delicate pads of a paw; his claws extended to form a furry fist. He knew she wouldn't get up to remove him. "Logan's a man of many personas," she whispered to her bored audience. Tiger yawned. "He's an English teacher, loved and respected by the boys and swooned over by the mothers. Good at his job, he's running the faculty like a sergeant major." Hana buried her face in her hands. "So who's the man I watched with Tama. He wasn't afraid, despite the strength and sheer angry power of the kid. It's Tama who showed fear and then attacked him from behind. I can't believe his family watched that play out and did nothing." Hana exhaled. "Why do I get this feeling Logan's in charge there? And driving home I felt I couldn't take any more of this Du Rose crap. Then he touches me and I can't get enough of him."

Tiger narrowed his eyes in a glare of rebuke and Hana bit her lip. "Yeah, sorry old man. You probably heard. What did I get myself into? It's a big mess." Hana reached across for her phone and weighed it in her palm. Her relationship with Logan cut her off from Anka. Cilla's reaction meant she froze out her church friends. That left nobody to complain to, nobody to tell. Except Bodie.

Hana ran through the possible conversation. "I'll say, Bo, they're weird. They watched Tama beat Logan with a crowbar and refused to call the cops." She sighed and stroked the edges of the device. "He'll say he tried to tell me and ask what I expect him to do about it. Then I'll say nothing. But he'll know he's right and never let me forget it." Hana dropped her phone onto the table, enjoying the dull thud. "I can't believe that damn lawyer took my phone!"

The cat jumped in fright, pitching sideways into the empty sink and scrambling out with his hair on end. "Serves you right," Hana told him. "You shouldn't be up there. Nobody listens to me." Self-pity shrouded her in a welcome cloak and she rested her chin on her forearms with a groan. "I bet Bodie's checked Logan out and that's what he wants to talk to me about."

A sound from behind made her sit up in shock. She clutched her chest. "Geez, Logan. You scared me."

He stood in the doorway rubbing his eyes with his good hand. The sling hung slack around his neck. His bare chest looked inviting and his navy cotton pyjama bottoms drooped on the side he couldn't pull up. "Who's checking me out?" he asked, his speech slurred from sleep.

"Me." Hana stood. "I'm checking you out. You look adorable." She stood to help him, slipping his head through the small space in the stretchy sling. As her fingers lingered on his bare skin, she fought to stop her mind wandering. Logan snagged her with his good arm around her shoulder, smoothing the back of her neck and kissing her temple. "Hey," he whispered into the silence.

"Hey," Hana replied and despite herself, lifted her mouth to respond to her husband's addictive kisses. Every nerve ending in her body fired and though her brain screamed out warnings, she ignored them all. "You're a conundrum," she whispered against his lips. His eyebrows quirked upwards in question. "One minute you're this gifted, capable teacher and the next, you're a farm boy riding a horse."

"Which do you prefer?" Logan asked, his fingers working their way into her robe.

"Both," Hana breathed, realising her own dilemma and sympathising with some of Caroline's. Where the other woman failed, Hana determined to learn to love both sides of Logan Du Rose.

"Good," he breathed into her neck.

Sunday evening seemed peaceful after the drama of the day. "I'm not hungry," Logan maintained, eating nothing to replenish his energy. He slept on the painkillers, napping on the sofa next to Hana as she read a book. The TV played in the background, a rugby game which she muted as Logan dozed. "Oh, what?" He pushed himself upright in confusion and snatched the remote. "I was watching that." The All Blacks stood on the podium collecting their medals and hoisting a coveted trophy. Logan rubbed his eyes looking disoriented. "But it only just started."

"No, it didn't. I muted it and you kept turning it up. You slept through more than you watched."

"What's the score?" Logan's bleary eyes searched the screen for clues.

"No idea. I'm not interested." Hana closed her book with a snap. "And the picture's too fuzzy. It jerks like an out of control fruit machine.

Logan rested his head on a cushion and closed his eyes. The cat stretched out in front of the blazing fire like road kill. Hana's first attempt at a decent blaze failed, only reviving under Logan's careful tutelage. A standard lamp illuminated the room, driving the shadows against the walls and back into corners. She tried to fix the moment in her memory, supernaturally aware a storm approached and not the meteorological kind. "What's wrong?" Logan muttered. "I can hear you sighing."

"Just worrying about tomorrow." Hana stroked the cover of her book. "I can't battle someone who wants to kill me when I don't know who they are or what they want, can I?"

The early morning alarm clock sent Hana diving back under the covers with a groan. "No!" she wailed in misery. "I can't do this anymore." Her fingers raked the mattress next to her, discovering it empty. She padded to the bathroom and found Logan shaving one-handed. He swore as the razor slipped and nicked his skin. "I'll get you a plaster," she sighed and looked for the first aid kit in the kitchen.

Hana's despondency increased as the moment for departure loomed. "Do we have to go?" she asked, dragging her feet and delaying. "Can't we stay here?"

"You can, but I'm supervising soccer trials at lunchtime." Logan wriggled into his jacket and buttoned it over his sling.

Hana attempted to herd Tiger into the lounge and failed. As she bent down to grab her handbag, she saw his black and white shape squeeze through the narrow gap between the door and frame. Logan jumped back. "Sorry. I thought you put him in the lounge."

"He wouldn't go!" Hana stamped her foot, watching as Tiger shot down the porch steps and into the bushes. "Fine then!" she shouted to the retreating fluffy tail. "I was trying to protect you." She scowled at the amber eyes peering from behind a kaka beak bush. "If you get squished on the road, don't come crying to me!"

She set the burglar alarm, locked the front door and deactivated the central locking on the Honda. Every action felt laboured and stole too much energy. Logan yanked at the passenger door, trying not to drop his briefcase full of marking. It tipped as he inserted himself into the car and papers flooded the foot well. "Oh, bloody hell!" Logan tugged at the stretchy sling and leaned forwards to retrieve them.

"Don't be daft, leave it." Hana leaned forward, gathering the sheets together and trying not to bend them. "Were they in alphabetical order?" she asked, slipping them back into the case and zipping it up. She stretched across him, her breasts resting against his knees and heard him inhale.

"Yeah," he replied, his tone edgy. "You know that offer of staying home?"

Hana sat up and shook her head, her lips close to his. "Rescinded," she said and kissed his lips with a slow, sensuous action. Logan groaned.

"What happens if I see you at work?" he grumbled. "I might disgrace myself."

Hana snorted. "You didn't before."

"Are you kidding me? Everyone noticed me staring at you, only now I know what you look like naked. It makes it worse."

Hana rubbed a hand across his thigh and smirked at his look of discomfort. "Stop!" she told her husband as she clicked her seatbelt in and his puppy-dog eyes begged for attention.

"But I'm hurt," he replied, pleading with his eyes.

"Tough!" Hana started the engine. "I wanted to stay home in bed but you made me get up. So now you have to suffer."

Hana enjoyed driving the Honda. It seemed an age since her test drive. She belted down River Road, jumping when Logan touched her hand to stop her indicating left into Powell Street. "No," he said. "Not that way. Go to the bottom and turn left. If we park off Frey Street, we can walk through the back of St Veronica's School."

Hana did as she was told, finally pulling up to the curb in a quiet street she didn't recognise. Getting out, she looked around. "Is there a parking restriction here? The last thing I need is to have my car towed away."

Logan shook his head. "There are no signs. It's a regular residential street. I checked online."

Hana locked up and followed Logan. She wanted to hold his hand, but the work case occupied his only free one. She made do with walking next to him. Coming to the end of a short alley, she halted and peered at the muddy floor of the gully. She turned to Logan with her upper lip curled back in a snarl. "Are you serious?"

He looked down at her high-heeled boots and winced. "Sorry. I'm not used to worrying about footwear."

Hana stamped. "I'll get to work filthy." She pouted, adding, "You'll have to carry me."

Logan's brow narrowed as he considered the briefcase and his broken arm. Hana watched his mind working through the problem and he wrinkled his nose, looking for a solution. She stepped forward and rested her fingers on his sleeve. "It's okay. I'm fine."

"I would've worked it out," Logan replied, his lips turning up in a smirk. "You didn't give me long enough."

Hana snorted and shook her head. "You're gorgeous." She reached up and kissed his lips. "It's one thing knowing you'd carry me and another letting you." She patted his arm and held her hand out for the briefcase. "I can't carry you but I can help."

Logan shook his head and directed her around his other side. "I'll carry the case but you hold onto my arm," he offered. He cringed at the leather boots on her feet. "And I'll clean your shoes at home tonight."

Hana stiffened as a group of students approached them in the alley, talking and laughing. Their uniforms looked defective, shirts untucked and jumpers slung around necks. One boy wore the wrong socks. They exchanged a series of smirks at each other, jerking their heads towards two staff members hiding in a city alley. Their eyes sparkled with the promise of gossip. "Hi, miss," a tall boy said, sizing her up from head to toe. His gaze roved over Logan and the expression dropped. Swallowing, he hurried past, the other boys putting their heads down and following. Logan cleared his throat and Hana watched the collective crowd tense and speed up.

"Boys!" he called and they stopped and turned, feet scuffing against the silty ground. "Uniforms." He raised an eyebrow and Hana watched in amazement as shirts disappeared into shorts, jumpers slipped over heads and the boy with the incorrect socks fixed a helpless look on his face. Logan groaned. "I don't care mate. Sort it out before I see you again."

They hurried away and Hana stared up at him. "How do you do that? Nobody else can control them."

Logan shrugged. "I bent all the rules at school but good men straightened me out."

"How?" Hana double-timed her footsteps to keep up with him as he set off.

"Boundaries. Kids need them. I set the rules out at the start and they know not to cross them. Then we're all good."

"Give me an example," Hana demanded as they rounded a bend

in the gully and she tried not to slip.

Logan paused while she righted herself. "I don't know how I do it, Hana. I just do."

"So, how did you introduce yourself on the first day?" she asked, turning to face him.

"I wrote my name on the board." He shrugged. "Then I marked the register and stared at each boy until I knew his name. If I couldn't work it out from reading it, I asked him to say it until I got it right."

"That sounds a bit freaky." Hana's brows narrowed. "I'd feel self-conscious if someone did that to me." She concentrated on her footing. "But it worked with them."

"Yeah." Logan's face creased in a smile which produced crow's feet in the corners of his eyes. "Then I put my foot up on the desk of the one I identified as a troublemaker and leaned my elbow on my knee. I kept it there until I saw him back down." He laughed as Hana gaped. "It's not rocket science, babe. They might be stronger, faster, cleverer or wittier, it doesn't matter. My will is unbreakable as far as they're concerned and it puts them at ease. The good kids know I've got their back and the bad ones know not to bother. Simple."

"Did you do that for every different year group?" Hana gaped up at him and Logan nodded.

"Course. Not much point otherwise."

Hana contemplated a particular science teacher who spent six hours a day screeching at the top of his lungs. "Grunge could use lessons," she said with a sigh. "They moved the whole learning support department away from his lab because the boys couldn't concentrate."

Logan snorted. "Yeah. Good job I don't run that department. Angus needs to cull a few dead branches."

"Maybe I'm a dead branch," Hana mused and Logan smiled.

"If you're considering it as a possibility then it's highly unlikely." He gripped her fingers tighter in the crook of his arm. They parted outside the music room at the back of the site and Hana watched Logan stride away. Glancing down at her cold fingers, the wedding band twinkled in the early morning sun and gave her comfort.

She missed the early staff briefing owing to the mysterious absence of Sheila. A tower of mail on her desk distracted her and made her miss the warning bell. Hana reached for the telephone and dialled reception. "Hi," she said, not waiting for an answer. "It's Hana from the student centre. Has Sheila called in sick? She's not here and you've put all her post on my desk."

"I just do as I'm told," the receptionist grumbled. "The principal told me to give everything to you. So I did." Hana heard a click and the line went dead.

Caroline came in, dumped a pile of folders on her desk and left.

Hana swallowed her nerves in a loud gulp. "Thank goodness, because I don't want to hear anything that comes out of your mouth," she whispered to the empty room.

The bell sounded for registration and staff dispersed to their tutor groups. Peter North blasted in through the common room whistling. Seeing Hana leaned over her desk, he grabbed her by the waist and swung her round. "Henrietta agreed to marry me!" His kiss on her cheek sounded wet and Hana hid her wince beneath a smile of congratulation. "Your wedding gave me the idea. It got me thinking."

"Well done!" Hana hugged him. "I'm pleased for you. What did Logan say?"

Pete bounced on the spot for a moment and then let her go. "He said we could have it at his hotel." His eyes danced. "Oh, well not his hotel." He twirled a finger in the air. "His parents' place." He stopped speaking, his excited face morphing into an ugly sneer.

Alarmed, Hana turned to face the direction of his gaze. Caroline occupied the doorway, her cheeks pink and her lips twitching. Her fingers clenched in and out of fists. "I hate you!" she hissed at Hana. "I bloody hate you. You'll pay for this."

The smile of congratulations slipped from Hana's lips and she glanced sideways at Pete. Caroline exuded such venom, Hana felt unsafe in her proximity. Pete pushed Hana behind him, showering her with a storm of dandruff. "Leave her alone!" he snapped. "And leave Logan alone. You made your choice and now he's made his."

Caroline let out a peal of evil laughter which echoed around the empty common room and bounced off the walls. "What's in a ring?" She sneered. "I've got something she can't give him."

Hana left via the rear door, not wanting to hear the rest of Caroline's bile. Doubt crept into her vulnerability, comparing her to the other woman's lithe body and blonde beauty and finding herself lacking. Life could be good without Caroline in it. Something told her a long line of people believed that.

She busied herself tidying the brochure racks, occupying tutor group time and returning to peep through the office window. Posters and notices obliterated the interior but small gaps offered a view of Caroline's desk. Hana saw her stand up and breeze through the common room, a mammoth blot on Hana's landscape but a tiny figure against the arched ceiling and vaulted beams. Pete left after her and slammed the office door. Hana waited with her nose pressed against the glass for a moment or two, just in case Caroline forgot something and returned. Glancing across at her own desk, she caught sight of her door key sitting on a tower of paper. "Noooo!" she wailed.

"Why are you looking through the window?" Pete halted in the final second before he bowled her over. "I forgot my burger. That bitch put me off my breakfast." He unlocked the door and pushed his way in, seizing the greasy wrapper with a grunt of satisfaction. He took it with him, biting into it like a vampire.

Hana tasted the residue of bitterness and hatred in the office. It hung like fog, damp and eroding in a place Hana once loved. She contemplated resigning but worried about leaving Logan to Caroline's devices. Her tendency to run brought other problems with it. "I just need to keep going until the end of term," she promised herself. "Then Rory will be back."

Angus' voice in the corridor made her jump and Hana swung into her chair and logged onto her computer. Four budget requests and a dubious invoice greeted her. "Thanks for that," she sighed.

The comforting, familiar hum of male voices in the common room lulled Hana into a false sense of security. She started an email advising the head of the technology department that Sheila wouldn't authorise the astronomical bill for a new extension out of her careers budget. Her fingers paused over the keyboard looking for polite wording. A hush fell over the common room and Hana turned her face towards the open door. Angus poked his head through. "All well, working hard? Good, good."

Hana nodded. "Yes thanks. Is Sheila sick today?"

"Aaahh." Angus twisted his expression into one of discomfort and he wagged his finger at her. "That's what I need to discuss with you." He pushed the door closed and plonked himself down on Pete's chair. Hana winced. An empty biscuit wrapper in her dustbin mirrored the mess left on Pete's desk and chair. And Angus' expensive trousers. In a facetious moment, she imagined herself slapping crumbs off the principal's bottom.

"Sheila," began Angus with uncharacteristic awkwardness. "Sheila won't be back this term."

The consequences hit Hana in the face like a brick and she swallowed. The colour left her complexion. "Don't say it, Angus. Please don't say it."

"Oh, no dear. She's not very ill." He leaned across and patted her knee. "She isn't dying. Just needs some space." He mouthed the final word of the sentence and Hana gaped at him.

"That didn't even occur to me," she breathed. "But when she went to Europe last year, Rory covered the careers role for her."

"Yes." Angus smiled. "Quite right. The Year 13 dean can take over that job on a temporary basis. So you understand what will happen?"

Hana leapt to her feet with her hand over her mouth. "No." She shook her head. "Actually yes. I understand, but I can't do this." The words escaped her lips without filtering. "I quit."

"What?" Angus stood and dragged her hand away from her

mouth. "You can't quit. I need you to fill in for Sheila."

"No." Hana snatched her hand away and reached into her bottom drawer for her handbag. "I've had enough, Angus. I can't do this."

Angus sat in silence while Hana divulged her sorry tale of woe involving Caroline Marsh. Then he shook his head. "So you think Miss Marsh singled out my school in order to get near to Logan?"

"Logan thinks so," Hana scoffed. "That's exactly why she's here!"

"It explains certain things." Angus nodded his head like a toy. "But I'm somewhat confused. I heard from another quarter she was involved with someone else." He frowned and his red eyebrows joined in the middle. "Don't concern yourself with that." He drummed his fingers on the table. "I'd like you to forget I said it." He smiled at Hana. "You say she makes life difficult. I need facts otherwise I can't help you."

Hana shook her head and her thoughts came back empty. "She's too careful to give me ammunition. She spilled tea on my work but that might look like an accident. Intimidation could be my perception of her. Today she told me she hated me, but only Pete heard. He's not a credible witness in the eyes of the trustees." Hana's shoulders slumped. "There is no evidence, Angus. I have to quit."

"I'm in a quandary," Angus stated. "It's usual for the Year 13 dean to step into the careers role during a crisis. The administrative running of the school is down to Donald Watson and the management team, in which case Caroline will be asked."

"My situation is already intolerable, without giving her even more authority over me." Hana bit her lip and ran her fingers over the tension headache beginning at the bridge of her nose.

"I know and in that case, the school will fail in its duty of care towards you. I think for now, the best idea is to do nothing." He raised his hand as Hana's mouth opened in protest. "I feel the end is in sight. Not Armageddon, just the end of Miss Marsh's employment."

"How?" Hana demanded. Angus put a forefinger to his lips and waggled his eyebrows. Then he patted Hana's hand as he rose and unlocked the door. He turned towards her at the last moment.

"It's a shame you weren't in briefing this morning dear Hana." She looked for a reprimand, but his eyes seemed kind. "The other staff took the news of your wedding with great enthusiasm. They wanted to wish you all the very best."

"Angus!" Hana's voice sounded croaky as she called out and he stopped with his fingers caressing the handle. "What did you mean at the reception?"

His shoulders slumped. "Old men say too much sometimes. I meant nothing by it. Forget it."

He closed the door behind him and before Hana's eyes, her life twisted and writhed in complication and upset. The more she knew the less she understood. Catching sight of Sheila's empty office, Hana threw her head back in irritation. "And he avoided telling me what's wrong with Sheila!"

Hana worked alone until eleven thirty when the bell rang for morning tea. She texted Sheila to ask advice about the science teacher's dilemma and received no reply. When he rang her for the fifth time, she lost the plot. "No!" she hissed. "Sheila's not here and I can't authorise a purchase that big. There's nothing written down and I don't recall any conversations about you building an extension and charging it to our budget." Hana rolled her eyes at his retort. "Don't even think about it. I'm emailing Donald right now and if that bill gets paid on the strength of a fake signature, you're toast!"

A permanent knot in her stomach tightened as she anticipated Caroline's return. She steeled herself for it, practicing clever sentences and intelligent responses to pretend arguments in her head. To her surprise, Logan walked through the door first. "Hey babe, please can you sort me out?" Pain filled his eyes and the sling hung slack around his neck. "I tightened it and now I can't get my arm back in. Bloody thing's killing my neck." He eyed the devastation on Pete's chair and elected to sit on the corner of his desk instead.

Hana opened her drawer and pulled out a packet of painkillers. She popped two into Logan's palm and handed him her bottle of water, watching as he swallowed. She resisted the urge to tell him how wretched he looked.

A Year 13 called in for a brochure and eyed Logan sideways. Boys proved perceptive creatures, spotting extra-curricular activity between staff with frightening clarity. Hana handed the brochure over with a smile, safe in her guaranteed immunity from accusation. "Sit in my chair," she told Logan as the boy left. "You've knotted it so tight, I'm not sure I can undo it." She wrestled with the sling and Logan pulled it over his head, mussing his dark hair and rumpling his shirt collar. He sighed with the pressure off his neck and rubbed his good hand over the reddened flesh.

"There, done." Hana pulled the two ends apart with a triumphant smile. Logan wrinkled his nose.

"You used your teeth. That's cheating."

"Didn't." Hana licked her lips and Logan snorted.

"You're such a liar. There's lipstick on the knot!"

Hana looked down and laughed. She admitted defeat with a toss of her head. "Fair enough." She pulled lint from her tongue and winked at Logan. "Hold still. I'll tie it somewhere different. Your neck looks sore here." She stood in front of him and leaned around, tying the sling below his right ear. The cast felt heavy in her hands as she laid it in the cloth and fixed a panel around the elbow with a safety pin.

Logan caught hold of her soft fingers and left a sensuous kiss on her wrist. It tickled her skin and she giggled. "Wait until I get you home," Logan whispered and his eyes blazed with desire. Hana bit her lower lip and checked the knot, freezing in position at the sight of Caroline standing in the doorway. Her stomach clenched and Caroline ignored them, breezing in like an ill wind. An unexpected wave of pity gripped Hana's heart at the look of despair on the other woman's face.

Despite the constant glances Caroline shot Logan, he ignored her and the atmosphere became heavy and painful. Hana felt her chest tighten and her lungs struggled to extract oxygen from the bitter fog. Logan appeared calm and unruffled, pushing his fingers through hers and kissing her fingernails. She suffered a momentary panic, seeing what it might feel like to find herself thrust from Logan Du Rose's inner circle. When the bell rang, he stood, gracing her with a smile. "That's me. I'm teaching Year 12 English now." He wrinkled his nose and brushed his lips across hers. "See ya later, beautiful." He put his mouth to Hana's ear and whispered, "Happy sixtieth-hour anniversary, gorgeous." He left with a smirk on his lips and a subtle backward glance at Hana. Her lips reacted to the veiled promise in his eyes, lifting in a smile of expectation. But Caroline's stiff back oozed a warning and the pleasure left Hana's eyes.

Pete walked in and gave her a hard slap on the back. Hana accepted it as affection. "I'll fetch the post," she said and bolted. Taking advantage of the empty corridors, Hana ran and sought solace in the post room. Her boot heels clacked against the wooden floors. Once inside, she sighed with relief at the blessed space free of human interference. The glass doors betrayed her and Ethel Bowman scuttled along the corridor like a tornado, spotting Hana's red hair from afar. She waved her photocopying in front of her while her voluminous dress billowed out behind.

Oblivious, Hana leaned against the glass and accepted a congratulatory hug from a classroom assistant. "I hope you'll be very happy," Barbara said, reaching up with her tiny hands and snagging her post. "Logan's gorgeous. There'll be a few disappointed girls now he's off the market."

Hana laughed, the sound dying on her lips as Barb's face morphed into Ethel's. The small classroom assistant peeled herself off the back of a locker door and escaped. Ethel planted her meaty hands on her hips. "I knew it!" she squawked. "Didn't I say you two would end up together? I want to know every last detail, particularly why I didn't get an invite."

Hana blanched. If she told Ethel anything, she may as well publish it in the newspaper herself. The elderly woman fired questions at her like a machine gun.

"When did you start seeing each other?"

"How did he propose?"

"Where did you get married?"

"When did you do it?"

"Why didn't you tell Aunty Ethel?"

Hana gave scant detail where possible. Her mind wandered to the hilarious witnesses and the surreal bubble of excitement surrounding her wedding day. Ethel burbled on about trivia and Hana tuned in at the name of her old street, followed by her house number on Achilles Rise. "What?" she asked, seeing Ethel's eyes narrow. "Pardon. Say that again."

"Well," Ethel said. "I told him, I've no idea where Hana Johal shifted to. I didn't even know you'd moved. You never said. Anyway, if you give me your new address, he'd love us to pop round. I think that's what he said." She cocked her head like an owl. "Yes, he said he would love to catch up with you."

"Who would?" asked Hana, interrupting as Ethel stopped to draw breath. The older woman grew coy and shy, her cheeks flushing pink. She rolled her eyes in an attempt at a seductive look. "You know," she whispered.

Hana shook her head. The whole conversation left her miles behind. "I don't."

"Our mutual friend, Mr Laval." Ethel's fingers fluttered across her painted lips and she gazed around the empty room. At Hana's look of confusion, she spread her hands as though explaining a trigonometry question to a thick student.

Hana shook her head again. "I don't know any Mr Laval. Sorry, but you've made a mistake." She turned to go but Ethel grasped her wrist and Hana let out a yelp.

"But he asks me about you all the time," she said. Her manicured eyebrows joined in the centre around a clump of wrinkles. "He knew you'd changed your car and got a young man. If I'd known it was our dear Mr Du Rose, I would've said so. Mr Laval knows all sorts of things from when he visited you before. He described your old house and we drove past it one day, but you weren't in. Give me your new address and I'll write it down for him." Mrs Bowman moved so close to Hana, her breath moved her fringe. "You see dear, after the untimely death of Mr Bowman some years ago, I've been rather alone. Mr Laval is my gentleman person." Mrs Ethel Bowman, mistress of the twisted English language, strained to find the words for what Mr Laval represented to her. She flushed at the words she chose and sweat beaded on her forehead.

"Friend?" obliged Hana and Mrs Bowman beamed.

"Exactly!" she said satisfied. "Now may I have your new address?"

She stood there with an expectant expression and Hana panicked. In a masterstroke, she blurted, "I can't remember the full address and postcode. I'll have to ask Logan." She excused herself and fled in a blur, sliding out from between Ethel and the glass doors. A dreadful realisation thudded in the pit of her stomach. Mr Laval was one of the men hounding her.

Hana's heart thudded as she ran back to the office. She entered in a rush and Caroline shot her an acid stare. Dragging out her phone, she dashed off a text to Logan. '

'Don't tell ANYONE our phone number or address. Talk later. It's important!"

With shattered nerves and shaking hands, she ran down the front steps to reception, aware of another person who knew her new address. Angus' personal assistant sat at her desk typing, huffing in irritation as Hana rushed into the room without knocking. "Excuse me!" The woman rose to her feet, her face clouding in anger. Her mood lightened as she remembered seeing Angus stroll across to the boarding house and she sat back down again. "He's not here." Her face took on a smug expression. "You can't see him."

"Have you typed out the new staff list yet?" Hana demanded, hopping from one foot to the other.

The assistant shook her head and adopted a defensive stance. "I've been much too busy," she asserted, bugging her eyes. Hana felt sick with the release of tension and her knees wobbled beneath her. She thudded into a seat on the other side of the desk.

"Please can you remove my address?" she asked. "It's important."

"I can't do that!" The woman pulled herself up to her full height. "You must be contactable. Staff regulations."

The thought slipped into Hana's head and exited via her lips. She regretted the words as she heard them. "We changed our plans," she said. "I'm moving into Logan's house in Gordonton. Leave his alone and just add mine to that address." A sense of cowardice flooded her veins and she prayed she wouldn't rain her present troubles down on an innocent household. The woman's eyes bulged in indignation until she remembered Angus' announcement at briefing and then she relaxed.

"Oh, that's right," she simpered. "Congratulations. You married that irritating Māori." Her blue eyes sparkled with mischief in expectation of a fight."

But Hana already left.

Back in the office Hana located everyone she needed to speak to,

Boris, North, even Henrietta and Angus. She knew she couldn't settle until she spoke to them all.

The final text went through the ether to Bodie's number.

'I know who the crooks work for. Call me tonight. Please. Mum. X

-5-

"I don't know if it's enough to go on." Bodie's voice crackled through the connection later that evening. "It might just be the name he gave her. I bet it's fake."

Hana's silence communicated her disappointment. She'd wanted him to be excited. Bodie went on, "A photo would be best really."

Hana despaired. "How can I get that?" He didn't see her pout.

"Is Logan there?" he asked, dismissing her in a single sentence. Hana went in search of her husband and found him in the garage. She handed the phone over and sloped off to run a bath. Her footsteps to the bedroom and back for her robe sounded despondent and heavy on the wooden floor.

Logan appeared as she turned off the tap, a gentle knock preceding his dark head. "You okay?" he asked. Hana nodded and watched as he walked in and perched on the edge of the bath, dangling his right hand in the foam. He looked thoughtful and she nodded and turned on the heated towel rail. The atmosphere grew tense as she stripped down to her knickers and blouse, hoping he left before she got naked. Her cheeks flushed with a self-conscious glow as his grey eyes studied her with interest.

"Oh, Hana." Hauling himself up, Logan pulled her close. Dark shadows ringed his eyes and the strain of his injuries clouded his expression. Hana shivered in the damp heat and his arm around her felt welcome. She lifted her hands and ran them through his hair, feeling it slide through her fingers. He'd removed the sling and a red mark showed where it spent the day rubbing his flesh. "It'll be okay," he said, sounding more confident than he looked. "Nobody will find us here."

"I want the cops to sort it out," Hana whined and he rubbed her back.

"I know. Bodie's doing his best but it's hard. He's too far away." Logan kissed the top of her head. "I'll get you a glass of wine." He bit his lip in concentration and his pupils dilated as he ran his good hand up her waist and along the base of her spine. He leaned in and kissed the side of her neck and Hana heard her small exhale betray her.

"Yes please," she whispered. "To the wine."

While he fetched it, Hana stripped off and dived into the bath, almost breaking her neck in her haste to cover the not-so-sexy parts of her body beneath the bubbles. Logan returned with two glasses of wine balanced in one hand, far too full to be a single measure and a terrible idea with painkillers. To her embarrassment, he sat on the stool in the corner and settled in for the long haul. "Hana?" His tone sounded serious. "Do you regret this?" He indicated the room with his outstretched arm, wine slopping from the glass in his hand. "What did Angus say to you at the wedding? I know he upset you."

Hana considered her answer. His heightened perception meant he'd know if she lied. "I regret nothing when it's just us." She took a swallow of her merlot. "When other people get involved, it's messy and I feel out of my depth."

Logan nodded. "I get it. Perhaps we should run away." The suggestion sounded half-serious. "Clean toilets on the Gold Coast or in Fiji, what do you reckon?"

Hana laughed and sank into the bubbles until only her face showed. Her glass teetered on the tile shelf next to the bath. "If we didn't just buy this place, I'd be booking the flights."

Logan grinned. "I like the way you included me in your crazy purchase." His brow narrowed and he took a hasty swallow. "Hana," he began, his voice sounding grave. "I need to talk to you about something." She peeped over the side of the bath, his gravity alarming her. "If I died…" Her face recoiled in pain and Logan put his glass on the floor and stood. "Look, I'm sorry, but we must talk about this. We just blended two separate families and it's important." Logan stared at a mark on the ceiling to avoid the horror in Hana's face. "If I die, you'll inherit everything I have." He took a slug of his wine and sat back down. "You have your kids. Maybe part of your son's problem is worrying you won't make sure it works out for them."

Hana sank back into the bath, her face ashen. "Nobody's going to die."

Logan sighed. "I did some digging of my own, Hana. There's more to this than the cops think."

"What?" Her eyes widened in fear. "What do you know?"

He shook his head. "Nothing worth repeating. Something is going on and I can't get to the bottom of it. I've asked around." He raised a hand. "I have friends in Auckland. I only asked questions, Hana."

She sighed. "But we don't have to talk about dying, Logan. I already lost one husband."

Logan shrugged. "Someone's going to a lot of trouble to find you, Hana. We must cover our bases. I just wanted you to know that I'll never lay claim to anything you brought into the marriage. Your kids can take it all. I suggest you make a watertight will and reassure your son."

Hana shook her head and bubbles moved in her hair. "It can't be the money," she said, her tone heavy. "I don't know what his problem is."

"He doesn't trust me." Logan sounded certain. "Just reassure him I'm not after your money."

Hana nodded and a lone tear worked its way down her cheek and into the water.

"Oh, sweetheart." Logan placed his wine glass on the sink and knelt by the bath. He slipped his good arm around Hana's wet shoulders and held her. "I'll take care of you," he promised, stroking her damp hair and kissing her temple.

Hana didn't sleep well, despite another glass of wine and an exhausting romp with her husband. She rehashed the conversation with Ethel Bowman, hatching unrealistic plans to trap the faceless Mr Laval. She toyed with the idea of setting up a meeting via Ethel and inviting the entire New Zealand Police Force. Hana turned on her side and faced the bare windows, watching a plane track across the sky with its landing lights flashing. "It might not be him," she whispered to herself. "But who else would know so much about me without having ever met?"

Tiger slumped on the end of their bed and Hana felt his weight on her feet. He snuffled around and she recognised the sound of him licking his bum. "Stop!" Hana moved her foot and heard the controlled thud as he got off the bed. He gave a little mew which translated as, 'Don't care - didn't want to be here anyway.' Hana listened to his bell tinkle down the hallway. At least he'd returned home after his outdoor adventure.

Only Logan bought into Hana's theory about Ethel's gentleman friend. Bodie had brushed it off without consideration. Powerlessness assuaged her, knowing she could do nothing. The connection felt like a viable lead, but the risk lay in following it and discovering a harmless old man in companionship with a lonely old lady.

Hana turned over for the hundredth time, unnerved by Logan's foray into a path of questioning she didn't understand. She hadn't asked who he'd spoken too, but felt too afraid to press. A niggling fear added to her multitude of worries. Logan thought changing her will might assuage Bodie's animosity, but she sensed her son knew something he wouldn't share. Hana squeezed her eyes tight shut and pushed her face into her pillow, sensing a dangerous storm coming.

-6-

Hana woke to the sound of a mug clattering against her bedside table and the clink of cutlery on a plate. She struggled to rouse herself. Her breathing felt tight, as though a truck rolled over her chest while she slept. Looking at the wall clock in the dim light from the hallway, Hana saw the hands pointing to just after six.

She rubbed her eyes and when she opened them, saw Logan standing next to the bed. He carried his left arm across his chest, but the other hand clutched a card and small present. The wrapping paper clung to the box, tape sticking out at odd angles like a child's attempt. Hana hauled herself into a sitting position. "Hi babe." She yawned. "How come you're up so early?"

"I wanted to make you breakfast." Logan's thigh clattered against the plate, almost sending the whole thing onto the floor. Hana faked a wooden smile, cringing at the acceleration of the widening age gap. "Happy birthday," he said. She sighed and looked down at her hands, feeling old and scruffy with her hair matted and her monkey pyjamas skewed over her shoulder. Logan's beautiful face accentuated her inadequacy, with his fluttering dark lashes framing striking grey eyes and his fringe bouncing with the force of each blink. Hana bit her lip and accepted his birthday card and gift.

"Thank you." She smiled and willed her tired fingers to pull apart the envelope. Inside lay a beautiful card, picked with thought. Logan's neat left-handed script showed he'd written the card before his injury.

'To my best girl, I always knew I'd find you. All my love, Logan x.'

Hana felt tears rise into her chest and blew out through her mouth. Her birthday never felt special and she expected nothing more of this one. "What's the matter?" Logan asked, sitting on the side of the bed.

She fondled the embossed card and sighed. "I can't even get to work without subterfuge. And Pete's probably already eaten my birthday chocolate. What's the point of having a birthday?"

"So I can shower you with love." Logan's lips quirked upwards revealing the dimple in his cheek. He pulled her into his side. "Open your present."

Hana wrestled the tape off to reveal a silver locket. She turned it over in her fingers, examining the circular shape of a koru. "It's stunning," she breathed.

"The koru is the unfurling frond of a silver fern," he said, his voice low. "It means new beginnings."

Hana swallowed her misery and clasped it to her chest. "Did you put a photo in it?" she asked, peering around the edge to look for an opener. Logan shook his head.

"Na. I thought you could put your kids in there. You can see my ugly face every day."

Hana snorted. "Logan Du Rose, you have no idea how gorgeous you are."

"I don't think so." He turned sideways and used his right hand to grab the plate containing scrambled eggs on toast. His face looked grey from the effort of making it one-handed. "Do you want the spotlights on or the main light?" he asked, standing so she could settle herself to eat.

"Main light please," she answered. "Otherwise I won't get up."

Nodding, Logan walked across the bedroom and flicked the switch. He turned with a smile and left the room, not seeing Hana's horrified reaction to the sight of his bare torso. The crow-bar didn't just break Logan's arm, it caused a long bruise across his left side which spread as far as his spine. The black and purple mark made her stomach roil. She remembered the sickening thud as the bar contacted Logan's body. The curved metal prongs cracked the bone above his elbow, but the length of it left a diagonal welt. Hana shook her head in disbelief and stared at her uneaten food. She forced it into her mouth to honour her husband's efforts, but it cost her.

Logan cleared up the kitchen with difficulty, refusing to let Hana help. "No," he protested as she bent to push her plate into the dishwasher. "You're the birthday girl today. I'll do it."

She tied a plastic bag over his cast so he could shower and helped him with buttons and cufflinks. He wouldn't discuss his conversation with the emergency doctor the day before and left her unsatisfied about whether he mentioned the bruising to his ribs. "But it's a mess!" she insisted and Logan covered her lips with his to shut her up. "I worry about you." Hana pursed her lips and he smiled.

"And I love it." He brushed his thumb across her top lip. "But I'm not used to it."

Hana drove and they listened to the radio on the way to work, taking the same route and parking on the side street. Hana wore stylish but sensible footwear and the journey through the gully proved easy despite light rain speckling the track.

"I love you, Loge." Hana smiled up at him as she navigated a puddle. Turning, she saw the faintest glimmer of pain cross his face and then he banished it like morning mist. "I know you're lying to me," she said with a sigh. "You're in agony. I can see it in your eyes."

On her desk, Hana found the elusive chocolate bar from the social club. Pete cowered like a whipped dog. "I didn't eat it," he said, looking pleased with himself. "But can I have it now?" He rubbed his stomach and eyed the bar in her hand.

"No." Hana's eyes narrowed. He sat down and she relented, breaking the packet open and snapping off a few squares.

Hana received texts from her children, but when her phone buzzed again, she didn't recognise the number. Opening the message with caution, she read the words on the screen.

'Happy Birthday, I hope this year brings you all the happiness you deserve. Wishing you all the best, your friend, Anka xx.'

Hana glanced at the other occupants of the room. Caroline argued with a Year 13 with a raised and angry tattoo poking from his shirt collar. Pete sat in his chair marking assignments with his eyes shut and his cheek resting on his desk. Hana texted back.

'Thank you – I miss you – where are you?'

Nothing came for a while, but after she gave up hope and tucked the phone into her drawer, she heard the muted signal. Dragging it free, Hana read the message.

'Don't laugh but I'm working as a chalet cleaner in Russell. I need space. Please don't tell anyone. Nobody knows where I am. You looked beautiful at the registry office. I'm proud of you.'

Hana replied, her fingers moving across the keypad at speed.

'I won't tell. I saw you there. Please stay in touch?'

Her phone beeped again before she could silence it. Caroline sighed and gave her a warning glare which chilled Hana's blood. The woman's blue eyes narrowed to angry slits and Hana turned away with anxiety budding. Angus wouldn't fire her for taking private messages, but Caroline might be keeping score and wouldn't be above fabrication.

The single lettered reply made Hana's heavy heart dance with delight.

'K.'

Hana powered through her work, leaving herself enough time to create a display in the foyer. Logan visited at interval with a coffee from the vending machine and Hana sighed with pleasure. "I could get used to you running around after me. I've tolerated that insipid brew all year and never considered bringing coins for the machine."

Logan grinned, the expression coy. He leaned forward to kiss Hana and she sighed and tilted her coffee. "Whoa," he whispered, a rushed, breathy sound. "You don't want to add to the stains on the carpet do you?" He raised an eyebrow and Hana stifled a snort which ended in a shudder.

"I don't want to think about what might be on this carpet," she said, wrinkling her nose.

"See ya later," he whispered. "We'll go home and stain our own carpet."

Hana hooted with laughter and shoved his thigh. He winked at her and left through the door to the common room. Her eyes tracked to Caroline, noticing her rigid spine and envious glare in her blue eyes. Both women watched Logan's outline through the misted glass of the rear door as he skirted the office.

Rattled by the atmosphere, Hana went into the common room to drink her coffee. She stood at the floor to ceiling window and watched Logan on duty in the courtyard, supervising boys collecting litter in red buckets. A group of prefects flanked him like bees around a honey pot, hanging off his every word with eagerness. He dispatched them in different directions as trouble arose, an orchestra conductor with a band of hundreds.

He glanced up once as a small boy bounced next to him while imparting some trivia only he found hilarious. Logan's smile looked polite but his eyes rested on Hana. She blew him a kiss at the same moment the bell sounded and the child departed to his next class. He raised his eyebrows and Hana saw the top of his dark head as he ran up the front steps and entered the building. The broken arm did little to hinder him and Hana gasped as Logan burst through the double doors a minute later. His quickened heartbeat told her he'd run as he pulled her into his chest. He bailed her up against the wall to the left of the window as noise filled the buildings around them at the sound of six hundred boys on the move. "You're a real bad girl," he breathed into her hair. "You'll get us both fired!" He pulled the huge curtain across the glass and kissed her, leaving her breathless as he strode away.

Hana hugged herself, enjoying the feeling of safety his presence imbued. The empty coffee cup tilted in her fingers and dregs dribbled onto the carpet. Logan glanced back once more at the entrance to the covered bridge across to the English building, a look of desire flashing in his eyes.

Hana jumped at the slam of the office door and watched Caroline pick up speed. Her blonde hair bounced as she ran towards the overbridge, her feet clattering against the wooden floor. "Logan!" she shouted and the contented smile slipped from Hana's lips.

"No!" Hana hissed, dropping the paper cup to the floor. She

gave chase, her self-defence reaction shrouded in guilt. She hid at the entrance to the covered walkway, letting the left of the wooden doors screen her from view. The stamping feet of boys grew closer.

"Come on Logan, you can stop this charade now. You made your point. We need to talk. You're delaying the inevitable because we're meant to be together. We both know that." Caroline's voice betrayed an element of pleading and Hana held her breath.

"Go away, your behaviour is unprofessional." Logan kept walking and Caroline jerked towards him, seizing his wrist in her hand.

"It's fine, I learned my lesson. Let's go back to the way we were. I know you don't want to be with the brainless bimbo. I don't understand why you married her but it doesn't matter. We can undo it."

Logan's face clouded in fury and Hana put a hand up to her mouth. "Leave me alone!" he snapped, shaking off her grip. "Hana's worth ten of you, so back off! I don't want you in my life, Caroline. You had your chance." His voice sounded clear and steady, devoid of awkwardness or doubt. Hana watched Caroline's hand reach for him again but he turned, leaving before it connected.

Hana's relief brought overwhelming nausea. She ran to the staff toilets and vomited, anxiety spreading like an infection through her system. Caroline wouldn't give up and Hana doubted her ability to win this fight. So far, Logan's ex fiancé had proved relentless. She waited before returning to the office, hearing Caroline bashing hell out of her keyboard through the closed door. "Enjoy the show, bimbo?" the blonde woman snapped as Hana walked towards her desk. The nausea overrode her again, bringing with it the stench of defeat. "You're nothing more than a minor distraction." Caroline turned to face her, eyes flashing as though sanity no longer lived there.

Colour flushed Hana's cheeks and she stiffened her reluctant backbone. "It didn't look that way to me." She narrowed her green eyes to slits. "From where I'm standing, you're the loser in this. Pity you forgot to show up for your own wedding." She waggled a shaking ring finger. "And now I'm wearing the band of gold which ties me to Logan." She forced a smile onto her lips. "I won't be taking it off anytime soon."

Objects spewed from Caroline's desk as she lurched for Hana. Taller, she glared down her nose and gave Hana a hefty shove backwards. Hana grunted as her ribs contacted the side of an open drawer of the filing cabinet and rage lit like a flame in her heart. Caroline set her face into its characteristic sneer, not expecting resistance. "You're such a fool!" she sniggered. "Women like you don't snag guys like him."

"No?" Hana took a step forward, ignoring the tightness in her left lung. "It sure looks like they do from where I'm standing." She shoved her finger into Caroline's face just millimetres from her nose, the unexpected action making the other woman take a step backwards. "I'll fight for what's mine and if you want to test me, let's start now!"

Caroline threw her head back and laughed, further antagonising Hana's redheaded temper. "Logan Du Rose belongs to nobody, darling. None of them does. He'll pick and choose just like his brother and one day, he just won't pick you anymore!" She prodded a sharp nail into Hana's chest.

Hana felt her heart detonate. She ground her teeth and her breath came in angry gasps. She pushed her body in close to Caroline's, enjoying her grimace as she stepped on her toes. "Logan picked me years ago, sister." She let her face crumple into fake dismay. "Oh, that's right. You weren't at our wedding so you don't know the whole story. Logan fell in love with me at fourteen, so whatever hold you think you had over him, he won't come back for seconds. We met in London, Caroline. Didn't you know that? Thanks for not showing up to your own wedding because we reconnected a few short weeks later. You can't win this."

Hana wrinkled her nose in disgust, stepping away from Caroline as though she represented a bag of trash. Her conscience quailed and then disowned her as she behaved so out of character, staking her claim at last. Caroline's face moved through a range of emotions from anger to misery, blanching at a part of Logan's history she never knew. The tiny redhead shook inside, but her calm exterior masked the lie as she pointed an index finger at Caroline's face. "I mean it! Stay clear of my husband and keep out of my way. Or I swear I'll make you sorry you ever learned his name!" Hana heard the bile in her own voice, fighting the urge to pin Caroline to the floor and pound her perfect cheekbones until she evaporated in a haze of steam and dust.

Caroline swallowed. Perhaps she recognised the narrow path between control and insanity in Hana's face. She grabbed a folder and left the room, not stopping to look over her shoulder. Alone, Hana sank into her chair, hating what she'd become. "Oh God!" she wailed after closing and locking the office door. "I just handed her every card in the deck; she'll get me fired." Worse than the fear of Angus' shock and disappointment was the realisation she'd plumbed depths of herself she never knew existed. With the addition of the wedding band to her jewellery collection came a change in her nature. She wasn't sure she liked the result.

Hana stared down the years at the nice little push-over she'd been, playing the poor victim for too many wasted years. It contrasted with the woman who stood in front of Caroline, unleashing threats she couldn't fulfil. Nausea bit again and she dry retched into the dustbin, aware of the hundred boys just metres away through the flimsy walls. Afterwards she tried to concentrate on her work, making a mess of a budget and having to redo it.

When Pete turned up at lunchtime, she blagged his car keys, borrowed a school uniform and cap from lost property and left the site unnoticed. Heading to the rest home, she unburdened herself to her old friend, Father Sinbad, who listened with his usual passive expression. When she finished her sad tale of woe, he put his head back and roared with laughter. "For pities sake, gal," he drawled in his thick Irish accent, "When I told youse to go and get some action, I didn't mean for youse to get everyone else's too. Well, you're a greedy gal ain't ya? Gawd love ya, youse gonna give me a conniption."

Hana failed to see the funny side. "Aren't you meant to give me Hail Mary's or something? I've been really bad! You just laughed at my confession. What kind of a priest are you? If you could see me now in my disguise, you'd wet yourself! Logan goes to great lengths to get me to work safely and then I drive up the road to see you. He'll kill me. So I'm wearing a scabby old shirt and jumper and a cap I think's given me nits!"

Father Sinbad roared again, lightening Hana's spirits with his jocularity. He waved away her anxieties about marrying a non-Christian. "It's too late now," he commented. "What's done is done. Every couple will stumble and fall in the harness of life. Being unequally yolked makes life harder but now you've accepted your place by his side, you need to run the race." The old man sighed. He'd seen enough dying parishioners encounter with the Lord Jesus himself in their last moments to believe he could and did, call whomever he wanted at exactly the right moment. "Och look gal. As an Irish Catholic, I've experienced abundant judging to last me a lifetime. I told ye what you needed last time afore ya weddin'. I've nuttin' to add."

Hana's sad inhale took in the scent of male body odour on the jumper and she grimaced. "Yes, you said it's my job to make my man happy."

"Aye." He turned his blind eyes to face her. "And de Good Lord's job to make him holy! Youse get on wit' your bit and mind yer own business."

Hana pouted and sulked. Sinbad's unfocussed eyes roved without control in front of her. "Ah, Hana, you'll be givin' me a heart attack to be sure." He fumbled air until his claw like hands clasped her wrist. "But it's grand to see ya living proper. I spend each day sitting in a chair by a window I can't see out of. I'm reliant on the kindness and duty of others and here is my favourite visitor telling me an exciting story."

"I'm glad you're entertained." Hana sounded grumpy and the old priest cackled.

"So what about dem men what's attackin' ya?" he asked, clearing his throat after a prolonged coughing bout. Hana patted his back, feeling the bones under her palms and jerking back in surprise.

"When did you lose so much weight?" she demanded and he shrugged her off with an expression of impatience.

"I'm an old man, Hana. 'Tis inevitable. Tell me about the men. Did Bodie catch them?"

"Oh, those men. There's nothing to tell. They almost ran me over, mugged me, did the home invasion and stole my car. They're still looking for me and the cops are useless." Hana gave one more rub to the sloping shoulders and perched on the edge of the bed. "Now I think I've married a man with a split personality. No wonder you're entertained."

"No more, no more!" the old man wheezed again as tears plopped onto his blanketed knees. Hana grew impatient.

"I'm beginning to wonder if you were ever a priest at all! All those years in the confessional and you're out of practice. It's shocking, Father, not hilarious. Stop laughing!"

"It's the way you tell da story," Sinbad chortled and Hana pouted.

"Izzie's having another baby," she said and the old man sobered. He cocked his head on one side and waited. "I'm pleased and I'm hoping she will be once she warms to the idea."

Hana bit her lip and resisted telling him about Bodie's little boy, although she suspected he already knew. If Bodie confessed to anyone, it would be him. She didn't want to take the risk and disappoint the old cleric, just in case. He adored Bodie. Hana knew the biblical rules on illegitimate love-children but didn't feel keen to test his resolve. She sighed and watched him cock his head. "That's all for today," she lied and his smirk spread.

"I should go." Hana checked her watch and winced. "If Donald Watson sees me drive into the car park dressed as a school boy, he'll have more questions than I can face." She kissed Sinbad on his bristly cheek, his uncharacteristic frailty making her worry.

He gripped her hand in a frantic, grasping movement and his voice wobbled. "Fight back, Hana. Your most dangerous opponent is this woman. We can replace possessions but not relationships. These men may steal from you, but what she takes will scar you forever." Hana swallowed and nodded, remembering he couldn't see her. "Don't let her, Hana." He squeezed her fingers. "Your mistake is to fight her in de flesh. So don't war with words. Pray gal, pray and I'll remember you to your Father in Heaven. Bind your mind to the mind of Christ, because He knows all things."

He released her wrist and turned away. His ramblings sounded pointless until Hana recognised the odd Latin word. She sighed, the sound heavy in the hush of the room. "You're right, Father. But I've lost my way."

"Ah, Anka." The white head nodded forward and back. "It's a normal reaction, gal. A Christian woman smashed up her home with her own bare hands and left it in ruins." His face drooped in sadness. "It takes so little effort to follow that pattern, Hana. Sin is subtle, an inching along process. Nobody wakes in the morning and decides this is the day they'll destroy their life."

"I know." Hana paused with her hand on the doorknob. "Caroline must be a great temptation for Logan. I pray he has the strength of character to resist her like never before. I could handle most things in this life, but not that."

Hana drove to school, abandoned Pete's car behind the gym and slipped off the shirt and jumper in the toilets. She ran her fingers through her hair, forcing submission after its gleeful escape from the cap. Sneaking into the back of the school shop, she placed the items in lost property, wrinkling her nose at the mix of her expensive perfume and eau de garçon. Entering her office whilst itching her head, she found it empty and heaved a sigh of relief. "First prayer answered!" she said with an exaggerated exhale. Hana dipped her head over her dustbin and scratched her scalp. "The second relates to any impending nit infestation."

Caroline's desk looked neat and tidy and Hana pouted, fighting the urge to mess it up on purpose. She sat on her hands to stop herself. "Happy birthday to me!" she exclaimed into the empty office, a tinge of bitterness in her voice.

"Quite right. Many happy returns!"

Hana squeaked and spun in her chair. Angus baulked at the state of Hana's hair sticking up on end like a bird's nest. He pointed to his receding hairline. "Is this a new style you're trying out? It's very intriguing." He paused and bit his lip. "You didn't look like that this morning. Hana, your hair looks like a squirrel's tail."

Hana put her hand up to her head, the patting turning to itching. "Sorry," she said with a grimace. "I think I've caught nits." Her cheeks and neck flushed bright red.

"It's an interesting style." Angus smiled and sat in Caroline's chair, repeating his description in case Hana didn't hear it. "Very interesting."

Hana panicked and attempted a flattening job with her hands. Angus shook his head and pointed at a few stray spikes. "I know," she said, her embarrassment growing. "I'll use this bottled water." She covered the end with her thumb to cause enough of a sprinkling to damp down the fire on her scalp and frizzling coils of hair.

"Oh!" Angus reached out a tentative hand. "That's lemonade."

Hana groaned. "I should've stayed in bed this morning!"

"Yes, it may have proved fortuitous." Angus stood and paced the room, touching things and causing a sheaf of papers to plunge to their death from a shelf. "Hana, Hana, Hana," he sighed and she stopped itching to cast a wary glance in his direction. "Ms Marsh came to my office this afternoon, in floods of tears and hysterics and claiming you threatened her. What, my dear, should I believe? Must I commence an investigation into the behaviour of one of my most trusted members of staff? Besides which, I count you as a friend." He pulled his bifocals further down his nose and Hana's heart almost stopped.

He waited as Hana sat in shocked silence. She reran Sinbad's warning against Caroline and shook her head, knowing she handed her the weapons herself. The old man spoke the truth. Caroline could prove more lethal than the blonde man and his accomplice. "Well?" Angus demanded, rocking on the balls of his feet and examining a stain on the carpet.

"I saw her," began Hana, speaking as though recounting a traumatic event. Sinbad never suggested play-acting as a tool but Hana decided to use her own skills while waiting for God. "I saw her run after Logan and make advances towards him at lunchtime, in public. I saw her on the bridge. She tried to take his hand and I heard Logan ask her to leave him alone." Hana rolled her eyes and attempted a look of pure innocence. Her wince of realisation ruined the effect as Angus raised an eyebrow. "I didn't eavesdrop," she said, widening her eyes in an angelic expression. "They spoke loud enough for their voices to carry." Hana turned away in the guise of reaching for a tissue and smirked at her ingenuity. "Even though Caroline knows we're married, she won't give up. She propositioned a married man! I'm shocked and I have to admit, I'm rethinking my position at the school. I need to speak to Logan but I don't see how we can stay. It's intolerable. She shouldn't be engaging in staff relationships at all, let alone tempting a man already married." Hana patted the frizz on her head, feeling the stickiness of the lemonade as her dignity crept out the door behind her.

Angus listened but his eyes widened in shock at Hana's overt threat. "You wouldn't leave! Not with Sheila off. Oh my goodness. I couldn't put Pete in charge!"

Hana shrugged. "Well, I don't know what the answer is then." The sentence damned her with the resounding truth of it. "And if I leave, Logan can't stay. I'm the only thing standing in the way of her devouring him like a…"

"I don't need an example, thanks," Angus interjected, raising his hand to block Hana's description. "I can imagine for myself. How can one woman cause so much trouble in a matter of weeks?"

"I don't know," Hana sighed. "What do you want from me?" She grimaced as a drip of lemonade slid inside the collar of her blouse and slithered down her back. Her hair felt like candyfloss.

"What exactly did you say to her?" Angus slumped into Caroline's chair and waited.

Hana told him the truth, although she changed a little of the emphasis to reduce the element of threat. The pricking of her conscience turned into full-blown stabs at the very different picture she painted.

Angus leaned forward in his chair. "What do you know about her and Chris Carter, the health and physical education teacher?"

Hana shrugged. "He comes in here looking for her sometimes and they go off together. I did intercept a text from someone who enjoyed a good night with her and wanted a repeat." Hana scratched her head without thinking and Angus winced at the movement. "Chris Carter's married, anyway." Hana's eyes widened. "Ohhh."

Hana saw the coffin lid closing over Caroline Marsh's teaching career at Waikato Presbyterian School for Boys. She faked an admirable look of concern and hoped they hammered the last nail in good and hard. "What a little slapper," she exclaimed, before clapping a hand over her mouth.

"Quite," Angus said, standing and leaving the room.

Hana punched the air. "Game, set and match, bitch!"

"I heard that, Mrs Du Rose," he said from the brochure rack outside the door."

An hour later, Hana closed up the office and sought out her husband. Sexual impropriety was definitely a coffin closer with the board of trustees. Chris Carter. Hana shivered. At least it explained the text and Caroline's hushed arguments with him the few times he'd come looking for her. "What kind of woman hunts down a previous lover and then entertains herself with another married man while she waits for the first one?" she asked aloud.

"A nymphomaniac," Pete supplied, wandering past Logan's office and slapping her on the backside. He bounced a basketball without skill and chased it as it escaped.

"No running indoors!" Hana hissed.

Pete smirked and threw a rude gesture over his shoulder. Hana shivered at the thought of Caroline's hands touching any part of Logan. Then the memory came without being called for and Hana saw another woman's hands in a different time and place. And her heart ached from the pain of it.

-7-

Walking back along the gully after school, Hana held hands with Logan and carried his briefcase. Darkness closed around them but Logan exuded safety. "Leave it alone, Loge!" She laughed at him as he let go of her hand and fiddled with the sling over his left arm.

"It's annoying!" he grumbled. Hana heard the sound of tearing material.

"Don't rip it!" She put his briefcase on the gravel floor and tugged at the white fabric. "I need a light to see what you've done. It's all rucked up underneath somehow."

"It's wound me up all day. Just let me rip it off." Logan's patience snapped and he pulled it from Hana's grasp. "And when I get home I'm cutting this thing off as well." He waved his cast in the air, grimacing at the instant pain in his elbow. "Bloody hell!"

"Poor baby." Hana played up her maternal side, soothing her husband as she won the battle with the sling. "Look, you tucked it under there wrong. And I won't let you cut the cast off." She narrowed her eyes. "It cost me forty bucks so technically it belongs to me. Did you teach sports today?"

Logan nodded and his lips turned down in a grumpy expression. Hana slid her hands around his waist and the sharp angles of his tense jaw softened. "How about I make it better at home?"

"Ok then." The sulk in his voice sounded pure play act and a smirk hung around the corners of his mouth. "Then I'm cutting this cast off."

"That would be stupid. It'll heal weird." Hana pressed her face against Logan's warm chest, his body heat radiating through his jacket.

"What like this?" Logan held up his right hand and Hana knitted her brow against the strange kink in two of his fingers.

"Yes like that! Keep it on."

"Or what?" Logan's lips pressed against Hana's as he issued the challenge and she felt the familiar flare of desire in her gut.

"I'll think of something!"

Logan let go of her with a hiss, the action abrupt. He reached into his pocket with his good hand and pulled out his phone, almost dropping it into the mud. It vibrated in his palm and he exhaled in annoyance. "She won't leave me alone!" he snapped.

Hana watched his expression morph into a frown of irritation. The rising moon dappled the scene, touching the dark reaches of the bush with a silver paintbrush. She held out her hand for the phone. Logan paused for a moment before dropping it into her palm. A gold message envelope flashed on the screen, unopened. The caller's name pulsed in the top left hand corner and Hana swallowed her bitterness. She pressed the keypad and opened the text message.

'She set me up! This isn't over!'

Hana read it aloud, her jaw stiffening in the effort to hide the spiteful smirk teasing her lips. Logan's brow furrowed.

"What's she talking about? She dumps me at the altar and then propositions me at work. I don't think I ever understood her."

Hana swallowed but didn't enlighten him. "Why does she have your number?"

Logan shrugged. "I got that sim card when I came back to New Zealand. What's that? Six years?"

"But you've still got hers." Hana's tone sounded flat.

"Don't read anything into it." Logan reached out an index finger and traced the line of her jaw. "Scroll up, Hana. Do you see my reply to any of her messages?"

Hana obeyed and nodded, the evidence of his truthfulness on the screen. "Fair enough," she agreed. "She's texted you hundreds of times." Her lips pulled into a tight, straight line as Hana flicked the screen with her finger and revealed Caroline's desperation.

"And I never answered." Logan bit his lip and concentrated on Hana's face, night shadows forming darkened areas beneath her elfin features.

Hana stared at the phone with hatred in her eyes, its green display ghoulish in the darkness. Logan reached out his hand and cupped her chin, bringing her face up so she met his grey eyes. "What does she mean, Hana? Is she talking about you? What did you do?"

Hana assumed a haughty expression, wearing it like a defensive shield. She tossed her red hair and the wind snatched it, puffing it behind her like a sail. "Angus thinks she's sleeping with Chris Carter. I gave him a little hard proof and he must have taken it to the trustees."

"Chris Carter? Are you sure?" Logan sounded more incredulous than hurt. "That can't be right. Carter's wife just had a baby girl. No idiot would risk losing all that."

"Why not?" Hana spoke softly, her voice sounding distant and swathed in pain. She directed her anger towards Caroline. "She only cares about herself! I hate women like her!" Hana's eyes misted over, an odd expression on her face and the phone still in her hand. Without warning, she turned and threw it into the deepest part of the gully where it contacted the sludgy water with a resounding plop.

"Hana!" Logan's eyes widened in shock. "Geez woman. You're a worry." Hana showed no sign of repentance and he bit his lip in amusement at the fiery redhead. Her hands rested on her hips and she flicked her head so her auburn hair cascaded down her back.

"I'm not sorry," she bit.

"Yep. I can see that." Logan shook his head from side to side. "You're a feisty little thing, aren't ya?"

Hana shrugged. "Maybe. That's for me to know and you to find out." She hefted the briefcase and her handbag back into place on her arm. "I'm sure you can remember the important numbers for your new phone." Her forced casualness made Logan raise an eyebrow in an effort not to laugh. He put his arm around her and edged her up the shallow incline towards the road.

"I'll have to now," he said, faking a look of annoyance which only lasted as far as the street. "Anyone ever tell you how hot you are when you're angry?"

Hana shook her head and conjured up Vik's face. "No," she said. "Not everyone appreciates it."

Caroline Marsh sat in her stinky rental room with her notice of termination in her lap. She reapplied her lipstick and waited. "Come on, Logan," she groaned. "You have to answer me this time. You hate injustice. Kick the little bimbo into touch." She ran her fingers through her short hair and gave herself a windswept look, comparing the shorn locks to Hana's amber tresses.

Her text reclined at the bottom of the gully, the phone filling with water as the connections fizzled and died. The stab in Caroline's warped heart felt physical, even though she didn't see Logan press his wife against the car and lean in for a kiss. Hana's laughter tinkled like tiny bells in the darkness. "I should get mad more often," she said with a sigh.

-8-

Friday night came around fast. Hana's comfort levels grew, the threat of attack almost unreal as Logan's safety precautions made them harder to trace. Hana relaxed and failed to notice her tendency towards sloppiness.

Work and the pain in his arm exhausted Logan and he slept after the long drive home under the influence of strong painkillers. One evening, Hana nipped into Ngaruawahia to the post office to post a letter to Izzie and ended up in the local supermarket, buying so much food her trolley overflowed. A packet of sanitary towels did a peculiar dance and hurled themselves onto the floor. As she bent to retrieve them, her fingers contacted the hand of a man in a business suit who also reached for them. Her fear rushed back like a burst dam. "Sorry." He sat the bright pink packet on the top of a cereal box and smiled at Hana. "Didn't mean to scare you."

Hana shook her head. "Thanks," she gushed, pushing the packet between a loaf of bread and a carton of milk. She resisted his attempts at small talk and moved away, smoothing her frown with tired fingers. The aisles of shopping closed in on her, reminding her of her foolishness and Hana felt her knees wobble beneath her. "Idiot!" she hissed and moved towards the cashier, glancing around her in fear. The businessman watched her from the end of the confectionary aisle and Hana felt her heart rate increase.

By the time the shopping left the conveyor belt for carrier bags, it wouldn't all fit into the trolley. A shop assistant accompanied her to the Honda with a second one. Hana thanked him and left tyre marks on the floor of the car park as she sped away, activating the central locking and breathing through pursed lips. The food clanged around in the boot as she made the steep climb up to the house.

Logan met her on the porch as the car revved up the hill. He rubbed his eyes and leaned his hip against the balustrade. "Where'd you get to?" he asked, his body foggy with sleep. Hana covered her face and burst into tears.

"This is nice," sighed Logan later as they sat at the kitchen table, polishing off a bottle of red wine. He wiped his top lip with his fingers, savouring the spaghetti Bolognese he helped Hana make.

"Want me to feed you?" Hana joked, her chest still hitching from her tearful outburst.

"Na, I'm full." Logan laid his fork down and stopped fighting the wriggling strands of pasta. "I don't need to tell you to be more careful, do I?" His tone grew serious and Hana shook her head.

"No." Her chest hitched again and Logan's face relaxed, forcing away the lurking hint of pain in his eyes. Hana twirled spaghetti around her fork and a stream of tomato sauce jetted across her face and into her eye. Logan laughed until he realised she hadn't joined in. She looked down, prodding a blob of sauce with her spoon.

"It's okay, babe," he whispered. "No harm done." He kicked her softly under the table with his bare foot.

A slow, rumbling vibration moved through the floorboards and they both froze in position. The monitor for the gate bleeped in the hallway and Hana's eyes opened wide. She stared at Logan, her breath catching in her throat. "It's not possible. They said nobody could get in!"

Logan shook his head, doubt flitting across his face. "They're not meant to."

They heard a vehicle labouring against the incline as the driver crunched through the gears. "The man at the shop, the man at the shop!" Hana squealed, casting around her in panic.

"What man?" Logan rose and pushed the chair back with the side of his leg. It skittered across the floorboards and hit the side of the sink. "What bloody man? You said he didn't follow you."

"Just a man, an ordinary man. But he must be one of them." Hana backed against the pantry door and attempted to flatten herself enough to disappear. Wrenching open a drawer, Logan's good hand settled on the trusty rolling pin. He hefted it right handed and wrinkled his nose.

"Better than nothing," he said.

"I used it to clout the man who hurt me at the old house," Hana whimpered. "It's still got dents in."

Logan looked at the long roll of pine and then back at Hana. "Do I look like I'm bothered?" he hissed at her. "I'm about to make more dents in it."

Hana bit her lip and put her hands over her face. "Oh," she moaned. "I'm sick of this."

"Lights out!" Logan snapped the order but found Hana already half way to the switch. He took a couple of air swings to get his balance. Hana watched him wide eyed as he shrugged in the half-light and looked at it in disgust. Moving out into the hallway, Logan flicked that light off too and the house plunged into darkness.

They huddled together, watching through the side window as the lights grew closer. Headlamps illuminated the house in an aggressive arc as the vehicle mounted the brow of the hill and settled on the flat section. Logan lowered the rolling pin and Hana reached for it, believing his arm gave way. "Don't worry, I'll do it." She sniffed in terror, stifling the sob at the back of her throat.

"Get off!" Logan whispered and lifted it higher than she could reach.

"Give it to me, I'll defend us!" Hana sounded irritated and jumped up and down on the spot with her arms in the air.

A car door slammed. Footsteps. The rattle of a key in the lock. Hana froze in position, one hand grappling for the rolling pin as the front door opened and the hall light illuminated the scene.

Bodie stood in the gap, letting in a family of moths who fluttered straight to the still warm light bulb. He looked at the welcoming committee in amazement. "Have I interrupted something?" he asked, his policeman's brain working overtime.

Hana's voice came out as a shriek, "What! Interrupted what?"

"Well," replied her son, "Why are you fighting over a rolling pin in the dark, covered in blood?" He narrowed his dark eyes and glared at Logan.

It took a while to convince Bodie that Logan hadn't beaten his mother. The drying spaghetti sauce stains proved convincing enough to make Hana's son furious. "But are you sure the gate is closed?" she demanded for the fifth time and Bodie closed the front door with his foot.

"They close themselves!" he bit. "Geez Mum, calm down!"

Logan sighed and shrugged himself back into his jacket one-handed. "Look, I'll walk down and check," he said, winking at Hana leaving them alone to talk.

"I said I needed to speak to you!" Bodie insisted, his voice becoming whiney as he repeated the sentence again. "I've transferred to Hamilton. I thought you'd be pleased."

"I am pleased." Hana tied her ponytail behind her head. "It's been one hell of a week."

Bodie rolled his eyes and jerked his head at the front door. "It looks like it. How'd he break his arm?"

Hana sighed and sank into a kitchen chair. "His nephew did it in temper as Logan tried to protect me."

"Is this the same randy nephew who had it away with Ivan's missus?"

Hana cringed at her son's bluntness regarding Anka. "Yes. Tama."

"Do you know where Anka is?" asked Bodie.

Hana shrugged. "Not really." But her green eyes betrayed her.

"Mum! Do you or don't you?"

"I do now, but I didn't then," she replied as Logan closed the front door behind him and kicked off his boots. He looked up at her and raised his eyebrows in a look of irritation at Bodie's aggressive tone. Hana examined the table with avid interest, determined not to betray her friend's confidence. "Why are you asking about Anka?"

Bodie leaned forward and his brown eyes filled with curiosity and concern. "Because her husband's filed a missing report," he replied.

-9-

"She's not missing," Hana said, her cheeks flushing. "She's in Russell."

Bodie shook his head. "Then you should tell someone. Her husband's going mental and we can't help him yet because she's a grown woman. She can go wherever she likes as long as we don't suspect foul play."

Hana nodded and sighed. "My last conversation with Ivan was horrible. He blames me." She baulked at Bodie's raised eyebrow. "Can't you just text him and say she's messaged me? I won't tell him where she is though. She wants no one to know."

"Fine. Show me the text as evidence." Bodie waited for Hana to find it and then snapped a picture with his phone camera. "I'll add it to the file and call him myself."

"Thanks." Hana twisted her lips into a pout. "So, tell me about this transfer to Hamilton. Is it permanent?"

"Yeah. I need to train with the fast cars and take a test to prove I can drive them. Then I'll launch my new career path as a traffic cop. There are more courses and probationary periods with other officers, but I'm hopeful it will be a better fit." Bodie smiled at Hana, his aura settled. Contentment clothed him like a good fitting jacket. "Can I crash here with you for a few days, before I move into the unit in town with the other single guys?" He raised an eyebrow in expectation. "I'll stash my gear in that tiny room next to the garage."

"It's fine. But what about Amy and Jas?" Hana asked.

Bodie heaved in a huge sigh and told her most of the story. She sensed he missed out the parts which might disappoint her most. "I fell in love with Amy at police training college. We carried on our affair back in Hamilton but it got complicated."

Hana's eyes narrowed. "As in a complicated boyfriend or

husband?" She swallowed back the fear he might have rejected Amy because of Jas.

Bodie blinked, caught off guard by her astuteness. He nodded, his high cheekbones flushing with colour. "Husband. Amy stayed with him, so I transferred north as fast as I could. I knew I couldn't cope with seeing her at work all the time."

"Oh." Hana nodded, a slow, cautious action blossoming with understanding. "That's why you left. You became so unhappy and then just disappeared. Because of Amy?"

"I honestly didn't know about Jas, Mum." Bodie leaned forward, his expression earnest. "She never told me I had a son. I found out by accident on my last visit home. Someone at the station said something about her taking a year off on leave after training college. I thought maybe she hurt herself as much as me when she broke it off." Bodie swallowed. "I needed to find out." He fiddled with the spout of the hot teapot, hissing in irritation when the brown pottery burned his fingers. Hana laid her hand over his to still the fidgeting and invited him to continue. "Amy's marriage dissolved because of the pregnancy. The prospective birth of a little quarter Indian baby would have sealed her fate anyway, even if her husband stuck around. He never wanted children and she knew the score."

"So she's managed alone?" Hana's brow knitted and she bit back her ready condemnation of Bodie.

He nodded and she saw the flash of shame and regret cross his eyes. "I didn't know," he repeated. "Her husband's a cop and he transferred out too. He remarried and lives in Wellington."

"So what's the plan?" Hana asked, releasing his fingers.

Bodie swallowed. "Jas is the priority now," he said. "I still love Amy but I don't know if we can ever get past the hurt and misery. It needs to be okay for the kid and I'll do whatever it takes."

"That's a good plan." Hana sighed and ran a hand through her fringe. "That makes me proud."

Bodie's phone chirped in his pocket and he peered at the screen, instantly distracted. Logan walked into the kitchen, his complexion white and a sheen of dampness on his forehead.

Hana looked at him in question and he waved her concern away. "I'm fine," he reassured her. "I went to the bathroom. Stop worrying."

Hana stood and refilled the kettle and Logan kissed the side of her face, closing his eyes against the pain of his injury. She saw Bodie's expression change to one of discomfort as he observed their intimacy. Logan's good arm snaked around Hana's waist as though staking possession in the gentlest of movements. Bodie ground his teeth and cleared his throat. "Too much public display, thanks."

Hana pulled back with a snort. "I suppose it's a huge leap for you, accepting I'm no longer just your mother."

"A bit." Bodie shifted in his seat and refused to engage eye contact with Logan. Hurt and betrayal bridled in his expression and made him spiteful. "I suppose eight years of widowhood is a decent interval," he snapped.

Logan opened his mouth and then closed it again, clamping his tongue between his teeth.

Bodie's phone rang and he looked at the screen, answering the call and standing. He moved into the hallway, still speaking. "Mate!" he said, his voice softer than usual. "Good on ya, son. That's awesome. A Gold Certificate! Show me tomorrow when I come round. How about we take Mum to lunch?"

Hana heard his footsteps pad along the hallway to the single bedroom near the back stairs. He kept talking, his tone light and carefree.

"Sorry." Logan's shoulders slumped as he leaned against the counter. He tried to fold his arms but jarred the cast and a look of agony fleeted across his face.

"No you're not." Hana raised an eyebrow at him. "But it's fine. I couldn't stay a widow forever just to please my son and I won't reject your affection just to please him."

"Still, it's hard for him," Logan acknowledged. His lips quirked upwards. "Especially now he's seen me wielding a rolling pin above your head."

Hana snorted. "My hero," she simpered and he laughed.

"I knew who it was anyway," he said, smirking at the look of disbelief in her face.

"No you didn't!"

"Did too," he countered. "I've been in enough tight spots to learn to think on my feet. After the initial panic, I remembered posting a key and gate code to Bodie before the wedding. I asked him to stay in the house and check on the cat before the party. It could only be him."

"Oh." Hana frowned in concession.

"Why did you fight me for the damn rolling pin?" Logan asked. He traced light circles on her back with his index finger.

Hana pouted. "I thought your arm hurt and that if I could get the rolling pin, I could protect you."

Logan laughed and realised his mistake as Hana looked offended. He tried to placate her. "Sorry. Nobody ever tried to take care of me as you do. That's the second time you've done that." He moderated the seriousness in his tone and tried to diffuse the tension using humour. "It's just as well you couldn't reach it, otherwise you'd be in a police cell right now. Not the best idea to bludgeon your cop-son with a rolling pin, especially when I gave him a key!"

"I guess not." Hana smirked.

Logan sighed. "I'm cross with myself, anyway. The Maglite in the drawer should have been my first thought. Not a bloody wooden rolling pin."

Hana nodded and stroked his wrist, the clamminess of his skin making her anxious. "You've had a lot on your mind recently," she soothed, narrowing her eyes. "Are you sure you're feeling okay?"

Logan frowned and dispelled her fears with easy platitudes.

Bodie left after breakfast the next day, eager to see his son's gold certificate. "He earned it for neat handwriting," he said with pride in his voice. "I'll check out my billet while I'm in town. I'll leave everything downstairs if that's okay. Then I can fetch it once I'm settled."

"It's fine, Bo." Hana smiled and waved to him as the engine started.

"Won't your husband mind?" he asked, an edge to his voice.

"No." Hana bit back a retort and walked up the porch steps, hating the growing antagonism between her men.

Logan settled in front of the lounge fire catching up on his marking. He balanced a tray on his knee and made scrawled marks on exercise books with a sketchy right hand. Occasionally he grunted in annoyance. Hana tidied around, fighting with a long tape measure and writing numbers on a pad. She measured every window and toyed with the idea of making her own curtains to keep the cost down. Logan discovered her standing on a chair in the bedroom with her arms stretched across the gap. "What are you doing?" he demanded, placing his hand in the centre of her back to steady her.

"Measuring for curtains," Hana said. "If you keep walking around naked, someone might see."

Logan snorted and lifted her off the chair with one arm wrapped around her waist. He lowered her to the floor. "Only if they use binoculars."

Hana slid along his body and gave a mischievous giggle. "Ah babe. Don't put yourself down."

Logan's brow knitted in confusion until he realised her meaning. Then he pinned her to the bedpost one handed and kissed her. "You have a dirty mind, Hana Du Rose," he sighed, breathing into her neck.

Hana giggled and a sound outside made her jump, banging Logan's arm. He hissed in pain. "Sorry," she whispered, the moment ruined.

"Why are you whispering?" Logan's hushed voice mirrored hers.

"I don't know. I wondered if Bodie came back for something." She slipped out from under him and ran to the window. "Just a sparrow in the eaves," she whispered.

Logan gave a slow shake of his head and chewed his lower lip. "You wanna make curtains?" he asked and Hana nodded.

"The money came from Achilles Rise," she said. "I can use that."

Logan shrugged. "I set up a transfer for half the mortgage fee plus additional for bills and food. It should have gone into your account yesterday. Did you check?"

Hana wrinkled her nose. "You didn't need to do that."

"We've had this discussion, Hana. I'm over it." Logan jerked his head towards the bedroom doors which opened onto the terrace. "Do you own a sewing machine?"

"Yep." Hana hugged herself with excitement. "It's years old, but it still works." She skipped across to Logan and placed her palms against his chest, avoiding the sling. "Logan," she mused aloud. "Now I've done the measuring and got an idea of colour, I feel desperate to go into town and buy some material."

Logan ran his hand through his fringe and eyed Hana with disbelief. "So you want to drive into Hamilton? Where you know there are people who want to hurt you?"

"But we've been fine this last week, Loge. Can we?"

"You have a short memory, babe." Logan turned and walked away. Hana skipped behind him. "You're safe because we've ducked and dived all week. You think I like walking through the gully every morning?"

"I guess not." Hana's shoulders slumped, her creativity leaking out through the soles of her feet. "Okay," she conceded.

She made Logan a coffee and took it to him, sitting on the sofa while he drank. "This room is annoying me," she stated. "It's the dirty grey walls and the furniture not pushed back against them." Hana sighed as she glanced around the room. The bare windows looked vast and the greyness of the day poured in uninvited. "It's depressing."

"No way!" Logan exclaimed. "You can't wear me down."

"Please?" Hana begged. "Just a tiny trip. There and back. I'll run in and out again."

"Look," Logan said, turning sideways on the sofa. "It's stressful enough having to take alternate routes to work every day, without trotting into town in your car and giving someone the opportunity to follow us home."

"What about the Huntly hardware place then?" Hana whined, putting her chin on his shoulder as she curled up next to him, "I'd settle for some paint." She gave a big sigh and stuck out her bottom lip in a sad face. Logan laughed at her, ruffling her hair but not giving in.

"I can't wallpaper or paint at the moment." He held up the plaster cast. Hana saw the skin poking out from underneath. It looked powdery and dry, starved of light and air. Logan's grey eyes watched Hana's disappointment and he reached out to stroke her cheek. "We don't know what Ethel Bowman told this guy. She may have heard the words Huntly or Ngaruawahia and sent him searching up here."

Hana gave a sigh of defeat. "It's not fair."

Logan stroked her cheek, sensing the beginnings of cabin fever. "Look, it's hard, I know that. It's not fair, I agree, but I don't know how to keep you safe any other way."

"I just have so much to do," Hana groaned, pouting.

Logan's shoulders stiffened and Hana felt him relent. Part of her knotted up and wished he wouldn't. She liked pushing against his boundaries and the devilment in her responded to his negativity with challenge. "What if we disguise ourselves and go north?" Logan asked. "Check out Te Kauwhata. That would be safer because we could go across country."

"Really?" Hana threw her arms around his neck, pulling back at his grunt of pain. She narrowed her eyes. "Do you need more painkillers?"

"I'm fine." Logan shook his head. "Grab the phone book and let's see what we can find."

Hana found a fabric shop listed in Te Kauwhata with a decorator's warehouse next door. "It's on the new industrial estate on the outskirts," she said, her eyes wide with enthusiasm. "I'll get ready."

She tied her long hair into bunches and found a black beanie to wear on top. A dark hoodie and tracksuit pants completed her ensemble. "Look, I've made an effort," she said, twirling in front of Logan.

He smirked. "You look like a burglar."

"Oh." Hana looked at her strange ensemble and frowned. "Should I change then?"

"No, come on. Let's get out of here." Logan pulled a baseball cap over his dark hair, still oozing testosterone despite the broken arm and the stiffness in his body. They locked up and left, Hana driving.

They headed north to the Tainui Bridge and across country to the little town of Te Kauwhata. Hana remembered the address but forgot to bring a map. By chance they found the decorator's warehouse first. The expedition cost them a small fortune as Hana fought her resolve to do one room at a time and steamed around the shelves like a game show contestant. "I don't know when you'll let me out again," she argued as Logan trailed behind her carrying her bargains.

"Probably never, at this rate," he grumbled under his breath.

Hana bought paint for the living room and hallway and twelve rolls of wallpaper to do a feature wall in each. Finding the fabric store, she behaved like a child discovering an unmanned sweet shop. "I love this place!" she gushed, wandering around with random swatches of material. Logan stumbled along behind, towing a heavy roll of calico.

"What's this for?" he complained.

"Curtain linings. I need it."

"Okay." Logan sank into a nearby chair. "You keep going and I'll catch you up." He waved her away and leaned his head back against the wall. His fingers worried at a loose thread on top of the roll and he remembered his mother with her old sewing machine, patching holes in their clothing with strange and inappropriate material.

Logan forgot he had Hana's phone in his jacket and jumped as it rang, fumbling one handed in his clothing. He winced at the pain radiating from his left side, dropping the phone twice before he could answer it. As he pressed the button, he heard it disconnect. The screen showed a missed call from Bodie, so he rang him back. "Your mother's around here somewhere. Oh, crap! I can't see her now."

Logan heard a child in the background asking questions and the noises of a busy, populated area. Bodie grunted. "Amy's gone on shift and I'm taking Jas to McDonald's. I'm ringing because I found something out. I called in to see an old mate in the criminal investigations unit and mentioned the name Laval in the course of the conversation. I told him about all the incidents with Mum. He acted real coy, but I'm telling you, his eyes went out on stalks at the mention of that guy's name. It looks like the link to Ethel Bowman's boyfriend is solid."

"Perhaps he used his real identity after all." Logan gnawed his bottom lip. "I guess he'd need his own name if the intention is to take money off Mrs Bowman. He'd need a legitimate bank account. It's got too hard to get cash or open cheques nowadays. Most people are too scam-savvy, although there's always the odd one."

Bodie coughed. "You know an awful lot about the subject," he bit and Logan sighed and shook his head. "I gave the detective enough to whet his appetite, knowing he'll come back for more once he makes the links, if they're founded. But I don't think it's a good idea for my mother to wander around the country."

Logan agreed, balancing the roll of calico against the chair and wincing as the weight shifted against his broken arm. "You try keeping her indoors," he grumbled. "She's buying curtain material."

Bodie roared with laughter. "Good luck with that, dude. I never had you down as a sucker. I still have mental scars from the time she made my bedroom curtains an inch too short."

Hana appeared from behind a shelf, trailing a tired looking shop assistant. She gave her husband a beatific smile. "I'm making them all myself," she announced. "On my sewing machine. It will take me ages."

Logan sighed, whipped out his visa card and paid the bill, hoping to goodness it did take her ages. "Make it last," he grumbled. "Because we're not doing this again."

"What's happened?" Hana demanded, but he raised his eyebrows to silence her.

The Honda pulled up the driveway without mishap or incident, but it took Hana a good fifteen minutes to unload the huge packets of material, wallpaper and paint. She saw Logan's exhaustion in his pale face and lacklustre grey eyes, refusing his help and sending him indoors for painkillers. "I'll be fine," she lied. "I'd rather have a cup of tea. Maybe you could boil the kettle."

The wallpaper proved heavy and the rolls slid around inside the massive carrier bag, but Hana hefted them up the front stairs and left them at the top. Then she brought up the paint and extra brushes and packets of paste, before dropping the Honda down the slope and into the garage. Back upstairs, she buzzed with excitement and wished she could clone herself and make curtains, paint and wallpaper all at the same time.

Logan looked dreadful. Hana squashed her overflowing enthusiasm for the project and turned her attention to him. "Hey, come out of the way," she said, shoving him with her hip and taking the kettle from his hand. He leaned against the kitchen bench, trying to swallow his tablets without water. "Idiot," she murmured, pushing him gently in the ribs.

The manner he jumped away from her and the grey look, which swathed his face, alarmed Hana. "What are you hiding?" she demanded. Moving the plaster cast aside despite Logan's protestations, she lifted his sweatshirt.

"Leave it!" Logan hissed.

Hana's mouth opened in horror. "Logan!" she exclaimed. The awful black and red bruise reached around his body, covering more than she remembered. It bled beneath his ribs and into his stomach like thread veins.

She thumped the kettle on the side and pointed towards the hallway. "Get back in that car!" she ordered.

-10-

Hana reached the outskirts of Ngaruawahia before remembering her phone languished forgotten in Logan's jacket pocket. Her stupidity slapped her in the face as familiar streets sped by, knowing she risked exposing herself to danger. She stayed as vigilant as she could with Logan grumbling to himself in the passenger seat.

"The wait-time is an hour," the doctor's receptionist droned, chewing her gum so that Hana could see it swilling around on her tongue.

Hana took a steadying breath and tried again. "You still have the paperwork from the cast you put on my husband, so I'd be grateful if you'd at least get a nurse."

"Nope," the girl intoned. "The wait time is an hour. I don't care what paperwork you have."

"Fine." Hana gritted her teeth and turned to the woman next in line. She rested a hand against Logan's chest as he propped himself up against the counter. "They're rubbish here," Hana said, jerking her head towards the receptionist. "Look what they missed last weekend." She wrenched up Logan's shirt to reveal his purple ribs. Blood threaded beneath the skin and he grunted and fought Hana's hand. Grey patches appeared in his complexion and Hana let him pull his shirt down and offered him an apology with her eyes. She maximised the attention she'd drawn from the waiting room. "I wouldn't bother waiting," she said. "How can they miss an injury that big?"

The seated members of the waiting room glanced around at each other. A mother with a small child in tow stood and lifted him onto her hip. "I already paid," she said, looking at Hana for guidance.

Hana glanced back at the counter to discover the receptionist gone. She jumped in surprise when an angry nurse appeared from a passage to the side of the waiting room. The gum-chewing girl slipped from behind her, sidled to her chair and sat down. She leaned around to Logan to shout, "Next!" Her grin at Hana showed courage emboldened by the presence of reinforcements.

"Come through!" the nurse snapped, aiming a glare in Hana's direction. Logan shook his head, too weak to voice the irritation in his eyes.

"Sorry," Hana hissed to his rigid spine.

The nurse looked at Logan's torso and called a heavyset male doctor with a crooked eye. He in turn left to make a phone call. When he returned, he looked sympathetic. "The emergency room is waiting for you. Can you drive your husband or should I call an ambulance?"

Logan swore and Hana gaped. "Hospital?"

The doctor nodded. "Yeah." He turned to Logan. "I could give you an ultrasound scan but I'd rather they did it. They have pain relief and the ability to take you into surgery if the need arises. All I can do is make it worse. I'll give you a shot for the pain, but they're waiting for you."

"Surgery?" Hana's voice rose an octave or three.

The nurse had lost her angry expression and rested a hand on Hana's shoulder. "Is there anyone I can call for you?"

Hana nodded. "Yes, please. Can you call the police station and ask for Bodie Johal or Amy? I don't know Amy's last name but someone there must. Please can you explain for me?"

"Bodie?" the nurse repeated and left at Hana's nod.

Logan lay on the gurney and glared at Hana. "This is a joke," he hissed and she licked her lips.

"I'm sorry," she repeated. "But I can see how bad that is."

The doctor nodded in agreement. "Yep. Broken ribs and perhaps a ruptured spleen. That's my educated guess." He shook his head at Hana and pulled her aside beyond the flimsy curtain. "I don't know how he remained upright, the mess he's made of his insides. Your husband must have an inhuman pain threshold!"

Hana swallowed and nodded. "He kept it hidden once he knew I saw it." She lowered her voice. "It's all my fault."

"No, it's not." The doctor smiled at her in sympathy. "What about the other scars on his body?"

Hana swallowed. "He had accidents as a child. One of them is a childhood hunting incident."

The doctor nodded. "I've checked and we don't have his notes. The hospital system recognised his name so perhaps they'll have more idea about what's gone wrong."

Hana shook her head. "He's from Auckland. I don't think he's ever been to the Waikato hospital."

The man shrugged. "Ah well. Maybe it's someone with the same name, but he's on their records."

"That must be it." Hana took a deep breath. "Tell me where to take him."

The drive into Hamilton proved torturous. Logan slumped in the passenger seat with a cocktail of drugs winging through his system. Hana battled with selfishness for forcing him to take her shopping earlier. She punished herself with odd little details, letting them merge into a damaging list. "I should have noticed you didn't manage a full plate of food in a week. This is my fault. I knew you hurt. I should have done something." Hana writhed in the driver's seat, guilt screwing her stomach into tight knots.

"It's fine," Logan gasped, gripping his side with a white knuckled hand. "I'm a big boy. I've had worse."

Hana parked and helped Logan into the foyer of the emergency room. She almost lost the piece of paper the doctor gave her for a fast tracked admission, finding it in the back pocket of her jeans at the last minute. The receptionist told them to take a seat and Hana gave Logan the last available chair. She paced up and down amidst the soccer and rugby injuries, worrying and berating herself.

Logan sulked, sitting with his head against the wall and keeping his eyes closed. When the patient next to him went through to the examination room, Hana plonked into the vacant chair. "I can't do this," Logan gasped, raising himself upright. "I need to leave."

Hana rested a steadying hand on his knee and leaned closer. "Talk to me," she whispered. "It'll take your mind off it."

Logan shook his head. "No, I can't stay here. You don't understand."

"So tell me!" Hana heard the exasperation in her voice and cringed.

Logan heaved in a breath. "My mother took me to Auckland General with my guts hanging out, Hana. They saw a brown face with a moko tattoo and treated her like dirt. They threatened to put me into foster care because they didn't believe her excuses for my injuries. A week later, they sent me home with a leaflet. Barry put the paper in the fire, which was a shame as it contained the date for a follow-up appointment. Jack took out the stitches in the barn with a scalpel and treated the infection with blobs of Manuka honey under swabs of cloth." He exhaled, his complexion looking greyer by the second. "Don't make me do this, Hana."

She ran the sleeve of her sweatshirt across his fevered brow. "You're sick, Logan. I'll stay with you."

His eyelashes fluttered and he snorted, a sarcastic sound. "Yeah, my ma said that. She bloody lied."

"I'm not your mother." Hana leaned closer and kissed his temple. "I'm your wife. I'll leave when they force me to and not before."

Logan's eyes rolled as he struggled to stay conscious. "He burned it. Barry burned it."

"I know." Hana rubbed his brow again, her sleeve becoming wet. "But you were kids."

Logan's head thrashed against the back of the seat. "My discharge notice. He put it in the fire. He hated me."

Hana opened her mouth to speak and then thought better of it. Logan sounded distressed and she sensed she only compounded his misery. His lucidity returned and he tried to sit up. "Ignore me," he said. "I don't need you to stay."

"Don't be daft," she admonished him. "I'll stay with you. I promised."

"I'll be fine, I always am."

"Logan." Hana's brow creased in concern at his obvious reluctance. "Whatever's wrong?"

"Nothing," he said and the shutters came down over his emotions, blocking them from view once again. Hana held his hand, feeling his fingers flex against hers.

The triage nurse came for him and Logan shrugged off Hana's attempts to accompany him. "I'll be fine," he said, his tone distant. "You go home and I'll phone you when I'm done."

Hana sat for two hours and Logan didn't return. Bodie arrived with Amy in tow and they sat in silence with her. Other patients left sporting casts on arms and legs, bandages swathing their bodies. Still no Logan. Bodie saw Amy to the door as she left to fetch Jas, calling at the reception desk on his way past. Hana saw him making polite enquiries and getting nothing in return. Bodie fetched a coffee Hana couldn't drink and sat with her for another two hours.

"Mrs Du Rose." A male nurse appeared from behind a closed door and looked around him.

"Here!" Bodie stood and waved him over. The man approached with a smile, finding Hana already standing by the time he reached her. "Your husband needed surgery," he said, his face radiating kindness.

Hana sank into the seat and felt the walls close in around her. "Oh, no!" she groaned.

The nurse squatted in front of her. "It's going well and he's expected out in the next few hours."

Hana nodded. "Should I just wait here?" she asked and the man shook his head. "The surgical ward closed to visitors an hour ago. I suggest you go home and get some rest."

Bodie snorted, a horrid, derisive noise. "Are you kidding me?"

Hana shook her head. "I'm going nowhere until I've seen my husband," she replied. Her response sounded more aggressive than she intended. She added with a tremble in her voice, "I'm appalled you'd even ask."

The nurse gave her directions to the surgical ward and the woman in charge let Hana sit in a tiny waiting room. She watched through enormous windows as lights winked on and off in Hamilton and traffic became sporadic. After a while, darkness left little of interest on the unchanging landscape. Hana tipped forward in her seat and buried her face in her hands. "I'm so angry at you, Logan," she whispered. "You didn't tell me how bad it hurt and now you keep me away from you."

Bodie patted her back in sympathy and made noises about leaving. "I need to go, Mum," he said, sounding apologetic.

Hana nodded, venting her anger in a different direction. "I want you to arrest Tama," she said, standing. "He caused this. I want him convicted."

Bodie shook his head. "Logan needs to make a statement. He's the injured party."

"But he won't!" Hana raised her voice. "Why won't you help me?"

Bodie backed away with his hands raised. "Don't complain to me now it's all going wrong." He stuck his jaw out and Hana resisted the urge to scream at him. "You chose this, Mum," he said, sounding victorious.

Hana shook her head and stared at the darkness outside. "You need to go," she said, her tone flat. "I'll find Tama myself and do some serious damage of my own."

"Don't do that." Bodie kissed the top of her head. "I don't want to arrest you."

Logan stayed in surgery until after midnight, wheeled into the ward looking grey and sick. Hana burst into tears at the sight of him, sobbing over his hand. She caressed the ink stains from his marking hours ago and wished she could turn the clock back. Logan gave her a lopsided smile but didn't speak. Monitors clattered around his body, adding to the sense of unreality.

As Hana stood back from the bed, the ward staff made it abundantly clear she should leave, tipping her out without ceremony into the deserted hospital. She drove back to Culver's Cottage to find the house lit up like a Christmas tree and Bodie's BMW on the driveway.

Bodie and Amy stared at her from the kitchen doorway as she kicked her boots off. "How is he?" Amy asked, her face set in a genuine expression of sympathy.

Hana sighed. "Poorly." Her shoulders slumped and she responded to Amy's gentle hand on her arm. "I'm glad you're here." Tears prickled behind her eyelids and she held her breath. Logan's jacket lay on the floor next to the pile of paint tins, wallpaper and fabric. Hana squeezed her eyes closed, but the tears tumbled over and bounced down her cheeks. "It's all my fault," she sobbed, covering her face with her hands.

The jacket condemned her selfishness and amplified her guilt. "I made him go shopping with me and he must've been in agony."

The thing Hana discovered about showing distress in the company of police officers is they automatically reached for the kettle. They demanded facts, not feelings as they dispensed practical help. Hana confessed the unadulterated story of Logan's injuries, adding her observations of the strange Du Rose family. Bodie shook his head. "I told you they were trouble," he said, his tone victorious. Gratified, Hana saw Amy kick him under the table.

"You certainly picked a dysfunctional family to join," he crowed. His orange juice slopped onto the table as Amy slapped him hard on the arm.

"Thanks! Define dysfunctional, asshole! Me and Jas have been a dysfunctional family by the world's standards!"

A look of shame crossed Bodie's face. He tried to improve the slight by including Hana in his generalisation. "I guess we were too really," he said looking to her for support. "You were a solo mum."

"Not by choice!" Hana let the indignation infiltrate her voice. "Logan has two parents. By your measure his family isn't dysfunctional."

Bodie shook his head and sighed. "I can't win this," he said. "I'll check on my son."

Amy smiled at his disappearing back, waiting until his feet padded down the hallway into Jas' temporary bedroom. "You're doing really well, you know. It must have been a terrible shock."

Hana exhaled. "I once heard a saying. It said, 'To lose one husband is an accident, to lose two is careless.' It almost happened again." She swallowed. "I can't lose Logan." Desolation snaked its spiteful tendrils around her heart and her chest hitched.

Amy cleared her throat. "I meant finding out about Jas. It must've given you a shock."

"Oh, yes." Hana ran a hand through her fringe, snagging her fingers in the tangled red coils. "I suppose so."

"I always loved Bo," Amy said and her face glowed when she said his name. "It seems we were victims of catastrophe." Her brow narrowed and Hana saw the years of regret in her face.

"Tell me about yourself," Hana said, craving distraction from frenzied thoughts of Logan's plight.

"I'm six years older than Bo," Amy said, a degree of challenge in her statement. "Does that bother you?"

"Not at all." Hana shook her head and sighed. "I'm older than Logan." Even saying her husband's name sent a dart of pain into her chest. The doctor said his prognosis was good, but a few days later, it might not have been the same story.

Amy continued, "I'm on reasonable terms with my ex-husband.

In a Christmas card sending kind of way."

Hana nodded. "I guess that's important for closure."

Amy agreed. "Yeah. It wasn't his fault I cheated." Her tone held regret. "I didn't intend to. It just happened."

"That's what they all say." Hana's comment sounded barbed and she held her breath. "Sorry, I'm making a mess of this."

Amy reached across the table and took her hand. "You look exhausted," she said, her voice soft. "Go to bed. We can talk more tomorrow."

Hana rang the hospital to check on Logan. The nurse on the other end of the call sounded harried and told her he'd slept since the operation. "He's having regular observations," she said with a yawn. "He's comfortable."

Hana jumped awake the next morning to a deafening knock on her bedroom door, followed by a high-pitched giggle in the hall. "Shh!" She recognised Amy's voice from the safety of her duvet.

She sat up and pulled her nightdress straight. "Come in," she called, greeted by Jas bounding through the door. He carried a cup of hot tea and Hana noticed a nauseating floaty scum on the surface. Amy followed, brandishing a piece of kitchen towel. The tell-tale brown streaks betrayed some heavy duty spillage along the hallway.

"Here you go." Jas placed his burden on the bedside table, clambering up onto the bed.

"Sorry," Amy hissed, lifting the cup to mop underneath. "He wanted to wake you up with a nice cup of tea."

"Morning Granny!" Jas beamed with enthusiasm and climbed under the sumptuous duvet. Hana's heart sank. Every time the child called her 'Granny' she cringed. The bouncy, four-year-old made up his own rules to this new game and Hana conceded she didn't like all of them. She held her arms out and he snuggled into her with a groan of pleasure.

"How about a competition?" she said, putting excitement into her voice. "Let's find the best ever name for you to call me? Everybody has a 'granny,' but I'd rather like something different."

"Sorry." Amy perched at the end of the bed and winced. "It never occurred to me."

Hana watched the cogs turn in Jas' little brain and his dark curls bounced as he wiggled his head in concentration. "Okay," he said with deliberate slowness. "We could have prizes and a naming party and I could ask all my friends." He got up and slipped from the bed. "I'll think of some good ones." He bounced around the room. "Granny, Nanny, Nonie, Oma." His eyes widened as he twirled on the spot. "There are heaps!" He bounded from the room to engage Bodie in his intrigue.

Hana rubbed her eyes and sighed. "I should ring the hospital and check on Logan."

Amy traced the pattern on the duvet cover. Her slender index finger blotted out a daisy. "This has been hard for you," she said with feeling. "I wanted you to know I really appreciate how amazing you've been over it all. You haven't judged us and I'm grateful."

Hana's body slumped in the giant bed. "I don't feel I've done anything worthwhile," she said. "Maybe I should let him call me 'Granny.' But I don't know if I can." Her smile seemed wistful. "The doctors say Elizabeth won't ever speak so I never considered what I might like to be called. Granny makes me think of a creaky hundred-year-old."

Amy patted Hana's shoulder. "You don't look it." She smiled and turned to leave the room, halting with something on her mind. "Don't drink your tea," she said, chewing her bottom lip. "Jas said it was English Breakfast Tea and I suspect he put peanut butter in it. I'll get you another one."

Hana sank into the covers, sliding her hand across to Logan's cold, empty side. After a week of sharing a bed, she adjusted to his presence with natural ease. She missed him with a tangible ache. "I can't even phone you because I ditched yours into the gully," she whispered into his soft pillow.

Hana sat up and reached for her mobile phone charging next to the bed. She fumbled the cup of tea and peered into the bottom. A brown scum littered the top and she crinkled her nose at the distinctive scent of peanuts. Staring at the screen until her eyes became unfocussed, she texted the message.

'Logan's in the hospital. Tama broke his arm and did internal damage. Keep away from him, Anka. Stay where you are. Bo says Ivan has filed a missing report for you. Be careful. H. x'

With no reply, Hana got up and used the landline to check on her husband. The nurse used that same word, comfortable, again. "Visiting hours start at eleven," said the disembodied voice on the other end of the call.

Hana disregarded the information, showering and dressing early. "I want to be there when the ward opens," she told her guests. "I need to see him for myself."

"How about I drop you off, Mum," Bodie offered. "We're sorting out my new room today."

"I'd be so grateful!" Hana gushed. "I hate that multi-storey car park."

Jas bounced around like a wind-up toy, shouting out possible names for Hana. Amy regained enough control to wash and dress him and settled him down with a drink at the kitchen table. He intermittently pestered Bodie. He called him 'Dad,' with great gusto and enjoyment.

Hana watched the child with interest. He reminded her of a younger version of his father. Despite the lack of contact, the mannerisms and idiosyncrasies fascinated her. As Amy took Jas out into the hall to get his shoes on, Hana reached out and held Bodie's forearm. "He calls you Dad," she whispered. "You need to get this right, Bo. You'll do him irreparable damage if you get it wrong."

Bodie nodded, putting his hand over hers. "I know, Mum. Whatever happens between Amy and me, I'll always be his dad and I won't trade that for anything. My dad screwed it up. I don't intend to copy him."

"What?" Hana's smile faltered. "He died, Bo. You can't hold him responsible for that." She put the bad memory to the back of her mind, brushing it off in her present turmoil and dismissing it as Bodie's amateur dramatics.

They travelled to town in Bodie's car, with Jas and Hana in the back. Jas bounced into the car, stuck his thumb straight into his mouth and went to sleep before they reached the gate. She thought again how amazing the child was. "Cute boy," she whispered and stroked his other hand, gratified when his fingers clasped around hers.

They spat Hana out at the hospital before eleven. She made her way up to the ward, joined by a queue of people waiting to gain entry. She pitied some of the unfortunates inside as she observed their visitors. One family ate an entire packet of grapes and a box of chocolates in the ten minutes by the sliding doors, entering empty handed. Another group contained a screaming toddler which showed no sign of letting up the dreadful wail. One elderly gentleman spat phlegm into a filthy hanky, without embarrassment.

As the guests filed past, Hana stopped to check the board showing patients' names and trying to locate Logan. A hand snaked around her waist, making her jump in fright. "Hey gorgeous." Logan pushed his face into her neck, breathing in the lingering scent of shampoo on her hair. Hana spun around and put her arms around his neck, tugging him into her. His hair felt wet and he wore yesterday's clothes. "I missed you so much." His voice sounded sultry and despite his ragged appearance, Hana found him as sexy as ever.

As she pulled away, she noticed the metal thing he held onto. Like a tall coat hanger with a bag of fluid dangling from the top, it bore another sack of awful red looking stuff. Logan pushed it around like a gruesome shopping trolley with horrid things clinging to its frame. The higher bag containing clear liquid sent a tube into Logan's hand, but the pipe from the red one disappeared under his shirt, ending somewhere inside. Hana felt appalled and the severity of it hit her afresh. "I missed you so much," she sniffed, trying not to tear up as they walked back to Logan's bed. He trailed his new apparatus without complaint and Hana tried to think of encouraging sentences.

"I brought you clean clothes." With trembling fingers, she unpacked the small black bag containing Logan's wash things, razor and a change of clothes and undies. Knowing the reputation of hospital food, she also produced an unopened packet of biscuits and some chocolate bars. "I thought you'd be flat on your back in bed." Hana's smile wavered as she fought for control. "I didn't expect you to be up and about already."

"Don't have much choice in here. They wake you up all through the night fiddling around with something and then start the real rattling and crashing around 6am. I think they want me out. Thank goodness a male nurse turned up to shower me." Logan wrinkled his nose. "There's no privacy in here, I hate it."

Hana gulped, guilt landing like a brick in her stomach. "I didn't have a choice, Loge. It was bad. You've had major surgery. It's not like I could have fixed it with a needle and thread! I did what I thought was right."

"I know," Logan conceded. "Apart from day clinics for minor stuff, I avoid these places."

"Oh. I'm so sorry." Hana bent to undo the bag, trying not to see the internal pain in her husband's eyes. "But I didn't see any alternative."

Perhaps a bed ridden, drugged up Logan might have been easier to handle than the hurt, angry man balling his fists next to her. "Hop back into bed," Hana suggested. "You're shivering."

Logan's face projected pure agony. He sat on the bed and tried to swing his legs around. As Hana struggled to work the pedal to raise the headboard, a nurse appeared with a plastic cup containing drugs. She pushed a different pedal to the one Hana wrestled with and the bed rose up with ease.

"Oh. Oops." Hana felt her incompetence flare in the face of such efficiency. The nurse gave her a wry smile.

"It's fine," she said. "There's an art to it."

Logan looked pale and his skin reflected a grey sheen from the effort of walking to meet Hana. "I can't believe I feel worse than before," he complained to the nurse, finding no sympathy with that line of conversation.

"You're lucky," she informed him. "You should have got help sooner."

Logan shrugged. "I want to go home," he stated. The tilt of the nurse's eyebrows told Hana it wasn't the first time he'd asked.

"What did the surgeon say?" asked Hana, remembering the conversation with the Ngaruawahia doctor the night before.

Logan lay back against his pillows, pulled a face and sighed as though bored. "Told me how lucky I was. They removed my spleen and stopped the bleeding. He called me an idiot and said I should have told the truth when they cast my arm. Blah blah blah."

"The doctor said you might have a couple of broken ribs," ventured Hana. She tilted her head. "That's meant to be really painful. How on earth did you cope all week in so much discomfort?"

"I've done worse." Logan gritted his teeth and made it clear he didn't want to talk about it. For once Hana kept quiet, not wanting to argue with her stubborn husband.

Logan rang Angus on Hana's mobile phone and she listened to the conversation. She heard him reassuring the principal. "Yeah, I probably won't be in work tomorrow but I might be all right for Tuesday."

Hana stood, shaking her head in disbelief. She gazed through the huge windows for a while, watching the world outside moving on, regardless of the agonies of people inside the hospital. The eighth floor window offered a spectacular view. To the west lay Hamilton Lake, shimmering and rippling in the steady breeze. A few brave and dedicated kayakers paddled on its surface like tiny, decorative figures on a cake. Hamilton city loomed out of the ground, the multi-storey buildings shaming their original counterparts. They crowded around like school children grouping together for a class photograph, the big kids pushing out the little ones.

Hana leaned her hands on a low windowsill and bent forward to see ground level. Pembroke Street seemed to head straight for the hospital, looking as though it went underneath. Hana knew it didn't, but the perspective seemed convincing and she leaned further forward than she should. A loud bang echoed around the ward as her forehead hit the window. "Ouch!" she hissed.

She turned with deliberate slowness, assessing her level of embarrassment. An elderly man slept in the bed opposite Logan and next to him, another man listened to hospital radio through headphones.

Relieved, Hana turned towards her husband. Dismay flitted through her heart at the way he held his stomach, his eyes creased in laughter. "I hope that bloody hurts!" she mouthed to him, seeing him roll onto his side. Logan ended the call and lay back against his pillows, clutching his stomach and groaning.

"It wasn't that funny," Hana snapped. "I only bumped my head!"

Logan laughed harder, a painful hitch in his breathing. Hana curbed her annoyance, knitting her brows and glaring. "Oh, help." Logan rubbed at his chest. "You crack me up."

Hana slumped into the visitor's chair with an indignant expression. "You're behaving so rude," she snapped.

Logan sat up with difficulty and Hana didn't offer to help. He held her phone out towards her. "How long ago did you put Angus' number in your phone?"

"Years ago. I think it was the day after Vik died. He came to see me. Why?" Hana glared at him.

Logan held the phone out to her so she could see the screen. Hana stared at the familiar contacts list and shook her head. "I don't understand."

"Look," Logan insisted. "Look at what's missing."

"Oh!" Hana's frustration disappeared, replaced by embarrassment. "Well, it was extenuating circumstances."

The small spelling error went unnoticed for almost nine years. Angus Blair was entered without the 'g.' In the grand scheme of things, it seemed minor, but in the face of a perfectionist English teacher with stitches in his abdomen, it proved vital.

"Argh, crap that hurt!" Logan slumped against his pillows, colour returning to his cheeks with the mirth.

"Serves you right!" Hana bit. "I didn't come to be insulted." She temporarily withdrew the sympathetic vote and ate the fruit salad Logan didn't manage for breakfast. Everything seemed to come wrapped in some way and Hana struggled with plastic, foil and shrink-wrap.

"I worked in a hospital one summer," she said, trying to lighten the mood. "They left me to do everything myself one day when they got short staffed. I think they regretted it. I had to do everything; cook, clean, wash up, the whole job, all by myself. The food arrived frozen and I put it into a big steel regenerator to heat. It needed to reach seventy-nine degrees centigrade before I could serve it. Otherwise, the patients might get food poisoning."

"A woman of many talents." Logan's lips quirked upwards, but he still clutched his stomach and pressed against the wounds to stave off pain.

"It was a dreadful day." Hana chewed an awkward piece of pineapple. "I burned a whole pile of toast because the nursing staff flustered me. They said the geriatrics injured themselves on my boiled eggs and my porridge looked like tile grout. The cereal went okay although not much can go wrong with cereal." Hana winced as her husband writhed in discomfort.

"Stop, woman! You're doing this on purpose." Logan clutched his guts and groaned, curling himself into a ball. At least he'd stopped demanding to go home.

Undeterred, Hana continued, "Once the ordeal of breakfast ended, I started getting ready for lunch. By the time the enormous steel shelving unit containing the frozen food arrived, I'd almost caught up, apart from the porridge saucepan which needed a few more hours soaking. The regenerator heated up and I started cooking the food. It's not an easy task. I might have succeeded if it wasn't for that one tray of mashed potato. It just wouldn't heat. After half an hour of bombing it in the regenerator, I'd pushed the special thermometer into the mixture so often it resembled the surface of the moon. The nursing staff wouldn't listen. They swooped on the kitchen like locusts and came back with empty trays and lorry loads of washing up. I've never been so glad to see the end of a day."

"Please stop," Logan wept. "It's not even funny. It's the way you're telling it." He breathed through pursed lips and straightened his legs with obvious pain.

"It wasn't funny," Hana said, hiding the fruit salad pot under the silver tureen. "The next day, my colleague came back and demoted me to washing up and cleaning. I've never felt more relieved. The trouble is, the ward emptied overnight. I'm sure the geriatrics all died in the early hours from my poisonous mash." Hana licked her lips, her expression serious. "For sure that's the scariest job I've ever had. After I married Vik, I stuck to working in a bar while he looked after Bo." She inspected a fingernail with forced interest. "I might be traumatised."

Logan took more painkillers and added the missing letter into Angus' name on Hana's phone. She sat in a squashy armchair and watched him. "What did Angus say?" she asked, wrinkling her nose.

"He says you have to stay off work until the end of term." Logan narrowed his eyes and handed her phone over.

"But why?" She sat up straighter. "You got hurt, not me."

"He thinks it's best." Logan lay back on his pillows and watched Hana from beneath his lashes. "And so do I. He says you've taken no sick leave for years so he's giving you two weeks off on full-pay."

Hana shook her head. "That's ridiculous. I'm busy at work. Sheila's still away, Caroline's gone and Pete doesn't do anything. There's nobody to run the office."

Logan smirked. "Pete is the teacher in charge of careers and guidance counselling as of tomorrow. He just doesn't know it yet."

"No. Way!" Hana moved skywards, jumping from her seat in consternation at the thought of Pete picking his nose over her keyboard. "He'll shed skin and pie crumbs all over my chair!" she wailed. "No, it can't happen!"

"It is happening." Logan patted the space on the bed next to him. "Sit here."

Hana popped onto the bed next to him, seeking comfort from physical contact. She started to protest again and he slipped his good arm around her shoulders and pressed his lips against her temple. "I can't kiss you," he said with regret. "I need to clean my teeth. All I can taste is antiseptic."

"I brought your toothbrush and paste," Hana said. "Want me to grab it?"

"In a minute." Logan sniffed her familiar hair shampoo and sighed with contentment. "This is good. A week of marriage and now I can't live without you."

"Two weeks leave?" Hana mused and he nodded.

"Yep. Two whole weeks to take care of me."

She snorted and pushed her face into his chest. A pipe moved beneath her hand and she jumped, remembering Logan's delicate state. "What's the real reason?" she asked, keeping her tone light.

Logan shrugged but Hana felt the tension in his body. "I told you."

"No, you didn't." She sat up and narrowed her eyes. "There's something else." She cocked her head and watched his reaction. "I'll find out, anyway."

Logan sighed. "Someone trashed the Gordonton House."

"What?" Hana clapped a hand over her mouth. "Oh, no!"

"Yep. We're sure now that someone in school is feeding information to the guys following you. Angus made sure you and I kept that address on the staff list and a couple of nights later, the place got done over."

"Did they take anything?" Hana's chin wobbled with emotion. "What made me put them at risk? I'm selfish."

"No, you're not." Logan smoothed her arm with gentle fingers. "We didn't imagine that would happen. The cops attended but found nothing of any use. It looks like whoever got in searched the place. They threw belongings everywhere and took some odd bits of cash left lying around. Henrietta's room took the worst of it. They didn't take laptops or electronics though."

"It's them, isn't it?" Hana's voice shook.

"Yep." Logan resumed the soothing motion. "So you're staying home with me for a while. You can play nursey." He buried his face in her hair and inhaled like an addict.

Bodie arrived with Amy and Jas to fetch Hana. Her face fell with disappointment at the position of the hands on the clock. "Already?" she complained. "That's not fair."

"Life's not fair," Jas replied, his gaze fixed on the array of pipes exiting Logan's body.

"This is true." Logan jerked his head in Bodie's direction. "Do you have a moment spare to walk me to the bathroom?" he asked.

"Can I come?" Jas asked and Amy grabbed his arm.

"No. Stay with me."

Logan heaved himself from the bed with difficulty and Bodie accompanied him along the corridor. "So," said Bodie, clarifying things in his head, "Mum's showing on the staff contact list as living at the Gordonton House and that's where they searched next. That makes sense if it's Ethel Bowman's boyfriend."

"Yeah," replied Logan. "Angus acknowledges it's someone at school. Nobody else gets access to that list. Someone needs to talk to Ethel Bowman."

"Yep," answered the younger man. "But it needs handling with care. Otherwise we'll never catch him."

They stood outside the toilet designated for patients and a nurse raised her eyebrows as she passed with a pile of sheets. Bodie inclined his head towards the door. "Do you need it then or not?"

Logan shrugged and rested his hand on the handle. "Now I've made all this effort to get here, I should."

Bodie shook his head. "You sound like a girl. Get a move on." He waited for him anyway.

Hana panicked when the bell sounded for the end of visiting hours. "The wards used to be open all the time," she complained. Her eyes grew wide and glittered with unshed tears. "This is stupid."

"Sick people need rest," Bodie acknowledged. "When the public had access all day, heaps of belongings went missing. It's better this way."

"But what should I do?" Hana demanded. "They open again at half past four. I don't know whether to go home and come back or hang around town."

"Hey." Logan reached for her fingers. "You don't need to come back again today. Visit tomorrow."

Hana's jaw dropped open in horror. "No! I have to come back." Her mind whirled with the realisation that this pattern would continue until Logan escaped the confines of the hospital.

Jas stuck close to Hana, wanting to hold her hand and stay close. He noticed her distress and became withdrawn. Logan ruffled his hair and gave him a forced smile. "Hey, mate. Can you take care of Hana for me?" he asked.

Jas nodded and squared his shoulders. "I will," he promised.

Logan accepted Hana's kiss and ran his thumb along her jaw. "Give yourself a break, babe," he whispered. "Don't come back again today. You look exhausted."

Hana inhaled and gritted her teeth. "I'll be back later," she said, ignoring his attempt to release her from obligation. She pressed her lips against his forehead and closed her eyes. "I miss you so much," she whispered.

Hana sat in the back of Bodie's car with Jas, her eyes sparkling with tears as she stared through the window. The little boy leaned sideways on his booster seat. "Can I show you my soldiers?" he offered. "You'll love my battlefield."

"That's a great idea," Amy said, turning to smile her agreement. "Come back to our house, Hana."

Bodie drove to Amy's period villa in the suburb of Claudelands. She made a lunch of sandwiches and soup as Jas took Hana by the hand and introduced her to his plastic platoon. "This policeman-Action Man looks like Logan," he informed her, nodding with approval. The house felt old and rickety, the wallpaper peeling away from battered walls. "This is my mummy's house," Jas informed her. "She buys it with her wages."

"That's awesome," Hana replied, not sure what else to say.

"My room is baby colours." Jas pouted and reached for a toy box full of Action Man figures. "I don't much like it." His fingers scrabbled inside the box. "Ah. Here he is!" He seized a male figure and hauled it from the box, detaching it from the arms and legs of all the others. "This one looks like Logan," he said.

Hana grinned. "It does a bit." She giggled and fondled the olive skin, smoothing the dark wavy hair which stuck up in random places. "He's even got a scar under his eye!" she exclaimed.

"Told ya," Jas replied.

Action Man's police uniform looked rumpled and very American. Hana pointed to a pink breast cancer support ribbon fixed to his chest. It took up most of the little man's torso. "What's this?" she asked.

"It's his medal," Jas replied, straight-faced. "He's a crime fighter. Like my dad."

Hana remembered Bodie and his Action Man adventures. "Your dad had the bungee-jumper," Hana mused as she turned the doll over in her hands. "His grappling hook got caught on an old lady's hat on the bus and whipped it off."

Jas giggled, especially when Hana added how it also snagged her wig. "Then during a christening service for a friend's baby, I noticed Daddy wailing during one of the hymns. I thought he might be singing, but then I saw the bungee jumper's hook stuck on his thumb. It pinched his flesh and I managed to dislodge it before the end of the hymn." Hana peered down at the little man in her hand. Action Man hadn't changed much over the years.

"That's so funny." Jas beamed showing rows of tiny white teeth. "My dad's a cool dude."

Hana knelt on the floor, feeling her knees object as the blood pooled in her joints. Jas slid across and plonked himself in her lap, popping his thumb into his mouth. Hana put her arms around him, enjoying the little-boy-smell of washing powder and shower gel which lingered on him. She tried not to sneeze as his fluffy hair brushed against her face. A sudden pop heralded the thumb's extraction and

Jas turned to face her. Seriousness filled his eyes. "I've got your new name," he announced.

Hana smiled outwardly, whilst acknowledging the cringe surfacing within. She gave him an encouraging squeeze and faked pleasure. "What is it?"

"I'll call you Hanny," he said with confidence. Hana noted he didn't ask permission. Relief flooded her heart.

"I like that," she replied. "How did you choose?"

"Well," he said, turning on her knees and paralysing her from the thighs down. "I always wanted a Granny, more than anything. I wanted one so bad. The other boys and girls get picked up by grannies from kindy and taken for treats. But you don't have fluffy white hair like them. And you don't have a stick. Granny doesn't suit you."

Hana detected the slightest lisp as Jas spoke. She appreciated his reasoning. "Yes," she answered, feeling happy. "I like it. Thank you. It's a great name." If a four-year-old could decide she wasn't yet over-the-hill, he earned the right to call her whatever he liked.

Amy peeked around the bedroom door a while later, looking for recipients of her sumptuous lunch preparations. Hana lay flat on the floor behind a cardboard box with an Action Man soldier grasped in her hand. Jas bounced up and down on the balls of his feet on the other side of the box, waving a somewhat battle-scarred Dr X. The doll's trousers looked too small, displaying rather a lot of bum crack for an action hero. Jas hurled rolled up paper bombs onto Hana's head, yelling, "Duck Hanny!" With an expert flick of Hana's wrist, Action Man soldier headed them like a soccer star.

-11-

Hana's afternoon with her new grandson passed before she realised. Bodie dropped her back at the hospital while Amy looked after a sleeping Jas. He stopped near the front doors and Hana thanked him. "I hate that multi-storey. Thanks so much for doing this."

"I'll be back around eight thirty," he said with an offhand shrug. "My room at the watch house still needs sorting. I'm expected at work tomorrow." Bodie gave a casual wave and pulled out into the traffic.

Hana found Logan asleep when she arrived. He looked peaceful, despite the grey pallor of his skin. A week of beard growth gave him a rugged handsomeness and she sat in the visitor's chair and watched his chest rise and fall. The air of calm left with the arrival of more visitors, bringing with them screaming children and loud greetings. Logan awoke with a start, finding Hana leaning on the windowsill. She occupied herself by watching an elderly man hold up the traffic on the main road. He held his stick out towards the stationary vehicles while he ambled towards the kerb. The geriatric resembled a tiny dot from Hana's vantage point, like a small bug creeping across a handkerchief. She nodded in acknowledgement of the man's courage in holding back a metal tide with nothing more than a wooden stick.

"Hey." Logan spoke to her and Hana turned and gave him a special smile. "I told you not to come back." He grunted and tried to sit up, clutching his stomach as red gunk oozed into his pipes.

"I rarely do as I'm told," Hana commented, fluffing his pillows and using the remote to raise the bed head.

Logan smirked. "I admit I'm relieved. It's boring in here."

"I missed you last night." Hana sighed and put her arms around his head, hugging him close into her chest. "You don't smell of you anymore. You smell of hospital." She kissed the top of his head.

"Sorry." He clasped his fingers through hers. "They won't tell me when I can go home."

"How do you feel?" Hana moved the chair closer and stroked Logan's fingers.

"Like someone shoved cotton wool in my brain. I can't think straight."

"That's the anaesthetic," Hana soothed. "Don't worry about anything. Just rest."

Speaking pained Logan and wore him out. Instead, they held hands and watched other patients converse with their visitors. It made fascinating viewing. Some talked without drawing breath and others sat and ate the food they brought for the invalid.

A nurse appeared at the doorway with a chart in her hand, making a beeline for Logan's bed as she read it. Another bag of clear liquid dangled from her hand and she switched it with the empty one and reconnected it into the drip. "Drink this, love," she said, handing Logan a plastic cup of water and a tub filled with tablets. At Hana's questioning look, she commented, "There's an infection. This is an antibiotic."

With a swish, she turned and left before Hana could ask anything else. Logan swung his feet to the floor and reached out for her. "Stop stressing. I can see your brain working and it's making me tired."

Hana nestled into his tee shirt, enjoying his nearness. She knew it would make her miss him more later when darkness and loneliness pressed in. "Oh." She sat up. "I haven't told your family. Am I supposed to?" She heard her own insincerity and shame pricked her cheeks with pink spots. The fear they might not care filled her with terror and loathing in equal measure.

"It's fine," answered Logan. "I'll ring Dad when I get out of here."

Noticing he didn't mention Miriam, Hana shrugged. She didn't challenge him, choosing not to meddle.

The few hours of visiting dashed by in a haze of antiseptic smells and patients stumbling around in hospital gowns. Logan managed a short walk along the ward and an hour in the television room. Hana didn't remember afterwards what they watched on the wide, cracked screen. Every set of steps cost Logan another bout of wrenching pain which left him sweating and ill. When Bodie arrived at just after eight o'clock, he looked shocked at Logan's appearance. "You look like crap," he said with unhelpful honesty.

"Geez, thanks bro'." Logan grimaced, his slate grey eyes standing out in his pale face. It terrified Hana how fast someone so vital and filled with life force could degenerate.

"Here." Bodie handed Logan a battered mobile phone. "Amy dug it out. I've topped up the credit, so at least you can text Mum if you want." He laid a pile of novels on the cupboard. "I raided Amy's bookshelves. They might not be your thing but I figured boredom might be setting in about now."

"Thanks mate. I appreciate it." Logan smiled, his face pale and sick. Beads of sweat formed on his forehead.

Hana left with great reluctance, sensing Bodie's growing impatience. "I'll come back tomorrow as soon as they let me in."

Logan smiled and accepted her gentle kiss. Then he dropped his bombshell. "I'm going home tomorrow, anyway."

Hana's face betrayed serious doubt and she looked to her son and then back to her husband. "Oh, I doubt it," she said, her expression one of confusion.

"I bloody am." Logan gritted his teeth and Hana avoided challenging his determination. While Bodie joined the queue for the lift, Hana sought the nurses' station.

"I'm Mrs Du Rose," she began, the name strange on her lips. "My husband thinks he's going home tomorrow and I wanted to check if that's true."

"I can't discuss his medical condition without his permission," the nurse answered, smoothing her fingers across a name badge with Selina in a spiky font.

"So, do I bring him clean clothes for sleeping or for travelling?" Hana demanded, her tone betraying her agitation.

"He won't go home tomorrow," Selina stated. "Or the next day." The woman bit her lip.

Hana sighed and ran a hand over her eyes. "This is so bewildering. Is there any way I can see Logan's surgeon and ask him to explain everything?"

Selina shook her head. "Doctors' rounds are at nine in the morning and visiting is at eleven."

Hana paused and stared at her, wondering if her English words emerged as Martian. "So, how do I see Logan's doctor?"

"You can see him at nine."

Hana cocked her head. "I can? I can come here at nine and speak to Logan's doctor?"

"No." Selina shook her head and her ponytail bounced against her shoulders. "Visiting isn't until eleven."

Hana inhaled, her frustration growing. Four buzzers went off in quick succession above the nurses' station. "Please help me," she pleaded.

"Look," answered Selina, "I'm on an early shift tomorrow. Come in around nine and I'll give you permission to sit with your husband while he sees the doctor." Hana looked doubtful, wondering if she lied to get rid of her. Selina inclined her head. "I'll be here. I'll remember." She accompanied the last with a broad smile.

"I'd like to hear everything explained," Hana replied, returning her smile with gratitude. "Logan won't talk about it."

Bodie drove Hana home to Culver's Cottage, checking the road behind him before turning into the driveway. "I think we should swap cars," he said as they pulled up to the house. "The tinted windows might give you some anonymity around town and you could see Logan when you wanted."

Hana smiled, touched by her son's kindness. Fear back-lit the gratitude. "I'm not the world's greatest driver, Bo. I'm too scared I might ding it."

Over a cup of coffee in the cheerful kitchen, Bodie reassured her. "It's just a car," he said philosophically and Hana gaped in surprise.

"Wow. I swear I thought you said your pride and joy was just a car." She smiled. "I'm hearing things."

"That's before I knew I had a son," Bodie said, leaning forward over his drink. "Now it doesn't seem so important."

Hana watched the look of pride cross Bodie's face at the thought of Jas. "He's a gorgeous little boy," she said, seeing his eyes light up with pleasure.

He grinned. "Amy's done a great job," he admitted. "He's adorable."

Bodie left as night extended its black fingers to exclude even the stars. Hana tried to settle in the huge, empty four-poster bed as time clicked over into the next day. She spent half an hour reading her bible, scanning the trials of David. It read like an adventure story and she drew parallels with her own predicament. "I'm not courageous or noble," she sighed. "But I am under fire."

She snuggled under the covers and prayed, settling her soul and trusting a higher power with control over her circumstances. Peace came, but sleep didn't. Hana padded to the kitchen in the early hours and boiled the kettle for tea. The curtain material lay where she left it, just inside the front door and she drank her hot drink and stared at it.

Hana finally slept around four o'clock in the morning, too exhausted to stay awake any longer. The alarm on her mobile phone roused her at six. The room seemed darker and Hana groped for her phone in confusion. She found it on the floor next to the bed. Switching on the lights in the bed canopy, Hana rolled over and admired the rich floor length curtains, cascading from the curtain track. She smiled and offered herself a mental pat on the back. "Not bad, Hana. Not bad at all."

The drapes still looked good in the half-light as Hana finished dressing. She hoped daylight wouldn't diminish the sense of satisfaction at the sight of the creamy swags. Her arms ached from heaving the sewing machine up the stairs from the garage in the dead of night.

She'd sewed for hours, focussing on creating a restful space for Logan once he returned home.

She almost toppled from the bedroom chair, hanging the heavy curtains at three forty-five that morning. Tiredness meant errors crept in, fortunately masked by the lining material. Her sewing expert mother always advocated hand-sewn hems. Hana lifted the material in the cold light of day and examined the machined line. Dying just after Bodie's birth spared Judith McIntyre the agony of witnessing Hana's fumbled attempts at home making. "Oh Mum," Hana sighed as she admired her handiwork. "I hope you're proud of me. I'm sure you would have ignored my mistakes." A heaviness settled on Hana's heart. "All of my mistakes."

The sumptuous curtains hung well. They met in the middle, despite the irregular line of hemming. Although exhausted, Hana gave a smug grin as she pulled them back after her shower, exposing daylight tinged with grey. She wrinkled her nose at the fronds of thread hanging from the bottom. "As long as nobody looks too hard, I should get away with it," she mused.

She drove into town early, snagging a good park and avoiding the multi-storey. Climbing the stairs to the surgical ward, Hana experienced a rush of adrenaline, a symptom of too little sleep. It propelled her onwards, so she arrived at the reception desk full of energy.

The dour-faced receptionist stamped on her optimism. "Ward doesn't open until eleven," she snapped, glancing up at Hana and then back to her computer screen.

"But Selina promised!" Hana protested, abandoning the fruitless argument ten minutes later when threatened with a call to security.

Filled with a sense of righteous indignation, Hana consigned herself to the dirty visitors' room and a droning documentary about oil wells. The sofa looked more ripped since the day before and someone had snapped off the channel changer. Hana rocked in her creaky chair and seethed. After a while, she got up and fidgeted, pacing herself up the corridor and back to the reception desk.

"Selina can't give you that authority," the receptionist said, enunciating her words in case Hana was stupid as well as early. "She's not in charge here."

"But she did," Hana argued. "I can't just sit there watching television while the doctor speaks to my husband about an operation I don't understand. Who can give me authority?"

"Nobody." The receptionist shrugged. "It's against the rules."

"But Selina did," Hana protested. "I'm not lying!"

She sat in the visitor's room and watched the surgeon step out of the elevator. He wore a blue turban and a serious expression. He marched onto the ward, flanked by a posse of white coated underlings.

Hana lost hope in the hour he spent walking through the ward, knowing she'd need to rely on Logan for second hand information. She tried and failed to bury the sense that things were worse than he acknowledged. A long while later, Hana watched the surgeon and his entourage head back towards the elevator. On a whim fuelled by exhaustion and annoyance, she ran after them.

"I refuse to discuss my patients in the corridor!" Mr Singh raised his voice and Hana blanched. She swallowed and forced out her words, indicating backwards with her outstretched hand.

"Then sit with me in the television room," she begged. "I just want five minutes of your time. Please."

The collective eyes of the entourage bugged as one, her bravery worthy of hushed lunchroom gossip later. Mr Singh's name badge winked in the light from the wide windows and he exhaled in an exaggerated sigh. "Five minutes!" he snapped.

The surgeon sent his collection of students and registrars ahead of him, sitting with Hana in the scruffy lounge. He maintained Logan's privacy while furnishing her with basic details. "As his wife, I can tell you that Logan sustained broken ribs which punctured his spleen and caused a bleed. He needed open surgery to remove his spleen. The last lot of tests showed the start of an infection and he's taking an antibiotic to counteract it. He'll take those tablets for the next ten days. My staff will remove the drains this morning and the drip came out last night."

His Indian accent and the paraphernalia of his Sikh beliefs soothed and comforted Hana. She relaxed. "So, he'll be okay?" she asked.

Mr Singh smiled. "I know he's threatening to discharge himself." Hana clamped her teeth onto her bottom lip and he waved away her discomfort. "Your husband is a terrible patient. He's healing as well as expected for someone with his condition. If you're willing to take responsibility for him, I can let him go but you must prepare for a relapse, in which case I'll readmit him."

A lump formed in the back of Hana's throat. Gratitude mingled with fear. "Thank you," she whispered. "I feel daunted. Logan hid the pain from me for a week. How will I know if he's in difficulty again?"

Mr Singh cocked his head. "I think you will. You brought him in before." He patted her hand and stood. Hana still wanted to push the nurse and receptionist through the eighth-floor window, but the doctor went some way towards restoring her faith in medical staff. He stood to go, turning back as he reached the door. "Oh, that cast on his arm is dreadful. I'll ask my nurse to redo it before he goes. I've written a script for pain relief, so make sure they give it to you before you leave."

"Doctor!" Hana stood in a sudden movement, halting him half way through the exit. "What do you mean by his condition? Are you talking about the spleen thing? Or something else?"

The doctor considered her for a moment. Then he shook his head and smiled. "Talk to your husband, Mrs Du Rose."

With a wave, he left. Hana spotted a familiar face in the doorway and Selina appeared like a genie. Hana stood, her body rigid with frustration. "I drove here all the way from Huntly this morning because you told me I could!" She jabbed her finger towards the lift as Mr Singh stepped onto it and the doors closed. "If that nice doctor hadn't bothered to sit with me, it would have been a complete waste of time!"

The nurse took a step back and Hana sensed how angry she must look. "Please leave me alone," she demanded with an exhausted sigh. She sat on the ripped sofa and put her head in her hands. The nurse slipped away and Hana noted she neither apologised nor let her see Logan. She looked at her watch and saw another half an hour left until the ward opened to the public. Craving coffee, she gathered her handbag and the goodies she brought for her husband and left.

Hana pressed the button for the elevator, her former burst of energy depleted by stress. She squeezed the bridge of her nose between her fingers and struggled to control the misery bubbling into her chest.

"Hana!" Logan battled with the door, the metal rack stuck against the skirting board. Its wheels pinioned him in the doorframe. Hana stepped back as the lift opened and a porter emerged pushing a patient in a wheelchair. She turned towards her husband. "Hey, don't cry," he implored her as he hauled the drip across the distance. Hana released the bridge of her nose and exhaled. Logan cupped her chin in his palm and tried to read her expression. "I only just heard you spent the morning in the waiting room. I could've sat with you."

Hana sighed and shook her head, pressing her face into the front of his shirt. "It's a disaster."

Logan nudged her with his arm. "You know they'll beat me if you upset them!"

"They told me to come and then wouldn't let me in," Hana sniffed into the front of his shirt and Logan stroked her hair.

"I'm sorry, babe. Fancy going for coffee? There must be a cafe or something in this hell hole."

"It's downstairs," Hana said, delving into her bag for a tissue. "It's too far for you."

"Oh." Logan's nose wrinkled in disappointment.

"If I leave you with this bag, I could nip there and back," Hana suggested. "Would you like that?"

Logan pressed his lips against hers and she tasted toothpaste. His beard grazed her soft skin and she sighed with contentment. "I won't be long," she promised.

Hana bought two cappuccinos from the vendor near the front doors and returned to her husband. She found him arguing with a nurse in the corridor. "I can sit here if I want!" He raised his voice and the woman backed away. Logan inhaled and licked his lips, regaining control. "My wife went downstairs and I'm waiting for her."

"I'm here now." Hana fled the elevator through half-opened doors. She rushed to his side slopping coffee over the tiles. "He's fine with me." She took up a defensive position, blocking Logan with her body. "I got him coffee." Hana narrowed her eyes and thrust the drink towards Logan. He took it with a smirk.

"Fine." The nurse put her hands on her hips. "You're on half hourly observations. Stay out here but don't go any further."

They sank into the ripped leather seats, Hana heaving out a sigh of exasperation. "Are you sure you're not in prison?" she demanded. "They're determined to keep us apart."

Logan rested his cup on the seat next to him and slipped his good arm around her shoulder. "I appreciate the lengths you went to trying to see me. Nobody's done that before."

Hana knitted her brows. "I find that hard to believe. You're gorgeous."

As the hour for visiting arrived, Selina appeared to commandeer Logan. She eyed Hana as though herding a dangerous animal. "You're not serious?" Hana snapped, already bridling. Her empty cup bounced onto the tiles. "You won't let me see him outside visiting hours and now I can sit with him, you're taking him away again. What did I ever do to you?"

"You got me in trouble with Mr Singh." Selina projected her petulance across the distance. "And staff nurse."

"Well, what did you expect?" Hana stood and the girl took a cautious step backwards.

"You need to come with me, Logan." Selina laid a plump hand on his brawny arm and Hana experienced a flash of jealous rage. Colour heightened in her cheeks.

Logan sighed with exasperation. "It's Mr Du Rose, to you," he corrected. "And the minute you're done, I'm leaving." He stood and shuffled towards the ward, casting an apologetic look at Hana over his shoulder.

Hana chatted to another patient, a middle-aged man with a hand injury who had no visitors. "I hate this hospital," he confessed. "I feel like a lump of meat."

Hana nodded in agreement. "My husband's just about ready to blow. I can't see him lasting the day." As the words left her lips, a commotion emerged from behind Logan's closed curtains. She excused herself and slipped through the gap to find Selina arguing with her husband.

"You can't go home, Logan, I mean Mr Du Rose! It's too risky."

"What's going on?" Hana demanded, giving Logan a chance to snatch his sweatshirt from Selina's hands. A bright blue plaster cast adorned his left arm and he looked grey and sick.

"I'm leaving!" he snarled. "I've had enough." The muscles forming his bare torso rippled and the livid scarring across his upper abdomen oozed. Pink stained piping lay in a tray on top of Selina's trolley.

"Patch him up, please," Hana asked, her tone sickly sweet. "Mr Singh said he could leave today if I took responsibility." She smiled and narrowed her eyes. "I'm happy to do that."

The nurse in charge forced Logan to sign a waiver, convinced his early discharge would herald a dreadful mistake. A porter arrived to wheel him out to the car and Logan sulked throughout the fifteen-minute journey. "This is ridiculous," he grumbled. "I'm not an old man."

"Stop complaining," Hana snapped. "Otherwise we'll leave you here."

The porter snatched the wheelchair away as Logan stood, leaving Hana to manhandle him into the low vehicle. He groaned in pain as his body folded in half to get into the passenger seat. "Wow, Super-cop loaned you his car?" Logan grunted, eyeing the walnut interior. "I bet he didn't put me on the insurance."

"Don't know," Hana answered, refusing to take the bait. "It doesn't matter. You can't drive for a while, anyway."

She stopped in Ngaruawahia to collect his prescription from the local pharmacy. Dashing to the cafe next door, she snagged coffees and took them back to the car. Logan lay back in the passenger seat with his left arm resting across his thigh. The effort of escaping the hospital exhausted him and dark shadows furrowed beneath his eyes. Pain washed out his olive complexion to a deathly paleness. With a fortune's worth of medication and a dent in her bank balance, Hana drove home to Culver's Cottage, carrying her precious load. She concentrated on not bumping the BMW too hard over the rugged driveway.

Logan slept for most of that day and the next. By Wednesday, he seemed more lucid and sat in the lounge admiring Hana's struggling fire. The television fuzzed in the corner, the terrible picture offering little entertainment.

"He's an awful patient," Hana confessed to Izzie over the phone. "The exact opposite of demanding. He asks for nothing. I fuss around him and I sense he dislikes it. I'm a rotten nurse!"

"Just think yourself lucky," Izzie retorted. "Marcus complains non-stop when he's sick and he speaks in this pathetic voice that makes me want to commit murder!"

"At least you don't get sick of the sound of your own voice," Hana mused. "I do."

"No!" Izzie snorted. "I get sick of his!"

The diabolical television reception gave Hana a headache. The rolling screen and horrendous snowstorm formed a black and white fuzzy picture that proved impossible to watch. In frustration, she phoned an aerial company in Hamilton.

"There's an additional cost for travel," the salesman told her. "It's outside our zone."

"Ngaruawahia!" Hana complained. "It's twenty minutes from Hamilton, not somewhere in the outback!"

The man attempted to blind her with technology and Hana gave up as the projected cost escalated. She texted Bodie in frustration. Half an hour later, he replied with the number of a local fitter who came recommended by a colleague.

An hour after her call to a mobile number, the aerial specialist drank coffee in her kitchen. "$150 all up, miss," he said, the job already complete. "You just needed a booster." He narrowed his bushy, black brows. "Them city blokes know nothin'. All piss and wind, bro'." He waved the home baked cookie towards the kitchen window. "My ma lives over that way, through the bush." He took a loud slurp of his coffee and helped himself to another cookie.

Hana straightened her spine, interest in her eyes. "Really? How far away?"

"Next door from here. Five minutes by road but twenty if you walk it. You'd get sore lost if youse didn't know the way. It's dense bush at the bottom with streams and ridges you can't see until you trip over them."

Hana gazed towards the forbidding darkness of the canopy with new respect. Hone continued, "Ma's stopped working but my stepfather still does building work. I'm surprised she didn't call by yet to say kia ora."

"I'd like that," Hana said, craving female company.

"What's them gates all about?" Hone asked, biting into another cookie. "Geez miss, these taste good."

Hana bit her bottom lip and focussed on justifying her extreme safety measures. "We work in Hamilton during the week. The gate's for security."

Hone nodded and expounded on a vast knowledge of the bush and Hakarimata Ranges. "I grew up playing in those mountains," he said with longing in his voice. "Most beautiful place on earth." After

another cup of coffee and four more cookies, he left with a cheery wave.

When Logan woke later and dragged himself to the kitchen, he discovered Hana with her sewing machine set up on the large pine table. She sang to herself and hemmed another set of curtains. Logan's entry made her jump. "Sorry." He leaned to kiss the top of her head. "I might watch the television for a while," he said with a sigh. "If I can bear it."

"About that." Hana's face shone with excitement. "Come and see." She took his hand and led him into the lounge. "Sit." She held his arm while he lowered himself onto the sofa. Hana used the remote to activate the picture, watching Logan's face as the crystal clear images scrolled across the screen.

"Wow," he said. "That's awesome. It gave me seasickness before with all that rolling and snow." His grey gaze settled on Hana's face. "You're so kind." He cocked his head in confusion. "I don't deserve it."

"You do!" Hana leaned forward and kissed his soft lips, trying not to jolt his fragile body. His self-deprecation resonated with an inner voice in her own head. She ran a finger along his cheekbone. "Logan, you're the best thing that's happened to me in years. You deserve so much more than a television aerial."

As the week progressed, Hana used the enforced confinement to decorate the house, painting and wallpapering while Logan rested. She sat with him in his waking hours, watching television or talking. He grew stronger as the days passed and the surgical scars lost their angry hue. The days seemed to lengthen without the restraints of a timetable and Hana relaxed into her new, sedentary life. A district nurse visited at the end of the week, buzzing the gate alarm for admittance. An older lady, she hailed from Rarotonga and showed gentleness and care over Logan's wounds. He lay on the sofa and allowed her to examine his stomach and ribcage as she chatted about the weather. "This looks good," she said, getting to her feet. "Keep it dry for another week or two. I'll keep checking it."

"Thanks." Logan sat up and yanked his dressing gown closed to cover his stomach. He made no attempt to chat and Hana experienced a flicker of embarrassment. She cleared her throat and distracted the nurse.

"Tea or coffee?" she asked and the woman nodded, her brown eyes widening in a meaningful expression. Hana swallowed, sensing trouble.

"Coffee, please." The nurse stayed to pack up her medical kit and joined Hana in the kitchen. She seated herself with a grunt. "I hate being on my feet all day," she sighed. "But I love my job."

Hana nodded and put the mug in front of her. She added a plate of muffins she made in the middle of the night when sleep evaded her. The nurse reached for the mug first. "That dressing should be fine until Monday. Any problems at all and you must take him to the surgery or back to the hospital."

Hana groaned. "He won't go, so it's pointless."

The other woman's nod looked slowed down. "Is he always that quiet?" she asked.

"He hates hospitals." Hana chewed her lip. "I think he's scared."

The nurse's lilting Pasifika accent sounded comforting and gave Hana confidence as they chatted. "That's understandable. He must be sick of them."

Hana sighed. "I know there's something wrong. Mr Singh refused to tell me and Logan won't discuss it."

The nurse cocked her head to one side in sympathy. "It'll be okay," she said, reaching across and smoothing olive fingers over Hana's. "It won't be anything you're imagining." She let go and reached for a muffin. "But tell me something." She took a bite and exhaled with pleasure. "Yum. But I know a fall down stairs when I see one and that ain't no injury from a fall."

Hana's mug wobbled and her tea spilled on the table. She watched a trail make its way towards a dip in the wood and form a pool. The weight of truth pressed on her, constricting her chest. Guilt at the official lie lay as heavy as the injustice of Tama's attack. "I'm not sure what to tell you," she began. "We filled in an accident form saying Logan fell down the stairs of his parents' hotel." Grinding her teeth gave her a splitting headache.

The nurse reached across, patting her hand. "I won't share anything you tell me," she promised. "But your husband's wearing a line around his body, like somebody struck him a hefty backhand with a thin, metal object. I can see where it contacted. With the angle of it, he's lucky to just lose his spleen and break some ribs. If it hit his kidneys, we wouldn't be sitting here sharing coffee and cake."

Her crime scene assessment finished, she sat back in her seat and supped her coffee. Hana's voice emerged as a whisper. "He used a crowbar, or a wheel wrench, same thing really. His nephew hit him from behind. I wanted to call the cops but Logan's family wouldn't let me." Hana sighed and let her head fall back on her neck, staring at the freshly painted ceiling through eyes that were blind and unseeing. She played out the scene with Tama like a roll of film in her head. "Logan tried to protect me and got hurt in the process." She let her head fall forwards again and met the nurse's steady gaze.

"Thank you for the truth," the older woman replied. "Keep a

close eye on your husband, Mrs Du Rose. He doesn't look so good and his temperature is high. I've recorded it in his medical notes so if you need help, they'll see it there." She popped the last piece of muffin into her mouth and stood. "Stay alert for signs of fever and higher levels of discomfort. And next time, lady, call the cops."

She left spare dressings with Hana in case and told her what to watch out for. Then she sped away in her tiny black car, powering down the drive at breakneck speed. Hana watched dust from the gravel rise above the trees and opened the gate from the lobby.

Sitting on the porch alleviated the stress which threatened to drown her. Late autumn turned the leaves to ochre and red in the expanse of bush between the house and road. Birds twittered high above her and Hana succumbed to the urge to seek solace amongst them. "I'm walking as far as the trees," she called through the open doorway, listening for Logan's reply and hearing nothing.

Strolling to the bottom of the front garden before the trees started, Hana peered at the only part of the road she could see. She heard the squeal of tyres and saw a flash of black, guessing the nurse had left the premises. Hana waited until she heard the gate clang shut.

In the half-painted living room, she found her husband lying on the sofa in his dressing gown and pyjama bottoms. He looked overheated, sweat beading on his brow. She plonked herself in front of him on the rug, leaning back against the seat. "You're too hot," she said, narrowing her eyes at the roaring fire. "You put more logs on."

"I'm cold." He stretched forward to kiss the back of her head, slipping his arm around her shoulders. Hana sat for a moment, recognising the character on the screen.

"Why are you watching SpongeBob SquarePants?"

Logan shrugged. "There's nothing else." He added as an afterthought, "I haven't seen this one. Pete's got the DVD's and this one isn't on it."

Hana half turned to look at him in disgust. He gave her a smile more like his old self and she let the worry dissipate. She turned side-on to the sofa, putting her head on the warm cream leather next to his chest. Logan cuddled her in closer and they stayed like that for a while, Hana relaxing at last. Logan watched SpongeBob's antics above her head, snickering at the behaviour of the little yellow man.

Logan ate soup for lunch and Hana's optimism gained traction. He went for a lie down and she attacked the wallpapering behind the fireplace. A bold print made life harder, but she kept going despite the level of difficulty. Their journey to the store the previous weekend seemed a lifetime ago. "Look, Tiger, you like it?" she asked the cat. He licked his paws and turned his back on her. The coving sported a gentle off-white paint, the wallpaper a mix of Tudor Rose interspersed with a filigree pattern of silver. It looked striking against the grey paint on the other walls. Hana cleared the kitchen table and used the tarpaulin, carefully carrying the wet wallpaper into the lounge.

She suffered two significant mishaps. As Hana carried one sheet of paper, folded back onto itself in its sticky state, it unravelled and stuck to the rimu floor. It tore as she tried to pull it free. "Oh no," she wailed as the glue welded it to the wood. Hana resorted to white spirit to remove the tacky residue. The house stank with a heady, chemical odour. The second mishap occurred as Hana climbed the ladder, trying to hold the folded paper aloft at the same time as watch her footing. She wobbled, failed at both tasks and put her foot clean through that sheet as well.

"Oh, bloody hell!" Hana stamped in fury. With the wastage, she made it to the end of the wall with only one sheet to spare. With glue in her hair, she stood back and admired the instant effect.

Exhaustion rushed over her soul like a tidal wash as she paused for breath. She'd created a marathon out of sewing, painting and wallpapering, in between caring for Logan. Her body ached and her sleep patterns seemed more messed up than usual. It left her with a disturbing sense of overwhelm. Shaking herself, Hana forced the knotty fingers of depression to release her heart. She persevered with her decorations until the part which television designers called 'dressing the room'. For her, that signified another climb up the stepladder.

When Logan stumbled into the lounge later, he just managed stop Hana plunging backwards off the ladder. Immersed in swags of silver fabric in front of the bay window, she resembled a tall grey ghost tilted backwards at a precarious angle. "Whoa," he shouted, jerking forward to stop her falling. "Why didn't you wait for help?" He reached up and placed his hand against the shrouded shape, which wiggled, beneath his palm.

"I'm okay," came Hana's muffled voice. "It's heavier than I thought. I just need to get these last few hooks in."

Logan grunted in reply, not daring to remove his hand as the shroud shifted under his fingers with Hana's movement. "Hurry up, babe," he groaned. "I need to put my arm down." His face whitened at the strain it put on his abdomen and he cursed under his breath.

"Heard that," Hana said with a giggle. "Logan, why are you feeling my bottom?"

"I'm not." He peered at the shroud, unable to distinguish any particular body part. "Not on purpose, anyway."

The activity continued and Logan heard clicking from inside the fabric as Hana fastened the hooks. With more wiggling and puffing, the material moved up Hana's back and over her head, as though she extracted herself from an extra-large pullover. She reappeared, hair on end and her clothes rucked up to her midriff. She wobbled regaining her balance and gave Logan a triumphant grin. "Ta dah!" she said and pointed at the silver swags.

Logan's lashes swished against his eyelids and he offered a quirky smile. "You're a twit," he muttered. "If you fall and break a bone, we're both screwed."

Hana shrugged. "I'm fine. I did the bedroom ones in the middle of the night alone. These are heavier is all." She spent the next few minutes pulling and tweaking the curtains into place. "I wanted to surprise you," she told Logan with disappointment in her voice.

He raised his eyebrows. "Oh, you did that. Finding you up a ladder wearing a curtain is beyond surprising. Alarming."

"You exaggerate." Hana gave him a sultry look. "I did the other one by myself with no issues." She turned away and winced, noticing the scuff mark on the floorboard where she reached too far and the ladder scooted out from under her. Hands on hips, she stood back to admire her work. "Don't you think they look wonderful?" she demanded, her eyes shining in victory.

Logan took the neat edge of the left curtain, drawing it back and forth across the window. "It works," he said, his eyes sparkling with mischief.

"Stop it!" Hana complained. "You're mocking me."

"No. I'm admiring." Logan stepped back and took in the fire glowing in the hearth. The grey paint and dramatic wallpaper gave a sense of home. "You're great at this renovation thing." He lifted his right hand and brushed his fingers through his hair. "You're talented."

"Not really." An embarrassed flush lit Hana's cheeks and she pursed her lips. "Home is important. I need to have a place I can go where I'm safe and the surroundings are peaceful and uncluttered."

"Me too." Logan nodded and their eyes met. "I've never found that until now."

"Never?" Hana held her breath as Logan shook his head.

"Never."

"Do you think we'll be okay?" she asked in a whisper. "Me and you."

Logan nodded. "More than okay, Hana. We both want happiness and security. I'll work hard to make it happen."

Hana swallowed and shoved the memory of the blonde man to the back of her thoughts. "I know," she said with a sigh. She tugged the new curtains closed over the bay window and turned. A late afternoon greyness edged across the paddock behind the house and lapped at the French doors. "I'll do those curtains another time," she said. "I don't have the energy today."

Logan followed her into the kitchen, watching as she packed the sewing machine away. He stopped her as she lifted it from the table. "Leave it up," he said, raising his eyebrows as Hana shook her head.

"No, it's fine. I know you hate mess. If I leave it on the table, I'll feel pressured to make all the curtains in one go, even when I don't have the energy." She carried it through to the back bedroom, refusing Logan's aid as it banged against her shins.

Making a drink later, Hana jumped as her mobile phone danced and vibrated around the counter. She picked it up and peered at the number. "I don't know who it is." She pushed it away from her, eyes wild in betrayal of her inner panic. Fear lurked just beneath the surface of her equilibrium as a permanent guest. It required little effort of late, to rise up and dominate her thinking. Snatching it up, she thrust the phone towards Logan. "What should we do?"

He took it and answered with a grunt. When his eyes rolled, Hana relaxed. "You threw us into a tail spin, idiot!" he snapped. "Try texting your new phone number before you ring us. Hana's phone didn't recognise it." Logan pulled the phone away from his ear and handed it back to Hana. "It's Pete," he growled.

Hana heard Peter North's nasal wailing without putting the speaker to her ear. She winced at the hysteria in his voice. "Where's that thing you do? I can't find it, I need it!"

"What are you talking about?"

"The thing! The thing! So I can pay for the drilling parts!"

A light went on in Hana's eyes. "Oh, is George from the tech department there?" she demanded.

"What the hell's going on?" No longer Pete's voice, but that of the gentle teacher who'd taught woodwork for over thirty years. "This clown doesn't know his ass from his elbow."

"What do you need?" asked Hana, avoiding the question. She heard Pete burbling something in the background, followed by George's heavy sigh of exasperation.

"Sheila gave us approval for a bench drill at the end of last year," he began, frustration in his voice. "I'm using it for the pre-employment classes so she said she'd pay for it. It arrived yesterday and I brought the invoice straight over. Now this idiot won't sign for payment." Hana heard Pete start to whine again in the background. "What am I supposed to do now? I can't send it back and I don't have the money in my budget."

"Right," replied Hana with deliberate slowness. "I remember Sheila approving it and I set money aside at the start of this year. Put Pete back on and I'll make him sign for payment. It'll be okay."

George muttered his thanks and Pete returned, still grumbling.

"Shut up, Pete and listen!" Hana snapped.

The conversation took so long, her mobile phone bleeped for

low battery. Her right ear hurt when she disconnected the call. "That man!" she complained to Logan. "Pete's happy to take extra money for running the department, but he didn't realise he needed to do any work!"

Logan laughed and gripped his stomach with a pained look on his face. "That sounds like Pete."

Hana plugged her phone into the charger and leaned back against the counter. "He's taken up residence in Sheila's office because he thought it might be a quiet spot for a nap. But it's too busy for him."

"What's the thing I heard him panicking about?" Logan asked, sipping coffee at the dining table.

Hana's eyes grew round. "My budget spreadsheet. I tried to tell him how to open it and then changed my mind. One wrong click and he'll mess it up for the rest of the year. He asked me how to turn my computer on and I knew that didn't bode well."

"Please don't make me laugh again," Logan begged, rubbing his hand across his stomach. His dressing gown parted and Hana eyed the dusting of hair disappearing into his pyjama bottoms. She lost her train of thought.

"Pardon?"

"What did you tell him to do with it?"

"Ooh don't tempt me," Hana bit, regretting her glib answer as Logan doubled over in pain. "Sorry, sorry," she said, rubbing his back. "I told Pete to sign whatever they put in front of him and I'll clear up the mess after. He wanted to know why I'm off work and I told him you'd been sick and in hospital."

"No, no, no. Please tell me you didn't say that?" Logan shook his head in misery and Hana baulked.

"He wanted details, but I gave none. And I asked him not to tell anyone else." A pensive expression masked a flash of naked fear. "He said Mrs Bowman keeps asking about me."

Logan lifted his head, suspicion in his eyes. "What does that mean? That sounds like more than a casual enquiry."

"He said she stops by to ask every morning. She wants to know when I'm coming back. Today she asked for my phone number. Pete says Angus took it off the staff sheet. She'll need to find an old sheet to get it now."

"She asks him every day?" Logan's eyes widened at Hana's slight nod. "Oh, crap!" he groaned.

"I told him to tell her nothing! I pleaded with him and told him it's crucial."

"Geez Hana!"

"It's okay. He agreed."

"Yeah, but on what condition?" Logan demanded and Hana

cringed. "Pete turns everything to his advantage, Hana."

She gulped. "Nothing I can't deal with by myself."

Logan's eyes narrowed. "Just tell me, Hana. Or I'll drive to school and bash his brains in."

"Oh, very civilised." Hana pouted and hardened her jaw.

"Just tell me." Logan stood, overshadowing her with his presence.

Hana sighed and traced the outline of his left pectoral with her finger. "He'll sign off invoices and text me. I need to log onto the school server and maintain the spreadsheet. He wants Angus to think he can cope."

Logan shook his head. "And?"

"That's it." Hana squirmed.

"Liar." Logan caressed her jaw in his strong fingers and Hana licked her lips.

"Can we go to bed now?" she whispered and Logan raised one eyebrow.

"Yes. But tell me first."

Hana sighed. "He did one of his ugly cackles. If I don't help him, he'll tell Mrs Bowman you got a vasectomy."

Logan shrugged. "Do I care? Don't help him, Hana. He's a twat."

"Let me just log on and enter this one amount and then I'll come to bed." Hana found her laptop in the sideboard and switched it on. Logan's strong arms encircled her as she leaned over the keyboard.

"Leave it!" he demanded, turning her body and pulling her away.

"I can't," she said, ducking out of reach. "I don't want Pete spreading rumours about you.

Logan smirked. "Whatever," he replied with nonchalance. He encircled her so she couldn't get away. "Like at school when he told everyone at the social I caught diarrhoea? Or the time I banged my head and needed stitches and he told them surgeons removed my brain? Or maybe the vasectomy story or the full castration? One day, he'll think of something original."

Hana smiled with her face pressed into Logan's dressing gown. Logan ran his hands down her spine, leaving a tingle in their wake. "You should have told him I'd break his legs if he repeated anything. He knows I mean it!"

The certainty in his claim made Hana uneasy, but she brushed it away. He led her to the bedroom and closed the door, cocooning them in the safety of each other. Hana breathed in the masculine scent of her husband and wished life could stand still for just a while. As her hands and mind explored the newness of their marriage, she sensed the tendrils of danger snaking nearer.

-12-

Hana woke, feeling groggy and out of sorts. The clock showed after nine and shocked her with its lateness. Logan slept next to her, drugged by painkillers and the dull, relentless agony he rarely complained about. The borrowed phone vibrated itself off the bedside table and onto the floor. Logan groaned as the sound dragged him from slumber. His right hand scrabbled on the floor, trying to reach it. A moan of agony escaped his lips and he clutched his side with white-knuckled fingers.

"Leave it, I'll get it," Hana sighed, dragging herself from the cosy bed and running round to retrieve it. "Hello?" she said, rubbing her eyes and hearing only the disconnect tone. "Damn, I missed them."

"It's a wrong number," Logan sighed, gingerly touching his dressing. "Oh crap, this leaked through again."

Hana sighed and sat on his side of the bed. "I'll change it if you trust me to try." She eyed the weeping mess and chewed her lower lip. "You don't think those men found us, do you?"

"Not through a random phone that's been in the bottom of a policewoman's drawer for over a year."

"So, you don't think I should call the number back?"

Logan shook his head. "No, Hana. If it's important, they'll call again." He yawned and lay back against the pillows.

"What if it is them?"

"It's not."

Hana struggled to stem her panic. She staggered first to the bathroom and then the kitchen. "It could be them," she muttered and Logan heaved out an exaggerated sigh.

"It's a wrong number," he snapped through gritted teeth. "I'm going back to bed."

Hana stood in front of the boiling kettle, watching the steam rise to the ceiling. As her eyes refocussed on the bush line, she spotted a moving shape trudging down the side of the paddock. Clad from head to toe in dark clothing, it slipped and slid in the cloggy soil. Hana drew back from the window in alarm. "Quick, someone's coming. Quick!" She rushed through to the bedroom, calling to Logan. Her eyes widened in terror as she looked for somewhere to hide.

Logan shifted onto his side and then worked his way into a sitting position, "Who is it?"

"I don't know, I don't know," Hana repeated. "You go, you go, please! Don't let him get me again." She fled from the room and Logan heard the click of the bathroom door locking.

He dragged his dressing gown over his pyjama bottoms and padded along the hallway. He rapped his fingers on the bathroom door. "Geez Hana, you can't do this every time someone visits!"

"I can," she squeaked from behind the wood.

Logan shook his head and responded to the sharp knock on the front door. The visitor eyed him through wide, brown eyes. "Kia ora," she said, grinning to display gaps in her front teeth. A woolly hat perched on her head and curly grey hair poked from beneath the tattered hem.

"Hi, kuia," Logan said, showing respect to the elderly Māori woman. He stood aside to let her in. She bounced across the doorstep after kicking her gumboots off on the porch. She hefted a bag of winter vegetables and wore an enormous smile.

"My boy, Hone fixed up your television aerial," she said, jerking her head towards the lounge. She indicated the dressing beneath Logan's ribs, clicking her tongue in sympathy. "He told me youse got sick."

Logan nodded and wrinkled his nose. His fingers pulled his dressing gown closed over his wounds as though embarrassed. The newcomer smiled in sympathy. "Don't be worrying, tāne. I bought veggies from the market to set you up with some of my soup." Shrugging, she padded to the kitchen in oversized socks and clattered around finding a knife and chopping board in the cupboards. Logan made an excuse and nipped to the bathroom. He knocked on the door and Hana opened it with deliberate slowness.

Her tear streaked face forced a groan from his lips and he pried the back scrubber from her fingers. "That's no good, idiot!" he said, pulling her into his chest. "The old lady from next door came to visit," he whispered. "She's sweet. Get dressed while I make her a drink."

Hana nodded and turned towards the tarnished bathroom mirror. She grabbed a swathe of toilet roll and dabbed at her tears. When she ventured to the kitchen, she found Logan sitting at the table and their visitor chopping an array of vegetables and stirring a teaspoon in the old brown teapot. She seemed able to do both at the same time. Hana swallowed and fought the hitching in her chest. "Hello. I'm Hana. This is very kind of you."

The woman turned with a beatific smile. "Kia ora. Ko Maihi ahau," she answered, giving her own name. She induced confidence and safety with her presence and Hana responded to the easy maternalism. "Youse both had a rotten time, I hear," she said, adding a taro to the broth on the stove. Hana darted a dark look at Logan and he shrugged. Maihi turned back to view their stunned silence with a smirk. "I know most things, kōtiro. I have whānau all over this town and down in Kirikiriroa."

"Hamilton." Logan translated the Māori name for Hana and raised an eyebrow in surprise. "Impressive, kuia."

The old lady chuckled. "I've a nephew with the cops and a niece who cleans at the police station on Bridge Street. They hear things and tell Aunty." She patted her chest with work-worn fingers and winked at Logan. Hana smothered a smirk as the old woman played him like a musical instrument. He deferred to her with such respect and deference, Hana watched in fascination. She experienced a strange mix of emotions, ranging through jealousy to confusion as they dropped into fluent Māori and she understood nothing of their conversation.

"Sorry, kōtiro," Maihi jumped to her feet and embraced Hana in a rough grip, sensing her isolation. To Hana's surprise, she cuffed Logan round the back of the head. "Speak English boy," she told him. "Or teach your wife Te Reo."

Logan's look of hurt made Hana giggle. He glared at her, resenting the female alliance taking shape before his eyes. "Cup of tea, for you." Maihi pushed a steaming cup of green water towards Hana and she peered into it. "Kawakawa," Maihi qualified. "Good for infection and health. If you lay the leaves over a wound, it tells what the ailment is by changing colour."

"Does it?" Hana's interest piqued. "It actually changes colour?"

"Yes!" Maihi's head bobbled on her shoulders with enthusiasm. "It turns many colours, including white. It can tell youse what's wrong."

Hana glanced sideways at Logan and he confirmed the fact with a nod. She smiled with the pleasure of learning hidden facts about her surroundings, satisfaction pinking her high cheekbones and lighting her eyes. "That's awesome," she breathed, peering into the hot tea with new interest.

So Maihi slipped into their lives, found a space and made herself at home. Logan admired a skill handed through the generations and longed to possess it. His paternal grandmother honed it to perfection and he hadn't seen the like since. As Hana sipped her tea feeling slightly bewildered, Maihi indicated the pan of boiling vegetables with a flick of her head. "Veggies," she stated, as though Hana might not recognise them. "From the Saturday market down town. You should get all your stuff there. It's good value. Meet your friends, have breakfast and do your veggie shopping. Perfect." She squeezed her wrinkled face into the cutest smile and Hana grinned back.

"It's kind of you," she responded. "We didn't know about the market."

"I came last week," said Maihi. "Just to be neighbourly. But I drove and didn't expect to see a gate blocking my way." She shrugged. "The last guy didn't have no gates."

Logan nodded. "Hana's son ordered the gate to help with our security issue. I'm glad he did now."

Hana watched in surprise as Maihi patted his hand. He let her, accepting the show of affection without protest. Hana tried hard not to feel like an outsider in their little Māori world full of mystery and lyrical speech she couldn't follow.

Maihi jumped up and slipped her coat around her shoulders. "I should go," she announced. She moved towards the stove and poked the vegetables with a sharp knife. "Not long now. Make sure youse watch it girly, so it doesn't catch on the bottom." Then she turned to Logan. "You can show me round now, tāne."

Like a meek little lamb, Hana's formidable husband led the wizened old lady around the villa. Hana smirked at the sight of his deference, struggling to line the image up with his usual hard exterior. She heard Maihi's exclamations of enjoyment as she saw the improvements.

"Goodbye, Hana!" Maihi popped her head into the kitchen again before she left. She nodded with approval at the sight of Hana peering obediently into the pot. "Youse make this house sing! Welcome to the Hakarimatas." She waved with enthusiasm and Hana noticed her own hand waving back, looking at it in surprise as though it belonged to someone else.

Logan returned, his fingers moving across the keypad of his mobile phone. "We exchanged numbers," he said. "She's awesome."

"She has a cell phone?" Hana asked in surprise and Logan smirked. "She's savvier than you might think."

"Do you think she rang before? The call we missed."

Logan shook his head and impatience flicked beneath the surface. "No, Hana. We just exchanged numbers then. Forget it!"

Hana felt the bite of his irritation, surprised at his vehemence. She remained silent as Logan poked in the saucepan with a wooden spoon. He placed a lid over the top and turned the heat to simmer. "What?" he demanded, responding to Hana's sideways glance.

Hurt made her spiteful and she drew her face into an expression of mock adoration. "Oh, come on Maihi, I'll show you round. Look at the bathroom. That's where I keep my slippers. Would you like to inspect my undies drawer? I can line my socks up on parade if you wish." Her voice trailed off at Logan's blank stare.

"She's an elder," he said. "We're brought up to respect the kaumātua."

"That's nice." Hana shrugged, mystified by the hidden code of honour in his culture.

Logan smirked and gave an exaggerated sigh. "You're such a Pākehā," he muttered.

Hana's lips parted in horror. "Did you just infer I stink like a whale?"

"No!" Logan dragged her to his side. "It's the word for European." Hana let her head relax against his shoulder. "And alien," he whispered, ruining the effect.

Hana shied away in mock offence, examining the broth through the glass lid. Pumpkin and kumara bounced against the movement of the water. Logan stroked her hair back behind her ear and dropped a kiss on her neck. Hana glanced at him sideways. "Stop looking at me like that. You're too sick," she told him, noticing the twinkle in his eye.

"I feel much better all of a sudden." His voice took on a seductive tone and Hana shivered as he ran his index finger down her spine. "It must be the kawakawa tea," he breathed onto her neck. "And I think Maihi put some into the stew."

"You're a very bad man. And what about the veggies?" Hana tried to dodge her husband's kisses.

"Turn them down," he whispered, his voice muffled in her hair.

Hana flicked the switch on the stove and the bubbling calmed. Logan pushed his fingers beneath her sweater. "No! Not here!" Hana squealed. "I bet you gave her a key."

Logan snorted. "No I didn't, but we should. She's trustworthy."

"Yeah, she'll also be shocked if she wanders in unannounced! You have the sex drive of a randy stallion! You're meant to be sick!"

"Get back to bed, wahine!" Logan ordered and Hana ran along the hallway giggling. She tried to shut the bedroom door against his onslaught but wasn't strong enough. Logan breached her pathetic efforts without breaking his stride. As he undressed her one-handed without losing eye contact, Hana sensed herself melt beneath his gaze. "You're such a player," she giggled as his rough palms caressed the soft skin of her spine. Logan smirked and brushed his lips across hers.

"I know," he replied with a wicked twinkle in his eyes. His gentle fingers released the zipper on her jeans and pushed them over her buttocks.

Later, Hana groaned as the hands of the clock moved towards midday. "I need to get up," she said with a sigh. Guilt laced her tone.

"Stay with me," Logan whispered, a sexy edge to his voice.

Hana sat up with a shrug and the sheet slipped to her breasts. "I can't. It feels wrong to stay in bed all day."

"What about when you lived by yourself?" The rumble of Logan's voice sent a comforting sensation along Hana's spine. "Didn't you lie in bed all day then?"

"No." Hana hung her head. "I still got up and put my makeup on, even though I might not see another person." She hugged her knees, the sheets spilling around her waist to reveal a soft, creamy stomach. Her empty weekends spread out behind her in the wake of cleaning, food shopping and remoting on to work via her laptop to stem the loneliness with unpaid labour. "Gosh, my life was dull," she breathed.

Logan ran his finger along the ridges of her spine. It tickled and she shivered. When he slipped his hand around her ribs and started to tug, Hana pulled away. "No, you bad boy. I need something to show for my day!"

"I can show you plenty." Logan's full lips quirked upwards and his eyes promised mischief.

Hana giggled. "I can't spend all day in bed! It's just wrong." She escaped into the bathroom, almost tearing the bed sheet in her haste.

Logan called to her retreating back, "What's wrong about it?"

Hana took a shower and Logan joined her, any sense of romance ruined by the plastic sleeve over his cast. "It kinda spoils your sex appeal," Hana said as she rubbed soap into his back, her fingers sliding over his olive skin with deliberate playfulness.

They ate the stew for lunch. It simmered itself to a pulp on the stove. "Will you tell Maihi we let it cook for too long?" Hana said, concern in her eyes. "I bet she checks."

"Yep, she'll check, but it's tasty and that's all she'll care about." Logan dug his spoon into the hearty mixture again and sighed. "It tastes like my childhood."

"Is that a good thing or a bad?" Hana licked her lips, waiting for his answer.

"This is a good memory." Logan's voice dulled. "Tasting this meant we had money for food. Or Jack's veggie garden prospered that year."

Hana nodded. "I imagined the mountain a great place to grow up, but sometimes when you speak about it, I'm not so sure."

Logan sighed. "Nor am I, Hana." The portcullis of his emotions descended with painful slowness and Hana feared exclusion. She rallied to change the subject.

"Can you manage another portion?"

Logan nodded and she rose to take his bowl. Gentle fingers clasped hers. "I love you, Hana," he whispered and she relaxed.

"Yeah, I think you do." The soft pad of her thumb grazed his stubbly jaw. "You rock my world."

Logan's grey eyes bored into her soul as he stroked her wrist. "You've upended mine," he admitted. Hana swallowed, not wanting to crush the moment. So much of him lay hidden beneath the surface, a fragile veneer of snow covering perilous rocks and sharp edges. Hana leaned forward to kiss him and felt lust and temptation mingle. with a fragile, fledgling sense of hope.

She pulled away and took Logan's bowl to the saucepan. "Maybe we can try the Saturday markets next week?" she mused.

Logan shook his head. "Not yet. Not until the cops catch those guys. Why lead them straight back here?"

"True." Hana's bubble of optimism burst and she quieted, the house crowding in on her like a prison again. "How did Maihi get onto the property?" she asked, a while later.

Logan shrugged and pushed his bowl away, swapping it for a glass of water. "Not sure. She mentioned an ancient path through the bush. She assured me only the very best tracker would find it."

He trailed off and Hana read his mind with frightening clarity. "You think we should learn the route?" she asked. "In case we need to escape."

Logan nodded. "Yeah. I do."

Hana sighed. "I'm tired of living my life looking over my shoulder. If the cops don't catch them by the time you return to work, I'm going back too."

Logan raised his eyebrows but said nothing. Hana veered between not caring, to panicking over nothing. He fingered the phone in his dressing gown pocket. Hana cleared the bowls away and checked the fire in the lounge. "I'll fetch more wood," she said, poking her head through the kitchen doorway. The wood basket clanged against the frame.

"Okay. Thanks. I think there's a movie on television. We can snuggle down and watch it." Logan turned in his seat and winced. Too much activity increased his pain. Bedroom antics counted as way too much activity. He waited for Hana to clump down the back stairs and withdrew the phone from his pocket.

"I wanted Bodie," he said when Amy answered his call.

"He took Jas to the park," she replied. "And forgot his phone again." She sounded fed up. "He might be gone for one hour or six."

"Sorry." Logan held his breath, not wishing for further confidence.

"It's fine." Amy sighed. "I should feel grateful. At least Hana wants you for yourself, not some advantage you bring with you."

"I didn't give her the chance," Logan replied and regretted it.

Hana didn't know what he brought with him into their marriage and he preferred it that way. For now. "Hana's going stir crazy." Logan steered the conversation away from dangerous ground. "I need to know how far the investigation's got. Nobody will tell me."

"Ask Odering," Amy replied. "And good luck with that. Guy's an ass."

Logan groaned. "You think I don't know that?"

Amy sighed. "We've both used Hana's car a couple of times. Just to see what happened. We each picked up a tail. A black BMW followed me and a beat-up Subaru stayed with Bo. Neither had an Asian driver or a blonde. Different men both times."

"But definitely following?" Logan demanded.

"For sure." Amy clattered cutlery in the background. "We ran both sets of plates."

Logan groaned. "Both stolen."

"You got it." Amy sounded tired, as though the rigors of crime in the city made her bone weary. "Both sets of plates stolen locally. Someone used one set later to steal petrol from a gas station in Rototuna. Same plates, different vehicle."

"Where does that leave us?" Logan demanded. "Why didn't you arrest the men following you?"

"How?" Amy snapped. "Prove they're following us. We arrest them, tie them up in legislation for a couple of hours for the stolen plates. Then the courts let them go with a slap on the wrist and three hours community service. That doesn't help you long term. There's something big happening. Odering's wheeled in more of his Auckland cronies. Just wait it out for now."

Logan snorted. "Wait it out? Easy for you to say."

"I know." Amy's tone changed. "The other alternative is to put Hana into witness protection. Maybe you should consider that between you."

Logan gritted his teeth. "I can't go with her. And we just married, Amy."

Amy sniffed, bringing the conversation to an end. "You know the choices, Logan. Go with her. Don't go with her. I think she should consider it."

Logan ran a hand through his hair. "This is crazy."

"I know," Amy conceded. She lowered her voice. "Bodie's planning to visit Mrs Bowman unofficially. He knows something but won't tell me. His mate on the investigative team let a piece of information slip and he's upset about it."

"What?" Logan demanded and felt Amy's attitude change. She switched from concerned co-conspirator to woman spurned.

"I don't know," she snapped. "Bodie only talks to me because of my son. I wish he never came back." She ended the call with an abruptness which made Logan wince.

Hana huffed to the top of the stairs with the wood basket, hearing the rumble of Logan's voice as he spoke to someone. Glancing through the kitchen doorway as she passed, she saw the phone pressed to his ear. He discussed his injuries. She heard the back end of the conversation as she placed more logs into the fire. "Na, I'm fine. It's not serious." He wandered into the lounge and watched her activity with unseeing eyes. "Hana's looking after me." She saw a vein tick in the side of Logan's neck as he grew agitated. "No, Dad, it's okay. I don't wanna hear about Tama. No, don't tell me. He's Mike's problem now. I don't want to know anymore."

The conversation ground to a halt with a grunted goodbye. Logan shoved the phone into his pocket with a jabbing action. He slumped onto the sofa and groaned at the impact. Hana raised her eyebrows and gave him a sad smile. "Problems?"

Logan shook his head, changing the action to a nod half way through. "Michael left. Tama's looking for me. He wants to talk." Logan's lips curled back from his teeth in a sneer.

"Did Alfred tell him where you are?" She held her breath.

Logan sighed and a strange look drifted across his face. "He can't tell what he doesn't know," he replied.

Hana swallowed, but the warning look in his eyes drove the question from her head. "You look tired," she said, her voice soothing. "Go and lie down for a few hours."

"No." Logan's jaw tensed. "Unless you come with me."

Hana resisted, alarmed by the greying look in his complexion. She turned the afternoon movie on and he slept within the first ten minutes. Muting the sound, Hana covered him with a furry throw, closing the curtains and dimming the lights. In the kitchen, she set up her sewing machine and made curtains for the French doors, finishing them quicker than expected. "I'm getting good at this, Tiger," she told the cat as he brushed past her legs.

Logan slept all afternoon and into the evening. Hana checked him at intervals, noticing how he shivered and adding another blanket over his legs. She hung the new curtains, drawing them against the darkness outside. Loneliness shrouded her as Logan's prolonged slumber forced her into a familiar isolation. She put more wood on the fire, realising as it hissed and spat that she brought up the wet stuff by accident. Evening shrouded the house with a black cloth and Hana resisted venturing out for more wood. "Stay away from it then," she said to the cat as he jumped back from the spitting fire.

Boredom drove Hana back to her fabric collection. She fingered the heavy navy material intended to tie in the colours from outside.

Deciding to continue sewing until Logan awoke, she began with the easiest window in the wide lobby, making both curtains in less than an hour. "I should do this for a living," she said to the empty kitchen. "As long as people just need hemmed rectangles with header tape."

Hana hung them to inspect and then removed them again, knowing she still needed to paint the walls. Making a wide curtain for the front door inadvertently produced her best work of the project. She shuffled a cute happy-dance in her socks and jiggled the reluctant cat around the hallway in her arms. "That's my best curtain," she whispered, smooching his black and white face into her neck. He put up with her affections for an acceptable length of time before mewing and wriggling free. His paws landed on the floorboards with a heavy thud. "Sshhhh!" Hana put her finger to her lips and he shimmied off, his tail kinked at the end in irritation. "You'll wake Logan," she hissed. Glancing at the clock, she pondered waking him herself. Loneliness made her selfish and desperate to tell someone about her success. Hana poked her head around the lounge door.

Logan still slept. The greyness gone, his complexion looked ruddy and overheated, a bead of sweat sliding along his temple. "Loge." Hana peeled the blanket away, surprised to find it damp to the touch. Her maternal instincts screamed alarm. Shaking fingers loosed his dressing gown cord to expose his torso and horror filled her green eyes at the pink and red seepage. It leaked through the white gauze and covered his stomach, dripping through the fabric of his dressing gown and onto the cream leather of the sofa. Hana hesitated, staring at the mess in front of her, her heart rate hiking as panic took hold. "Logan!" She shook his shoulder, grateful for the groan which escaped his parched lips. "Logan!" He muttered something incoherent in reply and Hana rested her palm over his forehead. Heat blazed through his skin and a clammy sweat stuck to her fingers.

-13-

"Logan?" Hana shook his shoulder again, her tone urgent. "Sweetheart, wake up. Logan?" Groggy and disorientated, Logan roused, pushing at Hana's fingers with weak, ineffectual movements. He clapped his hand over his mouth and leaned sideways with a groan.

Hana snatched the leftover paste bucket from her wallpapering and shoved it on the floor next to him, only just making it back in time. Logan tried to sit and threw up, red liquid spattering the remnants of paste. He reeled without control and Hana struggled to hold him in place. He pushed her hands away again as he vomited and she let go, backing off. "Sorry, Logan," she hissed under her breath. "Please forgive me." She reached into her pocket for her phone and slid it out, letting it rest in her palm.

Logan retched again and then plunged face first onto the rug, landing with a grunt. Hana dropped to her knees, pushing the bucket aside and calling his name. "Logan, Logan!" Hysteria bled into her voice and panic tightened her chest. He didn't respond as Hana patted his cheeks and called his name, her breath coming in terrified hitches.

The ambulance arrived ahead of Bodie. He ran from the passenger side of Amy's car and opened the gate using the keypad. The big truck moved through without waiting. Both vehicles laboured up the steep driveway to chaos. Hana appeared from the front door, tears streaking her cheeks. "I can't wake him up," she sobbed. "He threw up and lost consciousness." She spoke to her gathered audience, her expression pleading for help. Noticing her son climbing from Amy's car, she stopped in confusion. "Did they call you?"

"No, Mum." Bodie took a step towards her and saw the wild fear in her eyes. "Jas wanted to see you." He waved his arm towards the car as Amy moved it down the slope and out of the way of the ambulance. "What happened?"

The paramedics proved competent, moving with practiced calm and asking logical questions. They filtered Hana's panicked answers and assessed Logan's condition. "Set up fluids," the female officer said to her colleague after peering into the paste bucket. "Internal haemorrhaging."

Hana shook her head and forced out her words. "It's wallpaper paste," she said, watching as the male heaved Logan onto his back. The man shook his head at the pool of blood beneath him.

"Internal, external. It's coming from every-bloody-where."

"I'll set it up." The woman looked over his shoulder and waggled her eyebrows at the state of Logan's stomach. The male paramedic sighed and reached backwards into his medical bag. His colleague touched him on the shoulder. "You patch him up. I won't be long." She left the room, avoiding Hana as Bodie pulled her aside.

"Let them do their job," he told her, his tone calm and reassuring. Hana squeezed her eyes closed as the paramedic stripped the gauze from Logan's wounds and blood pooled in the cavity. Her mind tore her in two between wanting to see everything and keeping her eyes from witnessing the horror. Bodie spoke to the paramedic in low, professional tones, informing him of Logan's recent operation and discharge from hospital. They conversed without Hana's input. She stared at her new lobby curtains folded on the armchair and her small victory turned to ash in her mouth. She wished she'd spent the afternoon watching Logan instead.

The female officer returned to the lounge and set up a bag of clear fluids. She exclaimed as blood squirted from Logan's vein and stained her shirt. "Geez, you're a bleeder, Logan," she said, her voice jovial. "You trying to raise my laundry bill?"

"All good here." The male paramedic stood. "I've packed the wound. It's open. Something else is going on inside though. His blood pressure sucks."

Hana whimpered and Bodie shoved her towards the paramedics as they hoisted Logan's limp body onto a trolley. "He'll be fine, Mum. Go with the medics and tell them whatever they want to know." He gave her a warning look. "Tell them everything. I'll follow you in Amy's car."

Hana swallowed. "But Logan said something different on the form."

"Everything, Mum. Tell them how it happened. If it's important, they need to know."

Hana nodded, willing to betray Logan's trust if it meant saving his life. She heaped fresh curses on Tama's absent head as she climbed into the heavy vehicle and belted herself in.

Through the tinted windows, she saw Amy walk Jas up the porch steps and through the front door. The child clutched a card in his fingers and his face screwed up in misery. "I want my new poppa," he wailed, waving the blue card. Porch light scattered sparkles across his hair as Amy led him inside. Hana closed her eyes against the sight of his distress and jumped as the woman swung the ambulance into the slope to make the tight turn back onto the driveway.

Logan vomited twice more on the way to the Waikato Hospital and the tension in his muscles caused the wound to leak with more violence. Blood seemed to spray from inside and outside his poor body until the paramedic resembled an axe murderer. Desperation made Hana silent, staying out of the way while the competent paramedic handled each new crisis with clinical precision. He inserted pipes, tubes and needles into her husband, taking regular readings from a monitor above Logan's head. "He's burning up," he called to the driver and she put her foot down harder on the pedal.

Hana stared at Logan's pink cheeks and blame licked at her psyche. "I covered him up," she admitted, fear making her voice waver. "I lit a fire but got the wrong wood. I needed dry, not wet, but I didn't realise. It's all my fault. I caused this." Her eyes looked huge and frightened, like saucers in her pretty face.

The paramedic took pity on her. "You didn't cause this," he reassured her. "It's common after spleen removals and I suspect there's a sepsis somewhere. Did the surgeon prescribe antibiotics after the op?"

"Yes," answered Hana, as her mind did cartwheels with the information. "He took them. I don't understand."

The paramedic stopped listening and turned away as a machine to Logan's left bleeped out a frantic wail. He fiddled with the blood pressure cuff on Logan's arm. Then he leaned forward and spoke to the driver. "Put the lights on, Sal and warn them to get ready. Blood pressure is dropping. I'll try to get him stabilised but my guess is this guy's going straight into surgery."

As the driver pressed a button on the dashboard, Hana saw the red glow spin around her. The statistics he quoted and the ensuing discussion between the professionals went over her head as white noise. Hana concentrated on the strobe as it reflected off the river and the windows of silent houses. It felt surreal. Her throat ran dry and she coughed with the effort of swallowing. She knew how this scene played out and remembered the feelings of denial and loss. She lost one husband. It couldn't happen again. Her lips moved with a familiar mantra. "This isn't happening," she whispered. "This isn't happening."

Reaching the hospital reminded Hana of a game of Monopoly. Everyone wanted the card that entitled them to collect two hundred pounds and pass the square marked, 'GO.' Hana suspected she'd drawn that card as she skipped the crowded waiting room and Logan's gurney spun through the doors to the resuscitation area without stopping. Faces stared through the glass from the waiting room as patients nursed broken bones, cuts and headaches. Hana found herself surplus to requirements as medics surrounded her husband. One man barked orders and the room silenced for the paramedics to give their verdict. They squeezed her out towards the fringes, a frantic bystander as they poked and prodded Logan, asking questions he didn't answer. They behaved as though he did, nodding and continuing conversation with a man deep in unconsciousness.

"Just a wee injection, Logan."

"Let me know if that hurts, Logan."

"Stay with me, Logan."

"Logan, can you hear me? Logan…"

Hana couldn't bear to leave, but found it terrible to remain. She discovered a little stool in a corner and sank onto it, putting her head between her knees. The heat in the room coupled with her own fear made her sick to her stomach. Acid rose into her throat and she took deep breaths to stave off the nausea. Her mother's advice. She heard Judith McIntyre's voice speaking into her memory. She never sounded like other mothers. How could she form words she never heard? Hana felt the lack of a mother as a physical ache. She reached for Judith's facial features and saw only a dark haze. She owned nothing of her mother's, banished before Judith's death. No photographs, no keepsakes, nothing. Yet she remembered her voice. Stilted words spoken with love.

The memory soothed Hana, urging her to fight. She sat up slowly in response to a gentle hand on her shoulder. Her delicate stomach gave an angry lurch. "Mrs Du Rose?" The name sounded alien on the doctor's lips and sadness engulfed Hana. Her new name, spoken only by medics so far.

"Mr Singh." Relief swarmed through her veins at the sight of Logan's surgeon. No turban this time, but the same gentle face. She sensed he recognised the terror in her eyes.

"Your husband is very sick," he said and Hana knew she blanched even though she tried not to. "We'll put him in intensive care overnight once we've assessed him. I suggest you ask a family member to sit with you." He gave her shoulder a reassuring rub and moved away to deal with Logan. Medics swarmed around him like players in an orchestra, responding to his conductor's baton.

Hana ran through the day in her mind as a nurse offered her a drink of water. She accepted it with shaking fingers and spilled most of it. "He seemed better today," she said, hearing the appeal in her voice. "He ate lunch and watched television. I suggested he took a nap and this happened." Hana's eyes widened. "I thought sleep was good for you." Knowing her ramblings meant nothing, Hana silenced.

Her husband lay flat with monitors affixed to his body and numerous lines piercing his veins. Hana swallowed her water and listened to the medical terms and instructions without understanding. Mr Singh issued orders. "Be extra careful putting lines in. Is that Factor 8 here yet?"

"Factor 8." Hana moved the words around her tongue as a memory blossomed. She'd heard them before. Not heard. Seen them written down.

"Can I get someone for you?" a nurse asked and Hana nodded.

"Yes please."

Twenty-five minutes later, Pastor Allen blasted into the room where Hana waited with Bodie. The pastor's tawny hair stuck up on end and he wore his dog collar inside out, stuffed half in and half out of his old pullover. He kissed Hana, shook hands with Bodie and apologised for his appearance. "Painting the shelves in my study," he said, peering at the white streaks on his knuckles. "My tea is still sitting on the dining table and I left skid marks on the driveway."

Bodie leaned forward and jerked his head at the clerical collar. "Was it a passionate painting session?" he asked with a smirk. "Your collar is on inside out."

Allen looked down and shrugged. "Oops. No. It doesn't match this shirt. Visiting hours finished ages ago and they won't let me past the barricades without it."

"Like a holy warrant card?" Bodie asked and Allen nodded. He sank onto the seat next to Hana and put his arm around her shoulders, assuming authority over the situation.

"Hello, sweetheart." He crushed Hana into his side, bringing with his usual chaos a pervading sense of hope.

"I haven't made it to church for ages," she began, offering an apology for her absence. He brushed it off.

"It doesn't matter, Hana. No excuses needed. I'm here because you called. I'll always come." He rocked her like a small child against his raggedy pullover. "God knows. He has it all in hand."

"I don't understand what went wrong," Hana sniffed and the pastor kept a sturdy arm around her shoulders and winked at Bodie.

"I met Logan a while ago," he said. "He treated me to a blat on his motorbike. I've spoken to him a couple of times since. He invited us to your surprise birthday party, but it clashed with a deacon's meeting. I gather it proved more than just a celebration of your advancing years?"

Hana nodded. "Yes. Marcus married us. Kind of." She bit her lip. Everyone still assumed he married them, not that she'd eloped like a love smitten teenager and let a stranger put a ring on her finger.

"That's wonderful. But Logan always pops to see me or leaves a note. I didn't have a return address. When I called at Achilles Rise, the man who answered the door said you'd shifted and he wasn't sure where to."

"Yes, sorry. That's my fault." Hana sniffed and wiped her nose on her sleeve. "It's complicated."

Bodie let out a snort which Allen tactfully ignored. The pastor left them for a while and fetched steaming cups of coffee from a secret stash only he knew about. And he produced a wad of tissues from his pocket when Hana needed them.

Bodie wandered off on a pretext, embarrassed by Hana's lack of control. Fear and worry got the better of her and she felt his animosity hike. Allen behaved like she knew he would, listening to her angst with endless patience. She didn't mention her security issues, focussing on Logan's health and reliving her horror of the bleeding. "I should have spoken to you before I got married," she conceded, sniffing in tearful snorts of air. "But it felt so right and if I'm honest, I thought other Christians might want to talk me out of it."

"Ah, Cilla." Allen's slow nod betrayed a tense conversation. "That's why I visited Achilles Rise. I didn't like the half version and wanted the truth."

Hana shrugged. "What does it matter? I found true love after all these years and now I'll lose him, anyway."

Pastor Allen's brows narrowed to a single dark line. "Things aren't always as they seem, Hana. Much can be done."

A medic walked along the corridor and Hana jumped to her feet, bracing herself for bad news. He ignored her and kept walking, alternately dashing and raising her hopes without realising. Hana sank into her seat, her legs like jelly. Misery ringed her green irises. "They didn't care!" Hana turned towards Allen, her cheekbones pinked with distress. "Tama hit him from behind with a crow bar and they wouldn't let me call the cops or get help!"

"Ah, Hana." Allen's arm tightened around her shoulder. "You've had a terrible time. I'm so sorry."

She jumped up again as another doctor emerged from the room. Allen took her hand and pulled her back to a sitting position. "Stop, sweetheart," he whispered. "Let me pray for you." He soothed her with his gentle voice, infusing her with belief and assurance. Hana felt the overwhelming peace which surpassed human understanding. With it came the knowledge Logan would live to fight another day.

Bodie returned and paced while the pastor ministered to Hana. A side-glance told her he detested the intimacy. Faith fled her son the moment his father departed this mortal coil, leaving him believing God either didn't exist, or hated him personally. Muscle memory urged him to join in the prayer and Bodie fought it. But as the clergyman finished his whispered plea to the Almighty, Bodie's dormant spirit uttered a veiled Amen.

Logan went into surgery after midnight and Hana slept on the uncomfortable seating in the intensive care area. Pastor Allen stayed with her until the early hours of Sunday morning, squeezing Logan's limp hand as he arrived on the ward. Mr Singh dropped his facemask into the dustbin and smiled at Hana. "I cleaned his infected wound under anaesthetic. I also discovered another bleed into his stomach cavity. I want him in intensive care for tonight on ten-minute observations. The staff will page me if he deteriorates."

Hana thanked him, fighting a frightening sense of gratitude which threatened to render her speechless. "Can I stay with him?" she asked, bunching her fist around the sheet near Logan's face.

Mr Singh nodded and rubbed his eyes until the exhaustion looked painful. "Of course, Mrs Du Rose," he said. "Press the buzzer if you need anything." He turned towards the glass door and the promise of home, halting for a second before facing Hana. "Good luck," he said, his tone sober. Rich brown eyes quirked upwards. "Let's hope we don't find ourselves here again."

Hana nodded with enthusiasm. "Thank you doctor."

Bodie left with Allen, promising to return later with clothes and toiletries for Hana. "I'm glad he's okay, Mum," he said, sounding sincere. "I know you love him."

Hana sat on a two-seater sofa outside Logan's room, watching through a huge glass window as his chest rose and fell. A nurse checked his dressings and took his blood pressure while he slept. Nobody troubled her. "You can go back in now," the nurse said, leaving the door open for Hana to return. "He'll be in pain when he wakes as I've just reduced the morphine level. Call me if I need to raise it."

Hana sighed. "He won't complain. Logan will put up with it."

The nurse nodded. "They're the hardest sort to help," she replied. "I heard Mr Singh say he must have been in agony. I'm guessing your husband didn't mention it."

"No." Hana swallowed. Her mind drifted back to their energetic lovemaking and she blushed. "Not once."

Logan woke twice and Hana fed him water through a straw. At six o'clock, the staff removed the oxygen mask from his face permanently and took away the extra cannulas from his veins. When he woke five hours later, he found himself in a single room on a different ward. "You're out of danger," Hana whispered, stroking his hair away from his eyes. "The operation worked and the intravenous antibiotics kicked the infection into touch." The wobble in her voice betrayed her horrible night. "Why didn't you tell me how bad it hurt?"

Logan's eyes fluttered and closed, the answer dying on his lips.

Staff moved him again two hours later as lack of space bit. He shifted further away from the high dependency unit and nearer the dreaded surgical aftercare ward. Already exhausted, Hana felt tension hike in her chest at the memory of Selina and her dust up with the receptionist. When the moment came and a porter arrived to fetch a sleeping Logan, Hana panicked. "I can't do this again," she said, running sweating palms along her thighs. Tiny threads from her jeans stuck to her hands and reminded her of her uncleanliness. "You can't take him back there," she begged. "There must be somewhere else."

"Sorry." The porter shook his head and examined his sheet of orders. "Logan Du Rose to general surgical. That's all I've got." He took off at speed, forcing Hana to trot to keep up. At the elevator he paused and nodded to a colleague as another patient wheeled out first. A teenage boy lay splayed on a gurney, wires and monitors attached to every available part of his body. His face looked so smashed he seemed indistinguishable as a human being. Hana counted her blessings and stepped into the lift, unseen by the glassy eyed mother in the nightdress and slippers, who followed her broken son along the corridor.

Hana stared through the window for the hundredth time, turning as she heard Logan snuffle. He moved his head and his voice sounded hoarse and urgent. "Han! Han!"

Less than a metre away, she rose from her seat and gripped his hand. "I'm here," she replied and kissed his fingers.

"Where am I?" he demanded and pity rose in her chest, doing battle with overwhelming relief.

"Hospital," she whispered, her mouth close to his ear. "You got sick last night, don't you remember?"

"No, no, no, oh not again. Take me home; don't leave me here, please? They don't understand, help me get out." Logan struggled to surface, fighting the drowning lure of drugged slumber. "I need to tell you," he rasped. "You have to listen to me." The words wouldn't come. They slipped from his mind and he plunged back into the abyss.

Hana sighed and rested her forehead against his hand. The cast gripped the skin, reminding her of the beginning of the whole sorry mess. His other hand looked like a battleground, scarred with needle marks from IV lines and awful black bruises. Streaks of blood stained his wrist, so much blood for just a few needles. "You do have things to tell me," she whispered against Logan's fingers. "But will it be the truth?"

Hana closed her eyes and napped with her face pushed into the mattress. In calling for her when he woke, Logan allowed her to obliterate Caroline's influence for good. If he'd called for his former lover even in confusion, she didn't know if she could let it go. But he didn't. He wanted her.

A nurse popped her head round the door. "Mrs Du Rose, your son's here. Shall I send him through?"

"Yes, please." Hana sat up and looked at her watch. Visiting hour waned and dread snaked its fingers around her heart. When it ended, they'd force her to leave. Bodie appeared in the doorway, looking drawn and tired. His uniform shirt rumpled around his waist. "They wouldn't let me in this morning," he said, his dark lashes fluttering in distress. "I brought some clothes and a toothbrush. They wouldn't pass it on."

Hana let go of Logan's hand and hugged Bodie, feeling the tension in his shoulders. "It's okay," she said, "I know."

"I came back in uniform." He rolled his eyes. "But visiting hour started so they don't care now." Bodie focussed on the streaks of blood around Logan's mouth and wondered how to fill the void which opened up around them both. "Mum, we stayed at the house. Was that okay?"

Hana nodded and smiled. "It's fine."

Bodie swallowed. "Jas spent all day making a card for Logan. Amy persuaded me to come up with them. He saw you both get into the ambulance and cried himself to sleep." He ran a hand over his eyes. "I didn't know they could get like that. Kids."

"Things affect them," Hana replied, her voice soft. "Sometimes big things and other times, almost nothing at all. Jas seems like a child who forms attachments quickly. He likes Logan."

Bodie's jaw worked, creating lines through his cheek. He sank into the other visitor's chair and hoisted a bag from next to his feet. "Amy packed stuff for both of you," he said. "I hope it's what you need."

"It will be." Hana accepted the bag containing clothing and toiletries. She sighed. "Yesterday's shower seems a long time ago."

"Your phone's in there too. You left it behind. Izzie rang me in a panic. They gave her a scan yesterday."

"On a Saturday?" Hana's eyes grew wide and frightened. She put a hand up to her mouth.

"It's okay, Mum." Bodie stood and went to her, taking both her hands in his. When he squatted down in front of her, Hana went into panic mode. He raised a hand to force her to listen. "It's important, Mum. Don't go off half cocked. Izzie didn't feel great, so they admitted her for a scan. But the baby's absolutely fine, it's perfect." Hana's hands moved within his, sensing Bodie hadn't finished. "There was something not right though. It explained the sickness and bloating and why she's so darn grumpy. She's having twins."

Hana's jaw dropped and she waited for the punch line. Despite the smile on Bodie's face, she saw no teasing. A hysterical giggle rose in her chest, birthed by stress, fear and relief. "What a really bizarre weekend," she snorted. A month ago, I had one grandbaby and now I have four. Twins?"

"That's our Izzie," Bodie said with a hint of pride in his voice. "She does nothing by halves." He gave a cackle of laughter. "Marcus is walking around with a stupid grin on his face. He thinks it's proved his manhood."

Hana snorted and imagined the scene. Marcus always wanted a big family, but accepted it wouldn't happen. The news buzzed through her frazzled, tired brain, slowing her reactions and exchanging some of the fear for hope.

"What's all the fuss?" Logan's voice sounded hoarse and he hissed through his teeth. His lips cracked with the effort of speech. Hana jumped to her feet and reached for his hand.

"Hey, sleepyhead," she whispered. "Glad you could join us. Izzie's pregnant with twins."

Bodie nodded to Logan as the older man's eyes tracked towards him. "Hey Grandpa," he joked. "I don't think I've got to visit the hospital this many times in a week before."

Logan's eyes looked glassy, but he fought to stay awake and smiled at Bodie, a gormless, uncoordinated grin.

"I'm due on shift," Bodie whispered to Hana. "I'll come back later." He patted Logan's leg through the covers, the only part he dare touch for fear of hurting him. He left with a wave.

Hana drew the chair up closer to the bed and held Logan's hand. "You want some water?" she asked and he nodded. She found the straw from earlier on, but he sipped without taking much. He slumped against the pillows and fear stopped her altering the bed in case she damaged his fragile body. His face looked grey against the white sheets.

"I can't believe I'm back here," he groaned, lifting his cast to rub his eyes.

"It couldn't be helped." Hana tensed with the effort of defending her actions. "Get better and I can take you home again." She gripped his fingers and forced him to look at her. "And start telling me the truth about how you really feel. Then we won't keep ending up in emergency situations!"

Mr Singh walked through the door at the tail end of Hana's sentence. He nodded in agreement. "I concur," he said and jabbed a finger at Logan. "Your wife speaks sense and I'm sick of patching you up." He stifled a yawn with a brown hand, looking only marginally less exhausted than Hana.

"When do you sleep?" she demanded, covering her own yawn.

He waved his hand in dismissal. "Oh, you know, they stand me in a corner and recharge me like Frankenstein." His laugh sounded weary and Hana pitied him. Mr Singh peered at the scribblings on the clipboard at the end of Logan's bed, making more sense than Hana did earlier. He perched on the side of Logan's bed. "So, from what I just overheard, you have no comprehension of the reason for your admission last night?" He peered over his glasses at Logan and Hana sank into the visitor's chair, relieved someone else seemed willing to pick up the battle.

Mr Singh eyed the monitors surrounding Logan as they clicked, pinged and dripped. Then he pulled back the covers from Logan's stomach with a sigh. "Perhaps I can show you."

Yellow ink stained Logan's abdomen and chest and a fresh line of stitches hid beneath the dressing. The doctor pulled the pack aside and wrinkled his nose at its blood soaked state. Hana half rose to survey the damage, seeing the original wound ten centimetres longer than before. The whole area looked bruised and swollen. Mr Singh clicked his tongue and watched Logan's reaction. Nothing. Hana's heart sank as her husband eyed the doctor with an impassive expression, not allowing his words to touch him. "You know," Mr Singh tutted, "if you told your wife you hurt occasionally, things like this wouldn't happen. She thinks you ate well and yet I discover a stomach filled with blood. That tells me you faked it. I'm thinking you must have vomited blood for days. There's no shame in admitting you hurt."

Hana watched Logan's face and received the revelation as though he scrawled it on the wall. Admitting to pain invoked more shame than he could bear. She ached for him but couldn't remain a prisoner to his masked emotions. She experienced a flash of sympathy for Caroline, remembering Logan's lack of expression towards her. He'd stared at her hand on his wrist as though it meant nothing, yet he'd once taken her into his bed and produced an engagement ring. Hana stood, surprising both men. "I can't do this," she announced. "I can't live like this."

The doctor turned to Hana and his eyes widened in sympathy. "Mr Du Rose, are you comfortable for me to talk about your health with your wife present?"

Logan's jaw flexed. "Not really."

Mr Singh sighed and looked at Hana. She raised her hands in defeat. "Hey, don't mind me. I haven't slept properly since my wedding. I've spent most of my time here with a man who can't even tell me the truth. Just give me a moment to leave. I'm bushed anyway so I'll go home." She pressed a finger to her temple. "Oh, that's right. Silly me. I can't. I got here in an ambulance." Tiredness leaked from Hana's soul and she stepped over the doctor's feet, trying not to stand on his comfortable shoes. "Excuse me," she said and strode to the door, closing it behind her.

Once outside, Hana sought a change of scenery. She found a water heater and coffee cups in a tatty dayroom at the end of the corridor. Mr Singh found her there, sipping a tepid drink. "Mrs Du Rose," he said, sitting next to her. "It must be bad if you're drinking hospital coffee."

"It is." Hana took another sip and wrinkled her nose. "I don't know what to do."

The doctor blanched. "You need to speak to your husband."

Hana shrugged. "You saw him. He doesn't trust me."

"It's not that simple. Give him a chance."

Hana voiced her worst thought. "Whatever's wrong with him, can I catch it?"

"I promise you can't." Mr Singh patted her hand. "Absolutely not." He stood. "Talk to him."

Hana returned to Logan, her nerves frazzled and her mood plumbing the depths of misery. He didn't trust her and perhaps never would. "Logan, can we talk?" she asked, her lips forming a tight line.

Logan shook his head. "Later?"

Hana shrugged and took her seat to sit out the rest of visiting hour. Logan fell asleep again and she sensed he would stall as long as possible. She used the public bathroom to change her clothes and freshen up, returning to find him still sleeping. Hana watched Logan, studying him as she never could during his waking hours. Fingers never free from fidgeting lay in peace on the starched sheets and Hana stroked them, counting the cuts and scars until they numbered in the twenties. Logan's serious eyes remained shut, black lashes flickering against flushed, olive cheeks. "I love you, Logan Du Rose," Hana whispered. "Even if you are as stubborn and arrogant as one of your stallions." She stroked his cheek, feeling the dark stubble under her fingers and noticing how it grew lighter either side of his chin. Sadness filled her chest cavity with regret. She knew how it felt to be mistrusted and it hurt.

Nursing staff ignored Hana, working around her as she stayed through two sets of visiting hours. She sensed they wanted her gone but remembered her fuss from before. Bodie arrived after his shift and insisted she leave with him. She returned to Culver's Cottage to find Jas sitting by the fire in his pyjamas. He read a storybook while Amy made a scratch dinner from the contents of the fridge. Hana walked into the living room, halting in surprise at its newly decorated state. "I forgot," she murmured. "Yesterday seems a lifetime ago."

"Dinner won't be long." Bodie pushed her towards the child and the fire. "I'll shout you when it's ready."

Jas watched Hana's progress across the room, his expression serious. Then he patted the rug. "Sit with me and read my story, Hanny."

Tiredness ignited Hana's bones into a numbing ache but she didn't have the heart to reject him. "Okay," she said, hearing her knees creak as she sank into the soft threads of the rug. "Just until dinner."

"Good," he remarked with a satisfied nod. "I've waited all bloody day."

They sat around the kitchen table eating the leftovers of Maihi's stew. Amy used her culinary skills to turn them into a pie and jacket potatoes. Hana hadn't eaten for over twenty four hours, but the food refused to go down and she quit half way through. Amy looked at her in sympathy. "Why don't you grab a shower and relax?" she suggested. "You might feel like toast later."

"Thanks." Hana rose and pushed her chair underneath the table. She reached for her plate.

"I'll clear away," Bodie said, glaring at Jas as he grumbled under his breath.

Hana smiled her gratitude and took herself to her bedroom on leaden feet. She heard Jas voice his complaint and shook her head, allowing a smirk to lift her lips. "I don't get toast later when I don't eat my dinner!" he exclaimed. "I don't even get dessert!"

Hana closed the door against Amy's hushed recriminations.

After a disturbed night's sleep, she used Bodie's BMW to drive herself to the hospital. Queuing with the other visitors, Hana realised she didn't bring a gift, unless she counted toothpaste. Just before the ward doors swung open, she heard someone call her name.

"Hana!" Alfred waved to her from the back of the line and she motioned him forward. The woman behind her set up a fuss and Hana glared at her until she silenced. Alfred kissed her on the cheek and gave her a bear hug. "It's this bloody curse," he hissed into her ear. "The boy can't help it."

"Help what?" Hope burgeoned in Hana's heart as Alfred's lips parted and it seemed he might enlighten her. He shook his head and closed them again. "What's wrong with him?" she demanded and Alfred pinched his lips together and ignored the question.

Logan flicked an accusatorial look in Hana's direction at the sight of his father and her irritation grew. "Don't look at me, I called no one," she replied. "Don't mistake me for someone who knows what's going on." Logan narrowed his eyes and she avoided his gaze.

Alfred loped across with his uneven gait and embraced Logan, plonking a bunch of squishy- purple grapes on the bedspread. "I needed to see how you're doing," Alfred said. "Is it like the other times?"

Logan shot a concerned look in Hana's direction and Alfred silenced. Hana bridled and considered abandoning them to their ridiculous conspiracy. "I'll fetch coffee," she snapped. "I'll whistle on my way back and you can change the subject."

Alfred sighed in her wake and Hana heard him say, "You need to tell her, son. This ain't fair."

Hana gritted her teeth and made a vow to herself. "Oh, you'll tell me, Logan Du Rose. You're not making a fool of me any longer." She returned with two coffees, one laden with the four sugars Alfred requested.

"Where's mine?" Logan asked and Hana shrugged and ignored him. His eyes bored into her temple but when she stole a peek at his face, she saw his lips quirk upwards in approval at her spirit.

"How did you find us?" Hana asked, sipping the awful brew and wishing she'd handed it to Logan. Served her right.

Alfred jerked a finger at Logan. "He called me on a number I didn't recognise the other day. Tama did this fangle dangle thing with the buttons and found Logan's number. I got no reply."

Hana raised her eyebrows. "Tama?" Her lips curled backwards. "He's at your place?"

"He's whānau," Alfred replied in warning and Hana blanched.

Logan changed the subject. "I don't know where my phone is."

"Probably dead in your dressing gown pocket. I took it home last night." Hana struggled to regain her composure and still the feelings of hatred invoked by Tama's name.

"I called it again last night and a lady answered. She said you went to bed and she told me they took my boy to the hospital in an ambulance. I set off early this morning."

"Amy." Hana gave a slow nod. "She didn't mention it, mind you, Jas occupies most of her attention when he's awake."

Logan jerked his head upwards. "She'd tell you a guy called and you'd panic, anyway. She's probably still working out how to say it."

Hana rolled her eyes in mock self-deprecation. "I know. It's such a drag. You should take the ring back and call it quits."

Logan's jaw dropped open in dismay. He formed words and then swallowed them down. "Whatever," he replied, sounding hurt.

Alfred battled on in his deaf oblivion. "Yes, Mother sends you both her love." He delivered the second-hand affection with a smile and Hana grimaced. She bit back the question about Miriam's whereabouts. She sent her love but not herself.

As Alfred sipped his hot drink, two nurses arrived mob handed to monitor Logan. They consigned Hana and the old man to the smelly visitors' room with the broken television. Hana sank into the ripped seat with a groan. "Welcome to my life," she muttered, closing her eyes.

"This is stupid!" Alfred complained. "Damned useless health system. What does it take for them to let me sit with my son a couple of hours after he nearly died?"

"They do what they like here," Hana replied. "They tell me nothing and pen me up in here." Her eyes narrowed. "And I suspect Logan's at the back of it." She stood. "He married me for better or worse. We might not have said the words, but that's how it is. I deserve to know what's wrong with him." With a look of alarm, Alfred excused himself and walked to the nearest public toilet. "Traitor!" Hana muttered at his bent and retreating spine.

It took the nursing staff half an hour to refresh Logan's dressing and change his sheets. Afterwards, his mood seemed foul and Alfred squeezed himself into a corner seat and pretended to fall asleep to avoid recriminations. "I want to go home," Logan started and Hana sighed.

"What's the point? If your health condition is a big secret, you don't want to come home with me. You need to stay where knowledgeable people can take care of you."

"Don't say that." Discomfort made Logan squirm in the bed. "I don't want to talk about it."

"Fine." Hana sat on the side of his bed and folded her arms. "Stay here until you do then."

His slender fingers traced a line along her thigh, sending shivers down her back. She glanced sideways at Alfred and forced herself to resist his charms.

"Medical insurance!" The old man leapt to his feet so fast, the chair hit the wall with a crash.

"What?" Hana's eyes widened in shock.

"Bloody medical insurance!" He said it again and his lips widened to reveal missing side teeth. "Remember?" He appealed to Logan, dancing a jig in his excitement. "You still paying it?"

A little light went on in Logan's brain and a smile played on his lips. "Yeah," he replied. Hana looked from one man to the other without understanding, just as the bell sounded for the end of afternoon visiting time.

Later that evening, Hana grovelled in a cardboard box in the spare room. "Logan said it's in here." She waved an impatient hand towards Alfred, who poked around fecklessly in a banana box. "Aha!" She held up the white envelope in triumph. "Get out of jail free."

Alfred snatched it from her and disgorged the contents onto the bed. He peered at the date on the policy. "Bingo!" he shouted. "One month left before it renews. I always told the boy he wasted his money on this shite. Now he'll make me admit I'm wrong."

Hana gritted her teeth and pulled her phone from her pocket. "You should ring them." Her voice sounded sad. "They might ask me questions I can't answer."

Alfred dialled and walked away after giving the policy number. Hana heard him arranging to move Logan to a private hospital. The precious sheet of paper rested on the bedspread and Hana reached for it, reading the policy and schedule. The premium looked astronomical and she used the booklet key to isolate costs. Whilst it listed nothing personal, she deduced the insurance company considered her husband a substantial risk.

Bodie returned to the cottage with Jas, letting himself in with a key. "Amy's on night shift," he said, a sheepish expression on his face. "Can we stay here? I'm not quite sure what to do with him."

"Okay," Hana conceded. "But there's another guest.

Alfred emerged from the bathroom holding his nose. "You need an extractor fan in there," he complained. "Almost gassed meself."

Hana sighed and offered introductions. Bodie grunted in irritation at yet another Du Rose in his space, but Jas' enthusiasm reached new levels of hysteria. "Oh my!" he yelled. He counted off on his fingers. "I got a new daddy, a new Hanny, a new poppa and now a new old-poppa! Bloody hell!"

"Language!" Bodie pinked with embarrassment and Alfred ignored the child's error.

"I guess we're whānau." He scratched a hairy chin. "Not blood, but good enough."

"I remember you from the party." Jas bounced up and down on the spot. "You broked the lights."

"I remember you an' all," Alfred retorted. "You puked on the carpet."

"Did too. I don't appreciate curried egg." Jas patted his stomach. "Wanna read my book?"

"Na. I don't read so good." Embarrassment pursed Alfred's lips and Hana held her breath. "I didn't stay in school long. My brother kept getting us expelled."

"That's okay." Jas reached out for his gnarled hand. "I'll read it to you."

At eleven o'clock, Alfred accepted the fourth bedroom for the night with Bodie deeming it far too late for him to start the journey home. Hana excused herself, leaving her son and father-in-law chatting. She knew Bodie's game and his good-cop routine bored her. She wondered with a stab of bitterness if he'd fill her in the next day.

Bodie woke her early. He didn't mean to, but she heard him

whispering through the wall. Hating herself for it, Hana crept closer and listened, forming the muffled words into sentences. He spoke to Amy on the phone. "Logan's older brother died years ago from a blood disorder," he told her. "I wonder if that's what Logan has." He paused and Hana waited. "Yeah, the old man said one of the boys isn't his. The old girl must've cheated on him." Hana heard the disgust in his voice. "Family sounds a damn mess from what I overheard Mum saying to Pastor Allen the other night. I'm worried about her!"

The conversation ended with an abruptness caused by Jas. His wail of annoyance sounded loud through the wall and gave Hana enough noise-distraction to hop back into bed. "You're so loud!" he whined. "I'm trying to lie in! Get your own bed next time." The mattress creaked as Bodie scooted back under the covers and a tickling fight ensued.

Hana dressed and prepared to ring the hospital. Instead, they rang her. "Hello, Mrs Du Rose, this is Keely from the Bramwell Hospital. Your husband arrived this morning and you're most welcome to pop along and see him as soon as you wish."

"Thanks." Hana contemplated pumping her for information but sensed she'd waste her time.

Keely continued. "Mr Du Rose wanted you to know you're welcome to stay as long as you want. We don't have restrictions."

"Okay, thank you." Hana disconnected the call and chewed her lower lip. Another day of exclusion filled her with misery. Did he ever intend to confide in his own wife?

Alfred's constant presence ensured Hana gained no further insight and her disquiet grew to fever pitch. Her intimacy with Logan cracked under the strain of faking marital bliss while nursing a fatal sense of mistrust. Instinct told Hana to run. Instinct failed her once before. She ignored it.

Alfred stayed a few more nights and visited Logan each day. The old man confided some things, but nothing of note. "He bought that insurance policy years ago," he told Hana. "He hates hospitals after that hunting accident. They made him lay in a corridor for over three hours with his guts hanging out. The emergency room got busy and they kept putting him behind all the other accidents, so it became infected. Miriam complained but back in the day, brown skin was filth and the white nurses treated our women like second-class citizens. It's why she nursed Barry at home when he got real sick, because she didn't trust the hospital system to make him well."

Hana nodded, keen not to break his flow of confidence.

"Jack dealt with it," Alfred admitted. "He picked Logan up from the hospital and took his stitches out. Miriam gets sick when everything gets on top of her. She made a mistake. And we all paid for it."

Hana licked her lips. "You paid by losing Barry?"

Alfred snorted. "We paid by pretending her bastard was mine!" His grey eyes flashed and then calmed. "No matter, kōtiro. What's done is done."

Hana opened her mouth to speak again and he waved her unasked question away. "I'll leave the day after tomorrow," he said, stilting the conversation. "Need to get back and run the farm." He leaned across and patted her arm. "You take care of my favourite son. He's an ornery old git, but he's done more for me and his ma than any of the others put together. That boy knows loyalty."

Hana nodded, fitting the snippet of information into a file in her head. It made little sense against the other bits of history. She recalled the overheard conversation that afternoon as she returned from the shop with biscuits and coffee. Alfred's voice sounded raised from the corridor. "He turned up with a loaded .22 looking for you. Says he'll only talk to you. His boys are threatening the stockmen."

"All right," she heard her husband reply in a low voice. "I'll see him when I get out of here. It won't take me long to get over this and then I'll come. I'll sort it out."

"Well, I need you to," Alfred said, hatred underpinning his tone. "You started this. I never want to see that man's face again, not as long as I live."

"I said I'll do it! This is your bloody mess, not mine and don't you forget it!"

Hana heard the hardness in Logan's voice, astounded he expected to take on a man with a gun in a few days. The more she discovered about Logan Du Rose, the less she understood and it frightened her. She sensed that Logan and not Alfred ran the hotel and farm in the mountains. Did Alfred really visit his son out of concern, or to receive assurance of his forthcoming help?

Hana lay in bed that night listening to the moreporks and possums making their night calls. Her empty bed seemed vast with just her occupying one corner. Logan's scent faded from his pillow and she sniffed it, conjuring up his image. Warmth flooded her soul and added to her confusion. The darkness in him intrigued and terrified her. She fell asleep with the admission it was part of the attraction. He offered more than the good-looking English teacher from her sheltered, educational world. Logan Du Rose owned a metal backbone formed from emotional and physical hardship, pain and adversity. He could think on his feet and commanded respect in that other, mysterious world of family and hotel.

Hana met Jas and Amy at the Bramwell hospital the next day. Jas carried a dried blob of waxy, grey looking paper and Amy looked apologetic. "It's a horse," she told Hana. "He wants to give it to Alfred."

"Great-gramps!" Jas corrected her, his eyes wild. "It's not for you, Poppa Logan," Jas bobbed his head and Logan nodded with relief. "It's for him." He jabbed a finger at Alfred.

"Wow." Alfred took the blob and peered at it. "What is it?"

"A horse." Three people answered at once.

"It's got five legs," Alfred said, holding it up to the light.

"It's a boy one." Jas put his hands on his hips. "That's his thing."

Alfred's jaw dropped and Logan snorted. He clamped a hand over his stomach and groaned in pain. Jas glared at him. "Everyone's got one." His eyebrows narrowed in doubt and he pointed at Hana. "Not her or her." He looked at the women in disgust. "Everyone else."

"It's a ruddy big one," Alfred chuckled and Amy died a thousand deaths by embarrassment.

"Just shoot me," she muttered next to Hana. "Just bloody shoot me."

The women excused themselves to the corridor for the rest of the rather sexist presentation-of-the-blob-ceremony. Amy sighed. "I got called into his kindy yesterday," she whispered. "They think he needs a psychologist."

"Oh." Hana struggled for a suitable reply.

Amy spared her by continuing. "They don't believe a word he says. He's wanted an extended family for so long; they thought he made one up." Tears of mirth filled her eyes. "The principal expressed her grave concern about his imaginary family. I sat through twenty minutes of her suggestions."

"What did you say?" Hana drew closer for the punch line.

Amy snorted. "I told her the truth. She wrote down the number for a great counsellor."

"For Jas?" Hana shook her head in confusion and Amy's face creased into a grin.

"For me. She thinks I'm crazy too."

Hana laughed and clapped a hand over her mouth. "How rude."

Amy leaned against the wall and tucked a strand of her blonde hair behind her ear. "Yep. Wait until Bodie picks him up from kindy. I signed the form to give him access but they haven't seen him yet."

"They do look alike. The principal might need to apologise." Hana bit her bottom lip and imagined the scene. She inclined her head towards Logan's door. "Do you think it's over yet?"

Amy peeked inside and withdrew her head. "Nope. It might go on for hours. Be grateful he didn't have time to make you one. Fancy a coffee?"

An alliance formed without either woman meaning it to and Hana felt relieved. Friendship with Amy gave her access to Jas and bypassed either of their tenuous relationships with Bodie.

They left and Alfred's looming departure produced the taste of ash in Hana's stomach. She liked him but grew bored with the lengthy discussions about brood mares, sire fees and the state of the grass. Their speech lapsed into Māori, excluding her from their conversation. After a walk around the grounds, she bumped into an unexpected visitor. Pastor Allen held the front door for her as she ran up behind him. "Ah, I can see from your face things are better." He smiled. "I didn't stop praying for you both," he promised and his blue eyes twinkled.

"Thanks Allen," Hana touched his arm. "Logan's recovering well and his father came to see him. He should be able to go home next week."

"I figured I'd try the private hospital as Waikato's mortuary assistant didn't recognise Logan's name. Sounds like he's doing pretty well after the hospital-hop."

"Sorry. I should have let you know." Hana bit her lip and gave a guilty sigh.

Allen laughed and pushed her shoulder. "It's fine. I'm a detective in my other job."

Hana nodded and gave a slow nod. "You always catch me out."

"Don't I just?" Allen kissed her temple and waved his arm towards the stairs. "Take me to the patient."

Hana led him upstairs and the men shook hands. Logan's smile looked genuine. "Hey, thanks for praying for me. Hana said you did." His gaze strayed to his father and a look of discomfort flickered across his face. Alfred stood up with wooden precision and shook hands, intimidated by the dog collar.

"You a priest?" he demanded and Hana held her breath.

"Pastor," Allen replied. "Same difference, but I get away with more."

"But you don't do last rites and shite?" Alfred said and she closed her eyes.

"Not today." Unfazed, Allen winked at Logan.

Alfred jerked his head upwards. "Take my seat, vicar," he offered, shuffling towards the bed. "I'm going home."

"No, no, I don't want to disturb you. Just calling in." Allen waved his arm, including everyone in his apology.

"Sit!" Alfred insisted and Allen bumped his rear end onto the seat pad in fright, the smile wavering on his lips. "I'm leaving now, like I said."

The old man squeezed Logan's hand and nodded a goodbye. "You won't forget?" he demanded as though continuing an unspoken conversation.

Logan shook his head. "Have I ever?"

"I'll walk you down," Hana offered as Alfred nodded to his son.

"Thanks." Alfred straightened his back and headed for the doorway. His look back at Logan seemed pointed.

"I've enjoyed your company," Hana said on the front steps. "Thanks for coming."

"Aw, it's been a pleasure, kōtiro." He flashed her the classic Du Rose smile, a trace of a handsome, enigmatic man beneath the wrinkles. "And I got given a horse with a giant dick."

Hana watched the old man shift things around in his bag, trying to find a tape to listen to on the aged music player. Emptiness assailed her at the thought of sleeping alone at the cottage that night.

Alfred turned and hugged her, a mouldy cassette tape in his hand. "Haere rā, Hana," he said and rubbed his blunted thumb across her chin with affection. "Visit soon?"

She nodded and he took it as a promise. The weather broke, raining giant, uncomfortable spits of water as Hana watched Alfred battle the barrier arm for the private car park. She waved until she knew he couldn't see her, finality in his departure. Difficulty and a marriage based on lies faced her in the upstairs hospital room and her footsteps dragged.

Pastor Allen rose as she entered, refusing her offer of coffee. "No thanks." He watched her blank expression with concern. "I'd like to pray for you both before I leave."

Hana glanced across at Logan but got nothing back. "Yes, please. I'd love that," she said. "I'm sure God knows what's going on." She bowed her head, regretting her sarcasm in the face of kindness. Her gaze flicked up to peek at Logan and found him watching her. Shock made her giggle and she hastened to turn it into a fake cough.

The pastor left and awkwardness descended over the room. Logan shifted on the bed and stared through the window.

"I forgot to tell Allen you moved hospital." Hana picked at a hang nail and examined her shoes. "He rang the mortuary."

Logan gave an upward jerk of his head. "He said."

Hana heaved out a sigh and sat opposite, her back to the doorway. "What did you talk about?"

Logan settled a half amused look on her, his first spark of real enjoyment. "Nothing much. Just laying some cards on the table." As intended, his answer filled Hana with even more curiosity. But she daren't probe the vaults of his spiritual health without seeming rude and he knew it. Logan flicked the buttons of the television remote with his fingernail. "What gets said between a man and his priest is sacred."

Hana snorted. "Not just his priest it seems." She stood, her skirt flowing around her shins with the action. "And by the way, prayer got you through that second operation. Allen's prayers and mine. You might see a surgeon's hands but I see their maker's." Father Sinbad's words about unequally yoked marriages stopped her in her tracks. He'd never see things the same way as her.

She slumped back into the armchair and looked at her watch. Logan saw and his comment sounded barbed. "You can go if you want."

"What? And miss all the action?" Hana's sarcasm hurt her more than it did him and she curled her legs beneath her. Part of her brain urged her to run and she resisted, but only out of spite. A nurse appeared to take Logan's blood pressure and for once, Hana ignored his unspoken desire for privacy. She snuggled into the comfortable chair and listened to the gentle lull of the woman's voice as she chattered about nothing important. Rain drummed on the roof in a steady, soporific beat and exhaustion washed over her like a warm wave. After a valiant fight, her eyelids drooped and she slipped from consciousness.

She started awake in a fear reaction, her heart pounding. Her legs numbed beneath her and her spine ached from the unnatural position. Hana uncurled her body, unnoticed by the new visitor standing with his back to her. His coat looked damp, darker patches betraying a prolonged walk in the rain. His speech sounded ragged, interspersed with sobbing. Hana recognised his voice and shot up with a snarl of rage. "Get out!" she snapped.

"No, no!" He turned to face her, cheeks wet with tears. "You can't make me." His shoulders heaved and he wiped his sleeve across his eyes.

Logan shook his head and looked away, aiming the remote control at the television and hiking the volume. "Do what she says." He sounded calm, his tone level and unconcerned.

Hana held her breath, straightening her spine and readying herself for the rage building in her chest. Tama leaned over Logan. "Anka left me," he snivelled. "Why did you turn your back on me?" The tirade continued, fuelled by self-pity and accusation. Hana's blood pressure hiked, giving her a heady sense of drunken power. She scanned the room for something to hit Tama with as his voice rose against the volume of the television. Her eyes feasted on many metal objects but most of them were attached to Logan. Hana bent and reached for her weapon of choice. Her handbag.

Tama didn't see it coming but the thwack of the patent maroon handbag echoed out into the corridor. He ducked and the second blow landed with increased force. "Get! Out!" Hana yelled, losing control as she punctuated her words with heavy thuds to his head.

A jangle of metal heralded her keys and change spewing onto the floor as the bag hit its target with force and accuracy. Tama wheeled around to face her and Hana dropped the bag, shoving him with her hands instead. She pushed him around the bed and towards the door. Rage enlarged her pupils until they obliterated her green irises. "Get away from my husband!" she screeched, whacking him around the face with her open palm. Hana felt the hatred rise with every fibre of her being. Tama ruined her friendship with Anka. Tama wreaked havoc on her marriage from the start. Nothing survived around his toxic presence.

Tama ground to a halt in the doorway, proving his worth as a rugby first fifteen player. He set himself against the delicate waif of a woman, lifting her off the ground in a bear hug. With her arms pinned by her sides and her feet off the floor, Hana felt her own vulnerability and channelled it into further hatred. She kicked out hard and contacted Tama's shin, feeling herself drop from his grasp. As her feet touched down, she lurched again, clawed fingers reaching for his mocking face.

He disappeared from view. One minute he sneered before her and then his grey eyes and snarling lips vanished. Hana kept moving forward, halting as someone pulled her arms behind her. A strong forearm linked around her chest and pinned her against a hard body. "Enough!" Logan's voice sounded harsh and Hana inhaled with shock. Her foot contacted something and she looked down, seeing Tama sitting on his backside in the corridor. Blood streamed from his face and Hana smirked in satisfaction. She opened her mouth to speak and saw Logan's finger jab in his direction.

"Bugger off, Tama," he said through gritted teeth. "Or you won't get up after the next one." Hana's gaze followed the line of his finger to Logan's knuckles and the streaks of blood which covered them. Her heart sank and failure danced a jig on her soul. After all her scrapping with the giant boy, Logan felled him with one hit. Bedridden, injured Logan.

Anger lit her up from inside and Hana spun, aiming a punch at her husband. She met his open palm with an ineffectual slap. His fingers moved to her wrist without looking, his eyes staring over her head at Tama. He released her and rubbed his right hand against his hospital gown, leaving streaks of blood in its wake. His eyes resembled grey steel and his face wore an unreadable mask.

Tama hauled himself to his feet and staggered away. The sound of his soles pattering down the corridor came back to Hana as an echo. An alarm sounded from the monitor by the bed, the drip cable trailing along the floor and spilling clear liquid into a puddle. Blood ran in a rivulet from the cannula hanging from Logan's hand.

Hana reacted to the sight of the blood. The last few weeks

contained far too much of it. A strange warmth rose from her chest to her head and locked up her lungs, causing her to breathe out but not in. A tingling headache began behind her eyes. She heard a curious gagging sound and realised it came from her mouth as she struggled for air. Someone stole her legs and numbness drifted into her knees as the room spun past her vision.

"Geez, Hana!" Logan caught her and struggled to hold her up as she sank to the floor. She heard him grunting with the effort. Anger filled her mind at the sound of his voice, but exhaustion robbed her of the energy required to react. As Hana's cheek touched the floor, the nauseating scent of disinfectant added itself to the mix and nausea filled her stomach like a rising tide. Littered around her face, she saw the contents of her handbag. Lipstick, keys and odd bits of stationary occupied her outlook and she shied away from the thought of retrieving it all with her uncooperative body.

Her vision didn't blacken like on the movies. It faded away like a piece of music and the frantic need for air stopped. Relief overwhelmed her as if the fight for life belonged to someone else.

-14-

Hana regained consciousness beneath an oxygen mask, panicking at the restriction it provided. "Steady, steady," a female voice said as Hana tried to rip it off. It pinged back and slapped her in the cheek. "That's what happens," the voice soothed, like a teacher to a child. The nurse slipped the mask over her head and Hana looked down, finding herself in Logan's bed. She turned her face sideways to see her husband sitting in the armchair and another nurse waving a needle above his elbow.

"I don't want it!" Logan snapped. "Let me speak to my wife."

"She's just coming around," the nurse said, pushing the needle towards the crook of his elbow.

Logan dodged it and withdrew his arm. "I told you, I don't want it!"

"I need to get this in." The woman sounded as though her patience might be about to snap. "You messed up your hand pulling the last one out. I can't put it back in there."

"I don't want it at all." Logan put his hand behind his back.

"Did it just come out or did you actually rip it out?" she demanded, glancing up at Logan's impassive face. He shrugged and didn't answer. "You ripped it out then, didn't you?" The nurse sounded cross. "Hold this!" she put Logan's finger over a piece of gauze that soaked red in seconds. "I'll be back in a minute with more. Don't take that off!"

Hana turned her face away, feeling nauseous. Running a mental body-check, she discovered a weird tingle in her lips and a tightness around her face. A familiar male voice broke through her stupor. "I think she hyperventilated." Mr Singh felt the pulse in her left wrist while staring at his watch. He harrumphed and looked hard at her. "Your pulse rate is very low. Do you suffer from heart problems?"

Hana shook her head and pushed herself into a sitting position. "I'm fine, just embarrassed." The fog threatened to descend again and she sat for a moment, waiting for it to clear.

Mr Singh turned to Logan, watching as the nurse returned and tried to stop the bleeding on his hand with more packs. She glanced towards him. "I'll stop this and then try a different site." She held gauze with one hand and mopped up blood with the other. Mr Singh raised an eyebrow and shook his head.

"I shouldn't bother," he concluded.

Logan watched the nurse's ministrations with disinterest, his face a veil of frustration. She stopped her mopping with a look of confusion. "Don't bother stemming the bleeding or inserting another cannula?"

"Either." Mr Singh cleared his throat and paused until he gained Logan's reluctant attention. "I've completed the research and tests I began at the Waikato and have reached a conclusion."

Hana turned her face away, consciously breathing in and out in a steady rhythm as the doctor spoke. "You're an idiot, Mr Du Rose and I don't have time for this."

Hana watched Logan's neutral expression, but saw a vein ticking in his neck. He didn't answer and the doctor continued. "You haven't attended a clinic for your haemophilia for almost two years. Yet, you've required three infusions of Factor 8 in the last four months. You don't take care of your own body and expect us to patch you up when it all goes wrong. Would I be correct in that assumption?"

Hana's sigh sounded audible. Haemophilia. Mr Singh sounded capable and Hana hung onto his confidence as hers waned. "Your medical notes are incomplete, which doesn't help."

Logan's jaw worked through the rough skin on his face, the grey bristles intermingling with the black. Even unwell, he still managed to look handsome. "That's a breach of confidentiality," he growled.

Mr Singh shrugged and raised an eyebrow. "Slip of the tongue, Mr Du Rose. "So sorry." He bowed, a single, jabbing motion of the head. "Do you have brothers with this problem?"

Logan's jaw ground as he dealt with being bested by a skinny, tired man in a pink turban.

"How do they cope with it?" the doctor asked, unfazed by the dangerous look in Logan's eyes.

Logan bit his lip, stared hard at the man and answered, "They die."

Mr Singh ran a hand over his black beard. "Right then. You know the odds, don't you? When you decide you'd like my help, come find me." He placed a couple of leaflets on the end of the bed with careful fingers and strode away, stepping over the nurse wiping blood from the tiles with a paper napkin.

Hana swung her legs over the side of the bed and leaned forward, waiting to see if the nothingness engulfed her again. Part of her wished it would. The smart grey tiles danced towards her and away and she fought the nausea with valiant determination. "I'm leaving now," she said, hearing the wobble in her voice.

The nurse with the bloody paper towels grovelled under the bed after the contents of Hana's handbag. "Here," she said, piling them on the bedspread next to the upended handbag. "Check they're all there and I'll examine you before you go."

"Thanks." Hana's answer sounded wooden and she perched sideways on the bed, scooping the sundry items into the bag's depths without care. Logan faced her, clutching the gauze to his dripping hand.

"Hana, I'm sorry." He sounded chastened, like a naughty schoolboy.

Hana shrugged. "Why should I care? It's not like I'm your wife or anything, is it?" Sarcasm covered her disappointment and fear.

"Hana, it's not like that. I hate weakness. I didn't want you to see what it did to me."

"Save it!" Hana raised her palm in his face. "You don't want to share with me. Fine! Good to know where I stand in this relationship."

Logan's face clouded and he gritted his teeth. He reached forward as Hana fingered loose change and an earring. With his left hand, he picked up a metal box which clung to everything else on the bed. The fingers struggled through the restriction of his cast and he dropped it twice. He moved it around the bed as coins and a paperclip stuck to it, flicking everything off with his fingernail and then repeating the action.

Hana sighed and spoke to the nurse. "I'm sorry to be such a pain," she said. "I feel an idiot. I must be coming down with a virus."

"It's fine," the woman soothed. "How do you feel now?"

"Stupid. But better. I'll get out of your way. Please accept my apologies."

Logan revolved the metal box in his fingers, enjoying the smoothness of it as the nurse padded from the room. "That's what Tama said."

"What? He said what?"

"Please accept my apology."

"Oh." Shame lit Hana's cheeks red. "I didn't hear that part."

Logan smirked. "Hit first and ask questions later. Who knew, Mrs Du Rose?"

Hana's lips tightened and her face clouded. "Don't call me that if you don't mean it."

"I do mean it." Logan spun the box and dropped it, his broken arm failing him. His jaw worked beneath his cheek. "I wanted to tell you heaps of times, but not like this."

"How Logan? How else did you think I'd find out? It's not something you drop into a casual conversation, is it?"

He shook his head and avoided her gaze. Hana leaned forward to hear as he muttered under his breath. "The family say it's a curse."

"Is that what you believe?" Her brow creased and his answer mattered.

"No. It's genetic, courtesy of my mother." Logan inhaled through his nose. "But it weakens me. I didn't want you to see that."

"So you hid behind a smokescreen instead?" She shook her head and her red hair slipped forward over her shoulder. "You ask me to trust you but don't return the favour. Where does that leave us?"

Logan reached for her hand. "Better than before. You know the truth now." His grey eyes implored her to forgive him.

"But you're not sorry, are you?" Hana's eyes narrowed and Logan shook his head.

"No. For a little while, I enjoyed your belief in me. Now you see me as defective. Caroline said it made me weak."

Hana's snort forced him to meet her gaze. "Defective and weak? You? Give me a break." She snatched her hand free and ran it across her stomach, testing her resilience to movement. "You need to find better friends and I need to go home." She snatched up the metal box and shoved it into her handbag with the remainder of her possessions. The tiles felt solid beneath her feet and her equilibrium returned. She shoved the doctor's leaflets in her bag and turned back to Logan. "Why did you hit Tama if he came to apologise?"

Logan's eyes narrowed and he looked at his bleeding knuckles. Blood soaked gauze covered the back of his hand. "He touched my wife." His lips curled back in a snarl. "Nobody does that."

Hana swallowed at the vehemence in his tone. "Did I look like Miss Piggy, swinging my handbag at him?"

Logan's laugh sounded natural, the first time she'd heard it in days. "I found it sexy." He viewed her from beneath dark eyelashes and Hana felt her stomach respond with darts of pleasure at his approval.

"I can't work you out," she sighed, gathering up her handbag and jacket.

"You will one day." Logan got to his feet, almost tripping over the wheeled legs of the drip rack. His patience snapped and he kicked it, sending it flying into the wall. "I'm over this!" he shouted. "Wait for me. I'm coming with you."

Logan refused all forms of dissuasion and faced with his silent determination, the nursing staff gave in. Mr Singh added a complicated flourish to his signature and passed the prescription to Hana. "Your husband is more trouble than all my state healthcare patients put together! Make him listen to you. I don't want to see the inside of his guts again."

Hana gripped the what-to-do-if-it-all-turns-to-custard leaflet and gave him a lame smile. As the embattled pair stood on the steps down to the car park, the good Lord sent a watery sunshine to lighten their slow walk to the BMW. Hana settled Logan into the car, fussing a little too much to mask the nagging sickness in the pit of her stomach. She stowed his bags in the boot and slammed the lid, giving herself a moment of nose breathing to alleviate the nausea. Turning, she let out a yelp of fright.

Tama stood over her, his height blocking the sun. Hana took a step back, but he reached for her. Tears streaked his cheeks and his red-rimmed eyes betrayed his distress. She slapped his hand away. "Touch me again and I'll kill you," she threatened, not recognising the enraged woman's reflection in the side mirror of the car.

"Please. You have to help me." The impact of Logan's earlier punch left a bruise on Tama's chin and his lip oozed. Blood streaks on his sleeve showed his efforts to stem the flow. He looked scruffy up close, a day or two's worth of boyish beard covering his upper lip and the underside of his chin.

Hana took a step forward and jabbed her finger into his chest. "I don't have to help you with anything!" She raised her voice, the list of his offences forming in her brain.

"I'm sorry for everything!" Tama wailed. He brushed away the embarrassing tears as they dripped onto his jacket. "I didn't mean to hurt him." A shaking finger pointed over the roof to the passenger side of the car. "I don't have anyone else. You need to make him understand how sorry I am! He won't listen to me."

He reached for Hana's hand again, recoiling at the contact with her soft skin. Logan's words stood between them like an unwritten code and Tama got the message. He mustn't touch her. Despite her desire to kick him into next week, Hana's heart saw the small boy in a man's body. The tears didn't fit with the hairy face and masculine form. "I'll tell him you're sorry," she said and edged past him.

Logan's grey eyes watched the scene with a blank expression. The cast from his broken left arm rested on the roof of the BMW, his body still and the muscles of his upper body bunched. He said nothing but his interest paralysed both Hana and Tama.

Hana sensed her husband's powerful mana cover her with a sense of safety and peace. Tama halted and his eyes widened as he stared at Logan. Tired of the violence, Hana closed her eyes against the sickness and reviving headache. When she opened them, she gaped in surprise. Tama sobbed against Logan's broad shoulder and her husband rested his chin on the top of the boy's head.

"No!" Hana groaned, disturbed by the lack of forgiveness in her heart. Logan shrugged and gave a look of resignation.

"Whānau is whānau," he said, his voice a low rumble. "Forgive but not forget."

"Oh, for goodness' sake!" Hana exclaimed and climbed into the driver's seat.

-15-

"Where's your car?" Logan spun in the passenger seat with a wince. He directed his question at Tama as Hana drove through Hamilton.

"Head gasket went." Tama held onto the back of Hana's seat to lean forward. "I locked it up on a slip road off State Highway One. Can we fetch it?"

Hana glanced sideways at her husband, daring him to oblige. As Logan ran a hand across his stomach, she answered for him. "No. I'm taking my husband home to rest. You can make other arrangements."

Tama sat back against the seat with a thud and Hana saw his look of irritation reflected in the rear view mirror. "Kuia Miriam told me you went to the hospital. I hitched into town and couldn't find you at the Waikato. Geez man, I thought you'd died. I got upset, so they told me you moved to the Bramwell."

Hana hissed under her breath in annoyance. She struggled to fathom why her rear seat contained the man who half-killed her husband. Anka's attraction to him confounded her. Boyish stubble covered his chin like fine down and his scruffy appearance screamed his status as a child. Hana believed Anka trashed her marriage for a boy in a man's body, but the teenage acne dappling Tama's forehead challenged even that.

Tama gave an annoying whistle through his teeth as Hana turned onto the driveway and fumbled the remote to open the gate. "This yours Uncle Logan?" he demanded and Hana clamped her teeth together. She tapped an irritated beat on the steering wheel while the gate slid across with painful slowness. Logan studied her from the side, his brows furrowed with unfathomable emotion.

"He's not staying with us," she hissed in a singsong voice and saw Logan's head swivel back to face the windscreen. Hana shook her head against the tide of helplessness that single action caused.

She carried Logan's bag into the lobby and deactivated the burglar alarm. Tama's voice chattered behind her and Hana's impatience grew. She walked to the bedroom and flung the bag on the floor, collapsing onto the soft mattress with a groan. She daren't tell Bodie she drove home after fainting, especially not in his expensive car.

Hana lay on the bed with anger coursing through her veins. Tama's incessant chatter jangled her nerves, echoing along the hallway until it became white noise in her brain. Logan's body took a beating, but their marriage bent under the weight of his bloodshed. They needed time to talk and begin the healing process. Tama's continued presence ensured that couldn't happen. As the minutes ticked by, Hana craved Logan's reassurance. Her mind whirled with questions and she wondered if he stayed away on purpose. Instead of soothing her, he played happy families with a man who broke his body in a fit of childish pique and ruined the first weeks of their marriage.

Hana kicked off her shoes and pushed her legs beneath the blanket. Exhaustion claimed her within minutes and she slept. She dreamed she lay in Logan's paddock at the top of the mountain. The sunshine warmed her cheeks and he stroked her hair, undressing her with murmurs of desire.

Hana woke an hour later, the contented feeling dissipating in the empty, darkening room. The original pinch of betrayal and rejection replaced it. Staggering up, the sickness and strange headache returned, swirling through her senses and causing confusion. Her clothes felt restrictive and she stripped them off, clambering into her dressing gown. She fought to tie the cord and stumbled to the kitchen, finding it empty. Blundering around with the grace of a small elephant, Hana discovered the men in the lounge. They looked cosy in front of the television, a roaring fire in the grate. Jealousy rose in her breast at their easy possession of her property. Logan's passivity irritated her and she sensed he used Tama as a shield to deflect her questions about his disease.

"I'm ringing Bodie," she said, the casual tone belying the threat. "I'll invite him over."

Logan kinked an eyebrow in warning and they engaged in an unspoken battle. The void between them yawned wider. Hana hovered in the doorway and tried a different tack. She crossed the room and inserted herself between the men, ignoring the wince of pain on Logan's face as she attempted to regain possession.

A sideways glance at Tama found him ogling her bare legs and Hana recoiled in shock. She yanked the cord around her stomach, hiding her bra and knickers from view.

"Can I get you some food?" Logan asked, slipping his right arm around her shoulder. "You should eat."

Hana's jaw clenched in frustration. "No."

In a bizarre role reversal, he tried to take care of her. Hana's irritation bloomed to frightening proportions, creating a tremble in her hands as she balled them into fists. "Come to the bedroom with me," she whispered in his ear. "We need to talk."

She watched Logan's gaze track sideways at Tama. He knitted his brows and shook his head in a quick action.

"Ugh, old people shagging. Gross!" Tama made retching noises and pretended to stick his fingers down his throat. Hana acted as though he lit the blue touch paper on her firework and she lurched towards him, almost upending the sofa.

"Well, you'd know, wouldn't you?" she shouted in his face. Her heart pounded with an exultant surge of blood and it drove Hana to new heights of hysteria like a chemical high. "Anka's older than me so you must be an expert!"

Tama leaned back against the arm of the sofa, making himself small to avoid her flailing arms. Hana shoved at his chest, surprised at her own strength. "Get out of my house!" she snapped. Her dressing gown tangled around her feet as she stood and she gave both men an accidental flash of matching, lacy underwear.

As she stomped from the room, she caught Logan's low growl. "Quit being a dick, Tama! That's your last warning, bro'!"

Hana ran herself a bath and deliberately spent ages in the bathroom, hoping to inconvenience anyone requiring the toilet. The hot water raised her blood pressure and the nausea returned. She wasted half an hour of her life sitting on the side of the bath with her head between her knees. Deciding to pull the plug, she watched the hot water and luscious bubbles gurgle down the drain. Not wanting to face either of the men, she took herself to bed.

Waking in the night, she discovered Logan snuggled against her back. She gave him a shove, desperate for him to wake up and deal with her questions. He stirred and rolled onto his back, further denying her any kind of justice.

A primitive side of her bayed for blood, wanting to fight back from the rejection and sense of betrayal. "He almost died a few days ago, you stupid girl," she mouthed to herself in the darkness. "Now you're thinking of smothering him with a pillow."

She lay on her back with one hand on her stomach and the other over her heart. A magazine article suggested it helped with insomnia. Hana focussed on aligning the beats and realised how much rubbish she consumed from women's magazines. They all lied. It didn't work. Her starving stomach, thrilled with the attention, gurgled and put her off counting. She sucked in her stomach but holding her breath increased her heart rate and made her head swim. With a sigh of irritation, Hana abandoned the exercise.

The house felt cool as she padded to the kitchen. She moved without lights and closed the door behind her. At the flick of the light switch, a shape rose from the kitchen table and Hana clapped her hands over the scream. "You idiot!" she squeaked as Tama stood opposite her, his face streaked with tears. He wore a tee shirt and boxer shorts belonging to Logan. Without the bravado, he looked fifteen years old.

Hana softened, but wariness made her give him a wide berth. She'd seen him wield a crowbar. Skirting the table, she switched on the kettle and heaved out a sigh. She pulled the dressing gown closed enough to please a mother superior and tied the cord in a double knot. The clock ticked past two in the morning. Tama sat back in his seat, nursing a cold cup of tea. "Want another?" Hana fetched a mug from the cupboard and indicated his cup with her outstretched hand.

"Yes please." Tama held his cup up with a shaking hand, looking so defeated she struggled to muster up the hate. Only determination fought her natural maternalism in the face of the teenage monster.

She made tea in silence and fetched the toaster from the cupboard, filling it with bread. Setting two plates, knives, jam and butter on the table, she toasted the slices two at a time. Tama spread butter on his toast, watching as he put too much on and it slid onto the plate in a yellow lake. He seemed transfixed by the puddle on the smooth white surface. Hana watched him play in the yellow mess, trying not to crunch her toast. The harder she tried, the more she sounded like a horse eating a carrot. She choked on a crumb and a giggle rose into her throat. Tama stared at her and then he laughed. The tension snapped as they descended into juvenile snorts, each as bad as the other. Hana got herself under control and Tama started again. "Oh, stop it!" she giggled and Tama responded with a grin. It seemed incongruous that sniggering over crunchy toast in the middle of the night could dislodge such a powerful, mutual dislike.

"I know you don't believe me, but I loved Anka." Tama's words wiped the silly grin off Hana's face.

All humour disappeared. "So did her husband. And children. So did I once. Now we've all lost her because of you." Hana thumped the table with her palm, sending tingles through her fingers.

Tama pursed his lips. "I do know that." He sat for a moment, head down, contemplating the mess on his plate. "After it started, we couldn't stop. We got in so deep and now it's a mess." He looked up and stared into Hana's face, frightening intensity behind his grey eyes. "I'd never hurt her."

"No!" scoffed Hana. "But you attacked my husband from behind.

If that's what you do to the people who care about you, I pity your enemies."

Tama closed his eyes. Hana waited for a retort but none came. Shame hung his handsome dark head and prevented him meeting her gaze. Spoiling for a fight, she felt thwarted and anger bubbled in her chest. She stood and snatched his plate away, staying out of swinging range. "You wouldn't have the guts to hit him from the front!" Liquid butter spewed onto the table and she hissed in annoyance.

Tama visibly quailed, his cowardice unveiled in all its filth. "I didn't mean it," he whispered.

"Grow up Tama," Hana snapped, clattering the plates into the sink and squirting dishwashing liquid into the running water. "You want to be treated like a man. You want to have affairs with married women, but then weep over the consequences." She wheeled around, her hands soaked in suds. "You hit Logan because he prevented you bullying me into giving you Anka. The irony is that I didn't even know where she went." Hana balled her fists. "I can't believe he forgave you. You don't deserve it!"

She turned back to the sink, stunned by her own revelation. Its ugliness spread out before her and she discovered the flame beneath her fury. She couldn't forgive. A parade of other faces drifted through her memory and she gritted her teeth against them.

"I don't deserve it," replied Tama. "I know I don't. Uncle Logan is the only constant in my life and I hurt him. I'm glad he hit me at the hospital. He should've killed me for what I did."

Hana found no ready retort and reached below the belt. "He treated you as a son," she muttered, knowing the inference hit its mark when Tama sighed.

"You're right. I wish he was my dad."

Hana ground her teeth, grateful the disturbed young man held only the rights of a nephew and nothing more. She heard Tama's chair scrape the floorboards behind her. "I bought Anka a ring. I wanted to marry her."

She heard him leave the room and heaved a sigh of relief. The sight of the soapsuds on her wedding band reminded her of the irony and indicated another reason for the teenager to hate her. The door clicked closed and she turned to face him.

Tama opened his palm to reveal a small velvet box. The maroon colour absorbed the shadows in the room as he popped the lid with extreme care. Hana watched him hold his breath with sacred reverence. She leaned forward and grazed the diamond with her gaze. "It's beautiful," she said, her tone genuine. "And expensive."

"I didn't nick it!" Tama's eyes narrowed and he closed the lid on the sparkling beauty. "I've worked for Alfred every holiday." He looked so innocent standing in her kitchen in his boxer shorts, displaying his precious ring. His face reflected a mixture of pain and concentration. Tama opened his mouth to speak.

"No!" Hana cut him off. "I can't tell you where she is. If you pester me, I'll make you leave. Understand?"

Tama baulked at her firm tone, but conceded. "Okay," he replied. Hana watched him and saw the lie in his eyes.

She returned to bed and her sleep offered little rest, punctuated by disturbing dreams. Her efforts to speak to Logan the next day proved stilted. "I'll run you a shallow bath," she suggested. "We can control the water easier than the shower and you might feel better after washing your hair." Hana left the room before he could reply and busied herself with the activity.

Tama drifted past her in the lobby and Hana pointed to the back stairs. "Please can you go down to the garage and fetch wood for the fire? My son chopped some last week and it's in the cupboard next to the main door."

"Your son the cop?" Tama's upper lip curled back in a sneer and Hana took a step towards him.

"If you can't play nice, get out!" she snapped. "I asked you to fetch wood, not discuss my family."

Tama shook his head and gave a nonchalant shrug. "Sensitive," he muttered, loud enough for her to hear.

Logan slipped off his shorts in the steamy bathroom and stepped into the shallow water. His eyes closed in pain as he lowered himself to sit in the bubbles. Hana averted her eyes from the parts of his body which stirred her and concentrated on washing the blood from his right arm and around his ribs. "Keep still," she told him, nudging him in the back as he turned to look at her. She gritted her teeth and sponged soap along his spine. The iodine stained his skin yellow and proved harder to remove. "Try not to wet your dressings. I don't want to redo them."

"Get in with me?" Logan invited, his voice a whisper and mischief in his face.

"No!" Hana snapped, pushing his hand away from the zipper of her jeans. "Lean your cast on the edge of the bath and lean back so I can wash your hair."

She fumbled with the lid of the shampoo and rubbed the liquid into Logan's dark hair. He closed his eyes and enjoyed the massaging of his scalp. "What's wrong, Hana?" he asked as she lifted the jug to rinse away the soap.

She gaped in surprise. "I can't believe you're asking me that," she replied, a sneer in her tone. "You spring a disease on me and then allow your attacker to sleep in the only place I feel safe in this town. Is there any wonder I'm upset?"

Logan sighed. "No. I said I'm sorry."

"That's okay then." Hana smoothed her palm along the back of his hair to squeeze out the water. "I feel great now."

Logan tutted. "What did you expect me to do? You claim to be a Christian but don't recognise forgiveness."

Hana dropped the plastic jug into the water in shock. It clanged against the side of the tub and sent water into Logan's eyes. She took a step backwards, gored by his judgement on her shaky faith.

"Don't throw my beliefs back in my face!" she snapped, tears blossoming in her eyes.

Logan snorted. "It sounds like a pick and choose kind of faith to me."

Hana gritted her teeth and stemmed the urge to hit him on the head with the jug. Logan unearthed the unsightly blemish on Hana's character and she hated him for it. She swallowed and fumed.

Logan's expression softened and he struggled to stand, distracting Hana with his nakedness. "Tama's my whānau and he made a mistake. He apologised. What's the problem?" Logan's grey eyes gazed on her as dark, swirling pools of condemnation.

Hana shook her head, formulating her words in a dry mouth. "But I'm not your family, am I Logan. I will never fit in."

Logan exhaled and reached for her, his brow knitting as she moved backwards. "It's not like that," he said, his tone imploring.

"Really?" Hana backed towards the door. She balled her fists. "Yet there's so much you won't share. Why does your father want you to face a man with a gun?" She narrowed her eyes. "And why does it look like you run your parents' farm?"

Logan's jaw tensed and he shivered in the ankle deep, cooling water. "I don't. Dad runs it."

Hana scented the victory of a successful hunt. "No, he doesn't," she said, her voice turning to a snarl. "It's another lie. I've heard the way the farm workers speak to you. And Alfred can't read."

Logan struggled out of the bath, slipping and splashing the dressing they worked so hard to keep dry. Hana pressed her body against the door, reacting to the anger she saw in his face. "Hana!" Logan rasped. He clutched his broken arm across his stomach. "I can't tell you everything in one go?"

"Why?" A stray tear coursed down her cheek. "Because I'll leave you?"

Logan snatched up a towel and scrubbed the water from his body. The effort exhausted him and his pallor greyed. "Maybe," he sighed.

"You should have told me about the haemophilia!" Hana's tears back-lit her eyes with sparkles of reflected light and she stamped her foot. "You owed me that much." She spread her arms wide. "I don't know who you are."

Logan fixed the towel around his waist and Hana saw the pink stain spreading across his dressing. "Maybe I needed to find you trustworthy before I spewed my life into your hands," he answered through gritted teeth. Hana stared at him in horror, the hair rising on the back of her neck in warning. She grappled with the door handle without turning, her green eyes wide and gaping. Her fingers shook as she pulled the door wide and cold air rushed past.

"You should never have married me," she sobbed, her breath coming in heaves.

"Hana, I don't know what you want from me!" he called after her, his desperation raw. He wasted his breath as she ignored him. Running to the bedroom, she slammed the door and leaned against it. All sensible thought fled and she sat against the aged wood and cried until her reserves emptied.

When the weakness passed, Hana crawled to the bed and lay down. Numbness dulled the pain and she forced herself to release bunched fists and relax her tight muscles. Exhaustion rested over her like a shroud. Tama's presence in the house inflamed the situation and she couldn't make her thoughts coherent with him in her safe place. She regretted baiting Logan and reeled from his rebuke. It smacked of her marriage to Vik. He didn't trust her enough either.

Hana sat up as she heard her phone ringing somewhere else in the house. She listened for a moment, but abandoned thoughts of tracking it down. It silenced and she forgot it, closing her eyes and snuggling in against the greyness of another wasted day.

The click of the bedroom door roused her and she tensed. Her fragile sense of peace disappeared in an instant. "Hana?" Logan's voice sounded soft, his anger gone. "Can we call a truce?" he asked, venturing into the room.

Hana lifted her head and faced him, pushing herself up onto her elbows. He held a pair of white undies in front of him, flapping them like a flag. She exhaled and lay back against the pillows, no energy left to argue. "Yes," she replied.

Logan approached her side of the bed, clutching the pants against his chest. His good hand held up the failing towel around his waist. Hana turned on her side to face him and rested her cheek against her bent elbow. "Are they clean?" she asked, wrinkling her nose.

"No." Logan smirked. "I grabbed them from the laundry."

"Yuk." Hana pushed her face into her pillow.

Logan sat next to her on the bed, picking at a thread on her sock before pulling her feet across his knees. He massaged them in warm hands. "Hana." His tone sounded serious and she focussed on watching the pathetic knot at his waist give up its fight. "Hana?" He spoke again and she pulled her gaze away from the tantalising line of hair that disappeared beneath the towelling folds. "Some things are hard to explain and if you don't want me to spend my life lying to you, you need to learn to trust me." Logan's glittering grey eyes held solemnity and Hana found it impossible to look away. "I'm not giving up on us. I've got all the time in the world to work through the things we don't understand about each other."

Hana looked down and opened her lips to list her grievances, but Logan pulled her chin up and forced her to meet his gaze. "Besides," he said, a smirk playing on his lips, "I'm Catholic and we don't believe in divorce. You're stuck with me!"

"Don't tease me." Her tone held warning. "Don't trivialise my feelings."

Logan brushed his thumb across her lips. "I'm sorry. I don't mean to."

"But you do." Hana's eyes filled with tears and she hated herself for it. "I don't want Tama here because of what he did. Yet you let him stay."

Logan's lips pressed over hers, stopping her sentence and leaving it swirling between them. "I know. I understand all the reasons why you're upset. Just give me a chance to put it right, please?" Hana allowed Logan to lay on the bed beside her, not objecting when he cuddled her close. "I love you, Hana Du Rose," he whispered into her hair and she snickered with the ticklishness of it. "Do you want to see where my truce flag really came from?"

"I know where it came from," she grumbled and Logan tickled her with his good hand until she squealed.

"You need a closer look," he whispered and placed her fingers over the gaping hole in his towel. Hana gasped and pulled her hand back.

As the afternoon chilled, they snuggled beneath the duvet and Logan drew the curtains on the four-poster bed. Hana allowed the sense of safety to soothe her troubled soul as he removed her clothes. Logan's gentle kisses warmed her and revived their former intimacy and passion. He made love to her without breaking eye contact, whispering endearments in Māori and giving her access to his mysterious world. Hana lay in his arms and drifted off to sleep, her cheek pressed against his downy chest.

She woke with a start, unable to pinpoint a reason for her heightened sense of alarm. The house sounded silent and it struck her as unusual. The dull base of the television no longer vibrated through the wooden floorboards and Hana sat up. Not trusting Tama, she needed to account for his whereabouts. The silence seemed ominous

Hana poked her head through the curtains of the bed, tugging them aside to put her feet on the rug. Their bedroom door moved against a draught from the hallway and Hana looked down at her nakedness and swallowed. She remembered Logan shutting the door behind him and glanced across at his dark head on the pillow. He groaned in his sleep and rolled onto his back, pushing a hairy knee out of the covers. Hana snatched up her clothes and pushed herself into them. She moved faster without the pervading nausea, grateful for its absence.

She padded into the lobby and tried the front door handle, alarmed when it opened to her touch. On the porch, cold air bit into her bare feet and Hana walked around the deck calling Tama's name. She grew cross. "Tama, stop being an idiot!" she shouted. No answer. She checked his bedroom and nothing showed he ever existed. Panic vied with relief.

In the kitchen, Hana tripped over her handbag, wincing as she twisted her wrist against the table whilst trying to stop herself falling. Remembering the phone call, she fumbled in the open bag. A scruffy note in the middle of the kitchen table caught her eye. Hana read the boyish handwriting scrawled on the back of a power bill.

'Thanks for everything. Going home. T.'

Her shoulders slumped with relief. "Oh, thank goodness for that!" she exclaimed. She checked the rest of her handbag, finding nothing missing. Bodie's BMW keys still sat on the hall cupboard and the car nestled between the house and the top of the slope. She sank into a chair with a sigh.

The sound of her ringtone made her jump and Hana stared at her handbag in confusion. It came from elsewhere in the house. She tracked it to the lounge and the larger sofa, finding her phone singing to itself behind a cushion. She missed the call but a text message told her someone left a voicemail.

Hana blew out through her lips and listened to the stilted voice of her employer. Sheila Jennings hated the woodenness of answering machines. 'Hi, Hana. It's Sheila. Well, anyway. Hello. Pete said this was still your number but you aren't at work. I need to talk to you. Soon, actually. It's complicated but can we meet? Get back to me anyway. My phone number hasn't changed and I did get all your lovely messages. I just couldn't talk to anyone. Call me. Please?'

Hana chewed her lower lip and considered the prospect of venturing outside alone. Using Bodie's car increased her anonymity and she'd spent the week driving to the hospital and back without incident. Hana stroked the buttons and formulated a plan, deciding to text Sheila instead of ringing.

She clicked the button to create a new message, startled at what she saw written on the screen.

'Where are you?'

Hana swallowed. One of her frustrations with her ancient phone included the need to delete old messages from the text screen before she could send a new one. After so many years, she knew to delete as soon as she sent it to save time. "Where are you?" Hana repeated the message. "I didn't send that."

She hadn't used her phone all day. The call log showed it sent earlier while she romped with Logan in the bedroom. Hana scrolled down with shaking fingers and saw a missed call from Anka. "Hi," Anka's voicemail said. "Just checking in to find out how Logan is." Hana found it in an old message file, showing someone else listened to it.

She deleted the sent message with her heart in her mouth and responded to Sheila first.

'I can meet you in Huntly in an hour. There's a farmyard themed cafe at the end of the main street.'

Then she turned her attention to the spurious exchange with Anka. In her messages she found a reply, already seen by Tama, she presumed.

'Still working in Russell. Healing slowly.'

"Oh, no!" Hana ran her hands over her face and dialled Anka's number. No reply. Resorting to text again, Hana sent a warning, hoping her friend received it in time to ready herself for an unwelcome visitor.

She padded to the bedroom, desperate to talk to Logan about his errant nephew. He lay on his back in the big bed, one hand over his heart and his face turned to the side. Peace shrouded him and his breathing sounded regular and easy. Hana hovered in the doorway, recognising the imprint of healing and reluctant to disrupt nature's good work with her anxieties.

Instead, she used the bathroom, left a note for Logan next to Tama's, locked up the house and left.

It took ten minutes to reach Huntly on the back road. Hana wondered how Tama exited the property and half expected to see him hitching a ride on the long highway north. She braced herself, feeling relieved when she reached the outskirts of the small town without encountering him.

Snagging the last of the angled parking on the main street, Hana wandered to the cafe. She paused to admire a metal wall hanging moulded into the shape of a tulip in the window of her favourite shop. The owner noticed her through the window and waved from behind his counter. Hana returned his greeting and forced herself to keep walking.

The cafe hummed with the tail end of the lunchtime rush and Hana grabbed a table near the back. A scruffy wooden five-bar gate hugged the wall next to her, back filled with artificial flowers and grasses. The farming theme continued with pig ornaments along one wall. Hana ordered a pot of tea and added coffee for Sheila. The waitress grinned, displaying a blue jewelled tongue. "Is the coffee for that hot guy you often have with you?" she demanded, resting a hand on her ample hip. "He likes trim milk, doesn't he?"

"My son?" Hana cocked her head and narrowed her eyes. "The policeman?"

The woman pushed her hair behind her ear and licked her lower lip. Her smile displayed neat teeth and Hana's heart sank, placing her around her own age. "He's hot, but I meant the other one. Tall, dark, the sort you wouldn't kick out of bed for farting."

Hana's jaw clenched. "My husband."

"Oh." The waitress drew out the sound and realised her blunder. She backed away at speed with her order pad. "Yeah. I didn't realise. Lucky you."

Hana huffed out a breath of irritation. Despite his lack of confidence, Logan drew interest from women in all age groups and it heightened her sense of insecurity. Her fear of infidelity upending her fragile world grew with every such encounter. Sheila interrupted Hana's tortured thoughts by blasting through the front door and staring around her for a moment.

Hana rose to attract her attention and Sheila scurried towards her with her usual effervescent energy. Her handbag trailed behind her and a long coat flapped around her shins. "Hana!" She held her arms out and enfolded her in a tight embrace, not noticing Hana's gasp of surprise.

"What happened?" Hana exclaimed, taking a step back to admire her friend's new image. "You look amazing!"

Sheila primped her bobbed hair with red lacquered nails. A sly smile lit her face. "Dull Sheila's gone, Hana. Do you like?"

"Yes!" Hana marvelled. "But you didn't take leave for a term just to get a haircut and lose a ton of weight." She stepped back to scrutinise Sheila's trim figure and peer at the engorged breasts popping over a neat waist. "You got a boob job!"

"Shhh!" Sheila looked around and flapped her hands. "Don't shout it. Yes. I went to a surgeon in Auckland and he propped them up for me."

Hana thudded into her seat and shook her head. "Wow. I never saw that coming."

Sheila sat next to her and placed her handbag on the floor. "No, I've undergone a few significant changes."

The waitress delivered their drinks and eyed Hana sideways. Sheila's pert breasts nestled against the table edge like a pair of additional guests.

"Where have you been?" Hana demanded. She pointed at the boobs. "Apart from the obvious. You left me at the mercy of that she-devil."

"That's what I need to explain." Sheila sipped her coffee and gave a satisfied sigh. "Remember all the upset with the board of trustees a while ago?"

Hana shook her head. "No."

"Yes you do." Sheila patted her hand. "They started enforcing the ban on extra marital relationships with other staff members."

Hana thought of Caroline and Chris Carter and rolled her eyes. "Well, extra marital and all other forms of romantic involvement. I know Logan and I came under scrutiny."

Sheila sipped and nodded at the same time. Her plum lipstick left a rim on the mug. "Martin caused it."

Hana cocked her head in confusion. "I don't understand."

"After twenty seven years of marriage, the bugger cheated on me. Apparently it isn't the first time."

"Martin!" Hana gaped. An image of Sheila's flaccid husband rose into her mind, his unattractive comb-over and wobbling jowls an unwelcome picture. "Are you sure?"

"Did you know the board dismissed him?" Sheila waded on and Hana shook her head. "They caught four of them at it and terminated all their contracts!"

Hana let out a gasp. "Actually at it? Like an orgy! Of old people!" She pushed her cup away. "That's disgusting. Who knew? At a Christian school too."

"Not actually engaged in the act kind of 'at it', Hana." Sheila winced. "Just having affairs or involvements against their employment contracts." She pursed her lips. "That dreadful Caroline's gone. She had an affair with a sports teacher. You know who I mean. He wore stubby shorts and loved himself. I grew suspicious of Martin just after she arrived and thought for a while she might be his mistress. Perhaps even she wouldn't stoop that low."

"Did they fire Chris Carter?" Hana asked.

Sheila shook her head. "No. Angus took pity on him. The silly man claimed Caroline initiated it and he promised to undergo counselling. He won't get a second chance though."

Hana cringed. "I wonder if he gets a second chance in his marriage. I couldn't give him one." She swallowed. "Didn't his poor wife just give birth to a baby girl?"

Sheila shrugged. "I think so. They fired Martin and his mistress.

Angus said the board considered all the facts and decided a seven-year affair constituted gross misconduct. I suppose against the backdrop of that, Chris Carter's couple of indiscretions paled in significance."

"Seven years?" Hana's jaw dropped open. "With someone else at work?" Her voice rose an octave and other customers turned to stare.

Sheila nodded. "I felt such a fool. Annemarie Baggs from the social studies department is older than me." Her new image drooped. "A board member saw her and Martin at a golf club having dinner and followed them to a hotel. That's when they decided to enforce our employment contracts. The trouble is it's caused so much fallout."

Hana leaned back in her chair. "I thought they did it because of Anka."

"What about her?" Sheila finished her coffee.

"Nothing." Hana offered a sad smile. "Tell me how you are. What will happen to your marriage now?"

Sheila waved a hand in dismissal. "Over. Martin Jennings is history. I've sold the house and we signed the contracts on Friday. The lawyer halved everything and Martin didn't challenge it. I'm moving in with Rory." Sheila grinned at Hana's look of disbelief. "It's fine, Hana. We've done a lot of talking. They bought our house and I'm moving into the granny flat. We can still be separate but I'm there if they need me."

"What will Martin do?" Hana asked. "Where will he go?"

"Not with his fancy woman." Sheila snorted. "She lost interest as soon as he became available. It seems she likes her independence far too much to endure Martin's toenail clippings in the bath. That's the irony. She liked the affair because it meant she didn't need to commit. She only wanted a bit of company to break up the monotony, in return for the odd shag."

Hana sighed. "What a foolish man. I hope it proved worth it."

Sheila patted the table with her hand. "Martin bloody Jennings is not the reason I wanted to meet. I called into work on Friday and found a right mess. Pete's used my office like a bunk room and the department looked closed. I've promised Angus I'll start back on Monday. He said you're on sick leave but I can't manage without you. Do you think you could come back early? I figured Pete's leadership sent you off on stress leave. It's not something serious though, is it?"

Hana shook her head. The tale stretched out behind her, too long and complicated for a coffee meeting. Sheila leaned forward. "Please, Hana. George left me a hysterical voicemail about the woodworking equipment I approved. I'm scared of what I might find."

"I sorted that out." Hana sighed. "I remote onto the server every night and Pete's signing whatever they put in front of him."

Sheila clapped a hand over her mouth. "He can't sign everything! I'll have no budget left!"

"It's okay, I check it. I've said no to a few of them already." Hana licked her lips. "I'm not sure when I'll be back, Sheila. I don't have time to go into it all now, but I'm happy for you to speak to Angus about it." She ran a hand over her face and tiredness descended like a familiar cloak.

Sheila clasped her wrist. "You're not sick, are you?"

"No." Hana sighed. "It's much more complicated than that. I'll speak to my husband and get back to you. That's the best I can offer for now."

Sheila's chair squealed on the tiles as she scooted closer, her eyes widening in shock. She swore before demanding, "What bloody husband?"

-16-

Hana returned home to find a pair of bright red gumboots on the porch. She unlocked the door with a ridiculous degree of caution, catching herself sneaking into her own home. "It's me," she called, listening for a reply and hearing her pulse pound in her ears.

"I guessed." Logan leaned against the kitchen doorframe, his dark fringe over one eye. Sex appeal oozed from every pore. He'd dressed and the lack of pyjamas created an illusion of health. "Maihi's here."

"Cool," Hana replied, hanging her coat in the cupboard. She averted her face while she tried deep breathing to calm her nerves. "Idiot!" she rebuked herself. "It's not like someone broke in and bashed him after standing their wellies up neatly on the porch."

"What?" Logan's strong fingers seized Hana's shoulders and he kissed the top of her head. "Talking to yourself?"

"Yep. You married a crazy woman." Hana swallowed and bit her bottom lip.

"Come and say hello." Logan guided her towards the kitchen, rubbing her shoulders as he felt her trembling. "You okay?" he whispered and she nodded.

Maihi sipped herbal tea and Logan returned to mashing potatoes one-handed. Hana felt like an intruder. "Something smells good," she offered. "I'm guessing it's your handiwork, not my husband's?"

Maihi scuttled round the table and embraced her. "Haere mai," she breathed into Hana's cheek.

"Hey! I can cook," Logan grumbled. "I just haven't had the chance yet."

"Tēnā koe," Hana whispered, self-conscious of her faulty Māori. Maihi squeezed her arm and gave her an affectionate grin before leading her to the table.

"Sit with me," she said, keeping hold of Hana's hand. "What's the matter?"

Hana gaped at her intuition and then cringed as Logan looked around from his task. The air between them crackled and he dropped the potato basher into the pan. "What's wrong, Hana?" he demanded.

She raised her hand to still his ire. "Nothing," she replied, ruining the effect by chewing her lower lip. "Nothing with me," she conceded. "Anka rang me to ask about your health and Tama must have heard it. He checked my phone and intercepted her voicemail. He let her think she spoke to me and managed to discover where she's hiding." Hana swallowed. "By the time I realised, he'd already left."

"Stupid little shite!" Logan ground his teeth and went back to the mashed potato. His one-handed bashing took on new meaning.

"Youse need to text her," the older woman said into the uncomfortable silence. "Let your friend know he's coming. You'd want a warning, aye?"

Hana nodded and watched Logan's stiff back. "I did," she admitted. "She didn't reply."

Logan ceased torturing the potatoes and rubbed his good hand through his hair with rigid fingers. The long dark layers on top flopped forwards from his parting. "Bloody woman!" he hissed. "He's just a kid. She should've left him alone."

"It takes two, tāne," Maihi commented. "I think they both knew the odds." She patted Hana's hand and furrowed her brow with concern. "It's not this girl's fault."

Logan turned to face the women. "Did I accuse her?" he demanded.

"I'm not giving you the chance." Maihi raised her chin in defiance and gripped Hana's fingers. "She looks to me like a wahine taking the blame. What do you think?"

Logan's gaze strayed to Hana's blank expression and his shoulders slumped. "It's not your fault, Hana. It's mine. I let him come here and should have anticipated this." He stepped across and sat in the seat next to her. "It's not your fault, mate," he soothed.

"Good boy," Maihi said and Hana stared in surprise as Logan grinned with pleasure.

"Dinner?" he offered. He stood and pulled the door of the oven open to reveal glistening pastry. He looked at Maihi for an answer.

"Na," she replied, getting up with a grunt. "I gotta get back for me old man." She smiled, kissed them both and left, letting herself out through the front door. They heard her chasing her boots around the porch and cussing as one flopped down the steps to the driveway.

Logan leaned against the counter and stared at the bush. "Sorry," he said, without turning around. "We're past this. I know it's not your fault."

"Thanks." Hana wound her arms around his waist and leaned her cheek against his spine. He clasped her hand and she felt the abrasive cast against her skin as his body moved.

"I'm gonna bloody kill that kid," Logan muttered and Hana sighed. Sheila's news and the request for her to return to work paled in significance against Hana's need for Logan to love her. She breathed in his familiar scent and felt his strong body beneath her palms. Her fingers strayed to his shirt and she loosed the buttons and ran her hands across his muscular chest. A smile of mischief lit her pretty lips as Logan reached across to turn the heat down on the pie.

The bedroom curtains blocked out the remains of daylight as the clock ticked into evening. Hana snuggled into Logan's naked side and a sense of safety shrouded her. "The pie and mash will be cold," she breathed, tickling the hairs on Logan's chest. He twitched and stroked the back of her neck.

"Yeah. I'll reheat them."

"What will you tell Maihi when she comes back for her dish in a while?"

"I'll tell her I got busy doing something else." Logan turned on his side, wincing as he compressed his wound. "She won't come back tonight, anyway. It's a good twenty minute walk."

"Really?" Hana frowned. "She carried the pie all that way?"

"Yep."

"Wow!" Hana's respect for their elderly neighbour increased. "We'd best eat it then." She stroked the scar under Logan's eye and kissed the end of his nose.

"I'll get up when you do." Logan closed his eyes and pulled her closer. "What did Sheila want?"

"That's a hard one." Hana sighed. "I almost didn't recognise her. She's lost weight, changed her hair and had a boob job. And divorced Martin for cheating on her."

"At last!" Logan opened one eye and squinted at her sideways.

Hana rose up on her elbow. "You knew?"

"Yeah. Alan asked me to keep quiet."

"Dobbs? You call Dobbs Alan?"

"That's his name." Logan smirked. "Just because you call him rude names doesn't mean I have to."

Hana tossed her hair and hit him in the face with her ponytail. "Should I go back to work on Monday?" she asked. "You don't need me."

Logan pulled her into his chest and wriggled so she didn't disturb his latest dressing. "Yeah, I do." He sounded sulky.

"No you don't." Hana squeaked as he tickled her ribs. "I need to go back."

Logan pinned her arms by her sides and kissed her neck. "I don't want you to. It's not safe."

Hana's rebellion rose up and her desire for normality kicked against her enforced restrictions. "Sheila asked me," she complained. "I've got things to do."

Logan heaved out a sigh. "Hana, we park the car miles from school and walk through a gully. You can't do that by yourself."

"I've got Bodie's car," she argued. "They followed Amy and Bo in my Honda so they must think I got rid of it."

"They followed Amy and Bodie?" Logan's tone became serious and Hana cringed at her mistake. She opened her mouth to continue her case and he shook his head.

"I'm not talking about it now," he said. "I need a clear head. Let me think about it for a while, please?" He cradled Hana's head against his shoulder and sighed. "I'll ring Bodie in the morning and ask his advice."

"He doesn't know what to do," Hana mused. "I'm coming to the conclusion the cops are a bit rubbish."

Logan suppressed his uncharitable thoughts and nodded against his pillow. "Just leave it with me," he repeated.

Hana found her phone battery dead in her handbag and charged it in the kitchen. "Still nothing from Anka," she commented.

Logan closed his eyes and tried not to let her see his distaste even for the woman's name.

"What do you think will happen if Tama gets as far as Russell?" Hana asked, chewing her lip.

Logan's patience began to crack. "I don't know and I don't care, Hana. She made her bed and she can suffocate in it. Let's not get dragged any further into their stupid mess."

When the gate buzzer sounded in the lobby, Hana ran to the window. The house vibrated with the steady rumble of a car climbing the hill and headlights illuminated the porch. "It's the kids," she called and unlocked the front door.

Amy's old Civic laboured up the rise and Jas escaped before the car engine ceased. Hana met him with a rebuke at the top of the porch steps. "Please don't do that," she said, her tone stern. "What a shame to find a new grandson and then watch him get squashed on my own driveway." She watched as Amy rolled her eyes.

"But I've got stuff for you!" he complained. "I drew a picture of Poppa Logan in the hospital and bought you a necklace from Cambridge market."

"Thank you." Hana accepted the trinket from his outstretched hand. "It's beautiful. And so are little boys who do as their mummies tell them. They're more precious than gold."

"Are they?" Jas cocked his head and observed Hana through Vikram Johal's brown eyes. Hana shivered with the incongruity of his gaze, feeling as though ghosts walked across her grave. He nodded with satisfaction. "That's cheaper then, isn't it? If I behave good, I don't need to buy stuff."

"That works for me," Hana said and kissed the top of his head. "Hey," she said to Amy as the girl climbed the porch steps.

Bodie locked up the car and shook his head at Hana. "Kid's a nightmare," he muttered. Hana saw the colour rise on Amy's cheeks and felt the sting of Bodie's judgement. She swallowed her biting retort and smiled at Amy.

Hana heard Jas running through the house before his parents managed to kick their shoes off. "The beds are bare," he complained. "And my new-old Poppa is gone."

"Logan's nephew stayed overnight and I washed the sheets." Hana tried not to grit her teeth at the reminder of Tama. "And Poppa Alfie needed to go home."

"But I don't like it!" Jas stamped his foot. "I want it like it was before."

"Oh, Jas, stop it!" Bodie snapped, running his hand across his jaw and Amy pursed her lips.

"The sheets are dry," Hana said. "I'll put them on later."

"Now," Jas insisted. "I want to do it now."

Amy heaved out a sigh. "I'll do it with you," she offered, jerking her head towards Bodie. "Dad wants to talk to Hanny."

Logan made an expert one-handed pot of tea while Bodie sat at the table very still. Hana watched his agitation with growing unease. "What's wrong?" she demanded. She lowered her voice. "Problems with Jas and Amy?" Bodie shook his head and stared at Logan's back. Hana persevered. "Are you upset Tama stayed here?" she asked. "We didn't have much choice." Logan turned his head and raised an eyebrow. Hana bit her lip and corrected herself. "Well, Logan invited him. I didn't have a choice." Logan tutted behind her and Hana stuck her chin in the air in defiance.

Bodie shook his head. "No, it's not that. I'm not five, Mum. You can have other people to stay."

"Fine then." Hana slapped her palms on the table. "I give up."

"I went to see Ethel Bowman," he snapped, his sentence short and punctuated by an exasperated intake of breath. "She's a stupid woman."

Hana's brow furrowed. "That's kinda rude but also appropriate."

Logan plonked the teapot on the table. "Did you go in uniform?" he asked.

Bodie shook his head. "No, I'm not an idiot. I said I heard she asked about Mum and wanted to reassure her. I lied and said Mum went on honeymoon. She let me in the house and did her usual song and dance about caring. She asked me heaps of questions. When did you go? When are you back again?" Bodie's nostrils flared and he smirked. "She let me in and I drank tea, patted the cat and admired the knitted doilies. Then I dropped it into the conversation that Mum mentioned a boyfriend."

Hana's jaw dropped. "You made me sound like a gossip?"

"Who cares?" Logan sat next to Hana and leaned forward. "What did she say?"

"She behaved coy. I showed an interest and asked to see a photo. She said he didn't like his photo taken."

"Damn!" Logan leaned back in the chair. "Never mind."

Bodie raised a hand like a magician. "It's not over. I suggested he might not be real."

Hana gaped. "That's horrible!"

"That's genius." Logan tipped forward and back and nodded in appreciation. "Masterstroke. What did she say?"

Bodie's eyes widened. "She got mad. Bristled like a hedgehog. She said she knew my mother didn't raise me to be spiteful."

"I didn't," Hana retorted.

"Then she showed me a photo." Bodie grinned and held up his phone. "They drove to Rotorua for a day trip and she snapped a quickie on her phone to show her sister. I blue toothed it to mine when she left the room for a minute."

"Let me see," Hana demanded, holding out a shaking hand.

Bodie pressed keys on his flash iPhone and held it up to her. "You won't know him, Mum. He's a little old grandad with no distinguishing features."

Logan peered closer. "White hair, stick. He's generic."

"Yup." Bodie laid the device on the table. "But then I showed it to one of the detectives working for Odering." His eyes sparkled. "He lit up like a Christmas tree. This is the man they're looking for." Bodie's tone sounded serious, holding a myriad of hidden warnings and Hana blanched. "Look, he seduces and rips off vulnerable women. Ethel Bowman is the latest in a long line. The last one from up north lost everything, her home, savings, he scammed it all. His method is to produce dud papers from his company, claiming he needs a small cash injection of a couple of thousand. He goes to great lengths to make it look like he's drawing up legal papers, but they aren't real. Once the women are committed and he owes them a little, he asks for more and more until there's nothing left. Then he leaves them. He's acquired a decent income using that method, but with the last fraud he did something different."

"What?" Logan spat the word like gunfire, the urgency in his tone frightening Hana. She tensed from her hips and held her breath.

Bodie lay his phone on the table and Hana's gaze raked the photograph before the screen faded to black. The old man peered over the fence at the site of the Pink Terraces, concentrating on something in the volcanic water. He looked harmless but Hana sensed Bodie's veiled alarm.

"What did he do differently last time?" Logan demanded.

Bodie exhaled. "Odering thinks he killed her." Hana gasped and put her hands over her face. "She disappeared and Laval became the proud owner of everything. Her family called the cops in when he turned up with paperwork and tried to throw them off their farm." Bodie swallowed and his gaze sought Hana's. "I dived the Waikato for her a few months ago."

She nodded. "I remember. You stayed with me, didn't you? Did you know who she was?"

"No." Bodie exhaled. "We do so many body searches a year, I stopped taking notice of personal details. Easier that way." His wan smile hid a world of pain. "We searched major waterways over the summer and dived the Waikato, but didn't find her."

Hana reached for the teapot, but the hand pouring her second cup proved unsteady as she slopped brown liquid on the table. "Is Mrs Bowman in danger?" she asked, her voice a whisper.

"For sure!" exclaimed Bodie and Hana winced. "I've passed my information onto Odering, but she's not my problem, Mum. I asked her why he seemed so interested in you. She believes he knows you because he told her so."

"But I don't recognise him." Hana ran a shaking hand over her face. "What does he want with me? He might think I'm a vulnerable widow and want to take my money."

"No." Logan clasped her fingers in his, engulfing her shaking digits in his hand. "It doesn't fit. He seduces his elderly victims, Hana. You don't match the criteria. I can't imagine you dazzled by a pensioner and you're way too wary to fall for a scam." Logan fixed his gaze on Bodie. "Sending thugs after Hana makes this very different to his usual method. I agree with you there." His dark lashes blinked above rapid eye movements. "Hana's got something he wants or needs. Something else."

"The thing is," began Hana, avoiding Logan's gaze. She gulped. "I can't stay away from work forever. Sheila wants me back on Monday."

"No!" Bodie rose, even before she finished the sentence. He appealed to Logan with outstretched arms. "Absolutely not! Logan, tell her. She can't!"

Hana hissed out an exasperated sigh. She wanted her men united, but not against her. "You're not listening to me. I want to go back to normal. I'm fed up of this."

Logan leaned back and closed his eyes while Bodie thumped the table in temper. "You're not going!" He jabbed a finger into Hana's face. "And that's final."

Hana's green eyes flashed in challenge and she set her lips in a determined line. "You can't stop me! I'm a grown woman and I'll do what I want."

Logan remained seated and Hana sensed the strange vibe emanating from him. His influence prickled her spine and snaked into her chest like an overwhelming force. His voice sounded soft and deceptively gentle. "You're a married woman, Hana Du Rose and you'll do as you're told."

Hana gasped in a giant inhalation of air which contained too little oxygen. She turned to face him with her fists balled at her sides and met a wall of determination. Her anger flared as Bodie heaved out a sigh of relief. "Thank goodness for that!" he snapped. "Someone with sense."

"You can't tell me what to do!" Hana rounded on her son and his smugness infuriated her further. He jerked his head towards Logan.

"No, but he can."

Hana ground her teeth in temper and a spark in her chest rebelled. She reigned in her anger for the time being, having lost the battle but not the war. Rallying statements played on a loop in her brain, fortifying her against the men and building her confidence. Foolishness switched her focus from the need to protect herself to a desire to assert her own autonomy.

She slumped into her seat and turned her face away, seething inside. Logan reached for her hand, ignoring her resistance and obvious irritation at the roughness of his cast. She snatched her fingers away and with a grip of steel, he pulled them back into his lap beneath the table. Squirming proved futile against his iron grasp, setting an unexpected tone for their marriage.

Amy reappeared without Jas. "He's making a surprise in the bedroom," she announced, her gaze moving from one to the other. "What's happening?"

Bodie clenched his jaw and walked to the sink, tipping the rest of his drink down the drain. Hana watched as Amy stood next to him, their bodies touching. Her maternal radar went on high alert, distracting her from the need to extricate her fingers from Logan's hand.

Amy saw her expression and offered a tiny, secret smile, communicating an unspoken desire to fight for Bodie. Hana pursed her lips and nodded, the imperceptible motion shared only by the women. Her gaze flicked to her son, reading the intimate way he inclined his head towards Amy and raised his eyebrows. Hope soared in her heart at the prospect of seeing her problem child settled and happy.

Logan sighed and ran his right hand through his hair. He'd done it so many times in the previous half an hour his fringe resembled an excited rooster. His left hand still clamped her fingers, the plaster cast dragging against her thumb. Hana peeked beneath the table, noting the frayed edges of the cast in the shadows. "Are the cops interested in Hana now?" Logan demanded, the force of the question betraying the thought processes behind it.

"We were always interested!" Bodie spat and Hana felt Logan's body stiffen. She watched him through the corner of her eye and tried to release her hand again, without success. Straight to the point, her husband never wasted words.

"So where are the patrols making sure she's safe? Or are they invisible?"

Bodie sighed, an exasperated rush of air. "You have no idea what's going on."

"So enlighten me." Logan ground his teeth and Hana appreciated his self-control as he waited for the answer.

"It sounded dubious at the start. A mugging, broken windshield, an accidental shunt. It's only when you put the incidents together that you get a picture."

"What picture?" Logan unfolded his legs beneath the table. "And how does that help her?"

His grip on Hana's hand relaxed and she discovered she didn't want him to let go. She curled her fingers around his and his eyes widened in surprise. "What's going to happen next?" she asked and Bodie shrugged.

"Not sure. I handed everything over to Odering's detectives. They need to find a connection between you and Laval."

"Oh great!" Logan snarled with obvious sarcasm. "And how's that going for you?"

"Look, I know what you're thinking!" Bodie's brown-eyed gaze focussed on Logan. "Your people don't have a great history with the police. But it's not that way anymore. We aren't racists."

"No?" Logan leaned forward in his seat and his eyes widened. He radiated a vibe of intimidation. "You want me to forget how the local constable flogged my poppa in the street for possessing an apple? I ride my motorbike up the highway and I'm fine because they can't see my face. I drive my Triumph or something nicer and any road cop will stop me at least once. 'Bloody Māori, I bet he nicked that.' Nothing's changed, you just hide it better." Logan sat back in his chair so hard; it tilted onto its rear legs for a fraction of a second. He drew his top lip back in a sneer. "The minute your ma got involved with me, her case went to the bottom of the pile so don't kid yourself. What's wrong, mate? You too embarrassed to admit it's gone into a file with all the other multiracial domestic incidents?"

Hana held her breath as Bodie floundered. "It's not like that! I'm a bloody brown cop, man! I would know." He sounded hurt. Amy nodded her head in agreement, but slowly as though unsure.

Hana squeezed Logan's fingers, begging him with her eyes not to walk along a damaging trail of racist accusations they couldn't return from. He glanced at her and then shook his head. When he let go of her hand it felt spiritual as though he severed the union of their cultures. In protest, she leaned across his legs and seized his hand, gripping it in both of hers and glaring at him. "Stop!" she hissed. "Don't punish me for what others do."

Logan's eyes softened and ignoring their audience, he pressed his lips against hers. "Sorry," he whispered. Bodie's eyes narrowed and Hana felt his jealousy stretch across the room.

Amy broke the leaden silence. "What about Mrs Bowman," she asked. "Did you warn her, Bo?"

"No," he replied, his tone sullen. He scratched his chin and Amy watched his fingers move across his flesh with naked craving in her eyes. Hana ached for her. "I couldn't take the risk of her telling him anything. She's so enamoured of him, I suspect she would."

"Poor Ethel," breathed Hana. "Loneliness makes people vulnerable to any kind of affection."

"Is that right?" Bodie glared at Logan and Hana closed her eyes against the accusation. Tiredness filled her bones.

"Who will tell her?" Amy asked. She pursed her lips and looked at the floorboards. "She might not believe it."

"The investigators will visit her." Bodie chewed the inside of his lip. "They'll show her the evidence."

"She'll be traumatised. I hope she hasn't given him money yet." Hana remembered Ethel's coy excitement over her gentleman friend and the sparkle of hope in her eyes. "This sucks."

"She won't be the first or the last," Amy concluded with a sigh. She nudged Bodie's hip with the back of her hand. "We need to get our boy home," she said, her voice soft. "He's too quiet."

"I'll get him." Bodie left the room and Hana saw the unrequited love in Amy's eyes. She held her tongue and pondered on her son's odd behaviour. Amy's existence explained the hole in his soul and yet he resisted their mutual attraction with dogged determination. Hana identified the culprit in her own marriage. Lack of trust.

Bodie returned carrying Jas over his shoulder. "He put dried flowers on your pillows and fell asleep waiting for you." He winced. "What do I do now?"

"Put him in the car." Amy held her arms out and reclaimed her son.

"Sorry." Hana stroked the boy's hair back from his forehead and kissed his downy temple. "I'll look at them now."

Amy followed her down to the bedroom and Hana inspected the crinkled daisy chain on her pillow. Crunchy bits of flower leaf dotted the area like green dandruff and she admired the child's efforts with enthusiasm. "I love it," she declared, sniffing the decorations and inhaling particles so she coughed.

"I worked hard on that," Jas grumbled, coming alive on Amy's shoulder. He wiggled his feet to get down and strode across the room. "Can I sleep with you?"

"It's home time, Jas." Amy's firm tone met instant resistance.

"No!" he protested, dropping his knees and squatting on the rug. "Don't wanna!"

"Let's not do this right now," Amy implored, but the child scented victory and dug his heels in, setting up a loud protest about going outside in the cold.

Bodie appeared and took charge. "Come on mate, Hanny's tired and so am I." He led the sulking boy into the lobby.

Amy pushed his spindly arms into his jacket sleeves and bent to retrieve his boots. Jas bounced on the spot in temper. "I don't want shoes on!" he complained. "I don't need them." He toppled sideways and his foot slipped through the strap of Hana's abandoned handbag. He fell and the bag upended onto the floorboards.

"It doesn't matter," said Hana, bending to stuff everything back in. Her fingers touched the little metal box from her garage at Achilles Rise and she detached a coin from its surface.

"What's that?" Jas clambered up and rested his hands on her knee. "I like it."

On impulse, Hana handed it to him. "I think Daddy made it in metalwork at school. You can play with it if you do as Mummy tells you."

Jas fondled the box in his fingers, turning it over and over. "Okay," he conceded. He gave a tired, squinty-eyed smile.

Bodie peered over her shoulder. "That's not mine," he said,

shaking his head and shrugging. "You asked me about it once before. I don't know why you kept it."

Jas kept to his good behaviour bond and the little family left. Hana waved them off from the porch. Logan smiled as she returned to the kitchen and continued to load the dishwasher. "Sorry about before," he said. "I just hate how the cops aren't helping you."

"I know." Hana rested her hand against his back, feeling the bones of his spine move as he bent to load cups and spoons.

"I'm scared," she confessed and he turned to hold her.

"I know," he whispered into her hair. "But it'll be okay."

"How? This old man sounds nasty and the cops think he killed someone. I'm no match for them."

"No, you're not," Logan replied. "But we are."

-17-

Hana woke before dawn on Sunday morning. She lay in the darkness listening to the gentle breaths of her husband, feeling the mattress dip and shake as he shifted in the big bed. An austere grey light, filtered through the gaps in the bedroom curtains like cold fingers, exerting its hold over the day. Hana admitted defeat and got up.

She hugged a cup of tea at the kitchen table, swamped by boredom and a sense of imprisonment. "Oh, Lord. I can't live like this!" she exclaimed and pressed her fists to her forehead. "I'll go mad."

The sewing machine would wake Logan and she considered her limited options to fill the long hours ahead. She set off another load of washing and examined Logan's bloodstained dressing gown drying in the garage. "Dustbin, I think," she said, unpegging it and throwing it into the wheelie bin. "Two washes and it's still stained." The horror of the night rose up to meet her and she shivered against the memory. Catching sight of the paste bucket, she peered into it. No sign of Logan's haemorrhage remained after an earlier frenzy with bleach and the idea blossomed in her mind.

Hana set up her tools to wallpaper the lobby, trying not to make too much noise in the big open space. Pasting the navy and white paper on the kitchen table, she got to work. The large pattern made matching easy and Hana hung eighteen strips of paper before Logan surfaced. "Hey, babe. Look what I've done," Hana began.

Logan staggered from the bedroom, his pyjama trousers skewed to one side so the buttons rested over his left hip. He lurched into the kitchen, weaving and winding around the paste bucket and tarpaulin. Hana descended the ladder at the sound of water running and the clink of glass. "What's wrong?" she asked with dread filling her chest.

Logan fumbled with a foil packet of painkillers over the sink, his fingers shaking. A white pill popped out and rolled into the plughole. He swore and bent double, rubbing a hand over his dressing. "It hurts," he groaned. "It hurts bad."

Hana took the blister pack and popped two tablets into his hand, watching him chase them down with water. "I can ring the district nurse," she offered, concentrating on her breathing to keep her calm.

"No!" He shook his head and his eyes held warning. "Call no one." He slumped into a chair and rested his forehead on his arms, his body tense and rigid. Hana rubbed his back, trying to stroke out the stress and pain whilst praying in her mind. "It's still early days yet," she comforted. "If it gets too much, you need to tell me."

Logan remained listless and silent. Standing or sitting caused him pain and laying on the bed made him want to vomit. He agreed to a hot drink and then couldn't drink it, driving Hana's anxiety to fever pitch. "Where does it hurt?" she asked and lifted his tee shirt. He pointed to his lower abdomen but wouldn't let her press there.

Hana sneaked to the garage with her mobile phone and made a call. Speaking in hushed tones she sought medical advice. The receptionist at the doctor's surgery groaned. "Not again!" she complained. "You need to bring him into town and wait your turn."

"I can't lift him," Hana whispered. "And he doesn't want to come. Can I pay for a home visit?"

The receptionist scoffed and took her phone number, promising to ring back. "They'll tell you to call another ambulance," she said as her parting shot. Hana hung around for ten minutes, hanging washing on the line strewn across the garage and waiting for the call. It didn't come and she felt no surprise.

Upstairs, Logan curled into a ball on her side of the bed, his eyes closed and a hot water bottle clamped over his stomach. Her heart clenched in pity at his sorry state. She kissed the top of his head, holding his hand and resting her forehead against his shoulder. Her fingers traced the bold tattoo snaking around his upper arm. "Is this your genealogy?" she asked, trying to distract him while the painkillers kicked in. She followed the gothic tracks and swirls of the moko.

He looked up, his face drawn and grey. "Whakapapa," he answered.

"Is that the basis of your culture?" Hana asked, her voice wobbling at the tremors in his body. "Who you are, where you come from and how you got there?"

Logan nodded and crushed her fingers beneath his. "Yes."

Hana leaned forward and kissed its dark, woven centre, feeling Logan shivering as he tried to control the physical battering from inside. "Please let me help you?" she begged. "This is frightening me, Loge. It's happening again."

Her phone buzzed on the bed and she snatched it up, striding into the lobby to answer the call. The male voice sounded calm. "Mrs Du Rose?" he asked.

"Yes." Anxiety made Hana breathless.

"Are you related to Michael Du Rose?" the voice asked and Hana stilled.

"Why?"

A sigh. "I trained with him in Auckland and went to school with the brothers. Is Logan okay?"

"No. Please can you help him? I don't know what to do and if I call an ambulance, he'll divorce me."

The man laughed. "I doubt that. I've got your address here. I'm doing a stint as locum in Ngaruawahia. I'll pop up in about half an hour."

"Thank you!" Hana gushed, hugging the phone to her chest as he rang off.

He kept his promise and buzzed the gate thirty minutes later, blasting up the driveway in a sporty Mazda that spat out gravel like grape pips behind it. Thin, blonde and good looking, his movements oozed competence. Hana turned after the brief handshake to lead him into the house, keen to take him to Logan. "Wait." He held up a hand to halt her. "I need to know what happened. I've read the notes and they make little sense."

A flush of embarrassment crossed Hana's freckled cheeks and he drew his own conclusions. "He lied on the form, didn't he?"

Hana swallowed, not wanting to commit to the betrayal aloud. The doctor put his hands on his hips. "Level with me, Mrs Du Rose. I know your family and I need the truth, please."

"Someone hit him from behind with a crowbar and broke ribs, his arm and damaged his spleen." Hana spat out the list of injuries, her face blank. "A week afterwards they removed his spleen. A week after that, they repaired a tear and an infection. He was fine yesterday but I think it's happening again." She swallowed and struggled for control.

"It's okay." Blue eyes bored into Hana's as he nodded. "Where is he?"

Logan slumped at the kitchen table and the cooling hot water bottle lay on the floor next to him. Hana saw the kettle sitting in the sink where he tried to fill it. A sheen of sweat covered his back, the bones of his shoulder blades angled through the muscles.

"Hi Logan." The doctor smiled and lifted Logan's good arm around his shoulders, hauling him to a standing position. "Let's get you laying down. I'm Carlos. We went to the grammar school together. Do you remember me?"

Logan looked at him sideways and nodded. His affirmative reply sounded hoarse. Hana took Logan's other arm, wary of doing more damage to the break as she tried to support her husband. "Turn right," she told the doctor. "We'll lay him on the rug."

Between them, they lowered Logan onto the floor. "Stretch your legs out for me," Carlos instructed and Logan groaned. When the doctor pressed on his stomach, Logan shoved his hand away.

Hana stood on the fringe feeling useless. The doctor continued his examination of Logan's midsection, ignoring his patient's writhing. He tapped and pressed, unfazed by Logan's barrage of swear words. "Lie on your back with your knees up to alleviate the pressure on your stomach," he said, tapping Logan's shin. He looked up at Hana. "Where can I wash my hands?"

"Through here." Hana gave a nervous glance back at Logan as he covered his stomach with his hands as though protecting himself from an outward attack. She led Carlos to the kitchen and hovered in the doorway. The doctor used soap and water and dried his hands on a towel Hana indicated with a jerk of her head. "Should I take him back to the hospital?" she asked, a tremble in her voice.

Carlos smiled and his face lost some of the hardness. "No," he replied, his voice soft. "I'll fetch my bag."

He skipped down the porch steps as Hana checked on Logan. She heard the front door close again and the doctor's footsteps cross the lobby. "I won't be long," she promised her husband and he nodded without opening his eyes. She snatched up a blanket from the sofa and folded it next to his arm. "Put this on if you get cold," she whispered.

In the kitchen, Carlos scribbled words onto a prescription pad. He wrote a list of medications and added a flourishing signature at the bottom. "No charge," he said with a smile. "Logan is the better brother."

Hana accepted the paper from his outstretched hand and looked at the scribble. The Latin words confused her. Carlos lowered his voice. "His gut went into spasm because of the surgery. It's quite common. His discharge sheet says he left before they checked everything out. As long as nothing tears inside, he will get over this. The haemophilia makes it more complicated, is all." He released a megawatt smile that infused her with confidence.

"Did you know his brother died of haemophilia?" Hana asked and the doctor nodded.

"Yeah. I remember but it wasn't related to surgery. He fell from a horse and sustained multiple bleeds. His mother tried to nurse him at home without medical help. It could never end well. There were other complications too."

"So Logan doesn't have to die from it?" Hana heard the wobble in her voice and an embarrassed flush crawled up her neck.

"Not at all," the doctor replied. "I'm sure he manages it fine. The pharmacy should be open now. I'll wait with him if you want to fetch the medication."

Hana swallowed and her gaze strayed to the lounge. "Are you sure?" she asked.

"Yeah." Carlos scratched at an itch on his throat and gave a slow nod. "Logan Du Rose made my life at school bearable. Nobody touched me after he stood up for me." He jerked his head towards the front door and then checked his expensive watch. "Go. I've got half an hour before I need to get back to the surgery."

Hana ran to the lounge. She found Logan propped up against the sofa still clutching his stomach. "You don't need to go to the hospital," she said. "I'm driving to the pharmacy to get a prescription and then you'll be okay."

"You can't go alone," Logan rasped, groaning at another spasm.

"I'm fine." Hana stood and looked down at her scruffy tee shirt and shorts. She'd worn them to bed and then wallpapered in them and blobs of glue dotted the left sleeve. Carlos appeared in the doorway and she kissed the top of Logan's head, ran into the lobby and snatched up her bag and sweatshirt. Her boots looked ridiculous, but she grabbed the car keys and clattered down the porch steps. "I'll be quick," she shouted. The front door clicked shut behind her.

Hana flew along Hakarimata Road, making the journey into Ngaruawahia in less than five minutes. Sparse Sunday traffic afforded her an angled parking space in front of the pharmacy. The girl behind the counter took the prescription and her money before advising Hana about the twenty-minute wait. Hana groaned. "You should have said," she grumbled. "I could've driven to Huntly. My husband's at home with the doctor and they're waiting for this medication."

"Okay." The girl smiled and tossed her long, brown hair. She walked away from the counter and left Hana standing there alone.

Twenty minutes passed with no sign of Logan's prescription. Hana hopped from foot to foot and the tension around her grew. Staff worked in silence behind the partition, the sound of pills dropping into containers the only punctuation. Hana distracted herself using the testers on the makeup stand. She gave herself a makeover with foundation, lipstick and eyeshadow, feeling more human at the end of it. Whilst sampling the moisturisers and turning her hands into an oily mess, she noticed a rack of handbags near the window. A pale pink shoulder bag with large hyacinths dotted across the fabric captured her imagination. Hana wiped her hands on her shorts before counting the pockets and assessing the bag's possible usefulness.

Sudden movements on the street outside made her jump. A little boy stared through the window, pressing his face against the glass and pointing at a brightly painted wooden truck in the display. The decorative beach scene advertised sun cream and the dump truck's bed tipped sand onto the fake shore. Surfboards leaned at jaunty angles around a sea made from coloured foil. Hana waved to the child and he grinned and pointed at her as though she formed part of the display. As she savoured his innocent enthusiasm, the pharmacist called Logan's name and Hana gave the boy a last wave.

She felt the presence of the black BMW before it slid into a parking space across the street. Hana froze with fear as the brake lights winked out and the passenger door opened. She squashed herself against the handbag rack and shrank away from the window.

"Logan Du Rose," the pharmacist shouted, bringing Hana back to reality. She ran to the counter, reaching out to snatch the prescription.

"Thanks," she blurted and skirted the shelves until she reached the door. A million thoughts ran through her head, alongside the knowledge she had nowhere left to run.

"I need to check the address," the pharmacist called, walking around the counter towards her.

"Culver's Cottage." Hana glanced over her shoulder and fumbled for the door handle. No ready plan of escape formulated itself as she watched the blonde man step from the vehicle. He checked the street with casual interest. Her heart thudded like a mallet in her chest.

"Are you okay?" The pharmacist approached Hana as though she might be toxic.

Hana nodded and swallowed the panic enough to speak. "I need to get to my car," she squeaked, clinging to the handle. The woman peered into the street and reacted to the terror in Hana's eyes.

"Can I call someone for you?" she whispered.

Glancing back into the street, Hana saw the blonde man approach the cash point opposite and his hands moved as though he pushed a card into the slot. "Please don't tell that man you saw me. He'll hurt me."

Hana wrenched the door open and ran. She flipped the hood of her sweatshirt up and over her hair, turning away from the road as she shoved her thumb over the key fob. Praying for divine help, Hana sobbed with relief as Bodie's prized possession behaved as its expensive engineering dictated. The doors unlocked and Hana flung herself into the driver's seat. She fumbled with the central locking button, desperate to lock the blonde man out. Emboldened by the tinted windows, Hana craned her head to look at the wide street.

A central reservation separated the two lanes, planted with a stunning floral display. Hana glanced towards the end of the street, spotting the no-right-turn sign. If she wanted to escape, she needed to travel left onto the main highway and find her way home through the back streets. Without the presence of the black car, she would have turned at the end of the street and travelled back on herself. The thought of driving past the blonde man and the BMW sent her pulse rate pounding in her ears. "Think, Hana, think!" She hit the steering wheel and caught her breath.

Dithering too long in the driver's seat, she saw the blonde man finish at the cashpoint and walk towards the video store. He shoved his wallet into his back jeans pocket as he conversed for a moment with an elderly man on a bench outside. The old man shook his head and shrugged.

Hana covered her eyes and tried to think like Bodie. She formulated a plan to make him proud. Looking in the rear view mirror, she memorised the backwards registration number of the BMW. The Chinese man emerged and leaned against the driver's door, straightening his crisp white shirt and looking around him. Hana searched for distinguishing features and spied a tattoo of a dragon on his right wrist. The blonde man returned from the video shop empty handed and jerked his head towards the pharmacy. Hana gulped.

She saw the permanent sneer on his face as he strode across the single lane with confidence. The pounding of her heart sent the blood whooshing through her eardrums until it obliterated all other sound. Her body vibrated from the frantic motion of her arteries, a rhythmic pulse so violent she forgot to breathe.

The blonde man paused on the centre island behind her, waiting for a vehicle to pass. He tapped his fingers against muscular thighs and took an irritated stance. An old woman struggled with the gears of a green utility vehicle causing a temporary delay. Hana jumped into action. Forcing her shaking fingers to work, she snatched Bodie's sunglasses from the visor and clamped them over her eyes. They moved around on her face and she shoved the bridge over her nose. In the door cavity next to her seat, she seized a filthy drying rag. A bottle of interior polish fell back with a clunk. Hana pushed her distinctive auburn hair into the hood of the sweatshirt and scraped it back from her face. Then she tied the rag around her head like an old woman's scarf. Her eyes became slits with the tightness of the cloth and Hana's breath came in gasps. Her fingers shook tying the knot and she fumbled it twice. Checking her appearance in the mirror, she saw a land-girl from an English war documentary.

Bodie's expensive car started first time. "Thank you!" Hana breathed. She whipped the gear stick into reverse and waited for the green ute to complete its fifty-two point reverse manoeuvre. Someone honked a horn in frustration and the blonde man's gaze tracked towards an impatient people carrier. Spotting a gap, he left the centre island and made a run for it.

Acid rose into Hana's throat as he jogged towards her, slipping between her car and the one next to it. Hana heard the moan of panic escape from her lungs and she leaned sideways as though searching for something in the passenger foot well.

The blonde man tapped his knuckles on the bonnet of Bodie's car as he passed and Hana shoved a fist into her mouth to prevent the emerging scream. When she peered through the dark glasses, she saw him moving towards the door of the pharmacy. Flooring the gas, she reversed from the angled parking space and cranked the gear lever into drive. Her hands shook as she spun the wheel and her sweat-coated fingers almost lost control.

Hana's driving ability deteriorated as adrenaline coursed through her veins. Her wheels screeched against the road surface and she battled an overwhelming desire to flee without regard for other road users. She headed for the main road, keeping her eyes focussed on its promise of escape. The old utility vehicle lumbered along in front of her. A family stepped onto the pedestrian crossing and she fidgeted whilst willing them to walk faster. A mum and dad strolled across with two tiny children tottering next to them like ducklings, blindly following.

Shock hit Hana like a wave as inactivity frustrated her. Her legs turned to jelly and she couldn't press the pedal as the ute moved away. The car lurched and sputtered as she forced her muscles to behave. A squeal of rubber sent her over the pedestrian crossing. The family stopped to stare at her and Hana's rational mind screamed a warning. "Attention is exactly what you don't need right now!" she exclaimed to herself.

On the main road south through Ngaruawahia, Hana lost her bearings. She'd never gotten around to exploring her new area and the wide, tree lined streets confused her. Roads branched off towards the mountain, bisected by a railway line which lumbered towards Hamilton. In desperation as her half an hour ticked past, Hana did the only thing she could think of. She followed the green ute in front of her.

It turned right. So did Hana. It reached a roundabout and took the fourth exit. Hana followed. The Waipa bridge sped beneath her and she experienced a rush of exultation as the sign for Hakarimata Road loomed to her right. It swung from its post by one fragile metal stem, like a drunk on its knees. The ute rumbled towards the quarry and Hana made the turn. As soon as she hit the higher speed limit, she floored Bodie's car and pushed it around the bends toward home.

She checked her mirrors before turning into the driveway, staring at the road behind for the black car. Sunlight winked back at her from the empty road and Hana pressed the button to open the gate. She nudged her way through the opening without waiting for the motor to complete its circuit and another jab of the remote control set it closing behind her. The gate obeyed with a reluctant shudder.

The driveway seemed endless as Hana swept the car higher, desperate to escape anyone following her. Sliding to a halt at the top of the slope, she killed the engine. Sickness worked its way into her gullet and her lungs ached from holding her breath. She sat for a moment seeking her equilibrium before facing Logan and the doctor. The view of her face in the rear-view mirror sickened her further.

The dirty cloth slipped sideways over her left ear, streaked with dust and car muck. When she removed the sunglasses and fumbled them back over the visor, her face looked grey and aged without them. Freckles stood out like a starburst across her nose, the only colour in her face. Even her green eyes dulled with the strain of fright. With a sigh, Hana pulled the cloth from her hair, putting it back with the polish.

"What am I going to do?" she groaned, feeling the weight of the world rest heavy on her shoulders. "I can't do this anymore." Hana ran a hand over her eyes and wiped her fingers on her shorts.

"Mrs Du Rose?" Carlos tried the driver's door handle and Hana started and deactivated the central locking. "What's wrong?"

She licked her lips and forced out a smile. "Pharmacy kept me waiting." Her hand shook as she retrieved Logan's prescription from the passenger seat. "I'm sorry. I didn't mean to take so long."

"It's fine." The doctor's brow knitted over his handsome face and he gave her a smile. "I need to explain some of the medication and then I'll leave."

Hana gulped air and nodded, forcing her feet into the gravel and willing herself to stand. "Thank you," she squeaked.

Following Carlos up the porch steps, Hana glanced up at the lounge window. Logan stared back at her, his hair on end and his cheeks pink. He clutched his stomach with one white knuckled hand while the other rested on the windowsill. He communicated anxiety like a drum beat.

The doctor delayed his departure by administering an injection in Logan's backside. By that time, he'd vomited. "I need to stop him throwing up," Carlos said, scratching his head and replacing the syringe in a sharps' box housed in his medical bag. "He'll rip something."

"I'm fine." Logan propped himself up against the bath and Carlos released the blood pressure cuff.

"Always the hero, aye Logan?" The doctor smirked and Logan raised his top lip in a sneer. Carlos turned to Hana. "If this continues call an ambulance. If he won't go with them, call the cops. There's legislation to protect people from themselves." He nudged Logan's leg with the toe of his shoe. "Don't give her any trouble, mate."

Logan grunted and rested his forehead against his bent knees. The doctor smiled at Hana and shrugged. "We're unlikely to meet again," he said, holding out his hand. "I fly out to Africa in a few days. See if I can make a difference over there."

Logan raised his head and managed a bleary-eyed nod. "Thanks Carlos. Have fun curing sick people."

"I will." The doctor winked at Hana and left. As Hana pressed the gate release and watched his sporty car kick up gravel behind it, she heard Logan vomiting again.

"This is ridiculous," she groaned, leaning against the doorframe. "I'll call him back."

"No!" Logan leaned over the sink and ran fresh water into his mouth. "I feel better."

"You're a liar!" Hana exclaimed, watching his shaking fingers probe the drawer for something. "Let me do it." She retrieved a toothbrush and squeezed paste onto it. Logan's fingers trembled as he took it.

Hana stayed close while he brushed his teeth and rinsed out his mouth. He took huge gulps of air to steady himself, his knuckles white against the basin. "I'm fine," he persisted. "Let me sleep."

"You do that!" Hana snapped. "I don't suppose you want the medication I risked my safety to fetch from the pharmacy?"

Logan's grey eyes tracked to her face and his narrowed gaze stilled her blood. "What do you mean?" His body tensed. "Did something happen?"

Hana backed away shaking her head. "No. Nothing. Get into bed, you look horrible." She reached the doorway.

"You'll come and talk to me?" Logan winced and gripped his stomach.

"Yes, I promise. I'll bring hot water for your stomach. You might manage some of the tablets."

Hana escaped to the kitchen and boiled the kettle. She fussed around fetching mugs and making tea for herself, adding it to a tray. Tensing at the sound of the bathroom door clicking shut, she slumped with relief as Logan's footsteps shuffled towards the master bedroom.

After feeding the cat, Hana tidied the kitchen and then steeled herself to face her suspicious husband. The sun tried desperately to push its way through the clouds, bright shafts of sunlight speckling the kitchen table. Hana picked up the tray, squared her shoulders and set off for the bedroom.

Logan slept on his side, his face pushed into Hana's pillow. He lay on top of the covers and Hana put the tray on the bedside table. She felt his forehead, relieved at the coolness of his skin. His breathing sounded steady and a small snore escaped his pursed lips. Hana pulled a blanket over his bare feet, reluctant to swaddle him up after last time.

She pulled the sheets back on his side of the bed so he could climb in if he wanted and kissed his temple. Logan stirred but didn't wake.

Hana left his pills and water and removed the tray. The house seemed to thrum around her with the sudden silence. Boredom and loneliness hit her afresh and she took her tea onto the porch steps to drink.

Sunshine kissed the crown of her head and birdsong caused her to look upwards. A tui stared back at her from a native palm, cocking its head from side to side. It chortled and she smiled, squinting to look at his little white bow tie. The sun's rays caught the bird's feathers and colours leapt and twisted in the light, revealing an intense metallic blue. Her mind wandered back to the weeks following Vikram's death, afraid at how easily she could put herself back in those awful moments. His loss stretched behind her, raw and painful. Logan's illness and surgeries forced her to relive the powerlessness and terror the memory evoked. It proved the futility of relying on her own mortality. "Despite present appearances, God is in control." She recited the words of Father Sinbad, who believed them enough to convince her of their truth during her darkest hours.

Hana sighed as calm descended over her soul and felt grateful at the answering of her prayers. The men would find her. She knew that with certainty. "I need to work out what they want from me," she sighed.

She tipped the dregs of her tea over the side of the porch steps, wrinkling her nose at the weeds pushing upwards towards her. Growth sprouted forth from neglected flowerbeds, forcing its way into the gravel to take over the driveway.

As midday passed, the sun won its battle for a few hours and dominated the day. Hana checked on Logan and found him still sleeping. She cleared away the wallpapering paraphernalia and changed her focus. Needing to be outside in the sunshine, she grabbed tools from the garage and spent a good hour doing battle with the weeds. She discarded her hoodie and enjoyed the warmth on her bare arms. A sizeable mound of weeds mounted up in the wheelbarrow next to her as she forked through the bed, disappointed to find nothing of value. A flowerbed emerged, wrapped around the bay window of the living room and stretching beneath the porch. Any decent specimens died long ago, buried beneath the bindweed and scrubby grass.

Hana scrabbled around in the garage for remnants of a roll of weed mat and spent another hour laying it. She pinned it with a few stray metal rods and stood back to admire her work. Snapping a photograph, she sent it to Izzie. Her daughter texted back.

'What will you plant there?'

Hana wrinkled her nose and admitted it would remain bare. She ached for a covert trip to a garden centre, but the morning's antics drained her energy and she didn't dare. She moved to the slope and attacked its muddled edges, seeking to restore order to the chaos.

A noise made her start and Hana dropped her trowel. She retrieved it and stood, wielding it as a weapon.

"Don't get scared, girly." Maihi waved and walked towards her, nodding her head with understanding. "It's only me." She jerked her head at the cleared ground and the pile in the wheelbarrow. "Looks good," she said. "Ka pai."

Hana beamed under the spotlight of Maihi's admiration, like a child with a painting that pleased the teacher. "You got plants?" Maihi demanded and Hana's smile drooped.

"No," she admitted.

Maihi made suggestions, naming plants Hana didn't recognise. She laughed and held her palms outstretched. "You're cheating," she complained to the old woman. "I know nothing about gardens and you're using Latin names."

"You should learn," Maihi chuckled. "Know your surroundings, girly."

"I need to go to the garden centre." Hana pouted and looked around her. She jumped as Maihi snatched at her arm, digging her fingernails into her flesh.

"No! Not today! No!"

Hana looked down at Maihi's clawed fingers, frightened by the vehemence of her words. Maihi collected herself and released her, patting the red mark she left on the porcelain skin. "Lock up here and come home with me. We'll take cuttings from my place. I've thousands up there." She indicated the general direction of her home with an outstretched arm and waited for Hana to obey. "Lock your doors. Lock them tight."

Hana frowned. "I'm not sure. The doctor came out to Logan this morning. He's real crook." She deliberated and then shook her head. "Not today, but thank you."

"Check on him." Maihi jerked her head towards the door. "I won't keep you for more than an hour."

Hana looked up at the front door and then at Maihi. "What's the matter?" she demanded, cocking her head.

Maihi shrugged. "Come for a walk with me."

Hana kicked off her boots on the porch and padded to the bedroom to assess Logan. His head felt cool and his body lay in the foetal position. He'd woken and drunk half the cooled water and taken the medication and he looked peaceful. Hana stroked his hair back from his forehead and kissed his temple. "Won't be long," she whispered.

Grabbing her sweatshirt and house keys, Hana stuffed her phone into her pocket. She closed the garage door and locked up. "Are you showing me the secret route to your house?" she asked the old woman and Maihi nodded.

"Let's go," she said and beckoned with her fingers. They climbed the back fence into the empty paddock behind the house. Climbing the steep incline, they reached the bush line with Hana puffing and blowing.

"Wait a minute," she begged, putting her hands on her knees. She turned to view her home from the vantage point. "Roof looks nice," she said, running a hand over her damp forehead. "But the flat roof over the garage doesn't."

"Needs some nice plant pots," Maihi suggested, shielding her eyes from the sun. "You can make it nice."

Hana wrinkled her nose. "It faces west. I never noticed. That means it catches the afternoon sun."

"Sure does." Maihi nodded. She tugged on Hana's arm. "Come on. It's not much fun if we lose the light coming back."

"I never thought about walking back." Hana pouted. "Maybe I could come over tomorrow morning."

"You'll never find the path." Maihi set off walking again and Hana followed with a groan.

"I have a rimu garden table and bench seats in the garage," Hana said, puffing behind her. "I could lift that onto the roof garden."

Maihi stopped and raised a dark eyebrow. "Not on your own," she warned. "You'll hurt yourself."

Hana shrugged and shed her sweatshirt, tying the sleeves around her waist. "How much further?" she demanded.

Maihi chuckled and waved her onward. "Youse a wimp, girly," she called over her shoulder. "I'm an old kuia and even I don't puff like youse." She sprang over a line of barbed wire like a deer.

Hana tried many ways to cross the nasty wire. Climbing it sent the spiteful prongs through her gumboots and her running jump proved unsuccessful. Maihi watched, shaking her head and laughing as Hana disconnected her sleeve from its grip. "Do this," she said, pointing to a space between the barbs. "Look for the places where the sharps are bent down. Things aren't always as they seem."

Hana bent and peered harder at the lines of wire. Plier marks showed where someone created footholds. "Did you do this?" she asked, squinting up at Maihi. The old lady shrugged.

"Yep. It's an escape route for you."

"I won't remember the way." Hana peered beyond them into the bush, not able to see a way through the supplejack vines which twisted like spaghetti to head height.

"I'll think of how I can mark it." Maihi held out her hand to steady Hana as she scaled the wires. The bottom of her shorts caught on the nearest barb, almost causing her to face plant as she struggled to extricate herself. "You needed long pants," the old woman commented and Hana rolled her eyes behind her back as they set off again. "Don't disrespect me, girly," she flung over her shoulder. Hana halted before a line of supplejack.

"What? You didn't see that!"

"The tui told me." Maihi pointed up into a punga and Hana spied the white bow tie between the ferns.

"No he didn't," she grumbled under her breath.

"Did too. Watch your footing."

Hana stumbled along behind Maihi's stout figure. "Come on," the old woman urged her as though they ran a race. They climbed over and under the irritating supplejack vine, following the fence line and trying not to catch their skin or clothes on more barbs. Hana failed and her arms and legs sported ugly scratches.

"The gully is here," Maihi called back as the land sloped downhill. Rocks and mud crumbled beneath Hana's feet and she clung to the barbed wire fence and added her fingers to the list of injured body parts.

"How do I get back up again?" Hana squeaked as she slipped for the fifth time.

"You just will," Maihi retorted. Her head disappeared as she navigated a series of ledges alongside running water. Hana followed, clinging to the wire and snagging her arms. Pausing for breath, she glanced up and saw the height of the canopy, sunlight dappling the ground as it earthed itself between the silver tree ferns.

"Watch out for bushman's lawyer!" Maihi shouted over her shoulder as she reached the floor of the gully.

"Yeah, I already found it," Hana groaned, snagged on the talons of a horrid, spindly plant.

They crossed the water at its narrowest point, jumping over it and clinging to stalks of grass on the other side of the gully. Maihi sprang like a deer and Hana followed like a hippo in a ballet outfit. Maihi pointed to the bubbling stream as it coursed over rocks. "This fills your second water tank," she said. "It runs off the mountain."

"Logan installed a water filter," Hana replied and Maihi gave her a look of surprise.

"But it's fresh," she answered. Hana watched fallen leaves and a chocolate wrapper float past and nodded, deciding not to argue.

A wooden post and rail fence with a stile indicated the first sign of civilisation. It came after a gruelling upward climb and Hana panted at the top. Her palms bled and her fingers stuck together with orange mud. A herd of Friesian cows looked up from their chewing, eyeing the women with interest. Hana stuck to Maihi's back, watching the animals over her shoulder. She trod through their lunch with anxiety in her gut as they turned to face them and took a few tentative steps forward. "They're coming!" she hissed and Maihi gave a low chuckle. Hana gulped. "Are those horns!"

"They won't use them on you," she replied, her voice straining with the effort to hold in her belly laugh. "They just wanna see the white woman."

"Oh." Hana stopped and watched as the cows followed at a sedate and curious pace. Maihi's violent laughter drove her on, knowing she'd fooled her guest.

"White woman!" she puffed, embarrassed by her gullible innocence. "I can't believe you carried a casserole to our house," she called and Maihi turned with a nonchalant shrug.

"When youse done it often enough, it's easy." She parted her lips in her honest smile and Hana loved her for it.

A large house moved into sight on the downward. Made of faded cedar, it wore a light blue tin roof. Hana exclaimed in surprise. "I can see this roof from the kitchen window! I didn't know you lived here."

"And I can see yours," Maihi replied with a grin. "Youse are a bit higher than us."

They stepped onto a covered porch and Maihi kicked off her red boots, leaving them in a heap by a blue door. Hana kicked off her filthy boots and followed Maihi inside.

"Wow, what an amazing design!" Hana gasped. She stood in the open space and admired the bare wooden rafters flying overhead. Skylights allowed the fading sunshine to filter in and scatter its joy over rimu floors and chintzy furniture. A staircase in the centre offered access to a mezzanine floor with a balustrade and bedroom doors running off its length. "It feels like a log cabin," Hana said, admiring the wood. "I love it."

"Thought you might." Pride back-lit Maihi's brown eyes and she nodded towards a stool at the counter. "Put youse kumu down." She turned away and filled a kettle, placing it on an agar stove.

"Kumu?" Hana looked at her dirty hands.

"Ass." Maihi patted her own significant buttocks and sniggered.

Catching the scent of rosemary and sage, Hana searched for the source. Looking up, she tracked it to a rail of drying herbs above her head. She made a beeline for the sink instead and ran her poor fingers under warm water. The liquid soap on the windowsill made her hiss with the stinging sensation.

"Whatchoo do?" Maihi handed her a drying towel and tutted at the state of her hands. She rummaged in a cupboard and handed over a box of plasters before going back to her tea making.

Hana sat on a chintz sofa, clutching her hot tea in hands encased in fabric Band-Aids. A gentle calm filled her soul and she relaxed for the first time in too long. She squinted at a framed photograph on the wall. A younger Maihi laughed with her head thrown back. A man with an enormous handlebar moustache held her in his arms and her ivory wedding dress cascaded to the floor. Hana recognised the building in the background and saw the distinctive meeting house at Turangawaewae Marae.

Maihi tracked her gaze and nodded. "He's a great husband. I loved my first husband but counted myself fortunate to find love a second time."

Hana's breath caught in her chest and she pursed her lips. "You guessed."

Maihi snickered. "One broken wahine recognises another. Logan is a good man. Hold onto him."

Hana sighed. "I'm trying, but he possesses a death wish."

"Finish your tea," Maihi said. "Then we'll take some cuttings."

Maihi stood on the river aspect of her home and yanked out plants by the roots. Hana protested. "I don't want to kill them," she said. "I can't seem to make things grow."

"These will be fine." Maihi yanked up another green stem, its pink flower bobbing as she shoved it into a carrier bag. "Cape Daisy can grow anywhere. Just dump it into the soil and it will survive. I love it because it flowers all year round." Maihi stood up with a grunt. "There's a white one around here somewhere. Ah, there it is."

Hana followed her host around the property as the old woman selected suitable sacrifices to die in her neglected garden. "You ready for the return journey?" Maihi demanded as she shoved the bag of plants over her wrist at last. Hana's confident nod looked forced, a wooden action filled with doubt. The older woman narrowed her eyes. "Try to take notice," she ordered. "It's your escape route should it all turn to custard at your place."

Hana's face paled and she hurried after Maihi's determined figure. At the top of the paddock, the old woman paused, waiting for Hana to lurch after her. Letting her catch her breath for a moment, she pulled a length of string from her pocket. "I need youse to be able to find your way here and back," she said, her face stern. "I'll tie markers at various points along the way. They'll fade with age and the weather, so take care to note where I put them."

Hana nodded, her green eyes wide and frightened. She swallowed and her voice box jammed. Maihi reached out and touched her shoulder. "I don't mean to scare you, kōtiro. My niece works at the video store in town and our uncle sits outside when the sun shines.

Men came to town today, enquiring about a woman with red hair. My girl rang me earlier."

"Oh." The blood rushed to Hana's face and she sank her bottom against a fence post. The waves of panic from earlier overwhelmed her with increasing force. "Oh, no."

"Sit!" Maihi reached for her and forced her onto the wet ground. The beautiful view stretched out before her unseen. Hana put her head between her knees to quell the awful feeling of faintness. She felt the grass depress as Maihi sat next to her. "We gonna get wet asses, girly," she said as she put her arm around Hana.

"Too late," she replied, her voice muffled.

Maihi kissed Hana's temple. "She never told them, my niece. Said she never heard of you. Told them we don't gots no red haired women in our Māori stronghold. Then she phoned me. We don't betray our own, not here my girl. Not in the kīngitanga."

Hana heard the old woman's sincerity and nodded with gratitude. "Have you met the Māori king?"

"Course. He's my cousin. Stop changing the subject. You asked no questions, so I know you saw the men too."

Hana held nothing back. Desperation laced her voice as she recounted her loss of safety. The stronghold of Ngaruawahia threatened to give her up. Maihi laughed at the tale of the dirty headscarf. They sat together as the wet soil leaked through Hana's shorts and undies and made them as wet as Maihi predicted. "Come on girly," she said finally. "We can't sit here and hui all day!" She hefted Hana to her feet with a surprising grip and they progressed home through the bush.

At intervals, Maihi stopped to tie string to significant landmarks. The pale material disappeared into the landscape, but Hana struggled to memorise the route. Her survival may depend on it. Another hiker would never notice, but she banked on fear to recall it in an escape situation. Hana wondered as she fell over rocks and stumbled over roots, how she could possibly repay her neighbour's kindness.

They reached Hana's paddock and Maihi stooped to tie string to the area where she pressed the barbs flat. "A good tracker will find this," she said, dispelling Hana's temporary feelings of safety. "My niece thinks they're just thugs."

Hana swallowed back the tea rising into her throat and chased away the sense of doom with a change of subject. She waved her arm to include the expanse of land between their houses. "Do you own all that land? Is the gully national park?"

Maihi's snort sounded scornful. "I owned it once. Now you do."

"What?" Hana gaped. "No, I don't." She cast her mind back to her copy of the deeds to Culver's Cottage. Interested in the house, she never examined the surrounding land. She'd arranged to talk it over with Logan, but Caroline's intervention meant she dealt with the final stages of the purchase alone. She swallowed and pointed back the way they came. "I bought it from you?"

Stopping to tie another marker as the paddock doglegged sharply downwards, Hana pressed Maihi for answers. The old woman pursed her lips. "You own ten hectares of what once belonged to my grandfather and his father before him. My father built the house I live in. My husband died young and my son took drugs. He took out loans and they came after me."

Hana's lips parted in surprise. "Not Hone?"

"No, no. I forget you met him. No, my other son. He's in prison now. I sold the property to a Hamilton businessman to cover the debts and it left me bitter."

"I'm so sorry." Hana gnawed her lip and remembered Bodie's youthful antics following his father's death. A dark cloud threatened to settle on her shoulders and she shook it off. "Our kids put us through hell, don't they?"

Maihi nodded and her lips looked down-turned and sad. "It's good land. I miss having it. We reduced our stock to cope."

Hana tripped over another hillock and sighed. "The businessman went bankrupt, didn't he?"

Maihi jerked her head. "We still couldn't afford to buy it back."

"I'm not sure we'll get any animals, so why don't you graze here?"

Maihi stopped and Hana barrelled into the back of her, slipping as she grappled for her footing on the slope. The old woman watched her clamber upright again, a curious expression on her face. "Do you mean it?"

"Yes." Hana nodded. "It'll help me. I can't mow all this." They set off walking again. "I own land I don't need and you could make use of it. Makes perfect sense. It's the house and location I wanted."

"What is the rent?" Maihi demanded and Hana shook her head.

"Nothing. I don't want you to pay. You're a friend." The ground went from beneath her and Hana slid past Maihi on her backside, unable to stop. She picked herself up, brushing muck off the back of her shorts and dying of embarrassment inside. She spun on the spot and noticed a clump of grass stuck to her butt like a green tail.

Maihi waited until she stopped spinning and seized Hana by the shoulders. "I visited you to quell my bitterness and because it affected my mana so. I didn't expect to fall in love with you and your tāne but this is my reward." She suffocated Hana in her copious bosom and sniffed with emotion. Hana felt the unfamiliar glow of acceptance and kissed Maihi's cheek. The physical contact made her miss her mother with a jolt of pain.

Maihi let go and they slipped and slid down to Culver's Cottage.

The cuttings drooped in the plastic bag and the women planted them into the new flowerbeds. Hana cut slits in the weed mat with Maihi's pocket knife. "What's mana?" she asked as they worked side by side. "I kinda know the principle of it and I realise it sounds ridiculous, but I know what it looks like in a person. I know Logan has it, but not how he got it."

"Understood." Maihi plunged a daisy into the hole she dug with a small trowel. She rocked back on her heels. "It's linked to our spirit and increases depending on our standing within our community. It represents our prestige and authority. A person is born with a degree of mana which is linked to their whakapapa. If their ancestors were known for great mana, it passes to them."

"Ah, like Logan's grandmother?" Hana asked. "People still talk about her."

"Yes, like that." Maihi shoved the next plant into its new resting place. "You can accrue mana for yourself though, through your actions and behaviour. It's about what people say of you. Logan has great mana. You can just tell."

Hana nodded. "Yes, I know what you mean."

"The ethos and conduct of a group also raises the mana of those involved. Offering great hospitality will make people speak well of you and that's just as important."

Hana cocked her head and stared at Maihi. "You have mana. So does Logan. Can I get it?"

The old woman's eyes narrowed. "I don't know kōtiro." She chuckled. "He has enough to spare."

"Ain't that the truth," Hana muttered and Maihi nudged her arm with dirty hands.

"The secret is not to seek it, child. If you're meant to have it, it will find you."

Maihi left after the planting, refusing the offer of a hot drink. She said she wanted to go home and tell her husband the good news about Hana's offer of grazing. The air grew bitter cold as she set off up the slope and Hana went inside.

Logan sat at the kitchen table, looking refreshed. Hana put her cold arms around his shoulders and leaned her face against the back of his neck. She held her filthy hands away from him. "Hey gorgeous," she whispered into his warm skin. He smelled soapy and his dark hair dripped on her cheek. His fingers sought the back of her neck and he massaged it gently.

"The jug's hot," he said and Hana glanced at the steaming kettle.

"I'll wash my hands and make tea." She peered into his cup. "Do you want another coffee?"

Logan shook his head. "Na thanks." His eyes narrowed as he

stared at her back. "Hana! Your ass is disgusting! Did you go mud-sliding?"

Hana felt behind at the crusty mess and groaned. "No, I made a flower bed," she replied.

Logan shook his head in confusion. "With your backside?"

Hana left the kettle to boil and shook her head. "No. My hands. I'll grab a shower first."

She stood in the shower and let the hot water slap the back of her head. The door clicked as Logan let himself in. "I made you a cup of tea," he said and she heard the clunk as he put it on the sink. "How was your afternoon?"

"Good," she replied, turning off the water so she could lather herself with soap. "How do you feel?"

"Much better." Logan sat on the stool in the corner. "Those pills are good. They relaxed my muscles, so the pain is heaps better." He sighed. "As soon as I get rid of one problem, another appears around the corner."

"Thanks for cleaning the bathroom," Hana said, turning the water back on and missing Logan's reply. The scent of household cleaner overpowered the small room.

"I'm sorry about before," he said as she stepped over the side of the bath and swished back the curtain. Logan stood and wrapped a towel around her. He swaddled her up and pulled her against his chest. "I remember getting impatient with you. I shouldn't have."

"It's fine. You looked in agony. I forgive you." She closed her eyes against his chest and inhaled his musky scent. "I wonder how much the surgery will charge for the home visit." She chewed her lip and contemplated an astronomical medical invoice. "Carlos charged nothing for the prescription."

"Don't worry about it. I'm glad he came." Logan grabbed a smaller towel and used it to squeeze water from the ends of Hana's hair. His tender action melted her heart. "He's a good bloke." He kissed the top of her head. "Thanks for going to town for the medication," he said, his voice soft. "You put yourself at risk." Hana inhaled through her nose and then held the breath. She sensed the atmosphere change as Logan leaned back to look into her eyes. "Are you gonna tell me what happened?"

She blew out through her lips. "How do you know anything happened?"

He raised an eyebrow and shook his head. "Don't bother lying, wahine. You think I won't know?"

"I didn't want to worry you." She pouted and her lips formed a hard line. "The men turned up in town and I ran away."

"Tell me you called the cops?"

"No!" she snapped. "I tried to remember the registration number for the car but forgot by the time I drove home. They didn't believe me last time, so I figured they wouldn't this time either. The man with the Asian features had a dragon tattooed on his wrist."

"Bloody hell, Hana!" Logan raised his voice. "Did they follow you home?"

"No!" She gave him a rough shove, regretting it as he hissed in pain. "Sorry. I left you rolling around the floor in agony. I had different priorities at the time." Her towel slipped and she grappled with it, her fingers shaking as she covered herself.

Logan's face softened and he reached up to touch her damp curls. His complete change of subject floored her. "Hana stop hiding. You're beautiful."

"I've got stretch marks!" she retorted and stomped from the room. Logan heard the bedroom door shut behind her and bit his lip.

"Yeah, and I've kissed most of them," he sighed. He lifted his phone from his pants pocket and dialled.

Hana sulked in the bedroom and made her decision about returning to work. With the men as close as Ngaruawahia, it wasn't safe. Logan's reaction irritated her and she tried to shake it off. "It's because I care," he told her later, putting her cooling cup of tea on the bedside table.

"I texted Sheila," she admitted. "I won't go back yet."

Logan nodded. "I'm relieved." He smirked, one corner of his lip hiking upwards as a mischievous expression crossed his handsome face. "I can keep you busy here." He tugged at her pyjama shirt, wrinkling his nose at the faded monkeys.

"You're supposed to be sick!" Hana squealed as he attacked her pyjama pants. "You're insatiable."

"I want to show you what I think of those stretch marks," he muttered, rubbing his beard against her bare ribs.

-18-

Hana slept late again the next day and awoke feeling groggy. The sun peeked through a gap in the curtains and scattered light over her fiery hair draped across the pillow. Before she even fixed her feet to the rug, she decided to spend the day working on her garden.

In the kitchen, she found Logan on the telephone. He broke off his conversation to kiss her cheek and then ended the call. Already dressed, he looked healthier but still thin and gaunt.

Hana filled the kettle and flicked the switch, leaning back against the counter to face Logan. "Who was that?" she asked.

Logan shrugged. "My father." He jerked his head towards the window. "Maihi will be glad of the extra grass. He says it will be a bad winter this year." He seemed edgy and Hana watched his jerky movements with suspicion.

"What are you up to?"

"Me?" He smirked. "Nothing, babe."

"Whatever." Hana narrowed her eyes. "You know I'll find out." The cat shot under the kitchen table as she squealed. Logan chased her back into the bedroom. Tiger sat beneath Logan's abandoned chair and licked pork fat from his coat. He liked the men who arrived in the bush after dark. A ute dropped them off and they hiked the Hakarimata Trail before dropping down the ridge and tracking their way to the house. Expensive GPS guided their steps. They set up their camp with soundless expertise and killed a wild pig using a bow and arrow. The cat fed on the scraps from their meal as they took turns on watch.

Maihi's cuttings looked limp from their transplant and Hana watered them. Then she pottered around tidying other flowerbeds. Logan sat on the porch steps watching her and enjoying the sunshine on his face. "This is weird," he sighed. "I'm not used to sitting on my backside."

Hana turned soil with a pitchfork and defined the edges of the beds with a spade. "Enjoy it. You'll be back at work soon enough." She wrinkled her nose. "I wish I could visit a garden centre. I've run out of weed mat and it looks so bare."

"No," Logan said and Hana raised her hand in protest.

"I won't actually go," she replied, her tone barbed. "I'm not stupid!"

"Behave wahine," he warned her and Hana pouted. Logan rose and rubbed a hand across his stomach. "I'll take a walk to the bush line. I need the exercise."

"Are you sure?" Hana shoved her fork into the soil. "I'll come with you."

Logan shook his head and set off walking. "I won't be long and I've got my phone." He waved the device in his hand and disappeared around the side of the house.

Hana glanced up at intervals, watching Logan's progress up the right-hand side of the paddock. She saw him halt and waited, shielding her eyes from the sun. When he lifted his hand to his ear, she guessed he made a call. Reaching for her phone on the top step of the porch, she waited for him to ring her but it remained dark and silent. Hana watched as he continued walking and put her phone back with a shrug. When his hands swung loose by his sides, she guessed she imagined it. She looked up again and he'd disappeared.

Logan returned looking flushed and relaxed. "I enjoyed that," he said, running his right hand through his hair. The walk did him good. He went back inside to make a drink, kicking his gumboots off on the porch. Hana noticed fern roots in the grips of the soles.

"You went into the bush?" she called after him, receiving no reply. "Why?" Still no answer.

The sound of the intercom bleeped from inside and Hana screamed. She dropped the pitchfork, almost sending the prongs through her foot. "Logan!" Her voice broke and she tripped up the first two steps, landing on her hands and knees. "Logan!"

He met her at the top of the stairs, shocked by her white face and wide, staring eyes. His fingers gripped her shoulders. "It's okay, Hana. I know who it is."

She shook her head from side to side, her ponytail swishing against her back. "No! No, they've found us, Logan they've found us!" She writhed in his arms and he winced as his elbow responded with darts of pain.

"Hana!" His voice sounded sharp and she stared up at him in bewilderment. "It's. Fine." He spoke through gritted teeth and stopped her bolting at the sound of an engine struggling against the hill. She wriggled from his grasp and hid behind the front door as Logan shoved his feet back into his boots. Going down the steps, he walked to the top of the drive ready to greet the guest. Hana watched the flat backed truck labour the last of the driveway, stopping with a shudder at the top.

A man clambered from the driver's seat and shook Logan's hand. "Kia ora," he said with a wide smile. His tanned face oozed joviality. Despite the autumnal day, he dressed in stubby shorts and a muscle top. A boy around twelve years old emerged from the passenger side of the truck and helped to unload the wares. Hana ventured onto the deck as Logan's gifts waved in the breeze.

He turned to her with hope in his eyes. "Did I get the right stuff?"

"Yes. Thank you." She watched the unloading process and nodded to her husband. Small bushes and flowering plants came off the truck and sat around the driveway like a speechless audience. Hana ran a shaking hand across her forehead, feeling beads of sweat budding at her hairline.

"Can you let the guys out?" Logan asked and she nodded. Her vision blurred as she stepped back inside the house and listened to the truck engine roar to life. She leaned her forehead against the wall and heard the delivery driver's cheery goodbye. Counting to twenty before she pressed the gate release, Hana let go of the button and bent at the waist. Blood rushed to her head and she stemmed the feeling of nausea.

"I can't live like this," she groaned, forcing herself upright. The need to appreciate Logan's thoughtful gift drove her outside again.

"Want help to plant these?" Logan asked, clutching his stomach and moving the plant pots one handed. He glanced back at her, looking for her approval. Hana opened her mouth to speak but nothing came out. Her lips felt numb and her teeth chattered. "Hana?" Logan moved up the steps towards her, his face creased in concern. "Hana?"

She buried her face into Logan's sweater, reminding herself to breathe. Her face muscles refused to perform and express the gratitude he awaited. Nothing. The emptiness spread from the centre of her chest and tracked towards her head and feet simultaneously. Logan shook her shoulders and she felt the tugging motion, her head growing too heavy on her neck to respond.

Then it came. The nausea rose into her throat and the headache thrummed across her temples. Hana saw sunbursts behind her retinas and held her breath, praying it would pass. When the nothingness sucked her down, relief replaced her fear.

Logan grappled as Hana fell, managing to get his arms around her limp torso to break her fall. His broken arm couldn't straighten and it pulled his body sideways with a hiss of pain. She sank to the deck as a dead weight and her head hit the wooden boards with a dull thunk.

"Geez, Hana, what are you doing?" He knelt beside her, calling her name and rubbing her cheeks. "Hana? Hana, what's wrong?"

She twitched at the sound of her name but then remained still and silent. Her shallow breaths frightened him and the pulse in her neck betrayed a faint heartbeat. Logan scrabbled in his pocket for his phone and his fingers removed the screen lock with frustrating slowness. He cursed the restrictive cast on his dominant arm. Hana groaned and her eyelashes fluttered against her cheeks.

She opened her eyes. Thinking herself in bed, she gave Logan a sweet smile. The hard boards beneath her spine confused her and his face hovered above. Hana opened her mouth to speak and saw the blue sky above. "I'm outside," she said, surprise in her voice.

"Steady, steady." His voice cracked. She flailed in panic and Logan helped her to a sitting position, leaning her sideways against the balustrade where she slumped like a rag doll. A quick body check revealed a pervading nausea and leaning between the rails, Hana threw up over Maihi's wilted cuttings.

Logan rubbed her back as she retched, shock dilating his pupils to obliterate the stormy grey irises. "Maybe I shouldn't buy you stuff," he joked, a tremble in his voice. Relief coursed through him when she shook her head in objection. "I didn't mean to make you pass out."

Hana blew through pursed lips and her fingers grappled to hold onto the side rail. "Sorry," she whispered and her other hand streaked sweat across her brow. "I don't know what happened."

"You scared the crap out of me, that's what happened." Logan laughed but it sounded hollow against the backdrop of birdsong. He jerked his head towards the open front door. "Why don't you go and lie down?"

Hana shook her head. "I'm fine." She rubbed her eyes and willed the buzzing in her ears to leave. "The fresh air is helping."

"What do you think caused it?" Logan left his squatting position and sank onto the deck next to her. "Was it the delivery truck? You looked terrified."

Hana nodded. "I think that started it. My heart beat so fast and then it just didn't."

"What do you mean?"

Hana shrugged. "I don't know. Just let me sit here for a minute and then I'll do some gardening. I want to be outside."

Logan opened his mouth to argue and thought better of it. "Would a hot drink help?" He got to his feet as Hana nodded and kicked his boots off. She heard him pad to the door and closed her eyes. Without his concerned gaze unnerving her, she leaned her head against the railings and concentrated on regaining her equilibrium.

Logan fetched her tea and a sugary biscuit. Hana sat on the steps and watched him plant one-handed as she directed like an orchestra conductor. "How did you know what to choose?" she asked as he buried the roots of a rhododendron under compost. "And how did you think of getting compost and bark chips and stuff?"

"I gave them my credit card number and left it up to them." Logan patted the soil over the roots and stood. "You like what they chose?"

"Yeah!" Hana exclaimed. "It looks amazing already."

Logan eyed his wife sideways as he cut another cross in the weed mat. Her flushed cheeks and bright eyes faked vibrant health, but he'd seen her black out and recognised the physiological signs of distress. Hana put her empty mug down on the deck and rose, anxiety in her face. Once upright, her confidence grew and she took a steadying breath. "I'm okay now," she said, her voice rising in surprise. "I've no clue why that happened."

Logan stopped and leaned his cast across his legs. "Do you need to see a doctor?"

"No." Hana dismissed the suggestion. "I can't face any more doctors or hospitals. Perhaps I hyperventilated like Mr Singh suggested before. I need to catch it happening next time and remember to breathe." Pleased with her convincing tale, Hana gave him a radiant smile and ventured down the steps. "Here." She held out her hand for the trowel and took over, squatting to plant a healthy yucca whilst avoiding its pronged tips.

"If you're sure." Logan took her place on the steps and picked at the edge of his cast. His gaze strayed to the bush line high above them. "I need to get fit again," he commented. "That walk up the hill almost killed me."

"I saw you stop," Hana said, patting the soil. "You looked like you answered a phone call. Was it the plant man?"

Logan shifted in position. "I kept stopping to catch my breath. I might go up and down the hill a few times this week and see if I can get my fitness back. Then I can go to the school gym." He scuffed his boots against grit on the steps and his eyes held a faraway look.

Hana sat back on her knees, resting her bottom on her heels. "I'll come with you. I'm not doing enough exercise so we could go together."

Logan's brow furrowed for long enough to alert her to something amiss. He shook his head. "I might run some days. Can you keep up?"

"No." Hana shook her head and her tight expression betrayed the sting from his rejection. "You go. I'll never match your stride, especially not uphill."

Logan lay back on the deck and closed his eyes against the bright sunshine. When Hana finished planting, he pulled the hosepipe around from the side of the house and watered the flowerbeds. "Maybe you could walk up with me once a day and I'll run the other times." Logan gave her a wary smile, perhaps aware he'd hurt her.

Pique made Hana want to refuse, but she accepted the olive branch. "I'd enjoy that. Want to go soon? I can show you the markers Maihi left if you want."

Logan nodded his agreement and they locked up the house and activated the burglar alarm before setting off together. He clutched Hana's hand and pulled her towards the right-hand side of the paddock. She resisted. "No. We need to go up the left so I can find the first marker."

"It's fine." Logan gave her hand a tug. "It's steeper this side but easier to see the bush line."

"Why does that matter?" Hana peered across the distance to the dark spots beneath the canopy. "We don't need to see it." Her eyes widened. "Do you think someone might be watching and jump out at us?" She clutched her chest and Logan shook his head. Regret showed in the clench of his jaw.

"No babe. That's not why I suggested it." He squeezed her fingers. "If we go up one side and down the other we walk further. That's all."

"Okay." Hana blinked and raked the dark spaces, seeing nothing. Alarm began a patter in her chest, anyway.

The steepness of the incline affected them both and Hana stopped several times to bend at the waist and hug her knees. Logan cut the corner at the boundary and took a perpendicular line towards the other side of the paddock. Despite his surgeries, his fitness proved impressive compared to Hana's. "Can't we wait here for a second?" she begged, leaning against the corner post. "I'm knackered."

"No, come on," Logan called over his shoulder. "You need to keep going." He glanced up at the cloudless sky. "The weather is meant to turn today."

Hana groaned and turned her head to stare into the bush. Something caught her eye and before Logan could stop her, she climbed the fence. Her sweater snagged on a barb and she pitched forward, saving herself at the last minute. Exasperation flooded Logan's face as he turned and jogged after her. "Get back here!" he snapped. "What are you doing wahine?"

"Look." Hana crouched down and peered at the biscuit wrapper nestled in the supplejack. "Someone left rubbish." Her body tensed and she looked around her in jerky movements. "Do you think it's them?" She rose and her wild eyes searched the area.

Logan cleared the fence with an easy spring and he reached her fast, wrapping an arm around her shoulders. "Hana, it's blown up from the house." He dug at the wrapper with his toe. "You brought one of those for me last week. At the hospital."

"No, I didn't." Hana bent to retrieve it and Logan dragged her hand away.

"Don't touch it."

"Why?" Her tone sounded suspicious and she narrowed her eyes at him.

"Because it's dirty." The wrinkling of his regal nose indicated his disgust and he kept hold of her fingers. "Are you gonna show me these markers before it rains on us?"

A bird cawed in the depths of the bush and Hana gave a slow nod. She shivered and Logan reeled her in until she fit beneath his arm. "This place scares me," she admitted and he laughed off her fears.

"Na, the bush is beautiful. I'll take you exploring in the summer. You'll love it."

His confidence emboldened her and Hana's body relaxed. "Okay," she conceded. She squeezed his waist. "I love the top of your mountain. Maybe it's because you love it." Her rosebud lips parted in mischief. "Remember the first time you took me up there? You kissed me and I wanted more. We could christen this place." She looked around, seeking somewhere to lie down.

Logan hissed through his teeth and hauled her closer. "No, Hana," he said, lowering his voice. "Let's go."

"You don't like it here?" Her eyes widened in surprise.

"I love it," he answered, his eyes darting around. "I'm tired. Let's get going."

"Oh." Hana's face fell in disappointment and her lips turned down. "Okay."

"Another time," Logan whispered in her ear, leaning in to kiss her neck. "Not today."

Hana turned at a sound like the snort of a pig. She crashed into Logan's side. "Did you hear that?"

"No." He gritted his teeth and steered her towards the fence. Behind his back, he raised his middle finger and the snort sounded again.

"Is it a pig?" Hana demanded, clambering over the fence and landing on her backside in the mud on the other side. She scrambled up and moved backwards as Logan thudded next to her. Her eyes raked the speckled darkness of the bush.

"It's a great big fat pig." Logan raised his voice and Hana stared at him with a look of dismay. She tried to peer around him and he ushered her away. He didn't look over his shoulder, but sensed the hunter appear from behind a kauri trunk with a wide grin on his face. Logan felt the presence in his bones and longed to wipe the smug look from the man's grizzled face.

After only a couple of mistakes, Hana led her husband to Maihi's house. She swelled with pride at her navigation and looked back at Logan for approval. He seemed more relieved than proud. "Do you think you could do it in the dark?" he asked and Hana's face fell.

"No." She gnawed her lower lip. "Do I have to?"

Logan shook his head and forced a blank expression into place. "No. Just make sure you don't leave it too late if you walk to Maihi's during the day. Night draws in fast here."

"Okay." Hana sighed. "I'm tired now. Do you think we should call in or is it rude?"

"Na." Logan set off down the slope. "In our culture it's fine to visit without notice. Family is family."

"But we're not family." Hana slipped after his long stride, her hands flapping at her sides. "What if she's not dressed?"

Logan snorted and shook his head. "Who cares? She won't."

Maihi flung the back door open at Hana's tentative knock and hugged them both like long lost friends. "You want dinner," she asked, brushing off Hana's protestations with a wave of her hand. "Come, sit," she instructed and indicated the large dining table. They kicked their boots off on the porch and stepped inside. The room felt warm and cosy and the smell of cooking created the age old welcome.

"Gorgeous design," Logan said, looking up at the high ceilings and exposed beams.

A large man bounded down the central staircase and Hana jumped back in fright. He towered over Logan's six feet and four inches without effort, a veritable giant of a man. Broad shouldered and muscular he exuded pure strength. Hana recognised the handlebar moustache from the photograph, but age streaked it with grey and white. A full head of glossy black hair dated him as younger than his wife and Hana blossomed with gratitude at another point of similarity. "Guests?" he exclaimed and a smile lit his face.

"These are the people I told you about," Maihi said, straightening her shoulders as though introducing her own flesh and blood. "Logan and Hana."

"Hemi," the man said, making a beeline for Logan. They clasped hands in a firm grip and Hemi pressed his forehead against Logan's. The hongi felt intimate and power surged through both men as their flesh connected. Hana held her breath, only releasing it as they parted friends. Sensing her reticence, Hemi shook Hana's hand in a gentle action as though believing her crafted from fine china. He waved them both towards the dining table. "Sit, sit!" he commanded.

"I should at least help," Hana said and he protested and rested a heavy hand on her shoulder. Logan winked at her, easy in the family atmosphere. Maihi dumped a casserole pot in the centre of the table and Hemi set two more bowls. They made it feel natural and Logan lay back in his seat and relaxed. The hosts seated themselves and Hana watched as they clasped hands above the table. Maihi took Hana's fidgeting fingers from her lap and jerked her head towards Logan. "Let's say grace," she said.

He swallowed in surprise and accepted Hemi's outstretched hand. Hana smirked and looked away as the scales tipped the balance in her favour and produced something she understood. Hemi's karakia formed a gentle lilt in her mind as he thanked their Lord for the food on the table and good company. When he lapsed into Māori she kept her eyes closed and allowed the lyrical cadence of the words to wash over her soul. "Āmene," she agreed at the end of the prayer.

"Help yourselves to my wife's famous boil-up," Hemi declared, handing Logan a serving spoon first. Logan accepted it and his slender fingers filled a bowl of delicious pork and vegetables. Hana's stomach growled as the messages passed from her nose to her brain. Logan handed the bowl to her with care, offering her a smile as he filled his own bowl and passed the spoon to Hemi.

Maihi poured red wine and they drank as they ate. Hana felt tipsy after very little and Maihi grinned at her from across the table. Logan sipped a beer with care, not wanting to compromise his antibiotics. He refused a second beer as Hana moved onto her third full glass. "How will you get your cows over to our place," she asked, digging into a second bowl of broth.

"Truck them up." Hemi looked at Logan and spoke with his mouth full. "Can your driveway take a double loader?"

Logan leaned back in his seat and narrowed his eyes in thought. "A double yes, but not a triple."

"Are you running out of grass?" Hana asked, trying to sound intelligent in the realms of husbandry and failing.

"No." Maihi leaned forward. "But my husband purchased a big old bull and he's a little too efficient."

"At what?" Hana asked, closing her eyes with pleasure at the taste of pork in her mouth. "Where did you get this meat? It's gorgeous."

Logan chewed his lower lip and watched Hana's face. Hemi kept talking about truck sizes, digging into his food like a dump truck driver.

"A hunter shot a wild pig in the bush," Maihi said, glancing once at Logan. "And what purpose do bulls usually serve on a farm with cows?"

"Oh." Hana prodded the meat, her enthusiasm for it fading. Her cheeks pinked at the stupidity of her question. She compounded it by thinking up another. "How can a bull be too efficient?" she demanded.

Maihi snorted. "Because he's covering all the heifers too soon," she answered. "We want spring calves and this dude ain't waiting. We can move the ones he hasn't covered into your paddocks." She rolled her eyes at her husband as though resurrecting an old dispute. "Not that there's many still untouched."

Hemi stuck his nose in the air and huffed. "He came up for sale, wahine. I needed to grab him fast."

Maihi sniffed. "And you needed to pen him better too, but that's another story."

The peaceful atmosphere stuttered beneath a veil of brewing arguments and Hana stiffened. "It doesn't matter," she said. "You're welcome to use our place as a backup."

Hemi nodded and the storm left his eyes. "Thank you. We're grateful. The truck only needs to travel half way up the drive. I can use the gate to the paddock."

"What gate?" Hana's brows knitted and the hand with the wine glass wobbled. "Is there another gate?"

"Yep." Logan nodded and lifted Maihi's empty bowl into his. "Half way up there's a bend and a small pull in. Behind all that scrub is a gate."

"Oh." Hana closed her eyes and pictured an area half way up the long and winding driveway. She pulled in sometimes and used it to watch the main road before running down the last straight and exiting the property. It gave her a view of Hakarimata Road from the town end and provided a useful safety precaution. "I didn't know it had a gate there."

Logan stood with the gathered crockery and walked to the kitchen. Maihi followed with the tureen of casserole. "Dessert?" she asked, patting his shoulder.

He looked back at Hana and saw her scull the last of her wine. "Thanks. It's dark. We should probably find our way back."

"Hemi can drive you." Maihi looked at her husband and frowned at the fourth bottle of beer in his hand. "Bloody hell, tāne!" she groaned. "They weren't all for youse!"

Hemi looked down in surprise. "Sorry." A sheepishness slid across his expression and Hana giggled.

"We've all had too much. Except Logan." She quirked an eyebrow at her husband and her growing lack of coordination made the expression look painful.

"We'll be fine. Thanks for dinner." Logan kissed the top of Maihi's head and rolled his eyes at the occupants of the table. "Whose bright idea was it to put those two together?"

"That will be yours, tama," Maihi laughed. Her use of the word for son made Logan frown and she touched his arm. "What is it?"

Logan shook his head and shrugged. "A story for another time, aunty."

"Okay." She widened her eyes as Hemi reached for the red wine and poured Hana another glass. "Best get your wahine home." She raised her voice and spoke to her husband. "Hemi, get them a bike. They'll break their necks in the bush. You won't need it this week."

Hemi grunted in hearty agreement. He slapped the table with his palms. "Ah, yes. The bike." He stood and strutted to the outer door, flinging it wide and leaving it open to the elements. Hana snorted as Logan pulled her up from the table and pushed her arms into her sweatshirt.

"I feel a bit drunk," she announced and Logan shook his head.

"You don't say," he replied, sounding annoyed.

"I don't drink much," Hana whispered, spitting onto his hands as he did up the zipper.

"We can tell," he answered, hiding his smirk.

The fresh air hit Hana like a concrete block and doubled the effect of the alcohol. She weaved around the porch, struggling to keep her balance. The sound of a roller door moving on its runners disturbed the night and Hemi appeared, pushing a motorbike up the slope.

"Oh. I'm not riding that." Hana's legs buckled and she set down on the steps like a protestor.

Logan whistled with appreciation. He looked the machine over and nodded his head a few times. Hana couldn't understand his conversation with Hemi. She cocked her head in confusion, identifying a few mechanical terms and realising they spoke English. Logan squatted on his haunches and Hana giggled as his jeans pulled taut across his bum. She remembered Sheila's description of his buttocks as though from a different life and sniggered to herself. "My colleague said they were like two ripe peaches," she said to Maihi and the old woman stared at her.

"Logan and Hemi?"

"No!" Hana widened her eyes for emphasis and waved a hand towards Logan. "Logan's things."

"Oh, my life, kōtiro!" The old woman turned her face away to hide her grin. She raised her voice at her husband. "This girly needs to go home," she chuckled. "She wants fruit for dessert."

"We got fruit." Hemi stood up, the effects of the beer on his giant frame already worn off.

"Yeah, I don't think we got what she wants." Maihi waggled her eyebrows and Hemi shrugged without understanding.

Logan straddled the bike with his long legs, looking confident. He kick started the motor with a few powerful strokes. Hana jumped up and down on the spot, getting no nearer to arriving in the saddle behind him. Maihi burst into a series of undignified snorts. "Somebody help her," she cackled, waving her hands at her husband.

Hana felt the ground disappear as Hemi lifted her around the waist and plonked her behind Logan. "Youse weigh nothing," he exclaimed as Hana squeaked and gripped the back of Logan's jacket. She tried to wriggle off.

"I can't do this," she announced. "I can't stay married either."

"What?" Logan half turned in the saddle.

"Miriam said." Hana hiccoughed. She lowered her voice and adopted a terrible Māori accent. "Youse can't marry a biker and not get used to riding pillion."

"My mother doesn't speak like that." Logan sounded hurt and Maihi's laughter increased.

"I need a thingy," Hana demanded.

"A what?" Hemi and Maihi spoke at the same time.

"You know." Hana gesticulated to her temple and Logan groaned. "Helmet. She wants a helmet."

"My son's a cop!" Hana prodded Logan's spine and he heaved out a sigh.

"And don't we know it?"

"Who'll feed the cat if I die?" Hana demanded. She tried to lift her leg back over the saddle and kicked Logan's thigh.

"I'll feed the cat," Maihi promised, waving as Logan revved the engine to cover Hana's bumbling ineptitude. He gave a cursory wave and drove around the side of the house.

Hana screamed at the sight of the driveway. "It's steeper than ours!" she shrieked and Logan shook his head.

"Isn't."

"Is!" she wailed and he plunged down it, anyway. He navigated ruts and slips, bringing the bike to a sliding stop before a treacherous bend.

"Can you help me out here?" He turned his head and lowered the revs so Hana could hear him.

"To do what?" Her voice squeaked and she closed her eyes to the sight of the river glistening beneath the moonlight. The current whipped along at a surprising rate and Hana wondered about water dragons and taniwha.

"You're gripping my stomach. You'll bust my stitches."

Hana nodded and scrabbled around for something else to grip. She settled on a wrinkle in the front of his jeans. Logan grimaced. "Yeah. I don't want that damaged either, thanks."

"Stop complaining!" Hana snapped. She rummaged around and discovered putting her hands in his jeans pockets helped her stability.

Logan shook his head. "For goodness' sake, just don't turn me into a eunuch! And please stop screaming in my ear."

"I'm not!" She put as much indignation into her voice as she possessed. "It's the bike engine."

"Okay, Hana. We're travelling four kilometres. A rollercoaster ride is longer so stop panicking."

"They aren't illegal," Hana grumbled and hiccoughed again, ruining the effect.

On Hakarimata Road, Logan picked up speed. Hana saw her life flash before her eyes and realised she had little to show for forty-five years on earth. She pressed her cheek against Logan's back and dug hard into his jeans pockets. Then she contented herself with reciting under her breath, "Help, help, help." She resisted the bends, leaning opposite to Logan and feeling the wheels slew beneath them. He corrected it, wincing at the pain in his broken arm.

Stopping in front of their gate, Hana realised two things in quick succession. They didn't possess a remote to open it and she couldn't remember the number. A third issue sprang to mind, obliterating the other two. The driveway proved hazardous enough in a car and she suspected she might not survive on a bike. "I want to get off," she shouted in Logan's ear and he shook his head and clamped his fingers over hers to trap them in his pockets.

"No," he growled and pushed a code into the gate mechanism. Hana squealed again as the bike took off through the gap. Logan drove one-handed, clamping her fingers with the other. At the bend, he needed both hands and let go. By then, Hana kept her face pressed into his spine, feeling the vibrations of the track reverberating through her body as the trail bike ate up the driveway.

The three-minute ride felt endless and Hana's senses vibrated with the bike's roar, even after Logan killed the engine. He kicked down the stand and rolled it backwards, sliding off without sconning Hana in the forehead with his foot. "You can get off now," he said, smirking at her in the moonlight.

Hana groaned. "I'm welded here."

Logan supported her as she worked her jelly legs off the machine and wobbled towards the porch. He shook his head at her in disgust. "My mother's right," he said. "By the way."

Hana wrinkled her nose and stuck her tongue out at him.

"Aye!" Logan bent and stared at something on the side of the bike. "What the hell's that?"

"An indictable offence." Hana kicked gravel beneath the soles of her gumboot. "My foot's hot."

Logan ignored her. He huffed some more and then pushed the bike down the slope, using his key to let himself into the garage through the side door. Hana heard the roller door rise, followed by scraping and swearing. The garage lights lit up the slope. "Thanks for your help," she grumbled to herself and followed him, irritated by the gravel underfoot.

Logan parked the bike next to Bodie's car and squatted, prodding at something outside Hana's range of view. She pressed the switch to close the roller door and wrinkled her nose. "What's that rubbery smell?"

"I dunno." He stood and ran his right hand through his dark hair, leaving the fringe sticking up. Hana tripped over a paint can and a roll of discarded wallpaper with a volley of slurred swearwords.

She kicked off one boot, but the other stuck fast to her foot. "I can't get my welly off!" she complained, hopping around on one foot. "It's frozen on."

Logan rolled his eyes and left the bike clicking to itself as the engine cooled. "Sit down!" he told her, opening the internal door to the house and helping her onto the third step. "Give me your foot." Hana lay back against the stairs and sulked, waving her pink boot around in the air. "Keep it still!" Logan snapped and she closed her eyes. "And they're called gumboots here."

"Well, that's stupid," Hana grumbled. "Because Wellington is the capital of New Zealand. Wellington boots makes more sense."

"That's not the history."

"I'm tired," Hana whined as he hauled on her foot.

"No, you're a miserable drunk," Logan commented, adding an expletive as Hana's backside thudded down to the second step. "Bloody hell!" he exclaimed. "It is stuck."

"It's never gonna come off!" Hana wailed. "Angus will fire me for wearing one pink Barbie wellie for the rest of my life." The alcohol ran through her veins making everything worse.

"Oh, no!" Logan let go of Hana's foot and peered at his hands. Bright pink goo covered his palms and the bottom of his sleeve. He yanked her foot upward and Hana's butt thudded onto the first step accompanied by a wail of anger.

"Ow!"

"Hana!" Logan held his palms up. A distorted Barbie face stuck to his hand with a melted daisy up her left nostril. "Where did you rest your bloody foot?"

"I don't know." Hana sat up and peered at her foot. "Hemi just pointed and I did what he said."

Logan grimaced. "Yeah. I suspect he pointed at the footrest. Not the bloody exhaust pipe."

"Oh." Hana's bottom lip curled downward like a pouting toddler. "My Barbies are ruined," she wailed. "I loved them." She turned sideways on the stairs and buried her face in her sleeve.

Logan swore as the melted rubber coated his fingers and the boot disintegrated at his touch. Hana's sock became collateral damage as he discovered it welded to the inside. She went to sleep as he examined the bike and found pink goo dripping onto the garage floor. "Bloody marvellous!" he sighed.

He nudged his sleeping wife awake and half carried her up the stairs. She face planted on the bed and he stripped off her jeans and covered her. "You kill me, Hana Du Rose," he sighed, allowing himself a small smirk at her expense. "Never take up poker or drinking. You'd suck at both."

-19-

Hana awoke unscathed and Logan claimed the headache. "That's not fair," he grumbled. "You should have the hangover!"

"Don't be mean." Hana stretched and yawned.

Logan reached out for her and seized the bottom of her sweatshirt in his strong fingers. The veins on his arms stood out against his olive skin. "Get back here now and make it up to me." A tearing sound came from her waist and Hana whipped around, her open mouth betraying her shock. Logan hooted with laughter and took the chance to reel her in. "That's what you get for arriving home drunk and sleeping in your clothes." He rolled her over in the wide bed and relieved her of her knickers.

Hana spent another morning in the garden while Logan slept off his sore head. She unearthed more flowerbeds and tidied as far as the garage. As she pushed the mower up the slope, she eyed the damp lawn with disdain and prepared to get her trainers soaked and her feet wet.

The old mower refused to play the game as Hana huffed and puffed at pulling the starter cord. She only remembered to check the petrol chamber after kicking it four times and hurting her toe. Empty. "Blast!" she exclaimed and turned the machine around, pushing it back down the slope to the garage.

She hunted for the red petrol container and oil, wondering where Logan put it. She found it in a white storage cupboard in the corner. Yanking the door open without care, she wobbled the cupboard and car shampoo and other chemicals bounced onto the floor around her like an aerosol shower. A bottle of brake fluid jumped out last, hitting her square in the forehead.

Hana grabbed what she needed and turned to leave, catching her foot on the pole of a sun umbrella leaned up in the corner. It fell with a shuddering crash, sending paint cans and a packet of new brushes half way across the garage floor. Hana stamped in temper, tempted to leave the mess until later. She imagined facing the tidying exercise after fighting the lawnmower through the overgrown lawn and her shoulders sagged. "Fine!" she grumbled. "I'll do it now."

Hana battled with the folds of the huge umbrella, pulling the green cloth together so she could get both arms around it and heave it back into place. She wrestled it upright and let go, watching as it pitched away from her and back into the corner. The clang it created sounded loud enough to wake the dead and Hana frowned and took a step forward.

She peeled back the folds of cloth and peered behind it, discovering a blue tarpaulin fixed across a rectangular object. Poking further, she saw a tall, grey metal cupboard leaned against the wall. Hana tried the door but the sturdy lock held against her. "Weird," she muttered and examined it from a different angle. It rocked when she pushed it and the umbrella slid sideways, threatening to squash her under its weight. Inside, something heavy swayed and knocked the sides.

Hana stood back with her hands on her hips and temper flared in her green eyes. "What did you do, Logan Du Rose?" she growled. "You wouldn't do this without asking, would you?"

Without him there to defend himself, Hana pushed the matter to the back of her mind, dragging the petrol container and oil out to the reluctant lawn mower. But she didn't forget and the presence of the cupboard seemed to weigh her down. The mower chewed up the grass, spitting the shorn chunks into a messy line to one side. Some stripes looked almost even if she put her head on one side.

The scent of cut grass reminded Hana of summer and she longed for its return. This year she had someone to share it with. The cupboard popped into her memory and she grimaced. Its presence seeped into her happiness, filling her with dread. Perhaps she didn't make herself clear enough.

Pushing the mower back down the slope into the garage, Hana eyed the rimu benches and table. She stopped and ran her fingers over their wooden surface and imagined sitting outside on the roof garden with a glass of wine and a good book. Driven by an image of perfect bliss, she found the wheelbarrow and manhandled one of the benches into it, not sure how she'd drag it up to the roof. As she lifted the handles and pushed her cumbersome burden a few feet, a voice made her jump and she dropped the lot. The wheelbarrow tipped and the bench clattered out sideways. "Logan!" she shouted in temper. "Stop doing that!"

Logan leaned against the doorjamb. His casual stance suggested he'd watched for some time. His good hand rested in his jeans pocket. Solid muscle showed through his tee shirt and Hana turned away to avoid the distraction. She bent to retrieve the bench and clattered it back into the barrow with lots of grunting. "Don't be stupid." Logan sounded calm and Hana gritted her teeth.

"It's not stupid to want my furniture where it should go." She lifted the barrow and the muscles in her biceps let her down within a few metres.

"Is that right?" Logan appeared next to her and pushed himself between the handles of the barrow. "Don't lift that onto the roof, Hana. You'll kill yourself."

"You do it then." Hana pouted and Logan laughed and edged her backwards with his thighs. Looking down, she saw his cowboy boots and her heart sank. "You're going out."

"It's too heavy. Wait until I'm fit and I'll ask Hemi to help me."

Hana's image of sitting in the afternoon sunshine with a glass of wine melted before her eyes. "But I wanted to sit there today," she grumbled.

"Tough." He spun her around and pressed her into him. His belt buckle grazed her stomach and she put her arms against his chest to stabilise herself.

"Where are you going?" she demanded, narrowing her eyes.

Logan smirked. "Nowhere for you to worry about."

"But where?" Hana's panic grew. "You won't let me out but it's okay for you to ride around the country?"

"I'm not riding around the country." Logan bent and kissed her forehead. "I won't be long." He jangled the car keys and jerked his head towards the wheelbarrow. "Put that back and if I find it on the roof, I'll saw it up for firewood."

Hana's eyes widened. "You wouldn't!"

"Try me." Logan grinned and kissed her lips, leaving the taste of toothpaste.

Resentment crashed over Hana's head like an icy wave and she reacted. "You can't tell me what to do." She shoved at Logan's chest and he didn't budge. Fury lit the redheaded fire in her gut. She stepped backwards, forgetting the wheelbarrow until she fell over its handle and stumbled. Logan caught her forearm and held on while she floundered. The veins showed in his bicep like blue rivers seeking the estuaries of his heart.

"What about the guns?" she demanded, ire making her unreasonable. Hana tossed her hair and faced him down, determined to force him under her spell. She shook her hand free of his grip. "I hate guns."

Logan swallowed but never broke eye contact. "You hate them. I don't."

The fingers of fear snaked around Hana's heart, its fibrous

black hands making her feel sick and ill. She remembered Bodie in the hospital, his olive complexion replaced by a waxen sickness as the doctors fought to save his life. He looked dead, his features identical to Vik's as she'd identified his body on the mortuary slab years earlier. Hana swallowed. She thought often about the day Vik died, looking for moments of revelation which warned her about the forthcoming disaster. The day Vik lost his fight against an oncoming truck, she lay in bed sick. The day a gunman put a bullet through her son's stomach she sat at her desk. Another ordinary day. "Please don't go." She heard the begging in her tone and hated herself. "Please. I need to talk to you about the guns."

Logan's brow knitted and he lifted her chin with his fingers. "I won't be long," he promised, his voice soft. "Then we'll talk."

"But you won't get rid of them." Hana chewed her lower lip and her eyes flared in challenge.

Logan shook his head. "No, Hana. I want them here." He jerked his head towards the ominous gun cabinet. "I'll screw it to the wall once I can reach without busting my stitches."

"No!" Hana dug her heels in and protested, feeling the sense of futility grow. "I won't let you."

Logan cocked his head and narrowed his eyes. "Because it's your house, Hana? Do you really want to go there?" His tone held warning and Hana knew she should stop. She wiped her eyes on her sleeve and tried to pull herself together. Logan nudged her aside and grabbed the handles of the wheelbarrow. He pushed it into the corner and upended it, clattering the bench to the ground. Hana saw the muscles bunch in his back and sensed his anger as he righted it.

"Where are you going?" she demanded, her fists balled by her sides.

Logan sighed with exasperation. "Nowhere important, Hana!"

"Then don't go!" Her chin wobbled with the effort of fighting for composure. "Don't walk away and leave your guns here when you know I don't want them around me. You can't use Bo's car. He didn't give you permission."

She pressed the self-destruct button without really understanding why. It shouldn't have surprised her when Logan snapped, but she still jumped and took a step backward. "The guns belong to me, okay? They're legal and licenced and I know how to use them. I want them here and you need to accept that. I'm not arguing about it, Hana. This debate is over."

He yanked the driver's door of Bodie's car open and climbed inside, messing with the seat controls to admit his long legs. Hana stepped aside as he revved the engine and backed out of the garage. The car dropped onto the slope and Logan pushed it into gear and drove away. In his absence, Hana folded in on herself and sank to the floor.

Maihi rounded the corner and found her there, sitting amidst tears and snot. "What happened?" she demanded. "Did you fall?"

Hana told the old woman the truth, appreciative of the strong arms around her. They sat on the garage floor amidst the solidified pink rubber and Maihi laughed at Hana's blunder with the exhaust pipe. They shared confidences and Hana revealed more of her complicated past than she intended. Maihi held her and took on the role of mother figure. After a while, the old woman stretched her legs and leaned backwards. "I'm too old for this, kōtiro," she groaned. "My legs are going to sleep."

"I'm sorry." Hana jumped to her feet and helped haul her up. "Would you like a hot drink?"

They went upstairs to the kitchen and Hana made tea. The women sat around the table and debated Hana's situation. Maihi leaned forward and covered Hana's hand with hers. "It will all be fine, girly. He ain't going nowhere. He loves you."

"So why not tell me where he went?" Hana grizzled, wiping snot from her face with the back of her sleeve.

"We have to trust our men folk," Maihi advised, breathing wisdom into the situation. "Sometimes they keep secrets from us." She sighed and watched Hana fight through her thoughts. "You don't share everything with him, do you?"

Hana's complexion paled and she pursed her lips. "That's not fair."

"You told me." Maihi blinked as Hana stood and poured her tea down the sink. "Now you can tell him."

"No!" Hana threw the guard over her heart and saw the regret cross Maihi's face. "I'm not ready. I need to trust you to say nothing."

"Okay." Maihi's slow nod made Hana doubt and she panicked. "Please."

"I keep my promises." Maihi looked at her through the tops of her eyes and Hana felt the sting of her chastisement. She sought to take the subject onto less dangerous ground.

"Logan brought guns here," she complained. "He knows how I feel about them."

Maihi threw her head back and laughed. "We have guns at our place. So do most of the townspeople of Ngaruawahia!"

Hana sighed. "It feels underhand. How did they get here? I found them today and I know they weren't there before."

"Dunno, sweetie. Only he knows those answers. He'll tell you when he's ready." Maihi snickered and touched her nose with her index finger. "Learn to trust him, Hana."

"Do you mind Hemi shooting?" Hana asked, leaning her bum

against the pantry door. Maihi snorted.

"Girly, I'm a better shot than him! My Hemi can't hit a barn door at five paces. Man's blind as a bat!"

Hana ran shaking hands through the sides of her hair. "I asked him not to go out this afternoon and he did, anyway." She swallowed and felt the misery rise into her chest again.

"Learn to trust him," Maihi advised. "He's trying to take care of you the best way he knows how." She pushed her mug aside. "He told me about your fainting yesterday too. That's not right."

Hana waved off her concern. "It's the least of my problems right now."

"No, it's your priority." Maihi rose and dumped her mug in the sink. "Take care of that first." She kissed Hana's forehead and wrapped her arms around her. "I'm a phone call away if you need me. Or a twenty minute walk."

"I know. Thank you." Hana let Maihi's peppery scent wash over her. Kawakawa and rosemary filled her nostrils and gave her peace. "Thanks for checking up on me after last night. I'm not great with alcohol."

Maihi pinched her cheek. "Maybe cut it out for a while then," she suggested and Hana rolled her eyes.

"Yes mother."

The house fell silent after Maihi left and only the tick of the lounge clock comforted Hana. She sat in the sunshine on the roof garden with her legs curled beneath her and rang Bodie. "Why didn't you call me when you saw them?" he demanded and Hana sighed.

"The cops don't care and I'm not including you in that assessment." She watched a ladybird crawl across her stained jeans. "They think I'm paranoid because I sound it."

"We take it in turns to drive your car but nobody's followed it for days." Bodie's frustration leached through the phone and Hana felt a rush of gratitude.

"Maybe we could swap back?" she suggested. "They must believe I got rid of it. What do you think?"

"A few more days and then, maybe."

"Bo, thanks for everything." Hana paused, struggling with her words. "I appreciate that you believe me. I know you care."

"Course I do."

Hana sensed her son's embarrassment and let him go. She sat on the roof garden and watched the sun dip behind the mountain. The temperature dropped and the surrounding air grew still and frigid.

She padded through to the kitchen, surprised to find Logan cleaning the oven. The bench tops shone with streaks of spray cleaner and the table felt damp to the touch. His compulsive behaviour indicated a rise in his stress levels, so she opted to take a shower instead of rehashing their argument.

Logan sought Hana out in the bedroom as she moved around in her damp towel. He lay on the bed and studied her movements with his cool, grey eyes. She likened him to a deep lagoon. No matter how far she dived into the black water, she couldn't find the bedrock. She may have miles to chart or be about to break her neck on the bottom. "Are you still mad at me?" he asked into the silence and Hana shrugged.

She opened her arms to convey her confusion. "Logan, what do you want from me?"

He sighed and rolled onto his back. "I want you to trust me," he whispered.

"I don't know how." Hana sat on the bed and watched his shirt part to reveal a swathe of glorious olive stomach. A dusting of dark hair invited her to poke her fingers through the gap and she resisted. He turned on his side and reached for her, tugging her down onto the mattress.

"Let me show you," he breathed, kissing her. His tongue sought hers in a familiar dance and he prised the edges of the towel apart. Gentle fingers touched her skin and Hana melted. Savouring his intoxicating scents she drowned in the depths of him, finally understanding there could be no soft landing for her in this after all.

-20-

"Do you think it's compulsory to have sex in every room before you can stop calling yourself newlyweds?" Hana asked with a smirk.

"I don't know. I haven't been a newlywed before." Logan took a bite of his sandwich and eyed Hana sideways as she struggled to keep the blanket trapped between armpit and breasts. He balanced his plate on the coffee table. "Anyway, what's in a label?" His lips quirked upwards to reveal the dimple in his right cheek.

"Good answer." Hana watched the colours of the sunset dapple the sky with orange and pinks against the backdrop of cumulus clouds. The lounge window framed it like an artist's masterpiece. She sighed. "I hope our enthusiasm never wears off."

Logan's brow furrowed as the spectre of Hana's former husband invaded his thoughts and sullied any renewed sense of arousal. His sandwich turned to ash in his stomach and he leaned back against the sofa and stretched out his legs. "Shall I tell you where I went this afternoon?" Logan asked, smiling as mayonnaise dripped between Hana's breasts and produced a flurry of activity tantamount to a strip show.

Hana shook her head. "No. I don't need to know. As long as whatever you did won't hurt me."

Logan shook his head and his eyes turned a serious shade of slate grey. "I promise. I tried to help, not harm."

"Okay then." Hana shrugged and abandoned her food. When Logan lay down on the rug, she did too, snuggling into his armpit and pulling the blanket over both of them. "Will you teach me to shoot?" she asked, feeling her husband tense beneath her. "I'd like to beat Maihi. She's a crack shot."

He took a while to answer. "Okay. I'll get you something small to start with. Maybe a pistol. I thought you hated guns."

"I do." Her voice sounded grave. "I've seen what they do. But learning how to control a gun and understand how it works might give me a different perspective. I don't think I could ever use one on another person, but it might be good to demystify guns for me."

"Fair enough."

Hana ran a hand through Logan's hair, feeling its length slide over her fingers. "You're a mop head," she giggled. Her brow furrowed as she felt her own locks cascading over his shoulder. "And so am I." She inspected a tatty end and sighed. "I need to see my hairdresser. Do you think I could sneak into Hamilton and get my ends snipped?"

"No!" Irritation bled into Logan's tone, fading the easy intimacy between them. "It's not just that you might run into them in town. They're here in Ngaruawahia!"

"Okay, okay." Hana lost the battle and conceded. She ran a finger over the bruised yellow flesh below Logan's scar and he didn't flinch. He'd dispensed with the waterproof dressings and left it at the mercy of his flawed healing process. She dipped her head and kissed his ribs and Logan jerked and snorted. "You're gorgeous," she sighed.

"What, like an old saddle?" he replied without humour.

"No. Scars are sexy, which means you're sexier than most. Women naturally seek the hunter-gatherer gene and scars are an indication of valour. You're ahead of the game Du Rose."

"Are you done making me feel better?" Logan asked, his voice sleepy and Hana nodded. His lips formed a lazy smile. "Now I know where Jas gets his verbal diarrhoea from."

Hana snuggled into Logan's armpit and pondered the family likeness, her mind wandering to Tama and his infallible Du Rose genetics. Anger stirred in her heart. When he attacked Logan, he set himself against her. But they didn't need more enemies right then, not with the blonde man seeking her auburn hair across the Waikato.

Logan napped but Hana plotted, a crazy idea forming in her mind. Sunlight streamed across the floorboards, dappling the wood with light and shadows as the clouds scudded across the sky. It turned the brown to red and back again and Hana smiled. She slipped from beneath the blanket and covered Logan, showering and dressing before making a phone call. When she woke him with a coffee, his mood went from zero to ten and not in a good way.

"You did what? I said no!" Logan snapped. He groaned as he sat up and leaned his back against the sofa. Hana plonked his coffee on the table.

"It's not local," she said, tossing her hair. "And I'm going. You're welcome to come. I made you an appointment but I can apologise. Drink your coffee and hurry up. It'll take a while to get there."

"You're not going." Logan reached for his coffee and Hana

noticed he used his left hand. It wobbled but he forced the muscles to work inside the cast. "I hid the car keys."

Hana sniffed and gathered her hair into a baseball cap. "Yeah, but you're rubbish at hiding things." She pulled the keys from her pocket and dangled them in front of his nose. "Undies drawers are the first place burglars look."

Logan sighed and rubbed his eyes. "Ah, Hana."

"It's Te Kauwhata, Logan. They won't look there. It's too far out. The hairdressers is further up the road than the fabric warehouse."

"Fine!" Logan conceded. "But please, no more fabric and paint. Not today."

"Deal." Satisfied, Hana high-fived him and helped him up. Logan pushed his fingers through the belt loops of her jeans and hauled her against his nakedness.

"Or I could just keep you here." He pushed his face into her neck and teased the soft skin with his teeth.

Hana wriggled out of his grasp and fled, calling over her shoulder. "I'm leaving in fifteen minutes, mop head." She jingled the car key on its ring and laughed at Logan's groan of defeat.

Hana drove to the small rural town, her gaze stroking the sign for the paint shop as they passed. Logan narrowed his eyes at her and reinforced their agreement without words. Hana laughed. The hairdressing shop proved a flash affair for a tiny rural outpost. Upmarket fittings and trendy young women belied the image in Hana's head. Logan succumbed to the shampoo with great reluctance, used to dashing into his barbers and out again in under fifteen minutes. The women gave him extra attention and he cringed while Hana seethed.

A spark of jealousy began in her heart and she recognised a fire she would endure for as long as she remained the wife of Logan Du Rose. She saw him through their eyes, tall, handsome and oozing mana like a rangatira. He attracted attention through his stunning good looks but a glimpse of the strength beneath proved addictive. His lack of interest in the fussing women acted as an aphrodisiac and Hana seethed beneath the foil wraps and hair colour. They didn't leave him alone and every eye seemed focussed on him.

"I'm going to the coffee shop next door," Logan whispered, squatting next to her and lowering his voice. "This place is too girly for me. I don't wanna sit and flick through women's magazines while you finish."

"Okay." Hana tried to remove the frost from her tone. "Your hair looks more teacher and less bum."

"Thanks." Logan ran a hand through it with approval. "What are they doing to you? It looks like torture."

Hana snorted and rustled the magazine on her thighs. "I'm fine.

Just a few highlights to break up the red."

"Ah. Okay." Bemused, Logan stood and kissed her lips, avoiding the rustling foils dangling from her hair. "Text me when you're done and I'll come back." He patted the phone in his pocket and wrinkled his nose. "I should buy a new one. I need data for emailing and stuff."

"It's not urgent," Hana replied, panicking as the most interested of the women made a beeline for them. "You go. Enjoy your coffee."

Logan winked at her and made his escape as the hairdresser clacked across. She looked disappointed to see him leave. "Where did you find him?" she breathed in a conspiratorial tone. "And are there any more where he came from?"

Hana gave a dry smile in response, the expression not reaching her eyes. The woman inspected the foils and widened her eyes. "Not long now and you'll be a new woman."

Hana took another two hours. She emerged from the salon feeling nervous and steeled herself before walking into the coffee shop. She feared Logan's reaction, knowing how much he adored her red hair. He gaped as she walked towards him and his jaw hung as he searched for suitable words. Hana raised a hand to prevent his struggle. "I know what you're going to say." She sank into the chair next to him. "But it's a solution for now."

Logan shrugged. "It's your hair, babe." He studied her through narrowed eyes. "I like it. It's classy. It looks like lots of different colours."

Hana sighed with relief and reached for his fingers. The contact gave her courage. "She mixed lots of browns and caramels and reds. The regrowth will look hideous, but I'm hoping all this is over by then. She added blonde streaks and lighter colours to create an overall effect. I don't look like a redhead, which is the most important factor."

Logan squeezed her fingers and leaned closer. "You're still Hana Du Rose to me," he whispered and his lips looked soft and beckoning.

"Thanks." Hana gave him a beautiful smile and sniffed the air. "I'll grab a herbal tea and we can go home."

"Okay." Logan walked to the counter and returned with a take away cup.

Hana took it in confusion. "Sorry, are you sick of sitting here? Do you want to leave straight away?"

"Yes." Logan waited as she took a sip and stood. Her mouth burned on the heated liquid and she winced. "I didn't spend the whole time here. I found a shop in a back street and bought what we talked about. I need a particular sort of ammo for it and they didn't have it." He followed Hana into the street. "How would you feel about stopping by my parents' place? I know there's some there. You could have a practice."

Hana gaped in surprise. The colour drained from her cheeks at the thought of facing Logan's family, but the words stuck in her throat. She swallowed and gave a small nod but the effort cost her. "Okay," she agreed.

"Cool." Logan put out his hand for the keys and Hana shook her head.

"No, you're not insured to drive Bo's car." She bit back the rebuke about his jaunt the previous day.

"I have my own insurance," Logan protested and Hana refused.

"And a broken arm."

She cut across country at Logan's direction and in under an hour they reached the hotel. Bodie's car hated the rutted driveway and Hana's lower lip stung from biting it. Half way along, they bounced onto a proper road surface and the awful creaks and groans stopped. "They're creating a decent driveway?" Hana remarked and Logan gave an upwards jerk of his head. "Thank goodness," she breathed under her breath.

"Park in front of the steps," Logan said as Hana swung the car through the gates. A fresh coating of gravel kicked up dust.

"It's fine. I'll use the car park." Hana reversed into a space, surprised to see how many cars already sojourned there. "There are lots of guests for a week day," she remarked.

"Yep." Logan pushed the passenger door open. "The power of advertising."

The receptionist saw Logan appear through the main doors and reached for a radio handset. Miriam ran down the long corridor from the kitchen to greet him only seconds later. She behaved as though nothing happened and wrapped Hana in a firm embrace. "You look different!" she commented. "I didn't recognise you."

Hana gave a wry smile and wondered if her mother-in-law fancied her already dumped and history. "Bad luck," she muttered under her breath. Logan's ears twitched and she pursed her lips, realising he heard her biting retort. She shuddered at the memory of her last visit and watched Miriam for some acknowledgement of the events of that day. Nothing. Hana seemed trapped in a time warp where only she remembered Tama attacking Logan and the awful unmasking of the Du Roses' true face.

Miriam turned her back on Hana, freezing her out of a whispered conversation with Logan. "How are you?" she asked. "I couldn't come."

Logan shook his head and wrapped his arm around her shoulder. "It's okay Ma," he responded. "It's always okay." He released her and turned to walk up the main corridor. Hana trailed behind, sensing the receptionist's gaze locked on their progress.

"How long are you here for?" Miriam asked and Hana experienced a flash of shame as she heard the hope in her voice. Logan turned on the spot.

"Just this afternoon. I need to collect some stuff. Where's Dad?"

Hana noticed a tiny speck of hurt in Miriam's expression. She glanced up at Logan and knew he didn't see. His mother seemed to crumble inward and a memory of Indra rose unbidden into Hana's mind. They buried more than two decades of hurt and rejection in a single visit and Hana knew perspective made that possible. She searched for something in her heart which might allow her to connect with Logan's mother and found only the olive branch of peace.

"I might see Dad first." Logan backed away on the parquet floor and hesitated at the sight of Hana. "Would you mind?" he asked, glancing sideways at Miriam. "I won't be long."

Hana swallowed and ground her teeth. Dumped in the first five minutes. She wanted to tell him this wasn't the agreement, this wasn't the deal. But she didn't. She gave a wooden smile and nodded, releasing Logan to abandon her in the lion's den.

"Come." Miriam crooked a finger at Hana and bid her follow. She did as ordered, her footsteps growing heavier as they reached the fire door leading into the kitchen.

Hana sat at the table and watched Miriam dodge the kitchen staff as she made a pot of strong tea. Her hands wrung beneath the cover of the table and her heart rate hiked. The idea of conflict repelled her and she closed her eyes and wished herself elsewhere. The thud of the teapot on the wide table startled her.

"I know you think I'm a bad mother." Miriam's voice sounded huffy and Hana cringed. "I haven't left the property for twenty-seven years and it's too late to start."

Hana swallowed and her answer emerged with more bile than intended. "I won't judge you for your choices and I'd like the favour returned."

Miriam halted, surprise in her face. Her lips turned upwards and she nodded. "Fair enough."

Hana ate home baked cookies with chocolate chips that melted in her mouth. She gobbled up four before nausea stopped her half way through the fifth. The sound of munching inside her head acted as a brake on conversation and without it, the atmosphere filled with tension.

"Ooh, cookies!" An olive hand dipped into the biscuit tin and snatched up two. Crumbs littered the table. Hana held her breath as Michael stared down at her. "Guessing the little bro came to check on his kingdom." His barbed tone put her on red alert. Seeing her apprehension and the way her eyes strayed towards the exit, Michael moderated his attitude with the ease of a performer. He squeezed Miriam's shoulder. "Did you make these, Ma?"

She nodded and her grey eyes softened with pleasure. "Yes, tāne."

"Awesome. I love yours best." He settled into a chair next to Hana, his thigh brushing hers. She tensed every muscle in her body to make herself smaller and edged away from him. Michael leaned closer anyway. "I liked you better as a redhead," he whispered and Hana held her breath.

"My son is on leave from his important job as a doctor," Miriam said and Michael bit his bottom lip. His sideways glance at Hana conveyed victory, as though she'd rubbished Logan's teaching role without saying so. His wink confirmed her theory.

Blood pounded in Hana's ears and the familiar headache snaked up the back of her neck to grip the space above her ears. She released the held breath and focussed on controlling the episode, her sweaty palms leaving a dark patch on her thighs. Her inner coach began its mantra, reminding her to breathe, to calm down and focus. The sugary concoction in her stomach shifted from pleasure inducing to sick making.

Hana focussed on the sunshine outside and watched it create prisms through the long sash windows. A woman sliced carrots by the sink and the rhythmic chopping aligned with her heartbeat. Michael spoke to her, leaning across so she tasted the chocolate on his breath. The fresh air of the car park beckoned to her, offering freedom and space to breathe. Hana stood in a jerky movement and the chair skittered away across the tiles. Everyone stopped their activity to stare at her and Miriam's lips moved. Hana cocked her head, hearing only a hum in her ears. The world spun and she closed her eyes against the sickening rush of the roundabout it created. Miriam's face came and went like a ghoulish fairground attraction. Hana saw the edge of the table rise up to meet her and felt her knees buckle.

She woke up on the floor, one bent arm under her forehead and the other trapped behind her back. The pounding in her head dulled to a faint throb. Michael's voice sounded calm and unconcerned. "Heart rate is low and her blood pressure sucks."

"Logan's coming." Miriam's voice shook. "What will you tell him?"

"The truth, Ma. She fainted."

"I'm glad you caught her, tāne. Logan will be grateful."

Michael snorted. "I doubt that."

Hana groaned and dragged her forehead along her arm. The wetness on her cheek embarrassed her and she wiped her lips against her sleeve. She sniffed, trying not to cry and holding out for the promise of Logan's strong and capable arms to dissolve into.

Freeing the arm trapped beneath her, Hana rolled onto her back. The overhead chandelier of the ballroom glittered in her vision and she closed her eyes against threatening nausea. A strong hand slipped behind her neck and pressed a cushion under her head. She concentrated on her breathing; bringing it under control and hearing the rasping sounds disappear.

Running footsteps and the slamming of a door heralded her husband's arrival. "What happened?" he demanded and Hana heard only silence. She opened her eyes and found his face next to hers.

"Logan," she whispered. "Logan."

"Okay." He gathered her into his arms and Hana pressed her face against his chest. "It's okay." He rocked her like a child and she inhaled his scent.

Miriam spoke. "I think it's a sugar rush, Logan. She ate cookies and passed out."

Hana heard Michael snort. "I doubt she's diabetic, Ma."

"She's not." Logan spat his reply. "Thanks for taking care of her." He kissed the top of Hana's head. "What made her come in here?"

"Michael carried her." Miriam's voice wavered and Hana felt Logan tense against her. His muscles bunched in anticipation of something.

"You'd rather I laid her on the kitchen table?" Michael's sarcastic tone induced a sharp inhale from Logan. Hana felt her body leave the floor, tipping and rocking as Logan hoisted her into his arms.

"Don't be a fool!" Alfred's voice joined the melee. "You've a broken arm and stomach wounds. Let Michael take her upstairs."

"No!" Logan hissed through his teeth and Hana struggled to get down.

"I can walk," she protested, her voice cracked and her head spinning. "I'm fine." She looked at Logan's face and searched for an answer to the question in her eyes. Did he have the bullets? Could they go home?

To her disgust, Logan carried her upstairs. "Put me down," she grumbled. "I can walk."

Logan lifted his leg and balanced her against his thigh as he pressed the key code for his bedroom. Hana wriggled and he gave her a withering look. He placed her on the bed with care and removed her boots. "I'm sorry," he said, his expression cowed as he sat on the edge of the mattress and rubbed her feet in his strong fingers. "I just left you and I shouldn't."

"It's fine." Hana lay back against the pillows and closed her eyes. "It's a sugar rush, like your mother said. I pigged on biscuits so it served me right."

"What about the other day? And the time before that?" Logan

massaged her toes and Hana opened one eye to look sideways at him.

"What about it? Each incident happened in moments of stress. Sitting between Miriam and Michael counts as stressful."

Logan answered a knock at the door and Michael stepped over the threshold carrying a medical bag. Hana watched her husband's body tense. "I'll check her out while I'm here." Michael dangled the bag from his fingers and Logan gave a cursory nod of reluctant approval. "I took your blood pressure before. It's low. Did you know that?"

Hana shrugged. "No. But low is good, isn't it?"

"Not when it makes you faint." Michael sat on the side of the bed while Logan jammed his fists into his jeans pockets and hovered nearby. "Can I take your pulse, please?" Michael held his hand out and Hana placed her wrist into it, looking away while he measured her heart rate using his expensive watch. Next he shone a bright light into her eyes and Hana held her breath. The temperature gauge he shoved in her ear recorded a normal reading. "It's settling," he concluded. "Better than before."

Another knock at the door distracted Logan and Hana heard Miriam's voice. "What about some hot, sweet tea?" she asked.

"No, not sweet," Michael interjected. "Just in case sugar caused it."

Hana heard Miriam's voice lower. "Alfie said you didn't finish your discussion. He wants to talk to you in the stables."

"Not now!" Logan's irritation bridled and Hana tensed. Michael raised his eyebrows and looked over his shoulder, his interest piqued.

"I'm fine," Hana called, not wanting him to leave but hating the conflict. "I'll lie here for a while and then you'll need to drive home."

Logan's jaw worked and he ground his teeth. He jerked his head towards Miriam. "Not now," he asserted and closed the door against her protests.

"Nice." Michael's sly grin threatened to set Logan off and Hana closed her eyes against the sibling rivalry. She recognised their pleasantries at the wedding as fake. Hatred bubbled beneath the surface, borne of something deeper than she could uncover. Michael stood and spoke to Logan. "Your wife needs to see her doctor and let him run some tests."

"What sort of tests?" Hana lifted her head off the pillow and looked at Logan.

"Pregnancy tests for a start," Michael replied and Hana laughed.

"Yeah, okay."

"I'm serious." Michael raised an eyebrow and narrowed his eyes into a serious expression. "It's that or a heart problem."

Logan's unreadable expression sent Hana into a panic. "It's not that. It isn't. I would know. I'm not pregnant and my heart is fine. I pigged on sugar." Hana spun her body sideways and rested her feet on the rug. "Let's go home."

Michael shrugged his shoulders. "Stay here a while longer, at least until your colour returns. I'll check on you later."

"I'm not pregnant," Hana asserted, her cheeks flaring in response. "And my heart is fine."

Michael selected a box from his medical bag and closed the lid, locking the clasp with practiced fingers. He sat the box on her stomach. "It only takes once," he said with a lascivious wink. "I should know."

"Screw you, Michael!" Logan lurched for him and Hana gasped in shock. Her husband stopped long enough for his brother to escape, before slamming his way through the ranch slider onto the balcony.

Hana lay her head against the pillows and closed her eyes. Her body screamed with exhaustion and the tension in the house bore down on her like a lead weight. "Every time," she murmured.

"What?" Logan slid the door closed and ran a shaking hand through his hair. "Every time what?"

Hana exhaled. "Every time I come here there's drama."

"Sorry." He sank onto the bed and rested his elbows on his knees. His fingers tapped a beat on the tatty cast. "I need to get this thing off. My arm feels good now."

"It can't be." Hana watched the set of his shoulders and shook her head. "It's too soon." She fingered the pregnancy test on her stomach and it slipped onto the mattress. "Should I do this test, do you think?"

Logan collapsed like a puppet with its strings cut. "No!" His eyes widened in horror. "Don't!"

Hana watched his internal agonies with surprise, his vehemence seeming to condemn her. "It can't be positive. I'm too old and my periods aren't regular anymore. I told you that before we married."

Logan swore and Hana poked him with her toe. "Please don't Hana."

"Why?"

He rubbed his eyes with the back of his good hand and shook his head. "I don't want you to."

"This is ridiculous!" Hana seized the box and Logan made a grab for it. They tussled and she won. "Stop!" His behaviour confused her and anger pushed the headache and nausea away. She fuelled it further, seeking wellness. "It's my body. I'll do what's best for me." Avoiding further confrontation, she took herself into the ensuite bathroom and slammed the door, locking it behind her.

"Hana!" Logan rattled the handle and experience told her it wouldn't hold him.

She threatened him instead. "Go away, Logan. Your behaviour

sucks and I don't have the energy for it. Leave me alone."

"But Hana!"

"No!" She leaned against the door. "I'm right behind this door. If you do anything stupid, you'll hurt me." She sensed his defeat and heard his boots against the floorboards. The click of the bedroom door took the standoff further than she wanted and isolation crowded around her.

"Great!" Hana twisted the box in her fingers and shook her head. "It's a virus," she asserted, believing her own conclusion. In the back of her mind, a distant memory tapped away at her resolve. The awful conversation with Vik replayed on a loop. One night of crazy turned into Bodie and a hastily created union to limit the damage. "It's not that," Hana repeated, letting herself out of the bathroom.

Hana understood the weight of emotion that drove a two year old to kick and scream with abandon. A sense of rejection returned full force, leaving her tired and empty. The sound of clattering drew her to the balcony and Hana watched a horse trot from the stable yard. The figure astride it sat with easy confidence against the motion of the beast and Hana recognised Logan's jacket. He rode the white horse as if he belonged to her physiology and they covered the ground beneath them at speed. Not stopping to open the paddock gates, he cleared them without breaking their and disappeared into the bush.

Hana pressed her face against the cool glass and closed her eyes. "Screw you, Logan Du Rose," she breathed. The window fogged and she reiterated her sentiment with her index finger. Ashamed of herself, she wiped it off and turned away. Snatching up the cardboard box, she fumbled with the cellophane. "It's time I became master of my own destiny," she declared with more confidence than she felt.

Ten minutes later, Hana sat on the closed lid of the toilet. Her thumb smarted from battling the plastic wrap and gaining entry into the stiff cardboard. A paper cut bled onto her tongue as she sucked her finger to take away the sting. The instructions fluttered in her other hand and she stared at them. "I must be stupid," she sighed. "What line goes where?"

Hana pulled out her phone and ran an internet search. Her eyes bugged at some of the ludicrous results and she scrolled through, narrowing her questions to avoid the weirdos. "I can't be pregnant," she muttered. "I'm a grandmother."

Missed periods alerted her to Bodie's existence. Late on the uptake, Hana blamed the stress of university for a blissful four months before realisation dawned. She rubbed a hand across her face and fought the sense of foreboding. They hadn't planned Izzie either. "Not again," she breathed. "This can't happen. Nasty Michael. Why did he put the thought in my head?"

Reading the instructions one more time, Hana sorted herself out and performed the test. She sat on the closed toilet lid and waited. The ridiculousness of the situation sent a giggle bubbling into her chest. Damn Logan for running out on her just when she needed him most.

The first line appeared to confirm she did the test right. In a couple of minutes, she'd throw the box in the rubbish bin and continue life as normal. Whatever a normal life looked like. But Hana didn't need to wait.

The blue line appeared alongside its mate, growing darker as the moments passed. Hana waited anyway, giving it a chance to go away again. Then she waited just because she couldn't trust her legs to carry her anywhere. Her butt grew uncomfortable on the toilet lid and she wriggled to increase the blood flow to her legs. The pee dried on the stick and the lines looked darker than ever as a sense of inevitability engulfed her. She'd hopped into bed with Logan Du Rose like a filly on heat and shouldn't be surprised at the outcome. "But I'm a granny," she whispered, justifying her understandable lack of contraception. "It's not possible."

Four weeks of marriage streamed behind her like a battered sail. Four weeks of stress and trauma. The thought of being only a little bit pregnant made no difference to the effect it would have on her relationship. A knock on the bedroom door sent Hana scrambling to hide the test. She shoved it into a drawer in the vanity unit and stood on wobbly legs.

Dragging the bathroom door open, she screamed as she ran into Michael. "What are you doing?" she gasped, clutching her chest. "How did you get in?"

He shrugged his broad shoulders and towered above her. "Sorry, you didn't answer. I know Logan's code because I used to steal his lollies. I needed to check you weren't unconscious." He looked past her into the bathroom. "When patients collapse in hospital, it's always in the bathroom with their body wedged between the toilet and the wall."

"Why?" Hana took a step back and ran a hand through her messy hair. The scent of the hairdressing salon wafted outwards.

"It's a natural place to hide. Often collapse is preceded by a feeling of sickness." He stopped and looked down at his socks.

Hana edged past him and sat on the bed. She wrung her fingers before her as a stress reaction. Michael followed her with his eyes. "You did it then?"

"We got into a fight," she said with a sigh, rubbing her eyes. Exhaustion swallowed her whole and she lifted her legs onto the mattress.

"Yeah, I saw your idiot husband ride off." Michael sank into an armchair near the window and observed her like a butterfly catcher watching his latest victim struggle with the pin through its chest. He shared the best of Logan's characteristics and yet something else lurked beneath his handsomeness like a dangerous undertow. "Did he tell you I slept with Caroline?"

The question caught Hana off guard and she floundered. "No," she replied. "That's disgusting."

Michael jerked a dark eyebrow upward. "She's not all bad. Logan's so closed and she couldn't access that part of him she really wanted. She craved love and he didn't offer it."

"But you did?" Hana's face creased into a sneer.

Michael shook his head and a grin settled over his features. "I never made any promises. I loved the sex but not the consequences."

Hana swallowed and bit her tongue to halt the need to question him. She wanted to know, yet suspected it might harm her. Michael jerked his head towards the bathroom. "Logan always wanted kids."

Hana let out a snort of derision despite herself. "Oh, right. That's why he ran away from the idea. I mistook it for horror."

"You're wrong." Michael sighed. "Very wrong. Not wanting something and giving up on it are two very different things."

Hana felt pressure behind her eyes and dared the tears not to come, gritting her teeth and squeezing every muscle in her body until she resembled a statue. Michael rose and approached the bed. For a horrid moment, Hana imagined he might fumble an inappropriate embrace but instead, he reached for her wrist. "Stop tensing," he said, his voice gentle. "You'll make it worse." He pressed his fingers over her pulse and studied his wristwatch. Hana lasted half a minute before pulling her hand away.

"Please can you lend me money for a taxi?" she asked.

"No." Michael dropped his hands to his sides. "Give him a chance." He left the bedroom, closing the door behind him with a click.

-21-

Hana sat in the kitchen and peeled potatoes for Miriam. The mindless action stopped her fretting and the rhythm calmed her nerves. She practiced peeling the whole thing in one brown coil, failing at every attempt. Each new potato represented a fresh start. Hana dropped her latest victim into the pail with a thud. Miriam glanced across at her from her own pile. "You done?" she demanded, gratified by Hana's nod.

Logan's entry into the kitchen set Hana's heart racing again. Rejection flared her anger and she tensed, forcing a disinterested look on her face. Miriam turned to face him, taking in the dishevelled appearance and the black dust on his fingers. "You saw them?" she asked.

"Yeah, I saw them." Logan slumped into a chair next to Hana, his eyebrow rising at the way she scooted her chair aside.

"I'll fetch more potatoes." Hana spoke to Miriam and stood, ignoring Logan. He put a hand out and grabbed hers, folding her fingers into his palm with an iron grip. Left with no other choice, Hana sat again.

"Did you sort it?" Miriam persisted. Her face expression softened. "Youse got gun grease on your cast." She jerked her head towards the plaster encasing Logan's left arm and he scowled.

"Jack can saw the bloody thing off," he said, examining a space where it had crumbled near the edge. "A hacksaw should do it."

"Don't be a fool," Miriam snorted and wrinkled her nose. Logan pouted like a child and Hana hid her smirk behind a cough. She shook her fingers, but he didn't let go.

The leaden atmosphere became unbearable and Hana panicked. The gun residue on Logan's fingers transferred to hers and the association terrified her. He'd sorted the men with guns and she didn't wish to know how. When Miriam rose to add her potatoes to the mountain on the draining board, Hana gave an almighty yank of her hand and kicked Logan in the shin. "Get off me!" she hissed.

Surprise made him sloppy and he released her, swearing as Hana bolted for the door. Longer legged and faster, Logan knew the house and caught her in seconds. He pulled her into the empty guest lounge and closed the door behind him. Resting his backside against the scarred wood, he folded his arms and observed Hana as she regrouped and considered her options. "It's locked," he said, quirking an eyebrow as her gaze slid towards the outer door. "So you need to listen to my apology."

"Apology?" Rage back lit Hana's green eyes. "You think?"

Logan cocked his head. "Yeah. I think I need to apologise and I think you need to listen. So, that's an affirmative on both."

Hana eyed the French doors with growing interest. She noticed an old key dangling from a hook on the wall and her escape presented itself. Distracted, she wasted her opportunity as Logan's arms fixed around her. "I'm sorry. Let's do the test. I needed time to get used to the idea that's all."

"The idea I might be expecting your baby?" Hana replied, her tone laced with bitterness.

"No!" Logan countered. "Time to get used to the idea you might not be. I thought we'd never have kids. I wanted space to imagine what it could be like. I'm okay now. I can face it."

"You can face it?" She jabbed him in the chest. "I'm thrilled for you. Now let me out of this room before I scream the place down."

"Let's do the test." Logan's eyes burned into her soul.

"I can't," she replied, a sharp edge to her tone. She extracted herself from his grip and at the same time, noticed the raw skin on his knuckles. "What did you do?" She snatched at his hand and turned it over. "You're bleeding."

"It's nothing." Logan wiped his hand on his shirt and placed his palm against the door in front of her face. His arm kept it closed against Hana's attempts to pull on the handle. "Why can't you do the test? I can get another if it's broken."

"It's not broken." Hana sighed and rested her body against the wall. The jelly legs returned and she closed her eyes. "I used it."

"Without me?" Shame sent a pink flush up the sides of Logan's neck and his lips parted in dismay. "You didn't wait?"

Hana shook her head, hearing her hair swish against the thick flock wallpaper. "You forfeit that right when you walked out."

"I didn't walk out! I said I needed time." Logan's tone rumbled with a manic kind of danger and Hana tensed and opened her eyes.

"I'd love some time too," she snarled. "It's my body but when do

I get time to deal with it all? When, Logan?"

"It's positive?" The grin spread across his face and Hana wanted to slap him until he understood her powerlessness. He saw children and the possibility of an heir to his peculiar whakapapa. She saw risky months ahead in her ageing body and the certainty of disappointment. She turned away from his question. Her children and everyone else would know she'd spent the last month romping around the bedroom with her virile husband. Flashing her stretch marks and conceiving a baby. Hana leaned forward and rested her palms on her knees.

"I can't do it," she groaned.

"You can't have the baby?" Logan panicked and seized her shoulders. "You have to."

Hana slapped his hand away. The effort of explaining seemed to take energy she didn't have and she shook her head. A flicker of relief congratulated her that Logan wouldn't expect her to terminate the pregnancy. Like Izzie, she couldn't, anyway.

A single tear rolled down her cheek and she tried to suppress the sob which followed. Logan stroked her hair as she bent over the carpet and took deep breaths. "Do you feel sick?" he asked, his tone exuding sympathy and fear.

"Not in the way you think," Hana sniffed. She wiped her nose with the back of her hand. "Only in my heart. I'm too old, Logan. I can't carry this baby. It'll end in disaster." A tear plopped onto her jeans, creating a darker patch in the fabric. The liquid spread and Hana watched as another joined it.

"Oh, Hana!" Heartbreak poured from Logan's soul as he comforted her. "I know nothing about having babies or child rearing, but people in worse shape than you manage okay. It is daunting, but let's not write this little Du Rose off yet. We've got good genes."

Hana blew out through pursed lips and afforded herself a smirk. Logan's ego covered her in a sheen of confidence and he pulled her upright. When he gathered her into his chest, she didn't resist. His words hit the pit of her stomach like stones. "I can't believe I'll be a dad," he breathed. "My parents will be stoked."

"No!" Hana pulled away. "You can't tell anyone. Are you not listening to me?" Pressure built up behind her eyes and the buzz began in her forehead again. She scrabbled for a handful of Logan's shirt to prevent the faintness taking hold. His fingers around her wrist felt firm and safe. "You tell no one for another few months. Promise?"

Logan nodded with knitted brows and straight-lipped expression. "Okay. If that's what you want."

"It's what I need!" Hana swallowed and fixed him in a dead stare. "I mean it. Nobody. If the worst happens, I don't want to explain to everyone why I'm sad or ill. Do you understand?" Logan nodded again, a childish hope in his wide grey eyes.

"Okay. I promise."

Hana relaxed and let go of his shirt. Exhaustion nipped at her legs like an irritating puppy. Miriam's voice called along the corridor. "Hana! Want some kai?"

Logan opened the door and Hana slipped through the gap. "Just tea please," she said, hearing the tremble in her voice. Miriam gave a cursory nod and noticed Logan emerge behind his wife. Her eyebrow rose in a complete misinterpretation of their reason for hiding behind a closed door. She huffed and shook her head. "Like father, like son," she muttered.

They sat in the kitchen and Hana pushed weak tea down her throat, praying the nausea wouldn't reoccur. Michael's presence turned her stomach further, his admission increasing her sympathy for Logan. "How are you now?" he asked, staring at her with a doctor's eye.

"Better," she lied and averted her gaze.

Michael turned his attention to Logan, noticing his oozing knuckles. His lips turned up in a grin. "Who'd you slap?" he demanded.

Logan stiffened and replied in Māori. Michael shook his head. "English, dickhead. You know I hate that language."

Miriam turned and eyeballed Logan. "Don't start," she warned.

"Who did you hit?" Michael repeated his question and Hana saw the lie form on her husband's lips.

"Nobody you know," he growled and the cuts leaked as he balled his fists. "But you can be next."

Michael crinkled his regal nose. "Whatever dude. You should cover those grazes though. I can write you a private prescription for some of the stuff you snort. Cost you seventy bucks."

"Shut up." Hana rose to Logan's defence. She imagined Logan's pain at discovering Michael's indiscretion with Caroline and hurt for him. Nobody deserved that.

Michael shrugged. "You know the truth now then? Factor 8 deficiency is a bitch."

Miriam dropped a saucepan into the sink and the kitchen girls scattered. They fled the room on the pretext of fabricated chores. "All of you shut up!" Her rigid body seemed to rock in place and crabbed hands gripped the side of the Belfast sink. "Logan's fine. He can't have it so stop saying it." Wild grey eyes roved to Michael's face and Hana swallowed at Miriam's unhinged expression.

"Calm down Mother." Michael's retort sent Miriam into orbit and she attacked him with outstretched, clawing fingers.

"Shut up!" she screamed. "Shut up!"

Hana inhaled and pressed her back against the chair. She scooted, so it touched the cupboard behind her and hunched her body up small.

Logan blocked Miriam's attack and his mother wrenched herself free, hauling the heavy fire door open with gargantuan strength. He heaved out a breath as she left and rubbed the space on his stomach where their bodies collided. "Happy now?" He rounded on Michael and his brother laughed.

"It's always about Barry," he sneered. "I'm sick of it. She did nothing for us as kids. Don't you remember, Logan? Nobody came to parents' evenings, nobody saw us graduate. Not her, that's for sure."

"She can't help it. If you only came here to cause trouble, bugger off." Logan held his hand out to Hana and she saw his distraction. His eyes looked bright and happy like shiny grey pebbles. Hope rolled off him in waves at the thought of a child. She accepted his hand and left the kitchen.

"Your mother never acknowledged your illness?" she said on the main stairs.

Logan shrugged. "Would you?"

"I don't understand." Hana paused with one hand in Logan's and the other clasping the ornate bannister rail.

"It's genetic. Mum's a carrier and she passed it to Barry and me. It's largely a male disease but the females pass it on."

Hana closed her eyes. "She blames herself for your brother's death?"

"Yep." Logan's brows knitted and he glanced at her stomach. He swallowed but spared her the obvious deduction. Any female child ran the risk of carrying the gene for haemophilia. Hana's fingers released the bannister and strayed to cover her abdomen, defending a child she only just discovered existed. Maternal instinct kicked in despite her desire to remain unattached and protect herself from pain. Logan watched the movement of her hand and pursed his lips.

He put sheets on his childhood bed, forcing Hana to wait in the chair by the window until he finished. Then he lay on the bed next to her and stroked her hair. "It will be okay," he promised, his tone soft as Hana drifted into sleep.

She woke hearing Logan speaking into his mobile phone. He'd replaced his muscular chest with a pillow and Hana snuffled against the squishy surface. "Can you feed the cat?" she heard him say. "Your mother's door keys are in the hall drawer. Drop them in to the lady next door and she'll sort out the rest; I already spoke to her." His voice sounded soft and lyrical. "Yeah, we decided to stay here for a while." He noticed Hana watching him and blew her a kiss. "Oh, don't go next door in uniform. It won't go down well." When he finished the call, Logan sat on the bed next to her. "Bodie said he'll take Jas to ours. That means we'll arrive home to wilted flowers and odd bits of pebble on our pillows."

Hana pushed herself to a sitting position and leaned back against the headboard. "I feel okay. Let's just go home."

"No." Logan stroked her hair back from her forehead. "You don't look well and a few days away from the stress of hiding ourselves will be good for you."

Hana pouted. "I want to go home. Here is much more stressful."

"It won't be." Logan stood and answered a knock on the bedroom door. "Hi, Ma," he said, standing back.

"Does your hoa wahine want some kai?" Miriam poked her head through the door and Hana gave her a pathetic wave.

"Sure. I'll come down and fetch something." Logan closed the door behind him, leaving Hana alone. She climbed out of bed and used the bathroom.

Hana assumed the knock on the door heralded Logan bearing a plate of food. She guessed he'd leave the wine downstairs in view of her pregnancy news. "You were quick," she commented, opening the door. Michael's sanctimonious grin met her.

"Nobody's said that to me before."

"Ugh!" Hana let the door go and Michael dodged into the room before it closed.

Five minutes later, Logan stiffened as he returned with food for her. Michael clapped him on the shoulder as he left. "Don't worry, bro'. Just checking your chick's pulse and stuff."

Logan glared at his retreating back. "Yeah, it's the 'and stuff' that bothers me."

Hana sighed at the hiking tension. Logan's stiff shoulders induced an unwelcome sense of foreboding. "He did check my pulse. And my blood pressure. He knows better than to try anything with me."

"Ma sent casserole." Logan held the plate out to her and Hana spent the next ten minutes chasing carrots around it.

"I'm not hungry," she conceded. "And we can't stay here. I didn't bring any clothes."

Logan took the plate away and gave her a lascivious smile. "Doesn't matter to me." He dipped forward and nibbled her neck.

"Not just for night time. What do I wear tomorrow?"

Logan wrinkled his nose. "Liza left some clothes next door. Want to come and see?"

"Okay, but she's taller than me. It won't work."

Logan pressed the code into the keypad and pushed open the door. He flicked on the light. Hana followed, stepping into the room as though fearful Liza might jump from behind the door. "Are you sure she won't mind?" Hana whispered.

"She won't know." Logan opened the wardrobe door and rifled

through the hangers. "She doesn't visit often and probably can't remember what she left here."

Hana fingered a pair of jodhpurs on a shelf. "If we must stay, can we ride up to your paddock tomorrow? I can turn the bottoms of these over a few times."

"No way!" Logan dropped a pullover on the floor of the wardrobe. "Don't be stupid."

Hana stiffened and her green eyes flashed. "Don't you dare wrap me in cotton wool, Logan Du Rose." Her fists balled by her sides and she took a step back. "Fine. Take me home right now."

"No." Logan reached for her and she dodged his outstretched hand.

"It's my body and I will do everything I want to." Hana scowled. "I wish I never told you."

Logan swallowed. "But it's risky. You might damage yourself or the baby."

"Don't!" Hana raised her hand. "If this child isn't strong enough to hold on, it isn't meant to be. I refuse to allow you to hold me responsible." Her voice wavered as her courage failed. She spun from the room and slammed the door behind her.

She found an old tee shirt of Logan's to sleep in and snuggled under the covers before he returned. Dull clunks and thuds from next door betrayed his search for borrowed clothing. He went downstairs for a while and the click of the door startled Hana awake. "Sorry." He sounded miserable and Hana sighed.

"No, I'm sorry. I'm trying to stop you hurting if it all goes wrong." Hana rolled onto her back. "I'm forty-five years old, Logan. I have a granddaughter with Downs syndrome and I feel much too old to have a baby."

The bed dipped as Logan sat down. "But it's my only experience of being a father." He reached for Hana's hand beneath the covers. "Even if it doesn't last long, I want to enjoy it."

Hana clamped her teeth over her lower lip, holding her breath to prevent him hearing her desperation. Tears dripped down her face and into her ears. An immovable blockage lay in her heart like a lead weight concerning her child. She couldn't risk loving it when it might be short-lived. Hana sought to protect herself, knowing it was futile.

Logan heard her ragged breaths and slipped off his shirt and jeans, crawling into the bed next to her. He soothed her with gentle kisses and Hana snuggled into his arms. His boxer shorts felt soft against her palms and she pressed her body against him, desperate for distraction. The very thing which got her into trouble promised to offer a temporary reprieve and she clung to Logan, hauling his shorts over his smooth skin. She bent him to her will and he loved it.

Michael smirked the next morning as Logan treated Hana like china during breakfast. When she rose to leave the table, his brow knitted at the sight of Liza's jodhpurs clinging to her thighs. He glanced towards Logan's back, watching as his brother loaded their plates into the dishwasher. "Is that a good idea?" he hissed, jerking his head towards Hana's abdomen. She felt her cheeks flush.

"Don't be ridiculous." She glared at him and he pursed his lips and allowed a flash of respect to cross his face.

"It's your funeral," he breathed and Hana fought the urge to slap the smug expression through the back of his head. She left the kitchen ahead of Logan, forcing him to jog to catch up.

Jack met them at the stables. Sacha scraped the ground with a dinner plate sized hoof, a rope tied from her halter to the wall. She turned to face Hana and her ears flicked forward and back. A stocky bay pony tore hay from a rack and swished her tail from side to side. Sacha screwed her neck around and eyed the pony with a glint in her blue eye.

"Don't even think it!" Logan snapped and she blew out a warm breath. The glint in her eye remained.

"Where's Digger?" Hana asked, looking for the Appaloosa she favoured. Logan shrugged and refused to get eye contact. Jack tugged on Hana's hand and turned her towards the pony.

"You're kidding me?" Hana's eyes narrowed to slits and she glared at Logan. "Is this your idea?"

Jack tugged on her hand again and led her towards the pony. He made a series of grunts and pointed at the saddle. Slapping the pony's neck, he let go of Hana and hauled a stirrup iron into place.

Hana followed Logan up the steep paddock towards the bush line. She seethed under the success of his revenge as her mount plodded beneath her. "How big is this pony?" she demanded.

"Big enough." Logan glanced behind, dropping his gaze to her height. "Nobody ever fell off her."

"You use her for the kids' treks, don't you?" Hana didn't hide her irritation. She leaned down to see how far her feet hung from the ground. "I didn't need Jack's help to mount; I could have just swung my leg over from ground level!"

Logan grinned. "I don't know what you mean." The little pony snorted and picked her feet up as they went through the second gate into the bush. She stuck to the back of Sacha's heels, wise enough to remain just out of reach. Hana longed to blow the cobwebs away with a decent canter but Logan's circuitous route made it impossible.

Hana settled and behaved as the ride progressed. They reached the lookout without incident and Logan relaxed as her feet touched the lush grass. He turned the horses loose and joined Hana on the edge of the cliff. Her voice sounded lazy. "Remember the last time we came up here?" she asked, shielding her eyes against the bright sun.

"Yeah." Logan bit his lower lip to hide the smug smile. He leaned down and kissed her neck. "Want a repeat?" Hana gasped as he turned her body into his and his hands roved over the back of her jodhpurs. His voice sounded muffled by her hair. "I don't need to control myself this time." He slipped his fingers into her waistband and dragged them across her skin, searing the flesh with his touch. When he undid the button and released the zipper, Hana conceded defeat.

Sacha munched around them as they lay in the long grass. Hana stared up at the sky and pulled Logan's abandoned shirt over her goose pimpled skin. "She looks different." She squinted through one eye as the regal nose tore at grass stems near her face.

Logan sighed. "Nobody told me the Appaloosa stallion got out. She's in foal so I haven't ridden her hard. She can manage for a few months yet but it affects my confidence in her. This is her last ride out for a while."

Hana rolled away from him and leaned on her elbows, butt naked against the big blue sky. "I don't want it to be like this for the next eight months," she sighed. "It's not fair."

"What?" Logan traced lazy arcs over her spine.

"You know what. I won't let you put me out to grass until it all goes wrong."

"Have a little faith," he whispered and pushed her over onto her back.

Hana enjoyed the ride down. She accepted the slower pace with grace, concerned for Sacha's comfort more than her own. Arriving in the kitchen in the hope of food, her mood changed at the sight of Tama seated at the kitchen table. Hana stopped in her tracks in the open doorway, almost letting it go in Logan's face. Her body stiffened. "Why is he here?" she hissed and Logan shrugged and shook his head.

"Hi Uncle Logan." Tama rose, displaying a vivid black eye and a long cut down the side of his nose.

"Hey," he replied.

Hana's appetite abandoned her and she followed it, heading up to Logan's bedroom. She lay on the bed and sulked. Her hand strayed to her stomach and she wondered how far back her pregnancy dated. Despite her innate desire not to bond with a child with no future, Hana found herself praying for a girl. "You must be a girl," she whispered. "I threw up with Izzie but not with Bo." She sighed, remembering how she also suffered fainting fits in the first trimester. Something to do with an oestrogen increase with little girls, her midwife said.

Hana imagined Logan holding his own little girl, playing with her in the park and walking her down the aisle. She conjured up a dark haired, elfin child with grey eyes and fear snaked grizzled hands around her heart. Hana turned on her side and closed her eyes, forcing the thoughts away.

Instead, she focussed on Tama's presence, drumming up enough irritation to distract herself. Something about his visit to the hospital tugged at her memory and she sensed she'd missed an important fact linked to the blonde man. When her memory failed her, Hana prayed for clarity and protection over her unborn child. Even though she didn't deserve his clemency, she hoped God would listen.

Hana slept through the afternoon and woke feeling groggy and disoriented. She found a luke-warm mug of tea on the bedside table and drank it, kidding herself it wasn't cold. Too tired for a shower, she changed into Logan's tee shirt and snuggled into the bed. A knock on the door disturbed her and she waited, hoping the visitor got the hint. They knocked again. "I'm not dressed," she called, punctuating the words with a cough. "I'm sleeping."

The keypad clicked and the door creaked open. Hana's eyes widened in fear and she half sat up. "Who is it?"

Michael poked his head around the door. "Just seeing how you feel," he said, his eyes roving over her torso. Hana sank under the sheets.

"I'm fine. I don't need anything."

Michael ventured further into the room, a curious sadness hanging around him like a shroud. "I know you're pregnant," he said, standing next to the bed. "It'll be fine."

Hana snorted and pulled the sheets around her so the outline of her legs resembled a mermaid's tail. "Is that your professional opinion or a lucky guess?"

"Both." Michael smiled. "I envy my little brother right now." Hana cringed and gave him a warning glare. Michael laughed. "You've nothing to fear from me, Hana," he said, his tone light. "I don't intend to risk my relationship with Logan again. He loves you. Stick it out and make it work. He deserves something good in his life."

"Why did you take Caroline?" she said, not formulating the question in her brain before she expressed it. "Why such cruelty? What did he ever do to you?"

Michael shrugged. "I took her because I could." His jaw flexed in his face. "And I promised."

"Promised who?" Hana's eyes narrowed. "Who asked you?"

Michael licked his lips, regret showing in his eyes. "It doesn't matter. Family stuff. They weren't meant to be together, so I broke it." He sighed. "She got pregnant and aborted the child. It destroyed Logan even though she said it was mine. He would've accepted it but she didn't give him the chance. He's been a pawn for too many people in this family, Hana. Get him away from here and keep him away."

She held her breath as Michael gazed at her tousled hair. It lay across the pillow like a brown curtain. "Logan called you, 'The girl on the train.' He described you when he got back to the hotel. He changed that day. Caroline messed with his head and the disappointment of not finding you meant he let her." Michael leaned forward and took one of Hana's curls, wrapping it around his finger. "You shouldn't dye it," he said. "He always loved the red." The bedroom door clicked shut behind him and Hana released her breath.

The light outside faded as she snuggled inside her cocoon of duvet and blanket, abdicating from life for a while. A clatter against the door marked the arrival of both Logan and Miriam, bearing soup, bread and fresh drinks. Miriam's eyes looked red rimmed and puffy and Logan rolled his eyes heavenwards behind his mother, begging Hana not to ask.

Miriam fluffed around shutting curtains and straightening Hana's discarded clothes. Logan waited for Hana to sit up before setting the tray on her knees. "You should eat," he said, his voice low. "Keep your strength up."

Miriam cleaned the bathroom and avoided contact with Hana, her presence odd and unsettling. Hana ate half the soup, watching as her mother-in-law whisked the tray away. With her hasty exit, Logan collapsed onto the bed. "You chose the right afternoon to sleep through!" he exclaimed, running his left hand over his eyes and catching his brow with the edge of the cast. "Bloody hell!" He glared at the tattered plaster. "I want this off! Jack won't do it."

"Tell me what I missed," Hana asked, sipping her tea. She regretted the question as Logan regaled her with the events of a traumatic afternoon. Miriam sobbed over the loss of Barry, her tears ruining a batch of carrots. Tama sat in the kitchen, shooting smart comments in Michael's direction. "I don't know why I stayed," Logan grumbled. "I kept checking on you but didn't want to abandon you by leaving the house."

"Sorry." Hana covered a yawn with her hand. "I didn't mean to cramp your style."

"Hey." Logan squeezed her fingers and shot her a look of disapproval. "I didn't mean that and you know it."

"What happened next?" Hana asked.

Logan quirked an eyebrow. "Tama pushed too far and slagged off his mother. Michael flew across the room and pinned him against the wall." He shook his head. "Dickhead asked for it." His brow furrowed. "Michael said he loved her and she chose Kane. Then he gave Tama a slap and stormed out."

"I'm glad I missed that," Hana breathed. "Then what?"

"Tama burst into tears like a big sooky baby."

Hana wriggled her nose and put her empty mug on the bedside cabinet. She yawned and snuggled under the covers. "Did Tama leave?"

Logan yawned and shook his head. "No. That's the weird thing. Michael came back to apologise and drove Tama home."

"How did Tama get the black eye?" Hana asked. "Did Michael do it?"

Logan lifted himself onto one elbow, shaking his head. "He told Ma Ivan did it. I don't know who that is."

Hana groaned. "He's Anka's husband." She hid her face in the pillow. "I don't want to think about that now. I've got problems of my own."

"Nothing's insurmountable." Logan stripped his clothes off and clambered into bed. "Trust me, Hana," he whispered into her hair.

"It's so hard though," she replied, sleep stealing the end of her sentences. "Everything is a mess. I need the men to stop chasing me. I need our baby to survive. Nothing is within my control and I don't like it."

"I know." Logan drew her into his chest and held her as Hana drifted off to sleep. She twitched and jumped as her dreams swirled around her and significant features of her recent troubles slotted into place.

The nagging thread of understanding unravelled in Hana's brain, gathering events and factors into a different order with a click. She woke, knowing everything centred around the small metal box she handed to Jas. She lay in the darkness and listened to Logan's steady breathing. Testing the theory over and over, it fitted each scenario, yet she knew she wouldn't tell Logan. When it sounded so fantastic in her own head, she couldn't tell someone else. First, she needed to claim it back.

-22-

Hana worked her way through Liza's abandoned stash of casual clothes until Sunday. Then Logan called time on their impromptu holiday. "But I don't want to leave." Hana pouted and pushed her face into the pillow. "I want more gun lessons."

"You just need to practice now." Logan ran his rough palms along her spine and sighed. "You know what you're doing with it. Practice will help you control the kick back in your wrist."

Hana snuffed into the soft fabric. "I love it here. It's safe."

Logan kissed her cheek. "The longer we stay, the harder it gets to leave. And Maihi's walking to the house every day. It's not fair on her."

"Can we ride up to the paddock one last time?" Hana turned onto her back and Logan bit his bottom lip as her tee shirt rode up over her thighs. "One last look at the sea."

"Maybe." He pushed his face into her neck and nuzzled the delicate flesh. "I need to look at the accounts with Jack and I'm not sure we'll have time."

"Why do you look at the accounts?" Hana nudged his shoulder to distract him. "Is it because Alfred can't read?"

Logan sighed and rolled onto his back, the moment destroyed. He stared at the ceiling. "I studied accountancy at night school in England, Hana. I just help out." His fingers snaked across the mattress until he found her bare thigh. "Stop asking so many questions."

"You're different here." Hana let out a giggle at the tickling sensation of his fingers, sensing he sought to silence her. "The men are scared of you. Except Toby and Jack."

Logan snorted and his fingers strayed higher. "Nobody's scared, Hana."

"They are." She wriggled backwards. "You're scary."

He laughed, but it sounded hollow. "They know not to mess with me. My parents lost the plot after we all left and visits home found discrepancies in the accounting and cash flow. I sorted it out and fired a few guys. Grown men don't listen to a teenager, Hana. You make them listen. My reputation grew bigger than me that's all."

"Shouldn't Michael take it over? Or Liza? She's the eldest."

Logan shook his head, the action slow. "They don't want it. All they thought about was getting away from here and everything it stands for. It's a millstone, Hana. A money sucking pit of family history and tragedy."

Hana heard a latent sadness in his tone and sensed the delicate thread which kept him returning to the mountain. He couldn't escape and the thought caused conflict in her heart. If he couldn't abandon the stronghold, its ties might bind her to it also.

Logan's grey eyes turned the colour of dark, storm-laden skies and Hana jumped as he moved with surprising swiftness for a man with a stomach wound and a broken arm. He pinned her in place beneath him and hiked up her skimpy tee shirt. "No more questions," he whispered and covered her mouth with his.

Hana sulked as they packed up to leave; delaying the process by washing Liza's borrowed clothing.

"Hana!" Logan snapped, finding her in the laundry room loading jeans and a sweater onto the drying rack. "I said we'd leave an hour ago. Stop stalling."

"What's the rush?" she demanded, turning with a lonely sock in her hand. It hung limp and pathetic over her fingers. "I want to ride one more time."

"No." Logan leaned against the doorframe and ran a hand through his hair. "We need to get back. Are you up to driving?"

Hana narrowed her eyes. "No. I feel faint. You're not insured to drive Bo's car, especially not with a broken arm."

Logan shook his head. "I'll drive. I have my own insurance."

Hana turned back to the drying rack with a sigh and he leaned over her shoulder and snatched the sock from her fingers. "Leave that. Leslie will do it!" He threw it back into the laundry basket. Hana gasped in shock and glared at him.

"Stop bullying me!" She raised her voice and her hand went instinctively to her stomach. Logan's eyes tracked the action and fear budded behind his darkening grey eyes.

"I need to get back." He gritted his teeth. "I'm meeting someone."

"Who?" Hana stood up straighter. "You didn't say."

Logan turned towards the doorway and waved his right hand over his shoulder. "I don't need to chart my every movement with you, Hana. You're my wife, not my event convener. We're leaving so get your ass out to the car."

Hana ran to the door and jabbed a finger at his back. "Or what?" she shouted after him. "Or what?"

Logan's grin chilled her blood. "Or I count to five minutes and leave you here."

Hana inhaled and rage filled her lungs. "Damn you, Logan Du Rose!" she hissed under her breath.

"A few wahine have said that over the years." Leslie let herself in through the door from reception and eyed Hana's basket of wet washing. "Mr Logan asked me to sort out Liza's clothes. I'll get the girls to do it."

Hana gritted her teeth and fixed a fake smile onto her lips. "Thank you. But I wore it so I'll sort it." Her brave expression failed. "But please may you fold it and put it back in her room when it's dry. My husband says we're leaving soon."

"Yep." Leslie put her hands on her ample hips and looked at Hana through the tops of her eyes. "And your tāne is leaving now. Your vehicle's waiting at the bottom of the front steps. A coach almost rear-ended it."

Hana hissed through her teeth. "Bloody man!"

Leslie threw back her head and laughed. "Too true, kōtiro. But if he says he'll leave you here, then he will. Youse best run."

Thwarted, Hana jogged along the narrow corridor towards the reception area. She slowed to a walk as she skirted a spiral staircase and forced a casualness into her movements. Too late, she noticed Logan watching her from a pillar in the lobby. He leaned against it, arms folded across his muscular chest and his lopsided smirk of victory set a fire burning in Hana's guts. Stepping through a crowd of new guests, she kept her eyes fixed on his self-satisfied grin and balled her fists by her sides.

Logan shifted, turning to leave before she reached him. He winced as he unhooked his cast from its position resting on his other arm. He'd won and he didn't even allow Hana the dignity of waiting for her. She sped up, consumed by the desire to slap his face. If she could reach.

Hana didn't see the suitcase trailing across her path, pulled by a businessman in an expensive suit. He cut in front of her, his attention diverted by a shiny phone in his hand. Hana inhaled as her feet became entangled in the small wheels and saw the ground fly up to meet her. One hand went forward to break her fall and the other moved across her abdomen. The businessman swore and yanked his case free, compounding the problem and leaving only hard tiles in front of Hana.

Logan's arms wrapped around her torso, hauling her upward and saving her. He grunted at the inevitable pain in his elbow as he took her weight and stood her on her feet. Not letting go, he glared at the businessman and whirled Hana away from the man's apology. Frog marching her from the hotel, he opened the passenger door of Bodie's car and thrust her shocked body inside. "Geez, Hana!" he bit as he settled himself into the driver's seat. He cranked the seat controls to allow for his long legs and adjusted the mirror.

"It wasn't my fault!" Her wide green eyes channelled hurt and shock as she turned her face towards his rebuke. The effort of not crying in front of him made her face tingle. Logan pursed his lips and turned away from her, concentrating on making more adjustments to his seating. Hana faced the passenger side window and let the tears fall onto her cheeks out of his sight. Her right hand strayed to her stomach and she caressed away the frightening sense of what might have happened. A week of shooting and riding and she almost blew the game walking across a hotel reception. Anger and rejection fuelled her temper and she watched the mountain scenery pass without registering the beauty it put on show for her.

Pastor Allen said the danger with anger lay in the false sense of exhilaration it induced. He said people responded to it by choice and got sucked into the addictive emotions it bred. Hana pushed his wise words to the back of her brain, choosing to avoid eye contact or conversation with Logan as they rode home in silence. He responded by shutting her out of his psyche as surely as if he'd bolted the door in her face. Hana felt sick at her stubbornness. She started the foolish argument and powerlessness stopped her from finishing it. She wanted to trust Logan as he demanded, but hit a brick wall when she least expected it.

They travelled back to Ngaruawahia in silence, the atmosphere tense and strained. The weather punished her for missing the mountainous display and rain threatened from darkening clouds above. Once at Culver's Cottage, Hana broke out the vacuum and cleaning products, throwing herself into physical toil to dispel the growing sense of depression hanging over her head. Logan took the car and disappeared. The cat acted snooty in response to her prolonged abandonment and turned his nose up at the kibbles she put in his bowl. Three dead mice and a kingfisher sat on the flat roof above the garage and he twitched his tail in disgust at her sigh of irritation. "I know, I know," she said, scratching him behind the ears. "Sorry I missed your gift. Can we please not kill kingfishers? They're beautiful." She peered through the glass at the entrails leading to the door. "But at least I know why you aren't hungry."

A call to Izzie found her daughter in a church meeting and unable to talk. Hana's sense of isolation grew. She dialled a different number and the person on the other end sounded delighted to hear from her.

She made a decision, took a firmer grip on the reins of her life and settled into bed feeling more in control.

Eight hours sleep meant Hana woke feeling refreshed. Logan didn't disturb her with his arrival home or when he slipped into bed. His sleeping form seemed a million miles away from her and he didn't rouse as her phone alarm vibrated on the bedside table. Hana showered and dressed in the bathroom and closed the front door behind her. She counted thirty-one jerks of the seat handle to get it back into a position where she could see over the steering wheel. Thirty-one reminders of her irritation with Logan.

A sense of freedom overwhelmed her and Hana cheered on reaching the hundred kilometre sign on River Road. She cranked up Bodie's loud rock music on the stereo to cover the sound of the BMW's wiper blades shepherding sheet rain off its windscreen.

Hana parked in her rightful space and walked into school, trepidation in her heart. New hair and a new outlook vied with her desire to sink back into old comforts. She felt unguarded and vulnerable, waving to the staff in the front office with feigned happiness and avoiding conversation.

"Hana!" Sheila ran from the other side of the office and wrapped her in enthusiasm and welcome. "I can't believe you came!" She jerked her head backwards and surveyed Hana through narrowed eyes. "I love your new hair." Her gaze roved across the blouse hanging loose and the skirt cinched at the waist with safety pins. "Why are you so thin?"

"I'm dieting," Hana answered, brushing off Sheila's concern with a fake laugh. Her colleague let the issue drop, but eyed her with suspicion. Gratitude trumped the need for information and she let Hana hang up her jacket and began work, keen for normal service to resume. Out of sight, she measured her wrist with her other hand and frowned at the way her fingers overlapped. "Worry and stress," she whispered to herself.

Hana's desk resembled a veritable junkyard of paper and mail. Her keyboard languished somewhere underneath and attempts to find it sent a landslide onto the floor. Starting outwards and working in, Hana satisfied a need to keep busy and stave off the nausea building in her upper abdomen. She cleared and binned, resorting to cloth and cleaning spray once she found the shelves and table surfaces. Filling the empty brochure racks took an hour, punctuated by calls to colleges and universities for more stock. Boys filed in and out, as Sheila caught up with appointments.

"Thank goodness you're back!" Evie Douglas wrapped Hana in a relieved embrace. "Pete's useless. He flicked every enquiry on to the guidance counsellors. Last week he sent a lost parent to Paul for directions to the main reception. He had to leave a crying boy to point them in the right direction."

Hana squashed the sense of dismay bubbling in her chest. She adopted a professional expression and nodded. "I'm sorry," she said. "I'm back now. Once I've found my keyboard, I'll log into your calendar and sort it all out."

Evie glanced at the pile on Hana's desk and nodded, patting her shoulder with understanding. "Okay. I'll leave you to it." She left in a hail of perfume and hair spray and Hana's stomach reacted.

As Hana sifted and filed outstanding correspondence, Sheila emerged from her office with a lipstick in her hand. She reapplied it without looking. "Do you know what that stupid little man did?" she raged. "He told the Year 12s to treat it as a gap year! Thank heavens most of them ignored him and waited for me to come back. Tertiary institutions look at the Year 12 results because the boys apply in their final year. It's their last complete year of results."

"Oh." Hana winced. "Did any believe him? How do you find those boys?"

Sheila snapped her lipstick closed and waggled her eyebrows. "How did that man ever get a teaching qualification? Does he have any brain cells?"

Sheila retreated into her office to deal with the next boy and Hana sorted her desk. She skim read most things and put them into piles relating to urgency. Creating a folder of items that should have gone to Sheila, she noticed requests from parents for appointments that were weeks old. Polishing the wooden surface of her desk before lunch, Hana heaved a sigh of relief. Satisfaction went some way towards lifting her mood as she counted the neat piles on the floor at her feet. She knelt and gathered one of the piles into her hands.

A sudden click and heady draught preceded an almighty crash. The rear door smacked into the stock cupboard and Pete followed. "Hi." He stepped across the piles of paper, scattering them far and near. Staring at Hana, he kept walking, a flicker of recognition in his face. When he hit the filing cabinet, he swore and caught the printer which plunged to its death from the top. "Do I know you?" he demanded, dumping the printer on the floor. "Are you new?"

"It's Hana, you idiot!" Sheila spat a small boy from her office and hauled in the next one. "Put the printer back on top of the cupboard where you found it. And be more careful!"

Pete ignored the printer and left it on the carpet in front of the door. He walked towards Hana and peered at her face. "Oh, hello," he said. "I thought you were Hana's replacement." He leaned closer and sniffed her hair. "I don't like it. Change it back."

Hana sighed and stood, the blood rushing to her head and

faintness threatening. She reached out and righted herself using Pete's arm and he stared at her fingers in surprise. "Actually, don't change it." He screwed his face into a coy grin. "The old Hana never touched me." He fluttered his blonde eyelashes and moved closer.

Hana let go and took a step back. "You're forgetting I'm married to Logan Du Rose," she said, her voice sickly sweet.

Pete jumped away and looked around the office. "Where is he?" he demanded. "Is he watching?"

Looking down at the mess at their feet, Hana gripped Pete by both shoulders, facing him toward the scattered documents. "Pete, this is important. I'm trying to make sense of the budget and invoices from when you were in charge."

His eyes widened like large lemons in his pale face and he shuffled backwards, eyeing the mess with suspicion and fear. His lips formed a round 'o' of distress. "It's not my fault," he began. His voice rose at the end of his sentence. "The sleep deprivation almost killed me." Clutching his heart, he continued backing away. Hana jabbed a finger at the papers littered around her feet. "Touch these and I'll quit. I need total silence and tea every half an hour or I'm done." Hana put her hands on her hips and raised an eyebrow in challenge. "And I'm not kidding."

Pete gasped in horror and turned to make a run for it. The open space of the common room stretched before him. Bounding backwards like a squash ball hitting a wall, he contacted the bulky frame of the head of technology. "You can't come in." He pressed his skinny fingers against the man's robust chest. "The office is closed."

Hana bit her lower lip and watched Pete shuffle the man backwards through the doorway. When the door shut in her face, she clasped her hands over her eyes, cringing at the ensuing argument outside. She ate a pie from the tuck shop for lunch and didn't break from her spring clean. The constant ringing of her phone resulted in her turning it off and tossing it into her handbag in the bottom drawer. By the time the boys changed lesson for the last time that day, the office looked its usual organised space and Hana felt satisfied with her progress. Apart from the piles of paper stacked next to her desk.

The steady hum of chatter from the common room ceased and Hana expected to see Alan Dobbs appear in the doorway. He didn't.

"So this is where you're hiding." Bodie leaned against the doorframe, his police radio chattering against his Kevlar vest.

"I'm not hiding." Hana closed the cupboard door with a sigh of pleasure at its immaculate state. A glance past her son showed boys craning their necks to see if she might be in trouble. A rumble of curiosity ripped through the group which dropped its pretence at study. Hana gave Bodie a tired smile. "Am I under arrest officer?" she asked.

Bodie slumped into Pete's chair and leaned forward. "No madam, but your frantic husband is considering lodging a missing report for you." He chewed gum as he waited for her answer, growing impatient as she pushed paper around her desk and ignored him. "What happened? You disappeared for a week and turned up at work where I asked you not to go. Judging by Logan's call, he didn't know either. Where's your phone?"

Hana sat, her legs wobbling beneath her. It all seemed too hard to explain. "My phone is off because I'm busy." She tried to sound casual. "I needed to come back to work, so I did."

"Telling no one?" Bodie raised an eyebrow and leaned forward. His touch on her forearm felt like an electric jolt. "If the marriage isn't working out, I can help you. You've lost heaps of weight since you married Logan. Are you sick or is he hurting you?" He closed his eyes and ran a hand over his face. "What's wrong? Please tell me."

His sincerity cracked her resolve. "We argued," she said, lowering her voice. The boys' collective radar twitched on high alert. "I wanted to stay at the hotel because I felt safe but he booked a meeting in Hamilton."

"A meeting with who?" Bodie's body stiffened.

Hana shrugged. "He didn't say." She licked her lips and sighed. "It's probably innocent, but he hated me prying. I handled it wrong and we fought."

"But you don't know where he went or who he saw?"

Hana exhaled, realising her massive mistake as she drove the wedge further between her men. "It's nothing," she said. "We're tired and fed up of hiding. It gives me cabin fever and we both get snappy."

"How long did he go out for?" Bodie demanded and Hana stood, terminating the conversation.

"It's nothing. Please leave it." One more question and he'd ask if Logan used his car. As he opened his mouth to speak, Hana raised her hand. "Bodie, enough!"

Her son puffed up his chest but refrained. Hana heard the radio cackle through the earpiece he'd removed. The wire dangled over his shoulder like black spaghetti and he picked up the bud and slotted it into his ear. "Gotta go," he said, forcing a grin onto his lips. "Be careful, Mum." He placed a peck on her cheek and the nosey boys outside gasped. Hana watched him stride from the office with a confident step, knowing his warning extended to within her walls as well as outside.

Sheila let her leave early. "You're amazing," she cooed, looking around the office. "I thought we'd never get it cleared up."

Hana turned away and bit her lower lip at her use of the plural. Neither Sheila nor Pete put in any effort, leaving it all to her. "See you tomorrow," she said, gathering up her handbag and making her escape.

Using the door to the soccer field, Hana skirted the chapel and checked the car park before venturing into the open space. She jogged to Bodie's car and dashed into the driver's seat, shooting the button for the central locking. Sighing with relief, she started the engine and pulled out onto Maui Street.

Logan waited on the porch as Hana drove up the hill. Bodie's car strained at the incline and exhaustion shrouded her as soon as the gate clicked shut. She clumped up the steps to the porch, embarrassed by Logan's intense stare. He blocked her route into the house, tall and striking with a guarded expression. Damp hair from a recent shower clung to his forehead and Hana inhaled his clean scent. Pressing a kiss to her forehead, Logan said, "I made coffee."

She stepped across the threshold and the smell of freshly percolated coffee greeted her like a strong, brown wall. Whirling around, Hana shoved at Logan's solid chest and tripped over the threshold. She landed on her knees and pushed her face through the porch rails before vomiting over the flowerbed beneath. The poor daisies bobbed their pretty heads and rued their rotten luck for the second time that week.

"Sorry," she spluttered as Logan crouched next to her, rubbing her back.

"It's okay," he soothed as she retched. The scent of coffee hung around the porch, filtering through the open front door. Logan left her, emptying the machine and opening the windows before Hana could enter the house. Even in the bedroom, she still smelled it. The roof garden seemed like the only safe place for her fragile stomach. Logan's leather jacket covered her shoulders and she sat on the garden bench overlooking the bush.

"Hemi helped me lift the furniture up here," Logan said, indicating the pots and heavy table. "You can move things around where you want them."

"Thanks." Hana pulled the jacket closer around her. "It looks good."

Logan shifted next to her like a small child seeking her approval. She glanced down and saw his fingers writhing with discomfort. She fought the urge to reach out and offer reassurance through touch. His behaviour the previous day damaged her trust in him. A voice in the back of her head whispered dangerous suggestions about where he might have gone. Hana inhaled and pushed away Caroline's image. "I want to go to bed now," she said, her voice hoarse. It sounded more plea than statement.

Logan nodded and stood to help her inside. His brow furrowed and Hana yearned to press her face into his safe chest and forget her doubts. Shrugging off her tight clothes and snuggling into bed, she watched Logan open the window and close the curtains. "Is this what happens?" he asked her, his eyes filled with concern.

"I can't remember," Hana sighed. "I think so." She pressed her face into the pillow and closed her eyes.

"What did you eat today?" Logan squatted next to the bed and stroked her hair back from her forehead. A clip caught against his fingers and he struggled to loosen the clasp.

"I don't know." Hana screwed up her face. "Don't talk about food."

Her rejection of dinner meant Logan ate alone in the kitchen. Hana saw his loneliness and watched the chasm between them widen. She didn't trust him. She'd tried and failed.

Logan found an old portable television and set it up on the dressing table. "The aerial cable is flaky," he muttered, reaching to plug it into the socket. "I've taped it sideways, but we'll need to buy another. I think the wire inside is dodgy."

Switching to a news channel, Logan stood back to admire his handiwork. The fuzzy picture settled and he nodded with satisfaction. "Can I get into bed with you?" he asked, reaching up to touch his shirt buttons. Hana shrugged. Logan shed his clothing and climbed into bed, snuggling close to her back. His warmth infused her with comfort and the ice in her heart thawed a little. "I'm sorry you're sick," he sighed. "I missed you today."

"Are you angry I went to work?" she asked, rolling onto her back.

Logan's hair swished against the pillow as he answered. "No, Hana, I'm upset you didn't tell me."

Hana snorted and closed her eyes, striving for sleep to rid her of the nausea. "Then you know how I feel," she whispered.

-23-

The damp night air felt bracing and the frost made the tips of the grass slippery underfoot. Logan stood on the steps of the roof garden, his gaze towards the bush. He shivered despite his warm clothing and took careful steps on the greasy wood.

A flashlight caught his eye, moving down the side of the paddock at a steady pace. Logan cursed the frost beneath his boots as his balance let him down on the top step. He clattered against the bannister rail and glanced up at the house, fearful of disturbing Hana. Admitting defeat, he jumped down the final steps and landed on the grass with a muted thud.

The flashlight beam jerked forward as its owner slipped. Logan clamped his teeth down on his bottom lip to stop himself laughing. Faint curses reached his ears and he shook his head as the light bobbed with the effort it took the man to gain purchase in the dirt and get upright. The light continued its journey downwards and Logan met it at the back fence. "Screw you, Logan Du Rose!" an angry voice hissed. "This is the last time I'm doing this."

"You'll do as I say." Logan growled out the command and the light flicked off. The men met on either side of the fence like farmers discussing the weather. The other man didn't remove his camouflage hood and Logan's frustration showed in his tone. "Stay until after next weekend."

"No! Toby's over it too. We're done."

Logan's right arm whipped across the fence and the other man coughed against the chokehold on his collar. "I pay you to do as I say!" Logan enunciated each word and the other man winced.

"Fine, boss!" he spat. "Whatever you say. But we're gone after that and you can shove your cash up your ass. I quit."

Logan's push sent the man sprawling into the grass and he grunted with the impact. "Tell Toby you just talked him out of a job, dude," Logan hissed with a sneer. "I'm sure he'll thank you heaps." He turned and strode up the back steps, not glancing behind as he heard the man pull himself upright. Shaking his head, he closed the rear door and locked it with a silent click.

He banged his cast against the wall and waited to see if Hana responded to the dull thud. Hearing nothing, he ventured further into the inky darkness of Culver's Cottage. Logan left his boots in the garage and stripped off in front of the fire. The orange flames warmed his skin enough for him to return to his marital bed. He folded his clothes and left them on the bedroom chair, fumbling his way to the bed in the darkness. Hana stirred as he climbed into bed. "Logan?"

Her voice sounded strained and he heard the residual fear from her nightmare leaking into his psyche. "I'm here, babe," he whispered. "Go back to sleep."

"I know you don't really want me," she said louder, her voice rising to a sob. "It's because of the baby, isn't it?"

Logan ached at the pain in her heart and hated her late husband with a passion. "He never deserved you, Hana," he whispered, pulling her into his chest. "I love you and I love our baby. It's not the same, sweetheart. We're not the same."

"Logan?" She sounded more together the second time, as though sleep relinquished its hold on her. "Did you go somewhere? Why do you leave me?"

"No, babe." He stretched the truth as far as he dared. "I checked something out the back and it's all fine."

"Are you sure?" Hana struggled to sit up and Logan held onto her.

"I'm positive." He pushed her face into his downy chest and stroked her back. "Go to sleep."

Within minutes, Hana's breathing slowed and her body slumped in his arms. Logan sighed and cuddled her close while striving for his own slumber. It proved harder each night to relax after he checked in with his spies. As a younger man, he brushed off such exploits but age crept up on him and hampered his coping mechanism. He breathed in Hana's scent and centred himself in her presence.

As Logan stirred and stretched the next morning, Hana drove into the school car park. Despite the early hour, another car sat in her space. Bodie's car struggled to maneuver in the small car park and Hana grew fed up with its restricted turning circle. The female art teacher stood and watched her perform a twelve-point turn. "That's it!" Hana slammed her palms on the steering wheel. "I need my own car back." The spiky bottom of the driver's door caught her on the shin as she closed it and her temper flared again.

In the office, Hana examined her laddered tights. She found a dribble of clear nail polish at the bottom of her desk drawer and dabbed it over the hole to prevent a bigger run. Hauling her skirt further down provided small comfort as the ladder popped into view like a glaring white lamp in a sea of black stocking. Blood seeped from the cut on her shin.

Hana worked hard and Sheila left her alone. Pete stepped over and around her with extreme care, treating her as he might a venomous snake. Hana worked straight through morning tea and lunch, crouching over her computer screen or kneeling next to the paper mountain on the floor.

The boys reentered the common room after lunch, bringing with them a hubbub of noise and food smells. Hana excused herself in search of the bathroom and a strong cup of tea. At the washbasin, she ran her hand under the tap and wet her lips, realising tea might make her sick again. The dark lowlights of her hair shone against the blonde streaks, mingling with shades of chestnut beneath the glare of the ancient strip light. A cough came from the end stall and Hana cringed as the toes of Ethel Bowman's sensible shoes showed under the door. Hana fumbled to gather her keys from next to the tap and make a run for it, her heart pounding in her chest. Her hand made a frenzied grab for the door handle as Ethel's voice rang out behind her. "Mrs Du Rose."

Hana turned and her eyes widened at the state of Ethel. A ready, fake smile slipped from her lips. Ethel's lank hair looked unkempt and straggly, framing her face like ivy around a brick. The absence of her usual coiffed perm made her look diminished and Hana kept all thought of wigs away from the speaking triggers in her brain. The un-ironed tent dress hung from Ethel's shoulders like a funeral shroud, betraying the loss of enormous poundage in weight. Gangly and spare, she seemed lost beneath the floral fabric and all that remained of her famous triple chins was a tell-tale flap of skin. She sounded like a Jane Austen character, uttering, "I am undone, my dear. Thoroughly undone."

Hana's arm ached, frozen between her waist and the door handle. She looked at it in surprise, seeing her fingers making a half-salute. She recalled it to her side. "Are you okay?" she asked.

Another flush sounded into the small space and Ethel jumped in fright. Humiliation and dismay crossed her expression. Ethel bowed her head and washed her hands with meticulous care as the other woman left. Then she turned to Hana. "Will you make time to speak with me?"

"Of course." All sense of betrayal fled at the sight of Ethel's misery and Hana's kind nature prevailed. "I'm due a break and the staffroom should be empty now. Why don't we grab a cup of tea each and chat?"

To Hana's chagrin, she discovered Ethel's preference for coffee and prayed she didn't perform a spectacular up-chuck at the smell. Choosing a strong and smelly peppermint herbal tea, Hana seated herself opposite Ethel near the balcony. She prayed for grace and a strong stomach.

Ethel took a loud slurp of her coffee and leaned across the table. Hana tensed and tried not to breathe in sync with her. "I didn't know," Ethel whispered. "You must believe me." She sniffed and delved into her sleeve for a tissue. "I thought he wanted me, but he didn't." She lowered her voice to a nasal whine so the nearby sports teachers couldn't hear. The group of muscular men continued their loud meeting. "I met him at a Christmas tea dance. My sister encouraged me to go and Michael seemed so attentive and genuine. I liked him and he lavished me with attention, which I haven't had much of."

"You met him around Christmas?" Hana asked as Ethel took another slurp of her drink. Hana released the question and then held her breath, dreading a waft of coffee sated air.

"You want them?" Chris Carter jerked his head towards an untouched plate of biscuits between the women. His sporty companions rolled their eyes, knowing Ethel could eat a packet in one sitting.

"No." Ethel's blunt reply silenced them all.

"Not for me." Hana shoved the plate towards him and he stalked across the distance between the tables to collect his prize.

"You Du Rose's wife?" Chris pushed his groin nearer the edge of the table and Hana moved backwards.

"We're busy!" Ethel snapped, giving him the death-stare. "Go away!" She waited until he'd reached his colleagues before turning her attention back to Hana. "Odious little poser," she hissed. "Avoid him at all cost."

Hana nodded, agreeing with Ethel's assessment for once. She turned the conversation back to Laval. "You called him Michael?" she asked. "And you met him around Christmas?"

"Yes. At a tea dance. He called at my house on New Year's Eve and took me out. Nobody ever did that before. I felt like I'd won the lottery." Her eyes filled with tears. "Instead, I lost everything."

Hana's face fell and her lips turned down. "No. Not everything."

Ethel reached out and touched Hana's hand. Her wrinkled fingers shook and she struggled to keep her voice level. "Your son told me your story and I need to apologise. I've been the author of some of your distress through my naivety. It seemed like harmless chit-chat between lovers when his aim was actually to get to you. I believe I'm what's known as collateral damage, Hana. An easy pick."

"But how?" Hana put a hand over her mouth and closed her eyes. "How could he take everything?"

Ethel shrugged. "One small loan after another from a foolish old woman. He furnished me with contracts from lawyers who don't exist and showed photographs of a business he doesn't own. Once I'd parted with the first few sums, it seemed foolish to write off the possibility of getting them back. I should have cut my losses and walked away, but I didn't. I gambled on having at least some of it returned and only lost more instead." Ethel swallowed. "I took out a mortgage on my little villa and now own part of a large debt on a South African mining company I've never heard of. Your son is investigating with the other man." Ethel's pained smile flicked across her face and she patted Hana's hand again. "You raised a great man, dear. He must make you very proud."

"I didn't think Bodie could deal with it." Hana frowned. "He's with the road cops."

Ethel blinked back tears. "Yes, he arrived in a car with another man. I didn't like the detective." She wrinkled her nose in distaste. "He treated me like the foolish old woman I am, but your son didn't. I shall be forever grateful for that small mercy."

"What will you do?" Hana's voice sounded like a squeak.

"Sell my house and retire." Ethel inhaled and stared around the staffroom. "It's given me time to rethink my life. My sister invited me to live with her in Tauranga. She suffers from Parkinson's and I can care for her in our dotage."

"But what about the school?" Hana's brow knitted in concern. "What about the boys?"

Ethel's rheumy eyes settled on Hana's face and she gave her a sad smile. "I've spent far too long worshipping at the altar of this school," she said. "They'll point at my face on staff photographs and struggle to remember my name one day. Be careful where you put your time and energy, Hana. Put it into things that last, like family and legacy. Build your house on rock, dear, not sand like I've done."

Hana made sorry noises to hide her loss of words. Ethel's emptiness radiated across the table and into her soul. Logan's image floated across her inner vision and Hana ached to feel his arms around her.

Ethel snorted, distracting her. "I've spent my whole life trying to lose weight." She looked down at her empty dress and grinned. "So, every cloud has a silver lining."

Hana forced a smile on her lips, trying to see anything aside from a lost retirement fund. Ethel leaned closer and breathed coffee fumes into Hana's face. "I'm sorry for spying on you. I hope you can forgive me."

Hana nodded. "Yes. Of course I can."

Ethel rolled her eyes. "You see, dear, I always admired you. I liked the idea of him knowing you. I hoped we might become friends and wanted to impress you."

"Me?" Hana raised her voice in surprise.

Ethel nodded. "Yes, dear. Suffering your great loss and carrying on, bringing up those beautiful children by yourself. You always looked so serene and together. Then finding that gorgeous husband of yours. I envied you and wanted a little happiness for myself. I'm a silly old woman!"

Hana's frown grew deeper and she shook her head. "I'm none of those things, Mrs Bowman." She rose and bent to kiss Ethel's cheek, feeling the nausea bite at the scent of coffee. Ethel's shock radiated outwards in an arc which silenced the sports teachers at the next table. "You are precious," Hana whispered. "And fearfully and wonderfully made."

Ethel's eyes filled with tears as she recognised the words of Psalm 139. It seemed woefully inadequate to Hana, but all she could offer right then.

As the bell sounded for the home time, Hana left the table and bent to put her mug in the dishwasher. Forgetting the peppermint tea, she upended it and groaned as green liquid splattered down the side of a nearby cupboard. She dampened a cloth and bent to wipe up the mess, smelling coffee dregs and floor disinfectant.

The grip on Hana's sickness loosened and she breathed through pursed lips. Shouting came to her ears as faintness vied for attention and sent blood pounding through her eardrums. "Not now," Hana hissed, begging her body to behave.

"You shouldn't be here!" Sheila's voice raised to a screech as the argument entered the staffroom. The hum of male voices halted and one lone speaker uttered a curse. Hana recognised Chris Carter's voice.

"Somebody get Angus!" Sheila shouted and Hana heard chairs scraping back against the carpet. She forced herself upwards and inhaled.

Caroline yanked her arm free of Sheila's grasp and took a run at Hana. Only the counter between them kept her safe from the onslaught. "Where's Logan?" she demanded. "I need to see him."

Hana backed away, feeling the cool steel of the draining board through her blouse. Her lips moved but nothing came out. The nothingness stole her legs out from under her and she hit the floor like a dead weight. The last thing she remembered was the way Caroline ran a hand across her own stomach.

Hana woke up in the school's sickbay, the nurse standing in front of her. "Steady on!" She held a bucket under Hana's nose and rubbed a gentle hand across her back. "Feel better?"

Wiping her mouth with the back of her hand, she nodded and sat up. The nothingness threatened and she panicked and closed her eyes. "I don't know."

"Are you pregnant, Hana?" The nurse lowered her voice and Hana opened her eyes to shoot a nervous look at the door. "It's okay. I threw all the boys out and Boris is standing guard outside. He carried you downstairs."

Hana blew out through pursed lips and nodded. "Please don't tell anyone."

The nurse rested a gentle hand on her shoulder. "I won't. How far along are you?"

"I don't know." Hana's chin wobbled with the effort of not crying. "I could be one week pregnant or five."

"When was your last period due?" The nurse sat on the bed next to her.

Hana swallowed and shrugged. "I don't know that either. I used to mark it on a calendar but I lost it when I moved house. They're sketchy at best nowadays. I thought it might be the menopause."

The nurse nodded. "I can imagine. Your first scan will tell you the approximate age. Make an appointment with your doctor."

"Okay." Hana exhaled. "Can I go now?"

"Not yet. Your colour is very pale and your pulse slow. Lay back and relax and we'll see how you are after a rest."

Despite the breeze from a window near her head, Hana smelled boy-feet and sweat. Her stomach churned in warning and she lifted her blouse to cover her nose. The nurse handed her cool water and she sipped it with care, keeping her nose covered. The water slopped over her hand as Hana jumped in fright. Caroline's voice screeched outside the door. "Let me see her! She needs to know!"

A scuffle sounded outside the door as clothing and bodies shifted against the wood. The nurse whipped it open and Boris and Caroline fell through the gap. "What the hell is happening?" the nurse bellowed and Boris pinked to the tips of his ears. Caroline broke free of his grip and Sheila hung to the back of the other woman's sweater, stretching it into a thin line.

"Leave her alone!" she pleaded, her shoes slithering across the smooth tiles. Hana squeezed her eyes closed as hysteria threatened to reveal the funny side. Caroline pulled until she stood in front of Hana, hands on hips and towering over her.

"Go away." Hana sounded tired and accompanied her request with a yawn.

"I need to talk to Logan." Caroline gritted her teeth and avoided the nurse's outstretched hand with a violent jerk of her body. "Why isn't he here?" Her blue eyes flashed with danger and again Hana saw her fingers flutter across her stomach.

Hana closed her eyes and swallowed. She knew why the woman wanted to see Logan and it turned her guts inside out. Nausea of a different kind rose into her chest and at the sight of her bleached colour the nurse intervened. "Out!" she demanded. "Sheila, get off her. Someone fetch Angus."

"I'm pregnant!" Caroline hissed, bending to achieve the full force of her news. "Logan should know he's a father." Her lips curled back into an ugly snarl and Boris inhaled. His red hair stood up on his head like a flame as his lower lip trembled. Hana pulled her gaze away from his shocked expression. She put shaking fingers up to the bridge of her nose and squeezed, willing away the pounding headache.

"Oh, crap!" Sheila let go of Caroline's sweater and clapped her hands over her mouth. "Hana, I'm so sorry."

Hana concentrated on her breathing and fought the nothingness as it offered to bring relief.

"How pregnant are you?" Sheila demanded and Caroline pouted.

"Three months." She stuck her nose in the air and her lips straightened to give her a hard look. "Logan needs to know."

Sheila counted on her fingers. "So you slept with Logan after you came here?"

Caroline tossed her head. "Keep your eyes on your own marriage," she snapped. "If you minded your own business a little more, your husband might keep his wandering hands to himself."

Boris gasped and Hana pulled her fingers away from her face. Contrary to expectations, Sheila laughed. The action shook her body and brought tears to her eyes. "You're so out of touch, Caroline," she snorted. "That's old news sweetheart." All mirth disappeared from her eyes and she took a step closer. "Pregnant or not, if you don't leave my friend alone I'll knock you into next week. Now get out!"

Boris moved between the women and took Caroline's arm. "Come," he said, pulling her after him. Hana kept her sob inside, wishing with all her heart Caroline lay at the bottom of the gully with Logan's phone. The door closed behind them and Hana heard more raised voices outside. Sheila reappeared with Hana's handbag. "Let me drive you home?" she offered, her face sad. "If it's any consolation, I know how you're feeling." She rolled her eyes. "Not the pregnant bit, but the rest of it." Her hand patted Hana's shin. "You need to speak to Logan."

Hana nodded and swung her legs over the side of the bed. The nurse returned and halted the proceedings. "Sheila Jennings, I'm in charge here!" She bristled and stood in front of Hana. "I need to keep her here for at least another twenty minutes. Then I'll let you take her."

Sheila fluffed up like a chicken and then conceded, directing her answer to Hana. "Okay. Sit here for a while and then I'll drive you home." She backed from the room as though fearful the nurse might slap her legs.

Hana reached for her water and knocked it over. The nurse gave her a sympathetic look and fetched paper towels. "Did you expect that news?" she asked in a soft tone and Hana clammed up. Her rigid body answered for her. "Sit for a while," she told her and Hana nodded.

The woman's heels clicked along the corridor and Hana seized her moment. Snatching up her handbag and checking for her car keys, she bolted. Wobbly legs carried her as far as the chapel car park and she sank into Bodie's car with her heart thudding in her chest. Shock sent adrenaline through her veins and the light-headedness returned. Hana drove without thinking, finding herself on Amy's tree-lined road. The urge to cuddle a small, tousle-haired boy with a generous spirit lit a fire in her heart. Hana wanted to breathe in the scent of washing powder, baby shampoo and feel his butterfly kisses on her cheek.

"Hi, Hana," Amy said, answering the door with a wooden spoon in her hand. Red sauce flicked onto the doorframe and she grimaced. "Oops, watch your jacket." Her expression grew serious as Hana imploded. Her body shook and her breathing came in wracking great sobs.

Hana told her about Caroline, alternately swearing and crying as she writhed at the kitchen table. Amy stirred tomato soup on the stove and her jaw dropped open. "Get off the grass!" she breathed. "Does Logan know?"

"I don't know." Hana hiccoughed. "The longer I know Logan, the less I understand."

Amy snorted. "He sounds like God." She plonked a saucepan on the table and three bowls and turned the conversation to cold, hard facts. Between them, they worked out the dates of possible conception and Hana's heart sank.

"If Logan fathered Caroline's baby then he cheated on me." Her voice wavered and Amy patted her shoulder. When Hana's phone rang, Amy answered it, speaking for a moment before disconnecting.

"Sheila Jennings checking you're okay," she said, returning it to Hana's bag. "I told her you're with me."

"Thanks." Hana sighed at the speed with which Caroline's news would circulate the staffroom as juicy gossip.

"Jas!" Amy yelled down the hallway. "Dinner!" She turned back to Hana. "Hey, remember this Hana. Innocent until proven guilty."

"Hanny!" Jas appeared in the doorway with his dark curls pressed down on one side. "I didn't know you was here. I been sleeping." He yawned and switched the male doll in his hand to the other one so he could suck his thumb.

"Hey, baby. I need a cuddle." She held her arms out to him and the child clambered into her lap. He snuggled close and closed his eyes. Hana drank in his nearness, drawing strength from their blood tie. She thought of an elderly church friend who said grandchildren felt like her own, but loaned to sons and daughters on a temporary basis. Elizabeth's birth helped her understand the sentiment.

Hana squeezed Jas and he sighed and burrowed deeper into her jacket. "Luff you Hanny," he whispered. Then he disturbed the peace with a gargantuan fart. He snorted and looked up at her with amused brown eyes, only partly apologetic. Turning aside, Hana fought the laugh bubbling in her chest as Amy told him off.

"Go to the toilet," she demanded, frowning as the boy slipped off Hana's knee and clutched his bottom at the emergence of another one. "And apologise to Hanny for farting in her lap!"

Hana's body rocked with mirth and Amy ignored her as Jas replied from the bathroom. "She liked it. I warmed her legs."

"I swear that boy gets worse!" Amy grumbled. "I thought having his father around might improve things."

"Oh." Hana swallowed, doubt filling her mind. "Is it not working out?"

Amy opened her mouth to speak, closing it again as Jas returned. He walked with a cocky stride and winked at Hana, a gesture involving the whole of his face.

"I should leave and let you eat." She stood and Amy whipped around to rebuke her.

"No! Stay and get some food in you. Skinny doesn't suit you." She dumped a full bowl in front of her and narrowed her eyes. "Why are you so thin all of a sudden?"

"Stress." Hana picked up her spoon and dipped it into the soup. Her phone buzzed in her handbag and revived the thought of facing Logan. She exhaled and Jas popped off his chair.

"I'll get it," he announced and Amy stopped him.

"Hanny doesn't want it," she said and nudged him back onto his cushion.

Isolation crowded in on Hana and her appetite fled. She made a valiant attempt at eating the meal and Jas took over where she failed. "I should go," she said, sounding sad. "Thank you for the reprieve."

"Whatever happens you'll get through it." Amy smiled with sadness behind the expression. "We just do."

Hana helped clear up and left, hugging Amy on the doorstep. "Please tell Bo I'm ready to swap cars," she said. "These idiots following me are the least of my problems right now."

"If you're sure," Amy said. "Bodie said nobody followed him the last three times. Maybe they gave up."

Hana turned away and then paused. "Please don't repeat what I told you to Bodie? He's already looking for reasons to hate Logan."

"Yep." Amy didn't sound surprised. "I hear ya." She shepherded her fractious son indoors after waving Hana off into the dusk and the promise of a traffic jam home.

Logan greeted Hana with a smile as she walked through the front door. He knelt beside a roaring fire, prodding the flames with a poker. "It's cold outside, isn't it?" he said, sitting back and admiring the blaze. His brows narrowed. "Please can I borrow Bodie's car?"

"Why?" Hana's body stiffened. "Where are you going?"

"I need to see someone." Logan stood. "I made dinner and left it in the oven. Get a nice bath and I'll be home before you know it."

Hana's jaw tightened. "I already ate and I don't want a bath." She rubbed a tired hand across her eyes. "Are you seeing Caroline?"

"What?" Logan's eyes widened and his nose crinkled. "Hell no!"

Hana gave an upward jerk of her head. "You expect me to trust you and yet you won't tell me who you keep meeting."

"It's not important." Logan advanced, concern etched into his face. "What's wrong?"

Hana sat on the sofa in response to the tremor beginning in her legs. She put her feet on the seat to prevent Logan sitting next to her. "Talk to me." He squatted in front of her. Hana noticed marks on the cast where he'd tried to remove it himself and failed.

"I don't know what to say." She sighed through pursed lips and her hands writhed in her lap. Logan put a steadying hand over them.

"Start at the beginning." His voice sounded soft. "Why are you talking about Caroline? She left remember."

"But she didn't." Hana swallowed. "She came to work today looking for you. She's three months pregnant and telling everyone you're the father."

Logan's jaw clenched shut and Hana watched the bone work through his cheek. "And what do you believe?" he asked, a whisper against the crackling fire. He closed his eyes and did the maths in a split second. "You think I cheated on you?"

Hana exhaled and watched the movement of his face. A vein in his neck ticked a warning but his grey eyes remained calm. She felt her resolve crumble. "I don't know, Logan. We can't catch a break, can we? It's one thing after another." Hana shrugged and her voice wavered. "It doesn't matter. Everyone else believes it."

Logan exhaled and shook his head. "Bloody hell!" He sounded more annoyed than upset. Hana felt the air shift around her as he rose to his feet, not touching her. His eyes became the colour of storm water, dark grey pits of swirling emotion. Hana faltered and floundered under his gaze.

She swallowed. "She looked desperate to pin it on you. Maybe too desperate."

Logan raised his eyebrows and backed away. Hana struggled to read the blank expression on his face as the portcullis crashed down over whatever he felt. "What do you believe?"

Hana licked her lips and waited a beat to formulate her answer. "She hijacked me and I felt shocked and devastated." She raised her eyes and fluttered dark eyelashes. "Now I'm here with you, I believe she might be lying."

"Might be?" Logan ground his teeth. He jerked his head sideways as though not caring either way. Then he left the room, jangled the car keys and exited the house.

As Hana reached the porch, the vehicle's rear lights already bounced down the driveway taking her husband with it. Her hands crashed to her sides in frustration. "Thanks for that, Logan," she shouted into the darkness. "I backed you and you ran. As usual." She stood on the cold porch in her stockinged feet and leaned her head on her arms. The wooden balustrade felt slippery with frost. The soup roiled in her stomach and sickness returned.

An early night didn't help and Hana watched the portable television, registering nothing on the screen. When her phone rang, she checked the number before answering.

"How did it go?" Amy demanded. "What did he say?"

"He said nothing. Then he left."

"He left?" Amy's voice rose an octave. "Forever or just to think?"

"I don't know." Hana sighed. "He took nothing with him, so maybe just to think." Her heart felt like lead in her chest and she ended the call before Amy could speculate about where he went. She fell into a fitful sleep with the television playing in the background. Her nightmares included Caroline.

Hana woke as Logan crawled into bed. He smelled of night air and brought a cold breeze into the bed with him. She turned to look at him and Logan cuddled into her back. "No!" Hana snapped, pushing his hands away. "You left me alone when I needed you. Don't touch me. You're a coward!"

"Hana, stop!" Logan captured her flailing hands and sighed toothpaste over her face. Infuriated, she kneed him in the groin. He grunted in pain and smothered her body with his, holding her arms above her head. The light from the television flickered in his eyes and he paused long enough for Hana to see the pain behind his anger. "Hana, I love you," he whispered. His lips crushed hers, rough and seeking and she fought to release her wrists.

Her body responded with treachery and Hana reeled at its betrayal. She opened her mouth to Logan's tongue and let his body dominate hers. Afterwards she cried as he slept, warm tears plopping onto the pillow beneath her.

The next few weeks passed in a blur. She swapped Bodie's car for her Honda against everyone's advice, making her decision and sticking to it. The drive to work and back provided an oasis of peace as silence fractured her relationship. Logan behaved as though the conversation about Caroline's child never happened and it festered between them like a sore.

Hana battled with continual sickness, alongside the staff gossip about Logan and Caroline. She kept her pregnancy secret, her thunder already stolen. Boris became a trusted friend and attached himself to her like a bodyguard. He carried her bags into the office and visited her often during the day. His male presence offered comfort and a safe haven where Caroline didn't feature. Gossip in the staffroom froze Hana into an isolated world. She stayed in the office, keen to avoid the raised eyebrows and whispers behind hands. Moving around in a fog of despair, Hana dug herself an enormous hole and jumped in feet first.

Behind closed doors, her marriage became empty and superficial and balanced on a wafer thin equilibrium. Logan grew fitter, running up the mountain every day. He eyed Hana like a man trapped in a pit with a venomous snake. The threat of Michael Laval paled in significance against the backdrop of Hana's relationship tumult and her sense of safety grew by degrees. She visited Amy often after work, cementing her love affair with Jas and making up for lost time. When she threw up after dinner one night, Amy nailed her. "You're pregnant, aren't you?" she asked, handing Hana a glass of water.

Hana nodded. "What gave me away?" She clambered to her feet and the colour drained from her face.

Amy shrugged. "You've got baby-brain. You handed Jas a block of cheese and put Action Man in the fridge after dinner."

"Sorry." Hana ran a hand over her face and shivered. "I'm just tired."

"Did you speak to Logan about Caroline yet? It's on your mind all the time."

Hana shook her head. "I can't. He left me alone after a bombshell like that. I can't forgive him. I'm shrouded in numbness and I like it that way. It's the only way to cope."

Amy tutted. "You look like crap."

"Thanks. I feel like I've died and turned into a zombie."

Amy shoved her shoulder. "At least the undead don't get morning sickness."

"Morning, lunchtime, evening and bedtime sickness." Hana yawned. "When does it end?"

Amy sat down on the side of the bath and watched Hana's colour return. "Three months or birth. Take your pick."

"Three months, I hope." Hana rinsed her mouth with toothpaste and tucked her grandson into bed. Then she left, armed with a million pictures to send to Elizabeth in Invercargill. Hana suspected she'd eat them.

Logan shed the cast and stitches and returned to work. Hana lost her journey of sanity. She relinquished the driving seat and huddled as far away from him as possible. The weight continued to drop off and her clothing hung like curtains around her fragile body. She cried often in toilet cubicles, bathrooms and once in the fated cupboard half way up the stairs. Logan watched her with the same intensity as a geologist peering at the seismic warnings from Mount Ruapehu. Life rolled on and Hana plunged on with it, losing track of time, her marriage and not caring anymore.

Caroline reappeared like the proverbial bad smell one evening. She emerged from a vehicle parked opposite the Honda, immaculately dressed and sporting a budding pregnancy. Her vitriolic spite reached them from the other side of the car park and arrested the attention of exiting staff. "How can you just ignore me, Logan? Don't you care about your child?"

Hana watched as Logan ignored her. He unlocked the car and sat his briefcase on the back seat. The scene appeared bizarre as he closed the door, not acknowledging the banshee crossing the car park to shout in his face. "Excuse me," he said, his tone polite and impassive. "You're in my way, physically and metaphorically."

Caroline moved through shades of antagonism and fast-forwarded straight to hysteria. Other staff stopped to watch. "You owe me," she yelled. "I expect support for this kid. It started the minute you fathered this baby, so get your wallet out."

Hana felt the familiar nausea wash over her, induced by stress. She gripped the passenger door handle and leaned forward in an effort to suppress the need to retch. Logan glanced across at her and his eyes widened in horror as she pitched forward. In seconds, his strong arms gripped her beneath her armpits and hauled her upright. "It's okay, baby," he whispered. "Breathe, Hana, breathe."

Hana let him support her weight, the closest contact they'd had for weeks. The sensation of safety reminded her of happier times and she realised how much she'd missed him. "Just sickness," she managed. "It's nothing else."

He nodded with relief at her reassurance and cradled her in his arms. Caroline's accusations continued in the background. Exhausted, Hana waited for the nausea to pass, knowing it would. Unsatisfied, Caroline moved in for the kill, her face a livid flush of rage. She yanked at Logan's jacket, causing him to rebound into Hana and knock her off balance.

"Leave it," Hana hissed as she felt his body tense, clinging onto him to right herself. Logan's hands shook as he rounded on Caroline, pure hatred in his grey eyes.

"Do you want me to say it, Caroline?" he shouted, to the pleasure of the bystanders. "You're happy for everyone to know the terms of our engagement?" Caroline swallowed and lost some of her fire. Logan gripped Hana around the waist with his right hand. "You don't mind everyone knowing how you begged me for the Du Rose name and a place in my family? In return, I'd get a trophy wife and the freedom to live my own life. I haven't touched you for years, Caroline and I couldn't after what you did. You bought yourself a marriage of convenience and then backed out. That isn't my child and I pity the man it really belongs to. You're poison. Leave us alone or I'll take out an injunction. Do you want that?"

The spectators recognised the end of the performance and shuffled towards their vehicles as Caroline gaped like a stunned fish. Hana let Logan's outburst filter through her thick head and the nausea made a last ditch attempt at winning the war. "Logan, please?" A sob sounded in Caroline's throat as she turned her rage to pleading. "I need your help. I still love you. They made me do it. They stopped me going to the wedding. You don't understand."

"I want to go home." Hana inhaled and Logan's faded aftershave touched a trigger for her sickness.

Caroline yanked on Logan's sleeve again, buffeting Hana without regard. "Logan!" she snapped, her tone aggressive. "Listen to me!"

"Let go!" Logan moved sideways, attempting to release himself and support Hana at the same time. Left with a clear line of fire, Hana gave up suppressing the desire to puke and projectile vomited across Caroline's exquisite Prada shoes. Logan dived sideways but Caroline shrieked in horror. When she moved backwards, she left an outline of her pointy feet in the wet mess. Hana concentrated on breathing, counting the gulps of oxygen in and carbon dioxide out. She cared about nothing aside from getting home and into her warm bed.

"Come, Hana." A body squeezed between her and the car and Hana saw the passenger door open. Boris tapped her on the shoulder and spoke to Logan. "I have her. Get in ze car and take her home." Hana mouthed her thanks and sank into the seat, grateful for the hands which fastened her seatbelt and sat her handbag in the foot well.

Boris moved Caroline aside like a cop executing crowd control duties. His ashen face spoke volumes. Hana groaned at the revelation and laid her head back against the rest, closing her eyes and concentrating on her ragged breaths. "Stupid man," she sighed and relaxed against the motion of the vehicle. Her fingers fluttered over her abdomen and she prayed away the sickness.

Hana wound the window down at Flagstaff, gulping in fresh air. She covered her eyes with a shaking hand. "I can't believe it," she gasped. Caroline's revulsion as the vomit splattered across shoes equivalent to the cost of an average car, seemed hilarious with hindsight. A laugh bubbled in Hana's chest. She groaned and writhed in her seat as mirth vied with discomfort.

"What's wrong?" Logan swerved into a side road and jammed the handbrake on, leaning across to shake Hana's shoulder. "Are you okay? What's happening?"

"I puked on her shoes." Hana pressed her fingers over her lips. "What a shot."

Logan snorted and laid his head back against the seat. "Yeah, babe. Right on target." He sighed and ran a tired hand across his face. "Bloody hell, Hana, you were right. We just can't catch a break."

Hana nodded and remembered the expression on Boris' face. He looked like a man under a spell. It meant they weren't the only ones in trouble.

-24-

The holidays arrived at the culmination of an endless term. A very pregnant looking Izzie and a growing Elizabeth visited, filling the house with laughter. Everywhere they went, people asked Izzie about her due date, refusing to believe she still had four and a half months before her.

Jas spent a few nights out at Culver's Cottage without his parents, revelling in the connection with his new aunty and cousin. He cried when Izzie waddled back to Invercargill. Despite many late night talks and lots of time spent together, Hana managed to keep her pregnancy secret from her daughter. It wasn't deliberate, but the continued uncertainty in her relationship heightened her sense of foolishness. She hid her diminishing sickness and Izzie went home unaware. At the end of the first week, Hana realised the nausea came less, confirming her suspicion she fell pregnant as soon as Logan placed the ring on her finger.

Hana spent the second week at Amy's, looking after Jas. They baked, walked and played in the park, encouraging Hana maybe she could go round again in the parenting world. She met older mothers at the play park, women who excelled in their careers and left childbearing until later. They seemed patient and in control. Hana remembered her frantic parenting with Izzie and Bodie and wondered if she might make a better job this time. If 'this time' came to fruition. Fear still haunted the back of her mind and she pushed all thoughts of her infant out of reach.

While Hana minded Jas, Logan organised their hazardous driveway up the steep incline to the house. He found one company willing to concrete and they spent the second week of the holiday doing it. Logan fetched his bike from the Gordonton house and used that to commute between Hamilton and Culver's Cottage.

"The gate is back on," he told her one night, climbing into the spare double bed at Amy's. "The drive looks great."

"I didn't like the gate being off," Hana commented, bunching herself into a corner away from her husband. "Those men might turn up and wait for us at the house."

Tiredness hijacked Logan's patience and he snapped at her. "Bloody hell, Hana. The construction guys created a ditch filled with hard core from one end to the other. Nobody could get a vehicle up there and if your mates wanted to walk, they'd have a wasted trip, wouldn't they?"

Hana backed herself further into the corner and rested her bottom against the cold wall. Logan sighed, the sound echoing in the small room. "Hana, I hate this," he whispered. "Come back to me." He reached for her with tentative fingers and she slapped his hand in the darkness.

"No," she bit. "Don't. I can't deal with your crap at the moment. I don't know who you are anymore. Please, just leave me alone."

"Do you regret marrying me?" Logan's whisper channelled self-doubt.

Hana turned on her side away from him and replied, "I don't know. I can't live with your secret meetings with faceless entities and women crawling out of the woodwork with paternity claims. So maybe I do regret it, yes."

As Hana distanced herself from Logan, Jas gravitated towards him. "Poppa Logan, bounce me!" he demanded. "Poppa Logan, can we do spitting in the bath?"

The last night at Amy's, Hana tolerated the shrieks and giggles from the bathroom for too long before investigating. She stood in the doorway, frozen in horror. "What did you do?" she squeaked.

Jas popped up from a covering of bubbles and spat foamy water straight into Logan's face. "That wasn't fair!" Logan protested. "Hanny distracted me!"

"You can clear this up," she bit, staring at bubbles clinging to the ceiling. "Amy is on her way home." She retreated to the bedroom, an ache beginning in her heart at the glimpse of Logan's ease with the little boy. Curling into a ball on her bed, she cried, more confused than she'd ever felt.

Amy arrived home with a cut on her chin and a bruise spreading a blue hue across her cheek. "Don't ask," she said, raising a hand as Hana filled the kettle. "I've suffered worse." She cocked her head at the sight of Hana's puffy eyes and squeezed her shoulder. "This constant feeling that everything's messed up will pass," she promised.

Hana nodded, unable to speak. When Logan walked into the kitchen with Jas slung over his shoulder in a towel, she gave Amy a weak smile and bolted to pack up her belongings in the bedroom.

On the final Sunday of the holidays, Hana went back to her little church with Jas. Cilla greeted her with a warm hug and knitted her brow at the gold band on Hana's finger. But Pastor Allen treated her the same as always and instructed her to sit with his family in the pew. Jas cosied up to the eldest of Allen's sons, in awe of the bigger boy and copying his every move. Hana smiled at his antics, surprised when he followed Allen's boys off to Sunday school without a backward glance.

Charlotte and Gareth drifted in late and grabbed the last spaces next to Hana. During a hymn, Charlotte leaned across. "Gareth drove us," she said with pride. "He got his full licence last week. He takes me to tennis too."

"Congratulations," Hana mouthed at Gareth and gave him thumbs up. He rewarded her with a nod of acknowledgement, the same one he gave when she smiled at him at school. She wondered if Tama knew or cared about the damage he'd done. She doubted he gave it a second thought.

Charlotte removed her earphones after the service and Hana saw Allen smirk and turn away. She nudged Gareth. "Get me a biscuit?" she asked.

He nodded and stood, yanking his jeans up to hide some of his underwear, but not all. He shuffled after a moving plate of biscuits, his legs constrained by skinny jeans. Careful not to mention Anka, Hana asked, "Where's your dad this week?"

"Oh, he's gone out with Mum buying furniture."

Hana kept her face straight, willing Charlotte to say more. She didn't and Jas interrupted the moment. "Hanny!" he yelled from the other side of the room. "Can I get a gingernut?"

Hana gave a pained nod and held up one finger. Charlotte giggled and covered her mouth with a hand. Each nail sported different coloured polish. She looked sideways at Hana. "I thought he meant you for a minute." She frowned. "But you dyed out your red. I always liked it."

"I fancied a change." Hana swallowed the truth and searched amongst the crowd for Jas. Standing didn't help. He appeared from behind her, falling over Charlotte's feet and carrying a swathe of drawings.

"Here you go," he said, dumping them on the seat. "I made Jesus less boring." He wriggled free before she could catch him. "I'll get you a biscuit."

Charlotte snorted and sifted through the art, giggling as she held up a scribbly Jesus with multi coloured sheep. "Oh, my!" she sniggered. "He's made the shepherd's crook into an assault rifle."

"Give me those!" Hana shuffled them into a pile, noticing Jesus wearing a bulletproof vest and a pointy green hat. His halo resembled pizza slices speckled with pepperoni. She watched Jas' slow progress as an elderly matron circulated the biscuit tray above his head.

"How's Logan?" Allen asked as Charlotte joined the futile biscuit trail.

"He went back to work." Hana kept her eyes on Jas, watching as he clambered onto a pew and dived for the biscuit tray. He missed and the old lady kept going, oblivious of the frustration left in her wake. Allen's wife scraped Jas off the carpet and stood him upright.

Allen patted her hand. "Please tell Logan, I pray for his health and welfare often."

Hana fixed her wooden smile in place. "I can give you his phone number. Then you can tell him yourself."

Allen's brow knitted and he peered at Hana through the tops of his eyes. She felt like a pre-schooler. "I hope you both know I'm here if you need me."

Hana opened her mouth to speak. She ached to blurt everything onto his capable shoulders and leave him to deal with it. Instead, she offered a lame thanks and rounded up Jas. She caught him putting four biscuits into his mouth at once and herded him outside. They didn't make it before he coughed up runny gingernut mess onto the carpet. Hana banged him on the back, her eyes watering at the thought of childish vomit. "Oh, please," she groaned. "Not here, not here."

"Is everything okay?" Allen's wife put her hand on Hana's shoulder and the promise of escape looked shaky. A tiny, bird boned woman, she looked the opposite of her burly husband.

"I'm fine," Hana gasped. "I don't feel so good."

"That's a contradiction in terms." Allen took her arm and led her into the fresh air, a recovered Jas trotting in front of them.

"What about the mess?" Hana asked. "I should clean it up."

"We'll do it." Allen handed her a business card. "Keep hold of this," he said, slipping it into the pocket of her handbag.

"But I know your number." Hana frowned and reached for the card. Allen pulled her fingers away and patted the pocket.

"Logan knows where I live, but not how to reach me otherwise," he replied. "Please give it to him."

Hana drove Jas home, wishing she possessed the courage to tell the cleric the truth. But which truth? The one where her marriage crumbled beneath smoke and mirrors, or that she feared single parenting again. Or the worse truth of all that her infant may not survive long enough to know either of its parents. "I'm too old for this," she said aloud.

Jas peered at her through the rear view mirror and sighed. "Me an all," he said. "I didn't like that biscuit game."

Back at home, he sped around the house on a tricycle, bumping into walls and furniture. He cried when he pitched off the steps into the back garden and then claimed it as part of the trick. Hana comforted him with cuddles and promises, killing the call from Logan's number to her phone. "Help me make lunch," she asked and Jas dried his tears on her blouse.

They made a peculiar smorgasbord of sandwiches, all of which revolted Hana. Jas tucked in to Marmite and blueberry jam while Hana tried not to look at the brown stuff oozing between his teeth. "Do you remember the little metal box I gave you?" she asked and he shook his head.

"No." The way he rolled his eyes raised Hana's suspicion.

"Yes you do. The night you didn't want to leave my house. You fell over my bag and it came out."

"What does it look like?" Jas shifted on his seat and shoved half a chicken paste sandwich onto a peanut butter one. Hana looked away and described the box, even including a tiny dent in the top. Jas continued to deny all knowledge until she lost her patience.

"I know you remember." Hana sighed in frustration. "What's the problem?"

Jas leaned close and Hana held onto her breakfast as he wafted Marmite breath in her face. "Doctor X wants it. It's the treasure chest. He's got the place bugged."

"I'd like to see it," Hana whispered, taking part in the charade. "To make sure it's safe."

"It's safe," Jas hissed. He dropped to the floor and crawled beneath the table, sandwich in hand. Hana squeaked as he touched her leg.

"Get back up here!"

"No! Doctor X is listening."

Hana persuaded him to help her load the dishwasher as a cover. Then she found herself on her knees in the middle of Action Man's battlefield. "What are we doing?" she whispered as Jas segregated tiny green soldiers with red armbands.

"We need to look," he said. "Let's put everything away and get it all out again."

"Just show me the box." Hana winced as a green soldier dug into her leg and Jas squealed and rescued him.

"Careful, Hanny! He could shoot yer balls off."

"Too late!" Hana replied. "And don't be rude."

Jas rolled his eyes and rescued four more green soldiers from beneath her.

"Are you sure it's here?" she groaned, an hour later.

"No. I fink it's gone." Jas looked shifty, poking his tongue into the side of his mouth and moving from foot to foot. "Maybe Doctor X captured it."

Hana nodded, rolling the last of his little tee shirts and putting them into a drawer in perfect colour-coded order. Jas enjoyed the process, wrenching open a dark cupboard where more clothing lurked. "Ooh more, Hanny. Do these."

Hana knelt in the centre of the spotless room with her hands on her hips. "Did your mother ask you to clean your room?"

"I think so." Jas pushed his bottom teeth over his top lip. "I think this might be my last chance."

"Or what?"

"Or she flushes my army down the toilet."

Hana groaned. "The metal box isn't here, is it?"

"I can't remember." Jas made goldfish faces with his lips. "You need to polish now."

"Polish yourself!" Hana sank onto the bed.

"Okay." Jas returned with white foam in his hair and an aerosol of polish in his hand. "I done it."

Half an hour later, they lay back on the bed. Swaddled in a towel, Jas wiped a hand through his hair. "It still stinks," he announced and Hana groaned.

"Tough," she answered. "I'm gutted about that metal box." She turned, so her face pressed against his pillow, smelling his baby shampoo and floral washing powder. Pushing her right hand under the pillow, her fingers contacted something sharp and she felt the sting of broken skin. "Ouch!" She pulled her hand out, sitting up to assess the damage.

The paper cut smarted and blood pooled in the opening. Another round of nausea passed over her head like a damp cloth. "Oh no, not again," she groaned.

"Sorry, Hanny," Jas whispered, cuddling her around the waist. He buried his face beneath her arm. "I'm a very bad boy."

"Why? What is that?" Hana reached for the pillow, but Jas let out a squeal and got there ahead of her. He dragged out the little metal box and clutched it in his hand.

Hana gaped. "Why did you do that?" she demanded. "You made me clean up your whole room looking for it!" His eyes filled with tears as he twisted the metal box around in his hand. Hana shook her head. "Don't do that, Jas, it's sharp. Look what it did." She held out her finger to show the trickle of blood and he threw himself at her, crying and burying his face into her arm.

"Sorry, sorry, sorry!" he wailed.

Hana sighed and stroked his head, sucking her sore finger. She waited, sensing irritation would produce nothing of value. After a moment of tearful sniffing, Jas popped his head up and the list of complaints began. "But you gived it to me and I really need it! I don't want you to take it away. Everyone takes away from me."

"So, why didn't you say that in the first place?"

Jas puckered his lips and shrugged. "Nobody listens. Mummy doesn't listen, kindy teachers doesn't listen, Daddy definitely doesn't listen."

"You assumed I wouldn't?" Hana swallowed a ball of guilt and chose honesty. "You're probably right." She took both his tiny wrists in her hands and pulled him close. "I'm sorry. I won't take the box from you today, but I need you to understand something. It's possible I gave the box away by mistake and it could become important. I might need it to protect me."

"This little box?" Jas looked down and turned it over in his palms, a hush of awe descending over him. "Protect you?"

Hana nodded, her movements slow and exact. "Yes. I'd like to look inside today, but then I'll need you to keep it very safe in case it's needed. You can hide it from everyone except me."

The child's eyes lit up like Christmas baubles and nodded with enthusiasm. "Not let Doctor X have it," he stated. Jabbing his finger at an ugly doll on the dressing table, he shook the box. "See this?" He waved it in his hand. "You ain't having it."

Hana nodded and waved to the infamous Doctor X and then turned her attention back to Jas. He took her hand and turned it over, placing the box into her palm with care.

Hana wasted five minutes of her life looking for an opening. She found edges and corners and sides which might be flaps. The box didn't open. "I can't do it," she announced, sounding desperate. "Did you ever get it open?" She shook it for the tenth time, hearing the dull rattle from inside. "I don't remember it making a noise before."

"Don't shake it!" Jas protested. "You'll mess it up!"

"Mess what up?" Hana released the box into his hands and he turned away. Carrying it to the other side of the room, he scrabbled in a carton on the ancient dressing table. Hana stood and he waved her away.

"You can't look."

"Why?"

"Because I'm not sposed to have needles." Hana saw a flash of shiny metal and leaned sideways, watching as Jas poked a thin embroidery needle into a corner of the box. She heard a click. He turned back to her, the box dismantled in his palm. "See," he said, grinning in victory. "Easy peasy."

Hana's eyes widened and her jaw gaped. A mathematical net sat in the child's hand, delicate but simple. The single sheet of thin metal hung slack on its bottom, the sides leaned outwards like a circus trick. Its lid formed part of a long side, rising above the object like a claw ready to close. The whole container looked no bigger than a matchbox. "How did that happen?"

Jas strode across, his brow creased in concentration. His tone sounded irritated as though not comprehending Hana's intellectual dullness. "Easy." They bowed their heads over it and he pointed out several features. "This magnet keeps the lid shut. You need to push a needle through that teensy hole there to pop it off." Hana looked closer, seeing the miniscule dent which she'd mistaken for damage. Jas clicked it closed in his hand and licked his lips. His voice sounded strained. "What I like best about it is the stickiness." He walked over to a white board and swiped magnetic alphabet letters aside. "It sticks real good." The box seemed to leap from the child's palm and hurl itself to the board with something like glee. "Real good." Jas turned with his bottom lip hanging low with misery. "I don't want you to take it away."

Hana swallowed. "Just show me what's inside."

Jas reopened with the box and held it up to her face, so close that her eyes crossed with the effort of looking in. A tiny green rifle sat in the bottom with a miniature necktie. Jas heaved out a sigh. "You shaked it and messed it up. My commander got blowed up and I was taking his things back to his platoon."

"Oh." Hana sat back and felt the blood rush to her head with disappointment.

"I know. It's shocking." Jas snapped the box closed with practiced expertise. "Mum sucked him up with the vacuum. She made me open the bag outside, but it was too late. It chewed him right up."

"When I gave it to you, did you find anything else inside?" Hana's voice wobbled and disenchantment coursed through her veins.

Jas smiled in approval at her appropriate grief for a fallen hero and patted her knee. "Yeah. Papers and a wubber band."

"And where did you put them, the papers and the rubber band?"

"Dunno." Jas shrugged, his interest waning. "Lofty played with them."

Hana pictured the giant ginger cat and swallowed all hope of retrieval. "Can you help me find them again?" she asked, but Jas shook his head.

"Lofty can. But not me."

Hana closed her eyes and waited for the sense of defeat to pass. "Promise you'll keep the box safe?" she whispered and Jas grinned and stuck it to the magnet board. The alphabet letters edged closer as if moved by an invisible hand. Her gaze strayed to untouched corners of the room, desperate to take it apart and hunt for the contents of the box. Exhaustion overwhelmed her and turned her feet to lead. She needed help to move the furniture. She also needed Jas to be somewhere else when she did it.

Hana congratulated herself on solving part of the mystery. Someone hid a precious object in a box made by a schoolboy in metalwork. They stuck it to the underside of her vehicle. That scenario smacked of her car being in the wrong place at the wrong time. The next part of the intrigue could prove even harder. Whatever the box contained led to a woman's disappearance and turned Hana's life upside down. "It's important, but not urgent," Hana said and Jas glanced across at her.

"What is?"

"The papers in the box are important to someone, but not urgent enough for them to throw everything at finding me and reclaiming it. They're taking their time."

"They don't need it yet then." Jas crawled around the floor, placing his soldiers at strategic battle points. "They know they're gonna need it soon, but not yet. They've still got time."

"Time for what though?" Hana mused.

Jas gave her a knowing sideways look. "Time to take revenge on Mummy for killing the commander. I'm putting them in battle formation. If she comes in with ice cream, they won't shoot her but if she comes to tell me off, I'll turn them loose."

"Nice." Hana raised her eyebrows and tracked the trajectory from the green soldier's gun to the door. "So, you're playing at it for the moment then?"

"Yeah!" Jas snorted. "Course I'm playing. I'm a bit busy with other things at the moment and she might give me ice cream. It's maybe not a good time for a war."

"A bit busy." Hana mouthed the words to herself and realised the cold, hard truth. The blonde man saw her as a sideline, someone to hound and torture when he got bored. Or when he needed to.

"It doesn't fit," she told Bodie on the phone later. "There's no urgency for the blonde man. I'm actually not that hard to find. Michael Laval wants this thing enough to kill a woman and compromise himself with Ethel Bowman. But not the blonde man. He's stalling, putting in just enough effort to look good, whilst leaving the box in my possession."

Bodie chuckled. "Hell of a stretch, Mum."

"Maybe." Hana ran a hand over her stomach, fancying it protruded through her nightdress a little. "What if two separate groups want this thing? Has anyone considered that?"

-25-

The term started with a perfect winter Monday. A dense fog surrounded Culver's Cottage, making it impossible to see beyond the lawned garden. Logan moved aside as Hana reached for her jacket. "The weather forecast says the mist will burn off by midday. It should be sunny."

Hana acknowledged his words with a smile and nodded, turning away to get into the car. Filtered sunlight glistened off the frost on the new driveway and she perched in the passenger seat in silence. The concrete surface made the downward slope appear much less frightening.

Hana sought the sunshine at lunchtime, sitting on a bench in the sun after the boys returned to class. Bodie's phone call disturbed her. He found nothing of interest in Jas' bedroom. She struggled with the sandwich Logan made her, managing only half. She tipped the rest into a bin next to her and leaned back in the seat, enjoying the warmth on her face.

"I saw that!" Angus sat down next to her. Hana smiled but didn't look up. "I tell the boys off for biffing their lunch and then I see you do it."

"Not hungry," she replied. "Sorry."

"Boris is leaving soon," Angus began and Hana whipped round to face him.

"Already?" She did the sums in her head and sighed, realising they fast approached late July. He always planned to return to Germany to complete his teaching degree. "I guess he's due home," she conceded.

"I'm asking my secretary to organise a leaving gift for him. Would you like to contribute?"

Hana nodded. "Yes, please. Count me in."

"What about Logan?" Angus raised an eyebrow and Hana looked away and shaded her eyes with her hand.

"You must ask him." She floundered and stood to leave.

"Don't go." It emerged as a command and Hana froze in place, dreading Angus' next question.

"Have you noticed anything odd about Boris of late?"

Hana relaxed as the question avoided the sensitive sore of her marriage. "No. Why?"

Angus shook his head. "It's nothing more than a feeling. He's lost his easy going nature and it happened overnight. His mood seems rather dark and serious and I wondered if he'd confided in you." He raised his hand. "I won't ask you to break confidences, but if it's something major, I wish to know."

Hana blinked. "No. I see him in passing but we aren't close anymore. Sorry, I can't help you." She smiled to close the conversation and backed away.

"Did the police ever sort out your little mess with the chaps following you? You don't look well, Hana. Is it the strain or something else?" Angus' red hair fluffed in the breeze and his brown eyes bored into hers.

Hana swallowed and shook her head. "We still need to take care. I'm fed up of feeling a prisoner."

Angus released her with a nod and Hana bolted before his interrogation turned to Logan or worse, Caroline. She reasoned he must already know and it unsettled and embarrassed her. Logan's open-air statement regarding the exact nature of his relationship with Caroline did nothing to stem the flow of gossip. If anything, it exacerbated it and made him look even worse. Rumours of the car park altercation still circulated in the absence of anything better to talk about. Hana heard one version in which she allegedly fought Caroline and got herself arrested.

Pausing at the top of the stairs to watch a tui rest in the branches of a kowhai tree, Hana wondered if the blonde man observed her right then. Hopelessness and vulnerability washed over her. The half-eaten sandwich felt leaden and she rested a gentle hand over her stomach. A sound behind made her jump and she turned to see Logan leaned against the wall. His pockets constrained his hands and concern edged his expression. "You okay?" he asked, his tone casual. "Did you eat your lunch?"

Hana glanced back at the tui, fancying it judged the lie on her lips. "Yes, thank you. I'm fine and I loved the sandwich."

Logan's lips pursed. "I saw you throw it away. What did Angus want?"

"That's creepy." Hana raised her eyebrows. "You know all my movements but I'm not privy to yours."

"I've watched you since that first day in the car park. I love you and I don't lie to you, Hana."

She inhaled, tired of the constant sparring. "Don't you?"

"No." Logan's dark eyes narrowed to slits. "What do you want to know?"

"Nothing!" Hana hissed her reply, embarrassed as a group of boys clattered past. It pained her to do her dirty laundry in public. Not the English way.

Logan waited for the boys to pass, raising an eyebrow in challenge at one who dared to glance back. Then he removed his hands from his pockets and approached his rigid wife. She smelled his familiar aftershave and her heart gave a throb of pain. She missed their connection; short lived but passionate. Hana swallowed as the index finger of Logan's left hand caressed her jaw. Before she could move, his right arm snaked around her waist. "I can't stand this," he whispered. "I'll tell you anything you want to know. It's a one-time offer."

Hana opened her mouth to reply, something suitably barbed on her tongue. The sensation came from low in her stomach and she gasped and pressed her fingers over it.

"What happened?" Paternal terror flashed in Logan's eyes and stole away Hana's resolve. If she wanted to hurt him, she knew how. "What should I do?" His arm tightened around her waist, ready to hold her up if she needed it. The peculiar sensation continued a while longer and then ceased, leaving tears in her eyes.

Hana exhaled and tried to release herself from Logan's grip. "The baby moved," she said, blinking away specs of salt water from her eyelashes. They ran down her cheeks leaving a trail. "I've blocked it out until now." She sniffed and wiped her face on her sleeve. "It dislikes being ignored."

"Did it hurt?" Logan's brow creased and his childish innocence acted as a spear in Hana's side. The naked emotion in his face wasn't for her and it stung.

"No." She shook her head and pushed Logan's hands away, leaving the staircase without looking back. "Stick your one-time offer of honesty, Logan Du Rose," she breathed.

At her desk, Hana collected herself and focussed on the tumbling emotions the tiny, butterfly movements evoked. "I can't pretend anymore, can I baby?" she whispered. Her rational mind reminded her that thoughts of bringing a Du Rose baby into the world terrified her almost as much as not managing to.

The following week, Hana rang the doctor's surgery and made an appointment. Amy let her use the landline and watched her with a raised eyebrow. "Is Logan going with you?" she asked and Hana chewed her bottom lip.

"No. I won't tell him."

"Why?"

"I don't know." Hana sighed. "The Caroline thing I suppose. But also because he left the house again last night. He thinks I don't notice when he leaves after I'm in bed."

Amy plonked a drink in front of her. "You sound like Bodie and me." Her brow furrowed. "Always missing the connection." She waved a biscuit at Hana. "As long as you're not punishing him. Children aren't weapons."

Hana rolled her eyes. "You think I don't know that?"

Amy smirked and turned back to loading the dishwasher.

Hana worked through the week, fielding calls about the upcoming Expo and documenting everything in case she suddenly disappeared again. When her phone buzzed on her desk one morning, the caller shocked her. "Anka, hi." Hana kept her voice clipped and her friend responded with understandable awkwardness.

"Hi, Hana. Would you mind meeting me for coffee tomorrow?"

Hana gnawed on the inside of her cheek. The overwhelming need for female company made her crave Anka's friendship, while reality reminded her why they no longer enjoyed one. She agreed and told Logan, expecting him to kick up a fuss. He didn't. "Why don't I drop you at the cafe?" he suggested. "Then you can use me as an excuse if you need to escape. Just send me an empty text and I'll come."

He dropped her on a Grey Street cafe and Hana found Anka already inside. She walked towards her table with her heart creating a drum roll in her chest. Anka sat alone, chewing her thumbnail and flipping a sugar sachet in the other hand. She rose as Hana approached. "Hi, how are you?" she asked and Hana accepted the trivial chitchat as a starter.

"Great thanks. How are you?"

"Oh, you know." Anka shrugged, brushing off the question like water off wax.

Hana inhaled the scent of coffee, testing her stomach by degrees. A single bout of sickness early in the week ensured she remained wary.

Anka looked thinner, wearing a chic jacket a few sizes too large for her. She appeared tense and kept her eyes moving around the shop to avoid Hana's gaze. Hana flicked her coat over the back of the chair, hauling her blouse down to cover the open top button of her trousers. They sat and ordered drinks from a passing waitress before Hana turned to business. "Why are we here, Anka?" She waited, her face expressionless as Anka struggled. An awkward silence descended over them and Hana kept her nerve, refusing to gush and smooth over the cracks as she once would.

When Anka said nothing, she stood. "I should probably leave.

This wasn't a good idea." Hana reached for her phone.

"Don't!" Anka swallowed and her eyelashes fluttered. "Give me a chance. I know Logan's not very far away and I'm sure he wants this to fail." Her hands flapped in front of her. "Can't say I blame him."

The waitress arrived with their drinks and Hana sat again, her fingers playing with the straw in her smoothie. Anka took a sip of her latte and Hana held her breath for a number of reasons. "I want to apologise," Anka said. "I just don't know where to start."

"Oh." Hana's eyes widened in surprise. She expected justifications and the same stone wall she ran up against before. Its absence left her without a ready reply. "Thank you," she said after a moment of floundering. "I appreciate it." She bent her head and sucked strawberry smoothie up the straw.

Anka wasn't finished. "Ivan asked me to come home. He says he's forgiven me and we're trying to put things back together. It will never be as before, but I think it's what I want."

Hana raised her eyebrows and nodded. "Charlotte told me. Weeks ago."

"Ah, yes. I should've got in touch sooner." She tripped over her words. "I feel embarrassed about my behaviour and I put off meeting you for that reason." Anka closed her eyes and her expression radiated pain through the dark shadows of sleeplessness. "I have no excuses." When she opened her eyes, Hana saw tears glittering as they formed up to create a deluge.

"I accept your apology. We need not rake through it all." She screwed up the corners of her eyes and placed a hand over Anka's.

"I found the bottom of who I really am and I don't like her." Anka's whisper caused Hana to wince.

"Don't," she replied, shaking her head. "None of us are perfect. Do you remember what that pastor from Africa once said? 'I knew who I was when I leaned forward, because it came out of my mouth.' It's like that for all of us. We discover our worst faults under pressure."

"I didn't think I could be that diabolical though." Anka pursed her lips and Hana snorted. A combination of relief and brain freeze made her giddy.

"Sorry. That hits a bit close to home. I've behaved like a brat recently."

Anka nodded and her smile looked easier. "I know Ivan rang you after I left. I also know he blamed you and that wasn't fair. He'll apologise when he sees you."

"No." Hana waved a hand in denial. "Tell him not to. I want to forget all of it."

Anka reached for Hana's hand, holding it until the circulation struggled. Hana ground her teeth and hoped she let go before nerve damage started. Something in her friend's expression made her doubt. "It is over, isn't it?" she demanded, narrowing her eyes.

"Yes!" Anka let go of her hand, a small, telling action. "Tama followed me up north, got drunk and caused trouble where I worked. They fired me. I caught the bus to Mangawhai Heads. It seemed appropriate to go to the last place I remembered being happy."

Hana chewed her lip and thought about Anka's words, searching her own life for the last time she felt happy. She knew the answer. Her wedding night.

Anka swallowed another mouthful of coffee. "I sat for a day and cried my eyes out. What I'd done seemed so unbelievable. When I got to the very end of my rope, Ivan checked in. He won't say how he found me, but I think your son played a part." Anka licked her lips. "It's almost too fantastic to be true, but Tama turned up there. He looked so drunk; I'm amazed he made it. He said he followed the bus, but drove too far south before realising I already got off. He looked wasted."

"So Ivan gave him a black eye?" Hana watched Anka's slow nod.

"Yeah. Ivan didn't want to hit him, but Tama saw him and went crazy. He launched himself at Ivan with a tyre wrench in his hand."

Hana shuddered, wishing Liza let her call the police when Tama produced the crowbar and hit Logan. She sighed. "Is that the moment Tama remembered Ivan trained as a purple belt in Judo?"

"About then, yeah." Anka sighed.

Finishing her smoothie, Hana felt the discomfort growing in her belly and shifted around on her chair. "Could we go for a walk?" she asked.

Anka nodded and retrieved her jacket, also grabbing the bill for the drinks before Hana could reach for her purse. "My treat," she muttered.

Hana texted Logan from the bathroom, explaining they would walk for a while and return to the cafe. The smiley face he sent impressed her as opposed to his usual trick of reading and not replying.

The women breathed in the wintry air near the riverbank and Anka looked sideways at Hana. "You look happy," she commented. "I'm pleased it worked out."

Hana fought the urge to scream that it hadn't, blanching beneath the inaccuracy of the assumption. She didn't remember what happy felt like anymore. Happiness died the day after her wedding.

Logan picked Hana up from outside the cafe, giving Anka a cursory nod. The smile he gave her didn't reach his eyes. He neither wanted nor expected an apology. Hana waved as the car pulled away from the curb, sitting in silence during the car ride. "Did you tell her?" Logan asked, breaking the silence. "About the baby?"

"No." Hana shook her head, her tone sad in the darkness. "It's not the kind of friendship to share secrets in anymore." He nodded and pulled his shirt away from his scar. Hana furrowed her brow at the sleight-of-hand action, reminded of his constant pain and difficulty in healing. She often forgot that he bore the physical wounds from Anka and Tama's indiscretion. It put her self-pity into perspective. "Did you go to the gym at lunchtime?" she asked, attempting to make conversation.

Logan nodded and turned the car onto Hakarimata Road. His fringe bobbed against his eyelashes. "Yeah. I ran on the treadmill. No point trying to lift weights yet. I've missed all the soccer musters and grading games, anyway. There's no rush now."

"I'm sorry." Hana reached across and laid a tentative hand on his thigh. He jumped in surprise and the car jerked sideways. "I'm sorry for everything," she whispered. Tears pricked against her eyelids and she felt grateful for the strong hand which encased her fingers.

"It's okay," he replied.

The butterfly in her stomach began again, a steady insistent flutter. Hana's faith in her ability to achieve any level of happiness increased.

Gentle lights flowed from Culver's Cottage as timer lamps flicked themselves on with the growing darkness. Logan drove the Honda down the slope and under the opening garage door, avoiding exposure to the biting wind outside. "I'll turn the alarm off," he said, skipping up the stairs ahead of Hana. She knew he checked the house each night, searching for intruders despite the burglar alarm.

Hana followed, watching her footing in the yellow glow from the overhead bulb. Her trousers cut into her waist and the stairs felt endless. Logan clattered around in the kitchen and Hana called to him, "I'll get into my pyjamas. My trousers hurt." She yanked on her zipper, groaning with relief as it slid down and allowed her to breathe. She paused for a moment, measuring the gentle swell of her stomach. Turning towards the bedroom, Hana caught sight of something through the corner of her eye. The glass door to the roof garden blinked back at her, her view obscured by the darkness. "What's that?" she said, walking towards the door.

"What?" Logan stuck his head through the kitchen doorway. "Tea or water?"

"No!" Hana raised her hand to her mouth and knelt down. "Oh no!" A small shape slumped on the doormat, lit by the glow from the hall light. "It's Tiger!" Hysteria raised Hana's voice and her breathing hitched. "He's dead!"

Logan's long stride sent him to her side in a matter of seconds. He crouched next to her and pulled her hand from the glass. "It's a possum," he said, slipping an arm around her shoulders.

Hana looked at the glassy dead eyes of the creature and it stared through her, its matted fur on end in several places. Her mind flicked her back in time to the lifeless body of her husband laid on a mortuary slab in a clinical chapel. "Hana?" Logan squeezed her shoulder and looked down at her. "It's just a possum. They bait up here so the cat probably killed it."

Hana collapsed onto her bottom and heaved in a huge breath. "It's too hard." She gulped and Logan felt her body slump. "I can't do this," she gasped.

"Hana, it's okay." Logan supported her body as she reeled, sensing she meant more than the furry corpse on the doormat. Its eyes glinted. "Sweetheart, things have a way of sorting themselves out. I promise."

"No." Hana shook her head and twisted away from him. "It's all ruined. Everything is ruined. I need to get away from all this death and violence." Her hands caressed her stomach. "I can't do any of it."

Logan pulled her to her feet and held her, pushing her face into his chest and stroking her back. "I'll sort it," he promised. "I'll sort everything. It's all I've tried to do."

Tiger bounced onto the roof garden and plastered his body against the glass. He cuffed the dead possum with an outstretched paw and then danced backwards as though expecting it to stand and fight. Logan swore and Hana looked up. She opened her mouth to protest and he pressed a finger against her lips. "I'll get rid of it," he said. "Go to the bedroom."

Hana moved backwards at a snail's pace. Her gaze followed Logan as he unlocked the door and stepped onto the roof garden. He skirted the possum in his socks, swearing as he stepped in a pool of blood. Acid rose into Hana's mouth and she inhaled, only just making it to the bathroom before vomiting.

She sat by the toilet, listening as Logan locked up the back door. He ran down to the garage and the thought of the blood on his socks sent Hana back over the bowl. He reappeared as she rinsed her mouth under the tap. "Hey, I got rid of it." Logan waited until she sat on the side of the bath before washing his hands with soap and water.

"What about your socks?" Hana dabbed at her eyes with a tissue.

"Dustbin." Logan ran a damp hand across his face. "I'm sorry."

"Why?"

He shrugged. "I should've seen it first and saved you the upset. I let you down." He sat on the edge of the bath next to her. "I've done a lot of that lately." Olive fingers raked through his dark hair. "I never expected to suck at marriage so badly."

Hana nodded. "It's harder than it looks." She rubbed her eyes with her fingers, trying to remove the awful image of death which seemed burned on her retinas. "Are you sure the cat killed it?" she asked. "What if the blonde man found us and put it there as a warning?"

"He didn't." Logan took both her hands in his. "I promise. Will you trust me?"

Hana groaned. "Not that again. Logan, right now I can't even trust myself." She threw her head back and fixed her gaze on the ceiling. "There's too much happening."

Logan looked crushed, his irises dull and his lips turned down. "But I love you Hana Du Rose," he whispered. "I'll do anything to make it right."

"Yeah, I think you will." Hana looked into his face and ached for him. The wall between them lost a few bricks off the top and she shuffled closer. "Hold me?" she asked, sighing as Logan's arms wrapped around her. He breathed into her neck and didn't let go. His hand shook as he stroked her hair, teasing out small tangles and running the curls through his fingers.

Hana jumped as Tiger padded across the floor and wound his body through their legs. He jumped and butted the underside of her knee with his head, licking his lips and showing extreme pleasure with his conquest. Logan kissed the top of Hana's head and gave her a squeeze. "Let me help you into bed and I'll bring you a hot drink."

Hana nodded and staggered to her feet, testing out her sea legs before attempting to walk. She lurched through to the bedroom, stripping out of her clothes on the way. Dumping the bundle on the chair, she flopped into the huge bed, no energy left even for talking.

-26-

Hana stirred as Bodie raised his voice. "I know what you did!" he shouted.

"Don't fight." Sleep slurred her words and the dream whipped them around her head until she no longer understood them.

"He's talking crap as usual." Vik postured and Hana cringed. She knew what came next and exhaustion sapped her energy.

"Don't say it!" she shouted. "Don't tell him. Please, don't tell him." She shot up the bed, seeing the horror in Bodie's eyes.

Her feet felt glued to the mattress as she struggled to release them from the sheets. The cold air bit into her bare legs. Hana spun on the spot, trying to remember the way to the door and the voices ceased. "No!" she begged. "Please, no."

Groggy and disoriented, she weaved around the room, tracing the furniture with her outstretched fingers until she found the door. She pushed it, feeling it resist. "I need to get out!" She slapped it with the palm of her hands, panic rising into her chest. "Let me out!"

"It's okay, Hana. Let me do it." The arm around her chest felt strong and confident fingers pulled her away from the door. Logan gripped her wrists in one hand and pulled her towards him, feeling her body jerk in fright. "It's okay," he repeated, easing the door towards them. "It opens inwards, remember?"

"No!" Hana slapped at his hands in panic. The door opened out, not inward. She hated it, unable to slam herself into the bedroom and vent her disappointment and rage. Still, he held her and the bedroom filled with the noise of her rasping breaths. The house sounded silent and it confused her. "Where's Bo?" she demanded. "I don't understand."

"He's at home in bed." Logan's steady voice added to the sense of calm. "You're dreaming, Hana."

Grief washed over her like a breaking wave and the barriers around her heart failed her in the darkness. Hana sobbed and Logan held her like a delicate piece of china, fearing the break on the inside might permeate to the outer. "I wish you'd tell me," he whispered into her hair. Hana shook her head into his chest, remembering a phrase she heard the school chaplain use. 'Trauma is like a packet of frozen peas. We drag it from the freezer years after they were snap frozen and packaged. Unless we deal with them, the emotions will taste just as fresh.'

The bitterness and the overwhelming sense of loss never changed for Hana. Life dulled the sharpness of its cut, but when tiredness overwhelmed her senses and forgetfulness altered reality, she felt it. The knowledge hit her like the grind of a broken bone, as painful each time as the first.

Hana cried until exhaustion claimed her, sweaty and clammy in the wide bed. Logan held her, brushing her hair back from her damp forehead and aching for her. The night terrors grew in intensity with each passing day of the pregnancy and he lacked the expertise to prevent them. Something from Hana's past rose up to trouble her, but daytime left her tight lipped and in denial. She never remembered and he learned not to mention them. For weeks, her reliance on him to help her escape the room in her mind with the strange tricky door provided his only opportunity to demonstrate his love. Even if she blocked out his assistance during daylight hours. "Where do you go, Hana?" he whispered into her hair.

"Apartment," she replied with a sigh. "Vik." Her mind wandered back to the scruffy flat she and Vik barely afforded on their combined student loans. They brought the infant Bodie there at two days old, fumbling through the first year of a shaky marriage built on the foundations of an accidental pregnancy.

Logan sighed and stroked her back, jumping as Hana shot from the bed at speed. He heard her in the bathroom again and shook his head. Following, he handed her a wad of toilet roll to wipe her mouth once she felt the sickness ebb. She cleaned her teeth, trying not to look at the pale middle-aged woman staring back at her from the mirror. "I'm sorry," she groaned, leaning her forehead against the cold wall.

Logan settled her back into bed and tucked her beneath the covers. "I'll fetch you a drink of warm water," he said, his voice soft. "Will that help?"

Hana nodded and listened to his footsteps pad through the house. She rubbed her eyes and wished away the night terrors which threatened more frequently of late. Logan returned with two mugs and Tiger hot on his heels. The cat leapt onto the bed and clawed at the rucks in the duvet. "Thanks." Hana sat up and accepted the drink, holding it aloft so as not to spill as Logan settled onto the bed next to her.

"Did the possum cause the nightmare?" Logan asked, his expression thoughtful. "Or something else."

Hana set her mug on the bedside table and cuddled beneath the blankets. She pushed away the temptation to lie. "It started tonight's," she admitted. "My first nightmare happened after Vik's funeral and they come when I'm stressed. They've got worse lately."

Logan nodded and his eyebrows raised and fell. "I know."

"I can sleep somewhere else if you want me to." Hana chewed her lip and watched Logan's eyes narrow.

"You can try it," he said, his face growing hard. "But I'll carry you straight back into my bed."

Hana closed her eyes against the warm glow in her chest. His possessiveness revived a deep sense of longing. Logan reached out and stroked her hair. "You call for your husband." His voice sounded empty and lost. For the first time since she married him, she saw the spectre of her dead husband challenging Logan for her affection. She understood how that must feel. Vik's influence permeated further than Caroline's. She could tarnish her own reputation with her behaviour, but Vik couldn't. Death sainted him, yet he operated a long way from saintly during his lifetime.

Hana gritted her teeth. "It's not what you think, Logan." She inhaled and breathed out through pursed lips. "But I don't want to talk about it right now." Her hand sought her belly beneath the sheets and she steeled herself to confess at least part of her anxiety. "Bodie didn't find the contents of the box in Jas' room. It feels like the end of the road for me right now. I thought if I found the papers Jas tipped out, I'd have a bargaining chip for when the blonde man found me. Now I have nothing."

"Let's go to Amy's after work tomorrow," Logan suggested. "I'll pull the room apart." His long strokes across Hana's head made her grow tired as she relaxed. Guilt pricked at her at the memory of her doctor's appointment. Logan wrapped a curl around his finger. "What do you think?"

"I can't tomorrow." Hana swallowed and her body stiffened.

Logan sighed. "I work with teenage boys for a living, Hana. I spend my life listening to fabrications and blatant lies. Please don't insult my intelligence."

"I can't!" She hid her face in the pillow. "I'm busy tomorrow."

"Don't push me away, Hana. I'm in this for the long haul. You don't have to do this alone." His words, carefully chosen and well-aimed, resonated within Hana's psyche. He sounded desperate. "Please babe, I'm struggling here. I don't know what to do. You're the best thing that's ever happened to me."

Hana took his hand and pulled it beneath the sheets. She spread his fingers and lay them over her stomach. The tiny being fluttered and moved around in the unaccustomed wakefulness of the night. Logan inhaled and held his breath, connecting with his child as it halted and restarted its frantic activity. He shifted down the bed and kept his hand over Hana's belly, holding her until they both dropped off to sleep.

Logan awoke with a start, noticing daylight filtering through a gap in the curtains. "Oh, crap!" He swore and withdrew from Hana. "I'm meeting Angus before tutor group." He slipped from the bed and glanced back at her. "You look unwell, babe. Stay home. I'll tell Sheila you're sick."

"I've things to do at work," Hana complained, following him to the bathroom. The sight of toothpaste on his chin churned her stomach. She slumped onto the side of the bath. "Maybe I should stay home," she conceded.

Logan ran around like a maniac, dragging on clothes and hopping as he put his boots on at the front door. "I'll see you later," he said, dragging Hana towards him and kissing her forehead.

"I need the car!" Her eyes widened in realisation. "Please don't take it."

Logan stopped and examined her face. "Why?"

"If I get worse, I'll take myself to the doctor's." She blinked, knowing he saw straight through her fabrication.

"Okay. I'll ride the bike." Logan ran to the garage and slipped his leathers over his clothes, slamming his visor down to cover his suspicion.

"Be careful," Hana said from the bottom step. She gave a small wave and attempted to smile. The noise of the engine roared over her voice. "There's a head of faculty meeting tonight, isn't there?" Logan gave an upward jerk of his head and steered his bike under the open garage door. He glanced backwards but Hana couldn't read his face expression through the tinted visor. She dropped the garage door behind him.

Feeling conflicted about not going to work, Hana also enjoyed the opportunity to slow down. She took her time dressing and tidied up after Logan's mad dash around the house. His pyjama shorts lay on the hall floor and the bathroom looked like a bomb went off in the soap dish. The nausea pursued her from one end of the house to the other, assuaged by a piece of dry toast around ten o'clock.

Hana avoided the roof garden, shying away from memories of the furry corpse. She logged onto the school server for a few hours in the afternoon, answering emails from Sheila. She clambered into the bath at two o'clock, luxuriating in the deep metal tub and ignoring the phone when it rang. The child moved around in her stomach, disturbed by Hana's raised body temperature. She rested her palm over the tiny bump, knowing its movements would become visible soon, like the pitch and roll of an earthquake. "The doctor's appointment will make you real," she sighed. "You'll be written into my medical notes and other people will know about you."

Hana stepped out of the bath with care, pulling the plug and watching the bubbles exit. They fought their way down the plughole as though duelling for a fantastic prize instead of being first through the smelly pipe to the septic tank. She dried herself and dressed in clothing a doctor could poke around in, giggling at the lewdness of the thought. Twenty-seven years earlier, a naïve Hana stripped almost naked at her first antenatal appointment. Her sleeves proved too long for a blood test and her dress ended up hiked to her ribs. "Trousers and a blouse this time," she said, drawing a jacket over her shoulders.

Hana bent to collect her handbag from the floor next to the front door, shrieking in shock as the gate alarm sounded. Headlights bounced up the long slope and she looked around for somewhere to hide. When the house rumbled with the motor from the garage door, she peeked from behind the lounge curtains with one shoe on and one off.

"Hana?" Logan strode along the hallway in his boots, searching the rooms for her. She limped into the lounge doorway.

"Hi." She wrung her hands and guilt passed across her face.

"Are you leaving me?" He jerked his head at her outdoor jacket and single shoe, biting into his bottom lip. "I don't want you to."

"Did you flag the faculty meeting?" Hana slid past him and chased the other shoe with her toes. "I'm just nipping out."

Logan snorted. "What do you think? Of course, I flagged the meeting. Where are you going? I rang and you didn't answer."

Hana exhaled and muttered her destination. Logan stepped in front of her and rested his hands on her shoulders. "Where are you going, Hana?"

Her body sagged. "To the doctor's."

"You got sicker?" The concern in his eyes exacerbated her guilt.

"No. I need to get my pregnancy confirmed and set up antenatal appointments."

"Oh." Logan dropped his hands and stepped back. "And you don't want me there?" He swallowed and pain marched across his handsome features.

Hana felt the sting in her heart and held out the Honda keys. "Please would you drive?"

The doctor's surgery in Ngaruawahia heaved with patients and Hana missed the days when men offered their seats to women. The receptionist eyed Logan with dread and inspected him for a broken bone or hemorrhage.

"I have an appointment," Hana told her, offering her credit card before the woman could object. They lurked in the corner next to a fish tank and Hana watched the colourful bodies swim in lazy circles. When she snorted, Logan looked at her with narrowed eyes. "Rent a Tank," Hana said with raised eyebrows. "Is that like fish prostitution?"

Logan pursed his lips and looked away as thirty other patients turned their gaze in Hana's direction. His eyes laughed at her and she grinned like a child. "Is it?"

Hana grew irritated as the time ticked by. She grabbed Logan's arm and sought his watch for the fifth time. "My appointment started half an hour ago," she grumbled, fidgeting with the cord for the window blinds. The stopper came off in her fingers and her eyes grew round and frightened.

"Stop fiddling!" Logan rebuked and tied it back on. When a seat came free, he forced her into it and plonked a women's magazine in her lap. "Behave," he hissed.

When the doctor appeared and called Hana's name, she leapt up like a game show contestant. Logan hesitated, not knowing whether to follow or wait. Hana turned and read uncertainty in his furrowed brow and pursed lips. "Come on," she whispered and beckoned with her hand.

"Are you sure?" he asked, glancing sideways at the doctor.

"Yes." Hana offered him a smile and Logan nodded and followed her into the office. He bowed to allow his head to pass beneath the lintel.

"How can I help you?" The Indian doctor looked tired, dark circles underlining his brown eyes. "Sorry for the delay. Friday is always like this. Nobody wants to pay the weekend fees."

"I'm pregnant," Hana began. "And old."

The doctor threw his head back and laughed. "Those things aren't synonymous." He dipped his hand into his desk drawer and pulled out a tube. "Do a urine sample and we'll test it and take it from there."

Hana walked into the room after squeezing out another wee, finding Logan and the doctor chatting about soccer. "That was embarrassing," she grumbled. Logan turned to greet her and his eyes widened at the sight of the frothy mixture in the tube. "The lid went down the toilet." Hana pouted and handed it over. "And it wouldn't all fit in. Everyone in the waiting room watched me drip it across reception."

The doctor performed a dip test on Hana's sample over the basin.

He retained some for testing. Logan watched with interest. "Is it like making homebrew?" he asked and the doctor laughed. Hana glared at her husband, expecting a degree of decorum now she'd let him into her pregnant world.

Washing and drying his hands, the doctor invited Hana over to the bed. "Congratulations, it's positive. Let's take a look at you," he said.

Hana lay on the bed and lifted her blouse so he could palpate her stomach. "How is it going?" he asked.

"I'm still sick," Hana admitted. "I guessed at twelve weeks but it can't be more than that."

"Okay. Does this hurt?" The doctor prodded her kidneys and Hana groaned. The curtain at the end of the bed moved and Logan slipped between there and the wall. He jammed himself into the tiny space and glared at the doctor, daring him to elicit another groan from Hana. "There's blood in your urine. You might have an infection. That would cause excessive sickness." He pressed her stomach again, walking his fingers around her uterus. "It feels like the end of the first trimester," he commented. "I think twelve weeks is about right. The midwife will book you in for a scan." He pressed harder and Hana's eyes widened as a bubble of wind worked its way through her tubes. She feared she might let rip under the force of the doctor's fingers and give Logan's hair an unexpected parting.

Stepping back, the doctor pulled Hana's blouse over her stomach. "Sit up when you're ready," he said. "Then we'll talk." He swished the curtains closed behind him. Hana sighed and pulled up her zipper, standing and shoving her feet into her shoes. She glanced up at her husband.

"Are you coming?" she whispered, concerned at the curious expression on his face.

"In a minute," he replied, looking uncomfortable.

Hana sat in her seat and rested her hands in her lap. "I can't remember the drill," she admitted. "I had my older children over twenty years ago. You might have to explain things."

"Let's wait for your partner." The doctor glanced at his watch.

"Logan?" Hana turned in her seat when Logan didn't appear. She shot the doctor a curious look and walked back to the curtain. Yanking it aside, she discovered Logan fiddling with something on his leg. "What are you doing?"

Logan's body sagged. "I'm stuck."

The conversation degenerated as the doctor wasted time cutting a hole in Logan's work pants. "How did you do this?" he demanded, lying on his stomach with his face just centimetres from Logan's groin.

"There's a metal spike on the bed," Logan grumbled. "My pants got caught."

"I don't know why you went in there!" Hana paced the tiny office, watching her appointment time go past her allotted twenty minutes. "They'll make me pay extra out there. That receptionist is a pit bull."

"She's my step daughter." The doctor pursed his lips and Logan squeezed his eyes closed with the effort of not laughing.

Hana huffed and put her hands on her hips as Logan's pants ripped under the knife. The doctor cursed. "It's bleeding. I hope you don't have hepatitis."

"Nope. Not that," Logan replied, darting a look of mirth towards Hana.

"I must do an accident report." The doctor slid from the bed, pink splotches on his cheeks. His form filling occupied another half an hour.

Outside in the waiting room, an angry crowd gathered. They glared at Hana as she paid an additional bill for hijacking the doctor's time. She walked to the front doors without getting eye contact with anyone else, stuffing her prescription for antibiotics into her jacket pocket.

Hana drove home, watching as Logan kept his fingers over his pants leg. "How bad is it?" she asked and he shrugged.

"I liked these pants," he grumbled.

"Damn!" She slapped the steering wheel. "After all that, he didn't give me the name of the midwife."

"Sorry." Logan remained silent for the rest of the journey home.

Hana boiled the kettle in the kitchen and watched the outline of the bush through the darkened window. Her fingers scrubbed potatoes under the tap and plonked them in a pan on the stove to boil. Logan went straight to the bathroom and didn't emerge. His coffee chilled on the kitchen table and Hana grew concerned. She padded to the bathroom and knocked on the door. "Logan? Are you okay?"

"I'm fine." His voice sounded muffled, so Hana pushed against the door. It opened and she pressed onward.

"What's the matter?" The blood on Logan's leg drew her immediate attention. "Oh, goodness! You didn't say it was that bad."

Logan dabbed at the cut on his thigh, toilet roll sticking to the hairs. "Sorry," he said, sounding sad. Hana crouched in front of him and inspected the jagged cut.

"Why didn't the doctor stitch that?"

Logan shrugged and dabbed more. "I said it wasn't deep. He just wanted us gone."

"I'll take you back there." Hana stood and Logan grabbed her shin.

"Please don't. That bloody receptionist looked at me like I might have a body part hanging off. I'm not going back to prove her right."

"You're a worry." Hana sank to her knees and watched the blood pool on the tissue. "Will it stop?" She rested her hand on his leg and Logan nodded.

"I used my spray. Can you do butterfly stitches?"

Hana's eyes widened. "With a needle? No! I suck at embroidery."

"With tape, you egg!" Logan cracked a smile and it reached his eyes, crinkling the skin at the edges. "I superglue it and you cross tape over the top."

"Okay." Hana sounded dubious, but managed a decent enough job. She got the skinny tape stuck everywhere except where she meant to put it and sat back with a frown.

"Thanks." Logan stroked her fingers and yanked stray tape from her blouse.

"At least they gave you a tetanus jab in hospital," she remarked, leaning forward to examine her handiwork. "Not bad for a beginner. I always used Band Aids on the children."

Logan nodded and then paused, his face pulling into a frown. "What's that noise?"

"The potatoes!" Hana got up and ran to the kitchen, groaning at the splattery mess over the hob. "Why me?" she grumbled.

Logan hobbled into the kitchen in his shirt and boxers and found Hana attacking the starchy mess with a cloth. He confiscated it. "You'll burn yourself. I'll do it once it's cooled." He dumped the half-melted rag in the dustbin.

Hana leaned her back against the draining board. "Burned potatoes and beans?" she asked, quirking up an eyebrow.

Logan nodded. "Yum." He wrapped his arms around her and for once, she didn't push him away. "Sorry about ruining your doctor's appointment," he said. His voice sounded cowed and filled with regret. "Sorry about everything else too. I need you to trust me more than you can imagine."

Hana exhaled and closed her eyes against his shirt. "Everyone I trusted let me down, Logan," she sighed. "What makes you different?" She felt him shrug, his body nudging hers with the action.

"I'd die for you." Logan's fingers strayed to Hana's stomach and he caressed the sensitive skin. "I'd die for both of you."

Hana nodded and felt him relax. She pulled away to look at his face, following the curve of his sensuous lips and the regal angular nose. "You looked a right prat," she whispered. Dimples appeared in her cheeks as she fought the grin. "Standing there with your pants welded to that bed and the doctor cutting you loose." She sniggered. "His face was right near your rude bits. I kept imagining someone walking in."

"So did I." Logan closed his eyes and pursed his lips. "I want to be part of everything, Hana. This won't happen again."

She turned away, releasing herself from his arms. Her heart sank with the weight of the impossible pregnancy. She daren't say the words, terrified of stealing her husband's dream. But the responsibility cowed her. Hana turned back to her pan, stabbing the potatoes with a sharp knife and watching them slide along its hilt. "Maybe they're not burnt," she mused, stabbing another.

Logan let his fingers slide down her back, recognising the portcullis crashing over her emotions. He retreated to the kitchen table and examined the blood seeping through the tape.

"I want to let you enjoy it." Hana didn't turn around, speaking to the darkness outside the window. "But what if I can't do this? What if we both get attached and then I lose the baby?" Her voice shook and she didn't hear him move. His arms wrapped around her from behind.

"We can't predict the future, Hana," he whispered into her hair. "Atua numbers our days and I've squandered enough already. Let's enjoy what we have in our hands today. Planning for loss doesn't lessen the sting. It only makes you suffer before you need to." Hana sighed as Logan pushed his fingers beneath her hair. He loved feeling the curls shift like water and caressed her nape with gentle fingers. "Kaua e mate wheke mate ururoa."

"What does that mean?"

"Don't die defenseless like an octopus, die like a hammerhead shark. A Du Rose always goes down fighting, Hana. We are warriors."

Logan dipped his body and collected Hana into his arms. She inhaled in surprise and wrapped her arms around his neck. In silence, he carried her through the lobby and into the bedroom, closing the door behind him with his foot.

-27-

Hana slept late on Saturday, not stirring until after nine. She reached across the bed and her fingers contacted cold, empty space. Signs of a hasty breakfast included crumbs on the table and she wandered around the house looking for Logan.

As she reached the garage, Hana heard the gate alarm sound overhead. She hid on the stairs and watched the automatic door lift. The Honda swept down the slope and into the garage and she stood in her fluffy dressing gown and slippers feeling foolish.

"Hey, babe." Logan leapt from the car, seizing her in a hug and kissing her forehead. He smelled of fresh air and exuded triumph.

"Where did you go?" Hana wrapped her arms around herself, ready for his rebuff. Instead, he walked to the rear door of the car.

He produced tins of paint which clattered on the concrete floor. "Look," he said, smiling in pleasure.

Hana crouched and stared at the tint label, relieved to see a delicate eggshell textured cream. "This looks nice. Is it for the bathroom?"

Logan shook his head. "I thought I'd turn the room next to ours into a nursery," he said, his face searching for her approval.

Hana took a step back, shaking her head. "No, Logan! It's too soon. Stop pushing me!" Betrayal sent a stab of pain into her heart and ready tears collected behind her eyelids. She let him in and he stamped on her caution like the proverbial bull in a china shop.

Logan grasped her forearms and held her still as she wriggled. "The doctor said you survived the worst part. I want to get ready. Six months isn't long to prepare a house and our lives for a baby."

"You told your mother, didn't you?" Hana's top lip drew back in a sneer. She jabbed a finger in Logan's chest. "I asked you to respect my wishes."

"I told no one." Logan's eyes narrowed. "We made a deal."

Hana shook herself free and stalked off to bed, sinking beneath the covers in her dressing gown. She found a tissue beneath her pillow and sniffed into it. Logan's boots sounded on the hall floor and Hana waited for the thud of him shifting his purchases into the empty room. Instead, he poked his head around the doorframe. "Can we talk?" he asked. "We're at crossed purposes."

At Hana's reluctant nod, Logan shed his jeans and crawled into the bed. His fingers sought hers, not allowing her to snatch them away. Hana sighed in frustration. "I'm forty-five years old with a history of Down syndrome in my immediate family. There's so much that can go wrong and you have no clue about the worries and fears circulating in my head." A sob punctuated her final sentence and Hana pulled a hand free and rubbed her eyes. "I feel old, Logan. I'm middle aged and a grandmother. What if everything goes okay and I carry to full term and then can't cope? What then?" She let out a shaky breath. "I've encased myself in this bubble of protection because it's safer, but then I end up so damn lonely. It's an impossible situation."

Logan's face worked through myriad emotions, his grey eyes somber and his irises strangely light. "Caroline's accusations can't have helped. Are you ready to talk about it?"

"Don't! Don't even speak her name around me!" Hana pushed the covers away and tried to stand, tangling her legs in the bedspread and almost falling. "She's everywhere I look, Logan! Her influence over you makes me want to throw up. She's in my marriage and turns up at work whenever she chooses. I can't escape her and I won't do this again. I hate liars."

"What do you mean?" Logan sat up, his brow furrowed. "I haven't lied to you, Hana. I don't always tell you stuff, but I've never lied." The sheets tumbled away from his chest, the muscles hard and defined through his tee shirt in the dull light of a grey morning. Hana stared at the logo on his left pectoral, fighting the urge to press her face into her husband's strength until she forgot everything else. She slid sideways, heading for the door.

"Where did you go the night I came home and told you what that woman said?" Hana's jaw worked as she gritted her teeth and mentally left the room before her body followed. Already her attention turned elsewhere, expecting only lies.

Logan lay back against the pillows. "I needed to see someone."

His lame words grabbed Hana's attention and she focused, her feet level with the end of the bed as she sought escape. "You went to see Caroline?"

Logan shot up again, the sheets tumbling to the floor. "No! Geez is that what you thought?" Recollection and realisation came together. "Oh, crap, Hana. No, I'd never do that to you!" Hana dived towards the bedroom door, her feet still tangled in the trailing cover. She held onto the bedpost to extract her toes and Logan reached her before she escaped. "I didn't go to see Caroline. I should have stayed, I'm sorry."

"Where did you go?" Hana's tone sounded accusing and Logan swallowed.

"I'm having business problems. It's nothing to do with psychotic women and phantom pregnancies. I promise. I invested in something and I'm trying to keep an eye on it."

Hana relaxed. "What business?"

"A farming business. A family member got into trouble and I bailed him out. They keep paper records and I watch the books. I didn't go to see Caroline, Hana. I promise. I made the appointment and needed to keep it. I should have stayed."

"Is that where you keep going, to this business?" Hana's body felt rigid in his arms.

Logan nodded. "Mostly, babe. I have assets I need to protect. When everything is straightened out, we'll talk about all of it." He rubbed her back. "It feels minor compared to this other stuff at the moment."

Hana let her husband enfold her in his arms and breathe reassurances into her hair. "I want to believe you," she whispered. "I'm so tired of doubting you."

"Come back to bed," he replied. "Let me love you."

Tired, miserable and lacking the energy to fight, Hana allowed Logan to untangle her feet, pick her up and lay her on the bed. He banished everything else from her mind, all but the essence of him.

"I need to get that medication," she sighed later. "I'm not sure if I want to go back to the pharmacy in Ngaruawahia. They might remember me from last time."

"Where's the prescription?" Logan asked and yawned.

"In my jacket." Hana struggled up and Logan pulled her back into the bed.

"I'll get it," he promised. "You stay warm."

He returned with the prescription and a confused look on his face. "There's something else," he said, putting two papers in Hana's hand. "This looks like an order for blood tests. Why would he want those?"

Hana swallowed and slumped back, her newfound peace gone. Her colour paled and Logan climbed into bed and held her, waiting for her explanation. "He wants to check for irregularities. They do that anyway, but I'm an older woman so the risks are higher. This is the start of finding out." She ran her fingers over the black tattoo poking from Logan's sleeve, tracing the indelible strands and patterns. Her child would become part of his whakapapa. He or she already was.

"It's my baby." Logan savoured the words on his tongue. "I'll love it, anyway. Won't you?"

Hana nodded and relief surged through her. "Yes," she promised. "I will." She felt the dreadful weight in her heart lessen as Logan took up the slack and for the first time in weeks they pulled together.

"It will be fine," he promised, pressing his lips against her temple. "We can do this."

As Hana showered and dressed, Logan put his head around the door. "Hey, the lab at Rototuna is open until four today. Why don't I run you there to get the bloods done?" Hana felt a chill in her soul. Her silence made Logan venture further into the room. "Let's just get it over with," he said, raising a knowing eyebrow at her.

"Okay," she conceded. "It might help me regain control."

They climbed into the car and Logan reversed from the garage. "This is the plan," he said, reaching for Hana's fingers after putting the gear lever into drive. "I'll use the back roads to Rototuna and park away from everyone else. The blonde guy won't expect to see us around there so if we're vigilant, it should be fine."

Hana watched the side mirrors as Logan drove, seeing few other cars on the foggy route. Her anxiety hiked as Logan parked behind a fast food restaurant. "Are we allowed around here?" she asked, her eyes wide.

Logan shrugged. "There are no signs to the contrary. We shouldn't take long."

Hana looked around her. "It's nice and secluded," she admitted.

A door clanged and an employee emerged, dumping rubbish into a skip. He glanced across as Hana emerged from the car and squared his shoulders. "You can't park there," he began, striding towards the car. Logan stepped from the driver's seat and the man's face changed. "Oh, hi sir. I didn't see you there." His tone became kind. "You here for food?"

Logan gave him the kiwi upward nod of acknowledgement. "Hey Shaun, we need to nip over there. I fancy a burger though. Is it okay to park the car here?"

The young man pulled himself up to his full height. "Awesome sir and miss, it's fine. I'll take care of it for you. The manager lost his stereo in the main car park last week when someone smashed his quarter light. I let all my mates park round here." He bristled with importance. "Hey, if you want food, give me a yell."

Logan smiled and shook his hand. "Thanks Shaun," he said. "See you in a while." The young man walked towards the door, giving a little wave as he went inside. The door slammed behind him. Hana released her breath.

"I thought he might force us to move the car," she said, fear making her teeth chatter. "The last thing we need is a big fuss."

"Nobody makes me do anything," Logan answered, his tone harsh. "He's a nice kid actually, writes awesome poetry."

Hana peeked back at the door of the restaurant as Logan led her away. Nothing about the young man in the red uniform screamed 'poet' or 'lover of literature.' She shook her head to clear her brain and stifled a smirk.

They took a circuitous route in and out of parked cars, avoiding open spaces for as long as possible. Hana heaved a sigh of relief as they stepped through the automatic doors into the medical building. Logan peered at an information board. "Which is the pathology lab?" he asked.

"Over there." Familiar with the building, Hana used the first door on the right and read the notice. She placed her form face down in the tray. "Now we wait," she said with a wan smile, sitting in a red, plastic chair. She ignored the magazines scattered on a table nearby, choosing instead to hold Logan's hand. His capable, calloused fingers stroked calm into hers.

"Hana Du Rose?" A man wearing scrubs emerged from a nearby room and snatched up Hana's form, surprised to see customers on a Saturday. "This way," he said, inclining his arm towards the door. Logan's eyes widened and he assessed the male with a soldier's perception. Hana saw as he dropped his gaze to his hands, his face anxious and sad. Rejection oozed from the slump of his body as she stepped into the small office.

It comprised a small, white room with a man-sized giraffe taped to the wall. The phlebotomist busied himself at the counter with tubes and needles, indicating with a flick of his hand that Hana should sit in the only other chair. Hana sat, regretting her decision to leave Logan outside. The man affixed the sharp to the flexible tube, jumping in surprise as Hana ran from the room, abandoning her handbag. "Hey!" he called after her.

"Logan!" Hana reached him at a run, burying her face in his shoulder. He wrapped his arms around her and stroked the tension from her spine. "I'm pretending I'm not scared, but I'm terrified. Please can you come with me?"

Having established Hana's return, the phlebotomy technician went back to his bottles and tubes, sizing up Hana's paleness and anticipating difficulty. He twisted his lips at her narrowed veins. Logan's teeth grazed his bottom lip as anxiety rose to the surface. He stood in the corner of the tiny room, watching Hana's blood pool in the tubes with frustrating slowness. Everything about their relationship tested the concept of polar opposites, even their blood giving. Hana's vein swelled and the technician wrinkled his nose and removed the needle.

"You're not generous with your blood, are you?" he complained. He used a sphygmomanometer to confirm her low blood pressure.

"Sorry." Hana licked her lips and looked sick. Logan crouched next to her and rested his hand on her knee as the technician dug into another vein. By the time he finished, she bore two sore arms and a swimming sensation in her head.

"I suggest you drink sugary tea and eat something." The technician narrowed his dark brow at Hana's pale complexion. "The doctor's surgery is open next door if you feel faint."

"I'm fine." Hana stood and yanked her sleeves over the tape, reeling a little as she bent to retrieve her handbag.

Logan led her from the building, checking the car park for the blonde man. "It's safe," he said, fixing his arm around her shoulders. He crinkled his nose. "You're actually in more danger with me here."

"Why?" Hana stopped between two cars, trailing him with their fingers linked.

Logan jerked his head to indicate his tall body and rolled his eyes. "I'm quite distinctive, Hana. You got rid of your red hair but they'll recognise me."

Hana sighed and her lips quirked upwards. "Ever thought about going blonde?"

Logan settled her in the fast food restaurant under Shaun's watchful eye. He ordered her a sweet tea and jogged to the nearby pharmacy for Hana's prescription. He returned shrouded by cold air and ate chips and some dubious looking chicken nuggets.

"All good, sir?" Shaun asked, clearing a nearby table.

"Awesome mate. See ya Monday." Logan gave him a warm smile and the teenager blossomed under Logan's approval.

Hana leaned forward in her seat and stole a chip. "The boys love you, Mr Du Rose. What makes you different?"

Logan shrugged. "Boundaries. Boys need them. The devil makes work for idle hands." He waggled his eyebrows and Hana sensed his influence stretched further than his simple reply. Mana rolled off him in waves, creating a sense of awe. His dark, brooding expression gave him a mystique which made him someone that people wanted to impress. Few would succeed.

"I'm glad you chose me." Hana swallowed, wrinkling her nose as her stomach objected to the fat coating the chip's surface.

"Are you?" Logan peered at her from beneath black eyelashes, his grey eyes sultry and inviting. "Wanna go home and show me?"

Hana smirked. "I'm a little weak right now." Her teeth grazed her lower lip. "You might need to do all the work."

They slipped into Ngaruawahia, careful to check behind for any vehicles following. They fell into the wide bed and Hana used the last of her energy reserves. Exhausted, she lay back against the pillows, noticing how twitchy and unsettled Logan seemed. "Start the baby's bedroom if you want to," she conceded, conscious of his desire to keep busy. She soaked up the peace of the house and closed her eyes. Logan played the radio in the room next door and Hana dozed off to the muted strains of music. She enjoyed the unusual sensation of sleeping during the daytime and gave herself permission to move in and out of consciousness without guilt.

She woke as darkness pressed around the house. The tape and cotton wool from one arm stuck to her forehead and she pulled it off with a grimace of disgust. Her stomach gnawed on itself and she shivered in the icy cold of the house. Dragging a robe around herself, she stumbled next door. The door resisted her, jammed in place by an old sheet protecting the rimu floorboards.

"Hang on," Logan called, yanking the cloth free from beneath the door. He grinned at her, paint on the side of his nose and staining his hands. "What do you think?" he asked, taking her hand and leading her into the room. "I've painted the ceiling and two walls so far." His eyes creased in pleasure with his progress. He led her around the portable radio which played to itself on the floor.

"It looks amazing." Hana rubbed her eyes, comparing the cheerful cream surfaces to the brown plaster and filled cracks of the other walls. "I didn't imagine it could feel so warm. I love it."

Logan's grin widened. "I'm glad." His brow furrowed. "It feels like a little bit of me in the house. You did it all when I couldn't."

"Oh." Hana held her breath. "I never realised you felt that way."

Logan shrugged. "No matter. As long as you like it."

"I do." She exhaled. "But can we wait to buy furniture, please? I'm not ready."

"Deal." Logan reeled her into his chest, kissing the top of her head with paint-spattered lips. "This is a good day, Hana. Hold on to the good days."

Hana nodded against his chest, a flicker of doubt in her mind reminding her how fast life could spin into chaos. She inhaled Logan's masculine scent and felt peace descend over her soul. A passage from her Sunday school days rose to obscure her fears. Her father's voice spoke the words and they brought comfort as long as she didn't dwell on their last meeting. "For only a penny, you can buy two sparrows, yet not one sparrow falls to the ground without your Father's consent. As for you, even the hairs of your head have all been counted. So do not be afraid; you are worth much more than many sparrows!"

"Matthew," she whispered, seeking the scripture's origin.

"Na," Logan replied. "That's not a Du Rose name." He lifted her chin with his index finger. "But we'll talk about that another time." His lips felt soft and warm over Hana's. "I lit a fire in the lounge. Let me clear up here and we'll cuddle up on the sofa together."

Hana pottered in the kitchen making sandwiches. Logan joined her in the lounge and they watched television until it got late. After Hana clambered into bed, Logan continued work on the baby's room, finishing the other walls and adding a second coat of paint to the ceiling.

The next morning Hana went across country to church. She bickered with Logan about possible safe routes and rejected his offer of giving her a ride. "You won't come in," she grumbled. "You'll sit in the car outside."

"So?" Logan put his hands on his hips, not seeing the problem.

"You can drive me if you come into church."

Logan shook his head. "Na, thanks. I'm catholic, you know that."

Hana jabbed a finger in his chest and laughed, masking her annoyance. "Scared you might implode?" she snorted.

Logan waggled his eyebrows. "Hell yeah! That bolt of lightning will come straight for me."

Ivan and Anka sat together in the pews and Hana slid in next to them. Ivan stuck close to his wife, but Hana sensed the vibes of his animosity across the short distance. He still held her culpable and it stank of unfairness.

"How's that grandson of yours?" Pastor Allen asked after the service and Hana cringed.

"Sorry for the vomit on the carpet." She glanced around, trying to locate the offending patch.

"Don't worry about it." Allen waved an arm. "Five minutes of work." He jerked his head towards Ivan's back. "You okay? That looked uncomfortable."

Hana sighed. "If you noticed it from the pulpit, it must be obvious. He blames me for not telling him, which is unfair as I only found out the day before she left."

Allen squeezed her shoulder. "We often look for others to blame when we don't wish to look in the mirror."

Hana gaped, the parallel with her own marriage striking. She swallowed and closed her mouth with a snap. Allen slipped his arm around her shoulder and pulled her close, a smirk playing on his lips.

At Culver's Cottage, Logan finished the skirting board and stood back to admire his work. He heard Hana in the garage and walked down the stairs to meet her. "Come and see," he said, excitement budding in his chest. He glowed with satisfaction and exuded an infectious enthusiasm, dragging her to the bedroom by the hand.

"It looks perfect." Hana's hand strayed to her abdomen and she allowed herself a flicker of optimism.

"Please can I borrow the car?" Logan asked. "The shop owner is holding a blind for the window. I needed to measure it first. I'll nip and pick it up."

Hana nodded and continued to look around the room. She allowed herself to imagine it containing a cot and rocking chair, creating an idyllic nursery in her mind. Reality crowded in and she shook the image away. "That's fine," she said. "Want me to come?"

"Na, I won't take long." Logan kissed her forehead and borrowed the car keys, setting off for Huntly with a grin on his face.

He returned from the hardware store with a set of wooden slatted window blinds, a large rectangular cream rug and a chandelier style shade for the central bulb. Despite the dullness of the winter's day, the room glittered and sparkled with texture and light by the time he finished. Hope dared to burgeon in Hana's heart and she went to bed that night with an easier spirit.

As they left for work the next morning, Logan's mobile phone trilled. He stopped half way down the back steps to the garage and swore. "I'll come," he said, dragging on his wellingtons instead of his cowboy boots. His face creased with concern and he pressed the button on the wall to raise the garage door. "Stay here," he told Hana, his tone firm. "Don't come outside."

"Why?" she demanded, curiosity flourishing in place of fear. As the garage door finished rising, the house filled with the sound of a commotion.

Hana ignored Logan's instruction, rebelling against him telling her what to do. She edged up the slope and followed him around the side of the house. The noise grew louder, dividing into individual sounds of distress. A drum tattoo began in her heart and she should have returned to the safety of the house. Instead, she pressed on.

Logan ran up the slope and vaulted the post and rail fence, pausing long enough to get his balance on the top rail. Following it, he found a corner post and stood on it, waving his arms to someone further off. Hana gasped at the sight of over a hundred milling, distressed Friesian cows. They pushed and shoved in their efforts to escape a giant, hairy bull. It clambered up the side of the gully, snorting and lowing as it nosed the back fence out of its way. Hana heard the twang of barbed wire under tension as it snapped and rolled free. The bull kicked and bucked, its legs pinioned by the wire.

A few hefty stamps and the boundary posts collapsed, giving a dull thud as powerful horns knocked them asunder. A post on the bush line stuck up like a broken finger. The cows increased their panicked lowing and barged the back fence to the house. Logan wobbled on his post and shouted at them, waving his arms and seeing them veer away like a tidal wave.

Hana heard the quad and the motorbike before she saw them. Maihi rode the quad in a standing position, a shotgun waving in her hand. Supporting its weight involved the whole of her left arm and concentration darkened her expression. Hemi tore ahead on the motorbike, negotiating his way through broken wire and shattered wood. He made a beeline for Logan, navigating the cows which dived aside.

Hana's gaze moved to a single cow leaning against the garden fence. The rails shook with the trembling of its body. It stood prone and rigid, its eyes staring and black. Instinct told Hana why it strained, the muscles along its spine tense and bunched. Liquid dribbled from its snout like a line of wallpaper paste. "No!" Her shriek made Logan turn. His expression clouded with anger and he opened his mouth to rebuke her.

Hana's heels dug into the soft grass as she pointed towards the cow. Her finger shook. Logan's swearwords reached her ears like nails on a blackboard. The tiny, breathless body of a calf slipped to the ground with a small thud. Dead before its furry body slid into the grass, it represented the most hopeless thing Hana had ever seen and her heart broke. Its dam moved towards it and licked the lifeless body without effect. The baby would never raise its wobbling, oversized head or feed from the milk flowing into her udders. She nudged and lowed while the other cows milled behind, transfixed by her confusion.

Hana used her scarf to cover her eyes. She pressed her hands against it and constricted her breathing. The previous night's optimism dissipated in the face of nature's tragedy and she heard her own sobs.

"Sort out your wahine matua," Hemi shouted and Hana heard the thud of Logan landing on the grass.

His arms enfolded her and he led her away in her blindness. "It's natural, Hana. It's Papatuanuku's way. The animals don't see things like we do."

"They must do!" Hana sobbed, jabbing a finger back at the scene. The cow licked the dead body, bowing to maternal instinct while all hell broke out around her.

Logan bundled her away. "Let's get out of here," he said, sounding irritated. "I told you to stay indoors. Now they must manage alone."

"I'm sorry!" Hana's breath hitched in her chest and Logan pushed her into the passenger seat of the car.

"Stay there this time!" he demanded, returning to the paddock.

Hana sat in the car with her scarf over her face. She projected the cow's fate onto herself and sagged under the weight of responsibility. She cried until her makeup ran, leaving herself in a blotchy mess. Logan returned, brushing mud from his work trousers and changing his footwear. When he climbed into the driver's seat, he leaned across and wiped tears from Hana's chin. "It seems harsh, but you get used to it," he said, his voice soft. "Hemi shot another of the dams who broke her leg in the gully. She left a calf. He wanted you to know he'll try to give it to the one who just miscarried."

Hana sniffed, the sound ugly and undignified. "Is that what you'll do with me?" she bit. "Give me a consolation prize?"

"Hana!" Logan sounded exasperated and withdrew his sympathy. "You over think everything." He tried to take her hand later in the journey, but found it cold and still beneath his fingers. Hana sat in silence, leaving the car and walking towards the office in a daze. Logan shook his head and slammed the door after him. His work on the baby's room and the optimism it fostered, disappeared beneath the filth of circumstance.

"I can't bloody win!" he hissed.

Hana worked like an automaton, communicating little and achieving even less. Logan tried to speak to her during each of his breaks but she sent him away, knowing her ignorance infuriated him. At the end of the fourth period, she allowed herself a bathroom break. Looking at her face in the mirror, she recalled the tiny, defenseless body slipping to the floor amidst grass seed and flowery heads of common weeds. The closed eyes in its furry, mucus soaked head appealed to her morbid sense of fatalism. The mother's pathetic licks resonated with her efforts to shelter a child in her geriatric body. She dared to lay her hands over her belly and felt the nakedness of terror.

Sheila found her hiding in the bathroom and sent a boy to fetch Pete. "You poor girl. Whatever is wrong?" She tried to mop up Hana's tears, but wasted her time as more replaced them.

"I'm not coming in there!" Pete shouted from the doorway. "It's a girly room. It's not in my job description."

Sheila groaned and put her head outside. "Text Logan then!" she hissed. "You useless little man!"

"No!" Hana drew her legs up to her chest on the small chair and wrapped her arms around them. "He's cross with me."

"Why, Hana?" Sheila pressed, crouching down to look into her face. "What's happened?" Hana buried her face and didn't answer.

"Hana?" Logan barged through the door, banging it against the sink unit in his haste. His jaw worked in his face and Hana recognised fear. He pulled her feet off the seat and crouched in front of her, resting his arms along her thighs to prevent her blocking him.

"I can't do this!" she hissed. "It's too hard."

"It's different!" Logan took her writhing fingers in his and squeezed until she winced. "Listen to me."

"You should drive her home," Sheila whispered, sending away another member of staff needing the toilet. "It's flooded," she lied.

"Use the one downstairs." She shrugged as Logan caught her eye and jerked her head towards Hana's tears. "It kinda is," she said. She reached a hand through the gap and a resounding slap filled the space. "Get Hana's bag!" she instructed someone and Pete's grumbling split the air molecules.

"Why do you always hit me?" he demanded.

"Because you don't listen otherwise!"

Logan led Hana down the back steps and through Q Block to the car. Pete scurried behind carrying her handbag across his forearm like a woman. "I'll take you home," Logan said, pushing Hana into the passenger seat. He leaned across to fasten her seatbelt and she smelled his aftershave. He seated himself next to her and started the engine. The car braked hard and Hana heard a click. "What are you doing?"

"I'm coming with you," Pete grumbled. "I want to see your place."

Logan swore and sped off, turning left after the imposing school gates. "You tell anyone where we live and I'll break your legs," he growled. "And get my wife's handbag off your arm, ya weirdo!"

"No. I need it." Hana heard her keys shift around in her bag as Pete clutched it closer. "I don't trust you not to throw me out in the middle of nowhere. You can't if I'm holding her bag."

Logan exhaled, the sound loud and filled with exasperation. Hana covered her face with the scarf to avoid his sideways looks of concern.

While Logan led his fragile wife up the steps and into the hallway of Culver's Cottage, Pete scouted around the property with Hana's handbag still over his arm. Logan helped remove her shoes and led her to the bedroom. "I don't want to leave you." His jaw ground beneath his cheek and conflict warred in his eyes. "But I abandoned an English class. I left them watching a video."

Hana shook her head. "I'm okay now I'm home." Her eyes widened. "Is it gone?"

"I'll check." Logan wandered across to a bush-facing bedroom and returned with a nod. "Yeah. Hemi moved it. I can see him and Maihi in the top corner repairing the fence." He chewed the inside of his cheek. "Tell me what to do, Hana."

"Go back to work." She inhaled and looked around her. "Please take Pete with you."

"Okay. Need anything before I go?"

"Just my handbag." Hana shed her coat and dropped it on the floor next to the bed. She pushed her feet beneath the sheets. "Sorry for my meltdown."

"It's okay." Logan's brow knitted as though he didn't mean it. He picked her coat off the floor and Hana heard him load it onto a hanger and put it in the cupboard in the lobby.

He returned to press a kiss to her forehead, hanging around in the doorway as though wanting to ask her a question. Hana closed her eyes against his probing and heard him shut the front door. "Put the bloody axe down!" he shouted at Pete outside the bedroom window. "And bring that handbag here!" Hana heard his footsteps as he laid it on the lobby floor and the door closed again, accompanied by the jangle of keys.

She turned on her side in the empty bed and closed her eyes against the internal agonies flushing through her brain. Her hand strayed to her stomach and she prayed against her fears until the sleep of the exhausted claimed her.

Logan arrived home early and found Hana sipping herbal tea at the kitchen window. She wore the faded monkey pyjamas and looked skinny and pale. Her curls coiled down her back in a waterfall of chestnut and blonde. "You're right." She didn't turn to greet him. "They don't care." He kicked off his boots and joined her at the window, seeing the small herd moving around in an easy arc.

His hands felt strong on Hana's shoulders, kneading away the tension. "Hemi took her back to their place. She won't accept the orphan but she's okay. The vet looked at her."

Hana sighed. "I wish you'd lied to me," she said, rubbing her nose with the back of her hand. "At least I could sleep thinking it was happy ever after."

"I told you I wouldn't lie." Logan kissed the back of her head. "You read far too much into ordinary events. We face our own mortality every day, especially in farming. This has no bearing on you or our baby."

Hana kept her silence. She understood the sting of mortality. Life hung by a delicate, tenuous thread, taken away to leave catastrophe in its wake. Her head shook from side to side. She sensed Logan couldn't understand the depth of the mess Vik left behind for her to smooth beneath the carpet. She couldn't tell him then.

Logan made dinner and cosseted Hana. His sideways glances proved irritating until she remembered Miriam's confession. His mother's reluctance to leave the hotel smacked of the kind of behaviour associated with mental illness. Hana channelled her annoyance into reassuring him instead. "I'm fine now," she told him countless times. "Blame the pregnancy hormones." Her wan smile didn't fool him and he continued to watch her.

"I can't work you out, Hana Du Rose," he sighed, pulling her back against his chest in bed. "Sometimes you're like one of the fillies at the farm, skittish and afraid, trusting nobody. At other times, you're terrifying."

Hana smiled. "Like Sacha?"

"Exactly like her." Logan snorted.

"Are you admitting defeat?" Hana smirked, squealing as he flipped her beneath him. Strong fingers pulled her arms above her head and his pupils flared wide.

"No, Hana. I broke Sacha and I'll rein you in too." He planted a kiss on her ear as she shrieked and whipped her head sideways. His lips moved along her neck. "It might just take a while longer."

-28-

Hana minded her own business at work, avoiding the staffroom and enjoying the repetitiveness of her tasks. She found distraction in administration, making packs for boys and photocopying Sheila's endless worksheets.

"Please, can you make twenty of these?" Sheila asked, dumping a pocket file on Hana's desk. It obliterated her keyboard and prevented further typing. "Stuff them into wallets or the boys will lose the application form." She stalked back into her office. "They always do."

Hana sighed against the click of the door and examined the paperwork. She jumped as Sheila poked her head back out. "Oh, I need them for my next class." Click.

Hana dragged herself to her feet and rubbed the small of her back. It ached and she winced as she moved. The photocopier churned out twenty collated copies and Hana thought for a moment before requesting ten more. "Better to be safe than sorry," she mused. Her fingers worked at speed as she stapled and stuffed papers into wallets, reaching eighteen before the speaker in the foyer boomed out between lessons.

Sheila's head appeared from her office, looking disembodied. "What's happening?"

Hana opened her mouth, beaten to a response by a voice coming through the speaker. "This is not a drill. This is an emergency. Close and lock all doors and remain in the classroom. Stay away from windows and do not emerge until told it is safe."

Sheila ventured further from her office. "Are you sure it's not a drill? I refuse to go out if it is. Darn thing went off twice while you were away and it's freezing outside."

"It sounds like Dobbs. He said it's real." Hana looked down at her paper stuffing and sighed. "Lock the door and at least I can keep doing this."

The usual siren sounded, deafening and yet comforting in its familiarity. Hana relaxed. Sheila bounced across the room, making both doors secure. The empty common room seemed ominous. The voice began again, Angus replacing Dobbs. "This is not a drill. The school is in lockdown. Secure yourselves in classrooms, get under desks and stay away from windows and open areas. This is not a drill."

Sheila's eyes grew wide like oranges as the voice repeated the message at two-minute intervals. In between, the siren blocked out all other sound. Hana stuffed forms into wallets like a lunatic, relieved when she finished.

"There's someone outside." Sheila mouthed the words and stuck her eye against the keyhole facing the foyer.

"Where?" Hana demanded. "Come away from the door. We're meant to hide under the desk. What are you doing?"

Sheila waggled her eyebrows. "I want to see what's happening!" she hissed.

Hana rolled her eyes. "I'm blocking that up after you leave today," she said. "I'm gonna stuff tack in it."

"It's my peep hole!" Sheila whirled around, glaring at her.

"There's a window there!" Hana jabbed a hand at the long bank of glass facing the corridor.

"I won't see anything through there," Sheila grumbled. "It faces the wrong way. All the action happens out here."

Hana sighed and dropped to her knees. She grimaced at the dust on the carpet and crawled beneath her desk. "I'm doing as I'm told or Logan will growl me." She settled on her bottom with her legs crossed and jabbed an index finger at the door to the common room. "Actually, most of the trouble happens out there," she grumbled. An answering clatter against the door made her squeak and cover her mouth. She poked her head out from under the desk and flapped a hand at Sheila. "Get in here!" she begged under her breath. "They're out there, not out that way!"

Sheila turned her back on the coveted keyhole and dived for cover, not taking her gaze from the common room door. Her eyes widened in fear and both women watched, their bodies rigid. Someone tried the door handle and discovered it locked. The Yale mechanism meant no need for a keyhole and the women held their breath. Footsteps moved away and they hid further beneath their desks in case the intruder found their way into the corridor and peered through the side windows.

"Hana!" Sheila hissed and Hana pressed her face close to the join where two pieces of wood met. She spotted Sheila through the thin crack.

"What?"

"Can you see anything through the window?"

Hana sighed. "I don't know because I'm not looking."

"Please?" Sheila begged, her position beneath Pete's desk giving her no view of the glass frontage.

"No!" Hana grumbled. She felt a steady vibration and her eyes widened. "I think Logan's ringing me."

"Answer it then. He might know something."

"I can't!" Hana hissed. "It's locked in my bottom drawer and my keys are on the desk. I'm not coming out."

Both women screamed as something hard hit the rear door. It crashed open and bashed the cupboard behind it before slamming closed. Hana's heart almost burst through her chest wall and she held her breath and scooted backwards. A scream and the sound of a resounding slap got her attention. She poked her head out.

Pete's backside faced her, an ill-placed hole in his tracksuit pants. A pair of dirty grey briefs protruded through the gap. "This is my spot!" he demanded, tugging on Sheila's foot. "Get out!"

"Shut up, both of you," Hana begged. "Someone's outside."

Pete performed a three-point-turn and backed into Sheila's face. "They've gone. It's a dude with something in his hand."

"What thing?" Hana asked and he shrugged. Her face paled. "Did he look tall and blonde, quite muscular looking?"

"No. But I got my pie." Pete held up a paper bag which shed pastry flakes like confetti.

"Where from?" Sheila jabbed an elbow into his ribs as he settled himself beneath the desk next to her.

"I made Darnell pass me a steak and cheese through the tuck shop window. She didn't ask for the money." He grinned in glee and bit into the crumbled mess.

"What did you see?" Hana whispered. She jabbed a finger towards the common room door. "Out there."

Pete shrugged and spoke with his mouth full. "Just a guy. Short, fat with a gang bandana over his mouth. Oh, and some cops."

Sheila and Hana exchanged looks of alarm. "So it's real?" Sheila demanded.

"Yeah!" Pete sniffed and swallowed the results. Sheila cringed and closed her eyes. He turned his back on her and licked his greasy fingers like a cat.

Hana retreated beneath her desk and wished she'd gone to the toilet when her bladder first told her she needed it. Half an hour ago.

She managed another twenty minutes before poking her head out the front of her desk. Sheila looked across at her. "I need the toilet." Hana swallowed. "I'm desperate."

"You can't." Pete yawned and showed her a set of molars filled with dental work. "We're not allowed out."

"But you managed it," Hana replied in a loud whisper. "For a pie. Mine is a life or death need."

"Go in the dustbin." Pete shrugged. "I do it all the time."

Hana squeaked and pushed her plastic dustbin out from under her desk. A swift kick sent it spinning across the carpet, disgorging paper and a banana skin.

She spent the next ten minutes counting the seconds between each siren and the length of time Angus' emergency message took to read through. It didn't sound pre-recorded so wherever he managed to hide, he took the intercom with him. "I have to go."

"You can't!" came the chorus from beneath Pete's desk.

"I can!" shrieked Hana. "I'm pregnant! Ohhh!" Pain added to discomfort and she agreed with the doctor's diagnosis. Urine infection.

Pete and Sheila fought to evacuate the desk. Sheila won and poked Pete in the eye during their scrap. They scurried across to Hana on their knees and showered her with questions. Hana put her hands over her ears. "Stop talking," she begged. "I'll wet myself. Please tell no one."

In the first ever moment of agreement, Sheila nodded at Pete and spoke. "We'll all go."

Misgiving filled Pete's eyes seconds later. "I don't need it though," he said, attempting to back out. Sheila narrowed her eyes and he dropped his futile protest.

Like a line of ducklings following mother, they crawled towards the common room door. Sheila laid on her stomach to peer through the thin and draughty gap beneath. "All clear," she whispered. "This carpet is disgusting." She stood and unlatched the door, pushing Pete out first to check the area. He indicated after crawling some distance, jerking his head like a frisky pony.

"Stay away from the windows," Sheila hissed and Pete rolled his eyes.

"That's not easy. There are windows everywhere!"

"Just do your best," Hana groaned and he sped up. She tried not to laugh at his weird commando crawl, the hole in his pants bobbing up and down in front of Sheila's face. Hana pulled the door closed behind her and they filed towards the staffroom, negotiating three sets of double doors and a deserted corridor.

"What now?" Pete demanded as they reached the staffroom. He pointed towards the floor to ceiling windows occupying one massive wall.

Sheila jabbed him in the back. "Go behind the kitchen counter. We can get most of the way there without anyone seeing us."

Pete sighed and steered that way, complaining as his hand stuck to a dried splat of sticky coffee. Hana watched as he discovered a piece of biscuit lurking beneath the fridge, shoving it in his mouth as he passed. She groaned and made retching noises. Emerging from the other side of the counter, Hana raised her head too far and spotted a large group of police officers occupying the soccer pitch and vehicles blocking the school gate. "The armed response guys are outside!" she hissed. "If they shoot at me, I'll pee my pants!"

"If they shoot at you, we all will!" Pete grumbled.

"Not long now," Sheila promised. "Three more sets of doors and then we're there."

A one-minute walk took ten to crawl, checking every entry point for danger. Hana focussed on Pete's bobbing bottom and kept her nerve until they reached the bathroom opposite the locked door of the learning support centre. Her legs ached and wobbled beneath her as she crawled into a cubicle and yanked down her trousers and underwear. She groaned in relief, not caring if the others heard.

"My trouser legs are filthy," Hana whispered, emerging from the cubicle in a crouch. She avoided the window above her head and washed her hands at face height. "We can go now."

"No, we can't!" Pete shot through the door and looked around for somewhere to hide. "The cops are outside."

"That's okay." Sheila said, wiping sweat from her brow with a shaking hand. "We're safe then."

"No we're not!" Pete's eyes widened like boiled eggs. He jabbed his finger at Hana. "Her son's out there. We're meant to be in the student centre and I refuse to get rescued from a ladies toilet." He hurled himself into the tiny cubicle which served as a shower room and plonked himself on the floor in the corner.

Sheila followed him and yanked Hana's sleeve. "Get in here! Nobody make a sound!"

Pete opened his mouth to protest as the women crowded in and Sheila bent forward. Hana heard a slap and a grunt. With a muted click, the bolt slid across the door, closing them into the wet room. Hana perched on the slatted bench next to Sheila with a sigh. "Did they see you?" she whispered. Pete pursed his lips and shook his head. He made a gun with his thumb and index finger and Hana groaned. "They're still searching," she whispered to Sheila.

Pete positioned himself with his back to the wall, his feet sloping into the drain hole. He shut his eyes and put his head back.

"Thanks guys," Hana breathed and Sheila patted her hand.

"Tell me about this baby then," she whispered, leaning so close Hana felt her breath on her ear.

"Shut up, both of you!" Pete hissed and Hana glanced sideways at him.

She whispered in Sheila's ear. "Please tell no one. It might be okay, but I'm waiting for the test results to be sure."

Sheila nodded and squeezed her fingers. "I understand." She narrowed her eyes at Pete. "I'll hurt him if he breathes a word to anyone." The women jumped as Pete reached forward and patted Hana's knee with something like tenderness. She swallowed and felt tears prick behind her eyelids.

Then he ruined it. "I bet the sex was fantastic." He blinked in rapid succession as Sheila inhaled but Hana snorted.

"Brilliant," she whispered, cheering herself up at the thought of it.

They sat in the shower room for a further hour. The siren continued to belt out its warning, interspersed with Angus telling them all to stay where they were. Hana grew fractious, faced with the prospect of another crawl to the toilet and Sheila looked at her watch and groaned. "Can't take much longer to find one man!" she grumbled.

"It can in this place. I've worked here for years and I don't know half the cupboards and hiding places," Hana replied. "And don't forget the underground tunnels which end up in the gully somewhere."

"They're blocked up." Sheila shrugged. "Otherwise I'd use them right now. I'm missing a hairdressing appointment." She fluffed her bobbed hair and pointed out her regrowth.

"They're not all blocked." Pete grinned and Hana decided not to question him further. Sheila's slight shake of the head united them in deliberate ignorance.

Angus' next statement declared the situation over and he proposed a short interval followed by the resumption of normal school lessons. A muffled cheer reached their ears, a collective shout from six hundred cooped up boys ready to explode. The noise around the site rose to a deafening throb as boys and staff moved outside. Hana visited the toilet again while Sheila checked the hallway. "It's clear," she called to Pete, tutting as he delayed. "You need to get out of here!" she insisted. Hana emerged from the cubicle to see Sheila give him a shove through the open door.

Overestimating her own strength, she shot the thin little man across the hall and into the room opposite. Hana recognised the crash as he hit a metal filing cabinet on the far wall. "Oopsie!" Sheila called after him and slammed the door with a wicked chuckle. Hana shook her head and washed her hands.

The bell rang twice to honour the impromptu interval and the boys filed outside to the winter sunshine. "Are you ready?" Sheila asked, primping her fringe in the mirror. "Remember, if anyone asks, we stayed in the student centre and dashed straight here." She ducked forward as a stampede of desperate women filed into cubicles behind them.

"I'm a terrible liar," Hana hissed. "Let's just be honest, but not about the other thing. I'm not ready for people to know."

"Stick to the plan." Sheila waggled her eyebrows, squared her shoulders and pulled the door open.

"Geez, Hana! Are you okay?" Logan dragged her sideways, almost lifting her from the floor. "What the hell happened?" He searched her face for signs of distress and his dark fringe bounced on his eyelashes. "You didn't answer your phone." Hana smelled his aftershave and pressed her face into his chest. She sighed and he wrapped her in his arms and kissed the top of her head. Wolf whistles and lewd comments rang out from boys on the stairs and Logan ignored them.

"Where did they catch the man?" Hana asked, looking past Logan to the sight of Sheila shaking her head and drawing a line across her throat.

Logan reeled backwards and stared at her through narrowed eyes. "Outside your office." His voice lowered with suspicion. "Which you'd know if you were in there."

Hana swallowed and gnawed her bottom lip. "Could we talk about it later?" She shook her head. "It's complicated." Her eyes implored him for clemency.

Logan swung around to face Sheila and she failed to remove the grimace fast enough. He sighed. "Okay. Tell me later. I'm glad you're okay. It killed me sitting in a classroom with a group of rowdy boys instead of checking on you."

"I'm very surprised you did." Angus passed and slapped Logan's shoulder. "I'm glad I don't have to fire you." Hana pressed a hand against her husband's chest.

"I'm glad you stayed with the boys. You did the right thing."

"He did what I employ him to do." Angus halted opposite. "Now, Mrs Du Rose and Mrs Jennings. Our local constabulary have some intriguing questions for you."

Hana and Sheila exchanged nervous looks and Pete popped from the learning support office as though propelled by an unseen hand. "No need to push, Janice!" he yelled over his shoulder.

"Ah, the last musketeer." Angus seized Pete by the collar. "This way people."

"Help me!" Hana hissed to Logan, her eyes wide and pleading.

He gave her a satisfied wink. "This one's all yours," he said, giving Pete a narrowed, dangerous look. He strode away to deal with a bottleneck on the staircase.

Back at the student centre, a police photographer clicked away on an average looking camera. Several upended chairs alerted them to the drama which unfolded in their wake. "Damn!" Sheila cursed, her expression channelling disappointment. "I always miss the exciting stuff."

"Mum!" Bodie ran over to Hana and squished her into a bear hug. His uniform looked rumpled. "Where were you?"

Hana swallowed. "Toilet."

He glanced down at his open notebook. "But I'm here to take your statement."

"Oh." Hana watched Angus frog march Pete towards their office, Sheila tottering behind. She put a hand on her son's wrist. "Do you think the blonde man sent someone else after me?" She swallowed and her resolve crumbled.

"No." Bodie sounded so definite she exhaled the held breath. "I promise." He leaned closer. "This dude walked out of prison last night and came looking for his son. The receptionist sent him away, so he used a side door. His boy is a prefect so he found his way up to the common room. We heard reports he carried a weapon but unless he ditched it, we found nothing."

Hana nodded and watched as Angus turned to face her with a raised eyebrow. He jerked his head towards the office door and shoved Pete over the threshold. "I'm in so much trouble," she breathed.

Bodie smothered a laugh. "Is that because you disobeyed a lockdown order or because you smuggled a bloke into the girls' toilets?"

Hana gasped. "How do you know?"

"Security cameras, Mother." He shook his head. "Best laugh we've had all year."

-29-

"It's not funny!" Hana pouted as Logan laughed most of the way home.

"So they watched you crawl from your office to the toilet on the security system?" Logan's voice broke as he tried to control his mirth. "With Pete's bum in Sheila's face?"

"Oh, stop!" Hana buried her face in her hands. "We'll never live it down."

Logan checked the road behind before indicating left. A stupid grin split his face in half. He swept into the driveway and Hana screamed as the car slewed to a sliding stop. "Shit!" Logan cursed, almost rear-ending a white car parked in front of the gates. "Wait here!" he commanded, his body rigid as he climbed from the car and stalked towards the visitor. Hana's heart felt as though it crawled further up her chest, causing a tightness in her throat.

"Oh, no!" As the driver of the vehicle emerged, Hana's heart dived for the opposite end of her body, sinking into her boots. The thud of her blood pressure felt dull and strained. "Tama!" Hana spat his name through lips curled back in a sneer. She watched as the men embraced and foreboding hung over her like a shroud.

"It's okay." Logan clambered into the driver's seat and pressed the remote to open the gate. He glanced across at Hana, biting his lip in response to the look of thunder disfiguring her pretty face. "It's just for a few nights." He tipped an envelope into her lap. "I grabbed the post."

"No!" Hana exploded, "No, no, no, not for any nights, no!"

Logan blinked at her in surprise, almost fudging the steep final bend. He lowered his tone and employed the usual platitudes. "Come on babe, it'll be fine," he said, sounding dismissive. "He's my whānau."

"No. He's not my family and I don't care." Hana maintained her rigid stance, refusing to debate the point. She watched as Tama parked his car at the top of the slope, blocking their access to the garage. Logan tutted and negotiated the tight space, abandoning the car at the foot of the porch steps.

The icy air barely touched Hana, doing little to cool her rage as Tama hauled a duffel bag from the boot of his car. It hit the driveway with a thud. The surrounding atmosphere crackled and hissed with danger. Logan ignored her, skipping up the steps and unlocking the front door. He deactivated the burglar alarm and watched Hana stride past him. "I said no! Is anyone listening to me?"

"What?" Logan's brow narrowed in warning and Hana shook her head, stamping her foot in defiance. The sound echoed around the lobby.

"He's not staying here, Logan. Do you hear me?" His loaded silence should have frightened her but anger propelled her words. "He wrecked my small but significant honeymoon, ruined a friend's marriage, destroyed our friendship, put you in the hospital and read my private messages. He's a selfish little man and I want him off this property before I call the cops!"

"Cops?" Tama took a step back towards his car and his handsome face creased into a pout. "Uncle Logan, she can't threaten me."

Logan gritted his teeth. "Hana," he said in a reasonable tone, "I live here too and he's family."

"Not mine!" she countered, her tone hard and unyielding. She slammed the envelope onto the hall cupboard and channeled determination through her balled fists. Every fibre of her being resisted Tama's chaotic presence, reminding her of the isolation he brought with him last time. Hana's coat parted to reveal the tiny baby bump and Logan's pupils dilated. When she took a step towards him, he seemed mesmerized. "Send him away, Logan and if you don't like it, go with him!"

The words hit the freezing air invading the lobby and bounced back at her. Logan blanched and Hana sensed she went too far. He swallowed and gave a sad nod of his head. "My name means nothing to you, does it?" He jerked his head towards the envelope and Hana followed his gaze. The power company addressed the bill to Mrs H Johal and she looked away, not wanting to hear the rest of Logan's accusation.

"This is about a house guest," she said through gritted teeth. "Not whose name appears on the bills."

Logan shook his head. "It's about more than that, wahine. I'm your tāne but you don't respect me."

"Are you just the lodger, Uncle?" Tama's snort cut the air and Hana stiffened. He'd made it as far as the front steps and she turned and kicked the door closed in his face.

"I'm calling Bo," she snapped, pulling her phone from her handbag as she headed towards her bedroom. "I'm done with this."

She left Logan standing in the hallway, his angular jaw locked in a grimace. Her heart clenched in her chest as she walked away, not daring to look back at him. He'd leave because she offered him no reason to stay.

"You under the thumb, Uncle?" Tama's snarky shout and subsequent guffaw of juvenile laughter sealed the deal. He railed more comments at the closed front door and Hana put her hands over her ears as her world tipped on its axis.

She heard the slam of the front door and edged to the bedroom window, watching a side view of the men. Cracking the frame open gave her audio. "Why'd you antagonise her?" Logan shoved his hands in his pockets and rocked back on his heels, waiting for an answer.

Tama shrugged. "It's fun seeing you whipped by a chick, bro'. But I got nowhere to stay so tell her to let me in."

Logan removed one hand long enough to rub his left eye with the heel of his hand. "No. It's her house."

Tama's head jerked back on his neck, an action of disgust. "What? You not a man anymore, Uncle? You a pussy?" Hana watched Logan's jaw grind against his cheek and sensed the explosion rising in his chest. Tama pressed the detonation switch. "What do you see in her? Caroline's got legs up to her neck. That chick's a poisoned dwarf compared to her."

Hana closed her eyes and backed away from the window. Tama's comparison stung. Caroline's influence hung over her like a dense fog and she couldn't compete on any level. The woman even managed to get pregnant first. She sighed and sank onto the bed to remove her boots. Conjecture over Caroline's paternity claims heightened her nausea and Hana put her head between her knees. Logan promised he didn't father the child, but doubt trailed like a gossamer thread behind their marriage. Invisible, yet always there.

Hana heard a metallic clang and ignored it, changing into her pyjamas and hanging her clothes in the wardrobe. Her hand strayed to her belly and she rubbed it, gratified when the fluttering began. "Just you and me, kid," she sighed. "Somehow I don't think your daddy will stick around after that performance."

"Then you don't know me very well." Logan's voice made her jump and she turned to find him leaning against the doorframe. The gate alarm sounded from the lobby as Tama passed through the sensors. Hana swallowed, her face drawn and pale.

"Maybe I don't then."

"I sent Tama away." Logan looked down and winced at a cut on his knuckle. "I might need your help with the Band Aids again."

"You hit him?"

"Na, cut it open pushing him into his car." He walked towards her, holding his hand aloft. Blood seeped into his palm. "I listened to you," he said. "Eventually. Sorry. I don't mean to put the whānau first, but they've filled a gap for so long it's hard to break the habit."

Hana nodded and gripped the bridge of her nose to stem the rising headache. The child did another lap of her womb and age crept over her like a warm blanket. "I don't have the energy for this," she whispered.

"I know." Logan enfolded her with his good arm and kissed the top of her head. "I know."

Hana's realisation drove her to make changes throughout the following week. She filled in forms and visited the bank, changing all references to Mrs Hana Johal to Du Rose. Neither of them mention Tama again, but his existence haunted Hana like a curse.

On Thursday, she crept into the phone booth in the staffroom, waiting for the lunchtime rush to end. She phoned the doctor's surgery and asked for her test results. A single answer held the power to end or increase her sleepless nights and galvanise or ruin her appetite.

The receptionist answered. "We only give results at two o'clock in the afternoon," she snapped. "You should know by now."

Hana swallowed. "I didn't know. And I work in a school. It's hard to get privacy, especially then. That's right in the middle of lesson change. Please can I ring after four when everyone's gone?"

"That's too late," the receptionist snapped. "Two o'clock only." Hana stared into the handset as the line went dead. She groaned and rested her forehead against the glass.

She watched the clock for the next hour, growing more anxious as the hands seemed to slow to a tantalising snail's pace. Pete disappeared for his post-lunch nap and Sheila found herself called into an emergency meeting with other heads of department. "It's about the new chapel," she grumbled. "I don't know why they need me."

"Will Logan be there?" Hana asked, watching Sheila gather up a new, expensive handbag and plaster lipstick over her teeth without looking.

"It's all of us." Sheila rolled her eyes and tossed her head. "I'm sure he's got better things to do than discuss fundraising and planning permission. The building won't go ahead. It's Angus' latest pipe dream and we get sucked in." She slammed from the office amidst a haze of Chanel and Hana coughed and opened the window. Boy sweat wafted in and she closed it again with a thud.

Blessed with a few moments of privacy, Hana waited for the noise of lesson change to pass. At five minutes after the deadline, she phoned the doctor's surgery from her office phone and found it engaged. It stayed that way for another twenty minutes as the population of Ngaruawahia and Huntly sought their results. "Stupid system!" Hana griped, banging her fist on the table after pressing the redial button. The receptionist answered.

"Oh, hi. I'm ringing for my test results."

"Name."

Hana paused. "Johal, but I need to change it to Du Rose."

The receptionist sighed and Hana heard the click of her manicured nails on the keyboard as she spelled her name four times. "That's all done for you," the woman said.

"And my test results?" Hana held her breath and felt her heart rate reach thudding point.

"I can't give you those over the phone. The midwife does it."

Hana's voice sounded croaky. "Why? Is there something wrong?"

"No," the woman spat. "Midwives give the pregnancy results. Ask her." She hung up.

Enraged, Hana rang back again, stopping the receptionist mid welcome. She asked for her doctor.

She gasped when his voice came on the line, convinced the officious woman would guard his afternoon on the golf course instead of putting her through. Surprise made her stammer to explain the awful series of phone conversations with the receptionist. The doctor sighed and Hana heard the tick of his office clock in the silence. Not the golf course then. "She's right. The midwife gives those results." His fingers tapped as he checked his computer. "Ah, yes. Your pre-natal visit went somewhat downhill and I didn't give you the information."

"No." Hana closed her eyes against the thudding in her head. "I just need those results. The not knowing is driving me mad."

"My wife is one of our midwives. I'll get her to call you. Would that be okay?"

"Yes, please." Hana's groan of relief sounded indecent and she pressed a hand over her mouth. "Sorry." She ended the call and then fear worked its way back into her soul. She didn't have the results and someone else still had control over her future.

Sheila returned in a temper, flinging herself into a chair and recounting the meeting word for word. "We sat there for an hour while a boring architect burbled on about a building which looks more suited to a new age commune. What is Angus thinking?"

"Is Logan free now?" Hana half-stood, desperate to seek her husband's assurance. Acknowledging her need for his support felt like halving the problem.

Sheila shook her head. "He rushed off to supervise cross-country for the lower school." She stood and turned back. "And he asked me to remind you he's using his bike. There's another bloody departmental meeting after school tonight."

Hana groaned in misery and sank into her chair. She tried phoning him but he didn't answer. Cross-country meant a trip into the gully and nobody in their right mind took their phone down there.

School finished for the day and Hana glanced at her watch. "I'm heading off," she called to Sheila. "Don't forget your meeting." A grunted reply followed her through the door into the common room. She jumped as her phone rang and dumped her bag on a nearby desk to rummage through and find it. "Hey, Logan," she answered, confused by the long pause on the other end.

"Oh, hi. My name is Emma and I'm a midwife," a woman's voice said. "I hear you're desperate for some important test results."

"Yes, I am." Hana watched through the long windows as her husband rounded the top corner of the soccer field. Mud coated his legs and trainers and he chivvied up the runners at the back. A shower and change would make him late for the meeting. She turned away, listening to the gentle voice on the other end of the phone call.

"Let's meet," Emma suggested. "I've got your results here and we can have a proper talk about your pregnancy. I can be at your house in two hours as long as one of my women doesn't go into labour."

At home, Hana rattled around the house like a bag of nerves. She squeaked at the sound of the gate alarm and sized up the pretty Indian-looking woman speaking into the intercom.

Emma didn't disappoint. "I'm sorry for all the drama," she said. "The receptionist means well." Hana smiled, keeping her doubts about that to herself. Refusing a drink, the midwife followed Hana into the lounge and took a seat. "Now, I know you haven't signed with me, but I'm happy to do the initial meeting and you can decide afterwards."

Hana raised a hand. "I don't understand any of this process. My other children are twenty-five and twenty-six and I had them in England. Aren't you just allocated to me?"

"No." Emma smiled. "That's not how it works."

Hana grew desperate and her green eyes dulled in response to the panic in her chest. "You seem nice. Please can I just sign and have my results?"

Emma stood and joined her on the sofa. "Hey, it's okay." She reached for Hana's hand and the human contact made her realise how lonely and insular she'd become.

"I don't think I can do any of this." Hana's voice wobbled and Emma rubbed her fingers.

"Yes, you can," she assured. "We're women. We can do anything." She reached into her pocket and pulled out an envelope. Hana's brow knitted and she closed her eyes against failure and guilt.

"You're results are normal, Hana." Emma's gentle voice filtered into her locked up brain and she laid the envelope in Hana's lap. "An amniocentesis and scan will confirm that, but your bloods raised no alarm bells."

"Normal. All of them?" Hana's chin wobbled as her brain grappled with the unexpected. "Are you sure these are mine?"

"Yeah." Emma stroked an escaped curl behind Hana's ear and kindness radiated out from her. "Can I check you and the baby over?"

Hana nodded, her head unsteady on her neck. She lay on the lounge rug while her new midwife measured her from groin to ribs and located her baby's heartbeat with an ear funnel. "There it is," she said with confidence. "Nice and strong."

A rush of emotion squeezed tears from the corners of Hana's eyes as she lay on the carpet. She pursed her lips and closed her eyes. The midwife knelt next to her and pulled Hana's shirt over her stomach. "How pregnant am I?" Hana asked.

"Very." Emma offered her a hand and hauled her into a sitting position. "Thirteen or fourteen weeks. A scan will give more accuracy." She sat on the sofa and made notes on her phone.

"I don't want an amnio." Hana pulled herself backwards onto the sofa and wiped her nose with the back of her hand. "Logan and I talked about it."

"Fair enough." Emma smiled. "You're not twenty, Hana. I needn't hand hold you. If you'd like me as your midwife, I think we'll both enjoy it."

Hana nodded and accepted the various leaflets and documents relating to her pregnancy and the midwife service. She pressed the gate release for Emma and allowed a bud of excitement to flourish in her chest.

"Logan, I need to speak to you." She left him the voicemail when he didn't answer. A glance at the clock told her he might still be in the meeting. "It's good, not bad. Hurry home."

An hour later, she rang Sheila. "What time did the meeting end?" she asked, anxiety filling her voice. "Logan isn't home."

"That's weird." Sheila yawned. "He left before me on that damn bike of his." She paused. "Remember the rumours about Caroline Marsh?"

"No! He wouldn't see her!" Hana snapped, wondering when the woman's name would cease to plague her. "Thanks." She hung up.

Half an hour later her phone rang. "Mum?" Bodie's baritone seemed to fill the lobby where Hana paced.

"Is it Logan?" she demanded. "He didn't come home. I know it's only a couple of hours, but I'm worried."

"He's fine." Bodie exhaled through his nose, creating a hissing sound. "He's at Amy's. They followed him. Enough is enough. You both need to consider witness protection."

"What happened?" Hana's fingers strayed to her belly.

"He led them on a bit of a chase and lost them at Claudelands. He hid the bike in Amy's garden and rang me."

"Oh, my goodness!" Hana squatted in the lobby with her back to the wall. "How is he?"

Bodie snorted. "Amy almost smashed him with her nightstick. Probably not his best move to creep around the side of her house after dark. Control tasked the night shift to look for a dark coloured Subaru and they chased a few sightings, but lost it."

"What about Logan? Shall I drive down and fetch him?"

"No. I'm taking him to the Gordonton House to retrieve his truck. He'll be at yours in about an hour. His phone died. He said to tell you."

"Thank you." Hana rang off but couldn't settle. She shut all the curtains and sat in the lounge as television programs scrolled past her blank vision. Reaching for her former happiness gleaned little of its earlier buzz.

It seemed an age before the gate alarm sounded, followed by the roar of the truck labouring up the driveway. Despite the cold, she stood on the porch with her arms clasped around her, watching her exhausted husband step from the driver's side. Fatigue drained the olive from his complexion and his rucksack hung limp in his hand. He looked incongruous, descending from an all-wheel-drive in motorbike leathers.

Hana held her arms out to him at the top of the steps and he wrapped himself around her, breathing in the scent of her hair in giant gulps. "Everything's okay," he whispered. "I promise." Looking down at her bare feet, his brows narrowed. "Let's go inside," he said.

Hana shut the front door behind them, locking and bolting it with eager fingers. She waited for Logan to disgorge from his leathers. His tie looked adrift, his top button undone and his hair tousled. He'd aged since they kissed goodbye on the front steps and anxious lines crossed his forehead.

"Were you scared?" she asked, her eyes wide. "They terrify me."

Logan shook his head and his nose wrinkled upwards in a sneer. "No. I contemplated stopping and having it out with them." He shrugged. "A year ago that's what I'd have done." His gaze grazed her belly and he reached out a hand. "I've got more to lose now. I suspect they were armed. My phone died after lunch, otherwise I could have got myself some help."

"From the cops?" Hana's earnest face seemed to make Logan falter.

"Not quite," he replied, his expression guarded. "We'll talk about it another time, hey? I'm tired."

At the look of pure alarm in Hana's face, Logan coasted his fingers over her abdomen. "Who else can help you?" she asked in a whisper. "Who else is there?"

"Just people." Logan snaked his arm around her neck and pressed her face into his shirt. "This feels nice."

"What does?"

"Coming home to you and my baby. I've spent my life drifting and not caring about my own safety. Tonight felt different. I'm anchored."

Hana sighed into his chest and smelled shower gel and deodorant, mixed with his special, summer scent. "I'm glad," she sighed.

Logan's chest muscles tightened beneath her cheek. "I'm not riding round town like a dick again though. Next time, they'll get what's coming to them!" He jabbed his finger to punctuate his statement and Hana blanched.

"Maybe ride round town like a dick twice more?" she begged. "Then maybe the cops will pick them up and you won't get shot or beaten, or dumped in the river." Even the choices made her shiver with fear and a brick formed of terror lodged in her stomach.

Logan snorted. "The cops are overstretched. They couldn't catch a cold right now."

They sat at the kitchen table with mugs of tea and an air of defeatism surrounded them. "Help isn't coming, is it?" Hana said, her tone sad. "We need to go into hiding and leave all this." She looked around the comfortable room, her gaze straying outside to the darkened bush and Maihi beyond.

"I asked. It's not an option." Logan swallowed his tea and watched her beneath his eyelashes.

"But Bodie said we could." Hana jerked backwards in her chair. "He said we could go into a witness protection scheme."

"He still thinks we can." Logan ran a hand through his hair and guilt spiked Hana at the sight of a peppering of grey in his sideburns. "But we can't."

"Why?" Hana pushed her drink away, watching as it slopped onto the wooden table and soaked into the grain. "Why not?"

Logan ground his teeth. "Some of the late night meetings you resented involved me meeting with the head detective. I think you're bait for something massive. I asked him to take you into hiding and he refused." Hana put a hand over her mouth and Logan reached for her fingers across the table. "Hey, on the plus side, I can tick something off my bucket list."

"What?" Her voice wavered.

Logan smirked. "I razzed around the events' centre on my bike.

Always fancied doing that."

"How?"

"A guy on a mower left the gate open. Your blonde guy dumped his car and followed on foot, but I zipped through there so fast, I left him for dust." He wrinkled his nose. "I got airborne twice and dropped my bike off a low wall. I might need to get it looked at."

"What if the mower man took your reggo and you get a ticket?" Hana bit her bottom lip and worried.

Logan laughed. "Always the good citizen, Hana. Well, the bike is now at the home of a very scary policewoman. She can explain it away, can't she?"

Hana nodded and scraped her chair away from the table. She retrieved her phone from the hall table and dialled a number. "Hi, Amy," she said, her tone serious. "Please can we visit after school tomorrow? No, not for Logan's bike. It's probably safer there right now. Bodie looked for something in Jas' room a while ago and didn't find it. Remembering how he looked for stuff as a teenager, I think I need to do it myself." Hana raised a hand in placation, even though Amy couldn't see her. "No, Jas isn't in trouble, but I've lost something in there. It's best if he's not there when I visit. I might need to take the room apart."

-30-

Hana lay with her head cradled in the crook of Logan's arm, awake before the alarm chirped. Neither slept well, starting at every creak and groan of the old house. Tiger sensed their unease and prowled, getting into awkward places and knocking things over with a clatter.

Logan's breathing slowed as his sleep deepened and Hana lay still, watching the light change through the window. Exhaustion pressed her into the mattress. Logan's truck sat downstairs in the garage and she struggled to remember if the blonde man knew the registration number. Events tumbled through her tired brain as their chronology defeated her. They knew Logan's bike, but would they recognise his truck? Hana swallowed back the sense that the blonde man toyed with her like a cat teases a mouse.

Time ticked by as work drew nearer and doomed her. Sleep snatched her away, but the confusion went with her. Strange women with expanding pink flesh like marshmallow, gave her rotten advice in her dreams. Jerking awake, Hana reached for more obvious help through frantic, heartfelt prayer.

Using her imagination, she placed her insurmountable problems at the foot of a wooden cross. Scarred wood and huge nails held it together. She dropped her burdens at the bottom like pebbles one after another. The pile grew so high, Hana feared it might topple and crush her, anyway. It didn't and she dozed, her soul lighter.

The alarm sounded into the silence, frightening them both. Logan fumbled around on his bedside table to still the ringing. "I feel wretched," he groaned. Hana pushed herself into a sitting position and he snaked his arm around her waist and pulled her back down. He stroked her cheek with gentle fingers and she saw a distorted reflection of herself in his grey irises. "I'm stoked about the baby," he whispered. "We'll get through this."

Hana nodded and studied the chiseled contours of his face. Closing her eyes, she saw the teenage boy on the train who fell in love with a pregnant stranger after a single, chance meeting. "I don't deserve you," she whispered and Logan narrowed his eyes.

"Yeah, ya do," he said, pulling her into his chest.

"What's the plan for today?"

"Go to work," he replied. "My Year 13s are expecting an assessment and they need the credits." He kissed her forehead. "But you look shattered. Why don't you call in sick?"

Hana shook her head. "Can't. I've taken too much time off lately. And I hated wondering where you were. At least if I'm with you, we'll be in danger together."

"I don't like that idea." Logan's brow furrowed and he opened his mouth to speak. Hana pressed her fingers over his lips.

"You make tea and I'll grab the first shower." She dragged herself from the warm bed and braved the wintry bathroom.

Logan drove the truck, parking on the side street and entering the school grounds via the gully. He kissed her as she balanced on the front steps, leaving to find his tutor group.

"Ah, hi." The biology teacher from Hana's rental property on Achilles Rise met her at the office door. She jumped as he stepped from behind a brochure rack.

"Don't do that!" She clutched her chest and felt the ground tilt in her vision. "You scared me!"

"Sorry, sorry." His flaccid cheeks wobbled, an embarrassed flush rising beneath his many chins. He held his large paws out in front of him. One contained a set of keys. "My mother-in-law died last night." He swallowed. "I need a favour."

Hana unlocked the office and turned on the lights. Laying her handbag on her desk, she turned to face him. "I'm sorry for your loss. What can I do?"

He hopped from foot to foot with awkwardness and Hana waited. "We bought a kitten," he said, licking his lips. "It's against the terms of our rental agreement."

"It is?" Hana shrugged. "The agent handles all that. You should tell him."

The big man rolled his eyes. "I'd rather not involve him. I wondered if you'd feed it while we're away. We're flying to Christchurch at lunchtime today."

Hana gaped. "You want me to feed the kitten which you're not supposed to own in my house?"

"Yes." The man wrung his hands. "I'm sorry. Please don't evict us."

Hana sighed and ran a hand across her forehead. "You know this is messed up?"

He nodded. "If Margo hadn't died, you'd never know." He jangled the keys and Hana held out her hand.

"I knew you wouldn't refuse," he gushed and turned on his heel.

Hana stared at her old front door key and sighed. "Yeah, because I have the word 'mug' tattooed on my forehead."

Sheila barrelled into the room, handbag flying at ninety degrees from her body. "What's up?" she demanded, disappearing into her office.

"Nothing." Hana winced. "Yet." A conviction of her own stupidity gripped her as she contemplated confessing to Logan. She imagined the conversation and it didn't go well in her head.

Hana met her husband in the staffroom, hoping an audience might reduce his ire. Her heart fluttered as she caught sight of him at a table with Pete and the other sports teachers. He rose as she approached, his old-fashioned chivalry an instant aphrodisiac. "Sit with me," he ordered, pulling up a chair for her.

Pete took the opportunity to lean forward and snag Logan's toast, shoving it in his mouth whole. He gagged and Hana closed her eyes as the other members of the group gave a collective groan. Logan turned back to his plate and feigned ignorance, focussing on his wife instead. Chris Carter slapped Pete on the back. "You okay?" Logan whispered, leaning close.

Hana nodded. "Yeah. A bit rattled. What about you?"

"Na." Logan shook his head. "I'm over it. I want them to come after me again. Then they can answer my questions." He smiled and grazed her lower lip with his thumb.

Pete recovered enough to mock their whispered intimacy. "Get a room you two," he guffawed, drawing the attention of staff on nearby tables. "What do you think this is?" Sitting opposite Logan gave him a false sense of safety.

He yelped as Logan's leg moved beneath the table, administering a spiteful kick to Pete's groin. The skinny man bent double and smacked his face into the table. The other men smirked. As Pete rolled around in his chair, Logan spared Hana the effort of her confession. "There's another departmental meeting tonight," he said, reaching beneath the table for her hand. "I'll ask Pete to take you home."

Hana's eyes widened at the noise coming from across the table. "Is he okay?"

"He will be." Logan smiled. "Don't feed him. He's under strict instruction to take you home and leave. Besides, Henrietta arrives at Auckland airport tonight so he's got no reason to hang around."

"Okay." Hana nodded, grateful for her small reprieve. She could leave the argument until later.

Pete met Hana at the office, rubbing his groin with his palm.

"Your husband's an animal," he complained.

"Stop that!" Hana locked the door and turned to face him, the keys to Achilles Rise in her hand. "I refuse to go anywhere with a man who's fiddling with himself."

"Tell Logan then!" he griped and Hana shook her head.

"Tell him yourself."

Having established the unlikeliness of that scenario, they walked to the car park and Hana climbed into Pete's dustbin on wheels. She kicked a fast food tray and an empty drinks can into the foot well. "What time does Henri land?" she enquired and Pete gushed for a couple of kilometres about his larger-than-life girlfriend.

"She almost slept with me last time," he preened and Hana winced. "Yeah, she took her cardigan off," he said, offering definitive proof of her lascivious intentions.

"I need to nip somewhere on the way home," Hana said, sliding the location into the end of the sentence. She screamed as Pete slammed on the brakes mid traffic.

"No way!" he shouted. "Logan told me what happened last night. If I don't take you home, he'll kill me."

They argued all the way up the expressway to Achilles Rise. Hana won. "I won't take long," she promised as Pete crunched his car up the driveway.

"I'm not coming in." He cut the engine and folded his arms. "I protest against this whole, stupid idea."

Hana shrugged. "Please yourself," she said, climbing the front steps.

The revenue from the house rent covered most of the mortgage on Culver's Cottage, although the agent took a handsome slice for repairs and the ever famous administration costs. Hana stepped through the front door, remembering her last unfortunate visit to her former home. Her sense of detachment surprised her.

She felt like a stranger in the familiar house, her name on the property deeds but her heart elsewhere. Closing the door, she left it unlocked in case Pete abandoned his sulk in favour of kitten cuddles.

Hana searched the living rooms for the kitten, finding an empty food bowl near the ranch slider. Nothing horrid lurked in the fresh litter tray. She wandered along the empty hallway, peering in bedrooms which smelled of a new family. In the master bedroom at the end of the house, she discovered a dark brown ball of fluff in the centre of the bed. "There you are."

The kitten raised his downy head and mewed as Hana scooped him into her arms. She kissed his forehead and smoothed his furry face with her cheek. "Dinner time," she cooed. "Then I'll pop back tomorrow and check on you." He wiggled and she put him on the carpet, following his eager steps into the hallway. "I forgot to ask where they kept your food," she mused. "So I'll have to follow you."

The kitten nosed his way into the laundry next to the master bedroom and Hana followed. The cupboard beneath the sink revealed only washing powder and trays of seeds filled the sink and windowsills. Hana peered at the green buds poking from the soil. "He's dedicated to teaching biology," she told the kitten. "I thought they grew curriculum plants in the greenhouse at school."

The kitten retrieved a plastic ball from between the washing machine and sink and Hana bounced it along the hallway towards the kitchen. A process of elimination found kitten kibbles in the bottom of the pantry. Squatting next to his bowl, Hana shook biscuits into a mound and stood back for him to eat. He bent his body into an arc and she stroked the soft fur of his back, watching as he closed his eyes with the double pleasure.

The click of the front door made her smirk and she stood, readying herself for Pete's entrance. "Knew you couldn't resist," she said, the ready grin fading from her lips.

"I'm sorry," Pete mouthed, his face ashen. "I'm really sorry."

-31-

Hana groaned in pain on the cold floor. Her dress didn't keep out the chill pushing through from the icy surface. "Pull the cupboard out from the wall, Amy," she hissed. "We must keep looking." Nobody answered and Hana opened her eyes. "Oh, no," she whined as the mirage of Jas' warm bedroom faded, abandoning her on the garage floor of the Achilles Rise house.

Shadows lengthened from the walls and Hana pushed herself into a sitting position without using her right arm. Nausea bit as the bones in her elbow ground beneath the skin. Squinting in the half-light, she saw Peter North slumped in the far corner, unmoving. He sat on the concrete floor, blood seeping from a cut to his crown. His thin dusting of hair appeared translucent in the disappearing light and his head resembled a smooth, round, pale ball. "Pete," Hana whispered. "Pete, wake up." She swallowed against the dryness in her mouth, remembering the sound of the second crack on the head he didn't deserve. "Pete!" she called, but he made no response.

The coldness of the garage floor seeped through Hana's dress and tights, chilling her to the bone. The sun dipped behind the windowsill. She estimated the time around five o'clock and rush hour began in the distance. Steady creaking came from overhead, accompanied by the crash of china and glass.

Pete stirred and Hana called out to him to sit still while she made her way across. She crawled on her knees to stem the nausea, holding her arm against her side. "Keep still, Pete," she whispered. "Your head's bleeding." He moaned again and his heels ground on the concrete, thrashing and then stilling.

Hana knew without looking that her right arm had fractured just above the elbow. When she touched it with her left hand, it felt rubbery and unreal like it belonged to someone else. The pain seemed intermittent, veering between a dull, almost unbearable ache to the spasming, breath-taking throb resembling labour pains. Halfway across the distance towards Pete, the throb began again, leaving her sweating and praying for it to end.

"Henrietta?" Pete reached out for her like a child and Hana forced herself forward.

"No, Pete. It's Hana. Do you remember what happened?"

"I'm not sure." He spat out a mouthful of blood and reached a hand up to his crown. When he saw the gunky red stain in his palm, hysteria appeared in his eyes.

"Don't scream!" Hana hissed. "Please don't bring them back down here."

"Your arm." Pete pointed, noticing the odd way she carried her body and Hana nodded.

"An accident," she admitted, her tone rueful. "I tripped on the landing and the taller man caught my arm to stop me falling." Her voice cracked. "I could've lost the baby if I'd gone all the way down."

She sniffed and Pete patted her skirt with his bloody hand. "Is the baby okay?"

"I think so. It's moving around." Hana swallowed. "The way he yanked my arm pulled it between two corners of the bannister rail. I heard the bone snap."

"My head hurts." Pete put his hand to it again. "I feel so tired."

"Don't go to sleep," Hana begged. "This is all my fault. I'll get us out of here."

"Is it the same guys?" Pete asked and she shook her head.

"No. Different. But they want the same thing. They're pulling the house apart upstairs."

"They didn't look like thugs." Pete sighed and spat out more blood. "They looked like bankers."

"I know." Hana cast around her, seeking a ready exit. Nothing presented itself, but moving made the bone grind more and the heady sickness increased its grip. Blood soaked Pete's jacket and ran into his collar, speckling the surrounding floor in an arc. "I need to stop the bleeding," Hana said, her gaze searching the empty shelving in the distance. She forced herself to stand, tipping forward to control the jabs of pain stealing her breath. The nearest shelf unit revealed a pair of pliers sitting in the dust. Hana took them in her left hand. "I can't rip bandages," she grunted. "I need two hands."

Pete moaned and slipped sideways against the wall. His body slumped and Hana panicked as his eyes rolled backwards in his head like two boiled eggs.

Fingers shaking, she tore at her underskirt with the pliers. She groaned in frustration at the fumbling of her least dominant hand. Sitting on the cold concrete floor, she took a break while the pain from her elbow reached screaming pitch. By the time she crawled back to Pete, she trailed a ragged piece of elasticated underskirt.

"Pete, wake up." She pushed his shoulder and he slid sideways, his body limp. "Pete!" Hana's voice rose and she hushed herself in case the men upstairs returned. The blood ran slower from his gash as the platelets did their work, but the skin around the wound bulged. Without the cooperation of an extra hand, the bandage proved futile. It slipped off Pete's head before Hana managed a complete revolution. After the third failure, she leaned her head against the cold wall in defeat.

"Plan B," she muttered to bolster herself. Taking a deep breath, she wedged Pete alongside the wall, holding him upright with her knee against his cheek. Uncurling her painful right arm, she leaned on the end of the bandage and wound it around his head. It worked, even though the action jarred the broken bone and forced out countless gasps of agony. Sweat dripped from her hairline as she tucked the tattered end beneath the strip above his eye. It held.

Light faded from the garage and the crashing continued overhead. Hana felt her way around the walls to the small side window and peered outside. "We need to get away," she called over her shoulder. "I don't know what they have planned for us and I'm keen not to find out." If she pressed her face to the glass, she could see the road out front. The angle defied any attempts to contact the outside world. The neighbour's roof glinted under the streetlights, the solid fence between the houses obscured by ivy.

Hana opened the window and pushed, groaning as the security clasp prevented it opening wider than a few centimetres. "This used to unhook," she hissed, fiddling with the metal. Rust flaked onto the windowsill but it refused to disengage. It remained fast and the window proved useless as an exit.

Hana scrunched her cheek against the cold glass and craned her neck to the left. She saw the tail end of the hosepipe snaking across the path and sighed. "I'm so thirsty."

The growing darkness attacked all sense of hope and Hana gravitated towards the light switch next to the internal door. Beneath it sat the button to raise the garage door. The urge to push it and run formed a knot in her stomach. She couldn't leave Pete. They'd hit him twice and wouldn't hesitate to repeat it. Her voice broke. "This is my fault. I won't leave you, Pete, I promise."

Exhaustion settled over her soul and she rested her good hand against the wall. Despite her desperation, Hana resisted turning on the light. The yellow haze would flare over the side garden and attract attention from upstairs. Another crash overhead helped to motivate her.

"Pete, I need you to wake up," she urged, squatting next to him. When no answer came, she linked her fingers around his bloodied collar and dragged him towards the garage door. He left a streaky trail behind him and Hana's body strained against his dead weight. Blood obliterated the school logo on the back of his polyester tracksuit.

She paused for a break and squatted to dig in his pockets. "Where are the car keys?" she whined, panic making a resurgence. "Think, think," she told herself. "They pulled him from the car outside so maybe they're still in the ignition." The alternative wasn't worth consideration because it meant they confiscated them and locked up the car.

Hana made her plan. She needed to press the button, drag Pete outside and get to the car before the men intercepted them. They would hear the motor running and know within seconds. Logic told her she couldn't manage to outrun them, determination ensured she would.

She took a few moments to ready herself. Hana prayed for divine help then pushed Pete as near to the door as she dared. She adjusted his position twice, not wanting it to hit him on the way up. For the first time in their relationship, she ached for his irritating chatter to replace the unconscious silence.

Supporting her broken arm, Hana walked towards the switch. Her heart pounded in her chest, knowing as soon as she pressed it, she unleashed a storm of painful activity. "Come on, Hana. You can do this, girl," she told herself. She breathed out through pursed lips and pressed the button. Nothing happened. Memory told her that wasn't alarming. Sometimes it took a second to kick in. It didn't. She pressed it again harder. Still nothing.

"No!" Frustration consumed her and she stamped in anger. The jolt disturbed the broken bone and she panted until the pain subsided. She pushed the button again and the door remained closed. Moving her fingers upwards, she flicked the light switch, seeing not even a spark. Her heart sank as she realised they'd killed the power from the fuse box in the laundry upstairs.

Pete moaned from in front of the garage door and shifted. His trainers made a gritty noise against the concrete floor. A draught moved his wispy hair and regret sliced through Hana's chest. She'd worsened his position without meaning to. Walking back, she knelt beside him, shaking his shoulder and attempting to rouse him. "Pete, please help me. I need you to wake up."

He replied gibberish, shifting around on his back and smearing blood through the inadequate bandage. "Hurts," he groaned and Hana swallowed.

"I know, sweetie," she whispered. Her chest hitched with defeat.

"What would Logan do?" she asked and nobody answered. The thought depressed her further. Darkness engulfed the space as night laid hold and she knew he wouldn't miss her until after his departmental meeting. He knew nothing about the kitten and even less about her fool's errand.

Her only hope lay with Henrietta contacting Logan when Pete didn't meet her at the airport. She felt in Pete's pockets again, a fruitless exercise. He put his phone on charge when they got into the car.

She stood and peered through the darkness, trying to locate the emergency pull cord for the garage door. Her eyes strained to find the string with the red plastic toggle at the end. It wasn't where she remembered. She moved around beneath the motor, squinting into the darkness and losing hope. Then she saw it, flipped over the metal runner and far too high to reach. Their captors thought of everything. "I'm not quitting," Hana hissed. "Logan never gives up."

With nothing to stand on, she tried jumping to touch the toggle which lay just out of reach. The pain in her arm caused a feeling of faintness. Remembering the pliers with which she destroyed her dress, Hana snatched them up from the floor by the wall. It took precious moments to regain sight of the toggle in the darkness. A thud disturbed the peace as a drawer tumbled to the floor overhead and Hana steeled herself to rescue the situation.

Holding the very tip of the plier handles in her left hand, Hana dragged them along the metal runner until they contacted the toggle with a clunk. Keeping her arm above her head induced nausea and turned her good hand to jelly. Hana lost her temper. "I keep praying for help and getting nothing!" she raged. "Where are you when I need you?"

Ripping another length of cloth from her ruined dress with the pliers, Hana used it to tie her arm into a sling. It helped with the grinding of the bone and she regrouped and attempted to plan. "God please help me!" she begged. "I can't do this alone." She jumped, using the pliers to shove the toggle off the rail and groaned with satisfaction at the quiet thunk. It fell, bringing the string with it. Hana dropped the pliers with a clang and reached up for the string. It felt shorter than she remembered. She clasped the toggle and the knot at the end but her heart sank as she tugged and felt resistance. It had come down on the wrong side and wouldn't pull.

Hana stood on the tips of her toes and grasped the toggle. With a grunt, she threw it up and over, praying it didn't catch on the runner and stay there. It didn't. She allowed herself a breath of relief and seized the longer cord, tugging on it with everything she had.

A click betrayed the lock disconnecting. Hana saw streetlights glowing in the small gap between the bottom of the door and the concrete. "Hold on Pete," she huffed, grasping the metal strut and hauling the door upwards.

Hana managed to achieve a gap of a few metres, but no more. It proved enough. Crawling, she seized Pete's collar and hauled him outside. He resisted on the rough surface, reaching out to slap her as his hip grazed against the floor. His nails scratched the back of her hand and Hana let go with a hiss. "Pete, stop!" she begged, smacking him around the face. The passenger handle gave under her fingers and she yanked the door open. "Get in!" she urged, her voice rising. The chill night air revived Pete enough for him to drag himself upright using the remnants of Hana's skirt but he resisted her efforts to push him into the passenger seat.

A face appeared at an upstairs window and Hana screamed. It disappeared and she held her breath, knowing the man headed downstairs to the garage. With a gargantuan shove, she pushed Pete into the car head first and didn't stop to close the door after him.

Pain shot through her right arm as she ran around the car and hauled open the driver's door. Agony induced lights burst behind her vision and she flung herself into the seat despite them. The keys jangled against her right knee, still in the ignition. Her useless right arm burned in agony as she tried to grip them.

Panicking, Hana reached her left arm around the steering column and stretched, feeling the end of the keyring against her fingers. A little further and she managed to grip the key and turn it in the ignition. To her amazement and relief, the car fired to life first time. Using only one hand, Hana rammed the gear lever into first and jammed her foot on the clutch pedal.

The running lights flashed on as the engine started and Hana's eyes widened at the sight of the internal access door flying open into the garage. Three men rushed into the empty space and Hana gulped as the blonde man's eyes narrowed. "When did he get here?" she gasped, shoving at Pete. "Close the door, Pete! Close the door!"

Peter North balanced on the passenger seat, tipping forward. He'd blacked out again and Hana's breath hitched in her chest. She lifted the clutch and gunned the accelerator.

Two things happened.

The vehicle revved like a racing car but went nowhere. Screaming, Hana grappled for the handbrake and released it, feeling the car lurch. Then Pete plunged face first into the foot well.

Calamity followed as the car powered forward instead of backwards. Hana yelped and gripped the steering wheel as it bounced into the garage and not towards the road as she expected. The three men dived for cover and Hana glanced down, seeing the stick in first gear and not reverse. She looked up at the last minute as a man's body flipped over the bonnet and hit the windscreen.

Hana screamed and jammed on the brakes as Pete's door closed. The blonde man dived sideways and the car shuddered as Hana forgot to depress the clutch. Her left foot stood on the pedal in time to stop the car dying and she looked at the gear lever. Shaking fingers grappled with reverse and Hana lifted the clutch and gunned the gas, shooting backwards down the sloped driveway and onto the road. The man on the bonnet rolled off sideways somewhere on the journey and hit the concrete floor. Two men got to their feet in the garage, but he stayed crumpled in a heap.

A car shot around the corner and almost ploughed into them as Hana backed into a streetlight at speed. A horn honked, fuelling her need to escape. She found first gear again and made the change, relying on her left hand to do all the work. The steering wheel spun and she mounted the curb and careened along the street like a drunk. "Please call the cops," she begged aloud. "Please call the bloody cops."

Pete grunted in the foot well as Hana pulled onto Discovery Drive, inserting herself into traffic with a series of violent kangaroo hops. Another angry honk of a car horn reminded her to search for the headlights and she found them on the same side as her bad arm. A few dangerous swerves allowed her to lean across with her left hand and switch them from running lights to full, but she struggled to get the car any higher than second gear.

Flagstaff police station sat in darkness as Hana pulled into the car park. Unable to negotiate a parking space, she drove straight at the main doors. The front bumper rested against the glass and hopelessness flowed over her. The closed sign mocked her efforts.

With a sob of desperation, Hana pressed her forehead against the steering wheel. The old car's horn sounded impressive, booming into the evening like an ocean liner coming into port. Her left hand snaked across to assess the damage to her right elbow. Her fingers contacted skin that felt like it belonged to someone else. Until she moved her body. Then it became hers again in an overwhelming rush of agony.

Hana turned her face sideways and the horn offered a final toot as she closed her eyes. The unmarked police car slid into the car park behind her, quiet and unobtrusive in its response to a flurry of motorists' complaints. The officers slipped from their vehicle without sound and squared their shoulders to face a drunk. Or worse. They took a passenger each with a nod of acknowledgement and approached the battered car. The officer on the driver's side jabbed a finger towards the dent in the rear of Pete's car and the other man put a hand over his nightstick. Sirens split the air as colleagues rushed to their aid, bringing with them an aura of excitement.

Hana gasped as the door next to her clicked open. Cold night air rushed it to claim her breath. "No!" she wailed and scooted further away in her seat. The centre console bruised her hip as she reached across to grab Pete's upturned pants with her good hand. "Please wake up, Pete!" she sobbed and saw him bang his head on the underside of the dashboard. A dark space opened up next to him and a pale face stared into the vehicle.

"Miss," the cop said. "Please get out of the car."

Hana's bottom lip turned down like a child's and her chest hitched. "I can't," she whispered. "I just can't."

"Come out slowly," said the officer on her side. Hana blinked at the growing number of flashing lights around her, unable to discern the approaching shapes from each other.

"I can't," she repeated, crippled by the waves of pain radiating up her right arm and into her neck. Another screech of tyres sealed off the entrance to the car park. More strobing lights.

"Get out of the vehicle, ma'am." Hana slipped the underskirt-bandage over her head and felt the bone grind. Her stomach heaved and she supported her elbow and turned sideways in the seat. She bum shuffled along the cushion and the soles of her boots touched the gritty car park floor. "Out you come," the police officer said and reached for her forearm.

Hana remembered nothing after that. As the man wrenched her forward, she passed out from the sheer torment and her face smacked into the horn. The cop stepped back in dismay as her body slumped sideways, her arm hanging at a hideous angle to the rest of her body. The car horn echoed off the bricks and glass of the watch house as he lifted his hands in a gesture of innocence.

One officer pushed through the crowd and ran towards the sound, his mouth opening in a shout of utter horror.

-32-

Hana woke from unconsciousness without grace, gasping as though slapped by an unseen hand. The painless sleep ended like a douse of icy water.

"No!" she shouted as the hypodermic needle pierced her vein.

"Steady, steady." Logan's voice called to her from another world and the pressure of his fingers on her left hand seemed unreal.

"Hurting me," she wailed and a gentle hand brushed the hair from her face.

"It's pain meds," he whispered, his warm breath drifting across her cheek. "You had surgery, Hana."

Horror seeped into her confusing world and she tried to run her hand over her stomach. Pain shot through her right shoulder and her fingers didn't respond. "Baby," she groaned and Logan stroked her forehead.

"Not the baby, Hana. Your arm. It broke and the surgeons fixed it."

She turned her head in the general direction of her unresponsive fingers and saw a contraption suspended from a hoist. Her arm lay in a splint inside it, at the same height as her face. The volley of swearwords issuing from her lips forced Logan to turn away and cover his smirk with his hand. "Say what you really think, babe. Don't hold back aye?"

"It hurts," Hana snarled, slurring her words.

"I know." Logan's expression sobered. "I know it does."

Hana's brain did a mental body check and she wished it hadn't bothered. Her whole body sent distress signals. She forced her eyes to focus on Logan, at first just one at a time. He looked terrible. Dark circles ringed his grey eyes and his hair stuck up like he'd shoved his finger in a power socket. Hana's eventful evening drifted back by degrees. "Oh, damn. The kitten," she exhaled.

Logan's left eyebrow quirked upwards, often a sign of passion.

With anger falling into that list, it offered Hana no comfort. "Yeah, let's talk about the kitten," he said, leaning forward.

Hana groaned. "Let's not." Her eyes closed and then fluttered open. "Did it escape? I hope it didn't."

"No." Logan's voice lowered to a growl. "You and my child almost didn't either!"

Hana cringed with regret and the hunching of her shoulders caused more pain. She flapped her good hand at the retreating nurse. "Please may I have more drugs?" she begged. "Heaps and heaps."

"Sorry." The nurse gave Logan a rueful smile and pushed her trolley through the door. "Looks like you must face the music," she called over her shoulder.

"I don't like music." Hana pouted and Logan shook his head.

"We'll talk about this later," he said with a sigh of defeat.

"What's that noise?" she demanded, the robotic beat gnawing at the edges of her brain. "What is it?"

Logan's face lost its grey, haunted look. "It's our baby," he replied, his tone tender. "The surgeons monitored it during the operation."

Hana sniffed and then her chest gave an involuntary shudder. Tears rolled from the corners of her eyes and bounced against the starched pillows. "I don't deserve to have it," she sobbed. "I'm a bad mother and a terrible person." Memories of the man smashing against her windscreen flooded back and her eyes widened in terror. "I killed him!" Her voice rose to match the tumult inside and hysteria made an appearance.

Logan reached over to soothe her and Hana felt his stubble graze her skin. "Hana, the baby's fine with a strong heartbeat. As soon as the pain meds kick in, the nurse will take us for an ultrasound scan." His face hardened and his upper lip raised in a snarl. "The guy isn't dead yet. But five minutes with me and he'll wish more than a headache on himself!"

Hana cried, her distress communicating itself to the child. Logan's tone grew fearful as an erratic heartbeat drew staggered lines on the graph paper spewing from the machine. "Hana, it's not your fault," he said over the sound of her sobs. He used the cuff of his shirt to wipe the tears away. "Stop!" he told her and communicated seriousness through his narrowed eyes. "Enough, Hana. This isn't helping."

Her breath came in gasps and she grappled for control. Hysteria offered the easiest route, letting it run with her until she collapsed from the effort. Logan's earnest expression and the deep lines in his forehead drew her back, forcing her to face the consequences of her actions. "I've never got a speeding fine or a parking ticket." She hiccoughed as her lungs went into spasm. "Now I'm a felon."

"You're not." Logan ran a washcloth under a nearby tap and wiped her fiery cheeks and forehead. Hana gasped in shock at the coolness. "The cops are fine about it."

"Fine." Hana seized on his words and missed the point. "They'll fine me. What if I can't pay? I hit a man, a lamp post and a police station. What will I do?"

"Nothing." Logan ran the cloth under her chin and around her neck. The wetness distracted her. "I'll sort everything out."

"I should've said no to the biology teacher," she hiccoughed.

"Yep." Logan hung the cloth over the sink and let the side down on Hana's bed. He lay in the empty space next to her slender frame and rested his palm over her stomach. His proximity acted as a soothing balm and her chest hitched less. "Is this how you felt?" he whispered, careful not to jolt her body in reaching for the fingers of her left hand. "Like the world might end?"

"When Tama hurt you?" Hana turned her head so she could face him. "Yes."

"Then I'm really bloody sorry." Logan lifted her fingers to his lips and closed his eyes. "I get it now. I never want to feel like that again."

Logan kept back any confession of his desperate prayers. But he knew heaven responded and gratitude pricked at his conscience. Hana's God existed and it left him feeling more lost than before. Hana cried until sleep and the drugs claimed her. Her lungs hitched from the occasional memory of her sobs. Logan held her hand after a night of worry and exhaustion, dozing off next to her. A police detective visited and left without disturbing them.

The nurse saved Logan from falling backwards off the bed. She tapped his shoulder, jumping backwards in fright as he gripped her wrist with force. "Sorry!" he hissed, releasing her. She took a step back, rubbing the bone, her eyebrows narrowing in fear. Logan placed his feet on the tiled floor and ran a hand through his hair.

"I thought you might fall." The nurse backed towards the door and Logan shook his head.

"You startled me. I apologise." He turned towards Hana's sleeping figure. "How is she?"

"Doing better." The nurse plastered a fake smile on her face and Logan recognised her reluctance to approach him. He'd frightened her.

He rubbed his eyes and shook his head, the grogginess of sleep still heavy on his shoulders. The nurse took pity on him but kept her distance. "You're no good to her if you don't take care of yourself," she said. "There's a kitchen along the corridor. Make yourself coffee and I'll do her observations and check baby's heart rate. Your wife is due for her scan soon."

Logan took the hint and shuffled from the room, sending a glance back at Hana as he paused in the doorway. "Call me if she wakes?" He framed it as a question but the nurse heard the order beneath.

Logan returned with black coffee and found Hana stirring. The sound of the baby's heartbeat chugged along as background noise, the volume lowered. "Logan?" The panicked half-shout made him spill his drink and he dumped it by the sink to go to her.

"I'm here. You're safe."

"The men are coming. They're gonna hurt me." Her frightened jabbering made the nurse look differently upon Logan's earlier reaction.

"Nobody's gonna hurt you." He gritted his teeth and sat on the bed next to her. He gripped her fingers in his hand. "This is a private hospital, Hana. If they're looking for you in the state system, they'll come up empty."

"Promise?" Her wide green eyes struck pity and anger into his soul at the same time.

"Yes. The detective instructed the hospital not to give details about you to anyone. If they come looking for you here, the cops will know." He gritted his teeth. "So will I."

Hana nodded and accepted the beaker of water he held to her lips. She took a sip and gulped. "What about the cost though?" she rasped.

"I've covered it." Logan's brows narrowed and he felt the nurse watching him. Her stance softened as she saw him stroke Hana's fringe back from her eyes. "Don't worry about anything. Just get well so I can take you home."

Hana nodded and eyed the beaker again. Her tongue poked out and licked her lips. Without waiting for her to ask, Logan held it so she could sip, wiping the drops from her chin with his fingers.

"Mr Du Rose?" A male voice spoke from the doorway and Logan whipped around, opening his arms to shield Hana from the newcomer. The detective blinked, but made no comment at the dark aggression in Logan's eyes.

"It's just us," Bodie said, nodding to him as he walked to the end of the bed. "Hey, Mum. How are you?"

Hana swallowed. "I'm not sure." She shot a frightened look at Logan. "But I guess I'm in trouble."

Bodie shrugged. "I doubt it. It sounds like a mixture of self-defense and accident." He fiddled with the clipboard at the end of the bed. "I heard about the incident over the radio and knew when they mentioned Achilles Rise you'd be messed up in it somehow."

The detective stepped forward and Hana picked up a hint of antagonism between him and Logan. She watched her husband ball his fists and wondered.

"Your Achilles Rise house is cordoned off at the moment while the forensic team look through it."

"What about the man I knocked over?" Hana's voice broke and Logan reached out and rubbed her shoulder.

"I told you not to worry about it," he said, his tone menacing. "Liza's a lawyer, remember? But you won't need her." He squared his shoulders and glared at Odering with a challenge in his eyes. "Will she?"

Odering gave the nurse a pointed look and hesitated. Her eyes darted from one man to the other as though anticipating trouble. Bodie smiled at her. "It's fine," he reassured. "This pissing contest can go on all night, believe me."

"I remember it." Hana's chest hitched. "The sound as he hit the bonnet and the look on his face. Pete will never forgive me for banging up his car."

Bodie snorted. "Will he notice? The thing's a heap."

The nurse collected her medications' trolley and left. Odering cocked his head as though listening to it wheel along the corridor. "This whole thing is unfortunate."

"Unfortunate?" A sarcastic laugh issued from between Logan's lips. "Is that the new name for it nowadays?"

"What will happen to me?" Hana begged. "Will I go to prison?"

"No!" All three men answered at the same time.

"Excuse me." A man in a hospital uniform peered at a list in his hand. "I'm here for Mrs Du Rose."

"Who are you?" Bodie took a protective step forward and Logan winced and chewed on his bottom lip.

"It's okay," he said, reaching to clasp Hana's fingers.

Odering moved aside as the orderly unhooked wires and plugs from behind Hana's bed. His crisp detective's suit rustled as he wandered towards the window. Glancing at the machine monitoring the baby's heart, he looked back at Hana in surprise. "Well this puts a different complexion on things," he mused. He tapped the machine with an index finger and pulled his lips into a straight line.

"What does?" Suspicious, Bodie moved across to Odering and stared at the machine. "What's wrong? What's happening?"

Odering shrugged and dug his hands into his trouser pockets. He rocked back on his heels. "How is your baby?"

"What?" Bodie moved his face in front of the detective's, as though proximity might cancel out the unexpected announcement. "What baby?"

Hana blew out a breath of panic and looked to Logan. Her fingers trembled in his. He inhaled, ready to cover for her if she couldn't say the words. He sensed it should come from her.

"I wanted to tell you," she said, her green eyes wide like emeralds. "I'm expecting a baby next January." She looked down at her stomach and then across at her poleaxed son. "This isn't how I wanted you to find out."

"You're pregnant?" Bodie swallowed. The words sounded awful on his lips. "This is a sick joke right?"

"Okay. I might leave you and finish taking your statement another time." Odering nodded to Hana, ignored Logan and left the room. He didn't look back at the devastation caused by his calculated slip.

Bodie shook his head and the slump of his shoulders oozed betrayal. "You're a grandmother," he hissed. "What were you thinking?"

"Hey!" Logan's eyes flashed like gimlets and a flush crept up his neck. He bit his tongue to stop him commenting that at least they were married, unlike him and Amy. And to each other. Instead, he shook his head. "That's enough."

Hana watched as her son bolted for the door. "I need to go," he said and left without looking back.

The orderly made no comment as he pushed Hana into a darkened room. The wide doorway struggled to accommodate the machinery accompanying her. Logan looked more nervous than she'd ever seen him and she reached out to stroke his hand. "They took that heartbeat machine off," he whispered, fear in his eyes. "Is that okay?"

"It's fine," Hana soothed. "It's a monitor, not life support." She lay back on the bed and closed her eyes, listening to the plink of fluid dripping from an overhead bag. She imagined it seeping through her veins and removing the pain.

The female technician arrived and distracted Logan. Having missed the punk rock era whilst growing up at a private all boys' school, he stared open mouthed at her. When she dimmed the lights, her piercings glittered in the glow from the computer screen and her black lipstick appeared vampirish. He swallowed and widened his eyes at Hana. The technician's spiked hair moved little as she bent to dribble gel onto Hana's bare stomach. "I tried to warm it up," she said with a smile that displayed a tooth jewel. She moved the gel around with the end of the probe and then took a seat. "Let's take a look at this baby," she said with forced confidence.

Logan clutched Hana's slender fingers in both his big hands and Hana felt the moisture as he sweated in terror. Powerlessness filled her soul and added to the waiting sadness. She expected a negative result and hated herself for her defeatism. The technician peered and clicked and looked and clicked some more. Then she swivelled the screen to face them. "Is this your first scan?" she asked as Logan leaned closer to the confusing mass of dark movement. Hana nodded and swallowed. "Then meet your baby. Everything looks fine, but I'll ask my supervisor to review the photos just to make sure. Is that okay?"

Hana felt embarrassed for the tears which escaped onto her cheeks. A tiny shape moved around the screen, pulsating and changing angle as the technician moved the probe. Hana heard Logan exhale a long, ragged breath and spared him her scrutiny. "It's beautiful," she breathed.

"Sure is." The technician smiled. "Do you want to know the sex? I've got a great view."

"No." Hana shook her head. "I'll wait."

"Oh." Logan's lips turned down in disappointment. "I wanted to know."

Hana relented and agreed, but Logan changed his mind in the same moment. The technician laughed. "Yes or no? Which is it?"

Hana smiled at Logan. "You choose."

He squirmed in his chair. "I dunno now. What do you think?"

"I'll write it down and hide it in an envelope." The technician daubed Hana's stomach with tissue and then handed it to Logan to continue. "You wipe that and I'll get some paper." She turned off the monitor and stepped outside, leaving Logan dabbing around Hana's belly.

"You need to do it harder," she said, annoyance brewing at his futile wiping. The gel spread, sticking to her hospital gown and dribbling into the small of her back. Her ire subsided at the clench of Logan's jaw. The man who trained unpredictable mares and ruled over wayward, teenage boys, faltered at the risk of hurting his wife. "Sorry," she whispered and his brow knitted. "For everything. I wanted to see the kitten." She swallowed. "And the house."

Logan offered a curt nod in reply. "The baby looked like it sucked its thumb." His expression softened. "Is that normal?"

Hana nodded and confiscated the sticky tissue with her good hand. She spread the last of the mess around her stomach and then hauled the gown over her underwear. "Yes. I still catch Izzie doing it sometimes. Haven't you noticed Jas sucking his?"

"Yeah, but in there?" Logan pointed to her stomach and his pupils dilated in wonder. "It's amazing."

"It is." Hana's chest tightened. "I've come so far and then risked it all." She wiped her eyes with the back of her hand and blinked at the sticky gel which attached to her lashes. Logan used the bottom of his shirt to clean her face. The creases and rumpled appearance in the cloth belied his compulsive cleanliness. Hana used that fact to berate herself further as he stroked her hair.

"We are where we are," he whispered. "But let's not do this again. Impulsive and risk taking aren't my ideal traits in a wife."

Hana nodded and jumped as the door clicked open. The technician reappeared and handed a sealed envelope to Logan. He pocketed it and nodded to the man who followed her in. "This is my supervisor," the punk rocker stated.

"Everything looks fine." The man smiled. Clipped and professional in a pristine white coat, he contrasted with Logan's dishevelled appearance. "Baby measures at around fifteen week's gestation. Nice, strong heartbeat. Your blood pressure is low, Mrs Du Rose and I think there were some problems with that in surgery. That's not a bad thing for a pregnancy but keep an eye on it." He smiled and gave a perfunctory nod, aimed at terminating his required presence.

"What problems in surgery?" Logan's eyes narrowed and he lowered his head to look from beneath his lashes. It created a sinister illusion.

"Not sure. Orthopedic surgeries aren't my thing." The man gave a shake of his head and exited the room without looking back. The technician shrugged, a nonchalant, punk rocker kind of movement.

"Let's get you back to your room," she said, covering Hana's legs with a blanket and moving her equipment away from the bed.

The porter arrived to take her away and Hana felt exhaustion crawl through her nerve endings as the bed wheeled along a corridor and into a lift. She closed her eyes and allowed sleep to take her to pain free fields with psychedelic flowers.

Waking hours later in her hospital room, Hana roused without hurry. She watched Logan's strong profile as he stood at the window, his fingers rustling the envelope in his pocket. His muscle definition stood out beneath his shirt and his trousers fit snug against his neat backside. "I love waking up to you." Hana winced as her words slurred and he turned and gave her a smile. She sensed relief.

"Good," he replied. "You'll have years to get sick of me."

Hana sighed. "I want to go home."

"No bloody way!" Logan snorted and she pouted like a toddler. "Maybe tomorrow, but only if your arm shows no sign of infection and everything stays okay with the baby. I won't take any more risks with you, woman. Obviously you can't be trusted." He turned and leaned his backside against the windowsill. Folding his arms across his chest, he channelled determination.

"I didn't do this on purpose!" Hana grumbled. Logan's narrowed eyes and the forward tilt of his head shut her up.

"No, but you don't follow simple instructions. What did you not understand about the sentence beginning with, go home and stay there?"

Hana swallowed and gnawed on her bottom lip. She avoided the accusation in his eyes. Her gaze fell on her suspended arm and she sighed. "Why doesn't my arm have a plaster cast?" She lifted her head to peer into the splint, seeing bruising and dried blood around the visible skin.

"They need to see what happens after the surgery. They'll pot it up before they let you loose." His eyes narrowed and she sensed he held something back.

"What did the guy in the scan mean about problems?" Hana demanded and he shrugged. His irises glittered like diamonds.

"Not sure. It might be nothing. I spoke to the nurse while you slept and she read your notes. The surgeon thinks the anesthetic caused your blood pressure and heart rate to lower."

Hana sighed. "Mum had low blood pressure. She felt dizzy and laid down with her head lower than her feet. That fixed it." She sighed. "Her hair flowed over the arm of the sofa and I loved to play with it. I likened it to a red waterfall." Her face took on a faraway expression as though wishing for her might bring Judith McIntyre to her bedside. Her fingers flexed as though touching the remembered red tresses.

"Hey." Pete sauntered into the room without knocking. He'd shoved his hands so deep into his pants' pockets, his underwear showed above the waistband. Impressive black bruises lined his forehead.

Hana watched him in confusion as he mirrored Logan's stance against the windowsill, minus the folded arms. "I thought they hit you on your crown." She tipped sideways to inspect the large packing bandage adorning his head. Her elbow twinged and she sat up at speed.

Pete removed a hand from his pocket and jabbed a dirty finger at his forehead. "You did this!" he snapped.

Logan leaned sideways and lowered his voice. The air dripped with latent warning. "Watch your attitude," he whispered.

Pete pouted. "You put me in the car upside down." His blue eyes flashed accusation and Hana swallowed.

"I'm sorry."

"She rescued you despite her broken arm." Logan's low hiss made Pete stiffen. "You're lucky she didn't leave you there."

"It's her fault." Pete spun around so Hana could appreciate the size of the bandage covering his downy head. "She never does as she's told."

Hana hung her head, regret rendering her speechless. Logan's face remained dark and forbidding and the atmosphere crackled.

"I didn't get a nice hospital room." Pete chuntered about his hard-done-by situation as he inspected the plush room. "You came to the Bramwell and I get shunted through the state emergency room. They sent me home after two hours and I still couldn't see straight."

Logan smirked and looked away, sparing everyone his ready sarcasm about Pete's eyesight. His expression clouded as the skinny man continued his litany of complaints. Hana held her breath as

Logan's patience ran out. "Maybe if you looked after her like I asked you to, none of us would need hospital attention." His jaw flexed and Hana's eyes widened at the sight of his fists bunching.

"It's all my fault, I admit that." She rushed to shoulder the deserved blame. "I gave him no choice, Logan."

"She didn't," Pete squeaked. His eyes darted in Hana's direction like a cornered rat.

"Sweetie!" Henrietta squealed from the doorway. Hana winced, unsure whether the larger-than-life chef referred to her injured boyfriend, Logan or her. The relief on Pete's face showed his appreciation for the reinforcements.

"Logan's blaming me, Henri," he whined. He edged away from danger with tiny steps. His simpering stance made Hana recoil and shoot a glance at Logan. She found her husband exhibiting signs of major disgust in his grey eyes and the curling of his upper lip.

"Pussy," Logan mouthed.

To Hana's dismay, Henrietta bounced in her direction like an overflowing soup tureen. "Pregnant!" she screeched and Hana stiffened for the onslaught. Her elbow sent darting stabs of pain into her shoulder and wrist as the large woman slavered lipstick kisses over her cheek and eyelids. "Peetipoos told me everything," she intoned and Logan narrowed his eyes at his friend.

"What about me?" Pete whined as he tugged on his girlfriend's blouse. "I'm injured too."

"But not pregnant," Henrietta chuckled. She ruffled the remains of Pete's hair and planted a chaste kiss on his bruised forehead. Logan's face creased in mirth at the impression of rosebud lips left in the centre of the swollen skin. It looked like someone tried eating Pete's face.

"I want to leave," Pete complained, drawing his face into a toddler-worthy pout. "I've not had a good time of it."

Logan offered a tight-lipped smile and casual wave as Henrietta led Pete away by the hand. "Watch your back," Logan hissed after him. The remaining colour drained from Pete's face as he sped up and disappeared.

"Leave him alone," Hana sighed. "It's not his fault."

Logan raised his eyebrows. "If a bro' asked me to look after his wife, I'd look after her."

Hana cringed. "You might wish to rephrase that."

"Rephrase what?" Pastor Allen strolled through the open door, dangling a limp bunch of grapes between finger and thumb. He waggled them at Logan. "Got anywhere to put these? I sat on them in the car by accident."

Logan frowned and carried the squished purple orbs to the sink, dumping them into the porcelain and running cold water over them. Allen lifted Hana's left hand and kissed the back of it. "Not many bits left to kiss," he chortled. "Not decent ones anyway. Are you both competing for the most broken bones in the first year of marriage? It looks like it."

"No." Hana shook her head. "How did you know?"

Allen shrugged. "I have my sources." He winked at Logan and Hana frowned. Jealousy coursed through her chest at her husband's monopolisation of her friendship. Allen sat in the chair nearest the bed and grinned at Hana. "You're taxing our prayer chain, Mrs Du Rose."

Hana eyes widened and she pushed herself upright. The groan she released came from deep down as her elbow jarred. "You can't tell people. Nobody can know."

"I gave no details." Pastor Allen got to her pillows first and plumped them into a mound. Logan stood on her other side like a sentry. "All they know is that you broke your arm."

"I appreciate that." Logan swallowed. "This needs to stay out of the public eye. It's what the cops want." He narrowed his eyes at the pastor. "It's what I want."

"The prayer chain is like a gossip circle," Hana panted, closing her eyes against the pain. "They mean well but they can't help themselves."

Pastor Allen winced. "Only if you don't also run a secret prayer chain of elders and deacons."

Hana's jaw dropped open. "Oh my goodness!"

"Sorry, you're shocked." Allen's cheeks flushed pink and he retook his seat. "It is a little underhand."

"That's not why I'm shocked," Hana grumbled. "It's because all these years you left me on the other one. Why aren't I on the secret one?"

Allen smirked. "I thought you enjoyed games of Chinese whispers on a regular basis. What's not to like about the way some of those prayer requests end up? Remember the one which started as prayer for Mabel's floral group and ended up as Mabel's funeral? The kindness of our Hamilton citizens meant she didn't need to cook for months afterwards."

"It's not funny." Hana fixed her lips into a thin line. "I'm hurt."

"How about we pray now?" Allen asked.

Hana wished for the ability to fold her arms and display her irritation. "Is this the real prayer or the fake one?" she bit. "Because I wouldn't want to waste my breath."

"No prayer is wasted." Allen gripped the fingers of her left hand and held on. He winked at her.

"Will you shut your eyes?" Hana demanded, getting ready to stick out her tongue.

Allen faked shock. "And miss you sticking your tongue out at me?" He rolled his eyes heavenward as though for inspiration. "Of course not. They taught us in seminary to pray with our eyes open. It would be a shame to miss God when he does something amazing."

"Yeah, I wanna pray," Logan said. Hana glanced up at him and found him staring at the ceiling. His neck flushed with embarrassment. "I'd like to thank God for keeping you as safe as your stupid ass could allow. I'd also like to appeal on behalf of your guardian angels. Somebody deserves a pay rise."

Hana gave an indignant inhale but Allen cut her off, gripping her fingers and giving her a sideways look of rebuke. He launched into his usual brand of casual chatting with God and glancing at Hana, caught her watching. His lips curved upwards in a grin and he finished with a gentle amen.

Hana stifled a snort. Her head felt woozy and the situation pulled on a humorous thread. Allen took it in his stride having seen human nature at its best and worst. Hana started as he glanced sideways at her and darted towards the door. His crablike movement intrigued her and she watched with her head on one side as he closed the door and leant against it. "Now for the good stuff," he hissed.

Like a pickpocket, he opened his coat and disgorged two chocolate bars from within the lining. He dumped them on the side of the sink and reached in for a jumbo bag of crisps and three cans of soda. Two limp sausage rolls tumbled from his trouser pockets, leaving flakes of pastry on the tiled floor.

"Choice!" Logan murmured in approval. "I'm starving."

"I know aye," the pastor sniggered. "Praise the Lord for this overcoat!"

Allen handed over the loot and retreated with a wave. Logan shook his head. "That guy continues to surprise me." He laid into the chocolate and the crisps, popping open a soda can and slurping the liquid from the top of the lid when it fizzed over. "Want some?" he offered.

Hana nodded and waited while he fixed a straw through the hole. She sipped the sugary liquid and shivered. "Can I go home?" she asked again.

"No." Logan sighed and scooted onto the bed next to her. He slipped an arm around her waist and tried not to jolt her. "Not yet. Do you want to talk about Bodie's reaction to the baby?"

"No. Thanks."

"Okay. Whenever you're ready, I'm here." His eyes widened at Hana's unladylike burp. She clapped a hand over her mouth.

"I'm sorry. Where did that come from?"

Logan grinned. "I'm not shocked, babe. I lived with Pete remember?"

Hana's smile drooped. "Speaking of Pete, it wasn't his fault, Logan. I made him take me up there. He didn't want to."

"So why didn't he text me, Hana?"

"I don't know. In his defense, he put his phone on charge as soon as we got in the car. I think it died." She sighed. Resting her head against his shoulder, she looked up at his profile. Days of stubble covered his angular jaw and he chewed a square of chocolate with concentration. The grey streaks either side of his chin gave him a distinguished air and matched the increasing salt and pepper in his hair. Hana linked her fingers through his and squeezed. "I don't deserve you," she whispered.

Logan leaned sideways and kissed her temple. "I know. I'm sure you'll grow into your responsibilities." He quirked an eyebrow at her. "You need to behave though."

Hana inhaled. "Okay." Her eyes filled with tears and Logan saw. His expression grew serious.

"Hey, it's turned out fine, Hana. We'll get through this." His nearness comforted her, his musky hay and sunshine scent warming her bones. She breathed in his smell and allowed her eyes to close. The child entertained other plans and gave her a sharp jab in the stomach. Hana grunted and Logan's eyes widened in alarm.

"Just the baby," she muttered. The fizzy drink gurgled through her stomach causing a wave of nausea. A nurse appeared to administer a painkiller that wouldn't hurt the baby, pushing it through the cannula in Hana's hand. The vice of pain receded and she descended into an easy sleep, accompanied by the fluttery kicks in her womb.

-33-

The sleep lasted until a disoriented Hana tried to sit up in her hospital bed unaided. Drowsy and mindful of the urge to use the bathroom, she grappled around and yanked the cannula from her hand. A spurt of blood leaked across the white sheets and she spent valuable moments staring at it in confusion. "Logan?" She called his name and hearing nothing, panicked.

The ward sister discovered her wandering around the hospital, her gown open at the back. "What are you doing?" she asked, getting a garbled reply.

"I need to get out." Hana clutched her chest with her good hand and stared at the plaster cast on her right elbow. She remembered nothing of its arrival. Her heart pounded in her chest and she dipped forward to increase the blood pressure to her head. "I don't feel good."

"Let's get you back to bed," the nurse stated, calling for reinforcements. "It's just low blood pressure and you need your sleep."

They stuffed her back into bed after a detour to the bathroom. A doctor appeared like a genie in Hana's peripheral vision and administered a sedative and more fluids. She drifted back into a doze as the steady throb of her baby's heartbeat sounded into the room. "Leave the monitor on," the doctor said. "Check her and the baby through the night. Let's have her on fifteen minute observations. Surgery sometimes causes this, but the pregnancy makes it more complicated."

"Do we fetch her husband back?" the nurse asked, her tone brusque. Hana struggled to push herself up from the grasping waters of sleep to demand Logan's presence. She heard everything, but the sedative warred with her ability to respond.

"No." The doctor sounded positive. "It's not urgent and he looked knackered. When did you send him away?"

"A few hours ago." The nurse sighed. "He didn't want to go."

"Just watch her." The doctor's shoes scuffed against the tiles. "Only call him if you need to."

The clattering of trolleys along the corridor jolted Hana awake at seven with a bad headache. Her arm throbbed from the weight of her cast and it rested across her chest to constrict her breathing. She rejected food in favour of the wheeled medicine cabinet, opting for its tablet delights to remove the stabbing pain in her elbow. "I hate hospitals," she grumbled to a good-natured nurse wielding low-grade pain pills. "Why can't I have something stronger?"

The woman nodded towards her stomach and held out the two white tablets identical to ones available at supermarkets. "Doctor won't give you anything else because of the baby."

"I hate my life," Hana muttered.

"Yes, but look at the man you get to go home with." The nurse winked at her. "I'll swap him for the lard ass in my bed."

Hana conceded. "He's an amazing consolation prize." She lowered her head and glared through the tops of her eyes. "Hands off. I don't want your lard ass thanks." She held her good hand out for the pathetic tablets and forced them down with water.

To her dismay, the nurse accompanied her to the bathroom and waited like a sentry while she used the toilet. "This is so undignified," she grumbled. "I bet nobody dared do this to Logan."

The nurse snorted. "Lady, we formed a roster just to keep it fair."

"That's disgusting. I'm reporting you all."

The nurse laughed and adjusted the drip wheels so Hana could wash her hand at the sink. Hana splashed around one handed and glared at the tousled headed banshee in the mirror. Green eyes stared back at her. "I'm a mess," she complained. "I need a shower."

"Not today." The woman's brows knitted as an emergency call came from a buzzer overhead. "Damn. Will you be okay while I find out what's happening?"

"Yep. I'm fine." Mischief glowed behind Hana's smile, but the harried nurse missed it.

Hana heaved a sigh of relief as the woman rushed away and grinned at herself in the mirror. Wheeling the drip trolley back into her bedroom, she closed the main door. Then she scooted her bag of clean clothes and wash things into the bathroom using her foot. "Thank goodness for reliable husbands," she breathed, pushing her fingers through the zipper and finding enough supplies for a week.

The washing process proved difficult one-handed. Hana scrubbed where she could reach, using a stash of cloths from a shelf above the sink. The sense of cleanliness proved invigorating and she relished the thought of clean clothes.

She unfastened the robe using the necktie, screwing her body round to see in the mirror as she reached behind her. It slithered down her shoulders and came to an abrupt halt before the cannula in her hand. "Ah." Hana studied it like a complicated mathematical problem. Standing on tiptoes, she threaded the drip bag and rack through the armhole of the robe only to find it bottlenecked at the castors. It refused to go over all four wheels at the same time.

"Oh no!" Hana moaned, clasping her hand over her mouth to dull the frustrated cry. She assessed her new situation, crouching on the floor and pinned by her robe to a drip trolley. The clunky cast rested on her bent knee and Hana bemoaned its uselessness.

Backtracking, she rived the sleeve from its trapped position and threaded it back up the stem of the trolley. "Sparkling teeth and no knickers," she berated herself. "What use is that?" Her new focus involved remedying that situation.

Donning fresh knickers one-handed and catching the scent of floral washing powder, Hana felt more positive. She went a step further, hopping on alternate feet to get socks on. Confidence budded and she convinced herself she could do even better, hauling a clean bra from the bag. "You can do this," she hissed, sizing up the drip. A stupid idea formed in her addled brain and she wasted no time putting it into action.

Hana pulled the dangling robe back up over the rail at the top and stopped at the bag. "Genius," she breathed. Unhooking the bag of fluid, she lifted it down and held onto it. She pushed her arm and the bag through the hole and almost cheered as the robe fluttered to the tiled floor.

Hana fed her bra strap over her broken arm, wincing at the pain which moving it caused. She panted with her efforts and almost dropped the fluid bag, catching it at the last moment and wailing in agony. Trapping the swollen bag against her cast and chest, she wrestled her other arm into her bra. "Oh." She looked down at the sagging underwear and sighed, knowing nothing would enable her to fasten it at the back. Shrugging, she fumbled in the bag for a tee shirt.

The drip bag slipped onto the tiles with a whump sound and Hana squatted to retrieve it. Relief flooded over her that it didn't burst. The liquid inside bloomed pink and Hana watched as the tube filled with blood. She jerked it upright and her elbow complained, sending her back to her knees in agony.

"What happened?" the nurse shrieked, pressing an alarm on the wall and running to Hana's side. The sound of footsteps heralded other arrivals, including the doctor.

"Bloody hell!" he hissed. "What's she doing?"

"Putting my bra on!" Hana shouted. "Turn around!"

He grunted and turned his back as the women sorted her out. One helped her off the floor while the other fastened her bra at the back and shoved the tee shirt over her head. "That's the dumbest thing I've seen in a while," the nurse hissed and Hana closed her eyes against the rebuke. They at least let her step into her tracksuit bottoms before replacing the pink drip bag with a new one and forcing her into bed.

"I want to go home," Hana protested as one nurse pulled the blankets over her feet and another glared at her. "Look, I'm ready to go now."

"Do we need to sedate you?" she threatened and Hana glowered. "Yes please."

They left her alone, but not before threatening all manner of medical mayhem if she left her bed again. "I mean it!" the ward sister said, wagging her finger at Hana. "Behave yourself."

Bored, Hana entertained herself by flicking through the television channels. She settled on an English chat show and watched two lie detector tests and a DNA result. Four toothless men fought over a fat woman with tufty hair, flab piling over the top of her leggings. Hana shuddered and flicked to an infomercial advertising a revolutionary ladder. She watched as the man demonstrated different ways of using it and sighed in defeat. She almost fell off the kitchen steps hanging curtains. Logan wouldn't permit her to own such a contraption.

"Mum?" Bodie hovered in the doorway, the frown on his face conveying his uncertainty. He looked rumpled and careworn, dark shadows beneath his eyes.

Hana smiled and patted the bed. "Come and entertain me. I'm confined to barracks."

"So I hear." His smile didn't reach his eyes. He sank into a chair near the window, putting distance between them. Then he leaned forward, resting his forearms on his thighs and raking the floor with his gaze. Hana braced herself.

Her mind strayed back to Vik's funeral and she remembered her gangly son with his arm around Izzie's shoulder. He shielded his sister from the well-meaning, pitying glances of Vik's colleagues and friends. Marcus shivered and shook throughout the service, wounded to the core by the suddenness of the loss. Hana sighed, recognising the day she lost her son's confidence but not understanding why. She remained silent and waited, flicking the channel back to the chat show. The man with more teeth than the others won the prize; a set of defenseless children and a lifetime to ruin them.

"When's the baby due?" Bodie's voice sounded husky and cracked. Hana tensed.

"Around the end of January. I don't have an exact date yet."

Bodie sat up straighter and rubbed his hand over his eyes, pinching the bridge of his nose as though staving off a headache. He blinked in a series of rapid, jerky movements. "Is that why you married him? You didn't need to. I could've helped."

Hana swallowed and gritted her teeth. "I married Logan because I love him and no, the baby came afterwards."

A movement in the doorway caught her eye and Hana's heart sank. Logan leaned against the doorframe, his face dark with anger and his body language radiating danger.

"Hey." Hana spoke to warn Bodie before he made a worse mess of their conversation. He jerked his head up and his expression clouded at the sight of Logan.

"Does Izzie know about the baby?" he demanded.

"Not yet," Hana replied. "Please let me tell her." Her good hand strayed to her stomach as she imagined the conversation.

Bodie turned to gaze through the window. "Pete gave the detective heaps of information. He remembered the registration plate, type of car, and described your attackers down to the last freckle. Then he passed out. When he came around again, he remembered nothing. Fascinating. The guy is obviously more in tune after a bang on the head."

Hana winced at the memory. "I'm still sorry I crashed into that man. Do you know how he is? Will the detective take action against me?"

Logan stepped into the room and leaned against the wall next to Hana. He kept his hands shoved deep in his pockets and remained silent.

Bodie sighed. "Not unless you hit him on purpose. I know we get a hammering in the media, but we do know what self-defense looks like when we see it."

"But I didn't hit him in self-defense." Hana shook her head. She opened her mouth to finish the sentence but Bodie didn't give her the chance. He stood and held his hand up to silence her.

"Mum! If you're about to confess you did it on purpose, then don't! I would have to arrest you and I don't have the energy!"

"No, no," pleaded Hana. "It was accidental! I thought I put the gear lever into reverse and he ran towards me. I didn't know I'd found first gear instead until he hit the windscreen."

"Fantastic!" said Bodie, with an edge of nastiness in his voice. His eyes narrowed. "Dangerous driving is just as bad. Stop talking, Mum."

Images of prison drifted through Hana's mind as Bodie backed away from her. She covered her sob with a shaking hand. Logan moved so fast, Bodie missed the warning cues. In blue jeans and a denim jacket, he looked every bit the capable cowboy. "Get out!" he hissed, putting his body between mother and son. "You're done here."

Bodie shook his head numerous times before finding his words. "You can't make me."

Logan snorted. "Is that the best you came up with? Goodbye." His lips curled upwards on one side as he watched the younger man wrestle with his emotions. Hana covered her eyes and turned sideways in the bed.

"She's my mother!" Bodie gritted his teeth and his fingers balled into fists. He objectified the tall Māori into a monster capable of stealing away his surest anchor pin. The prospect of losing Hana terrified him.

"Then treat her with respect, man! You're behaving like a jealous little kid." Logan leaned forward for emphasis, not intimidated by the venom flashing in his stepson's dark eyes. "Grow up," he whispered. Shooting a glance over his shoulder, his face softened at the sight of Hana with her hand over her eyes.

"I don't want to have the baby in prison," she sobbed. "I didn't mean to hurt him. I messed the gears up."

"Hana, stop." Logan sat next to her on the bed and ignoring Bodie, pulled her head against his shoulder. "It's all gonna be fine," he promised.

Bodie blanched at the intimate moment, feeling like a boat which slipped its mooring and scraped along the harbour wall. He gritted his jaw and turned away from the touching scene, stomping from the hospital in a temper.

Hana's phone rang half an hour later and Logan answered it. He glanced sideways at her as she stared at the television through glazed eyes. "It's Amy," he said. "She's at work and needs to be quick."

Hana pressed the phone to her ear and sighed. "Hey, Amy. What's wrong?"

"It's Bodie," Amy whispered. "I just sent him home."

"Why?" Hana groaned. "What now?" Logan's body tensed and he slipped an arm around her shoulder.

"He slammed in here, throwing his gear around and I pulled rank. I sent him home sick. If he goes out on the road in that state, he'll end up on a disciplinary."

Hana's chest heaved in a ragged breath. "Okay. I don't know what you want me to do, sweetheart. He's a grown up. I've done my time in the headmaster's office with him."

"Yeah, I know." Amy sighed. "He found out about the baby, didn't he?"

"Yes and he's unhappy." Hana lay her head back against Logan's arm and closed her eyes. "I'm meant to remain alone and miserable. That's his plan for my life."

"Na, he's just thrashing." Amy paused the conversation and spoke to someone else in the background. "Gotta go. He wouldn't tell me what upset him but he's gone home to sulk."

"Thanks. Have a good day." Hana forced a smile onto her lips, communicating her gratitude without words.

"Hana?" Doubt crept into Amy's voice and Hana tensed. Her elbow twinged and she winced. "Be careful. He's entertaining strange ideas about what Logan might be involved with. He's threatening to do some serious digging and turn up dirt about him."

"But he won't find anything." A whine crept into Hana's voice and she felt Logan's gaze settle on her face. "My husband is a teacher. What dirt does he think he'll find?"

"Then don't worry about it. He'll get over it. Logan's good to you and he'll see that eventually." Amy bid her goodbye and ended the call, leaving Hana feeling confused.

"Just say it." Logan's sigh sent her mood spiralling lower.

"Bodie's determined to cause trouble." She sniffed and wiped her nose with the back of her hand. "I don't deserve this from him. I accepted his son and Amy without question. Why can't he do the same for me?"

"I don't know." Logan gnawed his bottom lip and his eyes narrowed. "He hates me, Hana. You need to get used to it."

"I want to go home." Her chest heaved against the return of the misery he soothed away earlier. She yearned for the peace and lofty isolation of Culver's Cottage. "I want to go right now." Her childish wail sounded like nails on a blackboard. She should have felt ashamed but the pressing need for escape overrode dignity.

Logan held her, kissing her temple and soothing her with gentle strokes of his hand against her hair. "You aren't ready to go home," he said, his voice quiet but determined.

"I helped you break out of here." Her lips turned down in a pout. "And the careers event is coming up fast." Hana turned to logic to reinforce her demands. "Sheila needs me."

"No. Sheila needs a two handed assistant who can type and take phone messages, Hana. You need time to recuperate." His fingers strayed to her stomach and he smoothed her tee shirt over the outline of his child. "And my baby needs you to take it seriously."

Hana pushed her face into his armpit in protest, breathing in the scent of him. "I still want to go home," she muttered and he snorted.

"No surprise there. But you're not." He pressed his lips against her forehead and Hana stuck her tongue out.

The sound of feet scraping against the tiles made Logan jump and Hana cried out in pain. "Sorry." Odering held his hands out in front of him and his face creased with guilt. "I need to clarify some points in Mrs Du Rose's statement." He flapped a piece of paper in her direction. "I made notes from what you said yesterday, but there might be gaps."

Logan's eyes narrowed as the man sidled to the visitor's chair and sat down. Odering rested the paper on his knees and picked lint from his trousers. "So, get on with it then," Logan bit and Hana stared sideways at him in surprise. The detective leaned forward, forearms against his thighs.

"We charged the injured man with kidnapping and assault. The other men fled the scene and our officers are looking for them. The damage to your property appears superficial and a friend of yours was putting it straight as I left earlier." He sighed and his gaze flicked to Logan. "I'll level with you but this must remain confidential."

Hana glanced at her husband and he conceded the faintest nod. Odering seemed satisfied for the moment and directed the conversation towards her. "The blonde man you've met a few times now is a nasty character. His nickname is Flick because of how often he uses a switchblade to make his point. Our investigations suggest after his release from prison last year, he started working for Michael Laval."

"Oh." Hana pursed her lips. "Mrs Bowman's gentleman friend. That's what we thought."

Odering pulled a notebook from his jacket pocket and flicked the pages. "Laval is linked to criminal activities involving vulnerable women. He's amassed quite a fortune and slipped through our net several times over the last few years. Changing his identity helped to add to our confusion, although in his latest few ventures he got sloppy and didn't bother."

"His last few ventures?" Hana's voice dripped with sarcasm. "You mean robbing Mrs Bowman?"

"And others. You might not think so, but your friend proved fortunate just to lose her house. A lady in Northland lost her life."

Hana nodded in silent agreement. Her brow knitted. "Why come after me though? I'm no longer a widow and never owned a fortune."

"From questioning Mrs Bowman and adding what we already know, his interest in you seems linked to something he thinks you're hiding." Hana's eyes flicked to Logan and she gnawed her lower lip. If the detective noticed the silent acknowledgement pass between them, he said nothing. "After your attempted mugging at the school back in February, another staff member identified the young man we arrested. We think he hid something on your vehicle, which is why many of the incidents involved it. He pleaded guilty to assault amongst other crimes but refused to implicate anyone else."

"What sentence did he get?" Logan demanded and Odering narrowed his eyes.

"You weren't informed?"

"No! Nobody tells us anything!" Hana snapped. "Your officers never return phone calls or keep me updated. I feel as if I don't matter."

"That's not the case, I promise." Odering licked his lips. "The boy received community service hours."

"Cleaning graffiti off toilet walls?" Logan swore and rolled his eyes. "Big deal. Who is the guy you arrested the other day? He broke my wife's arm. What will he get? Gardening duties for old ladies or more graffiti cleaning?"

Odering shook his head. "We just take the cases, Mr Du Rose. The court decides the sentences. He works for a local money guy. We're not sure why he subcontracted to Laval, but think it relates to a gambling debt he ran up." He turned to Hana. "Back to your car, I know our forensic officer checked it after you called them to a rear shunt at your address. We haven't ignored you, but the pieces don't fit. They will, but it takes time."

"Your guy didn't find the scratches underneath though, did he?" Logan pushed a pillow behind Hana and stood. Agitation showed in his jerky movements. "It looked like something was fixed to the underside. I imagined one of those plastic, magnetic boxes spent time fixed to the chassis, but Hana didn't put it there."

"When I moved house, I found a metal box in my garage." Hana's cheeks pinked with embarrassment. "I didn't realise its significance and put it in my handbag. Later, I let my grandson play with it."

Odering's eyes widened and he stood. The paper and his notebook fell to the floor. "You found it? I need you to give it to me. It's evidence."

Logan closed and opened his fist, ordering his words before he spoke. "We can't find it."

"No, I couldn't find it." Hana took the blame, watching the colour fade from the detective's face. "I searched my grandson's room and found the box, but it was empty."

Odering shrugged. "I still want it. It's evidence." He gritted his teeth and turned away from them, letting the rain against the windowpane distract him. "You don't understand. I've followed Laval from one end of this country to the other." He whirled around. "I'm getting desperate."

Odering's jaw flexed and he slapped his thighs, the slump of his body pitiful. "You need to find the contents of that box," he demanded. "And soon."

-34-

The detective asked numerous times for the address where Hana last saw the box. She refused. "No, I'll get it. I don't want you upsetting my grandson."

"I can get a warrant," he threatened and Logan stood.

"It's time you left. My wife is tired. We've told you we'll get it and I expect you to be satisfied with that." He moved close enough to Odering for the other man to take a step back. "If you interfere, we'll disappear and you're on your own." Logan's jaw worked in his cheek and Odering blanched.

"Okay." He side stepped Logan and nodded to Hana. "I'll see you soon, Mrs Du Rose," he said, his voice containing a veiled threat.

As his heels receded along the corridor, Hana slumped against the pillows. "I need to use the bathroom."

Logan helped push the drip stand into the bathroom and leaned against the wall. "How's your arm?" he asked, keeping his tone casual.

"Exhausted like the rest of me," she sighed. She yanked her pants and underwear to half-mast before pausing. "Turn around!" she insisted. "I can't pee with you watching."

Logan turned to stare at the door. "Don't be scared of Odering," he said. "I can see he's upset you."

Hana sighed. "I made a deal with Jas. He has such little faith in adults already that I wanted to prove some of us were different."

"You can't search his room," Logan mused. "I'll need to do it."

Hana nodded and hauled her clothing back in place one-handed. "Then let me speak to him on the phone or bring him here. I promised."

"I'll organise it." Logan turned around to face her and gave her a towel as she washed her hand. The slippery bar of soap plopped into the sink and she cursed. "I think you should recuperate at the hotel." He turned his head to gauge her reaction.

"No thanks." Hana spoke through gritted teeth. "I don't want to."

"Be sensible," he urged, increasing the pressure. "Mum and Leslie could help you and I'll know you're safe."

"No," she repeated with more force. "I'd rather meet Laval than become a captive of a different kind."

"You don't mean that!" Logan snapped and Hana swallowed, refusing to confirm her foolish point.

"I always help with the expo and I refuse to change my life because of a spiteful old man." She stuck her nose in the air and squared her jaw, daring Logan to challenge her.

"Yeah. Fair point." Logan slumped down onto the closed toilet seat. "Can't Pete help?"

Hana snorted. "You aren't serious? Last year, Sheila asked him to take photographs of the stallholders talking to boys. He went up to the mezzanine floor in the hall to get a better angle and dropped the departmental camera over the balcony."

"Ouch." Logan winced. "Did you retrieve the memory card?"

"Nope." Hana grimaced and amusement backlit her green eyes. "Because he dropped it into the power company's display tank. It soaked more than thirty people in a ten metre radius. It wasn't just water either. They stained it blue for effect. Sheila went mental."

Logan conceded for the moment but Hana saw the gleam in his eyes. She gritted her teeth and determined not to allow him to abandon her at the mercy of his weird family. As she battled tiredness, Logan kissed her pink cheek and left her to her dreams. "Tell Sheila I'm coming back to work on Monday," she muttered, not seeing him raise his eyebrows in disbelief.

"See you tomorrow," he whispered. "I love you."

Logan drove to Amy's house, his knock on the door answered by a hostile Bodie. "Sod off," the younger man said and moved to slam the door in his face.

Logan shoved the toe of his cowboy boot between the gap and barged the aperture wider, taking Bodie by surprise. "Don't play this game with me, son," he growled. "You might not know it yet, but I assure you it won't end well." He shouldered Bodie aside. "You can arrest me later if you wish, but right now I intend to take your son's bedroom apart. You can help me, or watch. I don't really care."

"I already looked!" Bodie postured, petulance creeping into the rigid squaring of his shoulders. "Who do you think you are?"

Logan stopped and turned, his grey eyes reading jealousy in the tilt of Bodie's head. "I'm the man who loves your mother, dickhead. And I'll keep her safe no matter what it costs. Laval wants his paperwork and it's here somewhere. Unless you want Odering to get a search warrant for this house and embarrass your girlfriend, I'd start helping real fast."

"Amy's not my girlfriend!"

Logan snorted. "Then you're more of an idiot than I suspected."

Bodie's jaw flexed in his cheek and Logan knew the moment he gave in. He jerked his head towards Jas' bedroom and followed Logan. They worked together to pull the room apart. Logan wrinkled his nose as he hauled a cabinet across the floorboards without emptying it. "Bring a bucket of water and some cloths," he grunted.

"Why?" Bodie stopped moving the bed and came to look at the covering of dust and fluff on the skirting board. "Oh. I don't think housekeeping is Amy's strong point."

Logan stopped and looked at him with his head tilted downwards. "Your kid sleeps here, asshole. Amy works full time and raises your kid single-handed. Get on your knees and clean it." He shook his head and sneered. "Take that as a life lesson."

"Or what?" Bodie snorted and his cocky expression flicked a switch in Logan's self-control. He grabbed Bodie's throat in his large fingers and squeezed, a smile breaking across his lips as the other man flailed. The length of his arm rendered Bodie's kicks ineffective. The young cop's nails scratched welts in his forearms as Logan drove him back against the wall.

"Or I'll clean it with your face," he whispered. He let go. Bodie choked and slid down the wall, anger and shame vying for dominance in his downturned mouth. His training proved useless against an unpredictable force like Logan Du Rose. The handsome Māori shook his head.

"Don't feel bad, kid. I've put down bigger guys than you. I tried hard not to hurt ya." Logan shrugged and hauled the cupboard free. Something caught his eye, trapped between the floorboards. He dropped to his knees and made a grabbing motion behind his back. "Get me tweezers or something to grab this with."

"Get stuffed!" Bodie rubbed his neck and turned his head from side to side.

"Fine." Logan shrugged without looking back. "Then I'll just rip the floorboards up and go under the house. Don't worry, I'll let you put it all back together after I leave."

Bodie fetched tweezers from Amy's room and Logan extracted the folded sheets from between the floorboards. Despite his care, the fold ended up battered and ripped, rendering large chunks unreadable. The men didn't speak again, but when Bodie fetched soap and water, Logan washed the skirting boards of the small bedroom and polished the floorboards until they shone. His stepson's arrogance galled him, but he decided the lesson would keep for another time. His kuia taught him that leadership often walked on its knees.

He found Hana without a drip when he returned to the hospital.

She'd plastered lipstick around her mouth with her left hand in an attempt to convince him of her good health. Instead, it served to make her resemble a vampire. A sling supported her arm and she maintained her intention to discharge herself. "I know Angus expects you back at work tomorrow," she said, rubbing her face and spreading lipstick into her eye. She blinked in surprise as it stung. "So I've told them I'll stay until school finishes."

"You're kidding? How will you manage at home?"

"My husband will help me." Hana's beautiful smile disarmed him. A wicked glint lit her eyes. "In return for certain favours."

He sighed and resigned himself to her inevitable discharge. His body looked leaden as he perched on the side of her bed and examined the scuffs on his boots. "I need to tell you something," he said, biting the inside of his cheek. "And you're gonna flip."

Hana sighed. "I already know. Amy rang me."

"Oh." Logan looked surprised, not imagining Bodie might be so candid about his throttling. "He told her."

"No, she saw for herself."

Logan's eyes narrowed in confusion. He left no marks on Bodie's body. Perhaps he'd lost his touch. "Saw what?" He smiled in innocence and Hana patted his knee with her good hand.

"You cleaned up Jas' bedroom and got rid of the mold on the wall. She said you found the papers."

"Oh, yeah." Logan relaxed. "Bodie helped with the cleaning. I took the papers and the box to Odering." He wrinkled his nose. "Jas kept his old teeth in the box. I nipped to the metal tech teacher at school and he gave me a spare. Some kid didn't bother picking it up at the end of last year. Jas might not notice the difference."

Hana sighed. "He did, but he's okay with it. He likes it better without the spikey bit in the corner. We talked and he's forgiven me for not telling him first."

"Cool." Logan dragged a hand over the bristles on his chin. Dark shadows ringed his grey eyes and Hana tuned into his tiredness.

"You should get some sleep," she said, running a hand through his silky hair. "Ready for me coming home."

Logan's phone rang and he looked at the caller's name, wrinkling his nose in disgust. "Odering!" he spat. "I'll take it in the corridor."

Hana knitted her brow. "You don't need to," she said to his retreating back.

Outside, Logan's tone remained clipped. "What?" he snapped. "You got what you wanted."

Odering's voice sounded tinny and detached. "You know what else I wanted, Du Rose. Did you give it any more thought?"

"No. Sod off. Leave Hana out of your plans from now on. We're done."

Odering clicked his tongue. "Forensics went through the Achilles Rise house and found Flick's fingerprints. He'd touched pretty much everything. Why wouldn't he act with more care?"

"How should I know?" Logan watched a nurse pad by and waited until she passed to continue the conversation.

Odering prattled on. "Apparently forensics needed to be quick because this fat chick followed them round with a vacuum cleaner."

"Henrietta. She volunteered to get the house straight for the tenants." Logan allowed himself a smirk at the image of Pete's girlfriend herding the cops from room to room at speed.

"The documentation appears to be land deeds," Odering said. Logan heard the sound of a printer spitting out paper in the background.

"Yeah, we worked that out. But paper records are outdated. Deeds transfer online every day of the week; they aren't worth killing over. Did you work out what that other document was? I ripped the official stamp as I pulled it from between the floorboards. It looked like a kid's drawing."

"The guys here say it's an engineer's report," Odering ventured. "It's dated around a decade ago. They're looking into it." He didn't see Logan's shrug of disinterest as he watched Hana negotiate her way to the bathroom. She stood outside the door and glared at the tie on her tracksuit pants as though it may undo itself.

"I need to go," Logan said, pushing himself away from the wall. The sole of his boot left a mark in the paintwork.

"Wait," Odering said. "The other thing is a handwritten will on a standard do-it-yourself form. The missing woman from Northland signed it. Her son verified a scan of the signature. We presume she's dead."

"Okay. Catch them now then," Logan replied. "I won't do your damn job for you. I'm an English teacher not a detective. I think you'll find our salaries reflect that fact." He hung up without saying goodbye.

He drove home, checking in his side mirrors every few seconds for anyone following. Retrieval of the documents might make no difference to Hana's situation. The blonde man needed to know she didn't have them anymore and Logan wondered how to make that happen. Culver's Cottage wrapped its cold fingers around him as he entered. Hana's absence left a gap in his world and he wasn't prepared to allow its permanence.

Logan arrived at the Bramwell early the next afternoon. He ran the stairs instead of using the elevator, checking in at the nurses' station and making his way down the plush corridor to Hana's room. He halted in the doorway at the sight of Angus occupying the visitor's chair. Hana perched on the bed holding court. She looked wired. "Told you I was going home," she said to Angus and the principal raised his bushy eyebrows.

"I didn't deny that fact, Hana," he said in his lyrical accent. "I said you shouldn't."

Logan nodded to them both and spoke to his wife. "I'll collect the discharge paperwork from the nurses' station. I won't take long." He reached out and stroked a lock of hair back from her face. Her wonky ponytail barely kept her curls in order.

"I'll come with you," Angus said, rising to his feet. "I haven't seen much of you lately."

Logan shrugged as the man followed him along the corridor, stopping at a mid-way point. "You don't need to see me," he said, quirking an eyebrow. "What's wrong?"

Angus clasped his hands behind his back in his characteristic thoughtful pose. He lowered his glasses on his nose and peered over them. "Caroline Marsh secured work at the girls' school. She's still in Hamilton."

Logan let out a sigh before he could prevent it and knew his body language betrayed his exasperation. "I don't care."

"She's pregnant and showing." He pushed his glasses up. "I'm told the child is yours."

Logan took a step backwards and his face clouded. "It isn't."

Past retirement age and shorter than Logan, Angus channelled determination as he took a step towards him. Piercing blue eyes held his gaze. "If I discover otherwise, Du Rose, I will not sanction the abandonment of a defenseless child." He jabbed a finger into Logan's chest. "I will find an excuse to fire you and hound you out of this city faster than you imagine."

Logan gritted his teeth. "The child is not mine."

Angus took another step forward, watching rage war in Logan's eyes. "Don't make the mistake of underestimating me, Du Rose! I know who you are. I've always known, son. Your connections don't frighten me and never have." He jabbed a finger back towards Hana's room. "But if you hurt that woman in there, I'll make it impossible for you to teach in this country ever again! Mud sticks, Mr Du Rose." Angus took a step back and smiled. "I'll stick it so hard to you, no self-respecting principal will ever employ you. I'll only need to hint about your associations and it will be game over."

Logan shrugged as though not caring and Angus shook his head. "Oh, you might not need the money, boy. But it's who you are; Logan Du Rose the effective teacher, good at everything you touch. You take away what matters to Hana and I'll return the favour. That's not a threat, boy. It's a promise!" He whipped round on his shiny shoes and clicked down the stairs without looking back, not even to witness the devastation he left behind.

Logan leaned against the wall, letting the coolness of the plaster sink into his scalp. Caroline's threat returned to bite him. She'd uttered the same words. "I know who and what you are!" He ran a shaking hand across his mouth, before letting it drop to his side. His fingers twitched as he passed over his credit card to cover the astronomical hospital bill. Shoving the receipt into his pocket, his disinterest halted the receptionist in her inane chatter. Gathering his wits and forcing a smile on his face, Logan walked back to Room 102 to fetch his wife.

Hana emerged from the bathroom, hauling her pants up around her waist. "Angus said Boris isn't leaving." She dug her teeth into her bottom lip. "He's applying for a visa extension to stay on longer."

"He never said." Logan shoved the discharge papers and a prescription into Hana's bag. He raised an eyebrow. "Although he doesn't say much anymore. I asked him the other day if he had issues and he bit my head off."

"That doesn't sound like him." Hana straightened her sling and clambered onto the bed. "Angus seemed rather keen to speak to you. Problems?"

Logan rolled his eyes and stroked her lopsided ponytail. "Nothing I can't handle, babe. You ready to come home?"

-35

Hana stared through the side window and avoided looking in Logan's direction. Caroline's image drifted through her memory like a curse.

"You shouldn't ask if you might not like the answer." His voice sounded cowed and distant. "You push me to tell you stuff and then punish me. I bloody hate it."

The sound of the tyres rumbling against the road surface filled the silence, lasting until the outskirts of Ngaruawahia. Hana battled her inner feelings of jealousy and fear. Even the mention of Caroline's name set her nerves jangling and the knowledge she'd stayed in Hamilton overwhelmed her. The woman could destroy her mood by proxy.

She sensed Logan stealing sideways glances at her and cringed. Another tear rolled down her cheek and she wafted it away with a hand which smelled of generic soap and hospital. He reached out and touched her thigh. "Sorry, babe," he conceded.

"I don't want to talk about it." She shut the conversation down, not wanting Caroline to claim any more ground in her marriage. But internalising the monster's existence gave it more power. Hana sighed at the irony.

"This is exactly why I said nothing." Logan shook his head in an angry movement. "But the jungle drums are still beating. Best you hear it from me."

"Stop!" Hana raised her good hand. "Please stop talking about her."

Logan shook his head and stared through the windscreen. "So much for honesty," he muttered.

Hana's homecoming lacked enthusiasm and Logan abandoned her to chop wood outside. The laden wood basket by the fire highlighted the lack of need for his activity and Hana drew her own conclusions. She wandered around, her heart leaden in her chest. A headache tugged at the back of her skull despite the heavy painkillers that coursed through her bloodstream. They took the edge off her physical hurts but couldn't numb the emotional trauma. Logan clattered around in the kitchen washing his hands and Hana padded in wearing one sock and her underwear. "Please can you help me?" she asked with forced politeness. The fingers of her good hand clutched the monkey pyjamas.

Logan wrinkled his nose at the tattered fabric and dried his hands. He channelled his irritation into the monkey on the front with its tongue out. Hana groaned as her awkward cast snatched and grabbed at the cloth sleeve, making her whole arm ache. "Stop!" she begged as it stuck half way up her arm. Logan ground his teeth and Hana baulked at the anger in his eyes. "It's hurting!" she pleaded. "I'm stuck."

Logan swore, loosing a series of hideous words. "I hate these things," he spat, jerking his head towards her pyjamas. Snatching the scissors from the drawer, he sliced around the cuff, ignoring Hana's wails of protest. The sleeve broke free and rolled up her arm, threads dangling from the severed fabric like nerve endings.

"Izzie bought me those!" she shouted, peering at the dilapidated sleeve. Her tear-filled eyes accused him of brutality.

Logan slammed the scissors back into the drawer and shut it with his hip. "Before or after God chucked Adam out of the garden?" His tone dripped sarcasm and Hana seized the bait.

"Is that a reference to my age?" Her green eyes widened, causing the tears to cascade onto her cheeks. She backed away, her knickers showing beneath the frayed hem of her shirt.

"Only to the pyjamas!" Logan raised his arms in an exasperated movement. "Stop reading into everything."

Hana ran from the room, turning late and colliding with the doorframe. She carried her right side with stiffness and refused to cry out, despite the pain. Logan's concerned voice followed her and she ignored him, running into the bedroom and slamming the door. When one slam offered no satisfaction from her physical and mental agony, she added two more, which didn't help either.

Hana climbed into bed and settled on her left side, balancing her broken arm across her hip. Even the weight of the sheets aggravated it. She heard the click of the door as Logan ventured into the room and she tensed.

"What's upset you most?" he asked. His footsteps padded across the floorboards and he paused beyond the bed. "I'm sorry I wrecked the monkey pyjamas. I'll apologise to Izzie and buy you more." He strayed closer, placing a scarred hand on the bedpost. Hana peered over her shoulder at his face, experiencing a jolt of satisfaction at the whipped expression. Her shoulders slumped at his next sentence. "It's not just about the pyjamas though, is it?"

Hana shook her head. "No. It's unfair that Caroline has the power to wreck things for us. I wanted to come home so much and now it's ruined."

Logan sank into the bed next to her and lay back against the pillows. His clasped hands cupped the back of his head. "It's only ruined because you let it happen. She's out to make life hard for me and every time we fight, she gets her wish."

"Do you think she's psychotic?" Hana sniffed into her wrist and Logan retrieved a handkerchief from his jeans pocket.

He shrugged. "Maybe. We never worked as a couple because it always became toxic. She operated in a world of mind games and attention seeking and I never understood."

"Why did you almost marry her?" Hana's voice sounded tiny in the big bed. She asked the question without wanting to know the truth. Logan's eyes took on an opaque quality.

"It's a long story, Hana. She needed cash and wanted the Du Rose name. It suited us both at the time but I'm glad it didn't happen."

"Did you ever love her?" Hana watched his brow furrow and he turned towards her.

"Would you think less of me if I said no?"

Hana swallowed and gauged her own reaction before speaking. "I think I would." She sighed. "There's no doubt Caroline loves you. I don't like to think of you sleeping with her and not at least feeling something." She closed her eyes. "I don't like to think of you sleeping with her at all."

Logan's lips twisted into a grimace. "I can't change that, Hana. I'm sorry." He turned on his side and reached out to coil a strand of her hair between his fingers. "I've spent my life on hold, waiting for you. Anyone else served as a distraction."

"So, I should feel flattered?" Hana wrinkled her nose and Logan smiled.

"Yeah." His brows knitted into a line. "About her baby Hana; it's not mine."

"Logan, I'm tired." She saw the expression of hurt cross his face as she denied him the opportunity to make his case. She struggled, pained by her inadequacy next to Caroline. Truth gnawed at her insides and she ached to share her suspicions with her husband and halve the burden. Taking a deep breath, she chewed her lower lip. "I think Boris is the father."

"What?" Logan sat up so fast he banged her hand. She cried out and he cursed his stupidity and stroked her hair as she tensed her body and waited for the pain to pass. "I'm sorry, I'm sorry," he breathed. "What can I get you?"

Hana dispatched him for tea and painkillers while she recovered. "You changed the sheets," she said on his return. "It smells clean."

"I'm house trained." He set her mug of tea on the bedside table and helped her into a sitting position. When he perched on the edge of the bed, she knew he sought an explanation.

"You want to know why I think Boris is the father?" Logan nodded and she licked her lips. "It's instinct and it's the best I can do right now. He believes he's the dad, even if he isn't."

Logan squinted at a speck of ink on his middle finger. "You think Boris would be so disloyal?" He gritted his teeth in a hard expression.

"Yes. I saw his face the day she accosted me at school. She mentioned pregnancy and he went white. When I puked on her shoes in the carpark, he helped to get me into the car so he could deal with her. He has a vested interest and I might be wrong, but he thinks the child is his." Hana pinched the bridge of her nose between her thumb and forefinger. She tried to interpret the dangerous look in his eyes. "Are you jealous?"

Logan snorted and jerked his head backwards. "Hell no!" He rolled his eyes. "But I don't appreciate disloyalty in my friends. He knew how she tried to sabotage us and if I find he still went there, I won't pull any punches."

Hana sighed. "He's a big boy, Logan. He behaved like a sweetheart when you and I weren't getting on."

Logan raised his eyebrows. "Really? Perhaps I underestimated his appeal with the women. Cunning bugger."

"It wasn't like that." Hana handed him her mug and slid down the bed whilst supporting the cast with her left hand. "You have a dirty mind."

Logan didn't smile and Hana grew nervous. "Do nothing, Logan. I shared this with you in confidence."

A vein in his neck twitched and he gave a small nod. "I won't go near him." His eyes narrowed. "You don't either."

Hana sighed and closed her eyes. "I'm stuck in bed, Logan. I won't see anyone ever again at this rate."

"You can see Pete." Hana squinted up to see Logan grinning.

"Why would I want to do that?"

"He doesn't want to live in the Gordonton house alone. He's asked to move in with us if Boris doesn't get his visa approved."

"What? No way! He moves in and I move out!" Hana scrabbled to sit up again and Logan rested a hand against her shoulder.

"Don't rip your nightie. I told him no."

"You already ripped it for me." She grumbled at his use of the colloquialism, glaring at her ruined sleeve.

Hana slept the evening away, sitting up only to swallow the medication Logan handed her with a glass of water. She woke in darkness, sensing the earliness of the hour. Laying on her back, her arm ached and her shoulder felt tight. The pillow she'd gone to sleep resting the cast on disappeared during the night and scrabbling with her feet didn't deliver it. Logan's gentle snores reminded her not to wake him.

The child did somersaults in her womb, kicking her full bladder without regard. Hana lay still and steeled herself for movement, anticipating the inevitable agony of getting up.

Cradling her arm with care, she tried to use her stomach muscles to sit. She failed and the jolt as she flopped back caused her to grit her teeth and gasp. Trying again, she swung her legs sideways but couldn't touch the floor. Her exposed feet felt the freezing air outside the warm sheets and she shivered. Scooting her bottom forwards, Hana turned her body and found the rug beneath her toes. She waited and weighed up whether to use her good arm to push herself upright or support her cast. For the first time since leaving hospital, she wished for the button which altered any part of the bed she required.

"Steady." Strong hands slipped behind her shoulders and supported her as she sat. Logan squeezed her upper arm. "I'll get your robe. It's freezing." Hana heard his feet pad across the floor to the wardrobe.

"Thanks." She yawned. "I need to pee."

Logan waited outside the bathroom while Hana coped with washing her hand. "You should come back to bed," he said, glancing at his watch. "I don't need to be up for another couple of hours."

Hana flexed her jaw and readied herself for a fight. "I'm going back to work early," she said and watched his eyes darken. "Today."

"Come back to bed. We'll talk about it later."

Hana shook her head. "I'm sorry I woke you. If you can help me get that plastic thing over my arm, I'll take a bath and wash my hair. You go back to bed."

Logan studied her face until Hana found his scrutiny painful. She looked away and he conceded. "I think I remember how it goes on."

Hana splashed around in the bath, not enjoying the experience once she managed to get in. Climbing out proved even harder. Logan hung around, appearing every time she decided she couldn't cope alone. He caught her shuffling in the empty bath on her knees, trying to work out how to stand up without the use of either arm. "Don't say it," she groaned as he raised an eyebrow at her predicament. "And don't laugh."

"I wasn't about to do either." Logan slipped an arm around her waist and hauled her upright. He kept hold of her wrist while reaching for her towel.

"Why?" Hana narrowed her eyes in suspicion. "It's not like you to pass up an opportunity to put me straight."

"Harsh." Logan swaddled her up in the fluffy towel and helped her over the side of the bath. "If you're done in here, I'll take a shower."

"Okay." Hana yawned and buried her face in the towel. She headed to the bedroom and shivered in the chill air. Half an hour later after several mishaps, she wore lipstick on much of her face and mascara in her hair. When she stamped in temper, she jolted her arm and wasted time bending double and holding her breath. "I bloody hate my life!" she grumbled.

"Charming." Logan walked through the door bearing a mug of tea and laid it on the dressing table. "What are you doing?"

"Getting ready for work." Hana stuck her chin in the air, fixing a defiant look on her face. Narrowed eyes invited him to challenge her.

Logan smiled at the mess on her face. Then he held his hand out. "Give me a wet-wipe and I'll clean you up. I can't promise that I'm a makeup artist to the stars but I'll do my best."

Hana pinked with embarrassment at the concentration on Logan's face. His fingers on her skin sent prickles of appreciation darting through her stomach. He took care to clean the mess from her cheeks and chin, reapplying the lipstick with care. A soft pink tongue poked from between his lips as he concentrated and Hana blinked at the love in his face. "I'm so lucky," she breathed as he brushed her eyelashes with mascara. "I don't deserve you."

Logan pushed the brush back into the mascara bottle and kissed the end of her nose. "No," he said, raising one eyebrow. "You don't. But if you tell anyone I did your makeup, we'll fall out."

Hana smirked. "I won't, I promise. But only because I want you to do it again tomorrow."

Logan snorted. "In your dreams, babe. That was a one-time-only event."

Hana's mood changed as she realised she needed Logan to help her into her clothes. He enjoyed sliding her into her underwear, a devilish smirk on his lips. "Stop it!" she complained as he smoothed his fingers over the clasp at the back of her bra in light, fluttery movements. "You're supposed to do it up, not enjoy a good grope."

"This is too difficult," he grumbled. "It's unfair." His fingers strayed around her stomach and over the bump of his child. "Let's stay home," he whispered, lowering his head and scratching her neck with his beard growth.

Hana turned into his embrace to protest and he bit the delicate skin beneath her jaw. She closed her eyes and enjoyed the thrill of his attention, feeling their marriage fight its way back to stability. His hands on her body communicated his need and she bent to his will, finding herself naked against his work pants and shirt. "I love you so much," he whispered, steering her back towards the unmade bed.

Hana looked in the mirror half an hour later, her hair in a wonky ponytail and a grimace on her face. "I look like a weirdo," she grumbled, staring down at her strange attire.

Logan shrugged on his jacket and smiled. "If you're determined to go to work today, you'll need clothes you can manage. You said you couldn't pull tights up and down one-handed and trousers are just as hard."

"You managed." Hana glared at him in accusation.

"Yeah, but I can use both hands better than you use your left." Logan bent to zip up her boots and Hana wiggled her toes against the lumpy socks trapping her feet. "I've broken enough bones to get the practice."

"I haven't." Hana peered at her long skirt and the denim jacket with its flapping, empty sleeve. "I look like a primary school teacher." She pouted and Logan laughed.

"Yeah, you do."

"I don't want to go dressed like this." She stamped her foot and watched a vein begin to tick in Logan's temple. He gave her a sideways smile.

"Don't go then. I'll see you tonight."

"No!" Hana trotted behind him as he headed for the garage steps. "I see your game, Du Rose!"

A watery sunshine rose over Hamilton as Logan drove along the expressway. He tapped the steering wheel in concentration. "I'll drop you at the main entrance and hide the car in one of the surrounding streets," he said. He raised a hand against Hana's protest. "Please babe, just do what I ask."

Hana climbed the steps to her office, the sling already aggravating her neck and her handbag clanking against her legs. Her email inbox overflowed with organisations desperate to secure a space at the expo. "I thought we already allocated spaces," she called to Sheila, clicking through the frantic messages on screen.

"We did!" Sheila bustled from her office, a worried expression drawing lines across her forehead. "But the council cancelled the local event and the presenters haven't stopped pestering me. They're trying to join ours and we don't have room."

Hana wrinkled her nose. "We could use the gymnasium and the new classrooms near the boarding house. Then you can allocate more spaces. What if we charged a fee for latecomers?"

Sheila's eyes glinted and a slow smile broke across her face. "What a great idea."

"The enquiries are all from companies. They shouldn't mind paying a last minute fee and they'll understand why we aren't charging the colleges."

"Awesome." Sheila's brain whirred with possibilities and she retreated to her office to thump numbers into her calculator.

The sound of the school bell jarred Hana's nerves and she tensed at the jolt against her sore arm. Noise surrounded her as six hundred boys moved around the site like a herd of elephants. An eerie silence followed the slam of the final classroom door. Hana rested her chin in her hand, knowing it would all begin again in an hour. Her head ached and she wished she'd listened to her husband and stayed at home. The stilted one-handed typing sullied her mood further.

Logan appeared half way through interval, carrying a take-out cup of steaming hot chocolate and a shop bought sandwich. "You didn't take lunch," he said, perching his neat bum on the corner of her desk.

"Thanks." Hana sipped the drink with a groan of gratitude. "I'm not enjoying today. Typing is impossible."

"Tell me about it," he said, waggling the fingers of his left hand. The movement looked sluggish as he flexed his arm. "I told you to stay home."

Hana shrugged. "It's no fun without you." She narrowed her eyes into a lascivious smile and Logan grinned. His wink reminded her of their passion earlier and she pursed her lips and blushed. "I need a hug," she said, placing her cup on the desk and standing. She pushed herself into Logan's body, drawing comfort from his proximity. He slid his arm around her left side and nuzzled her hair.

"If someone comes in, you'll jump in guilt and hurt yourself," he whispered.

"I don't care." Hana closed her eyes and rested her head on his shoulder. "I love you."

"That's a relief." Logan's voice against her neck sounded husky. "It's too late if you don't." He groaned at the sound of Pete's distinguishable screech drifting along the corridor. "Fantastic. Here comes trouble."

Before the door smashed against the radiator, Hana sat in her chair and resumed her drinking. Logan rested against the corner of her desk and eyed the doorway with suspicion. "It's the Du Roses," Pete yelled, throwing his arms wide. Sarcasm dripped through his words and Hana narrowed her brow, darting a startled look at Logan. Her husband folded his arms and his muscles bulged through his shirt. Pete ignored the warning and barrelled across to his desk, throwing objects aside in a pretense of searching for something. "Anything either of you want to say to me?" he demanded, glaring across at them both.

"Like what?" Hana looked from him to Logan and back again.

"Like sorry!" Pete's eyes widened in mock horror. "Sorry for getting me bashed on the head." His bony fingers fluttered towards his crown, gliding over his wispy hair and settling over a large piece of medical tape. He'd parted his hair at the back to accommodate it and from the front wore two wispy, straw coloured horns.

"I already said sorry." Hana's voice wavered and she stiffened.

"Did you forget, Pete?" Logan sounded casual and Pete's brow knitted.

"Maybe. Concussion makes you forget heaps. I'm sure if you say it again, it'll come back to me."

Logan rose to his feet and raised his arms above his head in a stretch. "Is that right?"

"Yeah." Pete took a step back. "I think so." Hana sensed static electricity in the atmosphere and shook her head at Logan.

"Please don't get into a ruck here." She glanced at Sheila's closed door. "I mean it."

"You remember how I asked you to drive my wife home?" Logan put his arms down and Pete's lips parted in fear.

"No. It's the concussion. I don't remember." He took a giant gulp and waved towards Hana. "I'm sure you must have apologised. It's okay. I forgive you."

Logan glared at him, his eyes as black as coals. He took a step forward, but a glance at Hana diverted his anger. "You'll keep," he hissed at Pete. "You won't always have women around you." He bent to kiss the top of Hana's head, drawing satisfaction from the way Pete scooted aside as he walked towards the door. Behind Hana's back, Logan made a throat cutting motion with his index finger and the colour left Pete's face.

"That was close!" Pete slumped into his chair and Hana pulled her lips back into a snarl.

"It serves you right!" she snapped. "I already apologised and you know it. You wanted to make me squirm and it failed."

Pete muttered to himself and Hana ignored him, clamping her earphones over her head and typing notes for Evie one-handed. It took her twice as long and she delivered the finished letters to the guidance counsellors' suite. She glossed over details of her injury and avoided further questioning by pleading busyness.

She spent the rest of the afternoon sticking dots to a floor plan under Sheila's direction and then peeling them off again. "Oh, bloody hell!" Sheila groaned, slapping her forehead with her hand. "Move the university to that room. Oh, no, put them in the hall. No, they can't go there because they draw too big a crowd and there won't be room for anyone else." She sagged in the chair and shook her head at Hana. "Let's look at this again tomorrow."

Hana nodded. "Yeah. I feel shattered. I'll think about it overnight."

Sheila stood and helped her shrug the denim jacket over her shoulders. "No, it's fine. You just concentrate on not falling down any more stairs."

Pete whipped around, his eyes bulging. He opened his mouth to speak and Hana's glare shut him down. "Don't worry. I'll take care." She retrieved her bag from the bottom drawer and picked her phone up from the desk. The back fell off and her sim card dropped onto a sheet of paper.

"I'll mend it." Pete leapt across to snatch it up and bumped Hana's arm. She cried out in pain at the same moment her desk phone rang.

"Let me get that." Sheila pushed past her to answer it. With a groan, Hana retreated. "Hang on, I'll fetch her." Sheila pressed the handset against her breasts, muffling the voice of the caller. "It's for you," she said, plucking the phone free and holding it out to Hana.

"All mended!" Pete yelled and dropped her cellphone into her handbag.

Frustrated, Hana nodded her thanks and took the phone from Sheila. Her clipped answer left the air molecules bouncing.

"Is this a bad time, Mrs Du Rose?" Odering asked. Expecting trouble, Hana sat down. Sheila trotted back to her office but Pete hung around, making a poor job of pretending not to listen.

"Hi." Hana turned to face the wall, letting her handbag fall to the floor. "How can I help you?"

"Can you talk?"

Hana avoided turning to look at Pete. "Not really. I'm listening." She heard Odering's lips smack and detected conflict in his voice.

"I'll keep this short then. Your husband isn't answering his phone."

"He's teaching all afternoon but school just ended. I can take a message."

"It's you I need anyway but I had trouble tracking you down. Aren't you meant to still be in hospital?" Odering paused. "We've found your vehicle."

"Oh. Logan dropped me off this morning and parked it somewhere. He said it would be safe." The colour drained from Hana's face. "He promised he didn't leave it in a short stay area."

"What?" Odering paused and static crackled across the connection. "Are we talking about the same car?"

"I don't know," Hana groaned. Pete's concerned face popped into her vision and she sat up straight. "Keep talking."

"Okay. Look, we found the car you reported stolen." He waited through Hana's hiss of awareness. "They torched it and hid it in thick bush over near Karangahake Gorge."

Hana leaned forward onto the desk so she could prop her cast on its surface and take the weight off her neck. The sling worked itself back into the groove it spent the day creating. "So there's nothing left then?"

"No, sorry." Sincerity crossed the distance between them.

"How did you find it?"

Odering paused for far too long. "Officers discovered it some weeks ago." He plunged through Hana's sharp intake of breath. "My colleagues over at Waihi sent the details through but local officers wasted time looking for Mrs H Johal."

"You're kidding me!" Hana blew out an exasperated breath. "It must be a joke!"

"I know, I know." Odering sounded apologetic. "It's a communication issue. The registered address for the vehicle is your Achilles Rise house and one department failed to make the link until all the drama last week."

Hana chewed her lip. "Oh for goodness' sake! I rented the house out before I got married. I just changed my name with the bank."

The detective cleared his throat on the other end of the line. "I can speak to your insurance company if you want to send me your details. They should pay out on the loss now."

"Yeah, thanks." Hana scribbled his email address in a sloping left-handed font. She glared at Pete as he tried to read over her shoulder.

Logan came looking for her when she didn't show up in the reception area. Still stinging from their earlier encounter, Pete stamped on his curiosity in favour of safety and left without saying goodbye. "I got worried," Logan said, eyeing Pete's dandruff laden seat and steering away. He reached for Hana's hand and clasped his fingers through hers. The tender moment revitalised them both.

"Sorry." Hana stood and looked around, noticing the absence of Pete and Sheila. "Oh. Everyone left."

"What's wrong, babe?" Logan drew her close and kissed her forehead.

"Too long to explain right now," Hana sighed. "I'm so tired."

"Yeah, you look beat." Logan picked up her handbag and slipped his other arm around her shoulders. "Come on, let's get you home."

-36-

Hana struggled to get comfy on Logan's bare chest. The heavy cast kept slipping back and yanking her shoulder. She sat up with a sigh and leaned back against her pillows, supporting her forearm across her chest.

Logan's eyes remained closed, his right hand resting on Hana's bare thigh beneath the covers. She wrinkled her nose and listened to the sound of his steady breathing. "Logan," she whispered, wincing in guilt as he opened his eyes and turned to face her.

"What?"

"Did you see Boris today?"

Logan scowled, ruining his handsome features with a brooding look. "From a distance. But no, I didn't go near him." He swore under his breath.

"Oh." Hana gave a watery smile. "That's probably best for now."

"Come back under the covers." Logan lifted the sheets and Hana smirked at the sight of his nakedness beneath.

"No. I can't get comfortable." She looked up at the darkening sky beyond the mountain. "I won't sleep tonight if I nap now."

Logan snorted. "I didn't plan on napping, babe." He patted the mattress next to him.

Hana shook her head. "Odering rang me at home time. The cops found my car."

Logan's eyes opened wider and his irises turned to granite. "When?"

"He didn't say, but because I left it registered in my old name, he says it confused things."

"That's crap!" Logan folded his arms behind his head and sighed. "Where did they find it?"

"The gorge on the way to Waihi. They burnt it out so there's no evidence."

"Geez, what a mess. Oh, I forgot to tell you. Henrietta popped in to see me this morning. She gave me the spare keys to Achilles Rise and said it's clean. When's the biology teacher back?"

"Angus said he's due home tomorrow." Hana sighed. "His wife is staying on with her father for a while. I'm not looking forward to telling him what happened."

"I already spoke to him on the phone." Logan stroked her thigh. "Henrietta said most of the broken stuff looked like crockery and I gave her the cash to replace it while you were in hospital. They tipped out drawers and emptied bookshelves and she put it all back."

"You spoke to him? What did he say?"

Logan snorted. "He wanted to know about his seedlings in the laundry. He's growing lettuces for some experiment with the boys. Henrietta said she'd watered them a few times and they're fine. He seemed happy with that." Logan rolled his eyes. "Biologists, hey?"

"What is that guy's name?" Hana closed her eyes and tried to force the memory. "I should know by now. I've spoken to him and signed a tenancy agreement with his name on it. It's not a weird name but it just won't stick." Hana pulled the duvet up to her chin and covered her shoulder. She frowned at the cast. "I appreciate you breaking the bad news to him." She sighed. "I'm so sick of my life."

"These troubles won't last forever." Logan pushed his face into her side. "Henrietta wants a kitten now. She's fallen in love with theirs."

"What does Pete say?" Hana wriggled against his warm breath on her skin.

Logan nipped her silky flesh. "He's allergic."

Hana sighed and closed her eyes. "Hey, thanks for not making me go to your parents' place."

Logan opened one eye and squinted at her, keeping his expression neutral. "How do you know I still won't?"

Hana bit her bottom lip and stuck her chin in the air. "I guess you could try." She squealed as he tickled her ribs.

Hana woke in real pain on Wednesday morning. She'd slipped down in the bed and woke herself up countless times by rolling over onto her right arm. "I should have taken the painkillers," she grumbled. "I haven't slept at all."

"Stay home," Logan argued as she banged into him at the sink. "Nobody would blame you."

"Sheila would!" she retorted, cleaning her teeth one-handed and spitting toothpaste onto her blouse.

Hana struggled into the Honda, refusing her husband's assistance and banging her arm twice. Logan remained patient, returning upstairs to set the burglar alarm that Hana forgot. She still managed to blame him. He dropped her at the main entrance of the school and drove back to the street near the gully, completing the twenty-minute hike back alone.

At the end of the first period, Logan ran into Boris in the corridor. The other man's scrawny appearance shocked him. "What happened to your face?" He peered at the black bruising beneath Boris' left eye and the deep cut on his lip.

"Ah, nussing." Boris waved a hand to flick him off and tried to move past. "Just accident."

Logan turned to watch as Boris limped away. "Oh, wait a minute." He strode behind him and caught him up. "The rumours about Caroline and me aren't true. I didn't father her baby."

"Nothing to do viz me." A flash of misery crossed the crystal blue eyes and Logan sensed Boris' inner agony. "Is your business."

"No, it isn't." Logan stepped in front of him and forced him to halt. "It's not my business, that's what I'm telling you." He dipped his head to peer into Boris' face. "Mate, what's wrong? I can help you."

Boris snorted. "No, you can't. Nobody can." His composure slipped and his eyes welled with tears. Anxiety leaked from every pore.

He leaned closer to Logan and his voice lowered to a whisper. "I've made a terrible mistake, zer bad, zer, zer bad! You can't help me now and you voudn't vant to." He whirled around, his body taut with pain. Logan opened his mouth to call after him but another sound grabbed his attention. From the other end of the corridor, a knot of boys gathered around a scuffle.

"Fight! Fight!" they chanted.

Logan projected his voice from deep in his diaphragm, causing the back row of spectators to peel away like a skin. "Enough!" he shouted and waded into the fray. He emerged gripping two flailing Year 10s by the backs of their jumpers. The crowd dispersed at the sight of his livid expression.

"Move on boys." Gwynne Jeffs arrived to back him up, brandishing his detention slips in one hand like a weapon. Lagging troublemakers slunk away at the sight of the flapping green pages.

Logan hauled the two boys into the nearest unlocked classroom, pushing them down into chairs before letting go. Gwynne followed behind, closing the door with his foot. "You okay, Mr Du Rose?" he asked, his tone casual.

"Yeah, thanks." Logan shot him a smile of appreciation. One boy clutched a bloody nose and Logan moved to the teacher's desk to retrieve tissues. "Here, take this. Keep your head down, no, down. Let the blood drain." The angry expression which steered them into the classroom left his face. It was an act perfected through practice. Boys fought. He knew that. But faced with an empty classroom and the presence of the adults, the seriousness of the situation sank into the culprits' indignant brains. Logan began, his voice soft, "So, you can tell me what this is about, or you can tell the Year 10 dean."

A look of shared horror passed between the boys. One of them groaned. "Not Dr Andrews, please sir."

The boys nodded in agreement. The doctor's propensity to counsel miscreants proved far more painful than punishment. It also took longer. They could kiss goodbye to every lunchtime for the rest of their lives, forced to sit in his office under watchful, bifocal eyes and talk about it. The boys eyed each other, neither wanting to crack first and get the story wrong.

Logan spun a chair around and sat astride it like a horse. He rested one arm across the back of the chair, his biceps straining through his shirt as he stared at them. His steel grey eyes bored into them one at a time. As the first one squeaked, the spell broke and they both called out at once. Logan held up his hand. "One at a time!" he exclaimed.

"You good here?" Gwynne asked, flapping his detention slips as he looked at his watch. Logan nodded.

"Yeah. I'll send these two to the dean in a minute."

Gwynne shook his head and left the room, muttering, "Poor buggers," loud enough for the boys to hear.

"We'll tell you," one boy pleaded, glancing at his partner in crime. "But don't send us to the dean."

What they said in their efforts to extricate themselves made the blood in Logan's veins run icy cold. Their tale drove him straight into Angus' office the second he dismissed them.

"You're joking?" Angus leaned back in his chair and let loose a torrent of swear words. "What a mess."

"I need to sort this out myself," Logan said, gnawing on his bottom lip and pacing the principal's office. "This runs too deep for the witless band of plods down at the Hamilton police station. I'll deal with it myself from here on in."

"You can't!" Angus protested. "There are processes, dear boy. They're there for a reason." He walked to his office door and poked his head through, summoning his assistant. "Ah, hello my dear. Please can you nip to the staffroom and send any aimless looking member of staff to Logan's Year 9 English class? He needs urgent cover."

She returned having dispatched Peter North. Her severe expression bore testament to Pete's reluctance, but her strutting walk indicated victory.

"Hana thinks Boris is the father of Caroline's baby." Logan squeezed the bridge of his nose between thumb and forefinger. "That's why he's staying in New Zealand. Plus the fact he's been looking mighty guilty."

"Ah," contributed Angus. He steepled his fingers against his chin but his expression gave nothing away.

Logan waited, expecting Angus to take the lead. Training horses taught him patience the hard way. Sometimes he drew on endless resources of the stuff from depths he didn't realise he possessed. It could take hours to get an animal to trust him enough to put a bit in its mouth or a saddle on its back. Logan stilled his body, forcing himself to play the long game.

Angus returned Logan's stare. "You're a mystery, Logan Du Rose," he mused. "You always were." He sighed. "I think I'm losing my passion for teaching. I can attest to the fact there's nothing new under the sun, but I'm rather tired of testing the adage."

Logan wrinkled his nose. "Hana's my priority, Angus. I care about nothing else."

The principal folded his hands before him on the desk. "What do you suggest?"

"We need to speak to Boris." Logan ran a hand through his hair. "That inconsequential fight turned into something sinister the second they mentioned my wife."

"No," replied Angus. "I will speak to Boris. I'm the principal."

Logan sat back in his chair. His jaw tightened as he gritted his teeth. "Fine. You speak to him now and I'll take him somewhere quiet and speak to him later." Logan stood to leave. He jabbed a finger at Angus. "Then I'll call my stepson to scrape him off the pavement and do some more talking with him!"

Feeling dwarfed in his chair by Logan's height, Angus stood also. He opened his arms wide. "Logan, I understand how you must feel. He put your wife in dreadful danger with his actions, but he already showed a disinclination to speak with you. I may have more success in the short term."

Logan stared the Scotsman down for a moment before acceding with a nod. He left the room and slammed the door behind him. Knowing Pete would struggle with the lively Year 9 class, Logan left him with them and headed up to see his wife.

Hana's office swarmed with activity. Logan stood in the doorway and watched her work. She knelt on the carpeted floor, bending over a huge piece of white cardboard. Tiny squares of coloured paper littered the surrounding area in an arc. She resembled a small girl with a complicated jigsaw and Logan experienced the dreadful weight in his chest that came with loving her. Her dark mahogany hair spilled from its clip, brushing her cheeks as she tipped forward. She reached out and moved a coloured square to another area. "That might work," she muttered to herself. Logan's heart clenched at her vulnerability.

Hana looked up, sensing his gaze. She started in fright and then smiled. He gave her a small wave, aware of the Year 13s studying behind him. "How's it going?" He pointed to the cardboard in front of her.

"It's a floor plan." Hana sat back on her heels and knitted her brow. "Don't you teach Year 9s this period?"

Logan grimaced and offered her his hand. She took it and hauled herself upright. "I love you," he whispered, running his fingers up the side of her face. "Promise you know that."

Hana nodded, distracted by the titter of laughter from the common room. Logan responded by kicking the door shut with his foot, raising a whoop from a Year 13 just outside. "I need to talk you." He kept his voice low. Hana sensed his alarm and stiffened.

"What's happened?"

"I'm taking you to the hotel this afternoon, Hana. You need to trust me."

"No!" She wriggled free, wincing at the protest from her arm. "You can't abandon me up there. You haven't even told your family about the you-know-what. Don't be ridiculous."

Logan slumped into Hana's office chair and put his head in his hands. "You still don't trust me."

Hana rested her good hand on her hip and Logan's eyes studied her. Her face hardened with determination and his stomach roiled in foreboding. He took in the gentle swell of his child, hidden beneath too-tight trousers. Instinct screamed at him to kidnap her and force her to submit to his desire to keep her safe. "I'm not going." She stuck her chin in the air. "You can't make me."

Logan stood and blew out a breath. "We both know I can, Hana." He closed his eyes to lock her out of the conflict in his head. "But I won't." He took a step forward and kissed her forehead, his lips tender as they lingered on her skin. "Stay inside, Hana. Don't leave this building. Promise?"

"Logan, you're scaring me." Hana's green eyes widened like jewels in her porcelain face. Even the dusting of freckles across her nose paled in her distress.

"Don't worry." Logan looked down at her lips and pressed a kiss to her cheek. His stubble grazed her flesh. "Please do as I ask. And trust me." With one last glance backward, he left.

Hana stood like a statue, perplexed at his worrying behaviour. "You gave in way too easily, Du Rose," she muttered. His footsteps faded in the silent corridor and she settled back on the carpet with her plan. Sheila changed her mind twice more about exhibitors and Hana tipped the squares onto the carpet and began again.

When the bell rang, Peter North emerged from Logan's English class with his wispy hair on end. Irritation and defeat replaced his usual languid expression. "Little bastards!" he muttered to himself as he stalked towards the tuck shop. He screamed when Logan stepped in front of him and his shoulders slumped. "I want a pie!" he groaned. "Get out of my way!"

"No!" Logan grabbed Pete's arm and dragged him against the flow of traffic. He looked up at the set of Logan's face and quailed. He'd seen that look before. Logan's determined stride made him afraid that this new crisis might run past interval.

"Can we go via the tuck shop?" he begged, trotting alongside to keep up. "If I don't get there fast, all the cheese and steak pies will go. Bloody greedy boys."

"No," Logan growled, leading him upstairs to the staff workroom on the first floor. Pete stumbled through the doorway and Logan slammed the door behind them. He turned to Pete with panic in his eyes. "The crap's hit the fan," he announced, running his hand through his hair. Pete bumped into a chair and watched Logan pace.

"Are you gonna hit me?" he asked, wincing in anticipation.

"No!" Logan balled his fists in exasperation and Pete whimpered. "Why do you always think that? We haven't fought since school."

"But I always lost."

"No, you didn't." Logan waved his arms. "Shut up. I need to think."

"So why am I here? I could be eating a pie right now." Pete shaped his hand into a pie holder and imagined steak gravy laced with greasy cheese running through his fingers. His brow knitted in temper. "Your Year 9s are a bunch of little gits. Next time you run out on them, get someone else to teach them." Logan ignored him, pacing between the door and the wall of windows. Pete contemplated an escape and then dismissed the idea. His pie hand folded and he peered at his shiny fingernails. Henrietta gave him a manicure before she flew back to Wellington. "It's not nail polish Peteepoos," she promised. "It's calcium hardener."

His nails still looked jolly shiny. He held his hands up high in front of him, the backs of them close to his nose and the fingers curled over like a dog begging for a treat. "Do these look weird to you?" he asked Logan.

Logan stopped his pacing and stared at Pete, his face a mixture of bemusement and disbelief. "What?"

"My nails. Do they look weird?"

Logan stepped towards him, peering at Pete's fingers. The door opened with a click and the geography teacher pushed his way in, loaded down with books and stationary. The sight of Pete begging Logan for something made him want to work elsewhere. "Weirdos!" he spat, exiting at speed.

"Yes, no. I don't know!" Logan exclaimed, peering at the shiny nails but unable to make a decision. "And right now I don't care!"

Pete sighed and turned his hands over, buffing his thumbnail with his tracksuit cuff and blowing off pretend dust. "I think the shine is too much," he complained.

Logan returned to his pacing. When he stopped and slapped his thighs in defeat, Pete looked up. "It's not the baby, is it?" he asked, genuine concern in the widening of his blue eyes. "I want to be god parent."

He looked so concerned, Logan experienced one of those rare flashes of realisation about Pete. Lazy, self-centred and unkempt, he could behave with utter sincerity. Logan pulled out a chair and sat, running his hand over his eyes. "Baby's fine," he said. "All the tests came back normal. But I have a massive problem."

It took a while to explain. Pete looked at his watch as the school grew silent after lesson change. The last sports class he abandoned went for a tour of the grounds including adjacent residential gardens. They threw rotten fruit at each other and Angus roasted him for negligence after complaints from angry mothers. He wondered how many last warnings he could sustain. He tuned back in to Logan's last statement. "So, you stopped a fight between two Year 11s."

"Yeah." Logan rubbed his eyes again. "Over a fifty dollar note."

Pete fought to stop his eyeballs bugging. "I'd love a fifty dollar note," he breathed.

Logan pulled it from his jacket pocket. "Well, here it is." He shook his head in disgust. "That's all it took to sell my wife's safety."

Pete reached out for the money and then withdrew his hand. "Oh, I guess it's evidence."

Logan nodded it and slipped it back inside. His fingers shook and Pete recoiled, recognising the signs of fury. "I don't understand this," he complained, turning his attention back to his fingernails.

Logan resumed his pacing. "The boys shared responsibility for delivering a message in exchange for fifty dollars. The dairy outside school refused to change it and they fought about who would keep it safe." He closed his eyes and Pete watched temper flare in his steely eyes. Logan shook his head. "They delivered the message to Boris."

"What did it say?" Pete leaned forward.

"Pay your debts or next time will be worse."

The colour faded from Pete's face, leaving him pasty white. "Oh, crap! It's about that internet gambling thing, isn't it?"

"What?" Logan whipped around, his face dark and suspicious. "You knew?"

Pete cringed like a whipped dog. "I knew he got into a little debt over it."

"Oh nice one!" Logan kicked a table leg, causing a heap of papers to cascade like a waterfall. He glanced at the mess and left it. "Well, one of the boys is Matthew Larne's nephew."

"Oh." Pete reared back in his chair, his lip curled in distaste. "The money lender?"

Logan balled his fists. "Even I've heard of him and I'm not a bloody local!"

Pete squirmed, standing and edging himself nearer the exit. "I didn't know Larne owned the debt though."

"Boris owes thousands!" Logan roared. "If Larne bought the debt, it's bad." He spun on his heel in frustration and then rounded on Pete. "Why didn't Boris go home to Germany? They wouldn't follow him there." His shoulders sagged at the memory of Hana's suspicion about Boris and Caroline, answering his own question.

Pete's eyes grew wide like saucers. "Can I move in with you? I don't want them turning up at home and hassling me."

"No," Logan snapped. "You can't." He tapped the toe of his boot on the floorboards. "If Larne is the local guy, then the men who attacked you and Hana the other day must work for him. Larne's helping Laval."

Pete pouted. "Larne lends his guys to all sorts of bad people. That's nothing new. This is nothing to do with Hana's safety. This is all about me. You have to keep me safe now. I've met Larne and he's evil."

"You were collateral damage, Pete. Don't flatter yourself. The next part of the message said, 'She's in Huntly. Get the address. No more excuses.' Why did it say that?" Logan ran a hand through his hair. The rigidity of his body heralded an explosion of temper. Pete gripped the door handle and started to turn it.

"You think Laval knows where Hana is?" He cocked his head, curiosity vying with fear. "It might not mean her. Larne's got no reason to look for her."

Logan closed his eyes and shook his head. "It's her! Who else does Boris know in Huntly?"

"I don't know." Pete's shoulders twitched. "It sounds suspect."

"I tried to talk to him earlier and he gave me a cryptic warning. If he's told them where we live, I'll kill him!"

"Nah. He never came to your new place. He won't know the address."

"You know it." Logan narrowed his eyes and Pete swallowed.

"I didn't tell him." He backed away. "He doesn't come home much. I think he got himself a woman."

Logan resumed his pacing. "Hana saw Laval's guys in Ngaruawahia. We blamed Ethel, but maybe Boris rolled over." A sudden thought made him stop and turn to Pete, "Hey, remember when someone broke into your place?" Pete nodded. "They searched it and took loose cash, didn't they?"

Pete nodded and his shoulders slumped. "They wrecked it but left no fingerprints. Henrietta wouldn't stay there for weeks in case they came back."

"What if Boris staged it?" Logan chewed his lower lip. "You'd expect his fingerprints to be there, anyway. What if his debt to Larne made him an easy blackmail target?" Logan tapped his fingers against his thigh. "I need to find out the link between Larne and Laval."

Pete hugged the door handle while Logan made a phone call. Logan said little but looked uneasy as he disconnected. Pete wrinkled his nose. "Does Hana know you talk to them?" he demanded. "She won't like it. Her son's a cop."

"Shut up!" Logan snapped. "Larne is a small time money lender and debt collector. My contact says he made some bad bets recently and lost a lot of money. He floated his existing debts using an Auckland player who goes by the name of Michael Laval."

"We should find Boris and ask him ourselves," said Pete, squaring his shoulders. Then his usual reticence returned. "I'll let you find him. You're better at hitting people."

Logan nodded in agreement on both counts. "You're right. We'll find him and sort this mess out ourselves."

"What about Hana's son?" Pete clung to the door handle, his knuckles white. "He could sort this out faster."

Logan winced and dragged his phone from his pocket. Bodie answered on the first ring, the sounds of a fast food place in the background. "What?" he snapped, over the sound of pop music and shouting.

"I've got a problem," Logan replied. He told the tale as fast as he could and waited for Bodie's verdict.

"It sounds suspect," he agreed. "I'll tell Odering. Do nothing for now."

Logan rolled his eyes and disconnected the call. "Do nothing? Who does he think I am?"

"You should listen to him." Pete gripped the door handle with one hand and his crotch with the other. Logan exhaled at his outward signs of distress.

"I'm looking for Boris," he said, pushing him aside. "Right now."

Pete groaned and trotted behind him, stopping at Logan's office to check Boris' timetable on the computer. "Gym," Logan concluded, following the codes on screen with his finger.

"He isn't there."

"How do you know?" Logan knitted his brow and Pete pointed

through the second floor window to the doors of the gymnasium standing wide open opposite.

"There's nobody there."

Logan shook his head. "We need to find him."

At the start of the next period, boys poured into the buildings and Pete admitted defeat. "He's nowhere," he whined. "Do you think he's hiding?"

"I don't know." Logan looked at his watch. "This is my free period. You go to class and I'll keep searching." He watched the bald patch at the back of Pete's head bob away in a tide of boys. Frustration drew lines in his olive forehead and he tried to plan his next move. Checking on Hana seemed obvious.

Logan experienced eagerness in the pit of his stomach as he crossed the common room. She drew him like a moth to a flame and his powerlessness terrified him. He enjoyed a mental illusion of her waiting for him at the hotel, a child on her hip as he finished some backbreaking endeavour on the farm. It represented a view of perfection and he nursed it in his heart.

He navigated through a queue of boys waiting to see Sheila and caught sight of Hana. She'd fought her hair back into the clip and her pink cheeks spoke of health and pregnancy. Her body arched as she peered over the floor plan still and Logan released the ready smile onto his lips. Then he froze.

Boris sat in Pete's dirty chair, legs crossed and eyes studying Hana's progress with the coloured squares. He laughed at something she said and they both jumped at the sight of Logan.

"Hey babe." Hana gave him a coy smile and her hand strayed to her stomach, fingers caressing the gentle swell. "Did you realise Boris never visited our new place? I said he should come for dinner one night."

Logan gritted his teeth and gave Boris a smile which didn't reach his eyes. "Yeah, what a great idea," he said, willing Hana not to say anything more.

"Do you know where it is, Boris?" he asked and the other man shook his head and paled.

"Oh. I'll write the address down for you," Hana said, reaching for a piece of scrap paper. "I never thought of that. Silly me."

"No need." Logan strode towards Boris and yanked him up by his arm. It took effort to make the action look more friendly than he intended. "I'll do it. Angus is asking for you, mate. I'll walk you down there."

"Okay." Hana gave a tiny wave and turned back to her map.

Boris got to his feet, looking unsteady as he gripped his ribs. Logan's fingers closed around his forearm like a vice. "Let's go," he hissed into Boris' ear. "Nice and quiet."

They walked down the main staircase, Boris limping ahead of Logan. The steps gave him difficulty and Logan jabbed him in the back twice to hurry him along. All vestige of friendship abandoned them as Logan played the game to win. At the principal's door, he ran foul of the personal assistant. "You can't see him," she announced, beating them to the opening. "You don't have an appointment."

"Don't need one." Logan shoved Boris forward and the poisonous woman pushed him back again. "Angus wants to see him."

"No, he doesn't," she insisted. "Or I would know about it."

"Ah, Mr Du Rose." Angus joined the fray and eyed the men with a calculated stare. "I see you found our esteemed colleague."

Logan ground his teeth in his jaw and shoved Boris forward. The assistant dived sideways as Boris lurched inside, but Angus stopped Logan from following. "I want to hear what he says," Logan snapped and Angus shook his head.

"No, Logan. Let me deal with this."

"But you don't understand!"

Angus spread his hands to prevent Logan following Boris, leaving the taller man with two clear choices. Either he barged his boss aside and slapped Boris into next week, or he did as Angus asked. The principal lowered his glasses to the end of his nose and peered at Logan over the frame. "Don't you teach a Year 11 class this period?"

Logan gaped in horror. "I'm not leaving."

"Yes, my friend, you are." Angus slammed the door in Logan's face in a swift, crafty movement. When Logan tried the handle, he found it locked.

"Don't even think about it!" The assistant dragged his arm away as Logan reached into his pocket. He dropped the metal pick back into its resting place. She slapped his hand. "I know what you're gonna do."

"What?" he snapped, his face screwing into a sneer.

"You're gonna break the door down," she stated, folding her arms. "Then I'm calling the cops."

"Do it!" Logan spat and she took a step backwards. A fog descended in front of his eyes and he recognised a rage bigger than ever before. Boris' behaviour threatened everything he held dear and it paralysed Logan in a heady mix of temper and terror. He retreated, determined to flush Boris out later. Angus couldn't protect him all day.

-37-

Logan taught his class. It pained him to listen to the terrible Shakespearean accents in an attempt to capture the essence of Hamlet. His mind remained elsewhere. He let the boys ramble through the text, impatient at their ignorance of iambic pentameter despite a term of teaching it. They picked up his veiled temper and acted up as though testing where the boundary might have shifted to. Logan kept his phone in his trouser pocket, pulling it out and checking for a message from Bodie that never came.

He ran a frustrated hand through his hair and cursed. When he looked up, thirty silent faces observed him with nervousness. He sighed. "You know what boys? I don't feel so great. Let's wrap this up for today. Take an early lunch and stay out of trouble."

The boys cheered and left without complaint. Logan slammed the classroom door, his hands shaking as he fought to lock it behind him. He ran down the back stairs three at a time. The assistant blocked him in front of Angus' office door. "He's not there."

"Where'd he go?"

She set her face in an expression of perpetual disdain, flaring her nostrils and peering through the corners of her eyes. "Never you mind!"

"Where is Boris?"

The assistant lost interest. "Oh. He left. Mr Blair got called to a sick child at the boarding house and Boris left." She fluttered her eyelashes and primped her hair. "Such a lovely young man."

Logan exhaled through his teeth. "Did he go back to class?" He eyed her computer, weighing up the risk of accessing Boris' timetable from there. She blocked him by walking around the desk and sitting down.

"I don't know. And, if I did, I wouldn't tell you!"

Logan clutched at straws. "When did he leave?"

Refusing to answer, the assistant pointed towards her office doorway with a jabbing finger, indicating he should leave. She ignored any further attempts Logan made to question her.

By the time the lunch bell sounded and the boys filed out into the fresh air, Logan reached the outskirts of Gordonton. At the end of the driveway to the rental house, a dark saloon car turned right across him and Logan almost T-boned it in his haste. He spun Gwynne Jeffs' truck onto the rutted driveway and put his foot down on the gas pedal. The sleek saloon slid out onto the main road and Logan ignored it.

He continued his journey, fuelled by an adrenaline rush. Too late, he wondered who the visitors might have been. The truck slid in the dirt and he forced himself to concentrate. Gwynne not only lent him transport, he also agreed to babysit Logan's Year 12 classical studies group if he failed to return.

Logan bumped down the familiar driveway, pulling up in front of the Gordonton house at speed. The front door stood open and the place felt deserted, a cool breeze fanning the leaves of a potted umbrella plant in the hallway. The timber groaned as Logan ran up the front steps. "Boris!" he shouted. "Get out here and face me."

He skidded to a sudden halt in the hallway. Boris lay on the floor, a pool of blood spreading along the rimu floorboards from a gash behind his head. His left arm splayed at an unnatural angle and his cheekbone swelled on the right side of his face. Logan's heartbeat shook him from the inside as horror coursed through his veins. He froze at the sight, his brain moving through myriad possibilities. "Boris," he breathed. "What the hell did you get yourself messed up in?" Logan stood in the doorway and hesitated, anticipating his DNA and fingerprints turning up as evidence. "Sod it!" he exclaimed and dropped to his knees beside his stricken friend, understanding he was probably too late.

Du Rose Legacy

A Sample from the next novel

CHAPTER ONE

Logan felt for a pulse on his friend's blood soaked neck and found nothing. His grip slipped in the red slick and he forced his index and middle fingers into the space beneath the left side of Boris' broken jaw. Closing his eyes, he waited. The weak, irregular beats forced a sigh of relief from his pursed lips. "Let's hope you're lucky, mate," Logan breathed. He reached for the phone in his pocket and dialled triple one for emergency, explaining his location to the efficient operator. "Yeah, it's bad," he said, casting an experienced eye over Boris' twisted body. "Multiple breaks and blood loss."

While the dispatcher chattered in his ear, Logan felt around Boris' limbs, finding a broken arm and perhaps dislocated knee. He snatched a cloth from a sideboard and balled it up, slipping it beneath Boris' head and wincing at the groaned response. "He's moaning, but not conscious," Logan relayed. The bloodied phone clattered to the floor as he leaned over the injured man's mouth. Guttural breathing rewarded him. "Come on, man. Help is on its way. They won't be long. What the hell did you get involved in?"

"Don't move him," the ambulance operator stated when Logan picked up the phone again. "Stay with him, monitor his vital signs and talk to him."

Logan hung up before the man could tell him to stay on the line and dialled Bodie's number. The young police officer let out a string of swearwords. "What the hell are you doing? I told you to leave this alone. You know what will happen now, don't you? Geez!" Logan heard the rage in his voice. Then Bodie's voice changed. "Did you get blood on you?" Logan looked down at his soaked fingers, the dripping phone and his bloodied shirt. He didn't reply. Bodie snorted. "Then you're an idiot and you get whatever you deserve. I spoke to Detective Sergeant Odering and he left half an hour ago to speak to Boris. If you'd stayed at work, you'd have an alibi!"

Logan ground his teeth at the hint of victory in his stepson's tone. "Way to go, Du Rose," he mouthed at his own stupidity. Boris stirred and he dropped to his knees, rocking the man's shoulder. "Boris, wake up, mate. Who did this? Did you know them?"

Bodie snorted. "Too late Du Rose. You put yourself in the frame and you can stay there for all I care. I'll take care of my mum and your kid." The call ended and Logan felt a flicker of fear. Sirens split the gentle, rural atmosphere and he checked Boris' weak pulse again. The sound of tyres on gravel heralded more than one vehicle.

About the Author

K T Bowes has worked in education for more than a decade, both in New Zealand and the United Kingdom and has been writing since she could first hold a pencil. She is married with four beautiful children who are all now making their own way in the world. She lives in the North Island of New Zealand between the Hakarimata Ranges and the Waikato River with a mad cat and often a few crazy horses.

Dear Reader

I hope you've enjoyed Hana Du Rose. Writing it seemed to take more of me than I wanted to part with and I hope the end result both intrigued and entertained you. I would be grateful if you would take the time to leave a review at your usual retailer. I often feature snappy review comments on my covers. My work is also ranked on reviews and your comments will allow me to reach a wider audience. It doesn't have to be an essay - I will be grateful for a few words.

K T Bowes is on social media if you'd like to follow her there.

FACEBOOK: https://www.facebook.com/NZauthorKTBowes/

TWITTER: @ktboweswrites

BLOG: https://ktbowes.com/blog

Other books by this author:

Logan Du Rose
About Hana - FREE digital copy
Hana Du Rose
Du Rose Legacy
The New Du Rose Matriarch
One Heartbeat
The Du Rose Prophecy
Du Rose Sons
Du Rose Family Ties

Free from the Tracks -FREE digital copy
Sophia's Dilemma
A Trail of Lies Gone Phishing

Artifact
Demons on Her Shoulder

The Actuary - FREE digital copy
The Actuary's Wife
The Actuary in Trouble

All Saints

Pirongia's Secret
Deleilah

Take a look at all K T Bowes' novels on her website:
http://ktbowes.com

Official Notices

This eBook is licensed for your personal enjoyment only. This eBook may not be re-sold or given away to other people. If you would like to share this book with another person, please purchase an additional copy for each recipient. If you're reading this book and did not purchase it or it was not purchased for your use only, then please return to the retailer and purchase your own copy. Thank you for respecting the author's hard work.

This novel is a work of fiction, entirely the product of the author's imagination. Any similarities to actual persons, living or dead, businesses and events are purely coincidental.
All rights reserved. No part of this book may be reproduced in whole or in part without the express written permission of the author. This work is the intellectual property of the author writing as K T Bowes.

www.ingramcontent.com/pod-product-compliance
Lightning Source LLC
LaVergne TN
LVHW040747250326
834688LV00034B/488